Aberdeenshire Library and Information Service
www.aberdeenshire.gov.uk/libraries
Renewals Hotline 01224 661511

D0411958

Black Hills

Black Hills

DAN SIMMONS

Quercus

First published in Great Britain in 2010 by

Quercus
21 Bloomsbury Square
London
WC1A 2NS

FT

A CIP catalogue record for this book is available
from the British Library

ISBN 978 1 84916 088 9 (HB)
ISBN 978 1 84916 089 6 (TPB)

Printed and bound in Great Britain by Clays Ltd, St Ives plc

10 9 8 7 6 5 4 3 2 1

This book is dedicated to my parents, Robert and Kathryn Simmons, and to my wife Karen's parents, Verne and Ruth Logerquist. It is also dedicated to my brothers, Wayne and Ted Simmons, and to Karen's brother, Jim Logerquist, and sister Sally Lampe.

Most of all, this book is dedicated to Karen and to our daughter, Jane Kathryn, who are *Wamaka-ognaka e'cantge* — "the heart of everything that is" for me.

Hecetu. Mitakuye oyasin.
So be it — all my relatives! Every one of us.

Black Hills

Along the Greasy Grass

June 1876

PAHA SAPA PULLS HIS HAND BACK SHARPLY BUT NOT BEFORE HE feels the rattlesnake-strike shock of the dying *Wasicun's* ghost leaping into his fingers and flowing up his arm and into his chest. The boy lurches back in horror as the ghost burns its way up through his veins and bones like so much surging venom. The *Wasicun's* spirit scalds a painful path through the nerves of Paha Sapa's shoulder and then pours out into his chest and throat, roiling and churning like an oily thick smoke. Paha Sapa can *taste* it. And it tastes like death.

Still expanding, the ghost spreads through Paha Sapa's torso and down and out, making the boy's arms and legs feel both weak and heavy at the same time. As the *Wasicun's* ghost fills his lungs with a terrible, expanding, thick-filling heaviness that shuts off all breath, Paha Sapa is reminded of the time, he was a child barely able to toddle, when he almost drowned in the Tongue. Yet even through his current terror, this boy just short of eleven summers senses that this—invasion—is something infinitely more terrible than mere death by drowning.

This, Paha Sapa thinks, is what Death feels like when it crawls in through a man's mouth and eyes and nostrils to steal his spirit. But instead of Paha Sapa's spirit being dragged *out*, this stranger's spirit is being forced *in*. Death acts here more as terrible intruder than thief.

Paha Sapa cries out as if wounded and crawls away from the staring corpse, tries to stand to run, falls, stands again, falls again, and resumes crawling away from the corpse, kicking and waving his arms and gasping as he rolls downhill across grass, dirt, cacti, horse shit, blood, and more dead *wasichus* in his blind eagerness to shake the ghost out of his body. But the ghost stays with him and grows larger inside him. Paha Sapa opens his mouth to scream, but this time no sound emerges. The ghost is filling Paha Sapa's gasping mouth and throat and nostrils as surely as if someone has poured hot liquid buffalo fat down his throat. He cannot breathe. The boy crouches on all fours and shakes like a sick dog but cannot force himself to vomit. Black dots swarm as his field of vision narrows. The ghost cuts into him like a scalping knife, slicing deeper behind his eyes, burrowing into his brain.

Paha Sapa collapses onto his side and rolls up against something soft. When he opens his eyes he realizes that he is only a finger's length from another dead *wasichu's* face: this bluecoat is only a boy, perhaps just five or six summers older than Paha Sapa; the dead *Wasicun* boy-soldier has lost his hat and his short-cropped hair is red, the first red hair Paha Sapa has ever seen; the dead boy's skin is paler than that of any *Wasicun* Paha Sapa has ever heard described and the small nose is dusted with freckles. Paha Sapa vaguely realizes that no breath issues forth from the cave of the soldier's mouth, opened painfully wide as if in a final scream or as if ready to lunge and bite into Paha Sapa's gasping, terrified face only a handsbreadth away. He also notices dully that one of the *wasichu's* eyes is merely a bloody hole. But Paha Sapa sees that the other eye, open and staring, is precisely the blue of the afternoon sky visible beyond the corpse's small, pale ear.

Gasping for breath, Paha Sapa stares into that dead eye, its blueness seeming to fade and pale even as he stares, as if seeking some answer there.

—*Black Hills?*

More warrior ponies thunder by, two of them leaping Paha Sapa and the *wasichus'* corpses, but vaguely—distantly—Paha Sapa realizes that one of the ponies has stopped and that a warrior has slid off and is crouched on one knee next to him. He vaguely, distantly, feels a strong hand on his shoulder, rolling him onto his back.

Paha Sapa loses sight of the red-haired boy's one-eyed corpse and is now looking up at the kneeling warrior.

—Black Hills? Are you shot?

The kneeling warrior is slender and paler of skin than most Lakota and has gone into battle as naked as the *heyoka* he is, wearing only a breechclout and moccasins, his hair tied simply into two long braids and sporting a single white feather. The lean man's body paint consists only of hailstones and a lightning streak, reinforcing the first impression that the thin man is indeed a living lightning conductor, a *heyoka,* one of the receiver-of-visions warrior-protectors who dares to stand between Paha Sapa's people, the Natural Free Human Beings, and the full fury of the Thunder Beings.

Then, blinking, Paha Sapa notices the pebble behind the man's ear and the narrow but livid scar stretching back from his left nostril—an old bullet wound, inflicted at point-blank range by a jealous husband, a scar that has left this *heyoka* warrior's lips slightly curled up on the left side, suggesting more grimace than smile—and Paha Sapa realizes that this is *T'ašunka Witko,* Crazy Horse, cousin to Limps-a-Lot's first wife.

Paha Sapa tries to answer Crazy Horse's query, but the ghost's pressure in his chest and throat allows only choking noises to emerge. Just the slightest trickle of air reaches Paha Sapa's burning lungs. Even as he tries again to speak, he realizes that he must look like a fish gaping and gasping on a riverbank, mouth wide, eyes protruding.

Crazy Horse grunts in contempt or disgust, stands, and leaps onto his pony's back in a single graceful motion, his rifle still in his hand, then rides away with his followers shouting behind him.

Paha Sapa would weep if he could. Limps-a-Lot was so proud when he introduced his first wife's famous cousin to his adopted son just four nights earlier in Sitting Bull's lodge, and now this absolute humiliation…

Still lying on his back, Paha Sapa spreads his arms and legs as wide as he is able. He's lost his moccasins and now he curls his toes and fingers into the soil in the same way he's done since he was a small boy when the first *touch-the-earth-to-fly* visions came. At once the old feelings flow in—that he is clinging to the outer surface of a swiftly spinning ball rather than lying on a flat world, that the sky hangs below him rather than above, that the hurtling sun is just another sky shape wheeling through the sky like the stars or the moon—and with that familiar illusion, Paha Sapa begins to breathe more deeply.

But so does the ghost. Paha Sapa can feel it inhaling and exhaling deep within him. And, he realizes with a shock that makes his spine go cold, the ghost is speaking to him. Or at least speaking to *someone* from inside him.

Paha Sapa would scream if he could, but still his straining lungs pull in only the thinnest trickle of air. But he can hear the ghost whispering slowly and steadily—the harsh-sounding and unintelligible *wasichu* words resonating against the inner walls of Paha Sapa's skull and vibrating against his teeth and bones. Paha Sapa understands not one of the words. He clasps his hands over his ears, but the internal hissing and whispering and muttering continue.

There are other shapes moving among the dead around him now. Paha Sapa hears the trill of Lakota women and with incredible effort he rolls onto his belly and then struggles to his knees. He has disgraced himself and his uncle-father in front of Crazy Horse, but he cannot continue to lie like one of the dead with the women here.

As he struggles to his feet, Paha Sapa sees that he has startled the nearest woman—a Hunkpapa woman he knows named Eagle Robe, the same woman who earlier this day he saw shoot the black-*Wasicun* scout named Teat whom Sitting Bull called friend—and in her fright, Eagle Robe lifts up the same heavy *wasichu* cavalry pistol with which she killed the black scout, raises it in both hands, aims it at Paha Sapa's chest from only ten feet away, and pulls the trigger. The hammer clicks on either an empty chamber or a cartridge that misfires.

Paha Sapa staggers a few steps in her direction, but Eagle Robe and three other women scream and run away, quickly disappearing in the shifting clouds of dust and gunsmoke that continue to roll across the hillside. Paha Sapa looks down and realizes that he is covered almost head to foot with blood—his dead mare's blood, the ghost-*Wasicun's* blood, and more blood from the other corpses, horse and man, that he has rolled across and lain upon.

Paha Sapa knows what he must do. He has to return to the corpse of the *Wasicun* on whom he counted coup and somehow convince the ghost to go back into the man's body. Gasping, still unable to wave or call to the half-seen warriors thundering by on their ponies in the dust, Paha Sapa stumbles uphill toward the dead man lying among dead men.

The battle is moving to the south again, and as the dust and gunsmoke begin to drift away on the very slightest of evening breezes coming over the ridgetop above—the high grasses dance and rustle to the wind's touch—Paha Sapa estimates that there are somewhere around forty dead *wasichu* horses lying in a rough circle ahead of him. Most appear to have been shot by the bluecoat soldiers themselves. There are about as many *wasichu* corpses as there are horse carcasses, but the human corpses have been stripped by the Lakota women and now stand out on the hillside like white river boulders against the tan dirt and blood-soiled green grass and darker shades of torn horseflesh.

Paha Sapa steps over a man whose scalped head has been smashed almost flat. Curds of gray have been spattered onto the tall grass that stirs in the evening breeze. Warriors or, more likely, women have cut out the man's eyes and tongue and slit his throat. His lower belly has been hacked open, and entrails have been tugged out like a buffalo's after a hunt—slick strands of gray gut wind and coil like glistening dead rattlesnakes in the bloody grass—and Paha Sapa notices that the women have also cut off the man's *ce* and balls. Someone has shot arrows into this *Wasicun's* opened body, and kidneys, lung, and liver have all been pierced multiple times. The dead man's heart is missing.

Paha Sapa continues stumbling uphill. The white corpses are everywhere, all sprawled where they fell and many hacked into pieces, most mutilated and lying atop great splashes of blood or atop their own dead horses, but he cannot find the *Wasicun* whose ghost now breathes and whispers deep in his own guts. He realizes that since he has been only semiconscious at best, it's possible that more time may have elapsed than he is aware of since he counted coup on the man. Someone, perhaps surviving *wasichus,* may have hauled the corpse from the battlefield—especially if the man was an officer—in which case Paha Sapa may never be able to get rid of this ghost.

Just when he is sure that the dead man is no longer lying among the scores of other corpses here on this bloody field, he sees the *Wasicun's* tall, balding forehead protruding from a pile of white bodies. The stripped corpse is half-sitting against two other naked *wasichus.* Some woman or warrior has slashed his right thigh open in the customary mark against the Lakota's dead enemies, but the man has not been scalped. Paha Sapa stares dumbly at the receding hairline and short-cropped light hair and realizes that the scalp was simply not worth the effort of the taking.

But what short stubble of hair there is looks very light, although as much reddish as yellow. Could this possibly be Long Hair? Could it be the ghost of Long Hair that Paha Sapa now carries like some terrible fetus? It seems unlikely. Certainly some Lakota or Cheyenne warriors would have recognized their old enemy Long Hair and treated his corpse with either more outrage or more honor than this all-but-ignored body has received.

Someone, probably a woman, has jammed an arrow far up the corpse's flaccid-in-death, forever plump, pale *ce*.

Paha Sapa goes to his knees, feeling expended cartridge shells ripping the skin of his knees, and leans forward, pressing both his palms against the *Wasicun's* pale chest, setting his hands near a large, ragged wound where the first rifle bullet struck the man's left breast. The second and more lethal bullet wound—high on the man's pale left temple—shows as a simple round hole. The corpse's eyelids are lowered, eyes almost closed as if in sleep, only the narrowest crescents of white visible under surprisingly full lashes, and this *Wasicun's* countenance, unlike so many of the others, looks composed, almost peaceful.

Paha Sapa closes his own eyes as he gasps the words that he hopes are ritual enough.

—*Ghost, be gone! Ghost, leave my body!*

As Paha Sapa repeats this gasping incantation, he presses down firmly on the naked corpse's chest, hoping and praying to the Six Grandfathers that the pressure will invite the ghost to flow back down his arm and hand and fingers and into the cold white form.

The *wasichu* corpse's mouth opens and the dead man emits a long, satisfied belch.

Paha Sapa jerks his hands back in horror—the ghost seems to be laughing at him from its safe nest inside Paha Sapa's brain—until he realizes that he's only pressed some last bubbles of air up and out of the dead *Wasicun's* bowels or belly or lungs.

His body shaking, Paha Sapa presses his hands against the cold flesh again, but it is no use. The ghost is not leaving. It has found a home in Paha Sapa's warm, living, breathing body and has no wish to return to the empty vessel lying there among the equally empty vessels of its murdered friends.

Sobbing now like an infant, ten-summers-old Paha Sapa, a sniveling boy again who thought himself a man just an hour earlier, crawls away from the heap of corpses and falls to the ground and curls up like an unborn thing, all but sucking his thumb as he lies there weeping between the stiffened legs of a dead cavalry horse. The sun is a red orb in the dusty sky as it lowers toward the uplands to the west, its crimson hue turning the sky into a reflection of the bloody earth beneath it.

The ghost continues to whisper and gibber inside his brain as Paha Sapa slides sideways into an exhausted state that is not quite sleep. It is still gibbering and whispering when Limps-a-Lot finds him sometime after sunset and carries him, still unconscious, back to the mourning and celebrating Lakota village in the valley below.

2

On the Six Grandfathers

February 1934

I T'S TIME FOR THOMAS JEFFERSON'S HEAD TO EXPLODE.

Visible in the rough sketch of stone is the parted hair, so much lower on the forehead than the hair above Washington's forehead immediately to the left and higher than the emerging Jefferson. And rising out of the white-and-tan granite below the hair and forehead is the long rectangle of a blocked-out nose, terminating just about even with the sharp line of Washington's chin. Also emerging are the over-hang of brows and the indentations of the eyes, the right eye more finished (if one can call a circular hole within an oval hole finished). But the two heads — one almost completed, the other just emerging — appear too close to each other for even the non-artist's eye.

Paha Sapa was resting in the shade of the powerhouse in the valley the summer before, carefully and slowly going through his dynamite box even though work on the project was officially in hiatus, when he'd heard two older tourist ladies arguing under their parasols.

— *That's George in front, so the other has to be Martha.*

— *Oh, no. I have it on good authority that they're putting only presidents up there.*

— *Nonsense! Mr. Borglum would never carve two men snuggled up to each other like that! It would be indecent! That's definitely Martha.*

So today, at four p.m., the first Jefferson has to go.

At four o'clock sharp the sirens sound. Everyone off the heads, everyone off the faces, everyone off the stairway, everyone off the rubble slope beneath. Then there settles in the briefest winter silence, unbroken even by crow call from the snowy ponderosa pines on either side and below or by the otherwise constant creak of the supply tram being hauled up or down, until suddenly three booms echo across the valley, and Jefferson's forehead explodes outward. There is the briefest pause as rocks fall and dust dissipates—then another blast as Jefferson's indistinct masses of hair and the overhang of brow explode into thousands of flying, falling granite shards, some as big as a Model T. This is followed by an even briefer pause during which more rocks clatter down the slope and crows whirl black above, and then Jefferson's nose and right eye and the remaining hint of his cheek erupt outward in half a dozen simultaneous final blasts that roll down the valley and echo back, diminished and tinny sounding.

The debris seems to fall and roll for long minutes, although the real work has been done in seconds. When the last smoke and dust drift away on the cold breeze, the rock face shows only a few subtle folds and minor spurs that will require burring away by hand. Thomas Jefferson is gone. It is as if he never existed there.

Paha Sapa, against all rules but with special dispensation, has been hanging in his bosun's chair out of view of the blast around the east side of Washington's massive head during the explosions, his feet set against a subtle ridge on the long expanse of virgin white rock that has already been blasted down to good stone in preparation for carving at Jefferson's new site. Now he kicks out, waves up to Gus, his winchman, and begins bouncing across the bulge of hair, cheek, and nose of George Washington, the winch crane above swiveling smoothly with him as he seems to fly. He thinks what he always thinks when he begins to move this way—*Peter Pan*! He saw the play performed on the Pine Ridge Reservation by a traveling troupe from Rapid City years ago and has always remembered how the young woman playing a boy flew around and above the stage on her all-too-visible wire harness. The steel wire that holds Paha Sapa hundreds of feet above the stone valley floor here is one-eighteenth of an inch thick, less visible than the girl–Peter Pan's was, but he knows that it could hold eight men of his weight. He kicks harder and flies higher; he wants to be the first to see the results of the fourteen large charges and eighty-six small charges he personally measured and drilled and tapped into place on Jefferson's head that morning and afternoon.

Balancing on Washington's right cheek, waving to Gus to lower him to a point level with the first president's still-being-worked lips and line of mouth, Paha Sapa looks to his left at his handiwork and finds it good.

All one hundred of the charges have fired. The masses of parted hair, eyebrows, eye sockets, eye, nose, and first hint of lips are gone, but no errant gouges or lumps have been left in the inferior rock where the first Jefferson carving was mistakenly started.

Paha Sapa is bouncing weightlessly from the right corner of Washington's chin, still some hundred and fifty feet above the highest point of the rubbled slope below, when he senses rather than sees or hears Gutzon Borglum descending on a second line from the winch house above.

The boss drops between Paha Sapa's bosun's chair and the remains of the first Jefferson rock face and Borglum glowers at the newly exposed rock for a minute before swiveling easily toward Paha Sapa.

— *You missed some little spurs there on the far cheek, Old Man.*

Paha Sapa nods. The spurs are visible only as the slightest hint of shadows within the patch of weak February light reflected from Washington's cheek and nose onto the now empty rock face. Paha Sapa feels the cold as the last of that reflected February light fades away on this south-facing slope. He knows that Borglum had to criticize *something*—he always does. As for being called Old Man, Paha Sapa knows that Borglum will be celebrating his sixty-sixth birthday in a few weeks but never mentions his age to the men and has no idea of Paha Sapa's real age; he will turn sixty-nine in August. Paha Sapa knows that Borglum calls him Old Man and Old Horse in front of the other men but actually believes that the only Indian he has working for him is fifty-eight, which is what the Homestake Mine records show.

— *Well, Billy, you were right about the charge sizes. I wasn't sure we should use so many little ones, but you were right.*

Borglum's voice is its usual dissatisfied growl. Few of the workers love him, but almost all of them respect him, and that's all that Borglum wants from them. Paha Sapa neither loves nor respects Borglum, but he knows that statement would be true about his feelings toward almost any *Wasicun,* with the possible exception of a few dead men and a living one named Doane Robinson. Paha Sapa squints at the clean rock face where the three-dimensional Jefferson sketch was half an hour earlier.

— Yes, sir, Mr. Borglum. Any more large ones would have cracked that fault open and you'd be patching for six months. Any fewer little ones and we'd be blasting for another week and buffing a month more after that.

It's the longest sustained speech Paha Sapa has given in months, but Borglum only grunts. Paha Sapa wishes the other man would just go away. He has a dynamite headache—literally a dynamite headache. Paha Sapa's been working with his bare hands in the cold all day, cutting, shaping, and placing the charges since early morning, and, as all powdermen know, there is something in dynamite, possibly from the nitroglycerine beading up out of it like dangerous sweat, that seeps through a powderman's skin, migrates to the base of his skull, and brings on these thudding, blinding headaches that make normal migraines seem insignificant. Paha Sapa tries to blink away the onset of the red film over his vision that the dynamite headache invariably brings with it.

— Well, it could've been cleaner, and I'm sure you could've used less dynamite and saved us some money. Be ready to set the new charges on the upper third of the new site early in the morning for the noon blow.

Borglum waves for his own winchman spotter, his son, Lincoln, to crank him up.

Paha Sapa nods, feeling the stab of pain and vertigo that the nod brings on, and waits for Borglum to reach the winch house before he will kick around for one last, closer inspection. But before the boss disappears up into the dark rectangle at the bottom of the overhanging winch house, he shouts down—

— Billy…you'd like to use enough powder to bring Washington down too, wouldn't you?

Paha Sapa leans far back with only the tips of his toes touching the rock, his body almost horizontal in the bosun's chair with only the one-eighth-inch metal cable holding him there in space two hundred feet above the valley floor, and looks up at the dark shape of Gutzon

Borglum hanging fifty feet above him, a small silhouette against the rapidly paling February South Dakota sky that is almost the blue of a dead *wasichu* horse soldier's eye.

—*Not yet, Boss. I'll wait 'til you finish all the heads before I bring them all down.*

Borglum coughs a laugh, signals his son, and is cranked up into the winch house.

It is an old joke between them and the question and answer, always the same, have long since been wrung dry of any remaining humor. But does Borglum ever suspect, Paha Sapa wonders, that his premier powderman is telling him the truth?

3

Along the Greasy Grass

June 1876

PAHA SAPA SIPS THE WARM SOUP. ALL THE FINELY SCRAPED buffalo hide walls of Limps-a-Lot's lodge glow orange from the multitude of fires burning in the village outside. It is very late, but a cacophony of singing and chants and the thudding of drums can be heard—cacophony to Paha Sapa's ears because it is a harsh and unusual mixture of celebrations and mournings, peppered throughout by screams of mourning women, exultant cries from celebrating warriors, and the continued rifle shots from both within the camp and from more distant shots echoing from the dark hills across the river to the southeast. Hundreds of warriors, many of them blind drunk by now, are taking turns trying to sneak up on the surviving *wasichus* surrounded up there, shooting at the soldiers whenever they think they see the dark shape of a head or body poke up from the dug-in circle of bluecoats cowering on the dark hilltop.

Besides Limps-a-Lot, there are three other older men in the lodge: *Tatanka Iyotake* (Sitting Bull), Foolish Elk, and an old Rock-dreamer *yuwipi* holy man named Long Turd. Paha Sapa, only half listening to the desultory talk among the old men, realizes that Long Turd is saying that he spent much of the afternoon's battle conferring with Crazy Horse, even going so far as to build a holy fire of buffalo chips to pray over during one of the pauses when Crazy Horse and his men were gathering fresh ponies. At the mention of Crazy Horse's name,

Paha Sapa flushes with shame. He hopes he will never have to see Limps-a-Lot's older wife's cousin again.

—*Black Hills, tell us what you have to tell us.*

It is Sitting Bill who gives the command. Even though most of the younger warriors have been talking and celebrating as if the day's work has been a huge victory, Sitting Bull sounds so sad that one would think it has been a great defeat for the Lakota and Cheyenne. And while Limps-a-Lot, Long Turd, and the younger Foolish Elk have all dressed more formally for the evening, Sitting Bull, who is old—he has seen at least forty-two summers according to Limps-a-Lot—is wearing his everyday outfit of a fringed buckskin shirt embroidered only with green porcupine quills and modest tassels of human hair attached at the shoulders, leggings, moccasins, and a red breechcloth. His braids are wrapped in otter skins and adorned with a single eagle feather set upright.

Paha Sapa nods, sets down his soup, composes himself cross-legged on the soft hide, and thinks about what he will say. Limps-a-Lot has told the other three men about the ghost—it is why they are here tonight listening to a boy rather than out celebrating or mourning or, in Foolish Elk's case, up the hill shooting at the surviving *wasichus*—and Paha Sapa knows that it is the identity of the bluecoat whose ghost he carries that most interests the two holy men and the warrior-friend of Crazy Horse here.

Paha Sapa closes his eyes for a minute to bring the afternoon's events out of the smoke and haze of the day's terrible memory. He hopes that when he opens his eyes to speak—and to speak as succinctly as Limps-a-Lot taught him as a small boy and as clearly as he can given the *Wasicun's* ghost's continued gibbering and throbbing in his mind—the few flat, emotionless words will emerge almost in the form of a monotone chant. But before he opens his eyes to speak briefly, Paha Sapa takes time to recall it all in detail.

———

HE HAD NOT COME TO FIGHT. Paha Sapa knew he was no warrior—his single, sad expedition against the Crow the previous spring had taught him that—but that afternoon, when the shooting started at the southeast end of the huge village of tipis that filled the valley, he and Limps-a-Lot ran out of the older man's lodge. It was very exciting. *Akicita* were trying to keep order, but the young warriors were ignoring the tribal police, shouting and leaping onto their mounts and riding toward the noise of battle. Other braves were rushing to put on their war paint, find their weapons, and chant their death songs. Although Paha Sapa knew he was no warrior at heart, he felt the excitement rise in him as the sound of shooting continued, the dust clouds rose from the east and from the bluffs across the river, and the men of all ages continued to ride out of the village in whooping packs.

— *The fighting is at the far end of the village.*

Limps-a-Lot pointed to the southeast.

— *I want you to stay here until I get back.*

And, carrying no weapons, Limps-a-Lot walked slowly away toward the shooting.

Paha Sapa tried to stay put, even when Wolf Eyes, Left Foot, and several other young men he'd met here at the giant gathering rode by, taunting him and shouting for him to find a pony. But they had ridden off to the south before Paha Sapa could decide what to do.

Then there was more shooting coming from the direction of the coulee there at the north end of the village, almost in the opposite direction of the original firing. Paha Sapa had looked up minutes earlier and seen a line of *wasichus* on horseback moving northwest along the line of bluffs. Was the bluecoat attack at the southeast end of the village merely a feint, Paha Sapa wondered, a distraction — with the full attack coming here at the opposite end where the women and children were gathering? Sitting Bull himself had told Limps-a-Lot only three nights ago that this was a strategy that Long Hair had used when the *Wasicun* war leader attacked Black Kettle's village.

A woman screamed that the bluecoats were coming down the coulee and crossing the river at the ford not far from Limps-a-Lot's lodge, close to where so many of the women and children had gathered. A group of warriors, their horses and their oiled bodies covered with dust from the fighting in the southeast, galloped north through the center of the village to face this new threat, scattering old men, women, and screaming toddlers as they came. A horse trailing that group was without a rider, showing a streak of blood on the blanket. As the riders paused briefly between the lodges to allow the scattering women to get out of their way, this riderless mare came almost to a stop at the rear of the mass of horses and shouting men, her eyes rolling whitely.

Without thinking, Paha Sapa leaped up onto the mare's back, wrapping both hands in its mane. When the mounted warriors forced past the screaming women and galloped toward the river, Paha Sapa hung on and kicked his heels into the mare's heaving ribs. It was unnecessary—the animal's blood was up and, like Paha Sapa's, its instinct was to run with the herd.

The sound of shooting still came from the long coulee that ran up to the bluffs from the river, and through the dust and smoke, Paha Sapa could see several bodies in the dirt there—some *wasichus,* several warriors from the village—but whoever was leading this band ignored the coulee and kept going northeast along the river, past bands of fleeing women and children, past the last Lakota and Cheyenne lodges, through the cottonwoods, until the thirty or so mounted warriors with Paha Sapa bringing up the rear splashed across at the second ford and galloped up a deep ravine toward the grassy bluffs above. Paha Sapa almost slipped off as the mare climbed the steep terrain but hung on to the mane with both hands and pressed his knees tight against the horse's laboring barrel chest as the wheezing, frothing mare, her lungs sounding like a leaky bellows, staggered up onto the grassy ridge.

Paha Sapa had time only for brief glimpses and scattered impressions—steep hogbacks to his right, warriors and *wasichus* on horseback there, another long ridge wreathed in smoke and dust ahead to his left, clumps of dismounted *wasichus* and disorganized bands of warriors shooting at one another there and struggling along the entire grassy stretch that rose toward another, higher ridgeline almost a mile to the northwest. Pulling himself upright, Paha Sapa glanced over his shoulder toward the valley but could not see the circles of a thousand tipis below due to the swirling dust and smoke.

He realized that the band of warriors he was riding with was as disorganized as the other clumps of men he saw scattered all over the hillsides here—his group was mostly Lakota, some Miniconjou, a few Cheyenne. Their leader, a man he had never seen before, looked to be Hunkpapa. The man shouted—*Hokahey!*—and the band of warriors, followed by Paha Sapa, kicked and whipped their ponies toward groups of bluecoat *wasichus* firing in dismounted clumps scattered up the hillside to their left. Everywhere in the smoke, *wasichu* horses and warriors' ponies were screaming and falling, some shot by their bluecoat owners to provide cover, others being shot out from under their riders or away from the soldiers who held their reins. The rattle of gunfire was constant but underlaid with a rising chorus of screams, cries, grunts, chants, and calls. Women on the hillsides were trilling their shrill tremolos of bloody praise as Paha Sapa followed the others out of the last high shrubs at the top of the ravine.

The next few minutes were largely lost to Paha Sapa's memory; he had blurred recollections of gunsmoke, jumbled impressions of waves of warriors on horseback flowing over and through and past dismounted *wasichus,* clouded images of warriors on foot encircling the bands of bluecoats and their dead horses, a nightmare sense of the horses — his mare included — simply stampeding back and forth mindlessly between men who were firing at them. He seemed to recall truly crazy sights, such as the *Wasicun* soldier galloping away with five Lakota warriors behind him. The soldier was getting away when he suddenly raised his revolver and blew his own brains out. Shocked, the warriors pulled their horses up, looked at one another, and rode south toward louder fighting; they wanted nothing to do with the crazy *Wasicun's* corpse.

Paha Sapa clearly remembered that at no point did he try to stop the mare so that he could retrieve a rifle or bow or spear or revolver from any of the dead men that littered the grassy hillside. He could not have stopped the mare if he'd tried. Her lathered sides were flowing with her own blood, and the boy realized that she'd been shot several times with rifle and pistol bullets and that there was an arrow sunk deep in her flesh just behind Paha Sapa's right leg. With each bound, the mare was snorting up larger gobbets and longer streamers of blood, which flew back and coated Paha Sapa's neck and chest and face, all but blinding him.

Then the warriors wheeled their horses left like a flock of geese changing course, and Paha Sapa saw that they were charging a band of *wasichus* that had dismounted on the long hillside below the crest of the ridge. As his mare stumbled forward—certainly she could not live through another charge—Paha Sapa decided that he would count coup. This was the reason he had come up from the village. He had no weapon, not even a knife or a coup stick, so he would have to count coup with his bare hand. Paha Sapa remembers now that he had been grinning wildly, perhaps insanely, when he made that decision.

In the midst of the dead and dying *wasichus,* a very few bluecoats were kneeling or lying prone or standing and firing. One man with his head bare, short hair, balding—the skin of his forehead so white that for an instant Paha Sapa thought that he had already been scalped—was standing and shooting calmly with a beautiful rifle. A cartridge jammed or he ran out of ammunition as Paha Sapa's band approached—waves of warriors were riding over and past these and the other dismounted and falling *wasichus*—and the bluecoat Paha Sapa had noticed now carefully set the rifle down, drew two pistols, and began firing one in his direction.

Paha Sapa's mare finally went down, her forelegs folding under her, throwing him over her neck and head. Incredibly, impossibly, Paha Sapa hit the ground running and kept running, never falling, almost flying with his dead mare's speed imparted to his own bounding legs, hurtling almost magically through the dead and dying *wasichus* as the warriors on horseback raced past on either side, screaming and firing arrows and rifles. Paha Sapa kept his eyes on the tall *Wasicun* now only twenty strides in front of him. The man saw him, whirled, raised one of the pistols, and was shot.

A bullet had struck the balding *Wasicun* high in the left chest, knocking him off his feet and backward onto a fallen horse. One of the man's pistols flew out of sight into the dust cloud, but he held on to the other and raised it, coolly aiming at Paha Sapa's bloody face as the hurtling, panting boy ran closer, closer.

A racing pony knocked Paha Sapa almost off his feet as the *Wasicun* fired. Paha Sapa heard the bullet buzz past less than a handswidth from his ear. Then he was upright and bouncing forward again, the *Wasicun* taking cool and careful aim at him, and at that instant some warrior fired over Paha Sapa's shoulder, striking the bluecoat in the left temple. The man's head snapped back, and his beautiful pistol fired harmlessly into the air just as Paha Sapa lunged forward and set his palm and five fingers on the white man's chest.

And the ghost leaped into him.

———

WHEN PAHA SAPA STOPS SPEAKING — he has condensed all those remembered details into a very few words — there are grunts and then a long silence. When Sitting Bull finally breaks that silence, he addresses himself to Limps-a-Lot.

— *When you return to your village, you must perform a Ghost Owning Ceremony with a very big giveaway.*

It is Limps-a-Lot's turn to grunt. Paha Sapa, ever sensitive to his stepfather's nuances, knows from this noncommittal noise that the old man does not agree with Sitting Bull that a Ghost Ceremony is the proper response to this spirit-possession.

Long Turd holds out his hand to bring silence and attention.

— *We will have to know whether this was Long Hair who sent his ghost into the boy. Black Hills, you saw the man die — do you think it was Long Hair?*

— *I do not know, Grandfather. The* Wasicun *had very short hair. I think he was an officer. He* did *have very beautiful guns, both the rifle and the two pistols. These were gone when I returned to the body.*

Foolish Elk cleared his throat, obviously hesitant to speak in the company of the three older holy men.

— *It is said that Long Hair carries a rifle with eight sides to the barrel. Did you notice that, Black Hills?*

— *No. Only that it was very fancy and that it fired faster than the other bluecoats' carbines.*

Paha Sapa pauses.

— *I am not a warrior. I am sorry for not observing such things more carefully.*

Sitting Bull grunts and waves his hand dismissively.

— *No one needs apologize for not being a warrior. You are still a boy and apparently do not wish to become a warrior. You are — and you will become — what* Wakan Tanka *wishes you to be. No man can change that.*

As if embarrassed by saying so much, Sitting Bull sneezes and says —

— *Hecetu. Mitakuye oyasin.*

So be it. All my relatives—every one of us.

Which means that the discussion, for this day, is at an end.

Sitting Bull nods to the others, gets heavily to his feet, and goes out of the lodge without saying another word. Long Turd and Foolish Elk take time to finish their pipes and then follow, pausing to whisper a few words to Limps-a-Lot.

When the other men are gone, Limps-a-Lot looks at his adopted son. His gaze looks weary, perhaps sad.

—*They are breaking up the village early tomorrow, but in the morning, if more* wasichus *do not arrive to save their friends, Sitting Bull and I will go up and try to find the body of the bluecoat who has infected you and we will try to determine if it was Long Hair. You will lead us to him.*

Paha Sapa nods. His hands have been trembling since he awoke safe in Limps-a-Lot's lodge this evening and he continues to clench his fists to hide the shaking.

Limps-a-Lot touches his back.

—*Try to sleep again, my son, despite all the crazy noise from the camp. We will leave before first light and while the other bands head west and north or back to the agencies—I think that Sitting Bull will take his people far away to the north—you and I will head east to home. There we will confer with the others and decide what to do about your ghost.*

4

Near Bear Butte

August 1865

PAHA SAPA KNOWS THAT HE WAS BORN DURING THE MOON OF Ripening in the Year the Lightning Struck the Ponies.

He knows that Lakota children are almost never named after places — his name, Paha Sapa, Black Hills, is very unusual and it made the other boys snicker — but he also knows that on the night that he was born near Bear Butte at the end of that hot, strange summer when the lightning struck the pony herd three times, the three most important men in the village — their war chief, Angry Badger; their old, tired *wičasa wakan*, Loud Voice Hawk; and their best and real *wičasa wakan*, Limps-a-Lot — all dreamed of the Black Hills.

In his dream, Angry Badger saw a white wolf running out of the dark hills surrounded and backlit by lightning and the wolf spoke with thunder and on the wolf's back was a crying and naked baby boy.

Loud Voice Hawk dreamed that he was young again and able to ride his favorite horse, *Pišco* — Nighthawk — who had been dead more than thirty years, and Nighthawk galloped so fast that he carried Loud Voice Hawk into the night air, into the lightning itself, and when the Black Hills were below him, a huge white *cetán* — a hawk like the one he had been named after seventy-four summers before — rose up out of those hills and the hawk was carrying a naked baby boy child in its talons.

Limps-a-Lot had not dreamed so much as had a vision. The thunder and lightning had wakened him and he had left his two wives and gone out into the hot, wild night—a night made wilder by the screams of Stands in Water dying as she worked to birth her child—and in the lightning to the north, beyond the hulking shape of *Matho Paha,* Bear Butte, Limps-a-Lot saw a baby boy's face drawn by lightning in the clouds above the Black Hills.

The morning after that fatherless boy was born and after the mother had bled to death and been prepared for burial by the women, Angry Badger, Loud Voice Hawk, and Limps-a-Lot met in a closed lodge for six hours, smoking the pipe and discussing their dreams and visions. They decided that—as odd as it would sound to all Natural Free Human Beings—the orphan baby, if he lived, should be named Paha Sapa, for the infant had come from the Black Hills in each of their dreams.

Paha Sapa has learned more about the details of his birth and about his dead parents than one might expect for a child who never knew his parents. He knows, for instance, exactly why his mother, Stands in Water, with only sixteen summers, died giving birth to him, and that her death was related to the fact that his equally young father, Short Elk, had been killed by Pawnee three months before Paha Sapa's birth.

He knew that Short Elk, who had not yet fully seen seventeen summers, had won Stands in Water in a raid on a Crow village where Short Elk had shown either much bravery or incredible stupidity. The Lakota raiding party had hit the Crow village, scattered their horses, and carried away several women—including Stands in Water, a Lakota who had been captive of the Crow for four years—and when the Crow warriors finally found horses, the twelve Lakota warriors had fled. But Short Elk had turned back, shouted *Hokahey!,* lifted his arms as if flying, and ridden through the Crow lines as they all fired and shot arrows at him. Nothing touched Short Elk. Then he rode *back* through the Crow skirmish lines, his eyes closed, his head thrown back, and his arms out to his sides. For his courage, Angry Badger and the other warriors had awarded him Stands in Water as his bride.

But then, three months before Paha Sapa was born, Short Elk—quite full of himself now, with six beautiful ponies to his name—had joined five older warriors on a raid on a large Pawnee village far to the west of the Black Hills. This raid was for ponies only, and Wolf Turning, the older warrior leading the raid, told the others that when they got the ponies, they would ride hard and not stop to fight. But again Short Elk showed himself a hero. Disobeying Wolf Turning during the wild ride back across the plains, Short Elk had slid off his horse, driven a stake into the prairie, attached a ten-foot thong to the stake, and then wrapped the other end of the thong around his waist. The idea was that he would not move from that place. Short Elk cried to the other five Lakota—

—*They cannot harm me! I see the future. The Six Grandfathers watch over me! Join me, my friends!*

The five older men pulled up their ponies but did not go back. They watched from a grassy hilltop two hundred broad paces away while fifty howling Pawnee rode Short Elk down and—in their anger at losing the ponies—leaped from their horses and cut the young, screaming warrior to pieces, gouging out his eyes while he lived and hacking off his arms, finally cutting his still-beating heart out of his body and taking turns biting into it. The five Lakota watching from the hilltop immediately left the stolen Pawnee horses behind and fled in terror across the prairie to their village.

Stands in Water had been in mourning—weeping, screaming, moaning, tearing at her hair, and slicing flesh from her forearms and thighs and upper arms and even from her breasts—for the full three months between Short Elk's death and her baby's birth.

Paha Sapa knew these things even when he was very young, not just because he had begun asking questions of his elders as soon as he could talk, but because of what he thought of as his *small-vision-backward-touching*.

Paha Sapa had used his *small-vision-backward-touching* since before he could speak or walk, and he was well into his running-around little-boy years before he realized that not everyone had the ability.

It did not always work. It usually did *not* work. But sometimes—and he could never predict when—the young Paha Sapa could touch another person's skin and receive a jumble of memories and voices and sounds and visual images that were not his own. It took him far longer to learn how to sort out these brief, powerful floods of *other-thoughts* so that he could make sense of them than it took him to learn to speak or walk or ride a pony or shoot a bow.

He remembers that when he was about three summers old, he touched the bare arm of Raven's Hair, Limps-a-Lot's younger wife (and Paha Sapa's wet nurse after his real mother died), and received a wave of confused memory-thoughts of Raven's Hair's own baby dying only weeks before Paha Sapa was born, of her anger at Limps-a-Lot for bringing this other infant into her lodge, of her strange anger at Stands in Water—Paha Sapa's dead mother—for grieving so terribly after her stupid boy-husband's death that she kept slashing her arms and thighs with her knife in mourning far beyond an appropriate amount of time for that sort of behavior, bleeding and weakening herself too much—especially if one is very small and with small hips and pregnant and not strong to begin with after a long captivity with the Crows, as Stands in Water had been.

At the age of three summers, Paha Sapa had seen through his *small-vision-touching* that his mother had come close to killing herself through this knife-slash mourning before he was born. Most Lakota women prided themselves on their relative ease of bearing children, feeling that *Wakan Tanka*—the All—had chosen them to be excused from at least a little of the pain and danger that afflicted all women everywhere. But at the age of three summers, touching Raven's Hair, Paha Sapa had *seen* his young mother, pale and weak and sweating, her legs apart and her *šan*—her woman's *winyaň shan*—open and ragged and bleeding, as Raven's Hair and Three Buffalo Woman and the other women used moss and warm clay and even strips of hide softened to the thinness of cloth to try to stem that terrible bleeding, even while other women held him, squealing his lungs out and with his umbilical cord still attached.

Paha Sapa had cried out and staggered away from Raven's Hair the day he had that touching-vision, and his stepmother—who had always treated him kindly, treated him almost as her real son—asked him what was wrong, what had happened, but Paha Sapa, at that age barely able to speak words in the language of the *Ikče Wičaśa*—the Natural Free Human Beings—had only cried and pulled away and been sick and feverish all that day and that night and all the next day.

After that, Paha Sapa both feared and wished for the *small-vision-backward-touchings* and slowly learned how to ask a question or direct a discussion to something he truly wanted to know about and then, as if by accident, touch one or more people near him, hoping to get the rush of their memories and mind-pictures.

Sometimes the magic worked; usually it did not.

But it seemed a shameful thing to Paha Sapa—like peeking under a tent flap to see a young maiden undressing, or deliberately watching Limps-a-Lot mating with Raven's Hair or his older wife, Three Buffalo Woman, on a warm night when the buffalo robes were thrown off—so he had not confessed his ability to his stepfather until he had reached his ninth summer, the year before the *Pehin Hanska Kasata*—the rubbing out of Long Hair at the Greasy Grass—that changed Paha Sapa's life forever.

———

IN HIS NINTH SUMMER, when he tells Limps-a-Lot about his visions, the holy man asks Paha Sapa several sharp questions about his *small-vision-backward-touching* experiences, seeking out lies or inconsistencies— obviously thinking that the boy has heard these things in other ways (since there is no privacy whatsoever in a tipi and very, very little in a band with only eighteen lodges). But when Paha Sapa tells of his *small-vision-touching* experience with Three Buffalo Woman, in which she remembered her time as a girl when she was captive of the Blackfeet and all the men took turns raping her and then burned the insides of her thighs with white-hot stones, Limps-a-Lot falls silent and his frown is fierce. Paha Sapa knows through the same *small-vision-backward-touching* that Three Buffalo Woman has never told anyone except Limps-a-Lot of those days, and that only once, many years before when Limps-a-Lot suggested (while they were gathering berries near Beaver Creek) that they should marry. The two never discussed it again or mentioned it to anyone else.

Finally, Limps-a-Lot says—

— *Why do you call this ability* small-vision-backward-touching *and not visions from the spirits, Black Hills?*

Paha Sapa hesitates. He has never lied to Limps-a-Lot, but he is afraid to answer honestly.

— *Because I know these*—glimpses—*are not my* hanblečeya, *Grandfather.*

Paha Sapa only calls his guardian Limps-a-Lot *Tunkašila*— Grandfather—at the most formal or most affectionate moments.

— *You know that is not what I meant, Black Hills. I am asking why you call* *these small visions* backward *visions. Do you touch people and also see* forward *in their minds and in time…do you see what will happen to them, to us, in the* *future?*

Paha Sapa hangs his head as if he's been caught touching his *ce.*

— *Han, Tunkašila.* Yes, Grandfather.

— *Do you want to tell me what* small-visions-forward-touching *you have* *had with me and others in our band?*

— *No, Grandfather.*

Limps-a-Lot says nothing for a very long time. It is late summer, the week of Paha Sapa's birth date, and the two have walked to a hill far enough away that the village lodges look like cloth girl-toy tipis under the cottonwood trees and the grazing horses across the river are mere black specks moving through the tan grass that rises to their bellies. Paha Sapa listens to the long, slow sibilance of the grass sighing and stirring in the breeze during Limps-a-Lot's silence. He will hear that sound again ten months later at the Greasy Grass when the shooting and screaming stop.

— *Very well, then, Black Hills. You showed courage by telling me these things.* *I will not press you to tell me about the* small-vision-forward-touching *visions* *until you are ready — but do not hesitate to do so if you see something that is impor-* *tant to the survival of our people.*

— *No, Tunkašila. I mean, yes, I will,* Tunkašila.

Limps-a-Lot grunts.

— *I will not tell Angry Badger or He Sweats or Loud Voice Hawk about your* *visions at this time. They already think you strange. But you and I should think* *about what this means for your* hanblečeya *in the Paha Sapa next year. Use this* *power carefully, Black Hills. Such a thing is* wakan.

Sacred. Filled with mysterious force.

— *Yes, Grandfather.*

— *It does not mean that you* must *become a* wičasa wakan, *a holy man like* *me, but it* does *mean that you have been chosen by the Six Grandfathers to be a* waayatan, *a man of vision who can see the future, like my young cousin Black Elk* *or your father's nephew in Good Thunder's band, Hoka Ushte. Waayatan often* *give their tribes* wakinyanpi *that may determine the band's fate.*

— *Yes, Tunkašila.*

Limps-a-Lot frowns at him in silence and Paha Sapa knows, even without touching the old man and receiving a backward-vision, that the wise *wičasa wakan* thinks that he, Paha Sapa, is too young and too immature for this *wakan* gift and that this vision-touching power might be bad for everyone. Finally Limps-a-Lot growls—

—*Hecetu. Mitakuye oyasin.*

So be it. All my relatives—every one of us.

NUMINOUS.

Paha Sapa learns the meaning of this *wasichu* word in English some forty-five years after *Pehin Hanska Kasata*—the rubbing out of Long Hair Custer at the Greasy Grass—and fifty-six years after his birth.

Numinous, the teacher and poet and historian Doane Robinson tells him, means everyday things charged and alive with spiritual or supernatural meaning surpassing all normal comprehension.

Paha Sapa almost laughs. He does not tell Mr. Robinson that his—Paha Sapa's—life was *numinous* up until the time it was taken over by *wasichus* and the *Wasicun* world.

The world of his childhood was literally alive with unseen meaning and connections and miracles; even the stones had lives and stories. The trees held sacred secrets. The prairie grasses stirred with truths half heard in whispers from the spirits that surrounded him and his band of Natural Free Human Beings. The sun was as real a being as his honorary grandfather or the other men walking past him in the daylight; the stars over the plains shivered from the breath of the dead walking up there; and the mountains on the horizon watched and waited for him with their revelations.

Numinous. Paha Sapa almost smiles when Doane Robinson teaches him that wonderful word.

But Paha Sapa's childhood was not all mystical portent and magical *small-vision-backward-or-forward-touching* of other people's memories or fates.

For most of his childhood, Paha Sapa was just a boy. Having no living parents was not a hardship for him—certainly not as large a problem as having such an odd name—since Lakota boys were not

taught, trained, punished, praised, and raised by their parents. All
Lakota parents were benevolently uninvolved with their kids to the
point of polite indifference. It was the other boys in the village who
taught Paha Sapa almost everything he needed to know from the time
he was old enough to toddle away from Raven's Hair's tit, including
where to go outside the village to take a shit and which reeds or grasses
it was safe to wipe his bottom with.

Lakota boys had few duties — other than watching over the grazing
pony herd in the daytime when they grew old enough for that — and
Paha Sapa played from early morning until after dark. After dark he
sat at the campfire as long as Three Buffalo Woman or Limps-a-Lot
would let him and listened to his elders there talk and tell stories in the
glow of the fire.

There were winter games and summer games for Paha Sapa to play.
There were games with sticks and games with hide-wrapped balls and
games with the river they almost always camped near and games with
hands and games that involved horses. Most of the boy-games that
Paha Sapa took part in involved shoving, pushing, the occasional fist-
fight, and more than occasional injuries. That was fine with Paha Sapa.
He might not be training to be a warrior — he was, at that time, not
sure yet — and did not spend much time thinking about whether he
would be *a wičasa wakan,* a holy man, like his beloved *tunkašila* Limps-a-
Lot, but he loved rough play and didn't mind facing down even larger
boys in a fight.

A lot of the boy-games were war games — preparation — and one
that Paha Sapa especially enjoyed was when the young boys, with a
few older ones, would go off onto the prairie on their own and make
their own boy-village, complete with grass tipis. And then they would
plan their raid on the *real* village. The band would have an older-boy
adviser, and that boy would send them off to steal some meat from the
village of the big people. This was serious enough to be exciting, since
the women — much less the warriors — would cuff and kick any boy
found stealing meat.

Paha Sapa and the others crawled on their bellies through the high
grass, just as if they were attacking a Crow or Pawnee or Cheyenne or
Blackfoot or Shoshoni village rather than their own, and then they had

to creep up on the meat (buffalo tongue was the best) hanging to dry or waiting to be cooked—or even steal it from someone's tipi—and then run away and get back to the boy-village without being caught or run down by an irritated warrior on his horse. Once back at their grass-tipi village, the boys would build their own fire and roast the meat while telling made-up stories of their bravery and their kills—kill-talks, the real warriors called such bragging—and often an older boy would hold the roasted and sizzling and dripping tongue on a stick, as high as he could hold it, and the younger boys would leap to bite off a piece. Those who could not leap high did not eat.

All the boys had little bows made for them by their fathers or uncles or some friendly warrior, but the arrows had few feathers and had blunt knobs rather than stone- or steel-barbed points on the end. Still, they hurt when they struck, and the boys spent much time stalking one another in groups along the banks of the river or in the willow groves or out in the wind-moving high grass. Decades later, Paha Sapa remembers the excitement of those boy-hunts.

When Paha Sapa got a little older—although he never grew very tall—he would join the oldest boys in their game called Throwing-Them-Off-Their-Horses. The boys were always naked when they played this game, and in many ways it was less of a game than a real battle without dead bodies at the end of it. They especially enjoyed playing it when there were several bands, most larger than Paha Sapa's little band under their leader, Angry Badger, pitching their lodges together near Bear Butte or in one of the better sheltered valleys.

The boys would group themselves in various teams, smear their naked bodies with berry juice, clay, and other stains approximating warrior paint, and then line their horses up and charge at one another, coming together with many shouts and yells and the crashing of rearing, screaming horses in the dust. The naked boys would seize one another and tug and pull and shove and elbow and strike out with their fists. When a boy fell to the ground, he was dead and had to stay dead. The last boy still on his horse was the winner of the battle and could tell his kill-stories around the boy-fires that night.

Sometimes Paha Sapa stayed on his horse during Throwing-Them-Off-Their-Horses, but more often—because he was short and slim—he was thrown heavily to the ground, once landing on a prickly pear bush. Three Buffalo Woman had spent hours that night carefully pulling thorns out of Paha Sapa's legs and back and belly and backside, while Limps-a-Lot smoked his regular smoking pipe and chuckled from time to time. The next morning, Paha Sapa went out to play the game again, although he did try to sit lightly on the horse's bare back, since his equally bare butt was sore and swollen.

There were other summer games like *Ta-hu-ka-can-kle-ska,* between the boys, ball games with balls made of scraps of buckskin wound into a wad and covered with more buckskin sewn together by sinew. Later, when Paha Sapa is playing on the Keystone baseball team that Gutzon Borglum has his men join each summer, competing with all the surrounding South Dakota towns and clubs—sometimes Borglum hires men to work on carving Mount Rushmore specifically because they are good at baseball—Paha Sapa often thinks of the small, hard hide *Ta-hu-ka-can-kle-ska* balls of his childhood. They were hit with specially prepared ash sticks—and hit while the boy was running—and the *Ta-hu-ka-can-kle-ska* balls were very hard and lasted as long as or longer than the Wilson and Rawlings hardballs that Borglum's baseball team plays tournaments with.

Both the boys and girls in Paha Sapa's band had as many games to play in the winter as they did in summer. Many of these were sticks-sliding-on-ice-or-snow games like *Hu-ta-na-cu-te* for the boys or *Pte-hes-te* or *Pa-slo-han-pi* for the girls. Sometimes when there were hills nearby, the older boys made sleds—called *can-wo-slo-han*—from the rib cages of buffalo or elk, with runners made from bone, and sometimes the boys allowed the girls to ride downhill or along the frozen river with them in their *can-wo-slo-han.*

During the many days and even weeks in winter when the hours of daylight were short and the weather was too snowy or blowing or cold to spend much time outside except for necessary duties, there were inside-the-tipi games that Paha Sapa and the others could play, such as *ta-si-ha,* where the game toy was made from the ankle bones of a deer and then strung on a buckskin string, narrow end down. At the end of that string, they tied little bones together. Paha Sapa remembers that they used about eight of these *ta-si-ha* bones in the game and that the other end of the buckskin string was tied to an eagle's wing.

When the boys and girls played together, they would take turns holding the eagle wing bone in their right hand and the tassel in their left, swinging the ankle bones out in front of them. If the other player managed to catch the first bone, the play went on. If he or she missed, they passed the *ta-si-ha* to the next person in line. Paha Sapa was very good at this game; his hands were fast and his eyes were good. After catching that first bone ten times, the teams would start on the second, third, and so forth, until all ten players would have caught the tassel. Other inside-the-tipi games, Paha Sapa remembers, included *i-ca-sio-he*, a sort of marbles game—although the marbles were almost perfectly round stones, which were hard to find. The boys prayed to the Six Grandfathers and to *Wakan Tanka* himself to help them find perfectly round *i-ca-sio-he* stones, and they were always found.

It was a silly game called *istokikicastakapi* that led to Paha Sapa's discovering his *touch-the-earth-to-fly* ability.

HE IS SEVEN SUMMERS and playing *istokikicastakapi* with a group of the younger boys, most his age or younger. The game consists of chewing rosebush berries, spitting the pits into your hand, and then wheeling to throw the pits into someone's face before he can duck or escape.

There is an obnoxious boy just Paha Sapa's age playing that day named Fat Frog—and the name is appropriate, for besides being fat he is a *takoja*, a pampered and spoiled grandson of the lazy old man named Feet in the Fire—and while they are running in their circle near the creek and playing *istokikicastakapi*, Fat Frog grabs Paha Sapa, pulls his head close, and spits in his face. There are almost no rosebush berry pits, just spit. Curds and slimy trails of Fat Frog spit all over Paha Sapa's face.

Paha Sapa does not wait to think; he balls his fist and strikes Fat Frog square in the middle of his fat face, bloodying his nose and knocking the boy backward into a prickly pear. Fat Frog screams and calls to his three older cousins standing nearby, boys who also live in Feet in the Fire's lazy lodge, and the three older boys leap on Paha Sapa and

strike him with their fists and feet and with willow branches, all while
Fat Frog is screaming and holding his bleeding nose and crying that
Paha Sapa broke it and that he's going to tell his grandfather, and Feet
in the Fire will come find Paha Sapa and *kill him* with the knife that
Feet in the Fire used to scalp ten *wasichus*.

When the three larger cousins are finished beating on Paha Sapa,
they kick him in the ribs once or twice and go away. Paha Sapa lies
there hurting, but he has no impulse to cry. It is all too funny, especially
the image of old, fat Feet in the Fire chasing him with a scalping knife.
He only hopes that he *did* break Fat Frog's nose.

When he gets up and dusts himself off, Paha Sapa realizes that he
has got blood—mostly his own, he thinks—spattered down the front
of his second-best deerskin shirt. Three Buffalo Woman will beat him
for sure when he goes back to the lodge.

Paha Sapa only shakes his head—still amused—and limps away
from the village, wanting to be alone for a while.

A little over a mile from the village, out of sight of all the tipis and
even of the horses and the boys and men who guard them, Paha Sapa
comes to a low, wide area where for some reason the prairie grasses
are low, almost like what he will someday learn is called a "lawn."
Paha Sapa lies down on this soft grass and soft dirt and kicks off his
han'pa—his moccasins.

He lies there on his back with his arms spread wide, the soles of his
feet turned down hard against the evening-cooling soil, and his curving, clinging toes—his *siphas*—curling hard into the dirt.

Paha Sapa almost closes his eyes, squinting through what seem like
tears even though he has not been crying, and looks up at a paling evening sky of a deep blue that seems disturbingly familiar to the boy. He
relaxes completely—first loosening the muscles in his tensed neck,
then letting his arms go limp, then releasing the pressure on his curving fingers and clawing toes, then uncoiling something deep inside his
belly. For some reason he cries out *Hokahey!* as if he is a warrior riding
into battle.

What happens next is very difficult for him to describe later, even
to himself. He will not tell his beloved *tunkašila* Limps-a-Lot about his
touch-the-earth-to-fly experiences until several more years have passed.

Paha Sapa senses the earth spinning as if it were a ball instead of a flat thing. He sees the stars wheeling in the evening sky even though the stars have not yet come out. He hears the song the setting sun is singing and can hear the answering song the grasses and plants are singing back to it as the light begins to fade. Then Paha Sapa feels his body grow cold and heavy and distant from him even as *he*—the spirit-self Paha Sapa—becomes more and more buoyant. Then his spirit-self floats up out of his body and away from the earth.

He rises for many minutes before he thinks to roll over onto his stomach in midair and look down. He is so high that he cannot see his body that he left behind, so high that the village is only barely visible as a scattering of tan tipis under tiny trees along a river receding from sight. Paha Sapa rolls onto his back again and continues to rise, higher yet, rising past the few scattered clouds showing pink now in the low rays of the setting sun, and then he is higher than all the clouds.

He looks and rolls over again. The sky above him grows black even as the clouds so far below begin to glow pinker and the shadows on the earth grow longer. Paha Sapa *knows* that it is terribly cold just outside his spirit-skin—colder than any winter air that has ever touched him—just as he *knows* that the air up here is too thin to breathe, but none of that affects his spirit-body and spirit-self. He ceases rising when the sky is black all around and when the stars are burning above the blue blanket of air below, and he looks down with eyes suddenly grown as sharp as an eagle's.

What he sees on that round earth—he can plainly see the horizon curving from where he silently floats—are the Paha Sapa, the Black Hills. The Black Hills are an oval between the Belle Fourche River to the north and the Cheyenne River, where the actual tribes of Cheyenne, driven out of the Black Hills and northern plains by the Sioux a century earlier, still live and hunt. The Black Hills, Paha Sapa now sees, are an oval inland island that he will later learn constitutes about forty-five hundred square miles of dark trees and hills, all enclosed by an almost sexual oval ridge of red sandstone that sets the hills off dramatically from the tan and dull green of the endless sagebrush prairie surrounding them. The Black Hills look like a woman's *winyan shan,* with pink, open lips. Or perhaps like a heart.

For the first time, seeing the geological rut and rim surrounding the Black Hills from this height, Paha Sapa understands why Limps-a-Lot has called that long, depressed, hogback-ridged oval that surrounds the Black Hills the "Race Track," because of a story of all the animals racing one another there back when the world was young. It does look like a track worn down by racing feet.

Paha Sapa also realizes why Limps-a-Lot and his people call the place *O'onakezin,* or Place of Shelter. The Black Hills, he sees, are the dark heart of the heart of this entire continent he can now see spreading away to either side until the haze near the curve of the horizon hides the details. It is the place where both animals and the Natural Free Human Beings can go to shelter when the winter winds howl too terribly on the plains and the game all disappears. This must be why Angry Badger and the other men also call the Black Hills the "Meat Pack." Paha Sapa, floating easily on his belly with his arms wide while he looks down at the evening shadows outlining the high peaks, understands that there will always be game and shelter in the Black Hills for his people.

Then he sees something moving in the Black Hills—something gray and huge rising up out of the black trees as if new mountains were being born. They seem to be human forms, four of them, and from their size even at this distance, they must be hundreds of feet tall.

But he cannot make out details. Suddenly the peaceful feeling he's had since lying on the ground is gone and his heart is pounding wildly, but he has the sense that the giants are pale *wasichus*—monster *Wasicun.*

Then the huge, gray forms lie down again and pull the earth over them like blankets and are again covered and hidden by dark soil and darker trees.

Paha Sapa begins to settle earthward. He does so slowly, the rays from the setting sun painting him bright red—he vaguely wonders if those in the village are looking up at him—but he does so with a heart and spirit that remain perturbed and disturbed. He is not sure what he saw below, but he knows it is not a good thing.

Paha Sapa opens his eyes and he is lying on his back in the little clearing in the sagebrush. Somewhere a coyote calls. Or perhaps it is a Pawnee or Crow or Shoshoni warrior in a raiding party making ready to fall upon the village with bows and rifles and tomahawks.

Paha Sapa is too tired and disturbed to care. He gets to his feet slowly and begins trudging back to the village. The coyote is answered by several other coyotes. They are only coyotes.

The next year, when Paha Sapa confesses about his *small-vision-backward-touching* to Limps-a-Lot, he refuses to tell the details of the few times he has experienced *small-vision-forward-touching* because he has seen forward to people dying. He will not mention his *touch-the-earth-to-fly* times because he begins not to believe in them himself.

When he gets home, Three Buffalo Woman does beat him (but with no real intention to hurt) for getting his second-best deer-hide shirt bloody.

5

George Armstrong Custer

*L*ibbie, my darling Libbie, my dearest Libbie, Libbie my love, my life, my everything, my Libbie —

  I need you, my darling girl.

 I have been lying here in the dark thinking of the time five weeks ago on May 17 — was it only five weeks ago? — when I led the regiment out of Fort Abraham Lincoln on this mission. You will recall, my dearest, that the day started cold and foggy before sunrise. I had the men eat hardtack and bacon, just as they would for the next month on the trail. Then General Terry and I marched the men through the rising mists to the fort — you always tell me that you wonder why our frontier forts have no stockades, my love — and then around the parade ground in columns of four so as to reassure the anxious wives and families and troopers we were leaving behind.

 But you were not left behind then, my darling girl, my love. The other officers had to bid farewell to their families outside the fort, but you rode along with us that day, along with my sister, Maggie, and my niece Emma. Do you remember as we passed Suds Row, the married enlisted men's quarters, all the women holding their babies and toddlers and even older children up and out toward us as they wailed? It made me think of a Triumph where the Roman general has returned in glory, only a bizarrely reversed one in this case, before any battles, where the wives of perfectly healthy troopers decide they are widows and treat their babes like orphans.

 We had more than seven hundred troopers in our line that day, thirty-one officers (most of them riding in the mass with you and me and Maggie and Emma), forty-five scouts and guides, and those three extra companies of infantry with that artillery detachment of four guns that followed those first days as an escort. (Yes, perhaps I should not have turned down the two batteries of Gatling guns Terry wanted me to take—but I'm sure you remember, my dearest, how those damned guns had slowed us down so on previous patrols, frequently pulling horses and men down with them when they tumbled into ravines or creek beds. A good cavalry unit has to travel light. No, if I were to do it again, I would still leave the Gatling guns behind.)

What a sight the regiment and its escort must have been that morning. The column stretched for more than two miles. I know that the regimental band was playing "The Girl I Left Behind Me" and "Garry Owen"—all through the War I loved that latter song, but I confess that I have been growing weary of it in these later years, my dear—but you and I couldn't really hear the music because of the clatter of our horses' hooves, the rumble of the hundred and fifty wagons, and the constant bellowing of the herd of cattle we'd brought with us.

It did not matter.

None of that departure matters except what happened thirteen miles down the trail, when it was time for you to turn back to the fort. Do you remember? I know you do, my love. The memory of it is what woke me from my cold slumbers here.

The group of us, including Maggie and Emma and my striker, Private Burkham, and the paymaster's old wagon with its small escort, rode back about half a mile behind the column for us to say our good-byes. You surprised me by dismounting and suggesting that we—just you and I—take a walk among the willows that rose along the river there. These were the only high trees and shrubs for many miles; all the rest, back to Fort Lincoln and forward to where we were headed, was flat, open prairie.

We'd walked less than fifty yards from Burkham and the wagon and the other women when you suddenly seized me and kissed me hard. You removed my hat and ran your hand over my short-cropped hair, smiling as you did so. You did not seem to miss what you always called my "lovely curly locks." Then you took the flat of your hand and began rubbing me below my belt buckle.

"Libbie . . ." I said, glancing back over my shoulder and over the thick willows to where I could still see the heads of Maggie and Emma, since they had remained mounted.

"Hush," you said.

And then you went to your knees, but not—I remember clearly—until you had swished out the skirt of your dress (you wore my favorite that day, the blue one with the corn silk little flowers on it) and your petticoats so they would not be stained by the damp grass.

And then you unbuttoned my fly.

"Libbie…"

But I could say no more, my darling, for you had taken me into your soft hands and then into your mouth, and I forgot Burkham and the waiting wagons, forgot my sister and my niece, forgot even the seven hundred men and hundred and fifty wagons and hundreds of cattle with the regiment now leaving me behind.

I forgot everything except the stroking of your hands, the warmth of your mouth, the movement of your lips and tongue upon me.

I arched my head back once, but I did not close my eyes. The blue sky — it had turned into a hot May day after the early morning fog and mist — disturbed me somehow, as if the color were a portent. So I looked back down at you and what you were doing with me and to me.

I always look, my dearest love. You know that. You know everything about me. Any other woman doing such a thing — I have never known any other woman to do such a thing — would, I would think, look bizarre, absurd, perhaps obscene, but when you take me in your mouth like that with your head bobbing back and forth, your hands still moving on me, your lips and tongue rapacious, and your lovely eyes glancing up at me from time to time from under those beautiful lashes, there could be nothing bizarre, absurd, or obscene in the gift you are giving me, in the sort of love you are showing me. You are beautiful. It makes me excited this very second, here in the darkness, to think of you, your cheeks pink with the sun after that long day of riding and also pink with excitement, the top of your lovely head, the sunlight catching individual hairs on either side of the part, moving faster and faster.

When we were finished — it had only taken a minute, I know, but it was a minute of pure joy and pleasure before weeks of solitude and care and hardship for me — you removed the handkerchief you had brought, dipped it in the stream, cleaned me up, tucked me in, and set the buttons of my tough blue cavalry trousers to rights.

Then we went back and said our formal farewells in front of Burkham and the others. We both had tears in our eyes, but neither of us could keep from smiling, could we, my darling?

When the wagon and you and the other women were mere dots receding across the prairie, Burkham startled me by saying, "It's hard, ain't it, General?"

Again I wanted to smile, although I forced myself not to. Remembering that Burkham might be one of those interviewed by the press — several correspondents came with us, you remember, and more waited in Bismark and elsewhere for every word of our punitive expedition — I put on my saddest, sternest face and said to him, "Private, a good soldier — and I have always been a good soldier, Burkham — has to serve two mistresses. While he's loyal to one, the other must suffer."

Burkham grunted, evidently not moved by my eloquence. He swung up onto his gelding and said, "Shall we get back to the other mistress, General, before the tail-end of it gets out of sight?"

Libbie, my darling girl. I know you do not mind my talking of such things with you, since I have written you so many letters filled with such intimate thoughts, and whispered them to you while we lay together naked. You have always been more open and generous with your passion than any other woman in the world.

Do you remember the time when I could no longer bear to be apart from you (and I had heard that cholera had broken out at Fort Leavenworth, where you were waiting), so I wrote you from my Republican River camp telling you to come at once to Fort Wallace, where my men would bring you to my camp on the Republican, but Pawnee Killer and the hostiles were swarming everywhere there in Kansas, and I realized, too late, that they would almost surely attack the rich wagon train you would be traveling in, so I ordered the men who would be picking you up to shoot you rather than let the Indians capture you — later, you told me that this was terribly sweet and that you took it as a sure sign of my undying love — but when the wagon train (which indeed had been attacked by five hundred or so Sioux and Cheyenne, right where Comstock, the guide whom the Indians call Medicine Bill, had predicted they would attack, but the hostiles were driven off) returned from Fort Wallace, there was no sign of you and I went half mad with worry and passion? I love you so much, my dear, sweet, darling little girl.

You will remember that they had sent Lieutenant Lyman Kidder out from Fort Sedgwick to find my column, and he and his ten men had dropped out of sight right in the territory between us and Fort Wallace where I had feared for your life. I called for a forced march to Fort Wallace — primarily out of concern for you, my dearest — and we found what was left of Kidder and his men, stripped and hacked and scattered all over a little hollow. Comstock explained to us what the tracks told — of how Kidder and his small party had tried to run, how Pawnee Killer and his band had caught them from the rear, run them down, shot them with arrows, then murdered and mutilated them. It was a July day, and the bodies and men's parts had been lying in that sun for days, and I took the lesson then—and shall never forget it—that when faced by any serious force of Indians, the thing to do is to stand and fight, using your far superior firepower to keep the savages out of arrow range. Kidder had galloped in panic for more than ten miles, and although our cavalry horses are faster than Indian ponies, the Indians are ingenious at swapping their tired mounts for fresh ones, and some of the Indian ponies simply never tire.

Never run from Indians *was the lesson I learned that July day nine years ago, standing there in the Kansas heat and stench watching the burial party inter the awful remains of Lieutenant Kidder and his men. And all that time I was sick with worry about you, my dearest—so worried that my belly constantly hurt and cramped with anxiety.*

Kansas was burning. Pawnee Killer and the other hostile Sioux and Cheyenne had slaughtered more than two hundred whites, including many women and children, in the area I was supposed to patrol on my first western expedition, and the cavalry had shot and killed only two of the redmen—and those had been killed by Kidder's party before they died.

So I called off the campaign and drove a hundred men and horses one hundred and fifty miles in fifty-five hours. Stragglers fell behind and were killed by Pawnee Killer's braves, but I would not go back to recover our dead or to chase the hostiles. You were all that I could think of. On July 18, I reached Fort Hayes and left ninety-four of the men there, taking only my brother Tom, two officers, and two troopers on a sixty-mile ride to Fort Harker, which we covered in less than twelve hours. There I left Tom and the four men behind and took the three a.m. train to Fort Riley, where—I prayed to God—I would find you waiting for me in relative safety.

Do you remember our reunion, my darling?

*You were in your quarters, pacing, wearing the green dress I had praised at Fort Hayes the previous month. You wrote me later that the vision of me when I threw open the door and entered the room was brighter than even the brilliant Kansas sun—*There before me, blithe and buoyant, stood my husband!*—you later told me that you wrote to your stepmother, but what you did not tell the dear second Mrs. Judge Bacon was that besides being visibly blithe and buoyant, I was also visibly aching for you, my sex as rigid and far more straight and much more in need of use right then than the securely sheathed saber banging at my leg.*

Do you remember, my darling, me—still dusty from the trail and railway—slamming the door and lifting you up and carrying you to the bed there in your quarters, smothering you with kisses and fumbling in your clothes while you fumbled at my buttons, then you unlacing your stays and lowering the top of your dress while I tore off your petticoats and pantaloons? Do you remember my spurs gouging the footboard of that bed that had been so carefully brought out all the way to Fort Riley while you rolled me onto my back, mounted me as I might leap onto Vic, seized me in your eager hand, and guided me into you?

You may remember that we were finished in seconds—our cries probably distracting the sentries on the ramparts—but, as has been our wont since our honeymoon, in minutes we started up again, tearing off the rest of our clothes even while we petted and kissed and stroked and suckled at each other.

I know I slept then, after the second bout of our lovemaking, slept for the first time in five hard-ridden days and more than five hundred miles, but you woke me two hours later. You'd had the orderlies and men carry in bucket after bucket of hot steaming water, them trying to tiptoe in their high boots past the bed where I snored naked under the light sheet (my clothes in disarray all over the floor, you not giving a fig what they might have thought), and when I woke, the curtains were closed and you were standing naked next to the bed, beckoning me to the bath.

Oh, the luxury of that claw-foot tub in that palace of a senior officer's visiting wife's billet in Fort Riley!

We had to leave by train that evening, taking you and your servant Eliza and the cookstove back to Fort Harker by rail so we could begin the long ride and wagon drive back to Fort Wallace, but that hour in the hot bath . . . Do you remember, my Libbie, my darling? Do you remember leaning back against me in the steam as I cupped your beautiful breasts and kissed your beautiful neck and your lovely ears and your luscious lips, kissing you again when you twisted around so that your lips could find me and so that you could turn and fall upon me, your hand going down in the hot water to find me again?

Oh, my darling Libbie—I remember my tongue against your sweet cunnie and your sweet mouth on my sex. We made love eight times that afternoon and you came ten times, both of us knowing even in our hunger and joy that it would be long days of hard travel and no privacy before we could so much as kiss again. I remember when we were dressing in a hurry to pay our compliments to the commander before rushing Eliza and the trunks and stove to the station—Eliza had taken and washed and ironed all my filthy clothes while you and I were alone and naked; she was used enough to that—and I started buttoning my fly, and you, in your corset and nothing else, the hair of the V of your sex still wet from the bath, stayed my hand and then went to your knees one final time. . . .

You'll remember, my sweet, that when I returned I was court-martialed for, among other things, abandoning my post. It was a year suspension without pay and reduction in rank. I would face a thousand courts-martial and suffer ten thousand suspensions for you, my dearest. But you know that. You've always known that.

I need you, Libbie. I do not know where I am. It is dark here, dark and cold. I hear sounds and voices, but they are muffled and seem to come from very, very far away. I am having trouble remembering the last hours, days, minutes, our march, the Indians, any battles we had… I remember almost nothing but the absolute verity of you, my sweetheart.

In truth, my love, I cannot recall where I have been or what has happened. My guess is that I have been wounded, perhaps seriously, although I cannot seem to gain consciousness sufficiently to know whether my body is intact, my limbs still attached. Sometimes I hear people speaking nearby, but I can never quite make out what they are saying. Perhaps I am in some hospital with German nurses. All I know is that I still retain my wits and my memories of you and our love here in this comatic darkness. I hope to God that it is mere sunstroke or concussion, which, as you know, has happened to me before, and that I will fully awaken soon.

You do not want your Autie damaged, your beautiful boy's slim body inordinately scarred or missing necessary parts. I have promised you… I promised you when I left Fort Lincoln… I have always promised you, during the War, before every campaign out here on the plains… that I will return and that we will be together forever and forever and forever.

Oh, Libbie…Libbie, my darling…my dearest girl, my sweet wife. My love. My life.

6

On the Six Grandfathers

August 1936

06 STEPS.

Paha Sapa pauses at the base of the stairway and looks up at the 506 steps he has to climb. They are the same 506 steps he has climbed almost every weekday morning for the past five years. It is 6:45 on a summer morning—Friday, 21 August—and already the sun has turned the air in the valley as hot as it gets here in the Black Hills. The air is filled with the sound of grasshoppers and the butterscotch scent of heated ponderosa pine. Because it's Friday, Paha Sapa knows, the crew coming down from the top this evening will play their "mountain goating" game—the 506 steps are separated into flights by some forty-five ramps and platforms, and the goal of the cheering workmen will be to "mountain goat" down by leaping from platform to platform without touching any of the fifty or so steps in between. No one has ever done this successfully, Paha Sapa knows, but no one has broken his neck or leg either, so the mountain goating will happen at the end of this long workday as well, the wild leaping accompanied by the shouts and cheers of the hardworking drillmen and hoist men and miners and powdermen released for their weekend.

Paha Sapa looks up at the 506 steps and realizes that he is tired even before beginning the climb.

Of course, he is seventy-one years old this month, but this is not the reason for his fatigue so early in the day. The cancer that Paha Sapa was diagnosed with just a month earlier—in Casper, Wyoming, so that no word would reach Borglum or the workers as it might if he'd gone to a doctor in nearby Rapid City—is already eating him from the inside out. He can feel it. It means that he has less time than he had hoped.

But Paha Sapa, even though he carries a forty-pound box of blasting caps and fresh dynamite on his shoulder, does not pause to rest on one of the forty-five ramps or landings on the way up. His strength has always been surprising for a man of his size, and he will not surrender to weakness now until it becomes absolutely necessary. And it is not yet necessary.

Paha Sapa has often heard visitors below estimate the height from the valley floor (where the parking lot and Borglum's studio are) to the top of the stone heads as "thousands of feet," but it's only a little over four hundred feet from the lowest point at the base of the talings of tumbled shards and boulders to the tops of Washington's and Jefferson's and (emerging) Lincoln's heads. Still, that's the equivalent of climbing the stairs in a forty-story building—something that Paha Sapa has seen in New York—and it takes the men about fifteen minutes to climb to the top of what is now called Mount Rushmore.

Of course, there's always the aerial tram—that open-topped, small-outhouse-sized box that is whizzing past Paha Sapa as he trudges up another flight of fifty steps—but even the new men know about the time some years ago when the A-frame tipi structure at the top of the mountain collapsed, sending the tram (and cable and A-frame and platform from above) hurtling to the floor of the canyon. Borglum was waiting to ride on the tram that day—he was always zipping up and down or hovering in it, studying some aspect of the work or hauling up VIPs—but the tram had just been loaded with casks of water, so Borglum waited and watched it fall. He still rides it daily.

But few of the other workers do, especially after a second accident earlier this summer in which the loosening setscrew had let go some two hundred feet from the top, sending the tram with five men aboard hurtling down toward the hoist house below. They'd rigged a hand brake since the first accident years ago, but the brake quickly overheated, so the only way they could slow the tram cage was by coming down in a series of spurts and jerks, pausing to let the brake cool, then spurting and jerking their way down again. Then Gus Schramm, who must weigh 225 pounds, pulled on the chain so hard that the brake arm broke off completely, sending the cage hurtling down the last hundred feet or so. Luckily, Matt Riley in the hoist house had the presence of mind to brace a fat board against the cable drum, which slowed them slightly, but the five men still went flying out of the tram cage at the end, three landing on the loading platform, another on a roof, the last man in a tree. Lincoln Borglum, senior man on the site that day, sent the five men to the hospital for observation, but six men ended up spending the night there. Glenn Jones, the man assigned to drive the others to Rapid City, decided to get a good night's sleep and some pain-killer at the hospital.

In the summer, the workers are expected to be at work at 7 a.m. (7:30 in the winter), but Paha Sapa and the other powdermen are usually there by 6:30, since they have to start early in preparing the dynamite charges that will soon be placed in holes being drilled that morning. The first blow of the day will be at noon, while the drillers are off the face having lunch. Paha Sapa knows that "Whiskey Art" Johnson is already up there with his assistant, cutting the dynamite into smaller segments—sixty or seventy short sticks for each shot—and that Paha Sapa's assistant will be there soon.

Reaching the halfway point on the 506 steps, Paha Sapa looks up at the three heads.

It has been a productive year so far, with more than 15,000 tons of granite removed—enough to pave a four-acre field with granite blocks a foot thick. Much of that rubble came from Washington's chest, which is taking shape nicely, but they've also cleared out many tons from beneath Jefferson's chin (where he now takes shape in his new spot to Washington's left, looking out from the Monument) and in roughing out Abraham Lincoln's forehead, eyebrows, and nose.

The majority of the rubble, though, came from the frenzied work on Thomas Jefferson's face, which Borglum is rushing to get ready for a possible visit and dedication in late August by no less than President Franklin Delano Roosevelt.

The presidential visit has been rumored for months, but now it seems certain to happen in just over a week—on Sunday, August 30.

Still climbing with the heavy box on his shoulder, Paha Sapa wonders if this should be the time for him to act.

Paha Sapa has no wish to harm President Roosevelt, but he still has every intention of blowing the other three presidents' heads off the face of the Six Grandfathers. And would it be more symbolic, somehow, if he eradicated these *wasichu* excrescences while the president of the United States sat in his open touring car below?

Paha Sapa knows that Borglum is planning a symbolic blasting as part of President Roosevelt's dedication ceremony. His son, Lincoln, has already been directed to find the best way to drape the huge American flag, now in storage, over Jefferson's face, the flag to be swung to one side by the long boom of the pointing machine atop the heads. There is to be a reviewing stand for dignitaries behind where Roosevelt's car will be parked, and live radio microphones and half a dozen newsreel cameras grinding. If Paha Sapa is successful in triggering charges on all *three* of the heads that Sunday, no one will be hurt, but the entire world will watch in movie theater newsreels the final destruction of the three heads on what would have been the Monument on Mount Rushmore.

Three heads.

There is part of the problem. Paha Sapa knows all too well Gutzon Borglum's plan for four heads up there, the last one being that of Theodore Roosevelt, tucked in between Jefferson and Lincoln. The stone experts are already drilling and coring to confirm that the granite there will be of adequate quality for the carving, and though many have protested Borglum's putting so recent a president up there — and another Republican to boot — Paha Sapa knows how stubborn Borglum is. If the sculptor lives (and perhaps even if he does not, with Lincoln taking over), there will be a Teddy Roosevelt head on Mount Rushmore.

Paha Sapa's Vision was of four *wasichu* Great Stone Heads rising out of the Six Grandfathers, *four* giant stone *wasichus* shrugging off the soil and trees of the Paha Sapa, and *four* of these terrible giants looking out and over the destruction of Paha Sapa's people and of the buffalo and of the Natural Free Human Beings' way of life.

Does he not have to destroy all four heads to keep this Vision from coming true?

More to the point, Paha Sapa realizes as he approaches the final flights of steps, does he now have *time* to wait for that fourth head to be carved?

The doctor in Casper said no. *A few months,* the white-haired doctor said solemnly but with no emotion, just another old Indian sitting on his examining table, *perhaps a year if you're unlucky.*

Paha Sapa understood that the "unlucky" referred to the pain and immobilization and incontinence this form of cancer would give him if the dying dragged on.

———

PAHA SAPA PASSES the wooden landing with a flat bit of graveled soil between the boulders where the men ambushed him each morning for weeks after he was first hired by Borglum five years earlier.

To their credit, they never attacked him all at once. Each morning they'd have another champion to beat the old Indian into submission, to beat him so badly that he would have to quit. One of the larger, more violent miners in the early attacks.

And each morning, Paha Sapa refused to be beaten into submission. He fought back fiercely, with fists and jabs and head butts and kicks to the bigger man's balls when he could. He sometimes won. More often he lost. But he always took a toll on his assailant, morning after morning. And he was never beaten so badly by the white men's single champion that he—Paha Sapa—could not lift his drill or crate of explosives and helmet and gear and continue the painful climb toward the powder shack, where he would begin work. And though they broke his nose and blackened his eyes and pulped his lips over those weeks, they never managed to disfigure his face so much that he couldn't don the filtration mask and go to work.

Finally, Borglum noticed and called all the men together in a meeting outside his studio on Doane Mountain opposite the work site.

—*What the goddamned hell is going on?*

Silence from the men. Borglum's usual roar of a voice became an even louder roar, drowning out the compressor that had just started up.

—*I'm goddamned serious. I've got a powderman who is obviously getting the excrement beaten out of him every day and two dozen other workers with missing teeth and rearranged noses. Now, I need to know what the goddamned hell is going on and I'll know it right* now. *There are thousands of miners and workmen and powdermen out of work, right here in South Dakota, who'll take your jobs in a fast minute, and I'm about fifteen seconds away from giving those jobs to them.*

The answer, such as it was, came from someone deep in the press of men.

—*It's the Indian.*

—*WHAT?*

Borglum's roar this time was so loud that the compressor actually stopped, the operator—the only man not at the meeting—obviously thinking that the machinery had seized up.

—*What goddamned Indian? Do you think I'd hire an Indian for this job?*

The question was answered by silence and a sullen shuffling.

—*Well, you're goddamned RIGHT I'd hire an Indian if he was the best man for the job—or a nigger, if it came to that—but Billy Slovak is no damned Indian!*

Howdy Peterson stepped forward.

—*Mr. Borglum...sir. His name ain't Billy Slovak. On the lists up at the Homestake, and the Holy Terror Mine before that, they had him down as Billy Slow Horse...sir. And he...he looks* like *an Indian, Mr. Borglum, sir.*

Borglum shook his head as if as much in pity as disgust.

—*Goddamn it, Peterson. Are you all Norwegian or did a little coon or Cheyenne or wop sneak in there? And who the hell* CARES? *This man I hired is named Billy Slovak—part Czech or Bohunk or whatever the hell it is, and why should I care?—and he was CHIEF POWDERMAN at the goddamned Homestake Mine when I hired him. Do you know how long powdermen usually last at the Homestake—much less at that Hell Pit that was the Holy Terror? Three months. Three...goddamned...months. Then they either blow themselves up, and half a crew with them, or become total alkies or just lose their nerve and go hunt for work elsewhere. Billy Slovak—and that is his* NAME, *gentlemen—worked there* eleven years *without losing his nerve or ever hurting another man or piece of equipment.*

The men shuffled and looked at one another and then at the ground again.

—*So either this crap stops or your jobs do. I need good powdermen more than I need stupid pugilists. Slovak's staying—hell, he's even playing first base on the*

*team when summer comes—and the rest of you can make up your own minds as
to whether you want and deserve to stay or not. I hear that finding a good-paying,
solid job like this in this goddamned year of our Lord nineteen and thirty-one
is a goddamned piece of fucking cake. So gang up on Slovak again—or anyone
else I hire—and you can pick up your week's wages from Denison and get out.
Now... either head for your cars or* get back to work.

As it turned out, sixty-six-year-old Paha Sapa didn't play first base
that first summer of 1931 or in the summers since. He played short-
stop.

———

PAHA SAPA FINALLY PAUSES to breathe and set down the crate of dynamite and caps and wipe the sweat from his face when he reaches the
top and walks over to the powder shed.

Can he be ready in eight days?

He has the explosives—almost two tons of them—stashed away
in the falling-down shed and root cellar in the collapsing house he
rents in Keystone.

Dynamite is much safer than most civilians imagine. *New* dynamite,
that is. Paha Sapa has trained his new powdermen to understand
that new, fresh dynamite can be dropped, kicked, tossed—even
burned—with little or no risk of explosion. It takes the little copper-
jacketed cylinders of the blasting caps, attached to each stick by a four-
foot electric wire, to set off the dynamite proper.

With fresh dynamite, Paha Sapa explains to his nervous new men,
it's the electric detonator *cap* that is dangerous and that must always be
handled with great care. They are touchy things at the best of times,
and accidentally closing a circuit or dropping a cap or banging it against
something will—even if the cap's not attached to the dynamite sticks
yet—blow off a powderman's hands or face or belly.

But the nearly two tons of dynamite (and twenty cases of detonator
caps) that Paha Sapa has stolen and hidden in his falling-down shed and
old root cellar in Keystone is *not* new dynamite. It was old (and abandoned) when he stole it from the closed-up Holy Terror Mine—named
after the owner's wife—where he'd once worked as chief powderman.
The owners of the Holy Terror had held life cheap, and the lives of its

powdermen were held the cheapest of all. The owners had carried over dynamite from one season to the next, something absolutely prohibited in any gold or silver or coal mine where safety is a consideration.

Paha Sapa always enjoys showing new powdermen how dynamite sweats — the nitroglycerine leaking through the paper and beading up on the exterior — and how one can take a finger and snap a bead of dynamite sweat against a nearby boulder. The new men always flinch away when that hurled bead explodes against the stone with the sound of a .22 pistol being fired.

Then Paha Sapa explains about the dynamite headaches.

But the old dynamite stacked and stored in his cellar and shed does more than sweat death. The nitroglycerine in most of it has gathered and clumped and crystallized until it's become so unstable that just shifting the crates — much less moving them in a car or truck or Paha Sapa's own motorcycle sidecar — would be the equivalent of playing Russian roulette with all six cartridges loaded. (Paha Sapa is tempted to smile when he thinks of President Roosevelt's caravan of cars on its way up here to the Monument on August 30, the president himself protected by Secret Service men, passing through Keystone and within thirty yards of Paha Sapa's shed and root cellar, holding enough unstable explosive to blow all of Keystone a thousand feet into the air.)

But, he thinks again, it's not the president he wishes to harm.

Even if Paha Sapa is able to get the unstable dynamite and the dangerous caps to the top of the mountain in the dark of night, past the few night guards Borglum has posted to watch over the tools and equipment, past the compressor house and hoist house and blacksmith shop and past Borglum's studio and residence itself — then manages to somehow get the two tons of unstable explosives carried up these same 506 steps he's just climbed — he'll still need to drill hundreds of holes into the three faces.

On a regular day such as this one in August of 1936 — normal except for the unusually brutal heat — there are already thirty or more men on the work areas of the three faces (and below them, a dozen men now on Washington's chest), drilling, drilling — the compressors howling, the drill bits screaming — and many more "steel nippers," workmen rushing up and down the cliff exchanging fresh drills and bits for old, sending the dulled bits down on the tramway to be sharpened at the blacksmith shop across the valley. Soon, Whiskey Art and Paha Sapa and their assistants will be swinging down onto the cliff faces and presidents' faces to join the drillers there as they load the preset drill holes with their hundreds of charges, then carefully tie the charges into an electrical detonator cord.

It's the loud, roaring work of scores—sometimes hundreds—of men, just for a minor blow at noon or four p.m., when the workers are off the face, to move a ton or two of stone. To kill the *wasichu* heads, Paha Sapa will have to do it all at night, with unstable dynamite in hundreds of holes all over the faces to move a hundred times as much stone as a regular blast, and do it all silently, in the dark, and by himself, alone.

Still—that's what he will have to do if he's to bring down the three heads already risen from the stone. And he has long since come up with a plan that may give him a chance. But now, between the news of his growing cancer and the confirmation of the date for Roosevelt's visit for the dedication, Paha Sapa knows he will have to do it by a week from the day after tomorrow, so that the "demonstration blast" in front of President Roosevelt and the gathered dignitaries and cameras will be the end, forever, of the stone *wasichus* rising from his sacred hills.

7

At Deer Medicine Rocks, Near the Big Bend of the Rosebud

June 1876

IMPS-A-LOT HAS NOT BROUGHT PAHA SAPA TO THE ROSEBUD AND the Greasy Grass to be there for the battle with the *wasichu* or for the rubbing out of Long Hair. They've ridden alone to the gathering of Sioux and Cheyenne for the giant gathering that Sitting Bull and Crazy Horse have called. Even though Paha Sapa will not see his eleventh birthday for another two months and thus is not quite ready for the manhood ceremony, Limps-a-Lot feels it is time for the boy with such special abilities to be introduced to Sitting Bull and Crazy Horse and some of the *wičasa wakans* who will be at such a gathering.

And Limps-a-Lot brings Paha Sapa to see the *wiwanyag wachipi*—Sun Dance—that Sitting Bull has sent word he will be performing.

The time is more than two weeks before the battle. The place is not at the Greasy Grass, where Paha Sapa will be infected by the *Wasicun's* ghost, but northeast of there, out on the dry, hot plains near the wide curve of the Rosebud River, near the Deer Medicine Rocks—odd, tall, freestanding boulders etched with carvings older than the First Man. Only the Lakota are to participate in this *wiwanyag wachipi*—the Sans Arcs and Hunkpapa and Minneconjou and Oglala and a handful of Brulé. There are some Shyelas—Cheyenne—there when Limps-a-Lot and young Paha Sapa arrive early in the Moon of Making Fat (the Shyelas also hold the Deer Medicine Rocks as *wakan*—sacred, powerful—but the Cheyenne are only observers for this event).

Sitting Bull performs this holiest of holies—this *wiwanyag wachipi* Sun Dance—for the *Ikče Wičaśa,* the Natural Free Human Beings.

That first day and evening at the Deer Medicine Rocks, Limps-a-Lot points out to the excited but nervous Paha Sapa the various great *Ikče Wičaśa* whom his *tunkašila wičasa wakan* wants the boy to know by sight and possibly to meet, but not to touch unless one of the men specifically asks for such contact.

As young as he is, Paha Sapa understands that his *tunkašila* wants these famous men to know of his *small-vision-backward-or-forward-touching,* but not for him to use the seeing ability—even if he were able to do so at will, which he usually is not—unless asked to do so. Paha Sapa bows his head in understanding.

All that day the famous men and their followers ride in from different directions. All the bands of the Lakota are present. From the Oglala come Big Road and Limps-a-Lot's first wife's famous cousin, Crazy Horse. From the Hunkpapa there are Gall and Crow and Black Moon and Sitting Bull himself. From the Sans Arcs has come Spotted Eagle. From the Minneconjou arrives Fast Bull and the younger Hump. Dull Knife has come up with the few Shyelas allowed to attend. (The other famous Cheyenne leader, Ice Bear, has chosen to stay at the larger village to the south.)

When Limps-a-Lot tells Paha Sapa each of the great arrivals' names, the older man cries out—

—*Hetchetu aloh!*

It is so indeed.

More than a thousand Lakota have already gathered. Paha Sapa thinks that this is the most magnificent assembly he has ever seen, grander even than the great gatherings at *Matho Paha*—Bear Butte— every second summer, but Limps-a-Lot tells him that this temporary village is only for Sitting Bull's Sun Dance and that even more Lakota and Cheyenne will continue to gather during the ceremony, the nights of the full moon, and the days beyond.

Paha Sapa watches the preparations for Sitting Bull's *wiwanyag wachipi* with a young boy's awe, but also with the strange sense of detachment that comes over him at such times. It is as if there are several Paha Sapas watching through his eyes, including a much older version of himself looking back through time while coexisting in the thin boy's mind.

First, an honored Hunkpapa *wičasa wakan*—but not Paha Sapa's beloved *tunkašila*—is sent out alone to select the *waga chun,* the "rustling tree" or cottonwood, that will stand in the center of the dancing circle.

When this *wičasa wakan,* an old boyhood friend of Limps-a-Lot named Calling Duck, returns with the news that he has found the right tree, many of the hundreds gathered bedeck themselves with flowers picked along the banks of the river. Several warriors chosen for their bravery then count coup on the tree, with the bravest warrior—this year a young Oglala follower of Crazy Horse named Kills Six Alone—being the last and loudest to strike the tree. Paha Sapa learns that Kills Six Alone will now hold a Big Giveaway in which he will give away almost everything he owns—including his two young wives only recently earned in battle—to the other men at the Sun Dance.

After the counting coup on the tall, proud (but not too tall or thick or old) *waga chun* standing alone in its high-grass meadow, several virgins with axes approach the tree while chanting a song saying that if anyone knows they are not virgins or that they are not virtuous in all ways, that man or woman must speak now or forever be silent. Then, when no one speaks, the virgins proceed to chop down the tree.

Limps-a-Lot leads Paha Sapa to the cluster of warriors and then boys and old men gathered to catch the tree as it falls; it must not, he explains, touch the ground. Six of the chiefs who were sons of chiefs then carry the sacred tree back to the site where the *wiwanyag wachipi* will be held.

Before the *waga chun* is stripped of its branches and erected, Limps-a-Lot leads Paha Sapa out of the grassy circle of the dancing place, and the boy (and the older man within him) watches while scores of warriors on horses gather around the periphery of this holy place. At a signal given by Sitting Bull, the young men rush to the sacred place at the center of the circle where the tree will stand, all of them pushing and shoving and fighting and gouging to be the first to touch that bit of soil. Amid the cloud of dust and flurry of hooves and rearing of horses and shouts from both warriors and their watchers, Paha

Sapa smiles. It looks like nothing more than a grown-up version of his own boy-game of Throwing-Them-Off-Their-Horses. But before the boy makes the mistake of laughing aloud, Limps-a-Lot touches his shoulder and whispers in his ear that this is very important, since the man who is first to touch the sacred place will not be killed in battle this year.

That evening they have a wonderful cookout closer to the river than to the Deer Medicine Rocks, and a very hungry Paha Sapa has his fill of buffalo meat and his favorite delicacy, boiled dog. The bands have sacrificed several puppies for this feast, so there is enough to go around. Then the warriors strip the chosen tree of its lower limbs and paint it blue, green, yellow, and red. Paha Sapa's *tunkašila* explains that each color signifies a direction—north, east, west, and south—and then a large willow sweat lodge and sun shelter is built near the center of this consecrated hoop, and the real prayers begin. A *wičasa wakan* takes tobacco and fills a pipe—in this case a unique *Ptehinčala Huhu Canunpa,* a most sacred Buffalo Calf Bone Pipe that has been in the Lakota nation for twelve generations—and reconsecrates the site and the tree and the event not only to the four directions of the flat, visible earth, but also to the sky and to Grandmother Earth herself, as well as to all of the earth's visible and invisible fliers and four-leggeds, asking each in turn to make this ceremony correct in each way so as to please them and to please Wakan Tanka, the All, the Great Mystery, the Father, the Grandfather of All Grandfathers.

Then the assembled men do what they have to do to turn the tree into a medicine lodge.

They raise the tall, thin *waga chun* to much deep chanting by the men and constant tremolo from the women.

They mark a circle around it with twenty-eight forked posts. From each of these posts they run a long pole to be bound up in the sacred tree, leaving only a special opening in the east by which the rising sun may enter.

Now, as everyone gathers around the tree-turned-medicine-lodge in the lengthening summer twilight, only women visibly pregnant are allowed to approach the *waga chun* and to dance around it. Paha Sapa understands that the All, *Wakan Tanka,* as well as the specific *wakan* of the Sun, loves fruitfulness, thus the pregnant women, as much as the spirit of the Sun loves dancing.

Paha Sapa looks east across the prairie—its grasses rustling now to the rising evening wind like ripples in the fur of a living beast—and sees the full moon rising. Limps-a-Lot has explained that such an important *wiwanyag wachipi* is always held during the Moon of Making Fat or the Moon of Blackening Cherries when the moon is full, banishing the ignorance of the black sky and making the summer night most like the radiant days so beloved by the spirit of the Sun.

Paha Sapa sleeps well that night. This night is so warm that he and his grandfather do not even raise a shelter of willow branches, but sleep in the open on the blankets and skins they have brought. Only once does Paha Sapa awaken, and that is because the full moon is shining too brightly in his face. He grunts and rolls over closer to his uncle-grandfather and goes back to sleep.

Early the next morning, as he eats, Paha Sapa watches a line of still-nursing mothers bring their babies to lay them at the base of the now-transformed *waga chun*. These boy babies will now grow up to be brave men and the girl babies will be mothers of brave men. Limps-a-Lot and the other *wičasa wakans* sit around the circle through-out the morning, piercing the ears of these babies. The parents of each baby so honored are expected to give away a pony to someone in need of one.

All that day, Sitting Bull and the other warriors involved in the Sun Dance purify themselves in sweat lodges and make ready for the important work to begin the following morning. During the preceding year—especially during the winter when food was scarce or loved ones were sick—many of the men and women gathered here took private vows to sacrifice at the sacred tree. Others preparing here are the boys, some not many months older than Paha Sapa, who will be dancing as part of their manhood ceremony.

The sacrifices will include slashing at one's arms or chest, or cut-ting squares of flesh from the same areas, or perhaps cutting off one's finger. But the most serious sacrificers here will undergo the full piercing ceremony and dance before the pole.

Thousands of Lakota have now arrived for the ceremony. The prairie near the Deer Medicine Rocks and on both sides of the Rosebud are bright with evening fires and glowing lodges.

The night before the dance begins, Limps-a-Lot takes Paha Sapa to visit Sitting Bull.

Even by the flickering light of Sitting Bull's small lodge fire, Paha Sapa can see that the man has been preparing for the ritual, which—according to Limps-a-Lot—Sitting Bull has performed many times since he was a boy dancing into manhood at his manhood ceremony. Several days before this, Sitting Bull washed off all paint, removed his feathers from his hair, and loosened his braids. Paha Sapa can see from his slow movements and slight air of weakness that Sitting Bull has been fasting. Still, the chief offers Limps-a-Lot smoke from his pipe after Paha Sapa has been introduced and as the two men talk about old memories. Sitting Bull's voice is low, his pace unhurried, when he finally turns his attention to Paha Sapa.

—*My friend Limps-a-Lot tells me that* Wakan Tanka *may have granted you the ability to see into human beings' past or future, Black Hills.*

Paha Sapa's heart pounds. He can only manage a nod. Sitting Bull's eyes are luminous and piercing.

—*I can also see into the future at times, little Black Hills, but I am granted a Vision only after much pain and effort and sacrifice. You have not had your* hanblečeya *yet, have you, boy?"*

—*No,* Ate.

The *Ate*—Father—is a term of respect.

Sitting Bull nods slowly, looks at Limps-a-Lot, and then returns his strong gaze to Paha Sapa's face across the fire.

—*Then these little visions you have had are not a true Vision. It may be some ability in you, given to you by the spirits or by* Wakan Tanka, *or they may be tricks done to you by some power that does not love the Natural Free Human Beings. Be very careful, little Black Hills, about trusting in these visions-which-are-not-a-Vision.*

Again, all Paha Sapa can do is nod.

—*You may know where these things come from when you perform your real* hanblečeya.

Sitting Bull looks at Limps-a-Lot and there is a question in his eye. Limps-a-Lot says—

— We thought perhaps next summer, when the whole band will be near the Black Hills again. It seems right that Paha Sapa does his hanblečeya *there because of the circumstances of his birth, but the band is now far from Bear Butte and the Hills, and it would be a dangerous time for the boy of ten or eleven summers to travel alone.*

Sitting Bull grunts.

— That is true. Long Hair and his wasichu *horse soldiers are on the march, as are General Crook and others. A boy traveling alone on the plains or with only his adoptive* tunkašila *would run a great risk of being captured or killed — especially if we have a big fight here along the Rosebud or Little Big Horn, as I hope we will, and if we kill many* Wasicun. *The other* wasichu *will want blood. But, Limps-a-Lot, I think you should send Black Hills on his* hanblečeya *sooner than next summer. Much sooner. No later than the Moon of the Colored Leaves or the Moon of the Falling Leaves. This … gift … of his may be dangerous. And not only to the boy. He needs a Vision, if the Father or Six Grandfathers will grant him one.*

Limps-a-Lot only grunts noncommittally. Sitting Bull leans toward the fire and Paha Sapa.

— Black Hills, I apologize for speaking about you as if you were not here. We old men do that sometimes when the young are about. Did you want to touch me to see if your small-looking-back-vision *or* small-looking-forward-vision *works with me?*

Paha Sapa is silent for a long moment. Then, through trembling lips, he says —

— No. Pilamaye, Ate.

He does not know why he added the "thank you."

Sitting Bull smiles.

— Washtay! Good. I would not have let you touch me for such a vision. Not on the night before my own Dance.

Sitting Bull swivels toward Limps-a-Lot and grasps his forearm.

— I am fasting, so I will not partake, but before you go, my friend, you and your grandchild will enjoy some hot pejuta sapa. *I found it on the body of a dead* Wasicun *only last week and I had my wife grind it tonight. And then we shall smoke together.*

Paha Sapa's eyes grow wide. *Pejuta sapa* — "black medicine," coffee — is one of the most magical drinks ever taken from the *wasichu*, second only in its power to *mni waken*, holy water, whiskey.

While Sitting Bull prepares the pipe, Paha Sapa drinks his cup of the *pejuta sapa,* sipping only when his *tunkašila* sips (out of fear that there may be some aspect to the ritual drinking of which he is ignorant). Paha Sapa has never tasted anything so strong and so black and so bitter and so wonderful.

Afterward, Sitting Bull and Limps-a-Lot smoke the special pipe — it is precisely the *Ptehinčala Huhu Canunpa,* the sacred Buffalo Calf Bone Pipe, used earlier in the preparing-the-tree ritual — long into the night.

At one point, when Sitting Bull has stepped out of the lodge to piss into the high grass, Paha Sapa whispers to his grandfather —

— *Can you just smoke this pipe as if it were...a pipe?*

Before Limps-a-Lot can answer, Sitting Bull replies from the darkness at the opening of the tipi, where he is tucking himself in.

— *Yuhaxcan cannonpa, el woilag yape lo. Ehantan najin oyate maka sitomniyan cannonpa kin he unywakanpelo.*

It is used for doing all things. Ever since the standing people have been all over the earth, the pipe has been *wakan.*

Then Sitting Bull adds —

— *And it is the best pipe I own for smoking tobacco.*

When they are finally finished and Limps-a-Lot and Paha Sapa both rise and step out into the smoke-smelling sweet darkness to go back to their own lodge — Paha Sapa does not feel the least bit sleepy — Sitting Bull steps outside with them and touches Paha Sapa on the shoulder, gingerly, with the curved end of his old coup stick.

— *Come watch my Dance tomorrow, Black Hills. Watch and learn how to ask* Wakan Tanka *and all the spirits for a real vision.*

— Han, Ate.

Then Sitting Bull taps him lightly and says softly, in a singsong voice —

— *Toksha ake čante ista wacinyanktin ktelo, Paha Sapa.*

I shall see you again with the eye of my heart, Black Hills.

8

The Black and Yellow Trail

December 1923

—*You don't mind driving, do you, Billy?*

—*No. It's a beautiful car.*

—*It is, isn't it? And almost brand-new. I picked it up in Rapid City in late October. I wasn't sure that I wanted a Nash—Fords should be good enough for a poet and historian, I think—but my brother-in-law knew the owner at the new Nash dealership and...well...it is an attractive vehicle, isn't it? I could have chosen the Nash 41 for almost four hundred dollars less. It's also a four-cylinder, but it's not closed. On days like this—the temperature must be only twenty or so out there—it's so much nicer to have a closed sedan, don't you think?*

—*Yes.*

—*Of course, for a couple of hundred dollars more, I could have bought a Nash 47, and it's certainly prettier, but it doesn't have any luggage rack or compartment at all. None.*

—*No?*

—*No. None. But then—if I wanted to really spend more, and the salesman certainly tried to convince me to do so, I could have gone up to the Nash 48 Touring Car or—although this is silly even to contemplate—the new Nash 697 Sport Touring version with six cylinders. Six cylinders, Billy! They would certainly help with these hills we've been climbing!*

—*The four cylinders seem to be doing just fine, Mr. Robinson.*

—*Yes, it does seem to handle the grades well, doesn't it? Of course, if I were dreaming of spending five thousand dollars or more for an automobile, I'd go for the*

LaFayette 134. It weighs more than two tons and—so I've read, at least—can travel at speeds up to ninety miles per hour. Tell me, Billy—why would any person need or want to go ninety miles per hour? Except perhaps at the Indianapolis Speedway, I mean?

—I don't know.

—But I'm no Jimmy Murphy, and anyway, I'd have to buy a Duesenberg to compete there and I'm happy with this Nash. Do you mind if I take some notes as we continue our discussion about the old days?

—Go ahead.

—Speaking of racetracks, Billy... I've heard mention on the reservation of the Race Track, but it's not a formation or place that the Park Service has on its maps or one that I'm familiar with.

—We drove through it coming out of Rapid City, Mr. Robinson.

—We did?

—The Race Track is the old Lakota and Cheyenne name for the valley that surrounds the Black Hills... the long, curving valley between the outer rim of red Hogback Ridge and the Hills themselves. If you went high enough in an aeroplane, perhaps you could see the entire reddish oval surrounding the Hills. That's the Race Track.

—Good heavens, Billy. My whole life lived near the Hills—me as head of the state history effort—and I never noticed that the valley goes all the way around the Hills or that your people had a name for it. Race Track. Why Race Track—because the sunken oval of the valley resembles one?

—No, because it was one.

Paha Sapa looks over at the older man as Robinson is hurriedly taking notes. Doane Robinson is sixty-seven years old (nine years older than Paha Sapa in this last day of 1923) and wears no cap in the freezing air—the Nash's heater is all but worthless—even though he is as bald as the proverbial egg. Robinson's ever-present gentle smile is matched by kind eyes only partially hidden this morning behind the circular horn-rimmed glasses.

Once a lawyer (who supported the Sioux tribes in some of their early lawsuits against the state and federal governments), Robinson traded law for literature long ago to become South Dakota's favorite humor writer and poet. He is also the state's official historian. Most important, Paha Sapa trades these occasional interviews about the "old days" — in which he reveals very little of substance and almost nothing personal — for permission to borrow books from the historian-writer's extensive home library. This arrangement has led to the majority of what fifty-eight-year-old Paha Sapa considers his personal and private "college education" in the past six years.

Robinson looks up from the notes.

— *Did the Sioux and Cheyenne used to race there?*

— *Before the Lakota and Cheyenne, Mr. Robinson. This may have been before the First Man and his cousins came up into the world through* Washu Niya, *"the Breathing Cave." The Park Service calls it Wind Cave.*

— *Yes, yes. I've long heard that the Cheyenne and Sioux and other Plains Indians believe that humans came into the world through Wind Cave. But why is it called "the Breathing Cave" rather than "the Birthing Cave" or somesuch?*

— *Because in the winter you can see the cave breathe through its various orifices. The warmer air comes out as regular breaths, almost identical to the breathing of a buffalo.*

— *Ahhh…*

Robinson scribbles away at his notes. Paha Sapa concentrates on keeping the broad-beamed Nash on the frozen mud ruts of the road. He turns right onto the Needles Highway. The Nash's engine is up to the climb, but the car's gearbox is putrid — not nearly as good as the Fords and Chevies Paha Sapa has driven — and he has to take care not to grind the gears of the historian's beloved new car.

Robinson looks up, and the sunlight gleams on his round glasses.

— *Did the buffalo and the humans enter the world at the same time, Billy? I've heard different reports on that.*

— *The buffalo came first. The first buffalo that emerged from* Washu Niya *were tiny — the size of ants — but the grass in the Black Hills was so rich that they quickly grew and fattened to their present size.*

Paha Sapa smiles at this, but Doane Robinson earnestly continues his note taking. When he finally looks up, he blinks at the approaching Needles formations as if he's forgotten they were in the Black Hills. The late-December sun is bright but weak, the shadows from the rock columns tenuous. Robinson taps his fountain pen against his lower lip.

— *So who raced on the Race Track if people weren't yet in the Hills?*

Paha Sapa shifts gears to go down a grade. The Nash's clutch does not engage until the driver's boot is almost against the drafty floorboards. Someday, Paha Sapa knows, the Needles Highway will be paved, but now it is a mass of frozen deep ruts that could high-end Mr. Robinson's Nash in a second if the narrow wheels slide off the high ridges.

— *The story goes that the winged and four-legged creatures of the world were competing to rule the world. They came close to warring to decide this, but finally decided to hold a Great Race around* Wamakaognaka e'cantge.

Robinson pauses in his note taking. When he speaks, his breath hangs in the air a moment as if the Breathing Cave were breathing here, only here their breath is also icing up the inside of the windshield and already-frosted side windows.

— Wamakaognaka e'cantge — *that means "Center of the Universe," doesn't it, Billy?*

— *Among other things. I prefer to hear it as "the heart of everything that is." But it all means Paha Sapa — the Black Hills.*

— *So the four-leggeds and the flying creatures agreed to decide who would rule the world based on a race around the Black Hills?*

The pen scratches. There is no other traffic on the road this New Year's Eve day. Beyond the thrust of the Needles, Paha Sapa can see the highest and most sacred mountain in the Black Hills, Evil Spirit Hill, which the *wasichu* have renamed Harney Peak to honor a famous Indian killer, and beyond Evil Spirit Hill, the long granite ridgeline of the Six Grandfathers, where he had his Vision forty-seven years earlier.

— *Yes. There are different versions of the story, but in the one my grandfather told me, the flying creatures put on magic colors to help them win the race. Thus the crow first painted himself black, the magpie used white earth and charcoal to make himself wakan —*

— *Holy. Sacred.*

— *Yes. The meadowlark trusted in yellow to allow him to win. So the four-leggeds and the two-leggeds, who were all flying creatures then but who agreed to keep their feet on the ground for this Great Race, rushed 'round and 'round the Black Hills a hundred, a thousand times, wearing down the ground there into today's Race Track. The buffalo and deer were the fastest of the four-leggeds, and the bloody froth that poured from their mouths and noses stained the rock red almost all the way around. They raced through days and nights and weeks and moons.*

—Who won?

—Magpie and Crow won, running on behalf of all two-leggeds, including us people who hadn't yet crawled up through the Breathing Cave. And by then the Race Track was as wide and deep and red rimmed as you see it now. Actually, my grandfather had another name for the red-rimmed oval that surrounds the Wamakaognaka e'cantge.

—What was that, Billy?

—Winyaň shan.

—Odd. For all my years recording Sioux words, I've never encountered that one. What does it mean, Billy?

—Cunt.

Doane Robinson screws the top on his fountain pen, removes his glasses, and cleans them with the handkerchief from the breast pocket of his thick wool suitcoat. Paha Sapa can see the line of red along the historian's cheekbone and is sorry that he's embarrassed the older man.

———

—Pull over here, please. At that turnout at the base of that column.

Paha Sapa stops the Nash. The dirt road here winds among the Needles—freestanding pillars of granite, some a hundred feet and more tall but most rising forty or fifty feet—and this turnout is to allow motorists to admire this particular fat finger of stone that rises immediately next to the shoulder of the road.

Robinson is fumbling with his new-styled door handle.

—Shall we get out, Billy?

—The wind's come up, Mr. Robinson. It's cold out there.

—Come, come. We're only young once. I want to show you something.

It is colder than Paha Sapa guessed. This part of the narrow road has been cut along the ridgeline, and there are no high peaks in the way to block the freezing wind blasting across the Hills from the northwest. Paha Sapa buttons his black-and-red wool coat and notices the blue-black storm clouds along the horizon far to the northwest. There will be a blizzard rolling in by midnight on this New Year's Eve. He calculates the time it will take to get Robinson back to his home and to ride back to his own home near Deadwood on the motorcycle. It will not be a night when he wants to be on that narrow, winding mountain road in a blizzard in the dark—especially since the motor-cycle has no headlight.

Doane Robinson is gesturing to the Needle column.

—*You've noticed, Billy, that there are dozens upon dozens—scores!—of these pinnacles within the newly established park.*

—*Yes.*

—*And you know of the Black Hills and Yellowstone Highway?*

—*The Black and Yellow Trail. Sure. We followed the painted bumblebee posts out of Rapid City and up into the Hills.*

Paha Sapa thinks of the crude dirt—only occasional gravel—main auto road that now cuts east and west across South Dakota and that the *wasichu* grace with the proud name of "highway." The black-and-yellow-striped roadside posts stretch across the prairie seemingly to infinity.

—*The highway connects Chicago to Yellowstone Park and was meant to bring tourists to the West, Billy. South Dakota's future will depend upon tourism, mark my words. If the economy stays this good, everyone in America will own a car someday and everyone will want to leave those crowded warrens in the eastern and midwestern cities and come out to see the West.*

Paha Sapa pulls his collar up against the freezing wind battling them. Doane Robinson's blush has been replaced with patches of red and white on his cheeks and nose, and Paha Sapa realizes he'll have to get the historian back in the idling car soon before the intellectual allows himself to get frostbitten. The man's not even wearing gloves on this subzero day. When an especially vicious gust threatens to tumble Robinson off the frozen dirt of the road down into the underbrush at the base of the granite column, Paha Sapa steadies him with a strong grip on his upper arm.

—*Have you ever been to Chicago, Billy?*

—*Yes. Once.*

Paha Sapa can still see Mr. Ferris's great Wheel rising above the White City at night in 1893, everything bathed in radiance by the thousands of electric lights. The authorities of the Chicago Columbian Exposition had decided that Buffalo Bill's Wild West Show lacked the proper dignity to be a recognized part of the Fair, so Mr. Cody had set up his show just outside the fairgrounds proper, thus drawing huge crowds while not having to share the profits with the Fair organizers. But the White City, with its huge Electricity Building and Machinery Building—the entire Court of Honor illuminated by those hundreds of electrical streetlights and spotlights through the bustling night—was one of the most amazing things the twenty-eight-year-old Paha Sapa had ever seen.

—*You have? Well, you can imagine then why the denizens of that overcrowded town are waiting and wanting to travel west and to breathe our clean air and to see our amazing sights. But South Dakota needs an attraction!*

—*An attraction?*

—*Yes, yes. It occurred to me only a few weeks ago that while Yellowstone Park has its geysers and its grizzly bears and its hot springs, certainly enough to bring someone out along the Black and Yellow Highway from Chicago or points farther east, the only attraction that our fair state has to offer the intrepid voyager is the park here in the Black Hills . . . and all the Hills have to offer are . . . well . . . hills.*

Paha Sapa can only stare at the state historian. Mr. Robinson's eyes are watering from the cold and his nose is running copiously. Every time a new gust hits them, only Paha Sapa's firm grip keeps the larger and older man from being blown down the hill and into the lodgepole pines and Douglas firs that cluster between the bases of the Needles columns. Paha Sapa can see from the shadows thrown that it's getting late—they will have to leave soon if he has any chance of getting to Deadwood before full darkness falls and the blizzard arrives. The air now smells of the approaching snow.

Robinson extends his free arm and opens his bare fingers in the direction of the granite spire.

—*And then it struck me, Billy. Voilà! Sculptures!*

—*Sculptures?*

Paha Sapa can hear how idiotic his repetition sounds, even though he rarely cares how he sounds in so un-nuanced a language as English.

—*These spires would be perfect for carving, Billy. I am quite sure that granite is the finest of all carving stone. So a couple of days ago, I wrote this letter to the foremost sculptor in America . . . perhaps in the world!*

Robinson fumbles in his inner pocket, under his blowing topcoat and wind-ballooned suitcoat, and comes out with a carbon copy of a typewriter-typed letter. A gust rips the flimsy paper out of Robinson's right hand, and only a lightning-fast lunge by Paha Sapa keeps the letter from disappearing forever into the forest.

— *We should read this and talk in the car, Mr. Robinson.*

—*Quite right, Billy. Quite right. I don't believe I can feel the tips of my ears or nose!*

Back in the Nash, Paha Sapa tries to turn up the car's primitive heater, but it's already putting out what little heat from the engine it deigns to share. He unfurls the now-crumpled letter over the top of the broad steering wheel and reads:

December 28, 1923

Mr. Lorado Taft
6016 Ellis Avenue
Chicago, Illinois

My Dear Mr. Taft:

South Dakota has developed a wonderful state park in the Black Hills. I enclose a brochure illustrating some features of it. On the front cover you will observe some pinnacles—we call them needles—situated high upon the flank of Harney Peak. The tops of those shown are more than 6300 feet above sea level. These needles are of granite.

Having in mind your "Big Injun," it has occurred to me that some of these pinnacles would lend themselves to massive sculpture, and I write to ask if in your judgment human figures might be carved from some of them as they stand. I am thinking of some notable Sioux such as Red Cloud, who lived and died in the shadow of those peaks. If one was found practicable, perhaps others would ultimately follow.

Pinnacles could be found immediately above the highway shown, that stand fully one hundred feet in the clear, above pedestals hundreds of feet in height, as seen from the other points of vantage.

This granite is of rather coarse texture, but it is durable. There are also in the vicinity

great blank walls upon which groups in relief
could be executed advantageously.

The needles shown are only suggestive of the
field, many others are trimmer—only a few feet in
diameter—and exceedingly showy.

I shall be pleased to hear from you, and if it
appears practicable we can, perhaps, induce you
to come and look us over.

Faithfully,

Doane Robinson

———

PAHA SAPA DRIVES THEM BACK toward Rapid City as fast as the Nash's
skinny tires will carry them on the frozen roads. He doesn't ask
Mr. Robinson if Lorado Taft, the sculptor, has responded to the letter yet, since there has hardly been time for that. He drives in silence
except for the banging four-cylinder engine and the loud but heatless
burr of the heater fan.

— *What do you think, Billy?*

Paha Sapa likes Doane Robinson; he likes the man's gentleness and
learning and sincere interest, however poorly focused, in the history of
Paha Sapa's people. And he *loves* Doane Robinson's library and the new
look at the universe it has given him. But at that moment, he also thinks
that if Robinson had shown him the letter to the sculptor *before* he mailed
it, Paha Sapa would have used the simple bone-handled jackknife with
the five-inch blade now in his pocket to cut the writer-historian's throat,
leaving his body in the woods along the Needles Highway and his Nash
in a ravine somewhere many miles away in the Black Hills.

— *Billy? What do you think of the idea? Do you think Red Cloud would be
the choice for the first Sioux leader to be carved into one of the pinnacles? Did you
know Red Cloud?*

Makhpiya Luta, Red Cloud, was famous for his victory in the Battle
of the Hundred Slain, but all that fighting had ended by the time Paha
Sapa was two summers old. Paha Sapa knew old Red Cloud primarily as
an agency Indian, someone who had surrendered the plains and lands of
the last Natural Free Human Beings, and Paha Sapa was near the Red

Cloud Agency at Camp Robinson in 1877 when a jealous nephew of Red Cloud's betrayed Crazy Horse, bringing him back to the fort to be murdered. Red Cloud outlived all the real warrior chiefs—Sitting Bull, Crazy Horse—dying as an old, old man only fourteen years earlier in 1909.

— *I didn't really know Red Cloud.*

— *What about Crazy Horse, then, Billy? Do you think it would be appropriate if Mr. Taft sculpted a huge statue of* T'ašunka Witko *here in the Hills?*

Paha Sapa grunts. Here on the east side of the ridgelines, the evening shadows are growing quickly and he has to drive extra carefully to keep the Nash from breaking an axle in one of the deep, frozen ruts. How can he tell this gentle man that Crazy Horse would have preferred to pull his own guts out through a hole in his belly—or to slaughter Doane Robinson's entire extended family—rather than allow the *wasichus* who betrayed and killed him to carve a likeness of him into Paha Sapa granite? He takes a breath.

— *You remember, Mr. Robinson, that Crazy Horse never allowed any of the frontier photographers to take a photograph of him.*

— *Ah, you're right, of course, Billy. He was obviously afraid of the camera "capturing his soul," as some of the Plains Indians feared. But I'm quite sure that a sculpture created by a great artist would not have offended* T'ašunka Witko's *sensibilities in that way.*

Paha Sapa knows beyond any doubt that Crazy Horse had no fear of a camera "capturing his soul." The warrior simply would never give his enemy the satisfaction of capturing even an image of him.

— *What about Sitting Bull, then, Billy? Do you think the Lakota would be honored if there was a monumental sculpture of* Tatanka Iyotake *here in the Hills?*

The highway is especially churned up into ridges and gulleys here, a Badlands in miniature, and Paha Sapa stays silent as he bounces the Nash across the least threatening patch of frozen road and shoulder. He remembers the time, only nine years after the rubbing out of Long Hair at the Little Big Horn, when Sitting Bull traveled east with Bill Cody's Wild West Show—this was eight years before Paha Sapa went to Chicago with the same troupe—and was so impressed by the numbers and power of the *wasichus* and by the size of their cities and the speed of their railroads. But Paha Sapa spoke to a missionary who had known *Tatanka Iyotake* upon his return to the agency, and Sitting Bull had said to the white holy man — *The white people are wicked. I want you to teach my people to read and write, but they must not become white people in their ways of living and of thinking; it is too bad a life. I could not let them do it. I myself would rather die an Indian than live a white man.*

Paha Sapa finds it difficult to breathe. There is a wild pounding on the inside of his rib cage and a pressure of pain in his skull that blurs his vision. Another man might think it was a heart attack or stroke happening to him, but Paha Sapa knows that it is the ghost of Long Hair gibbering and capering within him, pounding to get out. Does Long Hair hear these words through Paha Sapa's ears, see the Needles columns through Paha Sapa's eyes, and imagine the large sculptures of the Lakota men mentioned — Robinson has certainly not mentioned Custer for one of the sculptures — by seeing into Paha Sapa's mind?

Paha Sapa does not know. He has asked himself similar questions many times, but although the ghost speaks to him nightly, he has no clear idea as to whether Long Hair sees and hears through him or shares *his* thoughts the way that Paha Sapa is cursed to suffer Long Hair's.

— *Did you know Sitting Bull, Billy?*

Doane Robinson sounds concerned, perhaps embarrassed, as if he is worried that he has offended the Lakota man he knows as Billy Slow Horse.

— *I knew him slightly, Mr. Robinson.*

Paha Sapa makes his voice as friendly as he is able to.

— *I saw Sitting Bull from time to time, but I was, of course, only a boy when he fought and then surrendered and then was killed by the Indian policemen who came to arrest him.*

———

THE *WIWANYAG WACHIPI* SUN DANCE at Deer Medicine Rocks two weeks before they killed Long Hair lasted only two days.

The older boys and young men who had come for their manhood ceremony lay down at the base of the tall *waga chun* now bedecked with paint and poles and braided tethers. The boys and young men had been similarly painted by Limps-a-Lot and the other holy men, and did not move or cry out as the *wičasa wakan* then cut strips out of their chests or backs so that loops of rawhide could be pushed in under the strong chest or back muscles and tied off, usually to a small bit of wood. These loops were then tied to the long braids running up to the top of the *waga chun*.

Then the young men, streaming blood on their painted chests and backs, would stand and begin their dancing and chanting, leaning back from or toward the sacred tree so that their bodies were often suspended totally by the rawhide and horn under their muscles. And always they stared at the sun as they danced and chanted. Sometimes they danced the full two days. More often, they would dance and leap until the pain caused them to fall unconscious or—if they were lucky and *Wakan Tanka* smiled on them—until the rawhide and horn ripped through their powerful chest or back muscles and freed them.

Sitting Bull had danced this way many times before in his youth, but now, as Paha Sapa and Limps-a-Lot and two thousand others watched in this summer of 1876, he stripped naked to the waist and walked to the *waga chun* and sat with his scarred back against the sacred tree. Paha Sapa remembers noticing that there was a tiny hole in the sole of one of Sitting Bull's old but beautifully beaded moccasins.

Sitting Bull's friend Jumping Bull approached the chief chanting, knelt next to the man of forty-two winters, and used a steel awl to lift the skin on Sitting Bull's lower arm. Taking care not to slice into muscle, Jumping Bull cut away a square of skin the size of the nail on Paha Sapa's little finger. Then he cut another. Jumping Bull worked his way up Sitting Bull's right arm, cutting fifty such squares.

And during this, ignoring the streaming blood and never reacting to the pain, Sitting Bull chanted his prayers, asking for mercy for his people and for victory in the coming battle with the *wasichus*.

The cutting of the flesh from Sitting Bull's right arm, Paha Sapa remembers—thinking of the time now in *Wasicun* terms—took about forty-five minutes. Then Jumping Bull began cutting fifty more squares of flesh from Sitting Bull's left arm.

When Jumping Bull was finished with the slow cutting, when there was more red blood than ceremonial paint flowing down Sitting Bull's arms onto his belly and loincloth and legs and spattering the ground all around the *waga chun,* Sitting Bull stood and—still chanting and praying—danced all the rest of that long June day and all through that night of the full moon and halfway through the next humid, sweltering, cloudless, fly-buzzing day.

Sitting Bull's old friend Black Moon caught him when the chief was finally ready to faint. And then Sitting Bull whispered to Black Moon, and Black Moon stood and shouted to the waiting thousands—

—*Sitting Bull wishes me to tell you all that he just heard a voice saying unto him, "I give you these because they have no ears," and Sitting Bull looked up and saw, above him and above us all, soldiers and some of our Natural Free Human Beings and our allies on horseback, and many of the* wasichus *were falling like grasshoppers and their heads were down and their hats were falling off. The* wasichus *were falling right into our camp!*

And Paha Sapa remembers the cheering that had gone up from the camp at hearing this vision.

The bluecoat soldiers had no ears in Sitting Bull's vision, they knew, because the *Wasicun* had refused to hear that the Lakota and Cheyenne wished only to be left alone and that the Lakota refused to sell their beloved Black Hills. The women would drive their sewing awls through the eardrums of dead *wasichu* on the battlefield to open those ears.

And then the *wiwanyag wachipi* ended after only two days and after Sitting Bull's triumphant vision, and the thousands there moved southwest a few miles to the larger campground on the Greasy Grass, where Long Hair and his Seventh Cavalry *wasichu* soldiers would attack them and where Paha Sapa would become infected with Long Hair's ghost.

———

PAHA SAPA DROPS OFF THE HISTORIAN and the Nash just after dark. It is already snowing lightly but consistently. Doane Robinson follows Paha Sapa up the front walk to where Paha Sapa is pulling his oversize leather jacket, leather gloves, leather helmet, and goggles from the side-car. Snowflakes fly horizontally beneath the glowing streetlamp above them.

—*Billy, the weather looks bad. Stay the night here. That road up to Deadwood is terrible even in the daylight and when it's dry. It may not be passable in half an hour, even for a motorcar.*

— It'll be all right, Mr. Robinson. I have other places to stay along the way — if I have to.

— Well, it's a very handsome motorcycle. I've never really looked at it carefully before. American made?

— Yes. A Harley-Davidson J, made in 1916.

— At least it has a headlight.

— It does. The first of its kind to have one. Its beam is a little weak and shaky and, unfortunately, it's broken right now. I keep meaning to fix it.

— Stay with us tonight, Billy.

Paha Sapa throws his leg over the saddle. The motorcycle is a beautiful machine — long, sleek, painted light blue with the HARLEY-DAVIDSON lettering in reddish-orange script. Over the nonworking headlight is a stubby horn that works quite well. The intake manifold is curved, a piece of true sculpture in Paha Sapa's judgment, and feeds the reliable sixty-one-cubic-inch F-head V-twin engine. It is the first of its make to have a modern kick-starter. There's a plush leather passenger seat attached over the rear wheel (although no back for it), and though the sidecar is detachable, Paha Sapa keeps it on as a carryall for his tools and gear.

He reaches behind the engine and uses his key to switch on the magneto. Three kicks and the engine roars to life. Paha Sapa throttles it up and then down so he can hear the historian.

— Billy, it's beautiful! Have you owned it long?

— It's not mine. It's my son's. He gave it to me to keep for him until he came back from the War.

Doane Robinson is shivering from the cold. He rubs his cheek.

— But the War has been over for... Oh, my. Oh, dear.

— Good night, Mr. Robinson. Please let me know if Mr. Lorado Taft writes you back.

9

East of Slim Buttes Along the Grand River, Ninety Miles North of the Black Hills

———— •• ————

July 1876

PAHA SAPA AND LIMPS-A-LOT RETURN FROM THE GREASY Grass much more quickly than they traveled there, but word of the rubbing out of Long Hair has already reached their village, carried by the fast-riding young warriors from the band and by other groups of Lakota passing by. The word of the defeat of the Seventh Cavalry and of *Pehin Hanska Kasata,* the rubbing out of Long Hair, travels faster in that week through the world of the Great Plains tribes than it does through the *wasichu* army or telegraph lines.

For some days after his return, no one has time for or interest in Paha Sapa's tale of counting coup and catching a ghost.

Paha Sapa was always sorry that there had been no time that morning after his meeting with Sitting Bull, Long Turd, and the other men to go up the hill and show them the corpse of the *Wasicun* whose ghost had entered him. That morning there was a pillar of dust visible to the north of where Major Reno and his surviving men were still pinned down on the hill three miles from where Paha Sapa had touched his dying *Wasicun,* and while the *wasichus* feared that it was still more Indians, the scouts serving Sitting Bull and Crazy Horse and the other chiefs knew that it was a large detachment of mounted bluecoats, almost certainly General Terry's column coming from the same jumping-off point—the steamer *Far West* parked where the Yellowstone River meets the Rosebud—from whence Custer and his men had come.

Sitting Bull was too busy giving commands on breaking up the camp, leaving the honored dead in lodges, and arranging future rendezvous for the various groups of fighting men to go with Paha Sapa and Limps-a-Lot that morning, and when Paha Sapa led his *tunkašila* up that coulee in the sunrise, they saw the fresh *wasichu* troops on the northern horizon and quickly descended to their collapsed lodge and waiting ponies in the valley.

The huge village was broken down—except for those tipis and scaffolds left as lodges for the dead and tipi poles that some families simply had no time to carry with them, bringing only the tipi covers—within two hours, and by the time the *wasichus* descended into that valley in late afternoon, Sitting Bull had led all 8,000 or so Lakota and Cheyenne west toward the Big Horn Mountains and then divided the exodus into two columns, one heading to the southwest, the other—including Paha Sapa and Limps-a-Lot—to the southeast. From those main streams the bands and individuals broke off and scattered across the brown plains or toward the mountains.

In Paha Sapa's village near the Slim Buttes, the nights were much as the first night at Greasy Grass had been: a strange combination of mourning and celebration, but since only two young men from Angry Badger's band had died in the two big fights (the first fight with General Cook to the south, the second one with Custer), the late-into-the-night celebrations far outweighed the tremolo campfires and sunrise slashings of mourning.

By the early days of the new month, the Moon of Red Cherries, word arrives that while many of the warriors at the Greasy Grass are quietly returning with their families to the various agencies and reservations, Sitting Bull's people and Crazy Horse's warriors are still on the move, carrying on the fight. Some days after that, Lone Duck, a warrior from Angry Badger's band (and another cousin of Three Buffalo Woman's) who has ridden with Crazy Horse for three fighting seasons now, arrives to say that Sitting Bull and Crazy Horse have said their good-byes—the older chief's last words to the younger fighting man were *We will have good times!*—and Sitting Bull will be leading his many families and relatively few young fighters to winter in Grandmother's Country (the Grandmother being Queen Victoria) in the far north, while Crazy Horse, whose followers are almost all young fighting men, is roaming in the direction of Slim Buttes, killing *wasichus* whenever the opportunity arises.

But then word also arrives that the *wasichus* have been driven insane by the rubbing out of Long Hair and more than two hundred of his men. Soldiers are being marched everywhere. Warriors bring news that a band of Cheyenne has been attacked on the plains northwest of the Red Cloud Agency by elements of the Fifth Cavalry, who brag that they rode 85 miles in 31 hours to intercept the Cheyenne—who were not at Greasy Grass and who had nothing to do with Custer's death.

Scouts passing through report that what is left of the Seventh Cavalry has mostly gone to ground at their base camp at the head of the Yellowstone, awaiting orders and drinking great amounts of whiskey (which is being sent upriver by various steamships). Lakota and Cheyenne and even some Crow, who have always been friends of Custer and his cavalry, report from agencies that they fear reprisals from the white men.

Three Stars, the General Cook whom Crazy Horse had soundly beaten on the Rosebud nine days before the death of Long Hair, and Long Hair's commander General Terry are reportedly adding reinforcements to their fighting force and will soon be moving up the Rosebud Valley. What interests the Lakota scouts about this is that an old friend and enemy—a scout named Cody famous for shooting buffalo—has rejoined the army after many years to help Cook, Terry, and the others find the Lakota and Cheyenne and kill them.

All the men in camp agree that Cody is a worthy enemy and that his long, flowing hair—almost as luxuriant as Long Hair's once was—would be a fine addition to any warrior's tipi pole.

Despite his inability to sleep because of the ghost's constant talking and babbling every night, Paha Sapa almost hopes that his ghost will be forgotten by others in all the excitement and fear and nightly celebrations and comings and goings of men from other bands.

But it has not been forgotten. The irony is that the very presence of these other bands and chiefs and holy men now brings attention to Paha Sapa and his ghost.

———

PAHA SAPA SEES and feels the confusion flowing over his small *tiyospaye,* lodge group, as these events dominate the Great Plains. The leader of their band, Angry Badger, rarely lives up to his name. The badger is considered the most ferocious creature on earth by the Lakota and its blood has magical properties. (Peering into a basin of it, for instance, will allow you to see yourself far in the future.) Badgers have been known to seize horses and drag them down into their badger holes while warriors can only look on in horror.

Angry Badger is a short, heavyset man of about fifty summers. His face is broad, flat, almost feminine, and his expression is set into a permanent scowl, but it is rarely one of unsupportable anger. He is given to melancholy and indecision and has never been chosen to be among the Deciders — those chiefs chosen each year to oversee the hunt of all the Oglala bands and to appoint the *akicita* tribal police — but he is cautious when he finally does decide and he has always relied upon the wisdom of the leading warriors and hunters in his small band, and especially the advice of Limps-a-Lot over the old and increasingly impotent Loud Voice Hawk.

Now Angry Badger is all but irrelevant as famous warriors and their bodyguards and fighting bands sweep into the Slim Buttes and south fork of the Grand River area where Angry Badger has led his men to hunt for buffalo before winter arrives.

Angry Badger was a courageous warrior in his youth — the band has composed songs commemorating his deeds — but he is a poor leader, and the freshness of his youthful glories have faded with each autumn since he last went on the war trail. Paha Sapa, not quite eleven summers old as they approach his birth month, is amazed by the names and faces and personalities that stop by their *tiyospaye* or camp nearby for short periods. (Decades later, reading Homer's *Iliad,* Chapman's translation, borrowed from Doane Robinson, Paha Sapa again feels sympathy for Angry Badger as he reads of Agamemnon's jealousy in the presence of Achilles and other more-than-human heroes.

Among the famous fighters now within a few hours' or days' ride of their village is Crazy Horse himself—a charismatic warrior who now threatens to replace Sitting Bull as war leader, since the older chief is fleeing to Grandmother's Country while Crazy Horse continues to harass and kill *wasichus* every day—as well as some of Crazy Horse's feared and notorious friends and lieutenants, including Black Fox, Dog Goes, the intrepid Run Fearless, Kicking Bear, Bad Heart Bull, and Flying Hawk. Each of these men is a chief or leader of warriors in his own right and each now carries his own legends, as did Achilles with his Myrmidons. Along with Crazy Horse's subalterns are groups of his *akicita* tribal-police bodyguards, each more fiercely painted and countenanced than the last, and these include the Oglalas Looking Horse, Short Bull, and Low Dog, as well as the odd Minneconjou Flying By, who is so eager to share in Crazy Horse's growing glory that it is said that Flying By would ride east to try to capture the *wasichus'* White Father if Crazy Horse ordered him to.

Other *akicita* leaders coming up to the south fork of the Grand River area that sweltering, humid, stormy midsummer include Crazy Horse's close friends Kicking Bear and Little Big Man. This last man—named for his short but powerfully built physique (the Sun Dance scars on Little Big Man's chest are the most formidable Paha Sapa is ever to see, and Little Big Man goes shirtless until the snow is deep to show them off)—is especially famous among the Lakota, and the women and children and old men of Angry Badger's band crowd and jostle to see and touch him when he first arrives. (Paha Sapa listens to Little Big Man brag about his braveries at Greasy Grass around the central fire that first night of his visit and thinks that such an immodest manner is not nearly so becoming as Crazy Horse's silence and unwillingness to speak of his own victories, but the boy does see how the two friends tend to balance each other. Little Big Man is the threatener and corrector of undisciplined or unruly young warriors who follow them; Crazy Horse is the silent and frightening living legend.)

Angry Badger, who was not at Greasy Grass or at the fight with Cook on the Rosebud the week before, since he'd chosen to stay with his small band and lead them north after the last buffalo of the season, remains silent and glowering during these visits.

The story of the fight at the Greasy Grass and the rubbing out of *Pehin Hanska,* Long Hair Custer, increasingly dwells on the match-up between *Pehin Hanska* and Crazy Horse, and less and less on the leadership of Sitting Bull, eight winters older than Long Hair and too weakened by his Sun Dance flesh-cutting sacrifice to take part in the fighting that day. Sitting Bull's vision, Paha Sapa increasingly understands through Limps-a-Lot, will always be considered as wonderfully *wakan,* but Crazy Horse's leadership and fighting that day are becoming the material that gods are made of.

Inevitably, during his first four-day stay at Angry Badger's *tiyospaye* (another twenty lodges have been raised by the visitors here along the creek that runs near Slim Buttes, outnumbering the size of the original village), Crazy Horse hears that the boy Paha Sapa was infected by a ghost during the fighting at Greasy Grass, and the battle chief demands to meet with the boy in Limps-a-Lot's lodge. This terrifies Paha Sapa. He remembers all too well *T'ašunka Witko*'s look of disgust when the near-naked *heyoka* warrior found Paha Sapa lying unwounded and gagging for air among the dead that afternoon of the battle.

But as terrified as Paha Sapa is, the summons to Limps-a-Lot's lodge for his meeting with Crazy Horse has to be honored that second evening of the war chief's first visit.

It is intolerably hot and humid, and though the sunset has thrown long shadows from the occasional cottonwoods and tipis and horses and grasses, the twilight brings no relief from the heat. Storm clouds move heavily in the south and north and east. Even though the sides of the tipis are raised as high as privacy and propriety allow, almost a grown man's full arm length at Limps-a-Lot's lodge, no cooling air moves beneath the heavy painted hides.

Paha Sapa is surprised to see that his interrogators consist only of Crazy Horse, one of his lieutenants named Run Fearless, their own leader, Angry Badger, the holy man Long Turd, old Loud Voice Hawk, and Limps-a-Lot. The women have been sent away. Even though it's widely known that Crazy Horse loves his privacy and often goes off by himself for days or weeks at a time, there hasn't been a moment so far in his visit to Angry Badger's *tiyospaye* when the war chief has not been surrounded by his bodyguards, other chiefs, warriors, and Angry Badger's people. Somehow the fact that it is only Crazy Horse, Run Fearless, Angry Badger, Long Turd, Loud Voice Hawk, and Paha Sapa's *tunkašila* makes the boy even more apprehensive. His legs are shaking under his best deer-hide trousers.

Limps-a-Lot makes the introductions—although Paha Sapa was briefly introduced to Crazy Horse at the Greasy Grass—and then the six men and the boy sit in a circle. The tent hides have been rolled lower for privacy and sweat drips from the men's noses and chins in the thick, still air.

There is no pipe, no ceremony, no prelude. Crazy Horse scowls at Paha Sapa as indifferently and apparently as disgustedly as he did on the battlefield more than two weeks earlier. When he speaks, the questions are directed directly at Paha Sapa, and the war chief's voice is low but peremptory.

—*Long Turd and others tell me that you can see people's pasts and futures when you touch them. Is this true?*

Paha Sapa's heart pounds so wildly that he feels lightheaded.

—*Sometimes…*

He wanted to add an honorific to his answer, but *Ate,* Father, does not feel right with this fierce stranger. He leaves it off and hopes he does not receive a closed-fisted cuff for insolence.

—*And is it true that a* Wasicun's *ghost came into you near where I saw you lying and flopping around during the battle at the Greasy Grass on the day we killed* Pehin Hanska?

—*Yes,* Tasunke Witko.

Paha Sapa prays that using Crazy Horse's name with the proper tone of deference will be as respectful as an honorific.

Crazy Horse's scowl remains the same.

—*Was it Long Hair's ghost?*

—*I do not know,* Tasunke Witko.

—*Does it speak to you?*

—*It speaks to…itself. Especially at night, when I hear it best.*

—*What does it say?*

—*I do not know,* Tasunke Witko. *It uses many words and all in a harsh rush, but the words are all in the tongue of the* Wasicun.

— You do not understand any of them?

— No, Tasunke Witko. *I am sorry.*

Crazy Horse shakes his head as if angered by Paha Sapa's apology.

—Are there any words that the ghost whispers more than once?

Paha Sapa licks his lips and thinks hard. Outside, thunder rumbles from the direction of the Black Hills. Somewhere a child laughs and two women squeal as if they are playing a game. Paha Sapa smells horseflesh and horse manure heavy in the thick summer air.

— There is the word... Li-BEE *...* Tasunke Witko. *The ghost says it over and over.* Li-BEE. *But I have no idea what it means. It is as if he is saying it in pain, as though it were the source of a wound.*

Crazy Horse turns to Run Fearless, Long Turd, and Loud Voice Hawk, but neither the chief nor holy man has heard this *wasichu* word before. Angry Badger also shakes his head while looking irritated at Paha Sapa and this entire conversation. Crazy Horse's fierce glance moves to Paha Sapa's *tunkašila,* but Limps-a-Lot only shrugs.

Crazy Horse barks to Run Fearless.

— Go bring in the Crow.

When Run Fearless returns, he is shoving and dragging along a Crow captive. The man's hands are tied in front of him and his legs are hobbled like a horse's. Paha Sapa guesses at once that this is one of the Crow scouts for the Seventh Cavalry whom Crazy Horse's warriors captured and kept alive at the Greasy Grass; he has heard in campfire talk that there were three, but only one has been kept alive. This man is wearing torn and bloody clothes. His face is swollen with bruises, one eye looks to be permanently battered shut, and someone has been playfully torturing him — three fingers on his right hand are gone, two fingers on his left hand, and one ear has been cut away.

Not for the first time (or the last), Paha Sapa feels a strange reaction deep inside — a wave of disgust or disapproval, perhaps — but it is not *his* reaction. The Paha Sapa of almost eleven summers feels no compassion for this captured enemy. And it is certainly not his ghost's reaction — Paha Sapa receives no emotions or thoughts from his ghost, only talk, talk, talk in the *wasichus'* language. No, it is more as if there is another, perhaps older, but definitely a *different* Paha Sapa within Paha Sapa, always watching and reacting to things somewhat differently than does the boy named Paha Sapa. The effect is disconcerting.

Crazy Horse is speaking.

— *This is one of Long Hair's scouts. I only wish we could have captured those four who were closest to Long Hair — Curly, White Man Runs Him, Goes Ahead, and Hairy Moccasin. This one's name is of no importance.*

The Crow grunts as if in recognition of the other scouts' names. Paha Sapa sees that all of the man's front teeth are missing.

Crazy Horse turns to Run Fearless.

— *Ask him in Crow language if Long Hair knew anyone called…*

He looks back at Paha Sapa.

— *Did you hear a* wasichu *name in your ghost dreams? What was it?*

Paha Sapa's heart is pounding wildly.

— *Li-BEE.*

Run Fearless asks the question in Crow. Paha Sapa recognizes a few of the words — the languages of the Lakota and the Crow are not so dissimilar — and then Run Fearless repeats the question in different words.

The Crow slowly smiles, showing the dark gaps and broken stumps of teeth. He speaks a short sentence that leaves Run Fearless looking dissatisfied.

Crazy Horse is impatient.

— *What did he say?*

— *He says — Why should I tell you anything about Long Hair? You will just continue to torture me and then kill me.*

Crazy Horse removes his long knife from its beaded sheath.

— *Tell him that if he answers truthfully and with everything he knows, he will die quickly, like a man. If he does not, he will have no manhood to die with.*

The Crow's smile disappears as he listens. He barks a sentence, and Run Fearless repeats…

— *Li-BEE.*

Seemingly despite his pain and position, the Crow smiles again. Through his swollen lips and gums, he mushes out several sentences.

Run Fearless stares at the man for a second before translating.

— *He says that this word was heard a lot at the fort and on the march. This Li-BEE was Long Hair's woman… his wife. Elizabeth Bacon Custer. Long Hair called her Li-Bee.*

All the older men in the room, including the Crow, are silent for a long moment. They are looking at Paha Sapa in a new way.

Long Turd breaks the silence a second before renewed thunder rolls across the village. The noise is so deep and so loud that the tipi hides vibrate like the skin of a drum.

— *Black Hills carries the ghost of Long Hair Custer.*

Crazy Horse grunts and speaks softly to Run Fearless.

— *Take the Crow out and kill him. One bullet. In the head. Tell him that his body will not be mutilated but left in a proper burial scaffold. He has earned a warrior's death.*

The Crow appears to have understood Crazy Horse's words and is mumbling his Death Song to himself as Run Fearless leads him hobbling out.

Limps-a-Lot motions to speak.

— *Surely you do not believe that man, Tasunke Witko. The Crow has every reason to lie to you. Why would a lesser scout know the name of Long Hair's woman?*

Crazy Horse merely grunts at this. From outside the tipi there comes the short, flat sound of a single pistol shot. The constant noise of the village — as common and reassuring and unheard as the inevitable buzz of grasshoppers in late summer here on the plains — silences itself for a moment. Crazy Horse continues to stare at Paha Sapa.

— *The rest of you go outside now. I want to talk to the boy alone.*

Paha Sapa sees Limps-a-Lot's reluctance to leave and notes the look his grandfather gives him — he *sees* it but cannot understand what the holy man is trying to say with the look — but Long Turd, Angry Badger, Loud Voice Hawk, and Limps-a-Lot stand and file out, closing the tipi flap behind them.

Paha Sapa looks into Crazy Horse's eyes and thinks — *This man may kill me.*

Crazy Horse slides closer and grabs Paha Sapa by the boy's upper arm. The grip is ferocious.

— *Can you see into a man's future, Black Hills? Can you?*

— *I do not know, Tasunke Witko. I believe so. Sometimes...*

Crazy Horse shakes the ten-year-old until Paha Sapa's teeth can be heard rattling like seeds in a gourd.

— Can you, damn you? Do you see a man's fate? Yes or no?

— I think sometimes, Tasunke Witko, *that I can . . .*

Crazy Horse shakes him again and then grabs Paha Sapa's bare forearm so fiercely that the boy can feel the bones bending.

— Fuck "sometimes"! Tell me now one thing I must know. Will I die at the hands of the wasichu? *Just yes or no, Paha Sapa, or I swear to* Wakan Tanka *and the Thunder Beings whom I serve that I will kill you this very day. Will I die at the hands of a* Wasicun, *of the* wasichu? *Yes or no?*

Crazy Horse pulls Paha Sapa's open hands up toward the warrior's scarred, heavily muscled chest and sets the palms of those small hands hard and flat against him.

Paha Sapa shakes as if lightning has struck him. The air inside the tipi suddenly stinks of ozone. The boy's eyes roll back under his fluttering eyelids, and he tries weakly to pull away from the man, but Crazy Horse's grip is too strong. From a great distance Paha Sapa hears the roll of actual thunder and the equally low growl of Crazy Horse's demanding voice. . . .

— Will I die at the hands of the wasichu? *Will the white man kill me? Yes or no!*

———

IT IS LIKE THE OTHER VISIONS Paha Sapa has had — flashes of images, explosions of sounds, a strange lack of color, lack of context, lack of control, lack of understanding of what is happening when or where — but this black-and-white image is stronger, faster, and more terrifying.

Paha Sapa tastes Crazy Horse's fear and desperation. He recognizes faces and remembers names through Crazy Horse's careering, terrified, defiant, leaping thoughts.

They are in some sort of *wasichu* compound — a fort, a camp, an agency — but Paha Sapa has never been in such a place and does not recognize it, nor do Crazy Horse's increasingly desperate thoughts reveal the location. The heat is that of summer or very early autumn, but Paha Sapa cannot guess the year. He sees through Crazy Horse's eyes, but he also is above the shoving crowds, looking *down* on Crazy Horse and the others as if he, Paha Sapa, were staring through the eyes of a soaring raven or sparrow, so he can see that Crazy Horse looks much the same age as he does at this very instant, as he continues shaking Paha Sapa and pressing Paha Sapa's suddenly freezing-cold palms flat and hard against the warrior's chest and...

—*Am I a prisoner?* That is Little Bordeaux Creek, fifteen miles out, where the scouts joined the rumbling, rocking ambulance; there is stock grazing at Chadron Creek. Lakota on horseback. Now they are *in* the camp, amid the log buildings, two hundred, three hundred Indians, Lakota but also Brulé and others: Big Road, Iron Hawk, Turning Bear, the Minneconjou Wooden Knife, a *Wasicun*—the sounds Cap-tain Ken-ning-ton thud into Paha Sapa's brain like tomahawk strikes—and more Brulés: Swift Bear, Black Crow, Crow Dog, Standing Bear—Bordeaux, the interpreter Billy Garnett—and Touch the Clouds and his son there with Fast Thunder—Crazy Horse is being led, men are shouting, Crazy Horse is being pulled into one of the *wasichu* fort structures—where blue-shirted soldiers stand guard....

—*What kind of place is this?*

Is it Crazy Horse shouting? Paha Sapa cannot tell. He whirls above the masses of heads; black braided hair; wide-brimmed, sweat-stained hats; feathers; and now he is down behind Crazy Horse's eyes again as Little Big Man and Cap-tain Ken-ning-ton keep pulling Crazy Horse forward, toward and into the little house.

—*I won't go in there.*

Shoving. Shouting. A scout screams *Go ahead! I have the gun! Do what you want with him!* Crazy Horse is pulling away from grasping hands, leaping forward, away from the darkness, toward the opening and the light. Little Big Man is screaming *Nephew, don't! Don't do that! Nephew! Don't! Don't do that!*

—*Let me go! Get your hands... Let me... go!*

Blades are rising; rifles are rising. They are *wasichu* bayonets on rifles held by *wasichus*. Crazy Horse pulls out his blade for slicing tobacco, cuts Little Big Man's flesh between the thumb and forefinger. As the older man shouts, Crazy Horse slashes Little Big Man's forearm while he imagines cutting long strings of flesh away from a deer's white bone.

—Kill the son of a bitch! Kill the son of a bitch! Kill the fucker! Kill him! Kill him! Kill the son of a bitch! It is Ken-ning-ton screaming. It is the language of Paha Sapa's ghost, and Paha Sapa still cannot understand it. But he sees and feels and understands the spittle striking Crazy Horse's face as the *Wasicun* continues to scream at the blue-coated soldiers and guards with their rifles and bayonets raised.

Perhaps the *wasichu* soldier-guard behind Crazy Horse only means to prod with the bayonet, but Crazy Horse is pulling violently backward at that second, losing his balance, and the blade possibly meant to prod tears through Crazy Horse's shirt just above his left hip and keeps moving forward, piercing the war chief's lower back, Crazy Horse's own weight and movement driving the long steel blade deeper between his kidneys and into his bowels. Crazy Horse grunts. Paha Sapa screams but still hovers both as a bird above, beneath the roof but hovering, but also behind Crazy Horse's own eyes.

Redness descending, Crazy Horse grunts in pain. The *wasichu* guard pulls the bayonet out, the butt striking the log wall of the inside of the guardhouse, then—as terrified as all the others but gifted with terrible action—by the drill—*one, two, and three,* but silently—thrusts the rifle and bayonet forward again, the point going deep into Crazy Horse's lower back, between ribs, up into Crazy Horse's wheezing left lung—depriving the chief of wind and words for a moment—then the guard is grunting and pulling the long blade free again, the steel sliding slickly and obscenely out of Crazy Horse's bleeding flesh.

—Let me go now.

It is Crazy Horse, speaking softly amid the shouting and bedlam and shoving and screaming.

—Let me go now. You've hurt me.

The *wasichu* sentry circles, rifle extended, and lunges again, from the front this time, toward Crazy Horse's belly. But the steel misses under Crazy Horse's arm and embeds itself in the wood of the door frame. Little Big Man is holding Crazy Horse's other arm and is screaming for the *wasichu* to do something—to stab him again?

Crazy Horse's Minneconjou uncle Spotted Crow grabs the stuck rifle, pulls the blade free, and drives the butt of the long gun into Little Big

Man's belly, sending the short traitor whoofing into the dust on all fours.

— *You have done this before! You are always in the way!*

It is Spotted Crow screaming this as Crazy Horse falls backward into the arms of Swift Bear and two others. One of those three is saying haughtily, insanely, to the wounded warrior—

— *We told you to behave yourself! We warned you!*

Crazy Horse groans and finally leans, sags, and falls. The motion seems to take long minutes. Cartridges are being chambered and hammers clicked back on *wasichu* rifles all around. Crazy Horse holds both his bloody palms out toward the men around him, Indian and white man alike.

— ***See where I am hurt? Do you see? I can feel the blood flowing out of me!***

Closed Cloud, a Brulé, brings a blanket to spread over the dying chief, but Crazy Horse grabs at the Brulé's braids and shakes the warrior's head back and forth even as Crazy Horse jerks his own head back and forth in agony and fury.

— ***You all coaxed me over here. You all told me to come here. And then you ran away and left me! You all left me!***

He Dog takes the blanket out of Closed Cloud's hands, crumples it into a pillow, and sets it under Crazy Horse's head. Then He Dog takes his own blanket from his shoulders and spreads it over the fallen man.

— *I will take you home,* Tasunke Witko.

Then He Dog walks away across the parade ground toward a building there.

Paha Sapa shuts his eyes, inner and outer, so that he cannot see more. But he does see more. He screams so that he cannot hear what he is hearing.

He awakens to Crazy Horse bending over him on one knee, just as he did at the Greasy Grass—the warrior's face even more fierce than that time yet similar to the expression of disgust he showed weeks earlier. Crazy Horse is flicking water from a wooden bowl into Paha Sapa's face.

— *What do you see, Black Hills? Do you see my death?*

—*I don't know! I can't…It isn't…I don't* know.

Crazy Horse shakes him harder, snapping Paha Sapa's teeth together with the violence of the shaking.

— *Will I die by the hand of the* wasichu? *That is what I need to know.*

Crazy Horse's shaking and slapping have hidden those final memories from Paha Sapa in a way that closing his eyes and covering his ears failed to do. The boy feels like sobbing. It's not enough that he has become infected with a ghost that gibbers and mumbles all through his nights; now Paha Sapa knows that the flood of sensations and twice-removed memories that have poured into him during the contact with Crazy Horse almost certainly constitutes *all* of that weird warrior's memories, from his earliest childhood perceptions to those of his death just moments or seconds beyond what Paha Sapa has just witnessed. There is no doubt that the white soldier's wounding of Crazy Horse by bayonet thrust will be mortal.

— *I don't know! I did not see the…the final…the ending,* Tasunke Witko.

Crazy Horse throws Paha Sapa back into the hides and robes and jumps to his feet. His killing knife is in his hand and his eyes are not sane.

— *You are lying to me, Black Hills. You know, but you are afraid to tell me. But you will tell me, I promise you that.*

The warrior turns and stalks out. Paha Sapa does sob now, weeping into his forearm so that Limps-a-Lot and the others outside the lodge will not hear him. He did not see how long it will take for Crazy Horse to die from the bayonet wounds — and the glimpses *of* Crazy Horse he was able to catch showed a warrior not much older than the man who just left the tipi, a year perhaps, no more than two — but Paha Sapa *did* see an absolute conviction in the heart and thoughts of Crazy Horse when the war leader forced him to use his gift.

Crazy Horse is going to kill Paha Sapa whether the boy tells him his future or not.

———

PAHA SAPA HAS BEEN ASSIGNED a lodge separate from the village. Limps-a-Lot visits him there that night, late. Crazy Horse and his men have ridden away to their own *tiyospaye,* but the chief said that he would return by midday the next day, bringing Long Turd and other *wičasa wakan* to identify the *Wasicun* inside the boy and then to drive the ghost out, even if the ghost-driving-out ceremonies take weeks. Paha Sapa has been told to fast and to purify himself in the sweat lodge that has been erected near his isolated tipi.

— *Grandfather, I have seen that Tasunke Witko intends to kill me.*

Limps-a-Lot nods and sets his huge hand on Paha Sapa's thin shoulder.

— *I agree, Black Hills. I do not have your gift of forward- or inward-seeing, but I agree that Crazy Horse will kill you if you tell him that the* wasichu *will someday kill him and he will kill you if you say that they will not or even if you keep silent. He is certain that the ghost within you is Long Hair's ghost, and Crazy Horse is afraid of it. He wants the ghost to die with you.*

Paha Sapa is ashamed of his girlish tears earlier. Now he only feels empty and very young.

— *What shall I do, Grandfather?*

Limps-a-Lot leads him out of the tipi. Hundreds of broad strides away, the northernmost campfires of the village glow. A dog barks. Two young men on guard duty out among the horses grazing across the stream call softly to each other. An owl hoots in a cottonwood along that stream. Low clouds have moved in like a gray blanket to hide the moon and stars. Thunder continues to rumble from the south, but no rain has fallen yet. It is very hot.

Paha Sapa realizes that there are two horses standing there in the dark. One is Limps-a-Lot's favorite, the good-running roan he calls Worm, and the other is the broad-backed white mare belonging to Three Buffalo Woman. That mare is now piled high with carefully tied robes and gear, and Worm has Paha Sapa's own blanket, bow, quiver of arrows, lance, and other items on his back.

Limps-a-Lot points to the south.

— *You must leave tonight and take Worm and the mare that Three Buffalo Woman calls* Pehánska. *You are to ride* itokagata, *south, past Bear Butte to the Black Hills. Go all the way into the Black Hills, deep into them, but travel with care — Crazy Horse's and Angry Badger's scouts say that white men have poured into our sacred hills during the past few moons and even built new cities there. Crazy Horse has vowed before everyone to go to the Paha Sapa next week and to kill every* wasichu *he finds there.*

—Grandfather, if Crazy Horse and his warriors are going to the Black Hills soon, why are you sending me there? Would I not be safer if I rode north, toward Grandmother's Country?

—You would be, and I will tell Crazy Horse that I loaned you my horses so that you could go to Grandmother's Country.

—He will kill you for helping me, Tunkašila.

Limps-a-Lot grunts and shakes his head.

—No, he will not. *It would set the bands to fighting, and Crazy Horse wants to kill* wasichus *by the thousand this year, not other Lakota. Not yet. And you must go to the Black Hills because there you must have your* hanblečeya.... *Your Vision must come to you there and nowhere else. This I know. Do you remember all that I have taught you about purifying yourself, building the sweat lodge, and singing to the Six Grandfathers?*

—I remember, Grandfather. When may I return?

—Not until after your successful hanblečeya, *Paha Sapa, even if that takes weeks or months. And in both going south and coming back north, travel carefully—keep the horses off ridgelines, hide in willows and streambeds when you can, act as if you are in the middle of Pawnee country. Both Crazy Horse and the* wasichus *will kill you on sight. Our village will be somewhere between Slim Buttes and Arikara country to the north, but be careful even to the coming in when you return.... Hide and observe the village for a day and a night and a day to be sure it is safe.*

—Yes, Grandfather.

—Now go.

Limps-a-Lot swings the boy up and onto the back of Worm and hands him the hide rope for *Pehánska*, White Crane. The holy man peers into the midnight-black south.

—I think it will begin storming tonight and rain for many days. This is good. It will be very hard for Crazy Horse to track you, and he was never that good a tracker. But head west to where the stream runs south from Slim Buttes and stay in the river for as many hours as you can, then try to stay on the hard, rocky land. Hide during the day if you have to. Good-bye, Paha Sapa.

—Good-bye, Grandfather.

— *Toksha ake čante ista wacinyanktin ktelo, Paha Sapa.*

I shall see you again with the eye of my heart.

Limps-a-Lot turns and walks as quickly as he can back to the lighted village. Clucking the horses into silence, Paha Sapa turns their heads southwest and rides into the night.

10

George Armstrong Custer

Libbie, my dearest.

I have been lying here in the healing darkness thinking about how you looked that first time I met you—formally met you, since I had seen you as a little girl and even worshipped you from afar years before in Monroe—in 1862 at that Thanksgiving party at the girls' finishing school. Your dark hair, all in perfectly formed ringlets, fell down over your bare shoulders that night. Your pale face and exposed skin glowed like ivory in the candlelight. I remember how I was stunned by the dark slashes of your eyebrows above your daunting, expressive eyes, and by how even your slightest and most demure of smiles brought out those dimples. You were twenty-one years old that autumn, and your body had ripened far from the stick-figure girl in the blue pinafore I had glimpsed on Monroe's main streets in earlier years. The gown you wore that night to the Thanksgiving party was cut low enough for me to see your ample bosom. I could have set my hands fully around your slim waist and felt my fingertips touch.

Do you remember last autumn, when we spent our leave from Fort Abraham Lincoln in New York? We were so poor—in all my years of service and, some might say, of fame, I have never chosen to profit from my service to my country—so poor that we had to stay at the dreadful boardinghouse and take the freezing, drafty horsecars to the various receptions and dinners to which we were invited because we had no money for a cab. I had my one civilian suit. Only one. You had several lovely dresses for those balls and receptions, but they were dresses you had used and mended and made small changes on for many seasons and carried back and forth in your trunk across the prairie and continent with you many times.

You remember that forty times that cold autumn and colder winter in New York we went to see Julius Caesar *performed, not because either of us liked the play that much — I grew to despise it — but because the actor and our friend Lawrence Barrett always left two complimentary tickets for us whenever he appeared. We suffered* Julius Caesar *forty times those cold months because it was free and gave us an excuse to leave the loud, crowded, food-smelling boardinghouse.*

But do you also remember that December when, on a rare quiet night in our boardinghouse room when everyone but us seemed gone from the place, you and I lay in bed and talked about how we wished we had actually met when we were both children?

"What would you have done with me if you'd known me when I was a wee maiden?" you asked.

"Seduced you," I whispered. "Made love to you at once."

And then, you remember, my darling, you asked me to shave away your glorious thatch of black hair there, using my campaign razor and the hotel shaving soap. And you remember how I lit the extra candle and set the small mirror — at your request — so that you could watch the transformation even as it took place. Oh, how you trusted me, my darling. And how you shuddered and blushed when I kissed your now pale and hairless mons and continued kissing lower.

And how, when we were in the box at yet another performance of Julius Caesar *or arriving at yet another general's or politician's home for yet another reception — I was the Boy General, perhaps the most famous young general of the war, and much in demand, as were you for your loveliness — you would squeeze my hand without looking at me and blush most becomingly, and I would know you were thinking about the maidenly absence beneath your silk gown and petticoats. And both of us then could think only about the play or reception being over and of returning to our sacred little room at the odious boardinghouse.*

———

My darling Libbie.

I have been thinking about the autumn three years ago, just after my Yellowstone Campaign, when you finally came out to join me at Fort Abraham Lincoln. The frame house the soldiers had built for us there was beautiful; the first real home you and I had ever occupied.

That first Saturday you were there, you and I rose before dawn and rode far west out on the Dakota plain, leaving the fort far behind even before the sun rose.

You complained because decorum demanded that you ride sidesaddle, even though I know you prefer to ride like a boy. By nine a.m. we were far, far out on the prairie and we roughly followed the meanderings of that one small stream that curled east back toward Bismarck and the fort and the Missouri River, the few cottonwoods along that sad little creek the only signs of life except for the low-nibbled grass and sage and Spanish bayonet.

We came across a single bull buffalo and I told you to stay back while I shot it, but you rode along close behind, clinging tight to your saddle horn with your free hand as your horse galloped faster than any lady riding sidesaddle had a right to demand of the animal. The bull was old enough — and perhaps alone enough — that he quit his half-hearted loping within a mile and merely stood there on the prairie, head down, occasionally taking an absent-minded munch of the short-cropped prairie grass, acting as if we were no threat at all.

We both dismounted. You held the horses' reins while I removed my custom-made Remington sporting rifle from its scabbard. There was no tree or branch to use as a support, but I went to one knee and steadied the relatively short but heavy rifle as best I could.

The Remington No. 1 Sporting Rifle had become my favorite during my Yellowstone expedition, and I'd killed antelope, buffalo, elk, blacktail deer, white wolves, geese, and prairie chickens with it at distances up to 630 yards. (I confess to you, Libbie, that some of the prairie chickens simply exploded into feathers upon the impact of the 425-gram .50-caliber bullet backed by 70 grains of black powder.) The .50–70 had allowed me to bring down forty-one antelopes at a distance of 250 yards, so I had little doubt that it would serve for this single old bull bison at less than a hundred yards.

It took only one shot to the heart. The ancient bull dropped as if eager to leave its lonely world.

When you and I rode up to the fallen beast, you said, "What will you do now, darling?" and I replied, "Oh, send some of the men out to carve up the carcass, although I fear this old fellow will be tough chewing. But the head is magnificent."

"What would the Indians do?" you asked.

"The Indians," I said, surprised. "You mean the Sioux or Cheyenne?"

"Yes," you said, smiling sweetly at me as we sat there in the heat, the saddles creaking under us, flies already beginning to buzz around the dead bison's blood.

"The Indians would immediately cut its belly open and eat all or part of the poor fellow's liver," I said.

You slid off your horse and looked up at me. Your face, so radiant in the clear, warm autumn sunlight, held a new kind of excitement, one I had never seen before.

"Oh, let's *do that, Autie," you said.*

I remember that I stayed mounted and just laughed. "We would both be covered with blood," I said. "Hardly the way for the commanding officer's wife to return from a ride during her first week at Fort Abe Lincoln. What would the men in the regiment think?"

In response you began stripping out of your clothes. I remember glancing around anxiously, but the prairie was its usual tan and barren early-autumn void. Except for a low line of willows along the creek a mile to the north, only twenty miles of mid-morning flat prairie emptiness met the eye. I dismounted and rushed to disrobe next to you.

When we were naked except for our boots (the prairie is a living pincushion of tiny cacti and not-so-tiny thorns and stickers and quick-scuttling biting things), I took my long hunting knife from its beaded scabbard and slit the bison along the length of its distended belly. The mass of organs and connecting tubules and endless yards of gray-glistening guts slid out as easily as the dumped contents of a black and hairy purse. You couldn't believe it when I cut away the liver and held it up between us.

"Dear God." You laughed excitedly. "It's as large as a man's head."

"Larger than this man's," I said, and began slicing into the heavy mass. A fluid thick and black burbled up in the cuts along with the blood. "Do you want the first slice?" I asked, glancing yet again over my shoulder to make sure that we were alone and unobserved.

"No," you said. "Do not cut it up as if we were at a table, Autie. Let us take communion here as if we were Sioux or Cheyenne."

You took the liver—you were barely able to hold it up, I remember, and I had to help you steady it just above your face—and your perfect white teeth flashed as you bit deep. You gnawed *that chunk of the old bull's liver off and away and then chewed maniacally rather than choke. The blood and bile (or whatever that darker fluid was) spattered your chin and cheeks and bare breasts and the slight bulge of your belly.*

I would have laughed then, but there was something too ceremonial, too ancient, too physical . . . too terrifying . . . *in watching you take yet another bite of that liver, the blood now flowing down over your chin like a red Niagara.*

Straining, your shoulders and soiled upper arms showing muscles I'd never no-ticed, you handed the heavy, bleeding, seeping mass to me.

I managed to chew off three heavy chunks. I usually enjoy the cooked liver from bison, antelopes, deer, or cows, tossed in flour perhaps and fried up with bacon and onions, but this raw, thick-skinned organ tasted overwhelmingly sour. There was as much of the blood and heavy liquid in my mouth as there was meat.

I did not laugh. I chewed slowly, sacramentally, and then tossed the heavy liver back into the fly-gathering pile of guts and heart and stomach and more guts.

We both drank deeply from our respective canteens then.

I looked down at us—blood everywhere in streaks and rivulets and spatters and explosive patterns across my scarred flesh and your ivory-white skin, it looked as if I were wearing red gauntlets up to the elbow—and I said, "Now what, my dearest?"

Setting your canteen carefully back on your saddle, handling it gingerly so as not to leave more bloody handprints than necessary, you said, "Can we reach that creek on one horse?"

I looked toward the meandering line of willows to the north. "On one horse?" I understood her logic then. "There aren't many horses I would trust with that duty, but Vic is one of them," I said, and began removing his saddle and gear.

Leaving only the saddle blanket, I swung up on Vic's broad (but not too broad) back. The sorrel (Victory had the blaze face and white socks, you remember, my dearest Libbie) smelled the blood seeping into the ground and on us and he was skittish, but I pulled hard back on the reins and told you to stand on the saddle on the ground, reach up, and I would swing you up behind me.

"No," you said, that strange, radiant, laughingly mad and excited look on your face again, "in front of you, Autie."

"It would be more comfortable for you riding behind me and holding on with…" I began.

You laid your breasts and face against my bare leg and thigh. "In front of you, Autie," you whispered up. "Facing you."

And so we rode the mile to the hidden creek. Your breasts pressed against me, and the bison's blood flowed over them onto my chest and down. Your arms held me fiercely. In your left hand you held a wad of petticoats—our towels if we ever got to the stream.

I had Vic walking, but I spurred him to a canter and you set your hands on my shoulders and hitched yourself up higher against me, your blood-spattered white thighs rising and engulfing. I was already excited. Then you mounted me.

Your breath was hot against the side of my neck. "Faster," you groaned.

I spurred Vic to a slow, steady, but still violent gallop. I rose and fell in you with each downward pounding of his hooves and great, heaving trunk. I held you tight with my right arm, held Vic's reins with my left hand. The sorrel wanted to run hard. I let him.

We cried out together, I believe—both of us squeezing the other impossibly tighter and closer as we rose and fell, rose and fell to Vic's hard gallop. We could not have been closer. Both of us threw our heads far back at the same instant, shouting at the sun.

I remember the ecstasy as being so intense that it went beyond pain. The blood smeared across us, dripping from us, flying behind us as Vic galloped, seemed appropriate. Even the sour-blood-and-bile aftertaste of the slivers of buffalo liver were part of the pain and sunlight and release—a source of unbelievable and never-to-be-recaptured strength and passion.

And love.

There was a tiny bit of water left in the creek, enough to get the worst of the blood and gore off us, but we had to take turns lying in the deepest part, our bodies wider than the stream, each of us rolling and rubbing against the pebbled stream bottom like crazy otters. We ended up using the petticoats more as sponges than as towels and simply buried them in the mud and reeds when we were done.

When we came out of the willows to remount Vic, I shared my fear with you, my darling Libbie...that all of the Seventh Cavalry would be coming into sight from the east just as we mounted up, still a mile from your hobbled horse and our clothes.

That set us laughing. You were behind me riding back, your breasts full and insistent against my back, one of your hands flat across my chest but the other possessively on my inner thigh, and we could not stop laughing even as we dressed (your one remaining petticoat did little to fill out the riding outfit). We laughed most of the way back to the fort and when we managed to gain control of ourselves, one of us would glance across at the other and the laughter would start up again.

It was love, of course, Libbie, and passion for each other, but it was you yourself who later said it—"I have never felt more alive, Autie!" I had, but only in the heat of combat. I did not tell you that then and do so now only because I know that you will understand.

Sometimes, my darling, I wonder if this restorative sleep I am in now might not slip into coma and the coma inexorably into death, but then I remember moments such as that morning on the prairie and know that this is not possible. . . . I will not, I cannot, I shall not die before seeing you again. Before talking to you again.

Before making love to you again.

On the Six Grandfathers

August 1936

PRESIDENT ROOSEVELT IS DEFINITELY COMING TO THE BLACK
Hills.

Word on the cliff face and on the faces themselves is that
the president has given in to Borglum's endless pleadings and will include in his busy South Dakota itinerary a formal dedication of the
Thomas Jefferson head, probably on Sunday, August 30.

Less than a week's time, thinks Paha Sapa. He can be ready by then.

Work on Mount Rushmore continues at the fastest pace in the project's history despite the fact that this summer of 1936 is the hottest in
the *wasichus'* own recorded history.

Every day this summer, Paha Sapa listens to the other men talking
about the temperature and about the forest fires to the north and about
the Dust Bowl to the south. Average temperatures in July registered a
full ten degrees above normal and August has been worse. Out on the
plains where Rapid City swelters, midday temperatures hover around
110 and have touched 115 at least once. For Paha Sapa and the others
working on the Rushmore cliff face, it is like being in a giant white
bowl that focuses the sun's rays. Not only does a worker's back blister
from the sun, but the heat and light reflected from the increasingly
white layers of granite strike them like some sort of focused heat ray
out of a science-fiction magazine.

All this August, the stone has been too hot to touch with ungloved hands for the long daylight hours. Paha Sapa's and the other powder-men's placement of the dynamite has been riskier than ever, with even the new sticks and blasting caps less stable in the searing, focused heat, and the rock itself threatening to ignite any one of the hundreds of shortened and fused sticks as they are tamped into place. On some days this August, despite his overpowering rush to finish the Jefferson head, Borglum has ordered the men off the cliff face for hours at a time, at least until lengthening shadows offer some relief from the heat.

Dehydration is the serious threat. Paha Sapa's presumably cancer-ridden body feels it constantly, but now all the men are fearful of it. Borglum has set some men dangling full-time in their bosun's chairs just to keep delivering water to the men working on the drilling and polishing, but it seems that no matter how many times a man drinks, his body always craves more. Paha Sapa has never seen the workers as tired as these slouching, shuffling, dust-coated figures coming down the 506 wooden steps each evening. Even the youngest, strongest men shuffle like the red-eyed, white-coated walking dead they are by the end of the workday up here.

With less than a week to go before President Roosevelt arrives, Paha Sapa spends his hours crimping and placing dynamite thinking about how to deliver the ton or more of explosives he will need next Sunday to bring down all three of the presidents' heads in front of the horrified crowd (but not, he will take measures, down *on* them). But his epiphany on that matter the previous week makes Paha Sapa smile; all this time he's been thinking about the problem as if he were *planting* the charges in their predrilled holes—hundreds upon hundreds of them for a blast this large—requiring weeks or months of drilling, if nothing else. But this will be no careful, business-as-usual carving of the Monument; this is the *destruction* of it. There will be no follow-up polishing charges or drilling or buffing, only ragged stone left—blasted away to the bed-rock so that Borglum (or anyone) can never carve out sculptures here again. Paha Sapa smiles again at his own stupidity, bred by too many years working here as a faithful, skilled employee.

All he has to do by next Sunday is hide, in carefully placed and covered positions on and around all three heads, about twenty of the larger crates of dynamite he has hidden in his hovel in Keystone. One electric blasting cap and wire will do for each of the crates. If he prepositions the crates, he will be able to get them up the mountain and hide them and arm them on Saturday night—the flurry of work and activity on Friday and Saturday will be mostly cosmetic, buffing up the stone, especially on Jefferson's head, and arranging the flag with which Borglum plans to cover the head until the unveiling.

Paha Sapa shakes his head with the simplicity of the solution and his own opacity at not seeing it months—years—earlier. He can blame it now on the rare morphine injections he's begun to give himself so that he can continue working.

Six more days? Can his five years on the hill, those thousands of days, come down to six more days?

Paha Sapa will not see the aftermath—he plans to go out with the heads in the mighty blast that will be the headline in every newspaper and on every radio broadcast and movie newsreel for weeks—but he knows he will be seen as a villain. For a while he will replace the infamous Bruno Hauptmann, or perhaps that rising new German villain Adolf Hitler, as "Americans' most hated man."

Roosevelt, Paha Sapa has heard, is coming to South Dakota and the West purely for political reasons. (Do presidents and other politicians, Paha Sapa wonders, ever do *anything* for any reason other than political?)

South Dakota had been a Republican state since time immemorial, since bison and those red savages were the only (nonvoting) citizens there, but Roosevelt carried it in 1932 and has no intention of allowing it to go back into the Republican column in the 1936 election, now just two months and a dusty handful of days away. More than merely wooing South Dakotans amid the Depression and the forest fires and the record heat, this will be billed as the jaunty president's "Dust Bowl tour"—Roosevelt's first effort to get out and see the havoc that the increasingly perverse climate is wreaking on a huge swath of the nation he rules from Washington and shady Hyde Park—although, Paha Sapa knows, the president's destinations of Rapid City and Mount Rushmore are many hundreds of miles north of the northern boundaries of the actual, physical Dust Bowl.

While Paha Sapa cuts dynamite sticks into workable lengths—no gloves today for the fine work, so he will have a headache tonight—and prepares the fuses and blasting caps, he remembers his encounter with this so-called Dust Bowl.

———

BY SPRING OF THE PREVIOUS YEAR, 1935, work on the Monument was shutting down periodically for lack of funding. These funding gaps, often as imagined as real, and the brief work stoppages that came from them were a regular feature of work on Mount Rushmore, and the men were used to them, but this pause in the spring of '35 was more about Gutzon Borglum's battles with John Boland (Borglum's theoretical boss on the commission that oversaw the Rushmore carving) and Senator Peter Norbeck (the greatest supporter that the Monument ever had).

Borglum had never been able to tolerate "supervision" and he was poisoning his own nest that spring with his attacks on Boland, Norbeck, and his other most loyal supporters. So for a few days before Palm Sunday, 1935, Paha Sapa and the other men had neither work on the cliff nor pay coming in.

Then Borglum called Paha Sapa in to inform him that he and Borglum's son, Lincoln, and two other men would be driving to southern Colorado to pick up two submarine engines.

Paha Sapa had heard about the engines.

The compressors, drills, twenty-some jackhammers, winches, tramway, and other machinery on the mountain needed a tremendous amount of steam and electrical energy, and Borglum had "upgraded" the old powerhouse several times, first moving it from its original location in nearby Keystone to the valley here and then increasing the size of the steam boilers and electrical generators. But, in Borglum's view, there was never enough power, and recently the sculptor had accused commission member John Boland of shutting down the Insull Plant in Keystone not because it was worn out, as Boland had claimed, but for reasons of private profit.

Senator Norbeck informed Borglum that these sorts of wild attacks on Boland would get the entire project canceled, but Borglum persisted in both his attacks on Boland's reasons for shutting down the original powerhouse and his lobbying for larger engines, turbines, and generators in the new plant.

The response in the winter of 1934 was that the navy would donate two used but still-functioning diesel engines from a submarine they were decommissioning.

— *Probably two pieces of prehistorical junk left over from the Great War!*

Borglum had thrown the letter across the room.

Whatever shape the diesels were in, the War Department promptly shipped them to the wrong place. Rather than getting them to Mount Rushmore or to Keystone or to Rapid City, the navy sent them by rail to the Ryan-Rushmore Electrical Works at the Colorado Steel plant in Pueblo, Colorado. And there, on a siding, the two giant banks of engines had sat under a tarp for two months. The Navy and the War Department acknowledged their small error but said that it was Borglum's problem to get the monstrous things from southern Colorado to South Dakota.

Borglum seemed as distracted and angry as ever when he called Paha Sapa into his office at the studio on April 10.

— *Billy, Lincoln's going to take you and Red Anderson and Hoot Lynch down to Colorado in the pickup truck and the big flatbed Dodge we have on loan from Howdy Peterson's cousin's construction company. You're going to bring back those damned submarine engines.*

— *OK, Boss. Do we get paid for the trip?*

Borglum only stared at him with his most evil eye.

Paha Sapa started over.

— *I don't know how much a submarine engine weighs, Mr. Borglum, but I know we'll need a crane to get them onto that Dodge's flatbed. And odds are low to none that the Dodge's suspension will handle a load that heavy all the way back from Colorado.*

Borglum merely coughed his dismissal of that worry.

— *The diesel monsters are at a steel plant, Old Man. They'll have a crane, a ramp, whatever you need to load the things. Lincoln will take care of everything. He'll have some walking-around money for you and Red and Hoot during the trip. Consider it your vacation for this year. If you leave in the next hour, the four of you can get down into Nebraska tonight before it gets too dark.*

Paha Sapa had nodded and gone to find the other three.

They did get into Nebraska that evening, the two vehicles driving due south. Lincoln Borglum led in the Ford pickup truck, Hoot

Lynch and Red Anderson both crowded into the passenger side. The two were close friends and disliked missing conversations and neither liked Paha Sapa all that much.

Paha Sapa didn't mind driving alone, he preferred it actually, but the 1928 Dodge truck with its bug eyes and floating fenders and extended flatbed was a pure pig to drive. The whole vehicle was a dinosaur from earlier design days, including an opening slab of windshield that had to be battened down with brass clamps. The clamps were gone, the windshield never completely closed, and the result was that if they were lucky enough to find a patch of highway where they could drive thirty miles per hour, the cold air poured in over Paha Sapa. He was wearing his son's leather motorcycle jacket and his heaviest gloves, but his fingers were numb after just the first twenty-five miles, and the big truck steered so poorly that his arms ached abysmally from the exertion by the end of that first afternoon and evening.

Paha Sapa didn't mind the pain. It distracted him from the worse pain lower down.

They didn't drive very long after dark, since dust was blowing up with the Nebraska wind and Borglum had told his son not to drive at night if the dust storms were obscuring vision. They got permission to camp in a farmer's field that first night, hunkering the trucks down behind a lone line of pine trees put there a generation earlier to serve as a windbreak. They'd stopped by Halley's Store in Keystone — the better of the two general stores there (Paha Sapa always expected Art Lyndoe's store to go out of business, it extended so much credit to the miners and other locals) — and picked up some bread and bologna and canned goods for the trip.

There was no extra wood for a campfire, so they heated their pork and beans over cans of Sterno. It was a poor substitute for a real campfire, but they huddled in their sleeping bags — Paha Sapa had only two blankets — and tried to talk a few minutes before turning in to sleep at seven p.m.

With the wind and light dust storm, the talk invariably turned to the endless drought and the weather. Both of the Dakotas had seen their share of blowing dirt — just the year before, in '34, Mount Rushmore and the Rapid City area had had two days of darkness as uncounted tons of topsoil blew high over them in the jet stream, darkening the sun, that "duster" finally reaching New York City and the Atlantic Ocean—but it was Nebraska and states south that were really drying up and blowing away. At least South Dakota still had grass on its prairie.

Red Anderson cleared his throat.

—*I was talking to a CCC boss who says that President Roosevelt's got men out traveling all over the world hunting for the right kind of pine or fir tree. Roosevelt's got experts advising him that they could build a huge windbreak, just like this'n, only stretching from Mexico to Canada, and the farmers could huddle in its lee, like.*

Lincoln Borglum and Hoot chuckled at the image. Red frowned at them.

—*I'm serious. He really said it.*

Lincoln nodded.

—*And I bet they are considering such a windbreak, although where on earth they'll find a pine tree that can put up with this heat and these droughts, all the way down through Texas, I have no idea. And I heard from another CCC boss that the president was also being advised by his so-called experts to just save the expense and evacuate the south of Nebraska, major parts of Kansas, most of Oklahoma, east Colorado, and all of the Texas Panhandle down to Lubbock . . . just let the plowed-up topsoil blow away and hope the grasses come back in a generation or two.*

Hoot Lynch snorted as he scooped up the last of his beans.

— *Well, that's one shit-poor idea, if you ask me.*

Red shot his pal a glance, and Hoot sort of bobbed his head in the direction of Borglum's son.

—*Sorry, didn't mean to . . . I mean . . .*

Lincoln Borglum grinned.

—*I don't mind a little cussin', Hoot. If it doesn't get in the way of things. I'm not a Mormon.*

The other two men laughed at that, and Paha Sapa found himself holding back a smile. He knew that Lincoln's father, Gutzon Borglum, *had* been a Mormon—his parents Mormon, his father with two wives—and that the woman Borglum listed as his mother was actually his father's second wife, and his real mother had left the family after they'd moved due to persecution of the Mormons.

Paha Sapa knew this because he had had a confused glut of Gutzon Borglum's memories, including the direst secrets, in his mind since that day in the Homestake Mine in 1931 when Borglum had come to hire him, Paha Sapa, and then offered to shake hands when the deal was done. With that handshake, Paha Sapa had almost staggered back as all of Borglum's memories had flowed into him. Just as Crazy Horse's had back in the late summer of 1876.

Just as Rain's had that first night they'd kissed in 1893.

Luckily, these three people's lifetimes of memories (and Rain's was so sadly short!) were passive—there to confuse Paha Sapa at the time but not shouting out and interrupting and babbling away into the night the way the ghost of Custer still did.

Sometimes, Paha Sapa was sure that the bulk and weight and noise of these other memories, not to mention the ghost rattling its bars for almost sixty years now, were sure to drive him mad. But at other times he was glad the memories were there and he found himself walking through the corridors of Borglum's past or Crazy Horse's—more seldom Rain's, since it was so painful to do so—the way Doane Robinson might wander the stacks of a particularly fine reference library.

Lincoln said to Paha Sapa—

—*Did you attach the drag chain under the Dodge the way I said?*

—*Yes.*

They were coming down into the land of dusters and black blizzards now—there were twenty other names for these sudden, fierce, sometimes weeklong dust storms—and discharges of static electricity were a real threat. A truck's whole ignition system could be wiped out in an instant of white-static ball-lightning unless the drag chain grounded it, and then they'd be stuck for sure, a hundred miles from the nearest mechanic besides themselves. (It was the spare engine parts they lacked, although both vehicles hauled extra tires and wheels and fan belts and other parts in their carrying beds.)

The wind was rising, although it wasn't carrying that much dirt. Lincoln used a little water from one of their spare bags of water to at least go through the motions of cleaning the plates.

—*With a little luck, we'll be in a real bed, or at least a barn, tomorrow night, boys. Get some sleep. It's going to be a long few days of hard driving and there's nothing waiting for us at the end of this trek except two useless submarine engines that nobody wants, not even my father.*

———

LINCOLN HAD SPOKEN THE TRUTH in more ways than he knew. The submarine engines may have been the most abandoned- and unwanted-looking *wasichu* machines or devices that Paha Sapa had ever seen. The twin banks of diesel engines were the length of the Dodge truck's extended flatbed, taller than the cab, and amounted to a terrifying mass of early-1920s pistons, steel, oil tubes, conduits, shaft columns, rust, stains, and open metal maws. It was hard for Paha Sapa to believe that so many awkward tons of steel and iron had ever gone to sea.

They'd reached Pueblo, Colorado, on Saturday afternoon — April 13 — and quickly found the steel plant and its associated companies, huddled around like so many piglets nursing at the sooty teats of the great black sow of the steel mill itself. The place looked bankrupt and abandoned — ten acres of parking lot empty, tall smoke stacks cold, gates chained — but Jocko the watchman explained that the plant merely shut down on alternate weeks during these hard times and that some or all of the men would be back on the job come the following Monday. Jocko knew right where the submarine engines had been parked and led the four men to a rail siding behind another siding at the back end of an abandoned building just behind the slag heaps. The toothless old man had the style to shout *Voilà!* when Lincoln, Red, Hoot, and "Billy Slovak" dragged off the dust-covered tarp draped over the house-sized mass of metal.

Lincoln asked the watchman if they could get help loading the engines onto their Dodge flatbed. Monday, was the old man's reply, since the only one who could handle the crane-on-rails parked just over there by the sludge pond was Verner, and Verner, of course, was probably out hunting this fine spring Saturday and wouldn't even be *thinking* about work until Monday morning.

In the end, two relatively crisp twenty-dollar bills exchanged hands (Paha Sapa had not seen many twenty-dollar bills in recent years) — one from Lincoln to the old fart Jocko, another for Verner, who was probably drinking in a bar somewhere right down the street, to come in and transfer the engines from the flatbed train car to the Dodge's long and shaky platform.

Jocko promised that he'd have Verner there by five p.m., and Lincoln and his three tired and dusty workers drove deeper into the little south Colorado steel town to find a place to get a beer and another place in which to spend the night.

Paha Sapa had to admit that the thought of a real bed really appealed to him. (*Some Lakota,* were his thoughts—in English rather than Lakota, he realized, as if his *wasichun* brain was adding insult to injury.)

"You're getting old and soft, Black Hills," whispered Long Hair's ghost. "You'll be all white before you die and as round and soft as an albino sow with no legs."

—*Shut up,* Paha Sapa snapped silently. In the few years since he and the ghost had actually communicated—rather than the ghost babbling in the dark and Paha Sapa merely having to listen—Paha Sapa hadn't gained much from the exchanges. He couldn't imagine ghosts of murdered men aging, but this ghost was getting old and surly and sarcastic.

A town where half the population was made up of miners and their families (the mines were a few miles to the west, in the foothills) and the other half steelworkers and their families—a glut of Germans, Czechs, Swedes, Bohemians, and other odd lots—was sure to have good bars, and Lincoln and his boys found one within five minutes.

The first beers were ice-cold—the mugs actually refrigerated until ice rimned them—and Red Anderson couldn't stop grinning.

—*I could disappear into a dark little bar like this and not reemerge 'til the damned hard times are over.*

Lincoln sighed and wiped his upper lip.

—*Too many otherwise good men have, Red. We'll spend the night at that boardinghouse across the street, but there's no way I'm waiting 'til Monday.*

Red and Hoot looked at each other behind Lincoln's back, and their thoughts were easy for Paha Sapa to read even without touching them for a vision; the two would be happy to stay here for a week until the mythical Verner came back from hunting.

But one of the magical twenty-dollar bills brought Verner back just before sunset in time for the short, stubbled man to bring his railroad crane over from the main yard and get the great bulk of the submarine engines, pallets, tarps, and all, transferred to the Dodge's flatbed. That flatbed sank eight inches on its nonexistent suspension, but no tires blew or wheels flew off or axles broke apart. Not right then, anyway.

When the transfer was complete and the four men had lashed the engines down with more straps and ropes than the Lilliputians had used on Gulliver (one of the first books he'd borrowed from Doane Robinson's library), Paha Sapa drove the Dodge a hundred yards or so to a parking place outside the steel plant's chained gates — the Dodge moved, eventually, after a sluggish fashion, although he didn't think that it would climb any hill with a grade of more than 1 percent, and the steering had changed from difficult to damned near impossible — and the four left the mass there and went back to a café for dinner and then to the boardinghouse.

The last thing Jocko shouted after them was —

— *You four look like good Christians to me. Well, at least three of you do. If you're gonna stay over for Palm Sunday services in the mornin', I can show you the way to the Methodist and Baptist churches.*

None of the four looked back.

Lincoln showed the three men to their room — the Borglum largesse for this vacation didn't extend to private rooms for anyone but Lincoln, but rather to three cots crowded into a nonheated second-floor room where the blankets looked like they would get up and crawl away on their own if not nailed down.

Paha Sapa had brought in his own blankets and extra sleeping layers. Red and Hoot looked dubiously at the sprung cots and then out the window, where the few lights of Pueblo's modest but very serious about debauchery red-light district beckoned. (The bars still had their speakeasy false fronts and peepholes, even two years after Prohibition had been lifted.)

Lincoln Borglum sounded tired and dejected, or perhaps he was just as depressed by the dusty steel town as was Paha Sapa.

— *A beer or two, you two, but nothing serious tonight. We're leaving at dawn, and I'm going to have the three of you take turns tomorrow wrestling that Dodge east to Kansas and then north. It'll be a long day.*

Everyone nodded, but Hoot and Red tiptoed out in their stocking feet, carrying their boots, no more than twenty minutes later. Paha Sapa heard the stairway creak softly and then he pulled his thick and relatively vermin-free blankets up over his head and fell asleep. The last time he glanced at his wristwatch, it read 8:22.

Hoot and Red came stumbling in smelling of much more than whiskey and beer a little after five a.m. One of them was busy retching into a bucket that he carried with him. At 5:20 a.m., Lincoln Borglum not only rapped hard on the door, but came in and overturned the two slugabeds' cots. Paha Sapa was up, dressed, packed, and washing his face in the basin with what little water was left in a chipped pitcher that the management had begrudged them. The moans from the tangle of blankets on the floor were pitiful.

Lincoln and Paha Sapa ate alone and in silence at the small café across the street.

The pickup truck and absurdly weighted Dodge rolled east out of town a little before seven. The streets were empty. The air was very warm for mid-April. The sky was clear.

Something felt wrong to Paha Sapa all that long morning of driving northeast and into the afternoon. Of course, the slowly crawling Dodge with its mass of dead weight — if the load shifted forward, Paha Sapa would not even have time to jump free before the flimsy old cab was crushed — took up most of his attention as he literally wrestled it around the simplest turns and had to flog it up the shallowest of grades. Lincoln had sent Hoot back to share in the driving, and all that morning into the afternoon, Hoot snored and sprawled on the passenger side of the ripped old seat, waking occasionally only to open the door, jump off the running board, vomit into the weeds, and then run to catch up to the slowly moving Dodge.

What little traffic there was, even the oldest Model T's, swung around the slowly moving Dodge and its Ford pickup escort.

But through all the snoring beside him and the roaring of the over-taxed engine and his need to concentrate on the driving, Paha Sapa sensed something wrong... something wrong with the *world*.

The birds were flying south in an unnatural way. The few animals he saw — some jackrabbits, scurrying voles, one deer, even livestock in the dust-filled fields—were also rushing south. They were trying to *escape*. Paha Sapa could feel it.

But escape what? The skies remained clear. The air remained warm, too warm. The cab of the Dodge truck smelled to high heaven of the whiskey in Hoot's sweat, and for once Paha Sapa was glad that the windshield would not click shut.

This was country that gave the slightest hint of what would soon be called the Dust Bowl stretching a thousand miles to the south, but that hint was dramatic. Farms were abandoned. Even those farmhouses still occupied had had the last of their paint sandblasted off the walls. Sand drifted to the eaves of homes and outbuildings. Soil was so drifted against fences that Paha Sapa could see only a foot or less of the top of the fence posts poking up through the sand and soil. Farther south, he knew, farmers and ranchers said that they could walk miles on the dirt-buried carcasses of their livestock piled up against the buried fences, but even up here in the southeastern corner of Colorado, the dirt drifts were everywhere. Several times, Paha Sapa had to slow the Dodge to a stop while Lincoln, driving the Ford pickup, crashed repeatedly through heaps of reddish-brown soil that had covered the narrow highway like snowdrifts.

But for all the clear sky and warm day, Paha Sapa knew that something was *wrong*.

It was about two p.m., and they were nearing the Kansas state line when it hit them.

—*Hi-yay! Hi-yay! Mitakuye oyasin!*

Paha Sapa was not even aware that he had shouted in Lakota. He shook the snoring and snorting Hoot awake.

—*Hoot, wake up! Look to the north. Wake up, goddamn it!*

A wall of blackness rising three thousand feet or more was rushing at them like a tsunami of dirt.

Hoot sat straight up. He pointed through the open windshield and shouted.

—*Holy shit! It's a duster. A black blizzard!*

Paha Sapa stopped the Dodge immediately. Ahead of them, the pickup paused, then stopped.

There had been an intersection with a wide dirt road not a hundred yards behind them, and Paha Sapa almost stripped gears as he threw the overladen truck into reverse and backed wildly toward that crossing. Just before the intersection, he remembered seeing a dust-drifted little farmhouse set back amid the skeletons of a few trees.

— *What the hell you doin', Billy?*

— *We have to get these trucks turned around. Get the hoods and engines turned away from that wall of dirt. We'd never get them started again.*

Normally, backing that heavy load onto the dirt road and turning the Dodge around would have taken Paha Sapa five minutes of careful backing and turning. Now he made the turn in thirty wild seconds, looking over his shoulder at the advancing wall of blackness all the time.

Lincoln pulled alongside the Dodge and shouted across the wide-eyed Red Anderson.

— *That's one hell of a duster!*

Paha Sapa shouted back.

— *We have to get to that farmhouse.*

The ramshackle, tumbledown structure was less than a quarter of a mile ahead on the left as they drove back to the southwest. The only clues that it wasn't abandoned were the Model A in the driveway and two rusted tractors tucked under a shed overhang and half buried in dirt and dust. But both were so ancient that they might have been abandoned there with the house.

Paha Sapa didn't think they'd make it in time, and they did not. Beside him, Hoot was shouting the same mantra over and over, as if it were a religious invocation.

— *Holy shit Jesus Christ! Holy shit Jesus Christ! Holy shit Jesus Christ.*

Paha Sapa learned later that he would have seen this giant roller even if he'd stayed at Mount Rushmore. The cold front had slid across the Dakotas that morning, dropping temperatures thirty degrees in its wake and burying Rapid City and a thousand tinier towns in dust and howling winds. But the front was soon out of the Dakotas and rolling into Nebraska, picking up strength, velocity, and thousands upon thousands of tons of dust and dirt as it advanced.

Paha Sapa would also learn later that the temperature dropped twenty-five degrees in less than an hour when the west edge of the black-blizzard duster-roller passed by Denver. The width of the storm by the time Paha Sapa and his three fellow workers saw it approaching in southeast Colorado was more than two hundred miles and growing — advancing like a solid defensive line of brown-jerseyed football players — and it would be almost five hundred miles wide by the time it reached the real Dust Bowl states to the south and east.

None of this mattered as Paha Sapa floored the accelerator, getting the overloaded Dodge truck up to its maximum sprint speed of twelve miles per hour, watching in the rearview mirror and over his shoulder as the monster bore down on them.

Paha Sapa had spent his life on the Plains and it was easy for him to estimate the height of this black moving wall of dirt: the duster was coming over a low range of very eroded hills to the north and northwest, there were lower hills to the northeast — although the Dodge would have labored at the grade with the submarine engines on the flatbed — and just based on the size comparison with the hills, boulders, and the few pine trees disappearing into the black blizzard's maw, Paha Sapa knew that the wall was three thousand feet high and growing. Paha Sapa had also spent much of his life watching horses rushing toward or away from him on the Plains and could calculate speeds well; this moving wall was hurtling toward them at sixty-five miles per hour or more. The low range of hills it had appeared above was no more than twelve miles away. The duster wall of black had covered half of that distance in the past minute or so.

Watching Lincoln's pickup truck swerve into the dust-drifted driveway of the half-collapsed farmhouse, Paha Sapa glanced over his shoulder again and realized that the wall was black at the bottom, lighter more than half a mile higher at the top, but that strange, swirling, tornado-like columns of white were rushing in front of the solid wall, like pale cowboys herding stampeding cattle. Whatever those columns were (and Paha Sapa was never to learn), they seemed to be pulling the black wall along behind them and toward Paha Sapa and his truck with ever-increasing velocity.

He realized that Hoot was screaming something other than his former mantra now.

—*Jesus fucking Christ! We ain't gonna make it.*

To the farmhouse, no. But Paha Sapa had known that. There were a hundred yards yet to go to the shack's driveway, and time was up—the black wall was roaring behind them, audible now, and tactile as well, as the blackness blotted out the sun and the temperature dropped twenty or thirty degrees around them. Paha Sapa switched on the Dodge's headlights and then the wall was on them and over them and around them.

It was like being swallowed by some huge predator.

Paha Sapa found himself stifling the urge to scream *Hokay hey!* and to shout to Hoot across the storm roar and static—

—It is a good day to die!

But there was no use trying to shout now. The roar was too loud.

A white horse ran by from the direction of the fenced farmhouse field. Disoriented and made crazy by the outer wall of flying dirt, the horse was running blindly *toward* the storm. But what Paha Sapa noticed—and would never forget—was the aura of chain lightning, ball lightning, Saint Elmo's fire, and other static discharges that limned the horse in electrical flame. Lightning danced among the galloping horse's mane and tail and leaped along its back.

Then the static enveloped the Dodge and the truck's engine seized and stopped immediately.

Paha Sapa's long hair stood on end, the black tendrils writhing like electrified snakes. There was a brilliant strobe flash from beneath the truck and for a second Paha Sapa was certain that the truck's huge gas tank had ignited, but then he realized that it was lightning discharge from the drag chain attached to the rear axle. The flash lit up a fifty-foot radius in the sudden advancing darkness.

The truck rolled to a stop as blasts of dirt exploded inward through the open windshield and side windows. The dust was everywhere instantly—blinding them, choking them, flowing into their nostrils and closed mouths and ears. Paha Sapa grabbed Hoot's flapping flannel shirt.

—Out! Now!

They staggered out into absolute darkness punctuated by nonilluminating lightning crashes. The Dodge's engine seemed to be on fire, the hood thrown back, but it was only more electrical discharges frying everything there. Paha Sapa dragged Hoot forward—finding "forward" in the pitch-darkness only by feeling his way along the cab and fender to the bumper—and paused to grab the large canvas bag of water strung over the radiator. Paha Sapa tied his kerchief around his face after soaking it with water. He poured water in his eyes and felt the mud rolling down his face. With his powerful left hand, he kept Hoot from running while he handed the man the water bag.

Hoot had no kerchief. He tried to hike his shirt up over his mouth and nose while pouring water over both.

The darkness intensified even as the roar did. Hoot leaned closer and shouted into Paha Sapa's ear, but the words were lost before they were out of the man's mouth. Paha Sapa kept his grip on Hoot's shirt and dragged him into the roaring darkness beyond the truck, closing his eyes so that he could see the distance and direction to the driveway and farmhouse at least in his mind's eye.

Hoot seemed to be struggling, trying to break away—to go back to the truck?—but Paha Sapa dragged him onward.

Paha Sapa realized that the Dodge's headlights had somehow remained on, but they'd become invisible after only three or four steps into the roaring darkness. The lightning all around them still illuminated nothing. Paha Sapa wondered if they would be trampled by the fleeing white horse turned back toward its barn or field and had a sudden urge to giggle at the thought. He knew that he would never earn a newspaper obituary, but that would have been a great one after seventy years of life.

He staggered forward—it was impossible to stand upright, and even as they hunkered into a crouch, the wind threatened to throw them both down and scuttle them away across the ditch and fields like so much wind-tossed detritus—and then Paha Sapa decided that they should be even with the driveway, so he tugged the still-struggling and writhing Hoot left and let the wind shove them south.

Once they bumped into something unmoving and solid in the darkness, but it was only Lincoln's pickup truck, abandoned in the driveway. The driver's-side door was wide open, and Paha Sapa could feel the dust already filling the cab. They did not tarry there.

He found the front porch by tripping over the step. For a second as he fell forward in the howling darkness, he lost Hoot, but then he swung his arms out and around and caught a grip on the stumbling *wasichu's* hair and then his collar. Paha Sapa fell forward a few more steps. Already he could feel his lungs filling with the swirling, pressing, flying dirt—grains of sand and silica like so much molecule-sized sharp glass already cutting the insides of his nose and throat. Stay out here for thirty minutes of this, and their bodies, if they were found at all after the storm, would show lungs so packed solid with dirt that the autopsy doctor could compare them to vacuum cleaner bags that had never been emptied.

The front door! Paha Sapa felt it with the flat of his hand in the darkness and pounded around the edges to make sure. It was a door.

And it was boarded up.

Resisting the urge to laugh or cry or to call out to *Wakan Tanka* or to Coyote the Trickster in a dead man's glee, Paha Sapa pulled Hoot through the darkness as he felt his way along the house to the left.

They fell off the low and sagging porch together. Paha Sapa was on his feet in a second, lunging toward the side of the house. If he lost the house, they were dead.

For a short, sagging shack, the farmhouse seemed to go on forever. Paha Sapa felt boarded windows under his splintered palms. If there was no way into this house...

He left that thought alone and tugged Hoot along with him. The sturdy mine worker had fallen down and not regained his feet. Paha Sapa dragged him. Drifts were building around his legs as he moved. Paha Sapa suddenly felt disoriented, as if he were climbing a steep cliff—as if the flat, baked earth of this east-Colorado farmhouse were the vertical wall of Mount Rushmore, of the defiled Six Grandfathers.

Paha Sapa felt a sudden exhilaration welling up in him. He did weep then, the tears turning to clumps of mud on his eyelids, caking and sealing his eyes shut.

He would not have to be the cause of the Four Heads' destruction on the sacred mountain in the sacred Hills.

Wakan Tanka and the Thunder Beings had acted in his stead. Surely this terrible storm, this terrible *blotting out,* could not be resisted.

Lincoln and Hoot and Red had talked of President Roosevelt pondering abandoning all of the Plains states and the middle of America if no windbreak of pine trees could protect the farms and ranches and sandblasted ghost shells of the dying towns here and south of here.

Suddenly Paha Sapa realized that the gods of the Lakota and the All, and possibly the ancestral ghost spirits of his people, had already acted. For more than five years, the winds had blown and the topsoil had lifted into the sky and the farms had gone fallow and been buried in their own excreta and the ranches had counted their dead cattle in the thousands as the soil dried up and blew away, carrying the last remnants of overcropped grasses with it.

The gods were acting. Nothing on earth could resist a series of storms like this. Paha Sapa knew that this—this black blizzard, this booger of a duster, this big roller—could not be resisted by mere soft, fat, God-praying *wasichu*. Paha Sapa knew nature intimately, and this storm, all these increasingly violent storms he'd read about and caught glimpses of in newsreels and experienced in South Dakota's milder forms were not part of nature. No cycle of nature in the history of North America or the world had seen months of winds like this, years of drought like this, and screaming, wailing, roiling walls of suffocating death like this.

This was the gods of his people telling the *Wasicun* to leave forever.

Paha Sapa sobbed silently behind his kerchief, sobbed mostly from relief that he would not have to be the agent of the *wasichus'* destruction. He was old. He was tired. He knew the enemy too well. He wanted this cup to pass from him—and now it had.

Inside his heart and brain and chest, the ghost of Long Hair gibbered at him. Paha Sapa could understand the words now, of course—had been able to for most of the decades he had been alive, ever since Curly and the Seventh Cavalry and the battle at Slim Buttes—but he chose not to listen now.

Suddenly Paha Sapa's flailing left hand found nothingness...the back end of the house.

He tugged Hoot's body through high dirt drifts into the blessed lee of the house, away from the wind.

But the dirt swirled and intruded and compelled here as well, and it was no lighter. Paha Sapa took his free hand and held it a few inches in front of his mud-caked face even as he pried open his eyelids against the mud and stinging particles.

Nothing. He literally could not see his hand in front of his face. Lightning leaped and coiled all around him—from an unseen gutter to an invisible metal clothesline post, from an unseen pump to invisible nails in the porch, from the invisible nails in the porch to a never-seen metal fence or gate twenty feet away. The lightning and static discharged and displayed all around him but never illuminated.

Paha Sapa kept the rear of the house against his right shoulder as he pulled Hoot's body forward. Now that the wind neither shoved him from behind nor pushed against him as it had out on the road, he felt further disoriented. If it hadn't been for the farmhouse wall to lean on, he would have fallen on his face and not risen again.

He realized that there was a wild banging ahead of him, sounding exactly as if someone were standing in the roiling darkness and firing off a heavy repeating rifle or machine gun. Paha Sapa thought of his son.

It took the wildly flapping screen door hitting him on the head and almost knocking him out before Paha Sapa identified the source of the repeated explosions. He braced the banging screen with Hoot's body and tried the solid back door. Locked or stuck.

Paha Sapa threw his shoulder, his full weight, and the last of his energy into it.

The heavy, paintless door screeched inward, shoving against drifts and piles of sand within.

Paha Sapa bent over and tugged Hoot inside, slamming the door behind him.

The howl receded a few decibels. At first, Paha Sapa was sure that it was as dark and dust filled here inside the house as it had been out-side—and freezing cold—but then he saw what appeared to be the tiniest of glows. It was like a campfire glimpsed miles away.

Tugging the groaning Hoot, he crawled toward it.

It was a kerosene lantern on the floor of the kitchen not six feet away. The glow waxed and waned, but not before Paha Sapa saw the faces clustered around it—only faces, the bodies in dark, soiled gar-ments lost in the darkness—the faces of a whisker-stubbled rail-thin farmer and his thinner wife, their three children, and the wide white eyes of Lincoln Borglum and Red Anderson. They were all huddled around the low-flickering lantern on the floor like medieval worship-pers kneeling around some holy artifact.

The wide eyes had just enough time to register surprise at Paha Sapa's and Hoot's appearance in the howling space when the lantern glow dimmed and flickered out altogether. There was no longer enough oxygen in the air to sustain a flame.

Paha Sapa whispered— *Washtay, hecetu!* Good, so be it!—and collapsed onto the chipped and drifted yellowed linoleum. He couldn't breathe.

An hour later the deafening, unrelenting howl died down to a mere animal's roar. The lantern was relighted and held the flame. A second lantern was taken down from the counter and lighted by the farmer's wife. The glow now pushed six or eight feet or more into the swirling gloom. But the monster outside still banged and roared and shoved at the door and boarded windows to be allowed in.

The farmer was shouting something.

— Would y'all folks like something to drink?

Lincoln Borglum, his white eyes now red, nodded for all of them. Paha Sapa realized that he had been lying on his side, eyes open but unseeing, his kerchief choking him, for a long time. He sat up and leaned back against a cupboard under the kitchen counter. Hoot was on all fours, his head down like a sick dog's, and he seemed to be moaning along with the rise and fall of the wind's roar and moans.

The farmer stood, staggered in the whirlwind, and went to the sink. Paha Sapa could see things six, eight, ten feet away now, and his eyes marveled at the murky clarity.

The farmer pumped and pumped and pumped at a pump handle at the sink. Surely, thought Paha Sapa, a pump could not work now that the world had been destroyed.

The farmer came back with a single cup filled with water and handed it around, small sips for everyone, starting with the children, then the four guests, then his wife. It was empty when it came back to him. He seemed too tired to go refill it.

Thirty or forty-five minutes later—Paha Sapa was guessing; his watch had stopped in the first minutes of the sand's intrusion—the roar died a little more, and the farmer and his wife invited the four of them to stay for dinner.

—Mostly just greens, I'm afraid. And the Injun's welcome too.

It was the farmer's hatchet of a wife speaking.

Again, Lincoln Borglum spoke for them, but only after he pulled mud and more solid dirt out of his mouth.

— *We'd be much obliged, ma'am.*

And, after a minute's silence and still no movement from any of them save for the children crawling off into the darkness to do whatever they were going to do, Lincoln again.

— *Say, you folks wouldn't have any use for two really big submarine engines, would you?*

———

PAHA SAPA SMILES as he hangs in the blazing cliff-bowl of August light and heat. He is under Abraham Lincoln's roughed-out nose. It gives a little shade as the hot blue-haze afternoon thickens toward evening. He slides in the last of the charges. It is almost time for the four p.m. blasting after the men scurry off the faces.

Then Paha Sapa's smile dies as he remembers the lost exhilaration when he realized a year ago that those storms from the Thunder Beings, perhaps from the All himself, were not going to drive the *wasichus* out of the world of the Natural Free Human Beings.

It would have to be him after all.

President Roosevelt will be there in just a few days, this coming Sunday, for the unveiling of the Jefferson head.

Paha Sapa has much to do before he can allow himself to sleep.

12

Bear Butte

August 1876

PAHA SAPA'S ELEVENTH BIRTHDAY COMES AND GOES, BUT THE boy is too busy fleeing for his life across the plains toward the Black Hills and his *hanblečeya* to notice the date, which he would not have noticed even if he had stayed in the village.

Limps-a-Lot advised him to ride with his two horses during the night and hide from Crazy Horse and his men during the day if necessary, but that is not necessary. The rain that started pouring down on him the night he left the village at midnight does not and will not let up. For three days and nights it pounds down, accompanied by thunder and lightning that keeps Paha Sapa away from the few trees along the rare streams and causes him to hunker down even while riding, and even in the bright blur of daytime the visibility is only a few hundred feet as the gray curtains of rain roll across the soggy prairie.

Paha Sapa travels by both day and night, but he travels slowly and he travels wet. Never in his short life has Paha Sapa witnessed a Moon of Ripening Berries this wet and stormy. The usual end-of-summer month is so dry that the horse herds never stray from what little water is left in the streambeds, and grasshoppers proliferate until walking through the high, brittle, brown grasses becomes a matter of wading through waves of leaping insects.

Now, after three days and nights with no sleep, almost no food, and a constant diet of fear, Paha Sapa is totally disgusted with himself.

Any young brave his age should be able to find shelter and start a fire even in such a rain: Paha Sapa's flint and steel strike sparks, but he can find nothing dry enough to burn. Nor can he find shelter. The shallow caves and overhangs he knows about are along the streambeds, but now those banks are under three feet or more of water as the streams flood far beyond their banks. Despite his bundles of clothing and gear being carefully wrapped in layers of inside-out hides, everything he owns is soaked through. For a few hours each night, huddled beneath one of his horses, Paha Sapa clutches two blankets around himself, but they only make him wetter and more disspirited.

And then there are the voices.

The dead *Wasicun's* voice is more strident than ever, growing louder whenever the poor boy tries to sleep. But in the few days since Paha Sapa touched Crazy Horse and had all the man's memories flow into him—at times Paha Sapa feels that the violation was like being pissed on and being forced to swallow it—the gabble and gibber of all those memories that are not his have made Paha Sapa ill.

The *other-memories* are not as clamoringly insistent as the ghost's night babble, but they are more disturbing.

Paha Sapa is overwhelmed. He has only eleven rather uneventful years of his own to remember, while Crazy Horse thought himself to be thirty-four years old this summer when he poured all his memories into Paha Sapa's aching brain, and—somehow, despite his will not to—Paha Sapa's vision saw forward another year or two to Crazy Horse's death by bayonet.

Paha Sapa remembers nothing of his own parents, of course, since his mother died at his birth and his father months before then, but now he can remember the boy Curly Hair's, or Curly's, parents, his Brulé mother and holy-man father named Crazy Horse. He remembers clearly, too clearly, the time in Curly's sixteenth summer when, after Curly performed bravely in a raid against the Arapaho (and was wounded in the leg by an arrow, but only after killing several Arapaho, but it's *Paha Sapa* who now remembers the pain of that arrow), Curly's father, Crazy Horse, gave his son his own name and forever after went by the name Worm.

Paha Sapa's memories of his own recent childhood are now invaded by the false memories of Curly–Crazy Horse's years with his Oglala Lakota band, but Curly–Crazy Horse's memories are tinged red with memory-emotions of violence, near insanity, and a constant *strangeness.* Paha Sapa is the adopted son of Limps-a-Lot and hopes to be a holy man like his respected *tunkašila,* but Curly–Crazy Horse, the son of another holy man, wanted—has always wanted—to be *heyoka,* a dreamer and servant for the Thunder Beings.

Paha Sapa, cold, frightened, hungry, feverish, and infinitely lonely this rainy midnight, is setting off alone for his hopeful *hanblečeya*— alone—in the Black Hills, while in his intruding memories he sees Curly Hair's four-day ceremony, during which that boy-man's Vision was given to him. He sees Curly Hair being taught and helped and supported and his *inipi* interpreted by his pipe-bearing elders and relatives and holy men. Paha Sapa fears, deeply, that he will never receive a vision from *Wakan Tanka* or the Six Grandfathers beyond these invading, obscene visions of other people's ghosts and minds and futures, but now he has to suffer *memories* of Curly–Crazy Horse's successful *hanblečeya* and that strange man's celebration and acceptance as a Thunder Dreamer.

No men have chanted or will chant *Tunka-shila, hi-yay, hi-yay!* for Paha Sapa, as he remembers in these alien memories the band's men chanting for young Crazy Horse.

Paha Sapa has never touched a *winčinčala's,* a pretty young girl's, *winyaň shan,* yet in these new memories now echoing in the boy's feverish brain, he clearly remembers having sex with No Water's wife, Black Buffalo Woman, and half a dozen other women. It is…confusing.

Paha Sapa has never suffered an injury worse than the bruises and bloody noses of boyhood, but now he remembers not only Curly–Crazy Horse's war wounds, but also the sensation of being shot in the face at point-blank range by the outraged husband No Water. He tries to avoid the other-memory, but the sensations of the pistol ball sliding along his teeth, opening his cheek, and smashing his jaw are too strong to shut out.

Most disturbingly this endless black, rainy night, Paha Sapa's feverish mind tries to deal with the fact that he—Black Hills—has never hurt another person beyond rough childhood play, while the memories of Crazy Horse bring him the joyous-sick recollections of shooting, stabbing, lancing, killing, and scalping many—Crow, Arapaho, another Lakota, and *wasichus* almost too many to count.

Paha Sapa is afraid that he is dying.

His head aches so fiercely that he pauses every quarter hour or so to vomit, even though his belly has been empty for hours. The constant, solid rain makes him so dizzy that he has trouble staying on Limps-a-Lot's roan, Worm, and the mare, *Pehánska,* is acting more like a white snake, rearing and pulling the line and trying to escape, than like a white crane this terrible midnight.

Paha Sapa's head is full of pain, mucus, and memories that he does not want, cannot stand, and knows he shall never free himself from.

And to make the night more hopeless, he is sure now that he is lost. He thinks he should have reached the Black Hills after three days and nights riding, but in his stupid child-inexperience navigating in the rain with no real landmarks (or those few he knew flooded), he is sure that he has somehow missed all of the Black Hills, the Heart of the World.

It's at this midnight hour and one of the low points of his life that Paha Sapa sees a light far off to his left.

His mind, that small amount that is still his and not hostage to an angry warrior's memories, tells him to turn the horses' heads to the right and get away from the light. If it's a campfire, it belongs to *wasichu* who would kill him on sight or to Crazy Horse, who will torture and then kill him.

But he turns to the left, to the east, he hopes, and rides on in the night toward the tiny glow, waiting for the light to flicker out or disappear. Instead, between squalls that obliterate it from sight, it grows stronger.

After half an hour of riding through rain toward the light, his horse slipping and staggering in the deepening mud, Paha Sapa sees a large, dark shape above and around the small circle of light. It has to be *Matho Paha,* Bear Butte, which means that he is only a few miles north-northeast of the mass of the Black Hills.

But *Matho Paha* is a favorite camping place for Lakota bands heading toward the Hills, which is precisely what Crazy Horse was ready to do.

Riding up to this campfire may well mean Paha Sapa's death.

Teetering on his horse, keeping from falling off only by lacing his fingers through Worm's mane, Paha Sapa continues riding toward the light.

———

THE LIGHT IS COMING FROM A CAVE a few hundred feet up the northwest slope of the towering Bear Butte.

Knowing that he should back into the pouring darkness, Paha Sapa continues to lead his two horses up to the opening and through the waterfall of runoff pouring over the wide cave entrance. The cavern quickly turns out of sight, but there is a broad area just within the entrance where dry grass still grows. Paha Sapa ties the roan and the mare there, pulls Limps-a-Lot's feathered war lance from beneath wet straps on *Pehánska's* back, and proceeds, slowly, carefully, deeper into the firelight-brightened cave.

Immediately, Paha Sapa's stomach cramps and his mouth fills with saliva.

Whoever is back there, they are cooking something. It smells like rabbit to Paha Sapa. He loves just-cooked rabbit.

Paha Sapa stops and listens several times as the low-ceilinged cavern twists slightly, but the only sounds are a soft humming, the crackle of the fire, and, behind him, the constant munching and occasional shaking of mane and tail of his two horses. Have the people by the fire heard his approach?

Paha Sapa comes around the last turn, lance in both hands, and there by a roaring fire, in a broad section of the cave, an old man sits cross-legged, humming softly to himself and gingerly turning two spits over the fire, each holding a skinned and quickly browning rabbit.

Paha Sapa lowers the lance a bit and walks into the circle of firelight. The old man, his long gray hair tied in careful pigtails, wears a loose blue-print shirt that might have been made by *wasichus,* and his long pants are of some graying blue material that Paha Sapa first thinks is the *wasichu*-soldiers' sort of canvas trouser, but realizes is a different, more woven material. The old man's moccasins have traditional (and beautiful) Cheyenne-style beadwork. (Another pair of moccasins, of a sort Paha Sapa has never seen—they almost look to be made of green *wasichu* canvas—lies steaming and drying near the fire.) The old man's eyes, squinting up and across the fire at Paha Sapa now, seem absolutely black except for the reflection of the flames there. But there is no anger or fear in the old man's neutral but somehow pleasant expression.

When he speaks, it is in fluent Lakota with a strong Cheyenne accent.

— *Welcome, boy. I did not hear you arrive. My hearing is not what it used to be.*

Paha Sapa lowers the lance a little more but does not set it down.

— *Greetings to you, uncle. You are of the* Shahiyela?

— *Yes, I am Cheyenne. But I have spent much time with the Lakota. I have never been the enemy of your people and have taught many.*

Paha Sapa nods and does set the lance down, against the wall of the cave. He still has his knife, there are no signs of other men having been here—the sleeping hides and cooking utensils are all for one—and he doubts if the old man could rise quickly from his cross-legged posture. Paha Sapa, whose stomach is now actively rumbling at the sight and smell of the two browning rabbits on the spits, remembers his manners.

— *I am called Paha Sapa.*

The old man smiles, showing long, yellowed but strong teeth, with only one missing on the bottom. It is a lot of teeth, Paha Sapa thinks, for a man who looks so old.

— *Welcome, Paha Sapa. Odd for the Lakota to name a boy-child after a place. We shall have to talk about that. My name is Robert Sweet Medicine.*

Paha Sapa blinks at the sound of the man's name. He has never heard "Robert" before, even with Cheyenne names. It sounds *wasichu*.

The old man gestures to a hide unrolled across the fire from him.

— *Sit down. Sit down. Are you hungry?*

— *I'm very hungry, uncle.*

The sudden smile again.

— *That is why I cooked two rabbits tonight.*

Paha Sapa has to squint at this.

— *You said you did not hear me approaching.*

— *I did not, young Black Hills. I simply knew there would be another with me here tonight. There, it should be ready—there's a wooden bowl over there beneath that clutter. Just use your knife to cut what you want. The whole rabbit is yours.*

There's water in that jug there. . . . The smaller jug holds mni waken, *and you are welcome to it as well, as long as you do not drink it all.*

Holy water. The *wasichus'* whiskey. Paha Sapa has never tasted it and, despite his curiosity, knows he should not taste it now.

— *Thank you, uncle.*

He chews some steaming-hot rabbit, his face and hands instantly becoming greasy, and drinks some of the cold water. After a while, he wipes his mouth and speaks.

— *I have been to Bear Butte many times, uncle, but I did not know there were caves here.*

— *Of course you did. It was in a cave here that Maiyun gave my ancestor Mustoyef the Gift of the Four Arrows. It was in a cave here, before time was counted as it is today, that the Kiowa received from their gods the sacred kidney of a bear and the Apache the gift of sacred horse medicine. You Lakota — and I know you have heard this, Paha Sapa — say that it was in a cave here that your ancestors received the gift of the sacred pipe from* Wakan Tanka.

— *Yes, I have heard all of this, uncle — except about the Kiowa and the bear kidney — but I have never* seen *this cave or any other, although we boys have climbed and played all over and around* Matho Paha.

The old man smiles again. Each time he does that, a thousand deep wrinkles deepen around his eyes and mouth.

— *Well, then, Bear Butte still has secrets from us, does it not, Black Hills?*

Paha Sapa speaks through another mouthful of rabbit. It is excellent.

— *Did my people receive the gift of the sacred pipe, and your people the Gift of the Four Arrows, here? In* this *cave?*

Robert Sweet Medicine shrugs.

— *Who's to know? Or who knows if any of that actually happened? Once a place is considered sacred by any tribe, the other tribes hurry to find — or make up — some story of its sacredness to them as well.*

This shocks Paha Sapa. He assumed, when Robert Sweet Medicine said that he'd *taught* Lakota as well as Cheyenne, that the old man was a *wičasa wakan* like Limps-a-Lot and Long Turd and the others. Paha Sapa has never heard a real holy man admit that the old stories of the gods and grandfathers might be made up. Just the thought of that makes the boy dizzier. The gabble of his ghost and the awful memories of Crazy Horse buzz louder in his aching head.

—Are you all right, Paha Sapa? You look ill.

For a second, Paha Sapa has the wild urge to tell the old man the truth about everything—about his ability to touch people and to *see* into them and their pasts and futures sometimes (he has no urge at all to touch Robert Sweet Medicine), about the ghost of Long Hair (if it is Long Hair) talking and talking and talking in that ugly and endless babble of *wasichu* sounds, about Crazy Horse wanting to kill him, about his own fear (almost a certainty) that he will fail in the coming *hanblečeya*—tell the old man everything.

—No, uncle. I have a little fever is all.

—Take off your clothes, boy. All of them.

Paha Sapa's hand creeps to the hilt of his knife in its scabbard on his belt. He knows that some of these *wičasa wakan,* especially the recluses, are *winkte.*

Some *winkte* dress and act like women throughout their lives; some are rumored to have the organs of both men and women; but most *winkte,* according to what the older boys told Paha Sapa, prefer putting their stiff child makers up young boys' behinds rather than in lovely *winčinčalas' winyaň shans* where they belong.

Paha Sapa does not want to know what that feels like. He decides that he will have to kill Robert Sweet Medicine if the old *winkte* comes any closer.

The old *wičasa wakan* sees Paha Sapa's expression and looks at the shaking hand on the knife hilt and then Robert Sweet Medicine laughs. It is a deep, rich, long laugh, and it echoes slightly in and around the bend of the cavern beyond where they sit by the fire.

—Don't be stupid, boy. I'm not after your unze. *I have been married—to women—eight times. That's eight different women, little Black Hills, not eight wives at once. So unless you brought one with you, there are no* winkte *in this cave tonight. You're feverish and flushed. And shaking hard. All your layers are soaked through, and I think you've been soaked like that for days and nights. Get dry and stay near the fire.*

Paha Sapa squints at the old man, but he lets his hand fall away from his knife.

—Pull those two blankets up, boy. Get out of your clothes—behind the blankets if you wish—and set your wet things on this empty spit to dry. Moccasins as

well. Keep your knife if it makes you feel safer. The blankets are clean and free of vermin.

Paha Sapa blushes but does what the old man suggests, realizing as he does so that he's shaking so hard he can barely put his clothes on the drying rack. He clutches the blankets around him. They are scratchy against his wet skin but infinitely warmer than the soaked clothing he's just surrendered. He has kept the knife.

Robert Sweet Medicine wipes his mouth and sets the spit holding his browned rabbit, barely touched, on Paha Sapa's Y sticks. The boy is down to the bones of his rabbit. Few things, Paha Sapa has always thought, look as reduced and vulnerable as a rabbit without its skin and head.

— *Here, boy. I've eaten all I want. Help yourself to this.*

Paha Sapa grunts his thanks and begins cutting pieces off and into his bowl.

Robert Sweet Medicine looks to his right across the flames, toward the cave entrance.

— *How long has it been raining? Two days and nights?*

— *Three days and nights, uncle. No... wait... four nights now, and three full days. Everything is flooded.*

The old man nods.

— *On the day before the rain began, I met a* Wasicun *on the trail to the top of the butte. It was a sunny day. Some clouds later, but mostly sunny.*

Paha Sapa speaks through a full mouth.

— *Did you kill him, uncle?*

— *Kill who?*

— *The* Wasicun!

The old man chuckles.

— *No, I talked to him.*

— *Was he a bluecoat? A soldier?*

— *No, no. I think he had been a warrior once — I am sure of it — but no longer. He told me... no, that is not right; he did not quite tell me... but he let me know that he had once walked on the moon.*

Paha Sapa blinks at this.

— *So he was* witko — *crazy.*

Robert Sweet Medicine shows that long-toothed smile again.

— He did not seem witko. *He seemed... lonely. But, little Black Hills, have you never known a* wičasa wakan, *or some other sort of human with powers — a* waayatan *prophet, for instance, or a* wakinyan *dreamer who sees visions sent by the Thunder Beings, or a* wapiya *conjurer, or a* wanaazin *who shoots at disease, or a dangerous* wokabiyeya *who works with witch medicine, or a* wihmunge *who sucks disease straight out of a dying person with his own breath — who has spoken of leaving his body and traveling to far places?*

Paha Sapa laughs and takes a long drink of the cold springwater in the jug.

— Yes, uncle, of course I have. But I have never heard any holy man given powers who speaks of...

He pauses, remembering his own lying-in-the-grass experience (dream?) of rising so high in the sky that the sky grew dark in the daytime and the stars came out.

— ... of... traveling so far. *But are you saying, uncle, that* wasichus *can have Visions, just like real People?*

Robert Sweet Medicine shrugs and tosses more twigs onto the fire. Paha Sapa is growing warm and sleepy beneath his blankets. The second rabbit is now bones.

The old man's voice, strongly resonant in the little cave, seems strangely familiar to Paha Sapa.

— Have you ever noticed, little Black Hills, how all of our tribes — all the ones I've ever heard of, even those east of the Big River and west of the Shining Mountains and beyond the Never No Summer range, even those so far south that the plains are desert and no grass grows there — that all of us give our tribes names meaning the same as Tsêhéstáno, *the* People, *as we* Cheyenne *say; or the* Natural Free Human Beings, *as you* Lakota *call yourselves; or the* True Human Beings, *as the* Crow *say — and so on and so on and so on.*

Paha Sapa has forgotten the question, if there *was* a question, and is completely missing the point (if there was a point). He replies only by nodding sleepily and, remembering his manners, by belching softly.

— I am just asking, little Black Hills, why each of our tribes calls itself "the Human Beings" *and refers to no other tribe or group, even the* wasichus, *in that way.*

Paha Sapa rubs his eyes.

— I suppose, uncle, because our tribe is — I mean, that we are — *the real human beings, while others aren't?*

The answer seems a little inadequate even to the quickly warming and belly-filled boy, but he can think of no other at the moment. But he will revisit the question more than a few times over the next decades.

Robert Sweet Medicine is nodding as if satisfied by a particularly clever answer from one of his *wičasa wakan* students.

—*Perhaps, little Black Hills, when you learn the particular language of the Wasicun ghost now babbling in your brain, you will begin to understand this strange question of naming ourselves a little better.*

Paha Sapa nods sleepily and then snaps awake—*he has not told this old man about the ghost of Long Hair in him.*

Has he?

But Robert Sweet Medicine is speaking again.

—*You're going to the real Paha Sapa to perform your lonely* hanblečeya, *so you should fast after tonight's feast. The place you seek is only a day's ride from here if you take the proper paths in the Hills. I trust that your* tunkašila, *Limps-a-Lot, has instructed you well as to the preparations and sent along with you everything you need to do* yuwipi *properly?*

—*Oh, yes, uncle! I have learned what I must have, and for things that I cannot find in the forest, they are all packed away on my white mare you hear cropping at the cave entrance!*

Robert Sweet Medicine nods but does not smile.

—*Washtay! Limps-a-Lot sent with you the properly sacred pipe and the strong* canliyukpanpi *fine-smoking tobacco?*

—*Oh, yes, uncle!*

Did he? In four nights of rain now, Paha Sapa has not fully unpacked the bundles his grandfather sent with him, usually merely hunkering against the mare in the dark downpour and groping around for the dried meat or biscuits that Three Buffalo Woman packed away for him. Is the sacred, irreplaceable *Ptehinčala Huhu Canunpa*—the Buffalo Calf Bone Pipe that Sitting Bull had appointed Limps-a-Lot guardian of—*really* in his bundle of goods, or has Limps-a-Lot sent along the lesser but still sacred tribal pipestone pipe? Come to think of it, Paha Sapa has not seen in his various soaked bundles the red eagle feathers that adorn the priceless *Ptehinčala Huhu Canunpa*.

The old man is still talking.

—*Washtay, Paha Sapa. Stay away from the* wasichus' *roads—for the soldiers and miners will kill you on sight. Go to the top of the Grandfathers' Hill.* Yuhaxcan cannonpa! *Carry your pipe. Your pipe is* wakan. Taku woecon kin ihyuha el woilagyape lo. Ehantan najin oyate maka stimnyyan cannonpa kin he uywakanpelo. *It is used for doing all things. Ever since the standing people have been over all the earth, the pipe has been* wakan.

Paha Sapa shakes his head in an attempt to rid himself of the buzzing and confusion there. His fever fills him. His eyes are watering, either from the smoke or from strong emotions he does not understand. Still sitting cross-legged on the blanket while wrapped in two more blankets, he seems to be naked and floating inches above the cavern floor. Robert Sweet Medicine's voice booms in his head like *wasichu* cannon fire.

— *Little Black Hills, you know how properly to construct your* oinikaga tipi?

— *Yes, Grandfather . . . I mean uncle. I have helped Limps-a-Lot and the men construct many sweat lodges.*

— Ohan. Wašte! *And you know how to select the proper* sintkala waksu *from those other stones that might blind or kill you?*

— *Oh, yes, uncle.*

But *does* he? When the time comes in the Black Hills, will he be able to differentiate the special stones in the creek beds, those with the "beadwork" designs that show them safe for use in the sweat lodge?

Paha Sapa begins sweating and shaking under his blankets.

— *Has your grandfather's wife cut the forty squares of flesh from her arm for your* wagmugha *to go with the* yuwipi *stones?*

— *Oh, yes, uncle!*

Have Raven's Hair or Three Buffalo Woman cut the necessary bits of flesh for the sacred rattle or gathered the little fossil stones to be found only in certain anthills? How could they have? They have not had time!

The old man nods again and throws several scented sticks onto the already raging fire. The cave fills with the sour-sweet smell of incense.

— *You have been warned, little Black Hills, that once you are nagi, pure spirit essence, you will be visited — almost certainly attacked — by ocin xica, bad-tempered animals, as well as by* wanagi *and* ciciye *and* siyoko.

— *I am not afraid of ghosts, uncle, and* ciciye *and* siyoko *are boogeymen for children.*

But Paha Sapa's voice is shaking as he says this.

Robert Sweet Medicine seems not to notice. He is staring at the fire, and his black eyes are filled with dancing flames.

—*A* hanblečeya *Vision is a terribly serious thing to put on the shoulders of any man, my son, but especially upon the shoulders of one so young. You understand that sometimes the fate of the vision-seeker's band depends upon the Vision. Sometimes the fate of an entire people—more than a tribe, but a race—depends upon the Vision and what is done after that Vision. You understand this?*

— *Yes, of course, uncle.*

Paha Sapa decides that Robert Sweet Medicine is insane. *Winkto.*

— *Do you know why the Grandfathers, the gods, and* Wakan Tanka *himself exist, little Black Hills?*

Paha Sapa wants to say— *What are you going on about, old man?*—but he manages a respectful—

— *Yes, uncle.*

Robert Sweet Medicine looks up from the fire and stares directly at Paha Sapa, but the old man's black eyes still reflect the flames.

—*No, you do* not, *young Paha Sapa. But you* will. *The gods and the Grandfathers and the All himself exist because the so-called People exist to worship them. The People exist because the buffalo exist and because the grass grows free throughout the world we think is the World. But when the buffalo are gone and when the grass is gone, the People will be gone as well. And then the gods, the spirits—of our ancestors, of the place, of life itself—will be gone as well. Do you see, Paha Sapa?*

Paha Sapa can humor the old man no longer.

— *No, uncle.*

Robert Sweet Medicine grins his strong-toothed grin.

—*Washtay! That is good. But you will be the first to see, little Black Hills. Gods die as buffalo die, as people die. Sometimes slowly and in great agony. Sometimes quickly, unprepared, and not believing in their own death, denying the arrow or the wound or the disease even as it is killing them. Do you understand this, Paha Sapa?*

— *No, uncle.*

—*Washtay! This is as it should be now. What matters is not that you see how the buffalo and the people and the way the people live and the gods and the grandfathers and the All shall die and disappear, Paha Sapa—many of us with the gift of* wakan *have glimpsed this before—but what you* do *about it in the eighty summers and more remaining to you. What* you — *no one else* — *what* you *do about it. Do you understand this, Paha Sapa?*

The boy is angry now. Sleepy and feverish and ill and close to weeping and very angry. If he kills this old man now, no one would ever know it.

— *No, uncle.*

— Washtay! *You will sleep late and long in the morning, young Black Hills, and I will be gone.... The rain will abate just before sunrise, and I have business in the O-ana-gazhee, the Sheltering Place, far from here and the Hills. I will leave no food for you, and you must not touch yours. Your fasting must begin at sunrise.*

— *Yes, uncle.*

— *Your testing will not be over if and when you survive your terrible* hanblečeya. *That is just the beginning. You will never get word of your Vision back to Limps-a-Lot and your band. Your horses will be killed* — *not by Crazy Horse, who seeks you elsewhere and then forgets you in his lust to kill more* wasichus — *and your sacred pipe will be stolen and you will be stripped naked, but this is as it should be. Understand that while there is no Plan for the universe, there are specific crucifixions and new births for each of us.*

Paha Sapa does not understand that word — *crucifixion* — but the old man is making no sense with the words the boy does understand, so he lets it go.

— *I will not let that happen, uncle. I will die* — *as my father died, staked down and fighting* — *rather than surrender our tribe's sacred* Ptehinčala Huhu Canunpa *that Limps-a-Lot and ten generations of holy men before him have kept safe, never losing so much as a single red feather on it.*

Robert Sweet Medicine looks at him.

— *Good. Let me tell you now, Paha Sapa, that I am honored that you will name your son and only child after me.*

Paha Sapa can only stare at the old man.

— *It is time to lower the fire to embers, go to the cave entrance to piss and to see that your two horses are comfortable, and then to sleep, Paha Sapa. I will wake from time to time while you sleep to shake my own* wagmuha *to keep the ghosts at bay tonight.*

Robert Sweet Medicine shows him the ceremonial rattle that looks to be as old as time.

— *Paha Sapa,* toksha ake čante ista wacinyanktin ktelo.

I shall see you again with the eye of my heart.

With many groans and grunts, the old man slowly uncrosses his legs and manages — after several tries — to get to his feet, where he sways as old men do when seeking their balance. Robert Sweet Medicine's voice is very soft.

— Mitakuye oyasin!

All my relatives. It is done.

Together, slowly, the old man moving very slowly but the boy not helping him because he is afraid to touch him, Paha Sapa and Robert Sweet Medicine walk to the entrance of the cave where they check on the horses and piss — far apart, each looking into a different part of the darkness — out into the rainy night.

13

Jackson Park, Illinois

July 1893

ALL DURING HIS AFTERNOON ATTACK ON THE CABIN OF WHITE settlers, even after he is shot and killed by the arriving cavalry, Paha Sapa is nervous about the upcoming appointment with Rain de Plachette.

He also hates being killed. He hadn't volunteered for it, but Mr. C pointed to him and said that he'd be the one to be shot off his horse, so that was that. Almost every night, Paha Sapa has to nurse bruises or strained muscles or a sore left knee that never gets a chance to improve. There's an extra mound of soft dirt for him to fall onto, a heap that's supposed to be renewed each afternoon and evening, but the other warriors — in their very real excitement — often forget to clear a space for him to get to the soft dirt, and he has to throw his arms in the air and fall off the tall pinto pony onto the hard-packed arena dirt. Then he has to lie there, dead, while the tail end of his marauding band of mixed-tribe Indians pounds over and past him, then, immediately thereafter, try again not to flinch as the arriving cavalry horses come pounding and leaping by. Three times now he's been kicked by shod hooves and, being dead, he can never even react to it.

This getting killed every afternoon and evening is killing him. (At least he is allowed to survive the attack on the Deadwood mail coach.) His fallback plan is to get a smaller, lower, slower horse. That way he can live up to his name—the name the *wasichus* gave him seventeen years earlier—and if he *must* continue dying, he can at least guarantee that the fall will be as short as possible.

But this afternoon in July, in the four hours between the afternoon show and the longer evening program, it is the appointment with Miss de Plachette after the show that has Paha Sapa almost too nervous to think, much less die properly.

But, he reminds himself as he rushes to the men's bathing tent shared by the soldiers and Indians, it's not a *date*.

Paha Sapa just happened to be dropping something off in the outer office that morning when Mr. Cody and his friend the Reverend Henry de Plachette stepped out and continued their conversation. The Reverend de Plachette, whom Paha Sapa had met, was explaining that his daughter was here to watch the afternoon Wild West Show but wanted to go to the Fair proper afterward and needed an escort. He, the Reverend de Plachette, would be meeting her near the entrance to the Manufactures and Liberal Arts Building at the Grand Basin at six p.m. but would be busy until then. Mr. Cody said that it would be no problem; *he* would escort the young lady over to the Fair. Then Cody remembered that he had an appointment in Chicago after the afternoon matinee.

—*I would be honored to escort Miss de Plachette to the Court of Honor and wait until you arrive, Reverend de Plachette.*

For the rest of his life, Paha Sapa will not believe that he actually said those words at that moment.

Mr. Cody and the Reverend Henry de Plachette turned slowly to look at the small, thin twenty-seven-year-old Sioux they knew as Billy Slow Horse. Cody, who was wearing an expensive tan suit and had just put on his wide-brimmed Western-style tan hat in preparation to step outside, cleared his throat.

—*That's generous of you, Billy. But I'm not sure you would have time between the matinee performance and the evening performance, and perhaps it would be better if...*

—*No, no, William. I've talked to Mr. Slow Horse a few times and he has met my daughter, as you know, and I believe it's an excellent idea. I will, as I said, be meeting Rain no later than six o'clock, and that should give Mr. Slow Horse ample time to return and to get into his...ah...costume.*

Paha Sapa's costume consists of a breechclout, a bow and arrow, and a single white feather that he puts in his braided hair, his small way of honoring Crazy Horse's memory. But it made him blush that afternoon as he rode around the arena, thinking of Miss de Plachette looking at him almost naked, visible bruises and all.

Cody continued to look doubtful that morning, but the minister (and father) had obviously made up his mind.

—*Be so kind as to meet my daughter here as soon after your performance as possible, Mr. Slow Horse. I will inform her that you will escort her to the Fair. And I thank you again for your courtesy.*

The Reverend de Plachette nodded rather than offering his hand. Paha Sapa knew at the time that the man had decided to allow him to escort his daughter the short walking distance to the World's Fair out of a minister's liberal (and almost certainly shallow) sense of equality-of-all-men-in-God's-sight, but Paha Sapa did not care the least bit *what* the reason was.

After washing up as quickly as he can—all the while thanking the *wasichus'* god and the actual *Wakan Tanka* (the All who seemed so much larger, so much more complex, and so infinitely much more present than the Fat Takers' white-bearded deity) that he didn't fall on any horse apples when he fell dead off his horse in that afternoon's show—Paha Sapa rushes back to his tent and changes into the only formal clothes he brought on this trip east: a black, pinstriped, thick-wool, ill-fitting, and completely inappropriate-to-July suit coat and baggy trousers that he purchased in Rapid City.

He realizes, with some small shock, as he tries for the third time to knot the ribbon of the string tie, that his hands are shaking. Paha Sapa cannot remember any time when his hands shook, except when he was sick with fever as a boy.

While he is near a mirror, Paha Sapa tries on the straw boater he purchased during his second trip into Chicago proper the previous month. The little summer hat looks absurd with his black winter suit coat and his long black braids sticking out. He tosses the cheap hat onto his cot and returns to the washing tent to pomade the tips of his braids. Between every action, Paha Sapa nervously checks his pocket watch, kept in the pocket of his suit coat, since he has no waistcoat.

Finally it is time. His heart pounding in his ears, Paha Sapa walks to the main administration tent.

Miss de Plachette is waiting in the foyer and smiles in recognition as he approaches. Paha Sapa is sure that he has never seen any single sight so absolutely beautiful or so infinitely unobtainable. He also notices that he has already sweated through his shirt.

Miss de Plachette is wearing a silky tan blouse waist with the usual balloon sleeves, the blouse gathered at her waist, as almost all women's fashions seem to be these days. Even Paha Sapa has noticed that. Her skirt, which reaches the floor, is also a relatively light, summer, silky weight (for so much fabric), with stripes that continue the expensive tan of the blouse, the tan stripes alternating with rich green stripes bordered in thin gold. She is wearing a narrow-brimmed straw hat that looks as perfect on her as Paha Sapa's boater had looked absurd on him. She also is wearing thin tan gloves and is carrying a parasol.

Paha Sapa is glad to see the gloves. He has had fewer of the *small-vision-forward-touching* experiences as he has grown older, but those that have occurred, he knows, always happen when he touches bare skin. He is absolutely resolved not to touch Miss de Plachette's bare skin in any way even though he is wearing his only pair of dress gloves. He is pleased to see that she is also wearing gloves. Now no accidental touch will…

— *Mr. Slow Horse, it is a pleasure to see you again and I cannot thank you enough for escorting me to the Fair this afternoon so that I can meet my father. I apologize, but is it…Mr. Slow Horse? Or just Mr. Horse?*

Her voice is as soft and modulated as he remembered from their brief meeting two days earlier, when she'd toured the Wild West Show with her father. Mr. Cody introduced Reverend de Plachette and his daughter, it seemed, to most, if not all, of the hundred former US Cavalry soldiers and ninety-seven full-time Sioux, Pawnee, Cheyenne, and Kiowa that had come east with Buffalo Bill.

Paha Sapa finds himself tongue-tied first thing out of the chute. He expected it sometime during his escorting of Miss de Plachette into the fairgrounds, but not upon first encounter. He finds, insanely, that he wants to explain to her that "Billy Slow Horse," the name he's been known as to whites for seventeen years now, was a foul, stupid, insulting name that the Seventh Cavalry gave to him when he was their captive...scout...prisoner, and that his real name is...

He shakes his head and manages...

— *Billy, ma'am. Just Billy.*

His face is burning, but Rain de Plachette smiles and slips her arm through his, causing Paha Sapa to jump slightly.

— *Very well...Billy...then you must call me Rain. Shall we go?*

———

THEY STEP OUT THROUGH the Wild West Show's main gate into the heat and sun of high July. To the right of the gate a tall banner shows a full-color illustration of Christopher Columbus and proclaims PILOT OF THE OCEAN, THE FIRST PIONEER. The next-door World's Fair is, after all, officially known as the World's *Columbian* Exposition of 1893, even if it has missed the four hundredth anniversary of the Italian sailor's landing by a full year.

The banner on the other side of the gate, with an even larger and more colorful illustration of Mr. Cody in full, fringed western regalia, announces PILOT OF THE PRAIRIE, THE LAST PIONEER. But it is an even larger sign above and to one side of the wide entrance gate that says it all — BUFFALO BILL'S WILD WEST AND CONGRESS OF ROUGH RIDERS OF THE WORLD.

Miss de Plachette pauses just outside the gate to extricate her arm for a second and open her parasol, then she slides her arm through Paha Sapa's again and gazes back at the gate and long fence for a moment, the tiny holes in the parasol throwing Appaloosa speckles of light onto her pale face in the shade. Paha Sapa notices for the first time that there are also faint constellations of freckles across her small nose and flushed cheeks. How old is she? Twenty, perhaps. Certainly no older than twenty-one or twenty-two.

— *It's sad that Mr. Cody wasn't able to set up his performing arena and other exhibits* inside *the fairgrounds proper. Father says that the Fair authorities rejected Mr. Cody's application because the Wild West Show is — how did they put it? — "incongruous." By which they mean, I presume, too vulgar?*

Staring at Miss de Plachette's hazel-colored eyes, Paha Sapa has a terrible second in which he realizes he has suddenly forgotten all of the English he has been speaking now for almost seventeen years. He finds his memory and voice only when they begin walking east together toward Sixty-third Street and the Fair entrance.

— *Yes, too vulgar is what they meant, Miss de Plachette. They didn't want to sully the Exposition with Mr. Cody's entertainment, even though Mr. Cody had just returned from a very successful tour of Europe when he asked for the concession. But it's all worked out for the best.*

— *How's that?*

He realizes that she is smiling, as if expectant of hearing something interesting, but it is hard to think in words because all of his attention at that moment is on the slight pressure of her right arm in the crook of his left arm (she kept her left hand free for the parasol).

— *Well, Miss de Plachette…*

He pauses in confusion as she stops and turns and nods her head in — he hopes — a pretense of impatience.

— *I mean, Miss… ah… that is… when the Ways and Means Committee rejected the Wild West Show's concession bid, Mr. Cody got the rights to these fifteen acres here just adjacent to the fairgrounds. Not being an official concession, Mr. Cody doesn't have to share the profits with the Exposition and he can hold performances on Sunday — they're wildly popular — while the Fair doesn't allow shows then, and, of course, there's just the fact of all this room, the full fifteen acres, I mean, Miss Oakley, Annie, has a whole garden around her tent and cougar skins on the couch and a beautiful carpet from England or somewhere, not to mention electric lights and real furniture from Italy and…*

Paha Sapa realizes that after a lifetime of honorable, masculine taciturnity, he is babbling like a *wasichu* schoolboy. He shuts his mouth so quickly that the sound of his teeth clacking is audible to both of them.

Miss de Plachette twirls her parasol and looks at him expectantly, waiting. Is her small smile one of amusement or bemusement or mild contempt?

He gestures awkwardly with his free hand.

— *Anyway, it's worked out very well to Mr. Cody's advantage. I believe we're averaging about twelve thousand people per performance, which is far more profitable than any of the official concessions inside the Fair's grounds. Almost everyone who comes to see the Fair also comes, sooner or later, to see our Wild West Show, and some take the elevated train down just to see it.*

They walk in silence the half block from the Wild West Show's huge area bordering 62nd Street to the closest Fair entrance at 63rd Street. Paha Sapa does not have enough experience being around women — especially white women — to have any idea whether this is a comfortable silence or one signaling tension or displeasure on the part of the lady. Overhead, passing over the boundary fence, runs the Elevated Railway — the so-called Alley L, called that, Paha Sapa has heard, because it threads its way through alleys to get out of the Chicago downtown area, since speculators bought up other rights-of-way — constructed to bring the millions of visitors from Chicago proper down here to Jackson Park. Some of those yellow-painted "cattle cars" are rumbling overhead now, and as they pass, Paha Sapa glances up to see eager fairgoers hanging out the open sides in a most precarious manner. Attendees have managed to kill themselves at the Exposition in many ingenious and terrible ways so far, Paha Sapa knows, but none yet, he thinks, from falling out of the Alley L.

Admission to the World's Columbian Exposition is fifty cents, and those at the ticket counters like to tell grumpy fairgoers that if Mayor Harrison or Daniel Hudson Burnham, the man most responsible for the Fair, or President Cleveland presented himself at their gates, the gentleman would have to fork over fifty cents.

Paha Sapa pulls out a dollar, far too large a percentage of his monthly salary, but Miss de Plachette has freed her arm and is wrestling with a cloth purse hanging from her wrist by a string.

—*No, no, Mr.... Billy...my father left me money to cover the price of both our admissions. After all, you would not be attending the Fair today were it not for your gallant offer to escort me.*

Paha Sapa pauses, knowing that he hates the idea of her paying for the two of them, or even her paying for herself, but not knowing how to explain this important fact to her. While he dithers, the young woman pays, hands him one of the two tickets, and leads the way through the metal turnstiles. Paha Sapa grumbles, the dollar bill still dangling absurdly in his hand, but follows.

It is immediately after they enter the grounds and are passing a white towered building set near the western fence of the fairgrounds that something occurs that Paha Sapa is to think of many times in the coming years.

Suddenly Miss de Plachette whirls, looks at the windowless white building with its tall tower, and her demeanor changes completely. From being one of delighted, almost girlish animation, her expression has become one of alarm, almost horror.

— *What is it, Miss de Plachette?*

She hugs herself and, accidentally, hugs Paha Sapa's arm closer, but it is no act of coquetry. He can feel her trembling through the layers of his wool coat and her silk sleeves.

— *Do you feel that, sir? Do you hear that?*

— *Feel what, Miss de Plachette? Hear what?*

He looks back at the nondescript white building just within the fairgrounds fence that they've just passed. The structure has a series of black blind arches near the top, short white towers on the eastern corners, and a higher tower with perhaps an observation deck on the far, western side.

She squeezes his arm more tightly and there is no melodrama in her terrified expression. The lady's white teeth are chattering.

— *That awful coldness flowing from the place? The awful screams? Can't you feel the cold? Can't you hear the terrible cries?*

Paha Sapa laughs and pats her arm.

— *That's the Cold Storage Building, Miss de Plachette. I don't feel the icy air to which you're so sensitive, but it only makes sense it would be coming from the Exposition's main repository for ice. And I do hear the cries — very faint — but they also have a benign cause. There's an ice-skating rink inside, and I can just make out the happy cries of children or young couples on skates.*

But Miss de Plachette's expression does not change for a moment and she cannot seem to be able to take her eyes off the blocky white building. Then she turns away from it, but Paha Sapa can still feel the trembling of her body so close to his as they resume walking into the Fair.

— *I apologize, Mr. . . . I apologize, Mr. Slow Horse. From time to time I get these odd, dark feelings. You must think me a terribly silly goose. Women are a*

*strange species, Mr. Slow Horse, and I am one of the stranger members of that spe-
cies. I have no idea where in this grand Exposition they would choose to exhibit so
strange a non-fish, non-fowl, non-sensible specimen such as myself. Almost certainly
in a jar of alcohol or formaldehyde on the Midway.*

Paha speaks without thinking.

—*No, in the Palace of Fine Arts, Miss de Plachette. Almost certainly there.*

She smiles at him, knowing that she is being flattered (but not
knowing his deep sincerity) but not seeming to mind. Her old gaiety
flows back as they get farther from the Cold Storage Building, but Paha
Sapa bites the inside of his lip until he tastes blood. He dislikes men
who flatter women with compliments.

Four days later, on July 10, 1893, there will be a fire in the upper
reaches of the tall tower at the rear of the Cold Storage Building.
Firemen will arrive almost at once and rush up the wooden stairs to
fight the fire blazing in the cupola atop that tower, but the fire will already have crept down the inside of the walls and beneath that stairway
and will trap most of those firemen above. Two will survive by leaping
to a rigid hose and sliding down it sixty feet to the ground. Thirteen
other firemen, including the fire chief, will die horribly in the Cold
Storage Building Fire, as will four workers.

But none of this is known to them at the time—at least not to Paha
Sapa, for all his thought of being a sensitive *wičasa wakan* whose role
will be to predict the future for his people—and it is a hot, sunny day
where thoughts of fire and death have no place.

For a moment they do not talk as they walk northeast down the
wide avenue that runs to the left of almost a dozen pairs of railroad
lines that terminate in the Central Railroad Station. There are trains
leaving and arriving, but most do so in that odd, steamless muting of
usual train sounds that is a mark of these new electric trams.

In a sense, Paha Sapa and Miss de Plachette have come in through
one of the "back doors" of the Fair; the designers specified the formal entrance to be at the opposite end of this west-east corridor, at
the grand Peristyle that opens onto and from the Casino Pier that
runs almost half a mile out into Lake Michigan. Arriving from a ship
at the far end of the pier, one can, for the price of ten cents, take the
Moving Sidewalk (complete with chairs) the full 2,500-foot length of

the pier directly to the Peristyle. The World's Columbian Exposition was always meant by its designers to be first seen and entered from the Lake Michigan side, through the Peristyle and into the Court of Honor.

Back here, Paha Sapa feels as if he's in a stone canyon. To their left is the incredible mass of the Transportation Building (not the largest building in the world, that honor falls to the Manufactures and Liberal Arts Building that dominates the eastern end of this grand concourse now visible ahead on their right, but larger than anything in Paha Sapa's imagination, much less experience), and straight ahead is the white wall of the huge Mines and Mining Building. Miss de Plachette's arm still linked in his, Paha Sapa guides them diagonally to the right so that they emerge into the dazzling afternoon brilliance of the broad Grand Court of Honor that runs straight past the impressive domed Administration Building and along either side of the Grand Basin all the way to the Peristyle. Arrayed on both sides of this Grand Court are the incredible buildings: the tall and endless Machinery Hall to their right, the gigantic Agriculture Building farther east, the roaring Electricity Building to their left beyond Mines and Mining, and beyond it the behemoth, the leviathan of all buildings on earth, the Manufactures and Liberal Arts hall.

Miss de Plachette pauses and tucks a strand of her copper-tinted brown hair under her straw boater. Paha Sapa is grateful for a breeze blowing down the long Grand Court from the lake that begins to dry his soaked shirtfront. The lady with him takes a step away, puts a gloved finger to her chin as if considering options, and turns to look in each direction of the compass. She closes her parasol and lets it dangle from her wrist by yet another hidden strap or string.

— *Do you know what I think, Mr. . . . ah . . . I mean, Billy? Do you know what I think, Billy?*

— *What do you think, Miss de Plachette?*

The young woman smiles, and it is almost a girl's smile — unaffected, easy, seemingly prompted only by happiness.

— *Well, first of all, I think that this informality I proposed shall never work out. You will never call me Rain, will you?*

Paha Sapa does not actually shuffle his feet, but mentally he does.

—It is difficult for me to be so...ah...informal with so elegant a young lady, Miss de Plachette. It is simply outside my experience.

—Fair enough, then. I know that my brazen informality, while quite the thing in a Boston women's college, takes people aback elsewhere. So I shall be Miss de Plachette and you shall be...I can't remember. Did you tell me that it was Mr. Slow Horse or Mr. Horse?

—Actually, my name is Paha Sapa, which means Black Hills in Lakota.

Paha Sapa hears himself saying this to the woman but cannot *believe* he has said it.

Rain de Plachette stops all other motion and looks at him with great intensity. Paha Sapa notices that there is the slightest flaw of black in the hazel iris — it now looks green — of her beautiful left eye.

—I apologize for addressing you by the wrong name. When we were introduced...and Mr. Cody also referred to you as...

—No white person has ever known my real name, Miss de Plachette. And very few Lakota. I don't know why I just told you. Somehow, it felt...wrong...for you not to know.

She smiles again, but it is a grown woman's hesitant smile now, meant only for the two of them. She actually presses his scarred and calloused right hand with her gloved left hand, and he is glad for the gloves.

—I'm honored that you told me and I shall share the information with no one, Mr....Paha Sapa. Did I pronounce it correctly? The first A has almost a long sound, does it not?

—It does.

— Well, you have honored me with your secret, Paha Sapa, so before our walk is over today, I shall tell a secret that very few people know about me...why my mother, who was also a Lakota, you know, decided to name me Rain.

—That would do me a great honor, Miss de Plachette.

He has heard rumors in the Indian tent that the Reverend de Plachette's daughter is "half Indian." Everyone has. But each of the four Indian nations represented in the Wild West Show has claimed her.

—But later. In the meantime, Paha Sapa, would you like to know what I have decided that we should do?

— Very much.

She clasps her hands together and for a second, in her smiling enthusiasm, looks like a very young girl indeed. The strand of copper-tinted-by-the-sun hair has escaped from her boater again.

— I believe we should walk over to the Midway Plaisance and take a ride on Mr. Ferris's huge Wheel.

Paha Sapa makes a noncommittal noise and fumbles his cheap watch out of his pocket.

Miss de Plachette has already checked her watch—a tiny, round little thing, no larger than a cavalryman's red sharpshooter badge, that hangs from her blouse by a gold ribbon—and she waves away his look of anxiety.

— Not to worry, Mr. . . . Paha Sapa, my friend. It's not even quarter after four. Father will not be at the Grand Basin to meet me until six o'clock, and as much as Father demands punctuality from everyone else, he himself is almost always late. We have oodles and oodles of time. And I have been trying to work my nerve up to go on the Wheel for weeks now. Oh, please!

Oodles? thinks Paha Sapa. This is a *wasichu* word he has not encountered in his seventeen years of wrestling with the language.

— Very well, we shall go ride Mr. Ferris's Wheel. But I insist on purchasing our tickets. It's a long walk to the Midway, Miss de Plachette. Would you care to ride in one of those wheeled carriages that are pushed from behind?

— Not at all! I love walking. It is a short way to the Midway, and I have trod it a hundred times already in the three weeks that Father and I have been visiting our aunt in Evanston. Come, I will lead the way!

She sets a brisk pace, her arm still locked in Paha Sapa's, as they walk quickly north past the looming Transportation Building and then around a slight curve and then north again past the endless Horticulture Building on their left, with its domes and arches and bright pennants. All this time to their right is the huge lagoon, quite separate from the Grand Basin on the Court of Honor, in which the sixteen-acre Wooded Island (with its tinier, satellite Hunter's Camp Island to the south of it) holds center place.

Miss de Plachette is chattering away, although Paha Sapa does not hear it or think of it as chattering. He finds her voice melodic and delightful.

—Have you been on the Wooded Island? No? Oh, you must go there, Paha Sapa! It is best at night, with all of its fairy lanterns glowing. I love the maze of little paths—there are benches to sit on—a wonderful place to bring one's lunch and sit in the shade and relax, especially near the south end, where the view of the grand dome of the Administration Building is truly inspiring. I admit that the landscaping is not quite up to the high standards they set for it—the exotic trees they planned, the irregular flower gardens, the mosses and other low plants appearing as if they had been there for centuries—but it is still far superior to the small, rigid plantings of the Paris Exposition four years ago. Did you go to that, by any chance? No. Well, I was only fortunate enough to attend that exposition because Father was invited to speak at a theological gathering in Paris, and although I was only sixteen, he happily saw fit to bring me along for those weeks and the tower that Mr. Eiffel built! Many thought it vulgar, but I thought it grand. They had planned to tear it down as soon as the exposition there was finished—they called it an eyesore—but I do not believe they have as yet and sincerely hope they do not. All that iron! But Mr. Eiffel's Tower, as impressive as it is, does not move, *and Mr. Ferris's Wheel, which we shall reach in only a few minutes, most assuredly* does move. *Oh, I can smell the lilacs there on the northern plantings of the Wooded Island. Isn't that breeze from the lake wonderful? And did I mention that Father knows Mr. Olmsted, who is the landscape architect responsible not only for the Wooded Island's plantings but for the landscape design for most of the Fair? For this Fair, I mean, not for those rigidly planted and quite inferior little gardens at the Paris fair—such a disappointment!—as wonderful as Mr. Eiffel's Tower was and, of course, the foods there. French food is always marvelous. Are you hungry by chance, Paha Sapa? It is late for lunch, of course, and rather early for dinner, but there are some wonderful lunch counters here in the Women's Building, although some of them are set almost embarrassingly close to the large corset exhibit that... Why Paha Sapa! Are you blushing?*

Paha Sapa is indeed blushing—furiously—but he smiles and shakes his head as they turn left past the Women's Building. Miss de Plachette has not paused after her question but is informing him that the Women's Building was designed by a female architect and that the dimensions of the Women's Building are one hundred and ninety-nine by three hundred and eighty-eight feet, sixty feet or two stories high, and its cost was $138,000. One of the smaller buildings among the Exposition's architectural behemoths, it is still a massive thing, with its many arches and columns and winged statuary bedecking the upper walls.

She squeezes his left arm now with her free hand.

—*Have you seen the Fair at night, with all the thousands of electric lights illuminated and the dome of the Administration Building all outlined in lights and with the searchlights playing back and forth?*

—*No, I haven't been here on the grounds at night, but I see the constant glow and the searchlights from the Wild West Show's arena and tents.*

—*Oh, Paha Sapa, you* must *see the Exposition at night. That's when the White City comes alive. It becomes the most beautiful place on earth. I've seen it from a ship out on Lake Michigan and from the Alley L coming down from the city, and I want to see it from the captive balloon here on the Midway, but it doesn't make ascensions at night. The observation walkways atop the Manufactures and Liberal Arts Building, or atop the Transportation Building, are extraordinary viewpoints at night—the searchlights stab out and around from those very rooftops!—but the best place is on the Wooded Island, with all the soft-glowing electrical lanterns and the fairy lanterns and the clear view of the White City, especially the outlined domes to the south. But think how wonderful it must be to see all the blazing lights at night from high atop the Ferris Wheel!*

—*We need to ride it in the daytime first, Miss de Plachette. To see if one can survive at such altitudes.*

Her laughter is quick and rich.

———

PAHA SAPA WONDERS if this young lady would—possibly could—understand why he has spent almost all of his time during eleven of his twelve visits to the Exposition standing or sitting rigidly in front of only two displays. He realizes that it would be folly to discuss it with her, and he watches his tongue more carefully than he has with her to this point.

The two hundred cavalry and Indians, not to mention Annie Oakley and her husband and the small army of workers for the Wild West Show, arrived here in Jackson Park in late March, and Mr. Cody staged his first show on April 3, long before most of the actual Exposition's exhibits or Midway attractions were ready.

In May, President Cleveland and huge gaggles of more illustrious royal foreigners and local dignitaries officially declared the World's Columbian Exposition open for business by closing a circuit that started up the gigantic Allis steam engine and its thirty subsidiary engines in the Machinery Building, thus sending electricity to everything at the Fair that ran on electricity. Not long after that, Mr. Cody paid the way for all of his more than 200 employees — Indian, cavalry, sharpshooters, and tent-raising roughnecks — who wanted to see the Fair.

That one day of general fairgoing was a blur in Paha Sapa's memory: the taste of a new caramel-coated popcorn treat they were calling Cracker Jack; lightning leaping from Nikola Tesla's head and hands; a glimpse of an optical telescope larger than most cannon; a longer, more lingering glimpse — the other Lakota and Cheyenne were appalled — of a real cannon, of the *ultimate* cannon, the largest cannon ever cast: the 127-ton, fifty-seven-foot-long (from breech to muzzle) Krupp's Cannon, displayed in its own Krupp Gun Pavilion (which looked to Paha Sapa as foreboding as any real German castle, even though his experience with German castles was limited to picture books), a gun capable of throwing a shell larger and heavier than a bull buffalo some sixteen miles and penetrating eighteen inches of steel armor at the end of that screaming death arc.

But not even the giant Krupp's gun most interested Paha Sapa after that first long, long day he and the others from the Wild West Show had spent at the Fair.

That first day he had ended up, alone, at the southern end inside the huge Machinery Hall. And there he stopped and gaped at forty-three steam engines, each producing 18,000 to 20,000 horsepower, that drove 127 dynamos that powered all of the buildings at the exposition. A sign told Paha Sapa that it required twelve of these engines just to power the Machinery Hall.

Paha Sapa had staggered to the closest chair and collapsed into it. There he sat for the next three hours, and to that chair he would return for almost all of his next eleven visits to the Fair.

It was not just the noise and motion and whiff of alien ozone in the air that so mesmerized Paha Sapa (and, evidently, so many other males, white and foreign and one Indian, of all ages who gathered in the Machinery Building to watch the pistons drive up and down and the rotary belts whirl and the great wheels turn). Most women couldn't seem to stand most of the Machinery Hall, but especially not this southern end, where the coal-fed furnaces and steam engines and larger dynamos clustered—the so-called Boiler-house Extension area—and it was true that the noise in much of the hall was truly deafening. On his later visits, Paha Sapa solved the noise problem with two wads of wax that he kneaded until they were the proper softness and shape and then pressed into his ear canals. It was not the noise that drew him here.

This, Paha Sapa realized and knew in his heart, was the center and core of the *wasichus'* power and secret soul.

Oh, not just the steam and electricity, which Paha Sapa knew were both relatively new to the *wasichus'* culture and list of commandable technologies (although he'd seen the fifteen-foot-high statue of Benjamin Franklin holding his key and kite cord and umbrella at the entrance to the Electricity Building), but it was this demonstrated ability to harness the universe's hidden energies and secret powers—like children playing with the forbidden toys of God—that made the *Wasicun* so successful and so dangerous, even to themselves.

Since his three years of education at the hands of Father Francisco Serra and the other Jesuit monks at their failed monastery-school near Deadwood, Paha Sapa had understood both how important religion could be to most *wasichus* and how the majority of them could set aside their religion for everyday life. But these furnaces, these howling engines, this Holy Ghost of steam, this ultimate Trinity of motor and magnet and armature of miles upon miles of coiled copper wire, *this* was where the real gods of the *Wasicun* race dwelt.

Signs around the giant iron Westinghouse engine and its smaller acolytes informed Paha Sapa that *"power from these dynamos and generators runs the elevators in the tall Administration Building and elsewhere, furnishes thousands of Exposition exhibitors with motive force, sets in motion countless other machines here in the Machinery Hall, and, not of the least importance, drives the sewage of the Fair toward Lake Michigan."*

Paha Sapa had laughed at that last part...laughed until he wept. How perfect that the *wasichus* used the power of their secret gods, the secret powers of the *Wasicun* universe itself, to drive their sewage "toward" the lake a few hundred yards away. He wondered if and how the sewage made it the rest of the way, beyond the push of all these tens and hundreds of thousands of combined horsepower and volts and amperes of electromagnetism. And then Paha Sapa laughed again and found that he was weeping in earnest.

It was about this time that a blue-clad Fair guide of some sort, wearing a brimless little red cap, approached him and shouted at him.

—And these ain't even the largest dynamos at the Exposition!

Paha Sapa found this hard to believe.

—No? Where would the largest be found?

— Not too far from here, in the Intramural Railroad Company Building. You readum signums, chief?

— Yessum, sir, I cannum.

The man squinted, not sure if he was being made fun of, but continued shouting.

— Well, just look for the sign that says IRC or Power Plant. It's behind the Machinery Hall, back near the south fence of the whole Fair. Not many people find it or want to go there.

— Thank you.

Paha Sapa was most sincere.

The Power Plant was indeed tucked back close to the fence, beyond the Convent of LaRabida (which actually had something to do with Christopher Columbus) and beyond the totem poles and south of the Anthropology Building (in which Paha Sapa could have studied an exhibit of phrenology showing why American Indians were a less-developed race in Darwinian terms).

When he finally entered the IRC Power Plant building, which was all but empty except for a few bored attendants in coveralls and one old man with three children in tow, Paha Sapa had to find a chair quickly or collapse to the floor.

Here was the world's largest and most powerful dynamo. A yellowed placard announced— *"When it is considered that this railroad is six and a half miles long, has sixteen trains of cars in constant movement and this aggregate of sixty-four cars [is] frequently crowded with passengers, some idea may be formed of the energy sent forth by this revolving giant."*

And revolving giant it was, its largest wheel half-buried in its cement trough but the top of that wheel almost touching the rafters beneath the ceiling. The whir and roar here were deafening, the smell of ozone constant. The few hairs on Paha Sapa's arms stood on end and stayed on end. Rather than moving sewage toward the lake, this single dynamo moved every electric-powered train and car on the intramural railway that shuttled visitors around the perimeter of the Fair and from one end to the other. But, Paha Sapa knew, the purpose to which this invisible energy was being put mattered little; it was the ability to harness and direct it that changed the universe.

So each time Paha Sapa returned to the Fair after this, he would explore new sights for a while, spend a few minutes in the Electricity Building, spend hours standing near the roaring engines and dynamos of the Machinery Hall, and celebrate his last hour or two by sitting here in the remote IRC Power Plant building, watching and feeling this single dynamo. This last was like a forgotten cathedral, and the workers and attendants there soon came to know Paha Sapa and to tip their hats to him.

There was also another man there whom Paha Sapa saw several times during his visits—an older man in rumpled, expensive clothes and with a neatly trimmed beard and a bald head (which Paha Sapa saw gleaming in the light of the naked overhead bulbs when the gentleman removed his boater to mop at his pink scalp with an embroidered handkerchief). Even the man's walking stick looked expensive. Most of the time there were only the dynamo's attendants, as silent as acolytes serving a High Mass, and Paha Sapa standing or sitting in his chair, and the bearded gentleman standing or sitting in his chair some five yards away.

The third time the two saw each other there that May, the older gentleman came over, leaned on his walking stick, and cleared his throat.

—I beg your pardon. I do not mean to disturb you and I realize that my question must be presumptuous, if not actively offensive, but are you, by any chance, an American Indian?

Paha Sapa looked up at the man (who wore a soft, rumpled linen jacket on this exceptionally warm May day, while Paha Sapa sweated in his black suit). He could see the intelligence behind the older man's eyes.

— *Yes, I am. I belong to the tribe we call Lakota and which others call the Sioux.*

— *Marvelous! But I've compounded my presumptuousness by forgetting my manners. My name is Henry Adams.*

The man held out his small, finely formed hand. It was as pink as his scalp and cheeks above his beard.

Paha Sapa got to his feet, returned the handshake, and gave his false name of Billy Slow Horse. The bearded man nodded and said how delightful it was to meet a member of the Sioux Nation here, in a World's Fair dynamo room of all places. Suddenly Paha Sapa was filled with a great sense of old sorrow—not his own—but thankfully no other memories or impressions came through the contact of hands. With Custer babbling through his nights and the memories of Crazy Horse confusing him during the days, Paha Sapa did not think his sanity could survive another set of memories.

Little did he know what awaited him in years to come.

They both turned to look at the roaring dynamo again. Without steam engines, it was much quieter in the Power Plant than in the Machinery Building, but the noise from this machine, while lower, went deeper. It made Paha Sapa's bones and teeth vibrate and seemed to create a subtle but very real sexual stirring in him. He wondered if the older man felt it.

The gentleman's voice was very smooth, modulated—Paha Sapa guessed—by decades of polite but informed conversation, but also moderated by an almost but not quite audible sense of humor, an unexpressed chuckle that came through despite the sadness that Paha Sapa still felt flowing from the man.

— *When my friends the Camerons insisted that I come with them on this flying visit to the Fair—all the way from Washington, DC, mind you!—I was quite certain that it would be a waste of time. How could Chicago—I proclaimed in all my insular arrogance—how could Chicago do anything but fling its brash, new-earned millions in our faces and show us something far less than art, far less than business, even, but some demonstration less than either.*

Paha Sapa listened hard over and under the dynamo hum. If most men he knew were to craft sentences like that, Paha Sapa would have laughed or left or both. But somehow Mr. Adams interested him deeply.

The older man gestured at the dynamo and showed a broad smile.

—*But* this! *This, Mr. Slow Horse, the ancient Greeks would have delighted to see and the Venetians, at their height, would have envied. Chicago has turned on us with a sort of wonderful, defiant contempt and shown us something far more powerful even than art, infinitely more important than business. This is, alas or hurrah, the* future, *Mr. Slow Horse! Yours and mine both, I fear ... and yet hope at the same time. I can revel and write postcards about the fakes and frauds of the Midway Plaisance, but each evening I return to the Machinery Hall and to this very chamber to stare like an owl at the dynamo of the future.*

Paha Sapa had nodded and glanced at the little gentleman. Embarrassed, Adams removed his straw hat again and mopped at his scalp.

—*I must apologize again, sir. I babble on as if you were an audience rather than an interlocutor. What do* you *think of this dynamo and of the wonders of the Machinery Hall, where I've seen you staring even as I do, Mr. Slow Horse?*

—*It's the real religion of your race, Mr. Adams.*

Henry Adams had blinked at that. Then he put his hat back on and blinked some more, obviously lost in thought. Then he smiled.

—*Sir, you have just answered a question I have been posing to myself for some years. I have long been interested—in my distant, unbeliever's vague and insolent way—in the role the Virgin Mary played in the long, slow dreams that were the construction of such masterpieces as Mont-Saint-Michel and Chartres. I believe you have given me my answer. The Virgin Mary was to the men of the thirteenth century what this dynamo and its brothers shall be to ...*

At that moment another man entered, and Adams interrupted himself to welcome him. They had obviously arranged to meet there at that time. This other gentleman was very tall, with a sharp beak of a nose, pomaded dark hair slicked back, and with eyes so piercing they reminded Paha Sapa not of an owl but of an eagle. The man was dressed all in black and gray with a brilliantly white shirt, which reinforced Paha Sapa's impression of being in the presence of a predator, vigilant eagle in human form.

Mr. Adams seemed flustered.

—*Mr. Slow Horse, may I present my companion at the Fair today, the eminent Sher ... that is ... the eminent Norwegian explorer Mr. Jan Sigerson.*

The tall man did not offer his hand but bowed and quietly clicked his heels together in an almost Germanic fashion. Paha Sapa smiled and nodded in return. Something about the tall man made Paha Sapa afraid to touch his bare hand and risk learning about his life.

Sigerson's voice was soft but sharp edged and sounded more English than Norwegian to Paha Sapa's untrained ear.

—*It is a true pleasure to meet you, Mr. Slow Horse. We Europeans rarely get the opportunity to meet a practicing* wičasa wakan *from the Natural Free Human Beings.*

Sigerson turned to Adams.

—*I apologize, Henry, but Lizzie and the senator are waiting at Franklin's steam launch at the North Pier and inform me that we are all running late for Mayor Harrison's dinner.*

Sigerson bowed toward Paha Sapa again and he was smiling slightly this time.

—*It has been a sincere pleasure meeting you, Mr. Slow Horse, and I can only hope that some day the* wasichu wanagi *will no longer be a problem.*

Wasichu wanagi. The white man's ghost. Paha Sapa could only stare after the two men as they left, Mr. Adams speaking but not being heard by the young Indian.

He never saw the man named Henry Adams or his Norwegian friend again.

———

MISS DE PLACHETTE LEADS THE WAY onto the Midway Plaisance—a mile-long strip of attractions, private shows, and rides that extends away from the lake from Jackson Park to the edge of Washington Park, as straight as a broad arrow fired into the back of the Columbian Exposition from the west.

Ahead are scatterings of exotic structures on either side of the low, broad, dusty Midway boulevard: Old Vienna medieval homes and a Biergarten; Algerian mosques and Tunisian minarets from which alien music blares and voices screech; a Cairo street where Paha Sapa and his friends have seen the overrated belly dancer; glimpses of Laplanders and Samoans and two-humped camels and a small herd of reindoor being hurried across the boulevard by men in shaggy fur despite the heat;

the long water-propelled sliding railway; the Bernese Alps theater; a glimpse of the captive balloon far, far down the strip and to the right.

And in the middle of the boulevard and seemingly growing taller every minute, the 264-foot-tall Ferris Wheel, which, according to Miss de Plachette, boasts thirty-six contained cars or cabins (each larger than many log cabins Paha Sapa has known), with each car or cabin capable of carrying up to sixty people.

Paha Sapa feels a growing, if unfocused, anxiety. He is not afraid of the Wheel or of heights, but something suddenly seems perilous to him, as if he and this young lady he barely knows are approaching some point of no return.

—*Are you sure you want to do this, Miss de Plachette?*

—*Call me Rain, please.*

—*Are you sure you want to do this, Rain?*

—*We* must *do this, Paha Sapa. It is our destiny.*

14

In the Paha Sapa

August—September 1876

HE KEEPS TRYING TO RISE INTO THE AIR BUT FAILS EACH TIME. What once came so easily to Paha Sapa, like effortless play, now seems impossible, as if his soul has grown inescapably heavy. It is the ninth day of his *hanblečeya*, the ninth day of his total fast, and his weakness is matched only by his weariness and sense of defeat. He has come to believe that this quest for a vision was premature, presumptuous, and doomed to failure. Many braves much older and wiser than he have failed before this—no male of the Natural Free Human Beings is ever *assured* a Vision and those few who receive them often do so only after years of frustration and many repeated *hanblečeyas*.

Except first for the hunger, which has departed, and then the weakness of his long fast, this *oymni*—his wandering time—has been mostly pleasant. When Paha Sapa awakened in Robert Sweet Medicine's cave at Bear Butte, there was no sign of the old man—not his drinking or eating bowls, not even a trace of the rabbits they'd eaten—and Paha Sapa could almost have believed that the old Cheyenne *wičasa wakan* had been a dream. But Worm and White Crane were rested and well fed when he found them still hobbled in the entrance to the cave that morning, and though the sun had not come out, the days of downpour outside had changed to an increasingly heavy drizzle.

It was then, for a scrotum-tightening panicked moment, that Paha Sapa untied the bundle on Three Buffalo Woman's white mare, seeking wildly for the *Ptehinčala Huhu Canunpa,* the sacred and irreplaceable Buffalo Calf Bone Pipe that he, Paha Sapa, had foolishly told the old Cheyenne he was carrying to his *inipi* first real sweat lodge ceremony.

It was there, separated into its different segments, each segment wrapped in a red cloth, the red feathers intact.

Paha Sapa's knees went weak then, as he realized how easy it would have been for the old Cheyenne—if he had been more than a dream—to steal Paha Sapa's tribe's most sacred object. And then his knees *stayed* weak as the full weight of Limps-a-Lot's trust sank in. Paha Sapa was heading to the Black Hills, reportedly rotten with *wasichus,* soldiers and miners both, who would kill him and rob him on a whim, even while enemy tribes swarmed—as they always did—around those Hills, always on the lookout for a lone Lakota boy to kill and rob or enslave.

Paha Sapa wished to the depths of his heart that morning that Limps-a-Lot had sent with him only an ordinary stone pipe for his *inipi* and *hanblečeya* ceremonies, even if the chances for a true Vision were lessened by not having the more *wakan* and powerful *Ptehinčala Huhu Canunpa* with its special tobacco.

But the day's ride through occasional heavy rain into the Paha Sapa themselves was uneventful, Paha Sapa riding the gelding and leading the mare in a wide arc to the west to avoid the roads and heavily traveled paths the *wasichus* used to get to their mining town of Deadwood.

In later years, especially when taking his son on their own small *oymni* wandering time to the Black Hills and what was left of the open Great Plains, Paha Sapa will find it very difficult to explain what the world was like during these days of his people's proud years, when the Lakota gods still listened to their worshippers and when the earth was alive for them.

These days, entering the Black Hills and riding down streambeds and across long meadows between the trees, always being careful to avoid ambush, Paha Sapa and everything he perceives seem to exist and interact simultaneously around him and within him, and interact on at least two levels: the joyous physical level on which he feels the horse between his legs and the rain on his face and smells the wet aspen leaves and hears the breathing of the gelding and mare as well as the chatter of squirrels and cry of crows, and the overlapping, more stirring and soul-touching *nagi* level of himself and everything else existing and touching each other as pure spirit-essence.

He feels the *waniya waken*—the very air as alive. Spirit breath. Renewal. *Tunkan. Inyan.* The rocks and boulders are alive. And holy. The storms that move above the prairie behind him and mass against the hills rising before him are *Wakinyan,* the noise of the Thunder Spirit and language of the Thunder Beings. The late-summer flowers blooming in the high, wet grass of the meadows show the touch and color preferences of *Tatuskansa,* the moving spirit, the quickening power of the All. In the rivers Paha Sapa fords dwell the *Unktehi,* monsters and spirits both. Sleeping under his canvas shelter and warming robes, Paha Sapa hears the howl of coyotes and thinks of Coyote, who will trick him during his *hanblečeya* if he can. The glistening spiderweb on a tree bears unreadable messages from *Iktomé,* the spider man, who is a worse trickster even than Coyote. In the evening, when all of the other spirits are quiet and the sky is emptying of light, Paha Sapa is able to hear the breathing of Grandfather Mystery and—sometimes—of *Wakan Tanka* himself. And at night, during the rare times the clouds part, Paha Sapa watches the stars spread from dark horizon to dark horizon, his viewing undimmed by any light (he has no campfire), and in these minutes young Paha Sapa can trace the path of his life, past and future, knowing that when he dies his own spirit will travel south along the Milky Way with the spirits of all those Natural Free Human Beings who have gone before him.

This is truly the *maka sitomni,* the world over, the universe, and the world is never empty. More than forty-five years later, when poet and historian Doane Robinson teaches him the English word *numinous,* Paha Sapa will think back to these days and smile sadly.

PAHA SAPA HAS NO TROUBLE finding the mountain called the Six Grandfathers; its nearby peak, Evil Spirit Hill (which Paha Sapa will live to see renamed Harney Peak after a famous Indian-killer *Wasicun*) is the tallest in the Hills at a little more than seven thousand feet.

The south side of the Six Grandfathers is all crags and open, weathered, rocky face—good for nothing, not even climbing—but the north side has more gradual approaches up through the trees. There is a stream at the bottom there, where Paha Sapa makes his lower camp and builds his sweat lodge. The place he chooses is a sheltered bowl with the stream running through and where there is ample good grass for the horses. He retrieves the priceless *Ptehinčala Huhu Canunpa* from the large bundle on White Crane's back, the pipe's segments still wrapped in red cloth, as well as the *wasmuha* rattle that holds the forty small squares of Three Buffalo Woman's skin along with *yuwipi* stones.

It takes Paha Sapa a full day to find the *sintkala waksu* sacred stones for the sweat lodge, all that time spent wading through the ice-cold streams for miles around, seeking out the special rocks with the beadwork design. It makes Paha Sapa shiver to know that these very stones were once touched by *Tuncan,* the ancient and hard stone spirit who was present at the creation of all things. Then he has to find exactly the right sort of willows. It takes him another full day from dawn to late-summer sunset to build his *sintkala waksu* sweat lodge for his *inipi.*

After cutting down the required twelve white willow trees (and rejecting many more), Paha Sapa sticks the poles in a circle about six feet across. He weaves the pliable branches into a dome and covers that dome with skins and robes he's brought with him. Then he adds leaves to close all gaps. Inside, Paha Sapa digs a hole in the center of the little lodge and saves the dirt to make a tidy little path that the spirits can follow into his sweat lodge. At the end of the little path, he builds up a low mound called an *unci,* the same word his people use for "grandmother" because that is the way that Limps-a-Lot and Sitting Bull and the other holy men have taught him to think of the whole earth: Grandmother.

The opening to Paha Sapa's *onikare*—another word he uses for sweat lodge—faces west, since only *heyoka* may enter such a lodge from the east. In the center of his lodge he sets forked sticks firmly into the earth as a framework to support the sacred pipe, *Ptehinčala Huhu Canunpa*. Not having a buffalo skull for the entrance, Paha Sapa spends a day hunting in the pine forest, kills a large deer, leaves the carcass for the birds and other scavengers—he is deep enough into his fast that his belly is rumbling all the time now and he often has to sit and lower his head until his vision clears—and he flenses and cleans the skull, resisting the urge to nibble on the eyes, and mounts it near the entrance with six pouches holding offerings of the finest tobacco sent by Limps-a-Lot. This is for good luck.

Now Paha Sapa really misses the presence of his grandfather Limps-a-Lot and the other important men of the village. Were he doing this *hanblečeya* properly, the older men would have cut and woven the willows and prepared his *sintkala waksu* for him, and Paha Sapa would not have started his four days of fasting in the sweat lodge until everything had been made ready for him. But because of Robert Sweet Medicine's advice at Bear Butte, Paha Sapa has been fasting—from solid food at least—for almost six days by the time his sweat lodge is ready and his sacred pipe is filled and his gourds and pouches of water are ready to be poured upon the white-hot rocks in the center of the pitch-black and already sweltering lodge. At this point he is fasting from all food but may still drink water. During the actual vision quest in his pit, he knows, he must go at least four days without food *or* water.

And it is Paha Sapa himself who must chant the prayers here alone, as best he can, and gasp out "Ho, Grandfather!" each time he pours more water on the glowing *sinktala waksu* stones and feels the sacred energy flowing out of them with the explosions of steam. No man can take the blind, steaming interior of a sweat lodge indefinitely, and every hour or so Paha Sapa stumbles naked into the infinitely cooler August air outside, where he collapses gasping in the high grasses, sometimes startling his grazing horses, but always, after a few gasping minutes—during which he crawls to drink deeply from the teeth-numbingly cold stream, almost weeping with gratitude that he is still allowed to drink at this point—he stumbles back into the sweat lodge to smoke and to chant some more. He takes longer breaks only to bring more sticks for the fire and more water to pour on the rocks. Always a thin boy, Paha Sapa has lost any body fat that may have remained on his lean frame and bones.

For three long days he purifies himself thus, and although he welcomes a vision then, none comes. He knows that the sweat lodge is mere preamble, but he had hoped...

On the fourth day of his purifying, the ninth day of his fast, weak from hunger and shaking from the effects of the heat and steam and darkness and tobacco, wearing only moccasins and a single robe, he takes the sacred pipe and a bundle and makes the forty-five-minute hard climb above his sweat lodge to a spot near the rocky summit of the Six Grandfathers. There Paha Sapa finds a soft place between the rocky ridge and boulders. He clears this spot of pine needles and pinecones and digs a shallow pit just long enough to lie in. A red blanket, one of Limps-a-Lot's prized possessions, was in the bundle on White Crane, and now Paha Sapa uses his knife to cut the blanket into strips that he mounts on poles to serve as banners around his Vision Pit. Strings tied between these poles hold bundles of bright cloth holding still more tobacco—Paha Sapa wonders if Limps-a-Lot kept any for himself to smoke—and he cuts some small squares from his thighs and forearms to add to these sacred bundles around his Vision Pit.

The fifth pole rises from the center of the vision pit, next to his right arm as he lies on his back, and that final pole announces that—at least for the purpose of this Vision—this place is the center of the world and the locus of all spiritual power.

Paha Sapa has removed everything before entering the Vision Pit, even his breechclout and moccasins, since one has to wait for a vision in the same naked state one entered the world, but he does not lie in the pit all day. In the morning, when the sun rises in the east out beyond the faraway but clearly visible *Maka Sica,* the Badlands, Paha Sapa stands atop the rocky summit of the Six Grandfathers and holds the stem of his sacred pipe out to this most powerful visible form of *Wakan Tanka* while chanting greeting prayers and vision supplications to the spirit-behind-the-sun. All day he rises from the Vision Pit to repeat the gestures and chants and prayers, turning, at noon, to the south, standing at each pole he has marked with his banners, and singing the chants and supplications to the west all through the evening.

Paha Sapa watches everything carefully—the skies, the weather, the wind, the movement of the trees, the soaring of a hawk or owl, the distant padding of a coyote or raccoon—with the heightened awareness and expectation that the spirit of that thing or creature may be part of his Vision.

Everything is as it should be.

NOTHING IS AS IT SHOULD BE.

A decent *hanbleceya* is usually carried out under clear skies in the daytime and under starry skies at night, but it continues pouring rain for almost the entire time that Paha Sapa is in the Black Hills. When he wakes to greet the rising sun in the morning with his chants and prayers—only imperfectly remembered, and there are no *wicasa wakan* or elders here to help him chant or help him recall the words—the "rising sun" is a murky glow half-glimpsed to the east through thick drizzle. With the thick clouds above each day, he finds it almost impossible to tell when the sun has passed the zenith for his ritual facing-south and prayers, and the sunsets are no more visible than the sunrises. Paha Sapa continues holding the stem of the dripping *Ptehincala Huhu Canunpa* out to rain and grayness. Despite his efforts, the ancient and sacred red feathers on the pipe are soggy and molting from the damp.

Without the help from the older holy men and others, everything is wrong. Paha Sapa knows that his sweat lodge is not the elegant and proper structure it would have been if Limps-a-Lot or even Angry Badger had helped shape it. He feels that his selection of the sacred rocks was imperfect and, indeed, several cracked when he threw water on the glowing stones. He knows that his prayers and entreaties are sloppy and suspects that even aspects of his vision pit were wrongly done. Most important, the absence of other men and their chants and prayers in the pipe-smoking and other sweat lodge ceremonies makes Paha Sapa feel sure that the purification is incomplete and his *inipi* must be unpleasing to any spirits.

Finally, there is the fact that Paha Sapa is starving to death. Young men always begin their total fast *after* the last of the sweat lodge purification is finished, but Paha Sapa began his fasting—following the advice of a Cheyenne holy man at Bear Butte in what may have been only a stupid dream—even before reaching the Black Hills. Rather than start his total fasting on the first day when he dug the vision pit, that was Paha Sapa's *ninth day* without food and his body is now as shaky and unreliable as his mind.

But there are more compelling reasons than that to convince Paha Sapa that this entire vision quest is already a failure.

He realizes now, as he lies in his muddy pit atop the rocky ridge-summit of the Six Grandfathers with rain pouring onto his face, that Crazy Horse was right: no man infected with the ghost of Long Hair, or any other *Wasicun,* can be pleasing to the gods and spirits, much less to *Wakan Tanka.* And as Paha Sapa's body grows weaker and his mind more muddled, the ghost in his mind and belly gabbles on more loudly, as if eager to get out.

What will happen to Long Hair's ghost if I die here? wonders Paha Sapa. *Will both our* nagi *spirits fly out and up at the same time—his to whatever place* wasichu *spirits migrate after death, mine to the Milky Way and beyond?*

There is also the irritating fact of Crazy Horse's memories mixed in with his own. How can the spirits recognize his—Paha Sapa's—spirit if so much a part of his consciousness is given over to that fierce *heyoka's* violent and brooding memories?

He does have access to Crazy Horse's memories of his own successful *hanbleçeya,* back when the war chief was a young brave still called Curly Hair, but even those recollections discourage Paha Sapa. The Minneconjou boy had the full help of Thunder Dreamers such as Horn Chips and his own living father, then named Crazy Horse, as well as his entire band's certainty that young Curly Hair would receive a Vision from the Thunder Beings and become the *heyoka* and war chief they wished him to be. Even the memory of young Curly Hair–Crazy Horse's actual Vision is confusing, since it seems little more than a fuzzy dream of lightning flashing, thunder crashing, and of Curly Hair's *nagi* speaking to a spirit-warrior on a spirit-horse. Of all the people on the earth, Paha Sapa knows, only he and Crazy Horse know how fuzzy and uncertain that Vision was, although it began well, with a red-tailed hawk screaming for the boy's attention.

And it ended well, with the post-Vision purification with the older men in the sweat lodge again, and these elders and *wičasa wakans*— other Thunder Dreamers all—interpreting the dream as a valid Vision, anointing young Crazy Horse as a *heyoka* and *akicita* tribal policeman, and announcing to all that Curly Hair would someday be a great war chief.

Every time now that the thunder echoes through the Black Hills, Paha Sapa flinches and huddles tighter. He does not want to be a *heyoka*. He does not want to serve the fierce and warlike Thunder Beings. And at the same time he is ashamed of this shrinking back, this cowardice, this stubbornness in wanting to refuse his role in life if that is the will of the All.

But the Thunder Beings do not speak to him there on the summit of the Six Grandfathers, even while real thunder echoes and lightning flashes and Paha Sapa huddles in his muddy hole, fearful of lightning in such a high, exposed place.

He is, he realizes, not only a failure as a vision-seeker, but a cowardly failure.

ON THE NIGHT of his ninth day of fasting, Paha Sapa realizes that he soon will be too weak to hunt or find food even if a Vision does appear to him. That night he stumbles down the long, steep mountainside to the vale where the two staked horses still crop and drink from the stream and—with infinite and slow-motion labor—he makes four rabbit traps, which he sets in the trees and shrubs on the hillside. Then, seeing how his *sintkala waksu* sweat lodge seems to be melting in the continued downpour, Paha Sapa takes his robe and the pipe now hanging from his neck by a sturdy strap and makes the long, arduous climb and crawl back up to the summit ridge, arriving just in time to make offerings and prayers to a sunrise hidden behind clouds.

On his tenth day of fasting, Paha Sapa tries to fly.

He is so weak now that he spends much of his time sitting and leaning against one of the Four Directions posts as he offers the sacred pipe, but he is also so weak and light-headed that his *nagi* spirit-self slips easily from his body. (Afraid that it will not return, Paha Sapa entices it back with promises of a rabbit cooked to perfection over a crackling fire.)

His *nagi* leans into the slight breeze that blows up here most of the time, feeling the wind against his spirit-chest much as he used to feel the water in a deep part of a stream or river and be ready to kick off to float and swim, but—unlike so many times before when rising into the sky came so easily—the winds now do not bear him up.

Even his spirit is too heavy to soar.

Thus on Paha Sapa's tenth day of fasting and mumbling of prayers and heavy-armed offering of the stem of the *Ptehinčala Huhu Canunpa* to low clouds and rain, he thinks dully of admitting failure and going home.

Crazy Horse will kill me.

But certainly Crazy Horse must have moved on by now. The war chief was planning to lead his band against the *wasichus* in the Black Hills and then scout out the cavalry that were coming seeking vengeance for the rubbing out of Long Hair. The chance that Crazy Horse would still be with Angry Badger's and Limps-a-Lot's band camped near Slim Buttes is low.

And return a total failure, never to claim a vision, never to become a wičasa wakan *like my adoptive* tunkašila?

Better to be a failure than to be a corpse, Black Hills. You knew you were never cut out to be a warrior, a brave.... Now you know that you were not meant to be a holy man or an important man in the tribe.

Paha Sapa comes very close to sobbing. Sitting with his back against the western post, waiting for his sunset prayers, the red banner hanging thick, wet, and soggy above him, his sullen *nagi* aching in his chest, and the goddamned *wasichu* ghost always babbling in his aching brain, Paha Sapa decides that he will stay here on the Six Grandfathers for one more night, perhaps one more wet day, before surrendering his hopes and riding home.

If the traps have not captured a rabbit, you will die, unless you slaughter Worm or White Crane.

Shaking that thought out of his head, Paha Sapa closes his eyes in the rain as he waits for the approximate time of sunset behind the lowering clouds.

———

HE AWAKES LYING NAKED on his back near his vision pit. It is very dark, and the clouds have gone away. The sky is ablaze with the three thousand or so tightly packed stars he is used to seeing on such a late-summer night. For a moment he is panicked, thinking that he may have dropped the sacred pipe on the steep rocky summit, but then he feels the strap and finds the *Ptehinčala Huhu Canunpa* strangely warm across his bare belly.

Shooting stars scratch across the black between-the-stars night glass of the sky. Paha Sapa remembers that this time right after his birthing day has always been rich with shooting stars. Limps-a-Lot once told him that some elders believe that the falling stars celebrate some great battle or victory or Vision that has long been lost to the memory of the Natural Free Human Beings.

Paha Sapa is content to lie there on his back, half in his Vision Pit and half out, the cooling rock of the mountain strangely dry under his shoulders and head, and watch the stars fall.

Suddenly a shooting star brighter than all the others streaks from the zenith. It is so bright that it lights up the skies, lights up the summit of the Six Grandfathers, lights up towering Evil Spirit Hill and all the other surrounding peaks. The millions of dark pine trees in the Paha Sapa suddenly grow silver and then milky white in the light of this falling star turned hurtling comet.

— *Ooooh!*

Paha Sapa cannot help making the noise. It is the same noise he made as a tiny boy watching the late-summer falling-star showers when there was an especially bright one. But he has never seen any star falling with such dazzling brilliance as this one.

And, he realizes with a slow stirring of what might have been fear if he'd had more energy and presence of mind, it is headed directly for him.

The shadows of the direction posts and of the few stunted trees near the rocky summit leap away in all directions from the hurtling brilliance directly above him. Paha Sapa can *hear* the falling star now—a hissing, roaring, galloping sound as the star burns through the air.

Suddenly, silently, the falling star explodes, dividing into six different and only slightly smaller falling stars. They continue hurtling down toward him.

Paha Sapa realizes through his hunger and exhaustion, with something like bemused detachment, that he is going to die in a few seconds.

The six fragments of the Great Star hurtle lower. Each fragment is going to strike the Six Grandfathers; one, it seems, right here on the summit. At the last moment, Paha Sapa puts his forearm over his eyes.

No impact. No explosions. No noise whatsoever except for the slightest stirring of the ponderosa pine trees and fir trees in a slight breeze.

Paha Sapa lowers his arm and peeks out.

The six stars are all around the summit but they appear now as six shafts of vertical white light. Each shaft must be two hundred feet tall. Inside each shaft or upright cocoon of light is an old man who looks to be of the Natural Free Human Beings, and each old man is wearing a perfect white buffalo robe and has one white eagle feather in his gray hair. All of them are staring at Paha Sapa, and their gaze is unlike any human gaze the boy has ever encountered. He can feel the pressure of those gazes.

— *Will you come with us, Black Hills?*

Paha Sapa's head snaps around. He did not see any of their lips move. Nor did he *hear* the question, exactly. At least not with his ears. For many decades after this he will try to recall and describe their voices—certainly not sounds of the sort men make in their throats and mouths, or with their tongues and teeth, but more the subtle whisper of wind moving branches or the deep vibration of distant thunder felt or the slight bone-shake of approaching horse herds or buffalo such as the boy heard when, imitating the older men, he put his ear tight to the earth.

Except none of these comparisons is right either. He knows then and later that it does not matter.

— Of course I will come, Grandfathers.

One of the giant forms reaches out a hand encased in white light. Paha Sapa takes one step and realizes that all of him fits perfectly into the weathered palm.

They rise quickly and silently into the blazing night sky. Somehow, Paha Sapa can hear the sound of the stars — each star a voice, each voice a part of a chorus, the chorus of three thousand and more voices chanting a melodic prayer unlike any he has ever heard.

When they are many thousands of feet above the starlit landscape, the six forms cease rising and hover, Paha Sapa comfortable and unworried in the warm palm.

But when he finally leans over the edge of the giant, reassuringly cupped palm to look down upon the sacred Hills, Paha Sapa almost screams in terror.

The Black Hills are gone. Everything is gone.

Beneath him, beneath the hovering, cloudlike Six Grandfathers and him, an endless expanse of water stretches away to both of the distant, dark, and slightly curved horizons. The world is water without end.

Paha Sapa realizes at once that he is looking down on the world without form that existed before *Wakan Tanka,* the Mystery, the All, brought forth land and the four-leggeds and then man. This is the world before man, when *taku wankan,* the Things Mysterious, walked abroad in the spirit world: the *Wakinyan* Thunderbird, the *Tatanka* Great Beast, the *Unktehi* One Who Kills, the *Taku Skanskan* He Who Changes Things, *Tunkan* the Venerable One. All the pure *nagi* spirit-beings who walked the skies above a world still drowned in placental water and waiting to be born.

This is the all-water world that Limps-a-Lot has told him of in the Oldest Stories, but Paha Sapa has never been able to imagine it before this. Now the sea stretches out on all sides below him.

Paha Sapa realizes that the stars have been occluded by high clouds. Now there are gray clouds infinitely high above him and gray, almost waveless water infinitely far below him. He understands in his heart that the Six Grandfathers are allowing him to join them for the Birth.

Suddenly a single shaft of light — the boy knows at once that the light comes from the Mystery, the All — breaks the ceiling of clouds above and splits the intervening sky until it touches the sea below. The waters churn. Out of the World Sea rise, dripping, the hills and black trees and sacred stone of the heart of the heart of the world — the Black Hills. The shaft of light fades, but the Black Hills remain below, a tiny dark island in a vaguely glowing endless sea. For a while as Paha Sapa watches from the safety of the Grandfather's curled palm, the only sound is of the wind caressing the trees and grasses and wavetops so far beneath him. Paha Sapa understands that the winds he hears whispering are the hushed voices of other great Spirits existing here before the first men arrived: *Tate,* the Wind Essence; *Yate,* the North Wind; *Yanpa,* the East Wind; *Okaga,* the South Wind.

To all these winds has Paha Sapa prayed and chanted alongside Limps-a-Lot, training as a boy to be a holy man someday, and to all these winds Paha Sapa now silently prays again. Their presence makes him want to weep.

The sun rises. The sunlight paints dark strokes of mountain-shadows and pine-tree-shadows on the face of the Hills and throws more shadows of small hills and isolated trees on the long meadows. Then the waters around this island world recede farther, and the prairies and plains and *Maku Sichu* Bad Lands emerge glistening into the light. Solid land has now replaced the covering seas from horizon to horizon. The world has become mostly *maka,* earth, and it is ready for the four-leggeds and the two-leggeds to live on it now.

Paha Sapa wants to ask the Six Grandfathers why they are showing him these things, but his *nagi* spirit-voice is too weak — or the air up here too thin — for the word-sounds to reach the Grandfathers' ears. He can only look up and nod at the ancient, lined but friendly faces shifting slightly as towering clouds tend to shift in sacred winds.

Paha Sapa realizes that the Six Grandfathers have given him the *wanbli* keen vision of the eagle. When Paha Sapa looks to the southern wooded hills of the Black Hills, he can clearly see the opening of *Washu Niya,* "the Breathing Cave," that sacred place that the unseeing *wasichus* call "Wind Cave." He watches now with his *wanbli* vision as the first buffalo emerge into the light.

Paha Sapa laughs aloud, and that happy sound is louder than his weak *nagi* voice. Limps-a-Lot and Sitting Bull and the other *wičasa wakan* were right in their how-it-started stories! The first buffalo are tiny, hardly larger than ants, and just as numerous. But the rich, still birth-wet grasses in the Black Hills and wider great plains beyond soon allow the tiny bison to grow to full buffalo height and mass. Again, Paha Sapa laughs aloud. The Six Grandfathers are showing him aeons of time in these few minutes.

The sun rises higher, and now even the shadows of the bison grazing in herds on the endless windswept plains north and south of the Hills leap out in bold relief.

Paha Sapa looks south again.

The First Men crawl blinking from the Breathing Cave, rise on their hind legs, and immediately send up prayers to *Wakan Tanka,* to the Six Grandfathers, to the other spirits, and to the gift of Mystery itself, giving thanks for being led up out of the darkness into this new world so rich with game and alive with whispering, guarding, and sometimes wonderfully dangerous spirits.

Generations and centuries pass in minutes as Paha Sapa watches his people be born, hunt, marry, wander far, fight, worship, grow old, and die. He watches them hunt animals he has never seen or heard of before—great hairy, tusked beasts—and watches as the Natural Free Human Beings receive the gift of *šunkcincala,* the "sacred dog" miracle of the horse. He watches as his people spread far across the plains.

Once again Paha Sapa is able to see the Black Hills as the heart-shaped center of the endless green-and-brown prairies of the *obleyaya dosho,* the wideness of the world. Once again he sees the Black Hills as the entire continent's *wamakaognaka e'cantge,* the heart of everything that is. More than ever before, Paha Sapa sees the Black Hills as the *O'onakezin,* the Place of Shelter.

He can see the Sun Dance River to the north of the Hills, what the *wasichus* call the Belle Fourche, and the Cheyenne River to the south. Farther to the north he can easily see the meandering line the *wasichus* call the Missouri River. All of these rivers are in flood stage, but the Sun Dance River the most so.

In the distance Paha Sapa can see *Wapiye Olaye I'ha,* the Plain of the Rocks that Heal, and the *Hinyankagapa* Black Buttes and the *He Ska* White Buttes and the *Re Sla* Bald Place and back again to the *Washu Niya* Breathing Cave in the southern part of the Hills and half a hundred landmarks in the Hills and out that would take him days or weeks of walking or riding to reach.

He can see the Hogback Ridge of reddish sandstone that borders the sunken Race Track around the Hills, like a band of muscle around a pumping heart, and can easily see the broad *Pte Tali Yapa* "Buffalo Gap" that allows easy access both for the four-legged animals and for the Natural Free Human Beings when they go to the mountains for sanctuary. Directly beneath him is the Six Grandfathers, nearby the higher rocky summit of Evil Spirit Hill and half a hundred other gray-granite ridges and red-rock needles and spires thrusting up out of the soft black carpet of pines that covers the Hills.

It is silent up here as the sun rises quickly again and again, far too quickly to be in the harness of regular time or motion, and the shadows grow shorter so quickly as to be amusing. Again and again the sun hurtles into the sky, arcs across the perfect blue, and sets to the prayers of the Natural Free Human Beings. But suddenly that motion slows and there comes the wind-whisper, branch-murmuring, distant-thunder careful enunciation of the soft Grandfather voice in Paha Sapa's mind. The eleven-year-old boy suddenly feels as if he is in his and his people's future.

— *Watch, Paha Sapa.*

Paha Sapa watches and at first sees nothing. But then he realizes that there is a stirring and shifting among and within the rocks of the sacred Six Grandfathers mountain a mile or two directly beneath him, a trembling and vibration along the rocky ridge summit where he can still make out his muddy Vision Pit and his five direction posts with their wilting red banners. Paha Sapa's enhanced eagle-vision allows him to focus on things at will, almost as if he has one of the *Wasicun* cavalry officer's telescopes he's heard Limps-a-Lot describe, and now, as one of the Grandfathers points again, he looks more closely at the mountain from whence he came.

Small rocks and midsized boulders are shaking loose and sliding down the steep southern face of the Six Grandfathers Mountain. Paha Sapa sees the trees on the northern slope shake and shiver in unison. There rises a soft rumble as more rocks, large and small, tumble into the deeper valley on the south side of the sacred peak, and then Paha Sapa sees the earthquake in action as the very rock seems to become liquid, shimmering, and mile after mile of forest and meadow fold and rearrange themselves like a buffalo robe or furry blanket being shaken.

No, something is coming *out* of the stone.

For a moment, Paha Sapa thinks it is something erupting from the rock itself, burrowing up *out* of the stone, but then he swoops his vision closer and sees that it is the granite of the mountain itself that is reshaping, re-forming, emerging.

Four giant faces emerge from the south-facing cliff just beneath where Paha Sapa has been praying and lying for days and nights. They are *wasichu* faces, all male — although the first face to come out of the rock might be that of an old woman except for the bold thrust of chin. The second face to emerge from the granite cliff like a baby bird's beak and head from a thick-shelled gray egg is of a *Wasicun* with long hair, an even longer chin than the old-lady *Wasicun* on the far left, and a far gaze. He is looking up at Paha Sapa and the real Six Grandfathers. The third Head has a sort of goat beard that some *Wasicun* affect, but strong features and infinitely sad eyes. The fourth and final head, set between the far-looker and the goat-bearded sad man, has a short mustache above smiling lips, and around the eyes are two circles of what might be metal and glass. Limps-a-Lot has talked, rather wistfully Paha Sapa thought, of these third and fourth eyes that some *wasichus* put on when their own eyes begin to wear out; he has even given the *Wasicun* word for them: *spectacles*.

— *What*...

Paha Sapa has to ask the significance of these frightening heads, no matter how puny his *nagi* voice sounds to his own ears.

Paha Sapa silences himself when he feels the phantom touch of an invisible Grandfather hand on his spirit-shoulder as the mountain below continues to change.

The four heads are free. Then, in a way strangely familiar to Paha Sapa from earlier dreams, come the shoulders and upper bodies, clad in granite hints of *wasichu* clothing. Now the four forms writhe and twist — Paha Sapa can almost hear the grunting from exertion and *can* hear the rumble of boulders falling into the valleys and the flap and cry as thousands of birds throughout the Black Hills take wing.

The heads must be fifty or sixty feet tall. The stone bodies, when they rise from their fetal crouches, balance, and stand, must be more than three hundred feet tall — taller than the spirit Six Grandfathers in their columns of white light.

For a moment Paha Sapa is terrified. Will these gray stone *wasichu* monsters continue growing until they can reach the Grandfathers and him? Will they reach up and pluck him out of the sky and devour him?

The stone *Wasicun* do not continue growing and do not look up at Paha Sapa or the Grandfathers again. Their attention is on the earth and on the Black Hills all around them. The giants stand there on their massive gray stone legs, two of them are actually astride the peak of the Six Grandfathers, and Paha Sapa can see them looking around with what he interprets as the same sense of wonder held by any newborn, four-legged or human.

But there is more than wonder in those four gazes. There is hunger.

Again comes the wind-pine-rustle, distant-summer-thunder whisper of one — or perhaps all — of Paha Sapa's beloved Six Grandfathers.

— *Watch.*

The four *Wasichu* Stone Giants are striding through the Black Hills, knocking trees down in their wake. Their footprints in the soft soil are as large as some of the Hills' scattered small and sacred lakes. Occasionally one or more of the giants will stop, bend, and rip the top of a mountain off, throwing thousands of tons of dirt to one side or the other.

Paha Sapa has the sudden and almost overwhelming urge to giggle, to laugh, perhaps to weep. Are these *Wasichu* Stone Giants then mere *pispía* — giant prairie dogs?

Then he continues to watch and has no more urge to giggle.

The four *Wasichu* Stone Giants are plucking animals out of the forests and meadows of the Paha Sapa: deer from the high grasses, beaver from their headwater ponds, elk from the hillsides, bighorn sheep from the boulders, porcupines from the trees, bears from their dens, coyotes and foxes and their cubs and kits from *their* dens, squirrels from branches, eagles and hawks from the very air....

And everything the four *Wasichu* Stone Giants pluck from the forest and fields, they devour. The huge gray stone teeth chew and chew and chew. The gray stone faces on the gray stone heads show no emotion, but the boy can feel their unsatiated hunger as they bend and pluck and lift and pop living things with their own souls into their gray mouths and chew and chew and chew.

Paha Sapa's whisper is real, audible, formed by his *nagi* lungs and throat and mouth and forced out through his spirit-teeth, but it is also ragged.

— *Grandfathers, can you stop this?*

Instead of answering, the thunder-rumble, wind-in-the-needles whisper comes back with another question.

— *"Wasichu" does not mean "White Person," Black Hills. It means and has always meant "Fat Taker." Do you see now why we gave your ancestors this word for the* Wasicun?

— *Yes, Grandfathers.*

Paha Sapa did not know and never would have guessed that his spirit-body could feel sick to its stomach, but it does. He leans over the curling fingers of his protective Grandfather's hand and watches.

The four *Wasichu* Stone Giants are striding out of the Black Hills now, each moving in one of the four primary compass directions as if guided by Paha Sapa's poor little direction posts at his Vision Pit site. At first the boy cannot believe what he is seeing, but he uses his new eagle-vision to look carefully and his eyes are not deceiving him.

The *Wasichu* Stone Giants are killing buffalo and other plains animals now, using their giant stone heels on their *wasichu* stone shoes to squash the bison or antelope or elk before lifting the mangled carcass to their stone mouths three hundred feet above the green-and-brown-grass prairie. Somehow time has accelerated and the sun sets, the stars whirl above the Six Grandfathers and the crouching Paha Sapa, the sun rises again — a thousand times, tens of thousands of times — but the four *Wasichu* Stone Giants, roaming the plains to the horizon and beyond but always returning, continue to smash with their heels, to pluck and to lift, and to chew. And chew. And chew.

Then Paha Sapa sees something that makes him scream into the high, thin, cold air of the sky where he and the Six Grandfathers float as insubstantially and as impotently as clouds.

Even before they kill the last of the millions of buffalo, the four *Wasichu* Stone Giants are chasing the people on the Plains and in the Black Hills and even those living far to the east and farther to the west: chasing and catching Paha Sapa's Natural Free Human Beings and the Crow and the Cheyenne and the Blackfoot and the Shoshoni and the Ute and the Arapaho and the Pawnee and the Oto and Osage and Ojibwa, chasing the few pitiful remnants of the Mandan, sweeping up the Gros Ventre and Plains Cree and the Kutenai and the Hidatsa. All run. All are swept up. None escape.

Some of these little fleeing forms the four *Wasichu* Stone Giants tuck away in the stone pockets of their stone clothing, but others they throw far away, flinging the tiny, screaming, flapping human figures over the curve of the earth and out of sight forever. And some they eat. Chewing. Chewing.

— *Grandfathers! Stop this! Please stop this!*

The voice Paha Sapa hears next is softer than the one or ones he's heard before: low, musical, subdued, a combination of birdsong and water flowing around rocks in a stream.

— *Stop it? We cannot. You, our people, have failed to do so. Nor would it be proper to stop them. They are the Fat Takers. They have always been the Fat Takers. Do we stop the rattlesnake from striking its prey? Do we stop the scorpion from stinging the sleeping gopher? Do we stop the eagle from swooping down on the mouse? Do we stop the wolf or coyote from pouncing on the prairie dog?*

The words rattle in Paha Sapa's aching skull: *sintehabla, itignila, anúnkasan, hitunkala, šung' manitu tanka, šung' mahetu, pispía* . . .

What do these mere *animals* have to do with the slaughter and extinction of the Natural Free Human Beings he is watching below? What does the nature of a scorpion or wolf or eagle or rattlesnake have to do with the murder and capture of men by men?

On the wide prairies, the bison are dead, killed, eaten, removed. The lodges and villages of the Natural Free Human Beings and all their red enemies and allies and distant cousins are empty. The four *Wasichu* Stone Giants, fattened by their killing and chewing and taking of so much fat, are striding back across emptied grasslands to the ravaged Black Hills.

Paha Sapa leans so far over the edge of the giant palm and giant fingers holding him above miles of nothing that he almost falls. Instead, he finds his courage.

— *Grandfathers, Powers of the World,* Tunkašila *of the Four Directions and of the Earth and Sky, Oldest Children of the Great Spirit, please hear my prayer! Do not let this vision become true, Grandfathers! Do not make me return to Limps-a-Lot and my band with this as my Vision! I beseech you, O Grandfathers!*

Miles beneath him, the *Wasichu* Stone Giants have returned to the Paha Sapa, are lying down amid the shattered trees and tumbled rocks and burrowed mountaintops and are pulling the soil and stone over their gray granite bodies the way old men, after a feast, pull buffalo robes up over their shanks and distended bellies and old-men's shoulders.

Paha Sapa feels himself hurtling down — not falling, but hurtling lower still in the palm of the Grandfather bathed in the white light — but now the Grandfathers speak as one and their voices are very difficult to understand, so mixed are they with the wind and thunder rumble and rushing-stream sounds.

— *Behold, this was your nation, Black Hills. Your ancestors sang it into existence. Your generation shall lose it forever if you do not act. The Fat Takers are what they do, this the Natural Free Human Beings and all Our Children have known since they first saw the first Fat Taker paddling west in the day of your grandfather's grandfather. Lose the buffalo, lose your lodges, lose this world with all your songs and sacrifices, and you lose us and all the other spirits and deep, dangerous forces and names to whom your little voices have cried for ten thousand summers and more. Allow the Fat Takers to take all this away from you, and you lose Mystery forever. Even God cannot exist when all his worshippers are gone and all the secret chants forgotten, Paha Sapa, our son. A people who have no power are not a people. They are only food for beasts and other men.*

The six columns of light with the shadowy forms in them are flying low now. In a few seconds, Paha Sapa knows, they will set him down on the torn rocky top of the sacred mountain. Already the sun has set and time has slowed and the stars have faded and clouds are rolling in again.

— What can I do to help the Natural Free Human Beings from suffering this prophecy come true, Grandfathers? Please tell me!

It is the stream-and-small-birds voice that answers.

— This is not a prophecy, Black Hills. It is a fact. But you will be in a position to act. Of all Our Children who are now Fat to the Fat Takers, only you will be able to act.

— How, Grandfathers? When? How? Why me? Tell me how…Grandfathers!

But the great, warm hand has set his *nagi* back into his body, which lies faceup in the Vision Pit. The six forms in the six columns of light become shooting stars again and retrace their bright, flashing paths back up into the skies.

— Grandfathers!

The voice from the sky is only a whisper of wind.

— Paha Sapa, toksha ake čante ista wacinyanktin ktelo.

We shall see you again with the eyes of our hearts.

———

PAHA SAPA WAKES. It is a cold, wet, rainy sunrise. He is shaking so hard that even when he finds his robe to wrap around his nakedness, his body continues to tremble for half an hour or more.

Clutching the sacred pipe on its strap to his chest, Paha Sapa manages to stumble down the mountainside. Worm has somehow slipped his stake tether and hobbles but has stayed near White Crane. Paha Sapa is so weak that he knows that if the rabbit traps are empty, he may not survive.

There is a wriggling rabbit in one trap and the leg of a rabbit in another. Paha Sapa chants his song of thanks, kills the living rabbit, and takes the leg of the other.

His flint and steel are in the sweat lodge where he left them, along with some twigs still dry under a stack of robes. With shaking hands, he manages to get his lodge fire burning again. The winds and storm have blown away the leaves and some of the willow branches and blown off a robe, opening part of the little lodge to the sky and rain, but Paha Sapa ignores this as he huddles over the sparks, then breathes the tiny embers into flame. When he is certain that the fire will go…

— *Thank you, Grandfathers! Thank you,* Wakan Tanka.

...Paha Sapa skins and guts the rabbit, peels the hide off the leg, builds a crude spit with the fallen twigs, and begins to eat before the rabbit is fully cooked.

———

A DAY AND A NIGHT and a morning later, Paha Sapa is almost back to his village. He was in such a hurry to leave that his packing was careless; he left some robes behind at the sweat lodge site. He has not a moment to spare. He *must* tell Limps-a-Lot and Angry Badger and Loud Voice Hawk and all the other elders of his village this terrible news, share this terrible vision.... Perhaps the warriors and holy men will see the nightmare of the *Wasichu* Stone Giants rising out of the Black Hills as something not nearly so terrible as Paha Sapa imagines. Perhaps there are symbols and portents and signs in the dream that no boy of eleven summers could possibly understand.

Paha Sapa has never felt so young and useless. He wants to cry. Instead, deep into the morning of the second day heading north toward Slim Buttes, with the narrow river to his left now swollen into a torrent half a mile across (but he does not have to cross this to reach Slim Buttes and the village), Paha Sapa hugs the disassembled and blanket-wrapped still-red-feathered *Ptehinčala Huhu Canunpa* to his shivering chest and falls asleep while riding Worm.

———

HE WAKES TO HORSE SCREAMS hours or minutes or seconds later when the first arrow strikes White Crane.

Jerking upright on Worm, Paha Sapa looks over his shoulder, realizing at once how careless he has been. During his ride south to the Hills, he watched the horizons and hid himself constantly, despite the heavy rains. Now, with the clouds higher and occasional sunlight dappling the prairie, he has ridden on without looking back or around once, pregnant with need to get back home, arrogant in his carelessness.

Less than sixty yards behind him, eight Crows—all men, painted for war, screaming their war cries, heeling their war ponies on at top speed—are rushing at him. They are to the east as well as south. Paha

Sapa has no direction to run except northwest, toward the absolute barrier of the flooded valley with its quarter-mile-wide raging waters.

A second arrow hits White Crane in the neck and Three Buffalo Woman's beautiful mare goes down. Paha Sapa cuts the connecting strap a second before he is pulled down with the mare. Loud, terrible cracks and Paha Sapa realizes that two of the Crows have rifles. A small geyser of Worm's warm blood leaps from the gelding's straining shoulder and splashes Paha Sapa in the face.

He has no weapon with him other than his knife. The war lance and everything else went down with White Crane. Paha Sapa glances back again—the Crows have not spared even a man to plunder the dead horse's packs. All eight come on, screaming, their mouths black and wide, their eyes and teeth a terrible white.

They have him cut off now, three of the Crow warriors wheeling around to the northwest of him. He *must* wheel left toward the water. He does.

An arrow strikes between his calf and Worm's leaping rib cage, burying itself in the horse rather than the boy. A rifle bullet nicks his ear. Paha Sapa can hear a terrible whistling over Worm's labored panting as the good horse continues galloping hard even with bullet holes in his lungs.

Paha Sapa rides full speed into the advancing waters. The Crows scream more loudly, their cries as terrible as the chewing noises the stone giants made.

Two more shots and Worm's legs fold under him. Paha Sapa goes flying over the dying horse's head—it is just like the Greasy Grass, where he counted coup on Long Hair, only here he, Paha Sapa, will die!—and then the boy clutches the segments of the sacred pipe and strikes the water and swims toward the tangle of cottonwood branches and uprooted willows swirling in the current ahead of him.

The Crows ride their slathered ponies into the water until the current tugs at the horses, whirling them around, up to the thighs of the riders, but there they stop, still screaming and shouting, and take careful aim and fire bullets and arrows at Paha Sapa.

But Paha Sapa is being hurled downstream now faster than any bullet can fly. He holds the red-wrapped *Ptehinčala Huhu Canunpa* high, trying to keep it dry, even as his own head goes under the cold, muddy water and he splutters and gasps.

Something to his right, upstream behind him, it can't be a Crow… they wouldn't dare to…

Paha Sapa turns to look, still holding the pieces of the sacred pipe and feathers high, just as the onrushing cottonwood log strikes him in the head.

———

HE WAKES. Not drowned. It is hours later—either sunset or the next dawn—and he is lying mostly buried in mud at the western edge of the rushing and now half-mile-wide river. He has not even made it across to the other side. The Crows have him now if they still want him.

One of Paha Sapa's eyes is either gone or swollen shut. Several teeth are missing. A bullet has gone through his upper arm.

But these are nothing. The *Ptehinčala Huhu Canunpa* is gone.

Paha Sapa manages to get to his knees. He flails in the thin light, splashes water, somehow manages to get to his feet, wades, is knocked down, dives, dives again, barely manages to crawl out of the current, almost drowned.

It is gone. The *Ptehinčala Huhu Canunpa* handed down in his band from generation to generation, the most sacred item the tribe has, the heart of their mystery and their defense against the dark powers of the earth and sky, the pipe entrusted to him by Limps-a-Lot. Gone.

Paha Sapa is naked except for his breechclout, even his moccasins torn from his feet. He is covered with mud and horse's blood and his own blood. His one eye does not see well.

—*I still have to report the Vision to Limps-a-Lot and the elders. I still must tell them, then take my lifelong punishment for losing the* Ptehinčala Huhu Canunpa.

Hurting everywhere, Paha Sapa crawls out of the water and mud, pulls himself forward up the muddy bank by grasping grasses, reaches the top, and staggers to his feet.

Three Crows are standing just a few paces away. Paha Sapa cannot run. These are not the same Crows—they are older, larger, and they wear *wasichu* soldier shirts open over their tattood chests.

Behind the three Crows are about sixty mounted men, black against the sunrise, but obviously cavalry. One of the *wasichus* shouts something in the same ugly syllables that Paha Sapa hears from Long Hair's ghost at night.

The closest Crow, an old man with a scar running from his forehead across his nose and down his cheek, takes three steps forward, raises his repeating rifle, and brings the wood-and-metal stock down hard against Paha Sapa's forehead.

15

George Armstrong Custer

O f all people on this good Earth, my darling, you know that my reputation
as America's "Greatest Living Indian Fighter" is exaggerated. Under
my orders and following my lead, thousands upon thousands of Rebels
were killed, but it's not been my honor to kill many Indians.

Unlike the Rebs, the Indians are a sly and elusive enemy. The warriors fight at
a time and place of their choosing, almost never in a stand-up battle but with feints
and usually from a distance (except for their rushing in to count coup or to scalp
fallen whites), and then they flee, often running to hide behind the skirts of their
women and the rattles of their babies in villages. So the only time the cavalry usually
can surprise and bring the warriors to fight is when we attack one of their villages,
especially early, just after dawn. So it was at my Battle at the Washita River.

Those warriors, mostly Cheyenne, that bloody year of 1868 had been coming
up out of the Indian Territory and out of Texican country farther south to raid in
Kansas. That November, General Sheridan had showed me the butcher's bill just
since August — 110 white people killed, 13 women raped, more than a thousand
head of cattle stolen, and countless settlers' cabins burned and looted. The Kansans
were taking this rape, theft, and slaughter personally.

The Indians' violence flowed, as you know I believe, directly from the peace treaties we signed with Red Cloud and the others that year at Fort Laramie: treaties
in which Sherman gave the tribes everything they'd ever demanded and more, including the army's agreement to abandon our entire string of forts along the Bozeman
Trail and then, on top of that, acknowledging Sioux ownership of the Black Hills,

despite the fact that the Sioux were recent invaders there themselves and also in spite of the additional fact that white men—miners—were already following my surveying trail into those hills and building their own cities there. But Indians, like any worthwhile enemy, see concession as weakness, so it was little surprise that mere weeks after their chiefs signed these agreements, their braves were slaughtering settlers all over Kansas, then retreating to safe havens such as the Fort Cobb Agency on the Washita River in northern Texas country, where they took our beef, wintered over, and waited for good weather before riding off to slaughter more settlers.

You remember Phil Sheridan, of course, my dear. (And I remember you dancing with him at Fort Leavenworth when the general came out to take over Hancock's command.) General Sheridan was as helpful to my career as he was a bad dancer with you. He plucked me out of Monroe, where I was dying from boredom (except for the wonderful days and nights with you, my love), and on November 12, Sheridan and I were leading a mixed force of infantry and cavalry deep into Indian country.

The hostiles, with our help at such agencies disguised as forts as Fort Cobb, had short supply lines, but the cavalry always suffered from unacceptably long lines of supply, often all the way back to Leavenworth. Thus we built the Camp Supply depot on the North Canadian River near the Oklahoma panhandle. The hostiles were so used to their sanctuary there south of the Arkansas River that they'd grown smug and careless; this time, with Camp Supply as our logistics base, we were going to take them by surprise in the winter. (The old mountain man Jim Bridger argued that such a winter campaign couldn't be done—that cavalry would founder in drifts in a day and be dead in three days—but Sheridan and I knew better than that.)

I've told you, Libbie, about Phil Sheridan's unusual, almost nonsoldierly habit of using swear words (which I forswore forever on that same day in 1862 when I gave up drinking forever after you had seen me drunk in Monroe, just after I began court-ing you)—well, anyway, Phil's delusion that he was the first cavalry commander in the West to consider attacking the Indians in the dead of winter (many before him had done so) mixed with his swearing made for a fascinating briefing before my of-ficers and men and I set out in a serious snowstorm to the tune of "The Girl I Left Behind Me."

The snow helped our Osage scouts (who were eager to settle old scores with their enemy the Cheyenne), and on November 26 we crossed the trail of a band of Indians returning to their village in the Oklahoma country from what obviously had been a raid into Kansas. We immediately left the wagon train behind and followed that trail south for a day and a night.

I pushed the men hard, as you know I tend to do when on the real warpath, stopping only once for coffee and hardtack in the short, freezing day and longer, freezing night. It was the only stop my men saw from 4 a.m. to late into the next day. My 720 men followed me through the night, the only sound the crack of ice atop the snow as their horses' hooves broke through the crust. Finally one of the Osage guides called me forward to the crest of a hill, and I was surprised to see a river valley stretching away below us. I could see vague shapes moving about a half mile away, but I assumed they were buffalo.

"No," grunted the Osage. "Heap Indians. Ponies."

I whispered the query to the old Osage — why did he think they were Indian ponies? In the dim starlight, they could have been anything.

"Me hear dog bark," grunted the old guide.

I strained to hear but could make out no barking dog. For a second I thought I heard a bell . . . Indians sometimes bell the lead mare in their pony herds . . . but it was not clear enough. Finally I heard the thin, frail cry of a baby rise out of the dark valley. There could be no doubt now.

I ordered the attack to begin at first light.

I divided my forces, just as I did yesterday (was it yesterday?) at the Little Big Horn. I broke the column into four detachments — one to swing around to the far end of the village in the valley, two to sweep in from the sides, my own detachment to attack south from our current location.

I had no idea how many Indians were down there that night, of course, Libbie; it might have been a hundred; it might have been ten thousand. But I had seven hundred cavalry at my command, and no force of irregulars on earth could stand up to seven hundred US Cavalry fighting with surprise on their side.

Some of the members of the regimental band said after that battle that it was so cold their lips stuck to their brass instruments when they began playing our regiment's beloved "Garry Owen" at the beginning of the attack as I'd ordered, but they exaggerate. In truth, it was only their spittle that froze, soon sending the brass notes faltering and then stopping, but that was unimportant, since I'd already led the detachment down off our hill and into the valley and village at full speed, me at the lead (of course), sword out and extended in one hand, pistol in the other.

The Indians — it turned out to be a Cheyenne village, which pleased our bloodthirsty Osage scouts no end — were caught totally by surprise, but warriors came erupting from their tents and teepees within seconds, hurling lances, notching arrows, and firing repeating rifles. We cut them down where they stood. I have to admit to you the truth of war, Libbie—when an old man or old woman or, I saw early in the fight, a ten-year-old boy picked up a fallen brave's rifle or lance and directed it at my men, the cavalrymen cut them down as well. Many of these troopers had been chasing hostile Indians for two years or more, never catching them in a fair fight, only seeing the scalped whites, raped women, and burnt settlements in the hostiles' wake. The pent-up frustration on the part of my men was very great, the fighting—though brief, less than an hour with only the first half hour being a true fight—horribly intense.

The braves retreated from the village and tried to wade the Washita River, but we shot many of them down as they stood waist-deep in the rushing icy water. Those that reached the thick trees on the other side continued firing from vantage points there, but groups from all four of my converging detachments were sent in—the trees were not so tight that we had to dismount—and, one by one, the warriors were killed. Almost none allowed themselves to be captured.

Our own casualties were light—one of my officers killed and two officers and eleven enlisted men wounded. My second-in-command (you remember Major Elliott) and nineteen of his men had been seen chasing hostiles away from the river, and although we expected that detachment to return soon, it never did. We later learned that the Indians downriver had ambushed and killed Elliott and all his men.

Still, the victory was all but complete. I had fifty-three prisoners—mostly women and children who had remained hidden in their lodges during the fighting—and more than nine hundred Indian ponies. The women and children we would take back with us, but I ordered almost 850 of the ponies, mostly pintos, destroyed. I know how much you love horses, my darling, and knew when I told you upon my return that you were upset with the idea, but I believe you've come to understand that I had little choice. I let the women, children, and a couple of ancient men choose ponies for riding, but there was no way my troopers could herd the other 850-some Indian pintos all the way back to Camp Supply. Leaving them for the enemy to reclaim was unthinkable.

There are many memories for me from that battle along the Washita, but the screams of the ponies, the smell of the gunpowder mixing with the scent of the ponies' blood in the cold morning air, the sounds of their heavy falling in the snow and along the icy banks of that river... well, they are indelible.

By ten a.m., I'd learned who it was we'd fought. The band belonged to the Cheyenne chief Black Kettle—the so-called peace chief—the very same Black Kettle who'd somehow managed to survive Colonel Chivington's slaughter of his band at Sand Creek in Colorado. Black Kettle's sister told me, through my interpreter, that the old chief had camped here away from and farther north of the other Indian villages now strung out along the Washita down this long valley—encampments of Apache, Arapahoe, Kiowa, and even Comanche—precisely because he, Black Kettle, had been afraid of an attack by cavalry (a fear that none of the other Indians appeared to have shared, although none of the other chiefs had been at Sand Creek). Black Kettle himself had been killed, we discovered, in the first minutes of the shooting as the old man attempted to flee, not even staying to protect his family or grandchildren.

The intelligence of the thousands of Indians camping so near did not alarm me—this many cavalry troopers could have handled any number of warriors they sent upstream at us—but it decided me on shooting the ponies and withdrawing for the time being.

I know that you remember, Libbie, the outrageous newspaper articles that soon sprang up comparing this fair-fight victory to Chivington's massacre at Sand Creek. As we discussed at the time, this was not only untrue, it was libelous. Black Kettle's band along the Washita had been harboring many of the braves who'd been terrorizing Arkansas. We found white men's and women's scalps. We found photographs, weapons, clothing, utensils, and other loot from the burned cabins. More than that, Black Kettle's braves had two white women as hostages (one very young), and they cut the women's throats at the first sound of our attack. These were not innocent, peace-loving Indians, however much Black Kettle had liked to call himself the "peace chief."

Black Kettle's sister kept talking and talking and talking, blaming everything on the few "hot-blooded young braves" who had joined the tribe, babbling away, but I soon realized that she was just playing for time. By noon, the first hundreds of warriors from the many villages downstream were beginning to appear on the bluffs across the river. By late afternoon, there would be thousands there, and I'm sure that's exactly what Black Kettle's sister wanted—for us to still be in that indefensible position as thousands of Arapahoe, Kiowa, returning Cheyenne, Apache, and Comanche fell upon us.

During the last part of this harangue, just as the last of the ponies were killed and just before I cut her off so that we could mount up and ride, I could not help notice the beautiful girl—young woman of seventeen, actually—who for some strange reason had been holding my hand while Black Kettle's wizened sister droned on.

"What is this old woman doing?" I irritably asked my interpreter.

The interpreter laughed. "Why, sir, she's been marrying you to that squaw, named Mo-nah-se-tah. *I think you're duly and properly married by now."*

I immediately dropped the girl's hand and gestured Black Kettle's sister to silence.

I well remember that retreat out of the valley and upstream along the river, looking back in the early-afternoon winter light—the many hundreds of Indians along the bluffs there now looking like so many black vertical pegs in the reflected sunlight, looking, from the distance, like heathen Druid monuments to some forgotten sun god—and the valley itself alive with flame and smoke (we had burned all the tee-pees) and the snow there not only trampled, but red, for several hundred yards, from the blood of the murdered ponies.

I was later criticized both from within the Army and from without for retreating when I had so many Indians virtually at our mercy (our wagon train was coming up, and there was enough buffalo and other meat in the captured village to feed my seven hundred troopers for months)—not to mention criticized even more harshly for not tarrying and searching for Major Elliott and his men—but you know the reason for my so-called retreat, Libbie, my darling. Of all the people on Earth, you are the only one to know the full reason.

But sometimes I wonder what those writers-of-editorials who called me coward or "squaw killer" would think if they knew the truth.

———

Let us recall more pleasant (or at least amusing) things, my darling.

Mo-nah-se-tah.

How you used to tease me about her. She stayed with the Seventh after the Battle of Washita River and was either a guest in a tent near my tent, or was in my tent. It was a long, hard, cold winter. (You know that on the march—even those first November days in '68 when we were striking south toward the Antelope Mountains and the Washita River before the attack on Black Kettle's band—I often would not have my command tent erected when we paused, but would sleep the few, cold hours of the long, cold night outside, on a buffalo robe, with our two large dogs on either side of me. Later, when that endless winter campaign was over...no, wait, even during it, through our many letters, I remember now...you teased me unceasingly about my "Indian bride.")

I remember one early missive I sent you from the snowy wastes, one in which I described first the comic "wedding ceremony" along the Washita and then described Mo-nah-se-tah *herself to you in terms that no "ordinary" young wife would have found bearable, much less amusing:*

> She is an extremely comely squaw, possessing a bright, cheery face, a countenance beaming with intelligence, and a disposition more inclined to be merry than one usually finds among the

Indians.... Added to bright, laughing eyes, a set of pearly teeth, and a rich complexion, her well-shaped head was crowned with a luxuriant growth of the most beautiful silken tresses, rivalling in color the blackness of the raven and extending, when allowed to fall loosely over her shoulders, to below her waist.

That was in my letter for public consumption — and, perhaps, as I knew you would know, for later publication in the book of memoirs you and I had long planned to write together — but I knew how you would respond to it privately, and you did not disappoint me, my darling. I knew that you would tease me about the girl in a way that only a wife perfectly secure in her husband's love and adoration could tease her lover.

No more than a week later, somewhere on our freezing march through the panhandle of Texas and around back into Oklahoma, your responding letter caught up to me:

My Darling Autie,

Your second bride sounds ravishing, my dearest. As the victor in your lightning siege and burning of that Indian Troy, you certainly deserve this ravishing Helen whom you describe in such delightful (one might almost say "breathless") prose. Few white women have ever received a love letter of their own with such rapturous phrasings and felicitous paeons, so I have no idea how your Cheyenne Helen (whose name apparently sounds a little like "Minnesota," which is appropriate, since you took her, one might say, in the snow) feels about this praise. Can she read? Oh, that makes no matter, I'm sure, since while you must send *me* letters, I am certain that you need not even raise your voice to talk to *her* on these long, long winter nights. She does share your tent, of course? It would hardly be gallant of you if she did not.

So, my darling Autie, my dearest Beloved, what does our — *your* — *Mo-nah-se-tah* (and I see while actually writing the name, that she has much more "moan" than wintry state in her sweet name) look like *beneath* those soft and beaded doeskin dresses which I'm sure she wears only when *outside* your shared sleeping quarters?

Are *Mo-nah-se-tah's* ravenlike "luxuriant growth of the most beautiful silken tresses" matched by the richness of her escutcheon, my dearest connoisseur of all such luxurance?

I interrupt only to say that I remember when you first used "escutcheon" to describe what you are discussing here, my darling Libbie. It was in Monroe, when we were lying naked on our bed that summer evening after we'd bathed together and I was playing with the rich tangle of what I then called your maiden-hair and you asked me if your "escutcheon" was, as you whispered that warm afternoon, "too prolific?" I assured you then that it was not, that I loved the luxuriant growth of it, and then I ended any verbal argument by other means.

Your winter '69 letter continued, and I think I remember each word correctly:

Are your new friend *Mo-nah-se-tah's* attributes higher and firmer than mine?

I wrote you back that I had seen the lady bathing and that although she seemed to have almost no escutcheon, her seventeen-year-old's breasts were high and firm, but immediately assured you that they did not compare in attractiveness to your full, white bosoms. (I could have told you the truth, that Indian women's busts were almost always sagging, wrinkled old dugs before they were out of their twenties, caused, I presume, by suckling far too many Indian children and perhaps by never being supported by any proper undergarment, but I thought perhaps you knew this already. You were always put off by the appearance of old, wrinkled, sagging Indian women.)

You wrote more:

Is her skin a golden, dusky tawny all over (except for the parts that are pink on me)?

I assured you in the next mail that Mo-nah-se-tah's *skin was indeed a golden, tawny color, unblemished except for an odd tattoo carved into her left shoulder. Her nipples, I explained, were a light brown and thus not nearly as attractive or exciting as your pink tips, my darling Libbie. You then abandoned all subtlety:*

Do Indian maidens named *Mo-nah-se-tah* moan in your presence, my dearest Autie?

I laughed then and wrote you that the day before, the 14th of January, 1869, Mo-nah-se-tah *had moaned softly for hours. It was the day her baby was born, and during most of the time I had glimpsed her briefly naked in my tent, the small girl was grossly pregnant with some brave's child. I often wondered if we had killed the father of her child that morning of November 27 (odds are good we had), but I never asked* Mo-nah-se-tah, *and she never mentioned the warrior or his fate.*

The girl was always cheerful and never a drag on the regiment. Indeed, it was due to her excellent guiding that on March 15 of 1869 we found Little Robe's and Medicine Arrow's village in north Texas, thus ending a chase that had preoccupied us all that long winter. Since they had some white captives with them (the memory of those two dead white women in the burned village along the Washita, their throats so cruelly cut, had stayed with me), I chose to parley rather than immediately attack the village, but when Medicine Arrow proved especially recalcitrant, I seized four of their men as hostages and promised the chiefs I would hang these men at sunrise the next morning if they did not immediately hand over their white captives. Still, the recalcitrant Cheyenne resisted, so we sent the captives — after grabbing a few more — away to Fort Hays with a second ultimatum that these hostages would be freed only after Medicine Arrow and Little Robe brought their bands to the reservation and released the white captives. Luckily for us, the guards at Fort Hays killed two of these Cheyenne hostages, and Medicine Arrow released the captives and led his people to a reservation.

Then I returned to Fort Hays and you, and we had two of the most pleasant years of our marriage there, with you teasing me about Mo-nah-se-tah *at some of the most intimate moments of those two happy years. Why such conversation excited you, my dearest, I do not know, but your excitement always incited mine — and perhaps, to be totally truthful, the fantasy discussions of* Mo-nah-se-tah *did as well — so of all our little bedroom games, the* Mo-nah-se-tah *game may have been one of the most stimulating for both of us.*

---

*L*ibbie, *my darling, even while thinking these thoughts to you, I am overcome by a strange and deep foreboding.*

I am sure that I am merely dreaming, almost certainly in the arms of morphia, after being wounded at the Little Big Horn yesterday (or recently), but sometimes here in the darkness I feel insubstantial, no longer connected to my injured body or the world, in a word — untethered — except to you.

Even while I was reminiscing about the Washita victory and our ongoing Mo-nah-se-tah *game, another memory chilled me.*

Do you remember last winter in New York, when, weary of seeing Julius Caesar *for free (more than two score times, until we could — and did — recite all the dialogue from memory), we were allowed by our friend the actor Lawrence Barrett (the very same friend who'd left all those complimentary tickets for us to* Julius Caesar*) to sit in on the dress rehearsals for* Henry IV Part I *and* Henry IV Part II*?*

Neither of us knew the plays that well, but you were highly amused at the character of Henry Percy, the so-called Hotspur. When I failed to see the source of your amusement, you whispered, "Oh, Autie...Hotspur is you!"

I frowned at the martinet of a war leader strutting and fretting on the stage — the theater, I remember, being filled only with other actors and immediate family, was not heated, and we were shivering — and I whispered back, "I fail to see any resemblance."

"Oh, Autie," you whispered again, still giggling as softly as you could at the scene unfolding on the stage, "he loves his wife madly. Don't you see? But the two of them are always teasing and threatening and playacting toward each other."

At that very moment, the dialogue on stage was such:

HOTSPUR

  Away, away, you trifler! Love? I love thee not;
  I care not for thee, Kate. This is no world
  To play with mammets and to tilt with lips.
  We must have bloody noses and cracked crowns,
  And pass them current too. God's me, my horse!
  What sayst thou, Kate? What wouldst thou have with me?

LADY PERCY

  Do you not love me? do you not indeed?
  Well, do not then; for since you love me not,
  I will not love myself. Do you not love me?
  Nay, tell me if you speak in jest or no.

HOTSPUR

  Come, wilt thou see me ride?
  And when I am a-horseback, I will swear
  I love thee infinitely. But hark you, Kate:
  I must not have you henceforth question me

Whither I go, nor reason whereabout.
Whither I must, I must, and to conclude,
This evening must I leave you, gentle Kate.
I know you wise, but yet no farther wise
Than Harry Percy's wife; constant you are,
But yet a woman; and for secrecy,
No lady closer, for I well believe
Thou wilt not utter what thou dost not know,
And so far will I trust thee, gentle Kate.

LADY PERCY

How? So far?

HOTSPUR

Not an inch further. But hark you, Kate:
Whither I go, thither shall you go too;
Today will I set forth, tomorrow you.
Will this content you, Kate?

LADY PERCY

It must of force.

I remember it in such detail because I later read it in our newly acquired Compleat Shakespeare *volumes at least half a hundred times. It did indeed sound like a cavalry officer speaking to his beloved but too-inquisitive wife. How many times had you and I had similar conversations, Libbie? Always with me promising that wherever I was to be sent, I would summon you and we would be together.*

You also laughed that day, I remember, at this Hotspur's seeming similarity to me in the way he asked his officers for advice but then interrupted them, never listening. And Hotspur's temper and reckless boldness, you said, reminded you so much of me that you were considering calling me "My darling Hotspur" rather than "Autie" in your love letters.

But then Henry Percy, Hotspur, was cut down on the battlefield. (In single combat with that wastrel fop Prince Hal, which I did not believe for a moment.)

And then that fat, drunken bag of cowardly guts Falstaff gave his idiotic soliloquy about honor being "only a word, that is, nothing" and went so far as to slice Hotspur's corpse with his own sword and claim the victory over this fine warrior, lugging the body off stage. This dishonorable act, evidently much approved of both by Shakespeare and the crowd at the dress rehearsal that evening, so upset you and so angered me that we left early.

But the next evening, during the rehearsal for Henry IV Part II, *it was Lady Percy's eulogy for her dead husband—the other kings and royals and knights seem almost to have forgotten him—that caused you to start weeping. We stayed for the end of that interminable play, but I'm sorry we did. I don't think you ever forgot Lady Percy's widow's lament, and once, in the middle of the night, weeping hard even as I held you, you admitted that if anything ever happened to me, you would have to give the same speech, telling other members of the Seventh Cavalry and the ignorant public that your dead husband had been the miracle of men . . .*

> . . . and by his light
> Did all the chivalry of England move
> To do brave acts. He was indeed the glass
> Wherein the noble youth did dress themselves. . . .
> In diet, in affections of delight,
> In military rules, humors of blood,
> He was the mark and the glass, copy and book,
> That fashion'd others.

I told you then, Libbie (I almost said "Kate" there), each time you sobbed in the night that I would do everything in my not-inconsiderable powers to keep you from becoming the widow who would have to read Lady Percy's lines like that.

But tonight (or today, there is only darkness here in this semiconscious state), I worry and wonder if I can keep that promise. I know that you would be a fierce and loyal widow, Libbie, always keeping my memory alive and defending my honor from those honorless rogues (Major Benteen?) who have always wanted and tried to sully my reputation.

But I do not want you to be a widow, Libbie. I do not want to die.

Oh, my darling, my dearest—I hold fast to the memories of you and of us, and I lie here and wait for the light. I know that you will be there when I awake. I know it as surely as I know our love.

16

The Six Grandfathers

August 28, 1936

PAHA SAPA STEPS OFF THE BOTTOM STEP OF THE 506 STEPS down from the summit of Mount Rushmore and feels a wave of absolute exhaustion roll over him. He has to step aside and grab the railing just to remain standing. The other workers, most of them thirty to forty years younger than he, bound and joke and leap their way off the staircase, roughhousing, slapping, and shouting their way to the parking lot.

It is six p.m., and the direct sunlight has passed beyond the carved southern face of the mountain, but the waves of heat off the white granite hit Paha Sapa like a hot-knuckled fist. He has been up there all this long Friday, dangling from his cable and moving from site to site at the base of the three existing heads and the fourth field of white granite ready for carving the Roosevelt head, but only now does this absolute *tsunami* of fatigue and exhaustion strike him.

It is the cancer, he knows. The increasing and encroaching pain has been a factor, but one he's been ready for and can deal with. This sudden weakness...Well, he is seventy-one years old, but he has never been weak before. Never.

Paha Sapa shakes his head to clear it, and sweat flies from his long, still-black braids.

— *Old Man!*

The August cicadas are loud and there is a buzzing in his ears, so at first Paha Sapa is not sure the cry is for him.

— Old Man! Billy! Hey, Slovak!

It is Mr. Borglum, standing between the hoist house and the path to the parking lot. Paha Sapa lets go of the railing and raises a weary hand. They meet in the clearing near where the shouting, laughing men are lining up to pick up their paychecks at the office.

— You all right, Billy?

— Sure.

— You looked…well, I guess pale isn't the right word…fagged out. I need to show you something up on the mountain. You ready to head back up?

Paha Sapa turns his head toward the 506 steps of the stairway and wonders if he can climb them, even without his usual morning load of fifty or sixty pounds. His plan was to work all this Friday night to prepare and deliver the dynamite to a hiding place here—the site still to be determined—and then spend all of Saturday night placing the charges in time for President Roosevelt's visit on Sunday. Now he wonders if he can even stagger up the stairs in this heat.

Borglum touches his back but only briefly. Paha Sapa rarely sweats so that others can notice—it's been a long, bad joke on the site—but today his work shirt is soaked through.

— We'll take the tram up.

Paha Sapa nods and follows Borglum to the aerial tramway platform below the hoist house. Edwald Hayes is acting as hoist operator this Friday afternoon and touches his dusty cap as Mr. Borglum approaches.

Paha Sapa hates the tramway but says nothing as he and Borglum squeeze themselves into the upright, small-outhouse-sized space and Borglum signs to Edwald to start the ride up.

Paha Sapa knows that his fear of the tramway cage falling is foolish; he spends every day of his working life dangling from a one-eighth-inch steel cable, and the tram is suspended from huge pulleys running on a seven-eighths-inch cable stretched from the hoist house on Doane Mountain to the A-frame above the Roosevelt head thirteen hundred feet away and four hundred feet above the valley floor. The cage itself is propelled by a three-eighths-inch cable driven by a large drive wheel at the hoist house.

But Paha Sapa—along with all the other men after the accident with the tram—knows that while that drive wheel is supposed to be fixed on its axle by a steel key, and both wheel hub and axle contain key seats for such a steel key, in truth the wheel has always been fastened by only a single setscrew driven through the hub and into the key seat of the axle itself. That setscrew worked itself loose at least once, breaking the hoist shaft and sending the cage whizzing unstoppedly down the long wire while plucking the entire A-frame and its platform off the top of the mountain.

Gutzon Borglum was scheduled to be in the tramway for that ride but arrived a few minutes late, so Edwald sent a load of water cans up instead. Those cans were thrown over two acres of Doane Mountain and smashed to bits. If Borglum had been on time, the Mount Rushmore project would, most likely, have been shut down after the death of its sculptor.

Borglum shows no nervousness now as they rise higher and higher above the mountain, toward the basin between the three existing heads, rising directly toward the patch of smooth white granite that has been prepared for the Teddy Roosevelt head.

There is no breeze. If anything, the heat up here is worse than down below, with the white rock on three sides of them focusing and radiating the stored heat from the day's worth of blazing sunlight. The temperatures in Rapid City have broken all records; Paha Sapa guesses that it must be a hundred and twenty degrees or more here at the locus of all that white heat. He has been hanging and dangling and moving and drilling and working in it since seven a.m.

Borglum waves to Edwald far below, and the tram cage stops suddenly, swinging sickeningly back and forth. Both men hang on to the chest-high edge of the wooden cage itself, and Borglum has his hand on the guide wire. Now the sculptor reaches up and cranks down the emergency brake that Julian Spotts, the most recent bureaucrat to be put "in charge" of the project (Mr. Borglum is, always, the man really in charge), ordered added to the tramway system after another brake failure had sent some men hurtling to the bottom.

They are very high: past Washington, even with Jefferson's eye, looking across the rough mass of rock that delineates Abraham Lincoln's shock of hair from his forehead. The Theodore Roosevelt head has not been begun yet and is present only as a near-vertical swath of blindingly white granite awaiting the last careful blasts and then the carvers.

The tramcar quits swaying. Both men lean on the northwest side of the cage, looking down at the white granite.

To say that no work has been done on the Roosevelt head would be a lie. Over the past year, especially the productive four months of summer, Borglum has penetrated and had Paha Sapa blast away more than eighty feet of the original gray, wrinkled, rotten granite here on the south face of the Six Grandfathers. During all that blasting and carving away, only Borglum was confident that they would find carvable stone beneath the rotten rock. But they did, finally, and enough...barely...to carve the Roosevelt head.

If there are no mistakes.

The problem is that there is only so much rock left, and they have used most of it up. To any observer on Doane Mountain or in the valley below the heads, Mount Rushmore looks like a deep, solid mountain—one could imagine walking out onto the summit from the forest and mountaintop behind it—but that continuity is an illusion, as Paha Sapa knows from his *hanblečeya* there exactly sixty years ago to this day.

Behind the north face of the Six Grandfathers, behind the three presidents' heads now emerging from the granite and the fourth head ready to be carved, there is a long and deep canyon. This split in the rock begins just north of the Lincoln head and runs southwest behind the heads for about 350 feet.

The first three heads, already emerged from stone, had adequate rock behind them. The Teddy Roosevelt head, set so far back and near the hidden vertical cliff of this hidden canyon, has only thirty feet of rock left from which to carve this last president. Another ten feet of looking for carvable rock after the eighty feet he blasted away, Paha Sapa knows, and they would have had to give up on Roosevelt; there simply would not have been enough good rock there to work with.

Borglum takes off his white Stetson, mops his brow with the red handkerchief from his back pocket, and clears his throat.

— *We're within five feet of the nose, Billy.*

— *Yes.*

The heat from the white granite is palpable. Sickening. Paha Sapa tries to blink away the black spots swarming in his vision.

— *I've scheduled you to work both tomorrow and Sunday in preparation for the president's visit.*

— *Yes.*

— *There will be a lot of VIPs down there besides Roosevelt. Senator Norbeck'll be here*— *I don't know how he's lasted this long with that jaw cancer of his. Governor Berry, of course. Tom wouldn't miss rubbing up against a president, even if the president is a New Deal Democrat. A bunch of others, including Doane Robinson and Mary Ellis.*

Mary Ellis is Gutzon Borglum's daughter. Paha Sapa nods.

— *So I want the demonstration blast to go off really smooth, Billy. Really smooth. Five charges. I figure beneath the fresh granite here, cheating a little toward Lincoln so it'll be more visible. Who would you like to do the drilling for you tomorrow? Merle Peterson? Palooka?*

Paha Sapa rubs his jaw. Sensation there and everywhere is muted because of the pain throughout his body.

— *Yes, Payne would be good. He knows what I want for the charges even before I say it.*

Paha Sapa and Jack "Palooka" Payne have been working together almost every day of the blazing summer on both the Lincoln head and the granite field being readied for Teddy Roosevelt.

Borglum nods.

— *I'll tell Lincoln to assign Palooka to you tomorrow. Anything else you need? I do want this demonstration blast to go smoothly.*

Paha Sapa looks Borglum in the eye. The intelligence and determination he sees looking back is—has always been—almost frightening. *Is* frightening to most people.

— *Well, Mr. Borglum, this* is *the president of the United States.*

Borglum scowls. His displeasure at the reminder rolls off him in a wave that is as palpable as the late-August heat.

— *Damn it, Billy, I* know *that. What's your point?*

— *My point is that the president is usually met with a twenty-one-gun salute. Isn't that the protocol?*

Borglum grunts.

—Anyway, it wouldn't take that much more effort for me tomorrow, especially if I have Palooka and Merle as drillers, to rig twenty-one charges from just to the left of Washington's lapel all the way around to where we'll be blasting Lincoln's chin out someday. And I could rig them in a series, so everyone could tell there were twenty-one separate blasts.

Borglum seems lost in thought for a minute.

—They'd have to be fairly small charges, Billy. I don't want to blow Franklin Delano Roosevelt's eardrums out. I like the New Deal.

Paha Sapa knows that he should smile at this, but he's too tired. And too much is riding on Borglum's answer.

—Small charges, sir. Except for beneath TR and below Lincoln, where we do have to move some real rock. But they'll sound the same. And I'll pack enough loose rock around the charges that there'll be plenty of dust and rock fall.... The civilians always love that during a demonstration.

Borglum considers for only a second longer.

—All right, a twenty-one-blast salute it is, then. Good idea. But don't kill yourself—or Palooka and Merle—tomorrow getting the blast holes ready. This damned heat... Well, do your best.

Borglum squints up to where the sun is disappearing beyond Washington's head.

—I've told Roosevelt's people that he has to be here by noon. If he's not here by noon, I'll do the unveiling of Jefferson without him.

—Why's that, Mr. Borglum?

Borglum turns his fiercest countenance toward Paha Sapa.

—The shadows, of course. Any later than noon, and the features of the three heads will become somewhat obscured. Roosevelt has to see Jefferson and the others at their best. I told his people—damned bureaucrats—that if the president isn't here for the ceremony's beginning at eleven thirty, the president can go fuck himself.

Paha Sapa only nods. After five years with Borglum, he is not surprised or appalled that the sculptor thinks he can boss around the president of the United States. He also knows that Borglum will wait until dusk if he has to. In the end, Gutzon Borglum needs the patronage of the rich and powerful, and he does what he has to in order to get it.

As if to refute this thought, Borglum almost growls his next statement.

— Billy, let's skip that twenty-one-blast-salute idea. FDR's president, and I'm all for the New Deal, but five charges should serve. If they go off at once, no one can tell the difference.

— Yes, sir. Can I still have Palooka as my driller?

Borglum grunts assent and leans on the latched door of the cage, looking across and down at the white slope that will be Teddy Roosevelt. The air still ripples with heat.

— Old Man, you can see Teddy Roosevelt's head there, can't you?

— Yes.

— You know, Billy, you're the only one on this project, other than me, who can see the full head while it's still in the rock. Even my son…Lincoln…has to go refer to the new version of the models to understand just what we'll be doing, just what Theodore Roosevelt will look like when he comes out. But you, Billy, you have always seen the figures in the stone. I know you have. It's a little uncanny.

Of course he can see it. Of course he always has been able. Didn't he watch that fourth head and the three others — and their giant bodies — rising out of this soil and mountain like newborn giants clawing and chewing through their cauls sixty years ago? And, he realizes now, not for the first time, he has been one of the midwives for this unholy birth. By his own count, Paha Sapa has been personally responsible for blasting away more than 15,000 tons of rock from the side of the Six Grandfathers this shortened year alone. His own rough calculations have told him that in his five years here as powderman, Paha Sapa has moved and removed more than *five hundred million pounds of stone* — a good portion of the more than eight hundred million pounds of moved rock that the project will probably require before it is finished, including that which was moved before he came on the job — and every pound he has helped remove, every ounce, has felt to Paha Sapa exactly like carving into and removing the flesh of a living relative.

Mitakuye oyasin! All my relatives — every one!

The irony of the Lakota ending-discussion statement, the bonding statement that ends argument and planning and any further discussion of an issue, hits him harder than ever. He is betraying all his relatives, Paha Sapa realizes. Every one.

Suddenly, with a wave of nausea, he also realizes that he will fail in his mission.

For months, for years, he has planned this final blast—the one that will bring down the heads—but suddenly everything is rushed. He is out of time and out of energy. Just when he needs his strength, the gods are taking it away from him.

As Borglum drones on about future blasting on the TR site, Paha Sapa reviews his options.

His plan was to work all this night preparing and transporting the twenty crates of old, unstable dynamite he has stored in his shed in Keystone. Then hide it here on the site somewhere.

But where? He's scoured Doane Mountain and all the other areas. He can't place that many crates of explosive on the face of the mountain two days early—the crates would be detected for sure. There will be fifty men putting in unpaid overtime tomorrow, Saturday, rigging the huge flag that will hang over the Jefferson face for the ceremony, drilling, doing last-minute finishing work, working as Paha Sapa will be to prepare the demonstration charge for Sunday.

No, the crates have to be transported here tonight, Friday night, and hidden so that they remain out of sight until Saturday night, when—if his energy returns—Paha Sapa can get the dynamite up onto the mountain and out onto the faces and concealed the way he has planned, and rigged and wired to detonators and his master detonators for Sunday's final blast in full view of the president of the United States and the reporters and the newsreel cameras.

But he's found no hiding place that will work. There are no guards, per se, on the Monument site, but various people—including Borglum and his family—live in the cluster of cabins on Doane Mountain. Any arrival of a truck in the middle of the night or starting up of the equipment would be heard at once. And investigated.

And there is simply no place secret enough to hide the twenty crates of dynamite for the busy Saturday ahead. Paha Sapa has considered the various storage sheds, including the huge one holding the delivered but never-used submarine engines now rusting away there, but the place is too close to Borglum's and his son's living quarters.

Borglum drones on.

Paha Sapa moves closer to him and stealthily lifts the latch to the tram cage's door, hiding the motion with the bulk of his body. They are both leaning against that door now.

Paha Sapa knows how strong Gutzon Borglum is: the strength of the sculptor's powerful arms and body are second only to the strength of his personality. In his suddenly weakened state, Paha Sapa knows that he could not win a fight or wrestling match with the always wary *Wasicun,* but all he has to do here is swing open the door with his left hand and throw himself forward against Borglum, sending both him and the sculptor out through the sudden emptiness where the door and fourth wall of the cage had been. They are more than three hundred feet above the valley floor.

Paha Sapa tenses his muscles. He is sorry now that he has never composed his Death Song. Limps-a-Lot was correct in saying that only arrogant men waited to do this important thing. He could not sing it aloud now, but he could be singing it in his mind as he throws himself against Borglum and as the two fall, entangled, kicking and gouging, all the way to the gray boulder field below.

Will Borglum curse and fight? wonders Paha Sapa. *Will I scream despite myself?*

He hesitates. The carving of the heads is far along. Paha Sapa knows that Borglum anticipates never actually *finishing* the Mount Rushmore Monument; he sees himself working on it for another twenty years, twenty-five, thirty, for the rest of his life. But even with the addition of the ill-fated (until now) Entablature project and the Hall of Records in the canyon behind, a job almost equal to the carving of the Four Heads themselves, Paha Sapa knows that Borglum anticipates the bulk of the project being finished before the end of the 1940s.

Can his son, Lincoln, finish the project? Paha Sapa knows and admires Lincoln, so unlike his father in everything except courage and resolve, and thinks that he might well be up to the task. If the Park Service does not cancel the project for some unforeseen reason. If the federal money does not dry up.

But it has not dried up — at least permanently — through the worst the Depression has thrown at them so far. Current funding for 1936 and beyond looks strong, stronger than at any time in the project's shaky history. And this new supervisor, Spotts, is a man who gets things done. And if FDR arrives less than two days from now not only to be present during the dedication of the Jefferson head but to mourn the death of the sculptor behind this grand idea—Paha Sapa can see in his mind's eye the heads shrouded in black crepe rather than Jefferson covered with an American flag—the president could be so moved that he vows more money to complete the project, including the Hall of Records, ahead of schedule. And Lincoln Borglum would carry on his father's dream into the 1940s and...

The Hall of Records.

Realizing how close he is to falling out with Borglum even without the shove, Paha Sapa secretly slides the door latch back into place.

Borglum is speaking to him.

—*So let's go up and have a look.*

The sculptor reaches over his Stetsoned head and tugs down on the chain that releases the brake arm. Then he waves to Edwald far below.

The cage jerks and sways wildly for a moment and steadies itself only as they begin rising toward the top of the unstarted TR head. If Paha Sapa had not latched the cage door when he did, the swaying alone would have thrown the two of them out.

They glide through heated air above gouged granite to the summit of the Six Grandfathers.

PAHA SAPA FIRST SAW GUTZON BORGLUM through billowing clouds of steam and dissipating blasting smoke as the sculptor stepped out of the cage into Mineshaft Number Nine a mile below the surface near the town of Lead. The sculptor had come looking for a powderman listed on the Homestake Mine rolls as Billy Slovak.

He'd heard about Borglum for years, of course: the man wanted by the entire state of Georgia for single-handedly ruining their Stone Mountain monument; the arrogant SOB who drove his yellow roadster into South Dakota gas stations and expected the attendants to fill the tanks for free simply because he was *the* Gutzon Borglum; the fanatic who fielded the only baseball team in thirty miles that could take on the Homestake boys—and who treated baseball as a blood sport (in the Black Hills, Paha Sapa knew, baseball had always *been* a blood sport) but who had his team ally with the Homestake Nine when it came to beating the shit out of the vicious Cee Cee (Civilian Conservation Core) bastards.

This was the man Paha Sapa had heard and read about who was tearing the heart and guts out of the Six Grandfathers in an arrogant attempt to carve the heads of US presidents into a mountain sacred to nine Indian nations. And Paha Sapa had no doubt whatsoever that this Borglum person never even *knew*, much less cared, that Indians everywhere, and the majority of South Dakotan white people, for that matter, thought that carving mountains in the Black Hills was a defilement.

This was the man who stepped out of the steam and blasting smoke, his short, stocky torso backlit by work lights, the thin beam of light from his borrowed mining helmet weak in the fog of dust and smoke and powder, and began bellowing into the endless hole of shaft nine...

—*Slovak! Is there a Billy Slovak here! Slovak!*

Paha Sapa had taken the name for mining work thirty years earlier, when he'd moved back to the Hills with baby Robert after Rain's death, leaving Pine Ridge Reservation with no doubts or regrets. He needed money. The Holy Terror Mine had been open then—a death trap—and was still owned by the man who'd named the mine after his wife, who was indeed a holy terror. But the working conditions in that mine were so terrible—especially for powdermen, who lasted about three months—that the owner, William "Rocky Mountain Frank" Franklin, would hire, they said, even a redskin if the man knew how to set a charge properly.

Paha Sapa didn't know how to do that, but he learned quickly under one Tarkulich "Big Bill" Slovak, an older immigrant who said that he'd known six words of English when he came to America and started work as a seventeen-year-old powderman in the Brooklyn Bridge caisson under the East River in 1870, five of those words being "Run!" "Get down!" and "Look out!" Paha Sapa survived as Big Bill Slovak's assistant for thirty-four months, and somehow the name Billy Slow

Horse on the payroll became Billy Slovak, right beneath the older man's name. Then Big Bill had died in a cave-in (not of his own making), and "Billy Slovak" resigned before the Holy Terror was shut down for the first time in 1903 — not for lack of gold, but from insolvency due to all the lawsuits from families of all the miners killed or maimed in accidents there.

But Paha Sapa left that hellhole with memories of Big Bill's constant monologues about the building of the Brooklyn Bridge, with a work card with the name Billy Slovak on it, and with recommendations saying that he was an able powderman.

Borglum and Paha Sapa stood there talking in the roiling dust and smoke and steam and Paha Sapa's thought was *Why in God's name did the Homestake owners let you come down here to steal their men?*

But they had, and that's why Borglum was there — he had assumed that this "Billy Slovak" would instantly know who he was and what he was doing in the Hills — and he offered Paha Sapa the job as assistant powderman for four dollars more a month than the sixty-six-year-old Indian was making in the Homestake.

And Paha Sapa saw what he could do to the Four Stone Giants who were emerging from his sacred hills and he agreed on the spot — he would have agreed if Borglum had offered him no pay at all.

And then they shook hands on it.

It was not quite like the *flowing-in-vision* with Crazy Horse, but it was far more like that than the sudden *forward-seeing* visions he'd shared with so many others. Gutzon Borglum's life and memories did start flowing into Paha Sapa through that handshake, but somehow Borglum seemed to sense that something was happening — perhaps the man had his own vision abilities — and the sculptor jerked his hand away before all of his life, past and future, and all of his secrets, flowed to Paha Sapa the way Crazy Horse's had.

In the months that followed, when Paha Sapa had the time to open his own defenses to allow Borglum's memories in, he realized that, unlike with Crazy Horse, there were no future memories there. It would have pleased Paha Sapa if there had been. If Borglum, only two years Paha Sapa's junior, was going to outlive him — which would be the case if Paha Sapa succeeded in his plan — he could have seen his plan succeed in Borglum's future memories, the way he had seen the death of Crazy Horse. Paha Sapa would have seen his own death.

Instead, Borglum's captured thoughts and memories were all prior to the day the two men met and made physical contact in late January of 1931, and when Paha Sapa had the time and inclination, he picked through the sculptor's life like a man raking through the ashes of a burned-down home. Even the shards were complex.

Paha Sapa must have been the only man working for Borglum who knew that the woman whom the sculptor claimed as his mother in his already-published autobiography was actually his mother's older sister. It took some raking for Paha Sapa to understand.

Borglum's officially listed parents, Jens Møller Haugaard Borglum and Ida Mikkelsen Borglum, had been Danish immigrants. But they were also Mormons who'd made the trip to America with other Danish converts to live and work in the "New Zion" that Mormons were erecting near the Great Salt Lake somewhere in the desert of a territory called Utah. Jens Borglum and his wife, Ida, had gone west with the wagon trains, although they could only afford a pushcart.

A year after they reached Utah, they brought Ida's younger sister, eighteen-year-old Christina, over from Denmark to join them. As was the custom with the isolated, insulated Mormons at that time, Jens took Christina as his second wife. They moved to Idaho, where, in 1867, young Christina bore her husband a son, John Gutzon de la Mothe Borglum. Then, back in Utah, Christina had another son, Solon Hannibal de la Mothe Borglum.

But the railroad was connecting the nation and the railroad passed straight through Ogden, the city where the Borglums lived. And with that connection isolation ended and national outrage at the Mormons' practice of polygamy poured in. Congress, the newspapers, and an endless stream of newly arrived non-Mormons expressed their outrage over what they considered a barbarous, non-Christian practice.

Jens took his wives and children and headed east on that same railroad. In Omaha, knowing the discrimination that awaited them, Gutzon Borglum's real mother, Christina, withdrew from the marriage, stayed on briefly as a "housekeeper," and then left the family to go live with another sister. She later remarried.

Jens Borglum went to the Missouri Medical College, studied homeopathic medicine, changed his name to Dr. James Miller Borglum, and set up a medical practice in Fremont, Nebraska. There young Gutzon grew up in some small confusion, since his and his brother Solon's official and public mother was actually their aunt.

All this seemed unimportant but fascinated Paha Sapa as he allowed Borglum's childhood and young-adult memories to filter through in the months after they first met.

The first image that Paha Sapa was struck with was much more recent: the fifty-seven-year-old Borglum in 1924, already a self-proclaimed world-famous sculptor, high on the cliff face of Stone Mountain in Georgia, shoving large working models of General Stonewall Jackson's and General Robert E. Lee's heads to smash on boulders far below; the sculptor ordering a worker to take a sledgehammer to the huge twelve-by-twenty-four-foot working model of the seven figures of the famous Confederates (identities of four of them yet to be determined) who were supposed to fill Stone Mountain in what would have been the largest and greatest sculpture in the world.

The damned Georgians weren't going to fully fund him, they wanted to bring in another sculptor, and he—John Gutzon de la Mothe Borglum—would be God-damned to hell if he let those Southern redneck bastards have any of the fruit of his labors there.

Paha Sapa looked at these recent memories as if recalling a vivid, violent dream and watched as Borglum, finished with smashing and burning and destroying everything—working models, plans, maquettes, busts, designs for giant projectors and platforms, *everything*—then ran like a rabbit for North Carolina.

The state of Georgia still had warrants out for the famous sculptor.

So, in the end, Paha Sapa realized those first months of inhabiting some of Borglum's memories and old thoughts, Crazy Horse and sculptor Gutzon Borglum were very much alike after all. Both had been driven from childhood to achieve some violent greatness. Each saw himself as singled out by the gods for great deeds and accolades. Each had dedicated his life to goals of his ego, even if achieving those goals meant using others, casting them aside, and lying and hurting when necessary.

Borglum had never lifted another man's scalp or ridden naked through enemy fire, as Crazy Horse had done repeatedly, but Paha Sapa now saw that the sculptor had counted coup in his own way. Many times.

He also could see—thanks to his years talking to Doane Robinson and to the three Jesuits at the little tent school above Deadwood almost sixty years earlier—that while Gutzon Borglum's heritage was Danish, his attitude toward life was essentially classically Greek. That is, Borglum believed in the *agon:* the Homeric idea that every two things on earth must compete to be compared and then sorted into one of three categories—equal to, less than, or greater than.

Gutzon Borglum was not a man who would settle for anything other than "greater than."

In the fragments and shards of ego-distorted memory, Paha Sapa saw Borglum as a brash twenty-two-year-old would-be painter who went to Europe and studied under an expatriate American artist named Elizabeth "Liza" Jayne Putnam. Although she was eighteen years older than Borglum and infinitely more sophisticated, he married her, learned from her, and then discarded her and returned to America to create his own studio. Once in New York in 1902, Borglum opened his studio and promptly contracted typhoid fever and had a nervous breakdown.

Borglum's brother, Solon—the only sibling born from his own real mother, now unacknowledged and only the most distant of memories—was a renowned sculptor, so Borglum decided to become a sculptor. A *better and more famous* sculptor.

Borglum's discarded wife, Liza, now fifty-two, rushed to America to nurse her younger husband out of his illness and melancholia, but she learned that Borglum had already begun that healing by meeting a young Wellesley graduate, Miss Mary Montgomery, on the boat from Europe. Miss Montgomery—quite young, quite passionate, intensely well-educated and opinionated (but never so much that she contradicted Borglum or his ego)—was to be, of course, the Mrs. Borglum that Paha Sapa and all the other workers at Mount Rushmore knew so well.

Doane Robinson, who had come up with the idea of carving figures into the dolomite spires in the Black Hills to attract tourists, had seen the virile, aggressive, self-confident Gutzon Borglum as the salvation of his—Doane's—dream of massive sculptures in the Hills. But over the past five years, as more shards of Borglum's memory surfaced through the ash for Paha Sapa, he has seen that—especially after the debacle at Stone Mountain in Georgia—the Mount Rushmore project, enlarged and aggrandized as it constantly was by the sculptor, was actually the salvation of Gutzon Borglum.

In 1924, while the Georgia State Police were still hunting for Borglum and just after an innocent Doane Robinson had approached the sculptor (and, perhaps more important, just after Doane Robinson, South Dakota's Senator Peter Norbeck, and Congressman William Williamson had sponsored a bill appropriating $10,000 toward the project), Borglum was fifty-seven years old. In October of 1927, when the actual drilling on the mountain first began, Borglum was sixty years old. (Paha Sapa had heard that the sculptor, Borglum, had announced that the Washington head would be completed "within a twelvemonth" and that there "would be no dynamite blasting"... that all the carving of the mountain would be done by drill and by chisel. Paha Sapa had smiled at that, thinking of the tens and tens of thousands of tons of granite that would have to be moved just to find carvable stone. He knew even before Borglum did that 98 percent of the work on Mount Rushmore, if the project actually proceeded, would be done by blasting.)

There are hundreds of memories and powerful images that flowed into Paha Sapa that black day deep down in shaft nine of the Homestake Mine, before Borglum sensed some deeper connection in the handshake and abruptly pulled away (but did not rescind his job offer, whatever his temporary uneasiness), some of the memories, of course, explicitly sexual, some felonious, but Paha Sapa tries to avoid these, just as he long ago would have shut his ears to the lusty ramblings of the Custer ghost, if he'd been able to. Despite Paha Sapa's sacred gift of these visions, he hates intruding on other human beings' privacy.

Borglum is sixty-nine years old this August day as he rides to the summit of the mountain with the powderman he thinks of as Billy Slovak, just two years younger than Paha Sapa, and thus far three of the four great Heads have emerged from the stone, and these only partially. The sculptor plans to reveal much of their upper bodies and some arms and hands. And Borglum has more ambitious plans for the mountain—the Entablature, the Hall of Records. Gigantic projects in and of themselves. But Paha Sapa knows that Borglum has no worries about his age or health or about time itself; Borglum, he knows, plans to live forever.

———

THEY REACH THE TOP and step out of the cage and Borglum strides to where some of the boys have spent the day preparing the framework and armature of the crane that will drape the huge American flag over Jefferson and then lift and swing the flag back to reveal the head. The sculptor is talking, but Paha Sapa keeps walking along the ridgeline, past the crane and Jefferson.

From up here, one can see—feel—how very narrow the ridge of rock is between the blasted-in trough in which three of the four heads are emerging and the unseen wall of the canyon behind this ridge. When—if—the Teddy Roosevelt head is finished, the ledge between the carved face on one side and the vertical drop to the canyon on the other side will be narrow enough that it might make people nervous to stand on it.

Paha Sapa sees the crevice in the rock and the patch of soil where he dug his Vision Pit sixty years minus two days earlier. He continues along the ridge to the northwest.

Atop the heavily faulted knobs along the ridge above where the four heads are emerging, there's a small village of structures—wooden cranes, winches, winch houses, stairways spidering up and down the rocky knobs, wooden platforms, A-frame supports for the tramway and other devices, the vertical mast and the horizontal boom of the point-ing machine that translates the scale models in Borglum's studio below into the carving on the actual mountain. There is also one shack big enough for some of the men to crowd into during lightning storms or hail, outhouses, and various storehouses, including one set apart just for dynamite storage. (Paha Sapa has considered storing his extra twenty crates of dynamite there, of course, but the chances of it being discov-ered, even in just the one day he needs before deploying the charges, are simply too great. Alfred Berg, "Spot" Denton, and the other pow-dermen are in and out of there all the time.)

Far along the ridge, all by itself, is one small exposed post and steel winch platform. It's smaller than all the ones clustered above the heads and it's on the wrong side of the ridge, overhanging the vertical drop into the narrow dead-end canyon that lies behind the visible face of what the *wasichu* insist on calling Mount Rushmore.

Paha Sapa steps out onto the platform. The two-hundred-foot drop is precipitous and somehow seems worse than the exposure on the south face where the heads are emerging. The canyon below is narrow, claustrophobic even to look down into, and littered with massive tumbled boulders. The evening shadows have filled almost all of the narrow defile now, but Paha Sapa can still make out what he's come to see: on the opposite wall of the granite cliff, far below, there is a single square—no, a rectangle—of black, five feet tall by six feet wide, almost lost to the shadows.

Paha Sapa knows what it is because he helped blast it out the previous autumn: a twenty-foot test shaft for Borglum's future Hall of Records.

He suddenly feels the sculptor standing close behind him.

—*Damn it, Billy. What are you doing farting around over here?*

—*Just thinking about the Hall of Records, Boss.*

—*Why? We won't get to it until next year. Maybe the year after that.*

—*Yes, but I'm trying to remember all the things you said about it, Mr. Borglum. How deep it'll go. What'll be in it.*

Borglum squints at him. The sculptor is looking directly into the setting sun, but much of the squint is suspicion.

—*Damn it, Old Man. Are you getting senile on me already?*

Paha Sapa shrugs. His gaze goes back to the tiny black rectangle more than two hundred feet below.

But Borglum cannot resist giving a speech.

—*Next to the carvings themselves, Billy, the Hall of Records will be the greatest thing in America. There's going to be a grand stairway—broad, majestic, carved out of white granite—coming all the way up from the valley and into and up the canyon itself, with level areas with benches so that people can rest along the way and observe various statues and historical markers. We're going to have busts of famous Americans—some of you Indians included, Sitting Bull, Red Cloud, whatshername, the girl that went with Lewis and Clark—lining the grand stairway all the way up and into the canyon. It'll be lighted at night...glorious! Then, just when the people think it can't get any more glorious, they'll come to the Hall of Records itself... there, right down there where I had you and Merle and the others open that test shaft. The hall's entrance will be a single polished-stone panel forty feet high. It'll have inlaid mosaics made from gold and the world's best lapus lazuli, and the mosaics surmounted by a symbol of the United States of America...maybe it's a symbol of your people as well...a single bas-relief American eagle with a wingspread of thirty-nine feet. Then the door itself, the entrance... it'll be some twenty feet high by fourteen feet wide... they'll be cast-glass doors, Billy, transparent but as permanent as the mountain. Those doors'll open into the high chamber, which will be eighty feet wide and a hundred feet long. There'll be three hundred and sixty feet of wall space in that high chamber and all of it beautifully paneled and recessed to a depth of thirty inches. There'll be permanent indirect lighting there. It'll be beautiful day or night. Into those recesses will be built illuminated bronze-and-glass cabinets in which we'll place all the records of the United States... hell, of the Western World, of civiliza-tion itself... the Magna Carta, the Declaration of Independence, the Constitution of the United States, Lincoln's Gettysburg Address...all of it...and not just political stuff, Billy, but all the documents that show the glory of our civilization, show it to people and people's descendants a thousand and ten thousand and a hundred thousand and five hundred thousand years from now: documents of science and art and literature and invention and medicine. I know what you're thinking—that paper documents like that don't last thousands of years, much less hundreds of thousands. That's why all these documents, the Declaration, the Constitution, all of them, are going to be typed up onto and into sheets of aluminum and then rolled and protected in tubes of alloyed steel that'll last damn near forever. We'll seal those cabinets...hell, I don't know when, nineteen forty-eight maybe, or fifty-eight, or sixty-five, I don't care... but I plan to be here, trust me on that...and once sealed, those cabinets will be opened only by an act of Congress... if Congress lasts that long, which I heartily doubt. And on the wall above those cabinets, Billy, extending around the entire long hall, there's going to be a bas-relief, carved into bronze and plated with gold, that will show the whole adventure of humanity discovering and occupying and building up and perfecting the western world... us, our United States of America. And beyond that first main hallway there are going to be wide, brightly lighted tunnels going to more rooms and repositories, each one illustrated with its own murals, each one dedicated to a specific aspect of our time and glory...maybe even a room for statues of women who've made something of themselves, even just pests, like that Susan B. Anthony that those damned feminists keep demanding I carve there next to Washington, Jefferson, Teddy Roosevelt, and Abraham Lincoln. . . . I tell them the truth, that we're out of good carving rock there forever, Billy, but down here in the Hall of Records, for generations, for centuries . . .*

Borglum pauses, and Paha Sapa does not know if he's become self-conscious about the length of his speech or has simply run out of breath. He suspects the latter. But he doesn't really care. He just wanted the sculptor to go on babbling for a few minutes so that he could keep looking down into the now shadow-filled canyon and see the solution to his problem.

The test bore shaft for the Hall of Records. Only five feet high by six feet wide and twenty feet deep, but plenty of room in which to store his twenty crates of unstable dynamite tonight. And then, on Saturday night and into the wee hours of Sunday morning—with the help of just one winch operator, the dim-witted ex–Rushmore worker named Mune Mercer, already warned to be ready for some "special night work Mr. Borglum wants"—Paha Sapa will winch those twenty crates up here to the ridgetop, right here almost within touching distance of his Vision Pit, and then Mune will handle the winches on this side as Paha Sapa drops down on his cable, dancing in that unearthly gravity he's grown to dream about, the toes of his boots touching the faces only every twenty feet or so, as he places the twenty crates of dynamite in his pre-prepared spots and rigs the detonation wires that will blow the three existing Heads and the rock for the fourth waiting Head right off the side of this mountain forever. As Mr. Borglum has just said—there's no more good rock here to carve from, forevermore.

He turns and looks at the fiercely squinting sculptor.

—It's an incredible and wonderful vision, Mr. Borglum. A truly wonderful vision.

17

Jackson Park, Illinois

July 1893

PAHA SAPA RISES HIGH INTO THE AIR.

This does not alarm him. He's flown before. And this time he is being borne aloft in a device made up of more than 100,000 precisely machined parts, mostly of steel, including the largest axle in the world, which weighs—according to the Fair brochures—142,031 pounds. Paha Sapa believed it when he read that no single man-made item of that weight had ever been lifted before. And certainly not to its middle-of-the-wheel height of 148 feet.

The price of a ticket for a ride on Mr. Ferris's Wheel was the same as the price for entry to the Fair—fifty cents. But this time, forewarned, Paha Sapa had his dollar out and ready to pay for his and Miss de Plachette's tickets.

The Wheel, which opened for business fifty-one days later than promised just two weeks ago on June 21, is by far the most popular attraction at the Fair, but by some stroke of clever timing or pure luck, there are only five other people—an older couple who look like grandparents to the three nicely dressed children—in this car that can hold sixty people and which has swiveling seats for thirty-eight. And there is also one mustached, gaudily uniformed guard, sometimes called a conductor, who stands at either the south or north bolted door, both locks and guard there presumably to prevent suicide attempts, but who's also there to soothe those who discover their fear of heights during the ride.

Paha Sapa has heard through some of the Wild West Show's cowboys that these conductor-guards, each in his absurd uniform that looks to be part lion tamer's and part orchestra conductor's, have had to take instruction in boxing and wrestling and each also carries a three-pound bag of shot—a sap—in his pocket under that heavy tunic. Just in case fear drives a passenger insane.

Miss de Plachette—Rain—obviously has no such fear. Rather than sit on one of the thirty-eight round, tufted velvet chairs, the lady rushes to the almost floor-to-ceiling windows (each with its own wire mesh, also to prevent suicides, Paha Sapa assumes) and exclaims as the car begins to move slowly. Paha Sapa thinks he has seen the huge Wheel revolving in both directions, and today it is revolving east to west over the top. They are facing east as the car rises—the loading platforms are so cleverly arranged below that six cars can be emptied and loaded at the same time—and as they rise, Miss de Plachette watches the Midway Plaisance recede in size and the view of the White City beyond appear.

Her voice is sincerely and joyously breathless.

—*Incredible!*

Thinking—*This from the lady who has been up in the far taller Eiffel Tower*—Paha Sapa joins her at the window wall. He holds on to the gleaming brass railing, even though there is very little swaying. As if by instinct, the two of them have moved to the farthest corner on the eastern side of the mostly empty car, away from the quiet family and the conductor. The car, with its opposing north and south doors, each locked (the guard-conductor carries the key in his pocket), seems quite homey. There is a floral-pattern carpet and, in a corner, a huge brass cuspidor that is emptied regularly. The wire mesh in the large windows and door glass is so fine that it does not obstruct the view. Paha Sapa glances up and sees the glass-shaded rows of electric lights running around the perimeter of the ceiling and over both doors. He realizes that the lights are probably very dim so that they do not ruin the view at night and thinks that the view of the White City at night—with all of its searchlights and spotlights and thousands of electric bulbs illuminating the larger buildings and domes—must be as spectacular as Miss de Plachette had described. The lighted Ferris Wheel cars must also be a sight at night, seen from the Midway, with the bright carbide lights illuminating them from below and each carriage lighted from within by its own internal electric lights.

They continue rising.

One glance back over his shoulder toward the east through the opposite wall of windows makes him blink with vertigo. Looking *into* the spidery maze of spokes and steel girders at thirty-five other moving cars like their own, at the silhouettes of many hundreds of other people in those thirty-five cars, and at the giant turning axle with the truly gigantic support towers on either side makes Paha Sapa dizzy. The height is somehow magnified by looking *through* the giant wheel toward the more western exhibits along the Midway Plaisance so far below. And everything is turning, revolving, falling, and spinning at once. It is like being an insect caught inside a huge, revolving bicycle wheel.

Paha Sapa closes his eyes.

Miss de Plachette shakes his arm and laughs in delight.

The first of the two revolutions they are to receive for the price of their tickets is the slower one — their twenty-four-foot-long by thirteen-foot-wide car will stop at six different altitudes and positions on the wheel as more cars are loaded below. Their first loading stop is a quarter of the way up and when the car stops, it rocks ever so slightly back and forth on the horizontal bar that holds it, bearings and brakes below making the softest of sounds. Both Miss de Plachette and the grandmother at the opposite end of the car are also make squeaking noises — the older lady in terror, and Miss de Plachette, he is certain, in pure delight.

The conductor, who Paha Sapa heard introduce himself to the grandparent couple as being named Kovacs, clears his throat and gives a superior chuckle.

— *Nothin' to worry about, ladies and gents . . . and little ones. Nothing at all. These here steel posts we're hangin' from — trunnions, they're called — could hold ten times the weight of this fine car, even if we were fully loaded.*

The seven passengers watch silently as the car begins rising again and the eastern end of the Midway Plaisance and the domes of the White City appear. Beyond the domes, sunlight makes the band of Lake Michigan glow bright and visible above the trees and giant buildings. They see a cluster of ships in the harbor — mere masted points of

horizontal blackness from their exhalted position—and a ferry bringing more Fair visitors to the end of the long arrival pier.

Closer in, the Midway Plaisance stretches east beneath them, filled
with happy dark specks. Below and to their left are the red roofs and
forested grounds of the German Village. To the right of the Midway
rise the domes and minarets and odd spires of the Turkish Village.
Beyond the Turkish Village on the right is the large, round, strange
structure that holds the simulated Burmese Alps exhibit, and opposite
that across the Midway is the Javanese Village known as the Dutch
Settlement, across the street from the main Dutch Settlement.

Beyond these structures are the Irish Village on the left, with its
popular Donegan Castle and Blarney Stone; the round amphitheater
on the right for the animal show; and—farther down, marking the
east end of the Midway—the twin and opposing glasswork buildings,
Murano on the right and Libby on the left.

As he thinks the word *Libby,* Paha Sapa feels a dull stirring in his
skull and wonders if General Custer's ghost is watching through his,
Paha Sapa's, eyes, listening through his ears. Damn him if he is.

It is while they are stopped next, waiting for another six cars below
them to load quickly, that the little boy, no older than five, breaks away
from his grandparents and comes running around the car, waving his
arms as if he is flying. The boy's fingers brush Paha Sapa's bare wrist
above his gloves as the child flaps and flutters by.

He realizes then what an attuned state of sensitivity he is in, for at
once there is an *into-the-person* vision flash of images and thoughts from
the child. Paha Sapa has to clutch the railing at the window and close
his eyes as vertigo assails him again.

The elderly couple at the other end of the car, even now calling
the wayward child back to them, are named Doyle and Rheva. They
are from Indiana. Paha Sapa noticed that the man has a droopy left
eye and a strangely downturned mouth, and now—through the little
boy's unfocused memory—he learns of the stroke the year before that
caused it. Doyle has a long, thin nose, and Rheva, a slightly plump former beauty with full, flushed cheeks, kind eyes, and shorter-than-the-
fashion wavy silver hair, has always been embarrassed by her behind.
Everyone in the family—even the little boy—calls it the "DeHaven

Butt." It is Rheva's greatest secret, known only by the entire family, that she has never had to purchase or wear a bustle in order to be seen as wearing a bustle. The little boy does not know what a "bustle" is.

The boy's name is Alex and he has been so inspired by the exhibits at the Fair—especially Mr. Tesla's and Mr. Edison's—that his new goal in life is to grow up to invent a mechanical adding machine that can think.

Paha Sapa shakes his head to rid himself of these unwanted, swirling images and words and names and child-memories. His sensitivity to inward-seeing visions right now is as heightened as he'd feared, all because of his proximity to Miss de Plachette...and all the more reason to avoid any possible skin-to-skin contact with Miss de Plachette. He does *not* want to see into her mind or memories. It is very important to him that he does not do that. Not now. Not yet. With luck, never.

He realizes that she is whispering to him.

—*Paha Sapa, are you all right?*

He opens his eyes and sees that her gloved hand hovers too near his wrist.

He moves his arm away and smiles.

—*Perfect. Wonderful. I just discovered that I'm afraid of heights, is all.*

The guard-conductor with the waxed mustache, Kovacs, looks over at Paha Sapa suspiciously, as if this nonwhite passenger with the long braided hair may go berserk and begin battering the walls, shattering glass, and bending the iron of the door in his wild effort to escape, even though they are a hundred feet up, just as another height-crazed passenger was reported to have done just a week earlier. In that incident, so the newspaper accounts went, a woman finally stopped the crazy man by removing her skirt and throwing it over the man's head, immediately causing him to become docile.

Paha Sapa knows that such a blinding hood works with panicked horses. Why not with crazed Ferris Wheel passengers? More effective than the sap filled with shot purportedly in the guard's pocket.

Brakes release, the car wobbles again, and they resume their rise.

It is at the apogee of their circle—*apogee* being a word Paha Sapa learned when the three Jesuits at the tiny tent school on the mountain above Deadwood attempted for a year to drive Greek into his unwilling head—that Miss de Plachette does something...extraordinary. And changes his life forever.

The car stops suddenly at the top of the Wheel and begins rocking more noticeably than at their previous two stops. Rheva and her granddaughter let out moans. Little Alex shouts with joy at what he probably thinks to be their imminent destruction. Long-nosed Granddad Doyle pats the boy on the head.

The conductor's mouth slacks open. He cries out—

— *Miss!*

The shout is due to the fact that Miss de Plachette has suddenly moved to the center of the car, gathered her long skirt, jumped up onto one of the low, round plush velvet chairs, and is now standing there, balancing easily, very straight, arms full out from her sides, palms down, head back, eyes closed.

— *Miss, please...you mustn't, ma'am!*

The guard, Kovacs, sounds sincerely alarmed, but when he moves toward Rain, Paha Sapa instinctively steps forward to come between them. No man is going to touch Miss de Plachette while he is around.

Smiling broadly, head still far back as if tasting ocean air, Rain seems ready to leap forward and begin soaring out—magically, because of the glaze and wire mesh—through the windows into the blue Illinois sky. Instead, she lowers both arms and offers her right hand to Paha Sapa.

— *Your hand, please, dear sir?*

Paha Sapa takes it—grateful for his gloves and hers so that there can be no contact of skin on skin that might trigger any into-vision—and she steps down lightly and gracefully. The guard, Kovacs, returns to his post at the bolted south door and literally saves face by stroking his waxed mustache.

Miss de Plachette speaks softly, no apology audible in her voice.

— *I just wanted to be the highest person in Illinois — perhaps in the country — for a few seconds. I've got that out of my system now.*

The Wheel begins to move again.

Paha Sapa realizes in that second that he is going to love this woman for the rest of his life.

Paha Sapa says nothing. The two move to the west-facing windows now—the grandparents Rheva and Doyle and little Alex and the other two children giving the madwoman room, but also smiling.

Below them to the west, Paha Sapa and Miss de Plachette look down on the pretend turrets and towers of the Old Vienna attraction. Music from the multiple-domed Algerian Theater filters up to them. Farther up the Midway, a string of ostriches and reindeer from the Laplander Village mingle in wonderful but obscure mixed metaphor. To the north, there is a dark smudge above the city of Chicago and Paha Sapa realizes it must be from all the industry and smokestacks and locomotives and other machines there. He wonders how dark the sky gets in the winter with the hive-city's tens or hundreds of thousands of coal fires burning. Chicago, he has already seen, is the Black City to the Fair's pretend White City.

Miss de Plachette smiles and points to the captive balloon farther west along the Midway Plaisance and to their right. The balloon is at least a hundred feet up on its thick tether, but it's *below* them. (Three days later, on July 9, Paha Sapa will watch from the Wild West Show grounds as dark clouds gather, a funnel cloud appears, and then cyclone winds of more than 100 miles per hour lash the Midway, the Ferris Wheel, and all the buildings and exhibits. Huge glass panes will blow off the Manufactures and Liberal Arts Building and a forty-foot segment of roof will be torn off the dome of the Machinery Building. The sudden winds will catch the empty captive balloon before it can be hauled down and the beautiful mushroom of colored silk he and Miss de Plachette are looking at now will be ripped into nine thousand yards of silk rags, many scattered more than a half mile away. Mr. Ferris's Wheel, on the other hand, filled almost to capacity when the storm strikes it, will weather the wind's impact without a problem.)

They swoop down and start up again. There is no more loading or pausing. The second revolution is more wonderful than the first.

Paha Sapa knows that the boilers that provide the steam for Ferris's Wheel, for aesthetic reasons, are more than seven hundred feet away across Lexington Avenue, but he imagines as the great wheel accelerates that he can hear the boilers roar louder. He *knows* that he can hear the steam pressure in the giant cylinders of the thousand-horsepower engine at the base of the wheel rise in volume. One glance at Rain de Plachette's flushed features and bright eyes tells him that she hears this as well.

The rest is silence. Not even Doyle and Rheva and Alex and the other two children in the opposite corner make a noise. The conductor has turned his back to them and is at the door looking out his own window. The only hint of sound now is the whoosh of the large cabin through the air and the occasional creak of the cage shifting on the overhead trunnions or a low, almost inaudible grind from the gigantic central axle more than seventy feet from them.

The Wheel rises higher, higher, the White City in the east distance coming back into full view as they rise smoothly and silently. Paha Sapa looks out past the wooded island and lagoons and treetops, out to Lake Michigan, and sees the high afternoon sun break through the clouds and shine a single shaft of light down on the waters of the lake. The shaft of sunlight is so bright that everything else seems to fade and darken—the Midway, the White City, the trees and lagoons, the people, the harbor and lake itself—until there is only that powerful searchlight of pure sunshine pouring down on a limited circle of Lake Michigan wave tops far to the east.

Why is that image so hauntingly familiar? Why does it move him so?

Paha Sapa realizes and remembers just as the car heads up over the curve of the high arc, leaving the White City, Lake Michigan, and the prophetic shaft of light behind; then the car completes its voyage over the top and shows them all the western end of the Midway Plaisance and the distant prairies again. Even this view is striking, with the many shades of green and brown receding to the distant horizon—toward the prairies he knows so well a thousand miles west—but also with a web of train tracks and moving locomotives moving in toward Chicago, streaking the sky with their plumes of dark smoke.

But it is not the view that grips Paha Sapa and—he is sure, with no vision tricks necessary—Rain de Plachette on this second revolution and downward rush. It is the pure thrill and pleasure of speed and movement through space. Paha Sapa is surprised at the thought that strikes him next—*Only the* wasichu *can do such things. The Fat Takers are* wakan *in their own way, and it is a powerful magic.*

Then it is over and they are stopped and the guard has taken his brass key and unlocked the north door and they are all disembarking the cabin as mobs wait to board on the opposite, south side. The platforms and steps under girders and metal arches around and beneath the huge Wheel are an environment out of Jules Verne. (The friars at the Deadwood tent school, for some inexplicable reason, had English-language versions — he was sure the friars had translated them themselves — of *Voyage to the Center of the Earth, From the Earth to the Moon, Twenty Thousand Leagues Under the Sea,* and the newest, *Around the World in Eighty Days* hidden away in a trunk in their own tent, and Paha Sapa crept in and stole — borrowed — and read all of them within weeks of his learning to read.)

Miss de Plachette's expression is one of pure joy. She seizes his forearm in a death grip that shuts off all circulation.

— *Oh, Paha Sapa... I would give* anything *to experience that again.*

Paha Sapa removes from his pocket another dollar, a week's wages for him, gently takes her by the elbow, and leads her around through the Jules Verne world-of-the-future girder-and-metal-arch maze to the back of the growing line waiting to board on the south side. He surreptitiously checked his watch while they were still riding. They have time.

———

THEIR FIRST TWO TIMES AROUND, they were almost alone and hardly spoke at all. Their second two times around, there are at least twenty-five people in the car, but Paha Sapa and Rain de Plachette speak the entire time — softly, privately, secure in their own world somewhere between the Jackson Park–Midway Plaisance earth and the blue-sky-and-scattered-clouds Illinois heavens.

— *You'll pardon me for asking a personal question, Miss de Plachette, but isn't Rain an unusual name for* wa... *for white people? Beautiful... very beautiful... but I haven't heard it before.*

Paha Sapa's heart is pounding wildly. He is terrified of giving offense, of making her pull away from him — literally, as she rests her right shoulder against his left, but also in terms of offending her in any way. But he is aching from curiosity.

She smiles at him as they rise on the eastern part of their first slow revolution.

— *It is an unusual name, Mr.... Paha Sapa. But my mother also thought it was beautiful. The most beautiful word she'd learned in the English language, is what she told my father. When I was born and she wanted to name me Rain, Father didn't protest. He loved her very much. Did you know that my mother was Lakota?*

Paha Sapa feels a constriction in his chest and throat.

—*Yes. I mean, no... that is, I heard a rumor....*

She smiles again. The other passengers are making nervous noises as the large car sways and creaks on its trunnion when it stops, but they are veterans now.

—*Well, the rumor's true. Her name was White Shawl and I'm told that she was very pale for a Sioux... a Lakota. She was Father's choir director at the agency mission and they... Did I tell you that Father was doing mission work in Nebraska when they met?*

—*No. Please go on. Tell me more.*

Miss de Plachette looks out as the car stops and rocks again—there are afternoon cloud shadows moving over the trees and lagoon and walkways and giant buildings of the White City now—and he sees the slight blush beneath the freckles that cross the bridge of her nose and become fewer in number on her cheeks.

—*That's how Father met Mr. Cody, of course. Mr. Cody's new ranch was right next to the agency—reservation—where father spent five years as a mission-ary. There were several groups... tribes... there. Lakota and Shoshoni and a few Cheyenne and Creek and one family of Cherokee. It was a small agency, but the church had been there a long time, and the people came from miles around. Not just Indians...*

She blushes again and Paha Sapa smiles, encouraging her to go on. They are at the last stop before the high point of the wheel's circle. The crowded car is alive with oohs and ahhs and gasps and exclamations.

—*I mean, Mr. Cody and his ranch hands—some of them were Indians as well—of course you know that—would come over and the congregation was often more than a hundred people. Very large for that wild part of Nebraska. Mother was choir director, as I said, and she also taught all the children at the mission school there, and... well... Father and Mother fell in love and were married there.... Mr. Cody was Father's best man at the wedding, and the Reverend Kyle came all the way from Omaha to perform the ceremony. And I was born a year later and, so my Father tells me, it was raining the week I was born that June... the first real rain in more than seven months of drought... and*

Mother named me Rain, and then she died when I was four and we moved East a few months later and I've never been back.

Paha Sapa tries to imagine this—a *wasichu wičasa wakan* marrying a Lakota woman in 1870 or so. It is very hard to imagine. Perhaps, he thinks, the Natural Free Human Beings are—or were—very different in Nebraska. Then he thinks—*What are Natural Free Human Beings doing in Nebraska? Are they lost?*

He says aloud—

—And after you left, you lived in Boston and Washington and France?

— Yes, and elsewhere…and, Paha Sapa, I'm ashamed to say that I know much more of the French language than I do my mother's tongue. When Father and I have visited Mr. Cody's Wild West Show, I've tried to use my few words and phrases to talk to the Lakota there, but the men just smile at me. I'm sure I have everything wrong.

—I won't just smile at you, Miss de Plachette. Try out one of your phrases.

— Well, as I say, I only barely remember them, since Mother spoke English almost exclusively in the house when I was tiny, before she…before we moved…most probably at Father's request. But I do remember some of the Lakota men talking to her at church and asking her how she was.…I'm pretty sure I remember "Hello" and "How are you?"

—Say it. I will be your audience and noncritical coach. We still have ten minutes or more of this ride left. But let's don't forget to enjoy the scenery.

— Oh, I assure you, Paha Sapa, I haven't quit watching for a second. Even when I look your way, I am also looking beyond you to the south, or looking out at the prairie to the west. All right, "Hello, how are you?" in the Lakota I remember from the agency when I was four years old…Hau, Tanyan yaun he?

Paha Sapa just smiles. He can't help it.

Miss de Plachette curls her hand into a tiny fist and hits him hard on the shoulder. Paha Sapa's eyes widen—he's not been struck by a woman since he was a young boy—and then he laughs, showing his strong white teeth. Luckily—his world would end then if it were not so—she is also smiling and laughing.

— What was wrong with that, Paha Sapa? I have even heard your Wild West Sioux say that to one another!

—Nothing's wrong with it, Miss de Plachette…if you're a man.

— Oh, dear.

—*I'm afraid so. Did your mother not tell you that the Natural Free Human Beings have separate vocabularies and language rules for men and women?*

—*No, she didn't. I mean, I don't remember if she...I don't remember* so much *about Mother. Too much. I don't even know who the Natural Free Human Beings are...the Sioux?*

—*Yes.*

The young woman seems suddenly, strangely near tears, and Paha Sapa, without thinking, tenderly touches her shoulder.

—*The Lakota's name for ourselves is* Ikče Wičaśa—*which more or less translates to Natural Free Human Beings, although it means more than that.*

She smiles again. They have passed through the loading area and are rising in the east on the beginning of their second, faster, more exciting revolution. Other passengers squeal. Paha Sapa and Miss de Plachette grin at each other again, proud of their seasoned-Ferris-Wheel-traveler status.

—*I certainly understand about feminine, masculine, and neuter nouns and verbs and such from my French and little bit of German and Italian, although the idea of an entire separate* language *for men and women is almost shocking to me.*

Paha Sapa smiles again.

—*Oh, we tend to understand each other, the* Ikče Wičaśa *men and women, when we talk to one another. As well as the two sexes do in any language or culture is my uneducated guess.*

—*So how would I, a woman, say "Hello, Paha Sapa. How are you today?"*

Paha Sapa actually clears his throat. He's very nervous and almost sorry this particular discussion began. He knows almost nothing about courting, but *does* know that one does not impress or ingratiate oneself with a beautiful woman by laughing at her or giving her primitive language lessons. "*Courting? Is that what you think you're doing here, you moron?*" asks a voice in his head that sounds strongly and suspiciously like that of George Armstrong Custer.

He says softly—

—*Well, first of all, the* Hau *greeting is used only by men. And the* he *at the end of the sentence...*

He desperately thinks back to Father John Bertrand, the fattest and smartest and gentlest friar at the Deadwood tent school, and the Latin and Greek he tried to drive into 12-year-old Paha Sapa's thick skull...but all he can call back is the heat inside the tent in the summer, the strong smell of sun-warmed canvas and the straw that Father Pierre Marie used to lay down on the floor, as if the five boys there, two Mexican, one Negro, one white, and Paha Sapa, were barn animals rather than...no, wait...

—*the interrogative form, as it were, is also used by women and men informally, but if it were an official situation, talking in council, for instance, I'd...that is a male Lakota...would have to end the question with* hwo...*or* hunwo...*or so. Oh, yes,* Han *means "hello" for men but "yes" for women.*

Miss de Plachette sighs, but not, it seems, out of impatience, only at the first glimpse of the complexity of her mother's people's language. She is still smiling.

—*So you're saying that if a Lakota man says hello to me and I reply in kind, with the same word, I'm simply saying yes to anything the man has suggested?*

—*Well...ah...um...that is...*

She rescues him before his blush darkens his already dark skin too much further.

—*So how would I say "Hello, Paha Sapa"?*

—Paha Sapa, Han.

—*And how would a woman say "Hello, it is really good to see you" to a man? To you?*

—Paha Sapa, han! Lila tanyan wacin yanke. *Only you couldn't... wouldn't...come up and say that.*

Her smile seems almost teasing.

—*Really? Why not?*

Paha Sapa clears his throat again. His only salvation is that, true to her promise, she has not turned to look fully at him. She keeps watching the lake and the White City as the car rises quickly—too quickly—toward the top of its arc this second and final (forever for them together! he is sure) and too-fast-for-his-taste revolution of Mr. Ferris's amazing Wheel.

—*Because, Miss de Plachette, in the* Ikče Wičaśa *culture, women do not initiate conversations with men. They are never the first to say hello.*

—*Not even with their husbands?*

She is definitely teasing him. He opens his mouth to answer, realizes that his mouth stays open during the entire time it takes them to pass over the top of the arc of the wheel, and then manages...

—I've never been married.

Now she laughs out loud. The sound is so soft that it is almost lost in the loud exclamations and excited talk in the crowded car, but Paha Sapa will remember the pure tones of that easy, friendly laugh for the rest of his life.

She touches his forearm again.

—All right, I surrender. I won't learn the Ikče Wičaśa's *women's language during two turns of Mr. Ferris's Wheel. But is there a special term that Lakota women use to say hello to someone they really like...a special friend?*

Now Paha Sapa's throat feels so constricted he can barely get the syllables out.

She leans closer to him, her eyes finally turning from the scenery outside, and says very softly—

—Maske, Paha Sapa, lila tanyan wacin yanke...

It is still wrong because...it does not matter. The power of her intimate greeting and the "It's *really* good to see you"...she had stressed every syllable exactly as Paha Sapa spoke it earlier, except for that extra emphasis on the *really*...to hear her say this to him in *his* language...He will never forget it. He wonders then if it will be the last thing he chooses to think of before his death.

—We're almost down, Paha Sapa. I'm a greedy woman. I have three more requests for you before we go meet Father at the Grand Basin at six...

She consults the tiny watch on the ribbon pinned to her vest.

—...still ninety minutes away! Three greedy requests, Paha Sapa.

—I will do anything you ask, Miss de Plachette.

—First then, at least until we meet Father and the other gentlemen, please call me Rain, as you promised and did for a short while.

—Yes...Rain.

—Second—and this is just a silly woman's request, since you seem so...hot... with them on. Please remove those gloves after we get off the Ferris Wheel.

—Yes, Miss...Yes. Yes, of course.

—And finally, tell me what the Lakota word is for my name. For Rain.

—"Rain" is...magazu.

She tries it out. Says it twice softly as the view of the prairie is reduced, is eliminated, and the Midway Plaisance and loading platforms come up under them. Then she says very softly—

—Mother was right. It is prettier in English.

—Yes, Rain.

Paha Sapa has never more agreed with any statement. The car is slowing to a stop. The other passengers are growing louder in their laughter, exclamations, and praise of the ride.

—This qualifies as an extra request, Paha Sapa, but how do you say in Lakota—"I will see you later"?

Without thinking of gender language or anything else, Paha Sapa looks into her hazel eyes and says—

—Tokša ake wancinyankin ktelo.

—I asked for that phrase, Paha Sapa, because Father has decided that he must return to the missionary fields, and in September we will be moving to the Pine Ridge Agency in Dakota Territory. . . . I believe that is not too far from where Mr. Cody mentioned that you live.

All Paha Sapa has to say is *No, not too far,* but this time he can *not* get the syllables out.

The great wheel stops its turning. The car they're in rocks, creaks, settles. The conductor—with a tin badge saying something other than Kovacs; Paha Sapa has temporarily forgotten how to read English letters or words—opens the door for them all to depart before the next sixty people squeeze aboard.

———

THE NEXT NINETY MINUTES are delightful and infinitely rich for Paha Sapa, but they fly by like so many seconds.

On their way back to where they are to meet Rain's father on the steps outside the domed Administration Building on the west side of the Grand Basin, they take time to poke their heads into the Fine Arts Building, with its many art galleries north of the North Pond, then take an almost running tour of the gigantic Women's Building—Rain especially wants to stand in front of a huge mural by a woman artist named Mary Cassatt, the allegories of which would have been lost on Paha Sapa if she had not been there to translate them—and then they take their time strolling on the Wooded Island as the July afternoon slowly melts into a golden July evening. Paha Sapa is only sorry that they will not be together when all of the thousands of electric lights come on. What, he wonders again, would a turn in the Ferris Wheel be like at night?

It is on the Wooded Island, where they are sitting for a moment on a comfortable bench in the shade near the Rose Garden and having tall, iced drinks purchased from one of the ubiquitous canvas-covered refreshment stands, that Paha Sapa fulfills his promise by peeling off the too-tight, sweat-lined dress gloves and tossing them into the nearby wire wastebasket.

Rain laughs, sets her drink glass on the bench, and applauds.

Paha Sapa feels no anxiety about an accidental touch turning into an invasive contact-vision with her now. She has kept her own white gloves on and her long-sleeved blouse leaves almost no skin of her wrist exposed. Besides, it is only a few minutes until they are to meet her father.

Then she surprises him again.

—*Paha Sapa, Mr. Cody has told Father that you were a friend of Sitting Bull's.*

— *Yes. Not a close friend, he was much older than I, but I knew him.*

—*And you were with him . . . with Sitting Bull . . . when he was killed?*

Paha Sapa takes a breath. He does not want to talk about this. He feels it will only put distance between the young woman, her father, and himself. But he truly is at the point where he can and will deny her nothing.

— *I did happen to be there when he died, Miss . . . Rain. It was an accident that I was present. None of us had any idea that he might be murder . . . killed.*

—*Please tell me. Please tell me everything about it.*

Paha Sapa sips his iced drink to gain a few seconds to organize his thoughts. What should he tell this young *Wasicun* girl? He decides . . . everything.

— *It was three years ago, you know. Winter. December. I'd gone up to the Standing Rock settlement . . . and agency, really, a reservation . . . where Sitting Bull was living, because my* tunkašila . . . *not my real grandfather, but an honorary name for a man who helped raise me . . . was living there. He was there because he was an old friend of Sitting Bull's. Wait, this won't make any sense unless you've heard of a Paiute holy man named Wovoka and his teachings, especially about his advocating a sacred dance called the Ghost Dance. Have you heard these things?*

—*Fragments about them, Paha Sapa. Father and I were in France when all this happened, and I was only seventeen. I was more interested in grand balls in Paris than in the Ghost Dance that correspondents told Father about in letters. Please do explain.*

Paha Sapa sighs. It is not a happy sound. He catches a glint of light in the trees and realizes that it is one of the thousands of little colored "fairy lamps" — tiny lights of wick and oil — that turn the Wooded Island into a magical place after dark. He very much wishes that he and Rain could wander the Wooded Island under such lights, with the White City buildings blazing in light and the Ferris Wheel steel turning, painted white by huge carbide search-lights, in the distance.

— *The Paiute Wovoka's sermons and religious teachings were as confused as your scattered fragments. I heard him talk near the Pine Ridge Agency before I went to visit my* tunkašila *and Sitting Bull. The Paiute holy man had taken large pieces of the Christian story — he said a messiah had come to earth to save his children from the control and clutches of the* wasichus *and…*

— *Please, what are* wasichus, *Paha Sapa?*

He looks at her.

— *Fat Takers. White people.*

She blinks. Paha Sapa wonders if she feels as if he has slapped her.

— *I thought we…that whites…were called* Wasicun. *I seem to remember Mother using that term.*

Paha Sapa nods sadly.

— *That term was also used, but later.* Wasichus, *the Fat Takers, are what we called you…whites. But Wovoka was preaching that if his followers, of any tribes, all tribes, danced this sacred Ghost Dance, there would come a sacred flood that would drown all the* wasichus *but leave the red man alone. And then, when the whites were all gone, the buffalo would return and our long-departed ancestors would come back and all of us, Natural Free Human Beings and all the other tribes, would live in abundance and peace forevermore.*

Rain is frowning for the first time since they met at the Wild West Show.

— *Your ancestors would come back? Like ghosts?*

— *No, I don't think so. More like resurrected real people, like your Bible promises in Heaven. But not* nagi, *not spirit people, just people. We would see all our ancestors again, which is a promise that held tremendous power to us, Rain. And the return of the buffalo and the departure...deaths...of all the* wasichus *in our land, in the West. Well, you can see why this scared the whites, all the way up to President Harrison.*

— *Yes.*

Her voice is flat, emotionless, for the first time this day. Paha Sapa has no idea what she is thinking. He rubs his jaw with his bare hand and goes on.

— *Anyway, the summer of 1889, Ghost Dancers had appeared on all six agencies where the Lakota lived. They just...appeared. They wore shirts — special sacred shirts, Ghost Shirts, that Wovoka had promised them would stop any bullet. The whole idea was that the Ghost Dance itself, if all the Indians in all the tribes believed in it and danced it, would itself provoke the disaster that would take away all the* wa-sichus *and give the red men back their land, their old world, their universe, even their gods and protective spirits. And, if the* wasichus *tried to interfere, there were always the Ghost Shirts to protect the warriors....*

— *Did you believe in this prophecy and in the Ghost Dance, Paha Sapa?*

— *No.*

Paha Sapa actually considers telling her the reason he could not believe in it — his own Sacred Vision from 1876, the *wasichu* Stone Giants rising out of the Black Hills and consuming all the buffalo and the Natural Free Human Beings themselves — but then he comes to his senses. He knows he will love this young woman for the rest of his life, whatever that life brings him, but why have her thinking that he, Paha Sapa, is as crazy as that crazy old Paiute Wovoka?

He sips the last of his cold drink and goes on.

— *Anyway, the local Indian agents got very nervous — as well they should — and then the politicians got nervous and finally the army, the cavalry, got very nervous. The agents on all the reservations were ordered to use the tribal police to break up any gatherings of Ghost Dancers. The dance itself was outlawed on every reservation except little Standing Rock, way over on the Missouri River, where Sitting Bull and my* tunkašila *were living in little cabins rather than tipis.*

— *Did Sitting Bull believe in the Ghost Dance and the prophecy?*

Rain's voice is still flat, emotionless, save for curiosity.

— *I don't think so. I don't think he'd made up his mind about it. At least he hadn't said he had when I arrived there on the fourteenth of December, the day before they...the day before he died. But a lot of Lakota were sure that Sitting Bull was the messiah that Wovoka was preaching about. A lot of Lakota men were ready to follow Sitting Bull if the old chief had proclaimed himself that messiah. So, right at the end of November, Buffalo Bill showed up at Fort Yates on the Standing Rock Reservation with orders signed by Bear Coat... our name for General Miles... authorizing the arrest of Sitting Bull and...*

—*Mr. Cody arrest Sitting Bull? They were close friends! Mr. Cody talks about him with great respect and affection to this day! Father has always said that the two men were close.*

Now there is emotion in her voice... true shock.

—*Yes, well... perhaps that's why the* wasichus... *the agents and the president... sent Mr. Cody with the arrest warrant. Mr. Cody had just returned from the successful tour in Europe with the Wild West Show. But anyway, he arrived too drunk to carry out the arrest and...*

—*Mr. Cody? Drunk? I thought Mr. Cody never touched spirits or liquor. I am* sure *that Father believes this to be the case! Good heavens!*

Paha Sapa is not sure if he should—or can—continue. He starts to drink from his glass, sees that it is empty, and sets it down to consult his cheap watch. He is so disturbed that he thinks of checking the time in Lakota—*Mazaškanškan tonackca hwo?*—literally "Metal-goes-goes what?"

—*It is twenty minutes to six, Miss de Plachette. We should cross the bridge to the west side of the Great Basin just in case your father is early and...*

—*Oh, no. Please finish your story, Paha Sapa. I insist... no, no, I have no right to insist... but I beseech you. Tell me how Sitting Bull died. Mr. Cody was too drunk to arrest him?*

—*Yes. And the* wasichu *military men there* kept *him drunk for several days. Those officers were terrified that arresting Sitting Bull, much less hurting him, would cause the very catastrophe that Wovoka was prophesying about. Anyway, after about three days, Mr. Cody sobered up and headed down the road to arrest Sitting Bull. He was traveling with another Wild West Show fellow, whom we called Pony Bob...*

—*Oh, my! Father and I know Pony Bob. He used to come to Father's sermons.*

—*Anyway, Mr. Cody and Pony Bob ran into the agency's interpreter, a fellow named Louis Primeau, who lied to them... told them that Sitting Bull wasn't on the reservation. That he was on another road. By the time Mr. Cody and Pony Bob figured things out, President Harrison himself had... I'm sorry, what is the word for changing orders one has given? Reversing them?*

—Rescinded?

— Yes, that's it. The president himself had rescinded the arrest orders. Sitting Bull was safe. For the time being. That was around the first of December.

—But he died in December…did he not?

—He did. Bear Coat…General Miles…was so angry that his old adversary Sitting Bull was getting away that he sent the Seventh Cavalry in…

"Do not say anything to libel the Seventh Cavalry," rasps a familiar voice deep in Paha Sapa's skull.

Silence! The ghost is like a prisoner who gets out of his cell from time to time but can never escape the prison.

—Is something wrong, Paha Sapa?

— No, no, I was just gathering my thoughts. At any rate, I arrived at Standing Rock on the fourteenth of December. Sitting Bull and my tunkašila *were leaving with me and a few other younger men the next day, going back to Pine Ridge—and then planning to go to Rosebud—to visit these Ghost Dance leaders and finally decide what he thought, what Sitting Bull thought, of the whole prophesy thing. But he was skeptical. I know he was skeptical.*

—Didn't you say that the Ghost Dancers were banned from all the other reservations?

Paha Sapa nods. She is obviously paying close attention.

— That's true. The leaders Sitting Bull wanted me to meet with had taken about twelve hundred Oglala and Brulé to a place we call the Stronghold—a mesa way up in the Badlands part of the Pine Ridge Reservation surrounded by sheer cliffs on three sides. The Natural Free Human Beings have fled there in threatening times since before we had horses.

—And the cavalry pursued Sitting Bull there?

—No, he never got out of Standing Rock. The next day, the fifteenth, around six a.m.…we should have left earlier, but Sitting Bull was an old man and packed and acted slowly…the army sent more than forty local Indian policemen to his cabin on the Grand River. It was a very small cabin. My tunkašila *and I were sleeping in a sort of lean-to out back where Sitting Bull kept his horse.*

—So it was a tribal policeman…another Indian…who killed Sitting Bull?

Paha Sapa nods again.

—Sitting Bull at first said he wouldn't go with the policemen. Then he agreed. They let him get dressed. It had been dark when all the policemen rode up, but it

was getting light by the time the old holy man came outside. Others had gathered outside the cabin. Sitting Bull's youngest son — still a teenager — started mocking his father for submitting to the wasichu. *Sitting Bull changed his mind again and said he wouldn't go after all. There was pushing and shoving. Someone in the crowd shot a policeman, and that policeman, before he died, shot Sitting Bull in the chest. Another policeman shot Sitting Bull in the back of the head. When it was all over, there were six tribal policemen dead as well as Sitting Bull and six of his friends and followers.*

— *Oh, Paha Sapa. Oh, dear.*

— *It's time to go, Rain. We don't want to be late meeting your father.*

***

PAHA SAPA AND RAIN are five minutes early at the steps outside the Administration Building facing the Columbian Fountain set in the broad waters of the basin. Her father arrives twelve minutes late.

Miss de Plachette has said nothing since his story about Sitting Bull's death. But she looks even paler than she did earlier. He assumes that she has been put off by his story — all the sordid details, from Buffalo Bill Cody showing up drunk to betray his old friend to the very real violence threatened by the Ghost Dance and its Prophet. He knows he will always love her for...if nothing else...that moment of standing higher than anyone else at the top of the Ferris Wheel, looking as if she were preparing to fly the way his spirit-self had flown more than once in his life. No, not just for that. Perhaps not for that at all. Just because he does love her and knows he always will.

But she is, after all, a twenty-year-old *wasichu* girl, wise, perhaps, to the ballrooms and churches and embassies of Washington and Paris and the world, but having a four-year-old child's understanding of the West and of her mother and of Paha Sapa's world, where great warriors like Crazy Horse and rare *wičasa wakan* like Sitting Bull are cut down by little men no longer Natural Free Human Beings, little men neither natural nor free, little men on *wasichu* payrolls who wear oversized, flea-infested, cast-off cavalry blue coats and who kill the best of their own kind on *Wasicun* command.

No, she will never understand Paha Sapa's world. Even if she learned the language of the Lakota, he knows then, it would be as alien and adopted to her as French or German or Italian. More so, he realizes, since she has spent time as an adult or near-adult in those places, and remembers Nebraska and the West only in a distorted child's blur of half memory.

And he will not see her again, he knows. He is certain of this. As certain as if he *had* allowed another *small-vision-forward-touching* to occur. Miss Rain de Plachette may or may not move to the Pine Ridge Reservation with her father this coming September, but she and Paha Sapa will not meet again. Not after the terror and distaste and—*alienation,* he thinks, is the word in English—the *wacetug la* and *wo* he saw in her hazel eyes as he spoke.

It doesn't matter, he tells himself. Like so much else he's seen and experienced and survived since the Vision of the Stone Heads emerging from the Paha Sapa and the *wasichu* Stone Giants rising to finish the job that is all but finished on the Plains and in the Hills, this is just one more thing that does not matter.

Reverend Henry de Plachette arrives in a huffing hurry, accompanied by three men wearing very formal tails and top hats. There are introductions, but Paha Sapa does not hear or remember the names. None of the three men extends a hand to shake—they clearly see that he is Indian, despite, or perhaps because of, his ill-fitting suit and overly polished shoes.

But the Reverend de Plachette is extending *his* hand there at the head of the stairway to the dark waters of the basin. He is saying something.

—... so *much for escorting my daughter to our little rendezvous here, Mr. Slow Horse. It is much appreciated. I know that Rain enjoyed the diversion and I appreciate your gentlemanly offer to escort the young lady.*

Paha Sapa grips the old man's hand.

The world swirls, the Great Basin becomes a huge mural, a fresco, larger than the Mary Cassatt mural in the Women's Building, as the water becomes a vertical wall and the images and sounds and feelings rush in.

And then everything is black.

HE REGAINS CONSCIOUSNESS lying on the topmost step. One of the well-dressed men has dipped a silk handkerchief into the basin and is applying the wet cloth to Paha Sapa's forehead. His head is on Miss de Plachette's lap, and she is cradling him in her arms. *His head is on her lap.*

Paha Sapa realizes that tears are flowing down his face. He has been weeping while he was unconscious. He shakes his head.

— *Too much sun . . .*

one man is saying.

— *Perhaps the vertiginous effects of that infernal Wheel . . .*

another man is saying.

— *A problem with the heart, perhaps.*

This last is the Reverend Henry de Plachette, who has taken over the mopping with the wet silk handkerchief. A small crowd has gathered, and uniformed Exposition personnel are running toward them from the direction of Machinery Hall.

Paha Sapa blinks away the tears and looks up at Rain's face above him.

The images were few, fast, and terrible.

The prairie. Wind blowing. A winter morning.

The cemetery atop the small rise. There was one tree.

The grave with the plain pine coffin just lowered into it.

The Reverend de Plachette there, unable to conduct the funeral service. Surrendered to weeping.

And Paha Sapa there — seen through the old man's rheumy, tear-filled eyes — Paha Sapa looking older but not older enough. Paha Sapa taking the baby from the Mexican woman, a servant of the minister's. Paha Sapa holding the baby as he looks down at the first clods of dirt falling on the coffin of his young wife, Mrs. Rain de Plachette Slow Horse.

The image, from the Reverend's point of view, the Reverend who is also ill and who would give all he has ever had or believed in to take his daughter's place in that grave, the image of his Indian son-in-law, Billy Slow Horse, holding the distraught Reverend's dead daughter's only child — the baby who may have helped kill her in her weakened condition — the boy.

The boy named Robert.

Paha Sapa lies there on the top step of the staircase leading down to the Great Basin near the Columbian Fountain, too staggered to try to gain his feet again no matter how embarrassed he may feel at lying there with his head on this young lady's lap with the crowd gathering around.

Her hand is stroking his forehead now. Her bare hand. She has taken her glove off. Her bare hand.

Paha Sapa receives no vision from the contact, but he receives a terrible twin certainty: she loves him already and will do everything she must do so that they will be together; there is no escaping their fate-entwined destiny.

For the first, last, and only time in his life, Paha Sapa, inexplicably, ineluctably, gasps out three words that cause everyone except Rain to freeze in place.

— *Oh, dear Jesus.*

18

Near Twin Buttes

September 1876

PAHA SAPA IS RIDING IN THE RAIN. THE HORSE BENEATH HIM IS old, scabbed, and slow. And it is wearing a saddle. Paha Sapa has never ridden in a saddle before and it hurts his ass.

The hard rain keeps wiping the blood off his face, but the blood keeps returning. He does not even bother to blink it out of his eyes.

His eye. One eye is swollen shut or destroyed forever. He does not care which. The other eye sees only the blur of the fifty or sixty other men ahead of him and around him. He does not care that they are there. They are *wasichu* cavalry. He is dimly aware that he is their prisoner, to do with as they wish: torture, slow murder, whatever they want. He does not care.

Paha Sapa has been slipping in and out of consciousness for most of this long, wet day. He knows that he's riding with these dark forms and he knows that his head hurts more than any pain he has ever imagined. But he also knows that the Crow—the old man named Curly—did not strike him with the rifle butt in anything meant as a killing blow. After hours of half listening to Curly, who rides nearby and continues talking in his terrible, patchy language of the Lakota—the old man uses many words from the women's language, which makes him sound like a boy-who-decides-to-dress-and-act-like-a-woman *winkte*. Normally this would be terrifically amusing to Paha Sapa, but today nothing amuses him.

He wishes he were dead. He plans to be dead. In a real sense, he *is* dead.

He has lost Limps-a-Lot's and his band's *Ptehinčala Huhu Canunpa,* the most sacred Buffalo Calf Bone Pipe that was the most important and *wakan* object the band ever had. Oh, why had Limps-a-Lot entrusted the pipe to him, to Paha Sapa, to a miserable boy with no more sense or brains than not to look over his shoulder when traveling alone on the plains with the greatest treasure it was possible to carry?

Two great treasures, he realizes through the pain and rain. The *Ptehinčala Huhu Canunpa,* lost forever now to the swollen river, and the details of his Vision, granted by the Six Grandfathers. Limps-a-Lot and the other elders and chiefs and holy men will never listen to his Vision now, even if he were somehow to escape the *wasichu* cavalry. By losing the pipe, Paha Sapa has lost all credibility forever. He is sure of that. *Wakan Tanka* and the Six Grandfathers and all the spirits and Thunder Beings would *never* grant a man or boy such a Vision and then steal the *Ptehinčala Huhu Canunpa* from him. Such a loss is a statement by all the gods and powers and the All himself that Paha Sapa is not to be trusted as their servant and messenger.

His head hurts in unimaginable ways. He wishes he were dead. He plans to be dead soon. He welcomes it.

Each time Paha Sapa blurs out of his semiconscious, unhearing state, wobbling in the accursed leather wedge of a saddle, the old Crow, Curly, is talking at him. This old man keeps telling him how he, Curly, saved Paha Sapa's life by knocking him down before the Fat Takers' bluecoats shot him just out of meanness and misery — they have been lost and separated from their main detachment for four days now, terrified because Crazy Horse is said to be on the warpath nearby — and how he, Curly, the scout, told the *wasichus* that the almost-naked boy who had startled all of them by crawling up out of the mud and river was a Crow boy, probably a good scout but a little stupid, a little deaf and dumb and retarded, but it was worth keeping him alive anyway and giving the slowest horse, the one that had belonged to Corporal Dunbar before he was killed, to little Billy.

Billy?

Curly... When did he tell Paha Sapa his name? He cannot remember. Curly told the *wasichu* bluecoats that the near-naked and mud-covered boy's name was *Bilé*, which evidently is Crow for "water." The soldiers laughed, called Paha Sapa Billy, and gave him the dead corporal's old, scabbed, slow horse.

Paha Sapa, when he is conscious enough to form a thought, just wishes the stupid old man *psaloka kagi wicasa Absaroka* sonofabitch would just shut the fuck up. The words hurt Paha Sapa's head, which already feels as if he is spilling out his brains. Sometime later in that rainy, gray, miserable day, he realizes that he has been shot by the other Crows, the wild Crows, and there is a filthy bandage wrapped around his upper arm. The bullet wound throbs. His head is going to kill him.

He has lost the *Ptehinčala Huhu Canunpa*.

Curly. Paha Sapa remembers through his gloom and pain and blurred one-eyed vision and through memories not his own that *Tashunke-Witke*, Crazy Horse, had been called Curly Hair and then just Curly when he was young, before his father, Crazy Horse, gave his own name to his son.

But this garrulous old *psaloka* Crow looks nothing like the Crazy Horse Paha Sapa has seen several times this summer. The Lakota Crazy Horse–Curly is blade-nosed, scarred, thin-faced.... This old Crow's face is pocked with smallpox scars but otherwise unscarred by battle and is as round as the moon.

But he won't shut up with his continuous babble of bad Lakota mixed with lisping girl-man vocabulary. Maybe, Paha Sapa thinks through his pain, this old Crow is the kind of *winkte* who likes to fuck boys. Instinctively, reflexively, Paha Sapa gropes for the long knife at his belt.

It is gone. As is his belt. His breechclout is now held up by a piece of rope given to Curly by one of the soldiers. Paha Sapa's feet are bare in the idiot stirrups.

If this Curly tries to fuck him, Paha Sapa decides, he will gouge out the old army scout's eyes with his thumbs and chew off his ears. *But,* his bruised and mourning mind insists, somehow speaking in the *wasichu* babble voice of the ghost he swallowed less than two months earlier, *what if* all *the* wasichu *cavalry try to fuck him at once?*

Paha Sapa once heard from Limps-a-Lot that *Tatonka Iyotake* Sitting Bull had said that it is possible for a real *wičasa wakan* to will himself to die... to will his own heart to stop.

Paha Sapa concentrates on that now, through his pain and absurd saddle-bouncing, but fails. Of course he cannot do it. He is not *wičasa wakan* and now never will be.

He is nothing at all.

Not even a captured warrior. Just a boy who has lost his tribe's *Ptehinčala Huhu Canunpa* and who should be dead but has failed even at that simple act.

Curly keeps talking all through the long, raining, bouncing, ass-sore, head-exploding, arm-aching, endless afternoon.

This detachment of *wasichu* cavalry was part of General Crook's force of combined infantry and Fifth, Second, and Third Cavalry troopers that had broken off from General Terry's column to head east to cut off the Sioux and Cheyenne who had scattered after Custer's death on the Greasy Grass. Crook, champing at the bit (as Curly put it), had left his supply wagons behind weeks ago, taking along a mob of Shoshone scouts and a handful of Crow scouts such as Curly and his friends Three Weevils, Drinks from a Hoofprint, and Cuts Noses Off Frequently. Paha Sapa heard that a famous *wasichu*, a certain Buffalo Bill Cody, had returned from his Wild West Show back east to lead Crook's column, but he wasn't with this bunch.

The column was soon starving, unable to live off the land. They'd eaten all their packhorses, then shot and eaten many of their extra riding horses, and left hundreds of others behind. All a treasure to Crazy Horse and the other "hostiles" who are evidently trailing the cavalry that is supposed to be chasing them. Through his headache, Paha Sapa slowly understands why those Crow were on the warpath after him. The Great Plains north and east of the Black Hills have turned into an everyone-kills-everyone zone.

Five days earlier, when this full force tried to plod across the hills of mud that had been the Badlands, Crook sent this detachment of sixty-some men swinging south and east with the orders to scout for hostile braves and then meet up with Crook's main column near the headwaters of the south fork of Grand River... near two landmarks called Slim

Buttes. This detachment, as hungry as the main column despite their swing south and east to the Black Hills and Bear Butte area where game was always plentiful, is at least three days late for that rendezvous.

Despite the pain, Paha Sapa is beginning to focus on the situation when the bouncing, wet-wool-reeking *wasichus* reach Slim Buttes, his own destination, late that afternoon.

The Crow scouts are sent in ahead, and Curly gestures angrily for "Bilé" on his slow horse to keep up. Paha Sapa is eager to get there and he kicks the lazy nag as hard as he can with his bare heels.

The four Crows and one Lakota boy ride into the familiar valley beneath the low, wooded hills, and Paha Sapa sees at once that there has been a battle. No…not a battle…a massacre.

Most of the tipis have been burned, but the few still standing show long knife slits where women, old men, children, and even terrified warriors cut their way out of the backs of the lodges in their panic. The entire valley stinks of ashes and human and horse shit, but much worse than that smell is the overwhelming stink of death.

The four Crow ride on. Paha Sapa slides off his horse at the first sign of familiar tipis and faces.

The only thing that gives him hope is that the few intact tipis here — or shreds of tipis — sport designs that look more like old Iron Plume's *tiyospaye* rather than Angry Badger's village. Many of the bodies here are burnt — looking too small ever to have been human beings of any age or size — but some are mutilated but otherwise intact, bloated and blackened by at least three days of late-summer sunlight and heat. Insects cover them. Animals and dogs — perhaps the dogs of this very *tiyospaye* — have been busy at them.

But some are still identifiable.

Paha Sapa sees Angry Badger himself, the little fat warrior's corpse bloated to three times its normal size, lying on his back near the stream. His arms are raised as if in preparation to box. Paha Sapa somehow knows the gesture is only from a tightening of the muscles and tendons so visible where the dogs and coyotes and buzzards have been feasting. The bones of both forearms gleam white in the rainy gloom.

Farther on, where Limps-a-Lot usually set his lodge, Paha Sapa finds the blackened and knife-carved corpse of Three Buffalo Woman.

There is no doubt it is her, even though the *wasichus* cut off her large breasts. While most of her kind face is gone, he can still see the unhealed scars on her forearms and thighs where she cut strips of her own flesh to place in his *wasmuha* rattle for Paha Sapa's *hanbleceya* only days ago.

Centuries ago.

Thirty feet away is another woman's corpse with one leg and both arms missing, carried away, and the swollen, putrid face chewed off to the skull, eyes long taken, but her black hair, although pounded into the mud by the constant heavy rain, is still intact. It is Raven. Limps-a-Lot's younger wife. Where Raven's arms would have been is what is left of what was once an infant. Not hers, Paha Sapa knows. Possibly Loud Voice Hawk's new baby by the selfish old *wicasa wakan's* youngest wife, Still Sleeps. Paha Sapa can imagine Raven taking the child and attempting to save it, even during the madness of a full cavalry charge.

A few paces farther on, closer to the cottonwood trees, he finds an unburned corpse, facedown, face gone, whose bloated but somehow still-withered arms show the faded tattoos that Loud Voice Hawk was so proud of.

It looks as if everyone was killed here as Crook's cavalry charged through, burning and shooting and chasing down warriors and women and children alike. The entire valley is churned up with the hoofprints of hundreds of cavalry horses and hundreds of ponies.

Beyond this point, all the tipis have been burned, all the bodies reduced to blackened bird bones and charred flake-flesh. One of them might be, must be, Limps-a-Lot. He would not flee and leave his wives behind. Or his friends.

The four Crow scouts come back as Paha Sapa is attempting to mount the hard-leather-saddled horse they gave him. Curly is holding a repeating rifle, stock against his thigh as he reins up. His pony is mud splattered from hoof to hindquarters. Even the oversized pony's mane is matted and clotted with mud. Beyond him, the full detachment of cavalry has filled the valley and moved on along the ridge to the southeast.

— *Thinking of running, Bilé?*

Paha Sapa has *not* thought of running and now he wonders why. As if reading his aching mind, the old Crow laughs and says something in guttural Absaroke to the other three Crow scouts. They laugh. Curly spits and speaks again in his effeminate almost-Lakota.

—*It looks like General Crook and about a hundred and fifty cavalry from their main attachment did all this and finished their business with this village just a little ways beyond—there are more Sioux women's and children's bodies in the ravine just over that rise—and then the whole Fifth Infantry column arrived and bivouacked on a rise about a mile from here...oh...I'd say about three days ago, based on the state of the shit. But then the tracks show that about five hundred warriors arrived in a hurry from the south, your Sioux and Cheyenne both, most likely, based on the few corpses we found—the whole bunch almost certainly led by that bastard Crazy Horse—and while Crook's cavalry must have outnumbered the hostiles at least four to one, that crazy bastard Crazy Horse attacked... the signs are clear on that... and then fell back to repel Crook's counterattack. It looks like the tracks of the running fight continue on down the ridge for a couple of miles. Captain Shit-for-Brains here is pressing on to close up with Crook's main column, but we're sure that Crazy Horse is still out there somewhere, ready to pounce. Here, you may need this, Bilé.*

The old Crow tosses Paha Sapa a long-barreled Colt revolver. The thing is heavier than Paha Sapa could have imagined, and just catching it makes his head and arm throb worse and almost pulls him off the scabbed horse. He straightens.

Curly is saying—

—*I don't think Crook's people have any supplies left and they didn't have time to hunt before Crazy Horse's bucks attacked, so even if we catch up to them they won't have any food either and we...what the* fuck *are you doing, Bilé?*

Paha Sapa is lifting the heavy revolver, holding it steady in both hands. He aims it at Curly's fat, smug Crow face and pulls the heavy trigger three times.

The gun does not fire.

All four of the Crow scouts laugh until they're ready to fall off their muddy ponies.

Curly digs in his vest and brings out his fist, opens it. Half a dozen cartridges gleam ever so slightly in the dying gray light. Rain beads on brass.

—*When you prove yourself, Bilé—or when Crazy Horse has us surrounded and we decide to shoot ourselves rather than become his captives—then you can have these.*

The four Crows surround him, their Winchester rifles cocked on their hips or thighs, bandoliers across their scarred chests, pistols in their broad belts, and Paha Sapa's slow horse labors and wheezes to keep up as they follow the main column southwest out of the valley and along the hoof-trampled ridge.

———

THEY MEET UP WITH GENERAL CROOK and many hundreds of other men (Curly tells Paha Sapa that there are two thousand men in the main body), and do what they call "bivouacking"—since the *wasichus* are afraid to set up a real camp because of the presence of Crazy Horse and his warriors—which means hunkering down in the pouring rain with nothing but mud underneath them and their ponchos or rain gear over their heads, eating what little hardtack they have left (Curly gives Paha Sapa two bites), and trying to sleep while every fourth man takes turns holding the horses.

Paha Sapa now understands the word *infantry*, which Curly has used several times, not even attempting to put it into the Lakota language. Most of Crook's men are foot soldiers. No wonder, he thinks, they were so willing to eat horses.

Eventually the grumbling and idle chatter and cursing and farting die down until there is only the sound of the heavy rain on two thousand and more slickers, the nicker of horses spooked by the *wasichus'* stink of fear, and then the snoring. Curly and his three Crow scouts fall asleep quickly, lying in the mud with their heads on wads of wet wool—their horses still saddled and held by one of the *wasichu* troopers ordered to hold the reins through the darkness and downpour. But although Paha Sapa is more tired than he's ever been in his life, he does not even try to sleep.

He has to think.

Curly continued babbling at him right up to the second he started snoring loudly. Paha Sapa's head aches almost as much from the new information he's received in the past ten hours as from the rifle stock blow to his skull.

It seems that there are different tribes of *wasichus*. For some reason, young Paha Sapa, in his eleven summers, has never considered such a thing, and none of the wise men in his life, including Limps-a-Lot, has ever mentioned it. But, through Curly's effeminate gabbling, Paha Sapa knows it now and he thinks about this as he looks around on the hill-top at the hundreds upon hundreds of lumpish figures huddled under tarps and soaked blankets in the continuing rain.

Different tribes and different languages, according to Curly, al-though the tribe that speaks what Paha Sapa hears as "the In Glass lan-guage" seem to be in control, the way Sitting Bull and the Lakota were over the Cheyenne at the Greasy Grass. But there are also Fat Takers here in blue coats who come from tribes named (and who speak and think in) Ire Itch, Jure Man, Dutch, Pole Acky, Sweee 'D, Eye Talyun, and even a tribe called Niggers.

Paha Sapa saw these men from the Niggers tribe when the detach-ment joined up with General Crook's main body this evening, and when he saw the soldiers with brown and even black skin, with their nappy hair, he was reminded of the black-*Wasicun* scout named Teat whom Sitting Bull called friend. And he remembers that despite Sit-ting Bull's claim of protection for the wounded and slowly dying Teat at the Greasy Grass, back in the Moon of Ripening Cherries only two moons ago, the Hunkpapa woman called Eagle Robe shot and killed the black white man.

But Teat was respected in Lakota villages and, Paha Sapa presumes, as a scout for Long Hair and the Fat Takers. This makes it doubly hard to understand why he just saw some of the other *wasichu* cavalry and walking soldiers here berating and insulting the few buffalo soldiers he saw here from the tribe of Nigger. Certainly anyone with such black skin and hair that so very much resembles the kinky, tightly curled hair of the sacred *tatanka* buffalo bull itself must be considered *wakan*, holy, even by these Fat Taker savages. Do they not see the strange as part of Mystery and therefore sacred? Are the Fat Takers so ignorant of the universe that they don't see blackness itself — *sapa* — as a harbinger of holiness, as in the *paha sapa* to their south as they huddle here in the night rain?

Paha Sapa's head hurts.

But he does not allow sleep to come. Rather, he lets down some of the barriers he's kept up for two weeks now in his attempt to keep the flood wash of *Tashunke-Witke's* life memories separate from his own few years of memories.

Crazy Horse's violent thoughts, emotions, and memories threatened to overwhelm the boy and threaten to do so now. But he needs to look there. And something about the injury to his head and arm—or perhaps something left over from the terrible Vision he has had of the *wasichu* Stone Heads and Giants emerging from the Black Hills—has made it easier for him to sort through the mass and mess and morass of *Tashunke-Witke's* life thoughts, back to his youngest years, forward less than a year now, to five September, the Moon of the Brown Leaves, next year, when Crazy Horse will be killed while trying to surrender to this same General Crook at the Red Cloud Agency.

Somehow, Paha Sapa thinks, somewhere in this flood wash of dark thoughts and hatred and triumphs that made up the confused thoughts and future-memories of Crazy Horse at the time the war chief touched him, somewhere there is an answer to Paha Sapa's current dilemma.

Allowing Crazy Horse's memories to wash over him like this, even as the pounding rain does in the night, is painful. Paha Sapa leans against the wagon wheel he propped himself up against and vomits up the little bit of hardtack that Curly gave him. Now his belly is so empty, Paha Sapa thinks, that he can feel his belly button scraping against his spine.

First there are all the faces and names to glance at and thrust aside, the way a man elbows his way through a crowd: other *akicita* leaders like Little Big Man and Kicking Bear and He Dog. His father, called Worm now—Paha Sapa thinks of Limps-a-Lot's solid horse, dead from the Crows' arrows and bullets, another failure of his—and leaders Crazy Horse knew, only some of whom the boy knows, such as Man Afraid of His Horse and Red Cloud himself and Red Dog and Lone Bear and High Backbone.

That last name triggers other names associated with loss in Crazy Horse's jumbled memory—Rattle Blanket Woman and Lone Bear and Young Little Hawk and, above all others, They Are Afraid of Her.

Paha Sapa weeps silently, his tears mixing with and being swept away by the rain, but the weeping is not for his own loss, not for the terrible Vision or for the certain death of Three Buffalo Woman and Raven and Loud Voice Hawk and Angry Badger and the other corpses he has identified this day, or for the almost-certain loss of his beloved *tunkašila,* Limps-a-Lot, but for all those like They Are Afraid of Her whom Crazy Horse has lost to death.

Paha Sapa sees, not for the first time, that it is hard being a man.

Paha Sapa shakes his head to rid his mind of memories of rape and lust, of grown-man fury and of knife blades opening up bellies and cutting throats. He does not linger on Crazy Horse's smug memories of himself counting coup or riding, arms out, across firing lines of *wasichu* cavalry and infantry.

But it is in the battles that Paha Sapa now searches *Tashunke-Witke's* great grab heap of emotion-charged memories.

Paha Sapa searches for his own death in the coming hours and days, for Crazy Horse's memory of killing the boy who angered him so back in the village just weeks before. Not finding that, he searches Crazy Horse's memory of fighting the Fat Takers—so many fights, so much screaming of *Hokahey!* and of leading other warriors toward firing rifles and bluecoats—until he finally finds some memories of Crazy Horse and his men ambushing cavalry in the hills that must be east and a little north of here, of blue-coated *wasichus* falling that may well be Crook's cavalry.... One of the dead and falling bluecoats in Crazy Horse's memory may well be Paha Sapa himself.

In the morning, they rise before the gray dawn—everyone coughing and cold and cursing and shaking soaked blankets or ponchos and tarps—and while some brew up coffee and some troopers still have a few biscuits, Curly and the three Crow scouts merely chew on more cold hardtack. They offer none to Paha Sapa, and the boy realizes that they are going to starve him to death.

He feels the clumsy weight of the Colt revolver in his belt and prays to the Six Grandfathers for cartridges...but he knows in his heart that the Grandfathers are no longer listening to him. Perhaps they have deafened themselves to the prayers of all the Natural Free Human Beings.

—*Curly, I know exactly where Crazy Horse and his men are.*

The ugly old Crow repeats this to the other three scouts in his ugly Crow language, and all four men laugh. Curly spits into the mud. He is drying off his rifle with a long red cloth he has somehow managed to keep dry through the liquid night.

—You talk shit at us, Bilé... O boy made of mud and water.

—I don't. I know just where Crazy Horse is hiding with his four hundred men. It is less than three hours' ride on horseback from here.

The old Crow does not translate this to his fellows but just stares at Paha Sapa with those black, bulging dead-man's eyes of his.

—How could you know?

—I've seen him there. I've been with him *there. Everyone in our band knows that this is the-place-where-*Tashunke-Witke-*kills-his-enemies-from-ambush. Crow, Pawnee, Shoshoni, Paiute, Cheyenne, Blackfoot... even* wasichu *when they are stupid enough to follow him there. And you... General Crook... almost has followed him that far.*

—Tell me, Bilé, and I'll have Three Weevils or Cuts Noses Off Frequently give you one of the biscuits they've been hoarding.

Paha Sapa shakes his head. The motion almost makes him vomit or swoon. His skull still aches and his stomach is too empty. But he can speak.

—No. I know exactly where Crazy Horse is this morning. Exactly where he waits for Crook and the rest of you. Crazy Horse and his most important warrior-leaders—He Dog, Brave Wolf, Wears the Deer Bonnet, even Kicking Bear. But I will not tell you. I will tell Crook, through you.

Curly squints at him for a long, long moment. It is still raining. The old Crow's long braided hair is so soaked through that globs of bear grease stand out like yellow curds in it.

Finally Curly throws himself up onto his horse, pulls the reins of Paha Sapa's slow old horse from Drinks from a Hoofprint, and growls in his girly-language:

—Get on the horse. Follow me. If you say the wrong thing to the general or if you are wrong about where Crazy Horse is hiding, I'll cut your throat, scalp you, and cut your balls off myself. All while you watch, Water Boy.

PAHA SAPA has never paid much attention to individual *wasichus;* except for the black ones, they all sort of blur together in his vision and memory. In truth, the majority of *Wasicun* he has seen have been dead.

But General George Crook—he learns the full name only much later, as well as the nickname the Apaches had for him, Gray Fox—is somewhat more memorable than the corpses. The *wasichu* war chief has taken off his broad-brimmed hat to wring it out as lesser men prepare his mount for the day's riding, and Paha Sapa sees a tall man with short hair that's grown erratically into clumps on the narrow head. His face has been deeply tanned in his months in the sun pursuing Paha Sapa's people, but the forehead is startlingly white. Beneath the jug ears begin side-whiskers that soon leap off the man's face and down onto his shoulders, crawling almost to his chest. The general doesn't have a real beard, just those wild side-whiskers that have spilled down onto his neck and crept back to meet under that weak excuse for a chin. Crook's mustache is just an afterthought, a meek little bridge between two great statements of untended hair.

Crook's tiny eyes squint at his Crow scout as Curly, shuffling in abasement and apparent embarrassment, conveys Paha Sapa's statement that he knows where Crazy Horse is hiding this very minute.

The watery little eyes fix on Paha Sapa for a moment, and the *Wasicun* says something to Curly.

The Crow's Lakota is worse than ever as he mumbles to Paha Sapa.

—*The general wants to know what you want. Why you would tell him this. What do you want in exchange?*

Paha Sapa is so exhausted and starved that he looks at the *Wasicun* without fear. Just a few days ago—an eternity ago—he, Paha Sapa, stood in the hands of one of the Six Grandfathers and spoke to *them*. How can he fear a mere *Wasicun* general?

He tells the truth.

—*I don't want anything. I just want to let you know where Crazy Horse is waiting for you.*

Well, it is almost the truth. Paha Sapa *does* want something for himself—he wants to die.

He's thought about the ways. Limps-a-Lot instilled a great revulsion in the boy for the very idea of taking one's own life. Of course, Paha Sapa could just try to flee on his slow horse and Curly or one of the other Crows or perhaps a *wasichu* trooper would do him the service of shooting him dead. But this does not appeal to Paha Sapa. Not after the Vision of the Great Stone Heads.

Paha Sapa knows that he will die if he can escape and present himself to Crazy Horse somewhere about ten miles to the northeast—from the fragments of *Tashunke-Witke's* future memories, Paha Sapa is almost certain where the *heyoka* war chief and his warriors are waiting—but Paha Sapa does not want to die alone that way either.

But, *if* he tells this Crook the truth about where Crazy Horse is waiting, just beyond the citadel place where Lakota war parties looking for Crows so often camp, ten miles or so from here, Paha Sapa has no doubt that this General Crook and his two thousand men will attack Crazy Horse and his four hundred warriors. After all, isn't this the reason Crook and all these men have marched and ridden more than four hundred miles through summer heat and this odd, endless summer rain—to find and punish and kill Crazy Horse and the Sioux and Cheyenne who killed Custer?

And then, in that attack, Paha Sapa will ride near the front of the attack, with no weapons, slow horse and all. And then he will be cut down by Crazy Horse's men's bullets, even as Crook cuts down Crazy Horse and his followers.

It is a good day to die.

The general is speaking. Curly has said something. Paha Sapa looks at the old man inquisitively.

— *Gray Fox says*— *Where? Tell us!*

Paha Sapa tells them exactly where his memories of Crazy Horse's memories from what is still Paha Sapa's future tell him the warrior and his men are waiting. Just beyond the good camping place, less than ten miles to the northeast. Where the wooded hills begin, not far from the citadel camping place. Right where the rippled valleys begin running nothwest toward the Little Missouri River and northeast toward the Grand River.

Curly translates all this. General Crook does not call for a map or talk to any of his aides. The tall man continues squinting down at Paha Sapa.

Finally, as if making a decision, the *wasichu* warrior chief shouts two words in the In Glass language—

— *Mount up!*

Y EARS AND DECADES LATER, Paha Sapa will consider telling the story of these days and hours to his wife, Rain, or to his son, Robert. He never does, of course. He never mentions a word of any of it.

But he will compose some of the chaos of those days into a sort of sequence, and had he spoken of such personal things that he never would have spoken of, putting himself into the third person as was his mental habit, the explanation would have gone something like this:

Paha Sapa's eagerness to die that day actually did not have enough energy in it to be called "eagerness." He was so tired, so hollow, so beaten, so lost, that he wanted others to take care of it for him.

Decades later, he would hear others—whites and even many Indians from different tribes—say that Crazy Horse on his deathbed (and before that on the battlefield at Greasy Grass, where he had ridden against Custer) had shouted *"Hokahey!"* which, they said, meant "It is a good day to die!"

Bullshit, thought Paha Sapa when he finally heard this (showing off some of his new In Glass *wasichu* vocabulary). *Hokahey!* in a battle meant "Follow me!" and could also mean "Line up!" as in a Sun Dance Ceremony, or, with someone dying, could mean "Stand solid, stand fast—there is more to follow."

It did *not* mean "It is a good day to die," although this was said often enough by Lakota warriors. Having opened his mind to Crazy Horse's memories, he had far too many incidents of the warrior saying that to his men or hearing someone else say it. But in Lakota that phrase would have been something like *Anpetu waste' kile mi!*—and Paha Sapa did not have the energy to cry such a thing that day anyway.

He had failed at his *hanbleceya,* receiving the worst Vision imaginable and not even succeeding in taking it to his *tunkasila* and the other holy men and warriors of his village before they were killed. He had lost his people's *Ptehincala Huhu Canunpa.*

He had lost his people's *Ptehincala Huhu Canunpa.*

He wanted to die that day and if he could trick this strange-whiskered General Crook and all his starving *washichus* and Shoshoni and Crow scouts into dying with him by leading them into an ambush of Crazy Horse's, so much the better.

Could the future be changed? Could Paha Sapa's visions-forward be false...or at least be changed by someone, by him, who saw them ahead of time?

If so, he hoped that Crazy Horse would also die this day, in battle, shot down by one of Crook's two thousand soldiers or cavalry rather than by being bayoneted or shot twelve months hence — Crazy Horse's future memories were confused — while in the disgraceful process of *surrendering* to this same small-eyed, large-whiskered *wasichu* general at the Red Cloud Agency.

But the day dragged on much longer and more slowly than Paha Sapa could have imagined.

Two hours' or three hours' ride meant eight hours and more marching for these starved, exhausted foot soldiers. Crook sent cavalry ahead, of course, including two of the Crow scouts — Curly and Drinks from a Hoofprint stayed behind to guard *him* — but even though they marched at the rainy September dawn, the main body didn't come up to the natural citadel and amphitheater that Paha Sapa had in mind until midafternoon. Once there, Crook ordered a camp to be set up on the citadel — a natural outcropping with steeper, pine-topped crags on three sides. They started up cooking fires and buried one of the wounded who'd died in the jolting ambulance wagon that day.

Paha Sapa was half sleeping in the saddle, too exhausted even to climb down from his slow horse, when there came the rifle crack of Winchesters.

Crazy Horse had arrived.

Later, Paha Sapa understood that the war chief had mustered about five hundred of the Cheyenne and Lakota who'd been camping nearby and who had been roused by word of Crook's cavalry's attacks on the Minneconjou, Sans Arcs, and Hunkpapa villages — mostly against Iron Plume's *tiyospaye* — near Slim Buttes. Crazy Horse had waited in ambush right where Paha Sapa had "remembered" him being — just a mile or two beyond this citadel crag — but upon hearing that all of Crook's army had been brought up, delivered to him, Crazy Horse attacked, even with the odds more than four to one against him.

When he'd assembled his men, Paha Sapa realized, Crazy Horse had thought he'd be going into battle against only the 155 or so men under Captain Mills's detachment — the *wasichu* cavalry who'd attacked and burned the Slim Buttes villages, including Angry Badger's and Limps-a-Lot's *tiyospaye*. But now *Tashunke-Witke* found himself confronted by Crook's entire pursuing army. The *heyoka* attacked anyway.

Crazy Horse had beaten and humiliated General Crook on the

Rosebud and he tried the same strategy again here—a general charge to release Crook's Indian captives and to stampede the horses and captured ponies.

This time it did not work.

Crook committed his whole force. With the cavalry protecting his exposed eastern flank, the general sent his infantry and hundreds of dismounted cavalry directly at the wooded hills from where Crazy Horse's men were laying down a steady volley of fire.

Paha Sapa and Curly rode forward into the smoke and confusion. This was worse than Greasy Grass, Paha Sapa thought as he watched *wasichus* and Indians running and falling and writhing and screaming. It was certainly worse for Crazy Horse.

The range and accuracy of the infantry's long rifles was what made the difference—what made this outcome so very different from Custer's fate at Greasy Grass. The far right of Crazy Horse's line was the first to give way. Paha Sapa and Curly rode with the few cavalry and scouts advancing with the *wasichu* as they took the string of hilltops, wreathed as they were with clouds of acrid-smelling gunsmoke. The rain had relented for a few hours, but the air was so hot and humid and thick that Paha Sapa's new blue coat was plastered to his bare skin. The gunsmoke stung his one working eye.

He actually saw Crazy Horse then—riding his white horse, naked except for his breechclout and single white feather, waving his rifle in the air and commanding his warriors to fall back in order.

But as they fell back, Crook's infantry continued advancing, the *wasichu* cavalry lunging and harassing Crazy Horse's depleted band of warriors from both sides and the rear. For what seemed a long time that afternoon, the battle turned into a protracted, running duel with a no-man's-land of bullets and arrows filling a five-hundred-yard gap between the lunging, firing, swearing mobs of red man and white.

Paha Sapa and Curly had ridden to the left of the main advance just as there came a wild, brave Lakota charge at the Third Cavalry position there. The Indians—many on foot, those on horseback in clumps and disordered groups—charged forward, firing their own repeater rifles, probing for a weak spot in the Third Cavalry's dismounted defensive positions. Paha Sapa again was sure that it was Crazy Horse he saw riding back and forth through the thick smoke, urging on the attack, turning back Lakota who had turned to flee, always in the thick of the fiercest action.

Paha Sapa used his bare heels to kick his slow horse into some sort of advance—an awkward, reluctant, clumsy canter—and the boy rode out into the killing zone between the charging Lakota and the firing Third Cavalry. He rode straight toward the half-seen Crazy Horse on the horizon. Paha Sapa dimly remembered the unloaded Colt revolver in his belt and now he drew the useless weapon and waved it in the air, the better to get the attention of the rifle- and pistol-firing Natural Free Human Beings ahead of him.

The air was so thick with bullets that he could hear and feel them buzzing around him. *It's true what the warriors said around the village fire,* he thought idiotically. *Bullets sound like bees in the middle of a real battle.*

Paha Sapa was content. His only regret was that he had never composed his Death Song. But, he realized, he did not deserve a Death Song.

He had lost Limps-a-Lot's and his people's *Ptehinčala Huhu Canunpa.*

A bullet ripped through his sodden blue soldier coat under his arm but did not touch his skin. Another bullet plowed a shallow furrow in his upper thigh. A bullet struck the horn of the saddle, making his slow horse stagger and almost knocking Paha Sapa off the horse. The boy was certain, based on the sudden stab of pain, that a Lakota warrior had shot his balls off, but he stood in the stirrups and looked down, suddenly not so sanguine, and saw no blood. He rode on, waving his pistol and screaming at his fellow Lakota to kill him.

Another bullet creased his skull just above the swollen lump where Curly had clubbed him the previous morning. It did not knock Paha Sapa out this time, and he blinked away the new blood and kicked at the ribs of the slow, lazy, but terrified horse.

A bullet tore away part of his sleeve and the filthy bandage covering his earlier bullet wound from the Crows but did not touch him. Paha Sapa kept hearing buzzing, hissing noises and feeling his oversized blue coat leap up as if there were a strong breeze, but other than the new scratches on his brow and upper leg, nothing touched him.

Paha Sapa would think of this hour fourteen years later when the Paiute prophet Wovoka promised all those who wore the Ghost Dance

Shirt that bullets would not and could not touch them. Paha Sapa was wearing a flea-infested, sweat-and-wet-wool-stinking oversized dead *wasichu* soldier's blue coat that day, but bullets would not and could not touch him.

Crazy Horse and his surviving warriors were falling back. Crook's infantry was cheering and charging and firing as they went, and the Third Cavalry was sweeping in from the left, shooting the Lakota wounded and stragglers alike, taking no prisoners.

Paha Sapa's scabbed, slow horse would move no farther. At first Paha Sapa thought it had been shot—how could anything that large not have been shot in that air so filled with flying lead?—but the nag was simply being stubborn in its terror and had stopped to graze there in the middle of the killing field.

Paha Sapa kicked at the horse's ribs and sawed and tugged at the reins until the stupid beast turned around and began plodding back toward the line of firing *wasichu* infantry and dismounted cavalry that had not yet charged. Paha Sapa was still brandishing his unloaded pistol, now hoping and expecting Crook's soldiers to kill him.

Instead, the *wasichu* soldiers raised their rifles and cheered. And then they came at Paha Sapa and the retreating Lakota, some running, some of the cavalry trying to mount their panicked horses, with horses and would-be riders whirling in confusion, all their hunger forgotten in their sudden bloodlust to get at the retreating Lakotas.

Paha Sapa slumped in his bullet-shattered saddle and let the slow horse plod him back behind the lines. Finally the nag stopped to graze again, and Paha Sapa slid out of the saddle and landed on his ass, too weak and drained to stand.

Soldiers milled around him. Suddenly Curly was there, face distorted as he jumped off his pony. The old Crow stood over Paha Sapa seated there in the mud, his forearms on his bare knees, and the scout raised and cocked his own Colt revolver.

—*Lakota Water Boy,* Bilé, *Three Weevils and Cuts Noses Off Frequently are dead, killed in this ambush* you *led us into.*

Paha Sapa looked up then. And smiled.

—*Good. I hope their corpses are already filled with maggots and that their spirits stay in the mud forever.*

Curly grunted and aimed his big pistol at Paha Sapa's face.

This way, then, O Six Grandfathers? All right. I am sorry I did not compose my Song.

Horses slid to a stop, sending mud flying over Paha Sapa and the old Crow scout. It was General Crook, beaming through his idiot's whiskers, and a cluster of officers and the guidon carrier. The general was babbling In Glass *wasichu* talk at Curly before his horse was to a full stop—no one seemed to notice the aimed pistol.

Curly's round, stupid face gaped up at the *wasichu* war leader for a full minute before the Crow lowered the pistol and eventually lowered the cocked hammer gently down.

Then Crook and his men were gone.

Curly laughed the laugh of the not quite sane. He spat in the mud and looked at the pistol in his hand.

—*Gray Fox says that he knows you, Billy with the Slow Horse, are really Lakota, not Crow, but he welcomes you to be his scout for as long as he, Crook, Gray Fox, commands soldiers and cavalry troopers. He says your courage...*

Curly's face contorted as if the Crow were going to vomit, but he only spat again.

—*...he says he will never forget your courage today and only hopes his other scouts learn from it. Oh...and Gray Fox said to me that you are a skeleton and that if Drinks From a Hoofprint and I don't feed you well and keep you alive, he will hang us both from the first stout tree he finds.*

Curly laughed that insane-man's laugh again. Paha Sapa could only stare at him.

———

THAT NIGHT Paha Sapa slept, in the rain with no blanket or tarp covering him, for eight hours. Before dawn the bugles blew and Paha Sapa looked forward to another battle.

But no...despite the sound of continued shots between Crazy Horse's warriors and a rear guard of cavalry and infantry commanded by Bear Coat, Captain Mills...and despite almost six months of searching for the Lakota warriors, two months of that time without any food except horseflesh, and with the two thousand men dedicated to revenge after Custer's death...Crook was leaving the battlefield.

They'd crossed a wagon trail used by miners headed for the Black Hills, and now Crook put 1,700 of his starving men on that trail. Crazy Horse and his warriors pursued, sniping from the rear and sides day after day, making feints at night, but Crook refused battle.

Except for some two hundred Indian ponies and five thousand pounds of meat they'd stolen in the Indian camps they'd overrun at Slim Buttes, the long-wanted and long-awaited fight with Crazy Horse had shown no victory for Crook and his men. They'd come all the way from the center of Wyoming Territory, having left Fort Fetterman there on March 1 in a heavy snowstorm, and now, after all these months and miles...Crook kept refusing battle with Crazy Horse and the hostiles as the long column of men and horses staggered south into the Black Hills.

Paha Sapa entered his sacred *paha sapa* again with a growing sense of disbelief and disconnection. These muddy wagon roads and the stinking mining town of Deadwood near where Crook's depleted army finally came to a halt and camped had nothing to do with the Black Hills of Paha Sapa's world. The hairy *wasichus* here were tearing into the heart of the living hills to find their gold, just as Paha Sapa's Vision had shown him.

General Crook was summoned off to Fort Laramie for a meeting with someone named General Sheridan.

Curly and the other scouts now could beat Paha Sapa as much as they wanted, but they were still afraid to kill him.

Paha Sapa, on the other hand, was free to run away...leave his stupid slow horse and infected blue coat, steal a real horse, and simply ride back out onto the Great Plains to find his people. He could have avoided Crazy Horse's warriors and swung far west and then north to the white reaches of Grandmother's Country to try to find Sitting Bull and other survivors he might know up there.

He did not do that. He could not do that. He was without any people, without any family, without any *tiyospaye* of his own.

He had led Crook's army to Crazy Horse, and many Natural Free Human Being warriors had died that day.

He had lost the *Ptehinčala Huhu Canunpa*.

When the survivors of the Starvation March lined up again and rode and marched behind Crook to Fort Robinson south of the Black Hills toward the Nebraska River, Paha Sapa—Billy Slow Horse—went with them.

He was beginning to learn *wasichu* English—not In Glass—and the first word he learned from the troopers was useful, both noun and verb—*fuck*. Eventually that winter they trusted him with a knife, and he mastered the phrase *"If you try it, I'll cut your balls off."*

It was a long winter and spring and summer for Paha Sapa, and learning English meant that he now understood the lusty babblings of Long Hair's ghost in his mind every night. And there was no longer any doubt that the ghost was Long Hair—Custer himself. Paha Sapa did his best to seal off the ghost and to mute the words.

Paha Sapa was no longer with Crook and the Army on September 5 the next year—1877 as the *wasichus* counted years—when Crazy Horse came in to surrender and was bayoneted to death. He, Paha Sapa, had already seen that death too many times; he did not want to see it in person and he knew he could not change it.

That August—in the Moon of the Ripening again, around his birthday and the first anniversary of his Vision—Paha Sapa had left the army and Fort Robinson quietly. No one chased him. Curly had died of appendicitis two months before and no one else paid any attention to the presence or absence of an eleven- or twelve-year-old Indian boy.

Paha Sapa returned to the Black Hills, but not to hunt or camp or worship. He came back to the stinking mining town of Deadwood to find work or to steal.

And there, already in jail after failing at his first attempt to steal and probably facing death by hanging, he met the holy men who dressed in black like ravens or crows with their white collars and who had their absurd tent school on the hill.

And if he had ever told that story to Rain or to Robert, he would have added that while the *wasichus* talked of the Starvation March and of the Battle for Slim Buttes, the Lakota forevermore referred to that battle—that battle where young Paha Sapa had led General Crook straight to Crazy Horse—as *the Fight Where We Lost the Black Hills.*

19

New York City

April 1, 1933

PAHA SAPA IS READING ABOUT ADOLF HITLER IN THE MORNING paper as he comes into the city by train.

In Washington, FDR has been president for less than a month (and according to the majority of South Dakota voters, overwhelmingly Republican, already the outlines of that man in the White House's socialist agenda are becoming clear), and in Germany, Hitler has been Chancellor since January. The problem there, so it appears in this and other recent newspaper articles, is not socialism but the new chancellor's and his party's anti-Semitism. Jews there are protesting, says the *New York Times,* but the Nazis just voted into full power are responding to these protests by having their goons picket at Jewish stores and rough up shoppers who patronize Jewish-owned businesses.

Here in the city Paha Sapa is entering, a series of protest rallies on March 27 — just five days earlier — saw an overflow crowd of 55,000 at Madison Square Garden, where AFL president William Green, US senator Robert F. Wagner, and the popular former New York governor Al Smith all called for an end to the brutal treatment of German Jews. Parallel protest events were held in Chicago, Philadelphia, Cleveland, Boston, and more than a score of other cities.

In response to the weak protests of the German Jews and the loud protests in America, the Nazi propaganda minister — Goebbels — just announced a nationwide one-day boycott by "Aryan Germans" against

Jews in Germany. The *Times* has photographs of SA storm troopers with their signs preparing to block entrance to Jewish-owned businesses in Berlin. Paha Sapa has learned just enough German from the German miners and workers in the Black Hills to read the *Fraktur* script—*"Germans! Defend yourselves! Don't buy from the Jews!"*

Goebbels is quoted in the article as warning the Americans and others that if the protests against the Nazi behavior do not cease immediately, "the boycott will be resumed...until German Jewry has been annihilated."

Paha Sapa sighs and sets the paper on the empty seat next to him. The train is crossing a bridge to Manhattan and all the skyscrapers and other high buildings are painted in the rich, cold light of the April first sunrise. It's technically spring but the air outside is still chilly at night and there is frost on the window.

Paha Sapa wonders if Hitler and these Nazis could be the *wasichu* version of young Crazy Horse and the other *heyokas*—sacred clowns, Dreamers of the Thunder, spirit-possessed servants of the Thunder Beings whose failure to perform their duty meant death by lightning blast. Hasn't he read somewhere that the Nazi SS officers wear twin lightning slashes on their collars or insignia somewhere...? Yes, Lila Kaufmann at the bakery in Rapid City told him that when she was a secretary in the city government in Munich before she and her family fled the country, the typewriters there had a dedicated key showing the double-lightning symbol of the SS. (Paha Sapa has no idea what those letters stand for, but can imagine the art deco straight-lined double-lightning-bolt insignia. Crazy Horse and his *heyoka akicita* "peacekeeper" tribal police pals would have loved wearing such an emblem.)

If Hitler, Goebbels, and the rest of these unfunny clowns really are *wasichu* Thunder Dreamers, that would explain a lot, thinks Paha Sapa, including their obsession with rubbing out all of their real and perceived enemies. The Thunder Beings are sources of great power and staggering amounts of motivating energy for individuals and their tribes, but they are treacherous spirits, dangerous to everyone, even to their chosen Dreamers. The *heyoka* clown-warrior servants of the Thunder Beings are living lightning conductors and can strike their friends as well as enemies and themselves at any second with that terrible random ferocity of lightning.

Paha Sapa knows for a fact, after fifty-seven years of living with Crazy Horse's memories, that *T'ašunka Witko's* melancholy, sense of isolation, and frequent savagery were all manifestations of the Thunder Dreamers' tribal license to terrible excess. The Natural Free Human Beings even have a word—*Kicamnayan*—for that sort of sudden, unpredictable flash of lightning, the frenzied swoop of swallows ahead of a thunderstorm, an otherwise placid horse's sudden, senseless break into a panicked gallop, or the pitiless swoop and drop of the red-tailed hawk on its prey. *Kicamnayan* brought on by the surge of the *Wakinyans'* primal, unquenchable, and frequently violent spirit energies manifested in the frailer forms of mere living instruments as mere shadow of their cosmic rage.

Pity the poor Jews in Germany, thinks Paha Sapa, unless their long-quiet god with a capital G proves an equal to the *Wakinyan* Thunder Beings. Despite his reading and discussions with Doane Robinson—and even with the poor Jesuits in Deadwood—on the subject of Judaism, Paha Sapa has no real idea if the Jews believe in their god possessing them with the full *berserker* killing spirit. But he suspects that Hitler and his group know the joys, terror, and reflected power of that possession by fierce gods all too well.

Paha Sapa sighs. He has trouble sleeping on trains and is very tired after three days and nights sitting up on a series of hard wicker seats. He's glad when the conductor comes through the cars announcing that the next stop will be Grand Central Terminal and the end of the line.

———

PAHA SAPA HAULS HIS BAG the few blocks to the cheap hotel on 42nd Street that Whiskey Art Johnson told him about. The place has his reservation, but the room won't be ready until afternoon, so Paha Sapa takes an apple out of his bag, stores the bag with the clerk, and begins walking south along Park Avenue.

"Her apartment cooperative is only three blocks south of here, at Seventy-one Park Avenue. Will you stop?"

No. We agreed. The appointment is not until four p.m.

"But you'll be going right by her place...."

I'll come back at four. I have things and people of my own to see before then.

"But she might be home *now!* It's almost certain she is. She never goes out anymore, according to Mrs. Elmer. We could just stop, ask the doorman..."

No.

"What if we went the other way, then, up to One Twenty-two East Sixty-sixth Street, to the Cosmopolitan Club, where she used to..."

Silence!

The last is not a request but an absolute command. Paha Sapa has discovered that he can send the ghost back to his sightless, soundless hole any time he chooses.

If his hotel room had been available, Paha Sapa might have considered napping for an hour or two after his days sitting up on the train, rarely even dozing through the nights across the prairie and grain fields of the Midwest, then the dark wooded hills and tunnels of Pennsylvania and beyond, but he realizes a good, bracing walk is better. And it is a good walk.

He does glance at the apartment building at 71 Park Avenue, only three blocks south of his hotel, but does not linger. As such places in a city go, it is an attractive enough building. He feels his own anxiety over the imminent interview—it took almost two years to arrange—and can't even imagine the anxiety of his resident spirit. In truth, he doesn't want to know.

Paha Sapa smiles as he walks briskly down Park Avenue. He thought he was ready for New York City; he was wrong. The buildings, the myriad and maze of streets, the blocking of the early-morning sun, the countless automobiles and ice and delivery wagons, the streetcars and taxis, the constant flow of pedestrians. It's been almost forty years since he was in a city of any real size—Chicago during the 1893 Exposition—and the downtown of that Black City was nothing compared to any part of this metropolis. The effect on the aging and weary Natural Free Human Being—which translates as "rube" or "bumpkin" here—from the Dust Bowl western state is immediate and overwhelming.

At first the scale and pace of everything here are oddly exhilarating, making Paha Sapa almost dizzy on top of his fatigue, but within ten minutes all that scale and pace has become like a heavy pressure on every part of his body. (He thinks of Big Bill Slovak's caisson stories.) Everywhere else he's ever been, he's felt like a person—whether anyone knows his true name or not—but here he's just one of millions, and a pathetic one at that: a very thin and weary-looking Indian with long braids still black but dark circles under his eyes and wrinkles on his face. He catches sight of his quickly marching reflection in shop and restaurant windows—another pressure that he's not used to, this seeing himself constantly—and notes how ill-fitting and out of style his black suit and clumsily knotted dark tie and soft cap are. His rarely worn and highly polished dress shoes squeak with every step and are killing his feet. Smiling ruefully, Paha Sapa realizes that he's dressed for this trip in his going-to-funeral clothes, and that fact becomes more obvious in every reflective surface he passes. He imagines that he smells of sweat, cigar smoke from the train, and mothballs. Paha Sapa does not own a topcoat to go with this baggy old suit, and he has been cold since the train left Rapid City. . . . Spring is coming late this year on the plains and in the heartland.

Even though the sunny morning here in New York City is warming toward the promised low sixties he read about in the newspaper, he wishes he'd worn the thick leather jacket that Robert had left with him in 1917 and that he's worn everywhere except at work for the sixteen autumns, winters, and springs since. That and his comfortable work boots.

He strides down the broad Park Avenue from 42nd Street to Union Square and then follows Fourth Avenue southeast into the Bowery. He's soon south of all the numbered streets and passing through Little Italy, past Saint Patrick's Cathedral, past Hester Street, past Delancey and toward Canal Street, striding through all the teeming and seething immigrant neighborhoods that fed its second generation of laborers and builders to the rest of America. He muses that if he had been born American, rather than Indian, his parents might have lived in these tenements, in these neighborhoods, after coming in through Castle Garden from heaven knows where across the sea. (Doane Robinson once told Paha Sapa that before 1855 there was no processing point in America for immigrants. People moving here simply made a declaration—when they bothered to—to customs officials on the steamships or sailing ships and went on about their business in their new country. Robinson described how at Castle Garden, on an island off the southwest tip of Manhattan—also called Castle Clinton—the state of New York, not the federal government, had processed would-be immigrants until it closed in 1890. The government had taken over then and dealt with the immigration flow at a temporary center on a barge until Ellis Island opened for business in 1900. Since 1924, Doane told him, most would-be immigrants were once again being processed aboard the ships, with Ellis Island being the destination only for those who required hearings or some sort of physical quarantine.)

For some reason, Paha Sapa wishes he had time enough in New York City to visit all of these sites, even though immigration has nothing to do with him. Then he remembers the dead *wasichu* bluecoat soldiers littering the rolling hills above the Greasy Grass, their white and mutilated bodies so shocking against the green and brown grass. The majority of those dead men, he learned in his year as scout with Crook's cavalry out of Fort Robinson, were Irish and German and other immigrants fresh off the boat. The serious recession of 1876 had left signing up with the army an attractive alternative to starving in these very tenement neighborhoods Paha Sapa is walking through. Half of the micks and krauts in Custer's command, Curly told him in his *winkte* broken Lakota and even more broken English, hadn't understood their sergeants' and officers' commands.

There is no comment on this from the ghost sulking inside him.

The distance from Grand Central Terminal to the Brooklyn Bridge is not that long—less than four miles is Paha Sapa's guess—and walking between such high buildings, from shadow to sun and then back to shade again at each intersection, crossing to the west side of the street to get out of the chilly shadow when the buildings are lower, reminds him of canyons he has hiked in Colorado, Utah, Montana, and, to a much lesser extent, in his own Black Hills. But in Paha Sapa's part of the West there are only a few canyons, such as the one the *wasichus* are now calling Spearfish Canyon, deep enough or steep enough to give this echoing, stark-sunlight and then sudden-shade lower-Bowery effect.

The wind has a nip to it despite the growing warmth of the day. Usually Paha Sapa ignores high and low temperatures, but this year the cold has bothered him and this New York chill makes him wish again for a topcoat or Robert's leather motorcycle jacket. The streets are getting too narrow ahead, and he turns right and walks to the southwest along Canal Street back toward Broadway, turning left again onto Centre Street.

He can see City Hall Park ahead and...suddenly...he has arrived.

The Brooklyn Bridge stretches above low buildings and arches out over the East River. The rising sun is still low enough that the two towers and the elevated, arching roadway throw long shadows toward Manhattan, the closer tower—the so-called New York tower—shading the narrow waterfront streets and old warehouses on either side of the broad approach.

"This is what you came for?"

—*Yes. You and your wife were in New York the winter before you died. Weren't the towers finished then?*

"The Brooklyn tower was. The New York tower wasn't quite finished when we left in February. Both of them were a mass of derricks and scaffolds, but grand even so. There were no cables strung yet.... Look at that roadway! Look at those suspension cables! We could never have imagined that the finished bridge would look so grand!"

Paha Sapa says nothing to this. It does look grand. He's seen photographs of the bridge, but nothing could have quite prepared him for the reality. Even on this island of new architectural giants, the Brooklyn Bridge—even seen from the cluttered approach vistas here on the Manhattan side—has a grandeur and power all its own.

Paha Sapa could—but chooses not to—tell his resident ghost about the endless ten-hour workdays down in the dangerous blackness and dust and smoke of the Holy Terror Mine in Keystone and about his mentor Tarkulich "Big Bill" Slovak's constant talk, in that booming whatever-it-was Eastern European accent, the giant's shouts somehow carrying over the rattling of steam drills and the pounding of sledgehammers and the rusty screech and squeal and rumble of the mine carts squeezing past them in the midnight-dark chaos, and about his—Big Bill's—part in building the Brooklyn Bridge.

Having left the "Old Country" just a few steps ahead of the police after killing another teenager in a fight in some city that sounded
to Paha Sapa as if it had no vowels at all in its name, in May of 1870,
the 17-year-old Big Bill Slovak had arrived in New York and immediately hired on as a worker for the Bridge Company that had been
incorporated to build what was then being called the New York and
Brooklyn Bridge.

There were no towers or cables to be seen then. Big Bill admitted
that he had lied through his teeth when he applied—saying that he was
twenty-one years old, saying that he was a skilled worker (his only job
in the Old Country, wherever that was, had been as a herder of goats
for a crippled uncle), and—most important—saying that he had advanced skills as a powderman. (In truth, he had never lit a fuse attached
to anything more powerful than a Roman candle, but there were other
powdermen being hired that hot day in May, and Big Bill knew that he
could learn from them if necessary. It turned out that most of them were
lying about their skills as much as or more than Big Bill was.)

In 1870, as Big Bill said more than a few times down in the stinking black confines of the Holy Terror more than thirty years later, one
had to have some real imagination to see the New York and Brooklyn
Bridge. All that existed when Big Bill went to work was a huge caisson
that had been launched like a ship, floated down the East River to its
position near the Brooklyn shore, and deliberately sunk. That caisson,
filled with compressed air to keep the river out and the men working
inside alive, was going to be the foundation for the huge Brooklyn-side
tower built on it and above it. But first the caisson—and then its near
twin for the New York side—had to be sunk down through the river,
mud, ooze, sand, gravel, and stone until it was on bedrock.

Big Bill loved numbers. (Paha Sapa had often thought that if the
giant blasting expert had stayed in his Old Country and somehow
gotten an education, he might have become a mathematician.) Even
their first year together, Big Bill never tired of shouting the statistics at
his thirty-seven-year-old assistant (the Indian widower working down
there to make money to feed his five-year-old son, who was being
watched days and night shifts by Crazy Maria, Keystone's all-purpose
Mexican woman).

The caisson young Big Bill had worked in under the East River was a giant rectangular box, 168 feet long and 102 feet wide, divided into six separate chambers each 28 feet long by 102 feet wide. Both caissons, Big Bill said often, "were big enough to hold four tennis courts inside," which had amused Paha Sapa as he ate his lunch down there in the stinking gloom of the Holy Terror, since *he* had never seen a tennis court and he was damn sure Big Bill hadn't either.

There was no bottom to the caisson box, of course. The men walked and worked directly on the mud, silt, sewage, boulders, gravel, and bedrock at the bottom of the river. And it was the presence of these boulders around the descending edges of the caisson — the box was built to descend until it could go no farther and then the building of the towers *on it* would begin — that brought in Big Bill's fictional specialty of dynamiting.

The working conditions down in the Brooklyn-side caisson — and later in the New York–side caisson, which went much deeper — were horrific. Stinking mud, constant high temperatures, pressurized air so thick that a man couldn't whistle, literally couldn't force the air out of his body against the pressure, while each man's body and organs were daily assaulted by the constant descent into and climb up out of the high-pressure hole in the river.

Paha Sapa never did quite understand the math and science of the air pressure thing, but he believed Big Bill when the giant talked about the problems the men had with something they all called caisson disease and which others called "the bends." No one could predict whom it would hit or how hard, only that it would affect everyone sooner or later and that a lot of men would die horribly from it.

Colonel Washington Roebling himself, the chief engineer and son of the bridge's designer, John Roebling—who died of tetanus after getting his toes crushed on the site in the first days of work on the bridge—came down with caisson disease, and it ruined his health, turning him into an invalid for the rest of his long life. Big Bill said that the pressure-related disease wasn't so bad during the work in the first caisson, on the Brooklyn side, since that foundation box reached its lowest point at about 44 feet, but the New York caisson had to be sunk to more than 78 feet. The external pressure on the caisson and the corresponding air pressure on the workers inside were incredibly high. Men died of the caisson disease in both boxes, but the New York caisson, Bill said, was the real killer.

Slovak had been struck by the bends scores of times over his years working in the caissons and described the symptoms to Paha Sapa: blinding headaches, constant vomiting, overwhelming weakness, paralysis, tremendous shooting pains in various parts of the body, a feeling like one had been shot in the spine or stabbed in the lungs, and then, in many cases, blindness and death.

The worst cases, including Colonel Roebling when he was struck down after a day and night battling a slow fire in the Brooklyn caisson with all of his many rises and descents during that crisis, were treated with massive amounts of morphine just to relieve the agony until the worker either recovered or died.

Big Bill had had his own cure. However terrible the symptoms, he would drag himself down the stairs, into the air lock, and then plunge back into the darkness and pressure and smoke and sledgehammer crashes and plank-over-river-bottom-mud chaos of the caisson again. It always relieved his symptoms within minutes. Usually, he said, he'd work for an extra unpaid hour or two swinging sledges or priming charges while the caisson disease agony relented and then disappeared.

About twenty feet into the mud of the Brooklyn side of the East River, Big Bill told him, the caisson started encountering boulders too big to be broken up with sledgehammers and spikes and pry bars and sweat. Colonel Roebling conferred with Big Bill and two other new workers who, Bill thought, were also pretending to be experienced powdermen. Because the work of breaking up the boulders around the reinforced metal edge of the caisson—what they called the shoe—had moved from the almost impossible to the absolutely impossible no matter how hard the men labored down there in the heavy atmosphere in that box with the more than 27,000 tons of caisson roof and weights atop it, with tens of thousands of tons of weight of river and pressure above that, the workers were all for blasting.

Roebling had a few reservations. He explained to the three "powdermen" and the crew chiefs that in such a dense atmosphere inside the caisson, even a moderate explosion might blow out the eardrums of every worker in every room of the sunken box. Also, he explained, the compressed air in the caisson, already so filled with noxious gases as well as smoke and steam from the calcium limelights blazing at the end of their long iron rods, each torch throwing bizarre shadows and glare from its blue-white luminous jets, might become totally unbreathable when the smoke from an explosion was added to the mix. And the vibration from the blast, explained Colonel Roebling, might damage the doors and valves of the air lock—eliminating their only escape from the pressurized compartments on the bottom of the river.

Big Bill used to describe to Paha Sapa how the powdermen would look at one another so soberly after these explanations. But Roebling had an even greater worry.

The way rubble and sand were removed from the working area in the caissons was via water shafts—two huge columns of water that were being held in suspension *above* the spaces where the men worked merely by the great pressure of the air inside the caisson. The bottom of each water shaft pipe was open and only two feet above the pool of water they kept beneath it; handy for shoveling debris into and easy to send down a bucket through the standing column of water, but what—asked the Chief Engineer—would happen if an explosion inside the caisson to break up the boulders (and it had to be *inside* the caisson, of course) depressed that pool and allowed the air to escape up the shafts?

Big Bill said that he and the other work chiefs and powdermen had stared blankly.

Bill Slovak imitated Colonel Roebling's voice, distorted by the terrible air pressure there in the corner of the caisson where they had the discussion, and the effect was strange, with Big Bill's vocabulary suddenly enlarged, his voice distorted, and his accent lessened:

—*It would be a total blowout, gentlemen. All the water suspended in that tall shaft above us, more than thirty-five feet today, perhaps all the water in both shafts, would erupt like a twin Vesuvius, and the compressed air that keeps us breathing and keeps the East River out would follow after it. I think that the eruption, seen from the outside, would rise at least five hundred feet. Parts of those workers nearest the water shafts would almost certainly be part of the extruded debris fountain. Then the full weight of the caisson, held up now only by the tremendous air pressure here, would come crashing down, smashing and flattening all the blocks and braces and frames and the outer edges of the shoe itself. All of these interior bulkheads...*

Big Bill said that at this point the cluster of work chiefs and workmen, including the three "powdermen" so eager to light a fuse, had looked around them in the caisson, their wide, white eyes looking even wider and whiter in the blazing blue-white glare from the calcium limelights.

—... all of these interior bulkheads and supports would be crushed at once from the weight above. No one would have time to get to the air lock, or even to the narrow shafts serving the erupting geysers that were the water shafts until the blowout, and those fabrications of steel and iron—air shafts, air locks, water shafts, bracing, caisson shoe—would also be warped and crushed within seconds. And then the river would rush in, drowning any of us who might have survived the crushing force of the collapse.

The wide, white eyes, Big Bill told Paha Sapa (and sometimes five or six other listening miners) there in the black depths of the Holy Terror, then looked at one another a final time and turned back to Colonel Roebling.

—So, gentlemen, this new crop of boulders here is extruding outside the shoe beyond our reach and doesn't seem to want to surrender to our ministrations by sledge and spike. The caisson's own weight will continue to drop it deeper, and the shoe and framing will be inevitably damaged unless those boulders are removed. Shall we risk using explosives? We should decide today. Now.

To a man, they voted to try it.

But first, Big Bill Slovak explained, Roebling brought down his revolver left over from his service in the Civil War and tried firing it with increasingly heavier powder charges.

No one was deafened. The reports, said Big Bill, sounded strangely muffled in the hyperdense atmosphere of the caisson.

Then the colonel had Big Bill and the other two "experts" set off small charges of actual blasting powder in a remote corner of the caisson while others sheltered in the farthest rooms, slowly increasing the charge with each test.

The water shafts did not blow out, even as the amount of powder approached that necessary to break up the seemingly impervious boulders. The air locks were not damaged. The vibrations destroyed neither the inner bracings nor the workmen.

Big Bill said in the Holy Terror—

—The powder smoke, though, was a damned nuisance. We'd work for forty minutes or more in that thick, black cloud of smoke after each blast, not even being able to see the ends of our sledgehammers or pry bars, and I'd spit black phlegm the consistency of tar for weeks afterward.

But the results of a full charge were extraordinary. Boulders that would have held them up for days and damaged the settling caisson's shoe were blown to bits in seconds, the bits then being pulverized and sent up the water shaft into the open world.

It was he himself, Big Bill told Paha Sapa, who suggested to Colonel Roebling that they adopt the miners' technique of using a long steel drill hammered into the rock to create a hole for the blasting charge—the steam drill that they were all using at the Holy Terror in the Black Hills 1900 to 1903 hadn't been invented yet in 1870 to '71—and then the charge would be gently tamped in and set off. Big Bill, his hands twice the size of Paha Sapa's, even at the decrepit old age of forty in the Holy Terror in 1902, had been in charge of the setting and tamping in the caissons.

In one eight-hour watch, said Big Bill, he and his two partners may have done twenty blasts. The other workers grew so used to the explosions that they—and the powdermen—would just calmly and slowly step into an adjacent chamber to escape all the flying rock and debris when an explosion was triggered.

Instead of descending six inches a week, as had been the case when they were breaking up boulders by hand, the Brooklyn caisson now dropped twelve to eighteen inches in six working days (everyone took Sundays off). Colonel Roebling raised Big Bill Slovak's and the other powdermen's pay twenty-five cents a week.

In March of 1871, when the Brooklyn caisson had reached its permanent home of solid rock 44 feet and 6 inches beneath the surface, Roebling had Big Bill and the men pump cement into it. The caisson had now become the foundation for the Brooklyn tower of the future bridge. Sunk that deep into the ancient Mesozoic bedrock of the East River, where no sea worms or other borers or normal agents of decay could get at them, Colonel Roebling had suggested that they—the caissons—might last a million years.

In May of 1871, when the New York caisson came sliding down the shipyard stays, 18-year-old Tarkulich "Big Bill" Slovak was riding on top of it like a sailor, helping guide it downriver to its final resting place in September. A year later, when the New York caisson had reached its own final depth of 78 feet and 6 inches—at a loss of many more lives to caisson disease due to the much greater pressure difference—Big Bill was the next to last man out as the cement pour to fill the interior was almost finished, offering his huge hand to help Colonel Roebling up as the air lock door swung shut a final time.

Many of the caisson workers took their low wages and went home after that, but Big Bill had then gone to work first on the Brooklyn Tower and, when that tower was completed in May of 1875, over to work on the New York Tower until its completion in July of 1875. He explained to Paha Sapa that he had swapped the blackness and pressure of the caissons seventy feet and more under the river for work dangling up to 270 feet *above* the East River. They used no safety harnesses. Their survival depended upon their sobriety and sense of balance and a simple bosun's chair dangling from cable or scaffolds. When they worked atop the rising towers, they labored and lifted all day with their backs to a two-hundred-foot fall to the concrete-hard water below.

And then the dangerous spinning and spanning of the thousands upon thousands of miles of wire cable began. Big Bill Slovak learned that skill as well. He loved nothing as much as crossing the footbridge—a swaying, pitching four-foot-wide catwalk made of open slats swooping up to each tower at an angle of 35 degrees and more, all 200 feet and more above the river—and on the first day they'd begun spinning the strands of wire cable across, he and his boss, E. F. Farrington, had run back and forth across the entire river span of 1,595 feet and 6 inches of swaying footbridge at least fourteen times that one day alone.

Tarkulich "Big Bill" Slovak had loved every hour and day of his work on the Brooklyn Bridge, he'd told Paha Sapa a hundred times, and when the rest of New York and Brooklyn and America went crazy celebrating the official opening of the bridge on May 24, 1883, Big Bill had wept like a baby.

He was then thirty years old and had spent more than thirteen years of his life working for Colonel Roebling and the dream of the bridge. Suddenly...he didn't know what his future held.

After six months of heavy drinking in New York, he'd finally headed west to the goldfields in Colorado and then the Black Hills. Every gold mine needed a good powderman. The pay was good in towns like Cripple Creek, he said, but the cost of whiskey and whores was correspondingly high.

The night Big Bill died in a cave-in—caused not by one of his own infinitely careful explosions but by sloppy work by some of the didn't-give-a-fuck day supervisors on framing up the new support timbers on Horizontal Shaft Number 11 — Paha Sapa was working a different shift. Instead of clocking in the next morning, he resigned, waited just long enough to be one of the few workers (and one Mexican woman) at Big Bill Slovak's funeral in the windblown cemetery outside of Keystone, and then Paha Sapa used some of his money to buy a horse and took his young son and rode off north past Bear Butte onto the Great Plains.

———

PAHA SAPA WALKS OUT onto the wooden pedestrian promenade deck with the stone towers rising before him. To the right and left below him run the trains. Big Bill said that Colonel Roebling had put in cable cars like those in San Francisco, which ran by simply clamping onto an endless turning wire rope beneath them, but those had been super-seded in the following decades first by regular trolley cars and then by train cars of the sort that ran everywhere else in New York and Brooklyn on elevated tracks. Glancing at the trains whooshing by into their steel-and-wood protective coverings, Paha Sapa guesses that it won't be many years until they too are removed and the automobile traffic lanes widened from two lanes in each direction to three.

Even with only two lanes in each direction, the autos are mak-ing a roaring racket below and to each side of the promenade deck. Paha Sapa has to smile when he thinks of Colonel Roebling—and his father, John, in the 1850s—designing this bridge for pedestrian and horse-and-carriage traffic, only to have erected a structure so sturdy that it could handle millions upon millions of Fords and Chevys and

Stutzes and Studebakers and Dodges and Packards and trucks of all sizes. The traffic is heavier this morning, Paha Sapa notices, coming *toward* Manhattan than it is going out.

The seemingly endless promenade deck is busy but not crowded. Even here the majority of walkers—men holding their hats against the light breeze, the far fewer women occasionally clutching at blowing skirts much shorter than is the style among *wasichu wiyapi* in South Dakota—are coming toward the city.

It's a perfect day to stroll on the promenade of the Brooklyn Bridge. Even with the wind, it's warmer out here away from the building shadows. Paha Sapa glances at his cheap drugstore watch: a little after eight a.m. He wonders what kind of jobs these men are hurrying toward that would start so late.

Just as a range of mountains, say the Tetons or Rockies, is best appreciated from a distance, farther away from the occluding foothills, so the skyline of New York City becomes more impressive the farther he walks out away from it. All the high buildings from the downtown running north along the river's edge gleam gold in the morning light, and some of the higher skyscrapers behind that first line of structures rise so high and are so reflective that they appear to be columns of light themselves. Paha Sapa sees the light reflecting brightly from a very tall building farther north and wonders if it's the new Chrysler Building that some in South Dakota think is constructed completely of steel.

Ahead of him, the first of the two towers rises 276 feet and 6 inches from the river's surface. How many times did Big Bill Slovak repeat all these facts and precise numbers to Paha Sapa down there in the dangerous dark hole of the Holy Terror? Paha Sapa did not mind at the time; a repetition of certain facts and figures can be *wakan,* a sacred thing all by itself, a sort of mantra.

The East River and all of Manhattan are now festooned with bridges, fifty years after the completion of this first one, but these others—including the Manhattan Bridge so visible just to the northeast and the Williamsburg Bridge upriver beyond it—are made of steel and iron. They are, to Paha Sapa's eye on this beautiful first day of April, actively ugly compared to the graceful but eternal-looking twin stone towers that suspend the Brooklyn Bridge.

He knows that these are not just the highest but the *only* such stone towers in North America, but it's with some small sense of shock that he realizes that no other stone monuments to the human spirit, beyond these Roebling stone towers with their double gothic arches, exist in America other than Gutzon Borglum's emerging stone heads in the Black Hills.

It's a busy season of blasting there—Borglum is ready to give up work on the sketched-in Jefferson head to the left of George Washington (as one looks up at the monument) and is already blasting away rock to the right of Washington in search of better carving stone for a replacement Jefferson—and Borglum threatened to fire Paha Sapa when he asked for the six days off.

"So, are you satisfied? Can we go back to Park Avenue now and see if she's home?"

—No. Be silent until I say you can speak again. The appointment is at four p.m., and Mrs. Elmer in Brooklyn was very clear to say that we should not present ourselves—myself—before that time. So . . . silence. If I hear another word from you before I ask for it, I'll skip the appointment and take the train home today and save myself several days' pay.

No response. The only sounds are the rush of the trains, the hum of traffic on the bridge pavement, the slight whisper of wind through the giant cables and countless suspending bridge wires, and the constant honk–rumble–muted roar from the city behind them.

Paha Sapa hears voices and goes to the railing of the promenade deck. Four men in coveralls are on a scaffold strung below, smoking cigarettes and laughing, while one of them makes a halfhearted display of passing a paintbrush over the scrolled metalwork descending below the wood floor of the deck.

Paha Sapa clears his throat.

—Excuse me. . . . Can any of you gentlemen tell me if there's a Mr. Farrington working on the bridge today?

The four look up and two of them laugh. The fattest one, a short man who seems to be in charge of the work detail, laughs the loudest.

—Hey, what's with you, old fellow? Are those braids? Are you a Chinaman or some kind of Indian?

—Some kind of Indian.

The short, fat man in the stained overalls laughs again.

— Good, 'cause I don't think we allow any old Chinamen to cross the bridge on Saturdays. Not unless they pay a toll, anyways.

— Do you know if there's a Mr. Farrington still working here? E. F. Farrington... I don't know what the E or F stands for. I promised a friend I'd look him up.

The four men look at one another and mumble and there's more laughter. Paha Sapa doesn't have to work hard to imagine what Mr. Borglum would do if he came across some of his workers smoking on the job, only pretending to work, and treating visitors to the monument with this disrespect. As Lincoln Borglum once said to him — *After a while, everyone realizes that my father wears those big boots all the time for a reason.*

A tall man with a straggly mustache — Jeff to the fat crew leader's Mutt (Paha Sapa had always gotten the two comic strip characters mixed up until he met a tall, skinny, mustached worker at the Monument named Jefferson "Jeff" Greer, not to be confused with "Big Dick" Huntimer or Hoot or Little Hoot Leach) — gives out a strange giggle for a grown man and says —

— Yeah, well, Chief, Mr. Farrington's still working here. He's up on the top of the nearest tower. He's one of the bosses.

Paha Sapa blinks at this news. If Farrington had been thirty when Big Bill Slovak met him in 1870, he'd be ninety-three now. Hardly the age for someone to be employed and still working atop one of the towers here. A son, perhaps?

— E. F. Farrington? Master mechanic? Older man or young?

More inexplicable giggling from the men below. It's the Mutt crew chief who answers this time.

— Farrington's a mechanic, yeah. And he's as old as Moses's molars. Don't know about the "master" part, though. You oughta go up and ask him.

Paha Sapa looks up at the looming stone tower. He knows there's no stairway inside or on the outside of the solid-stone double-arched monolith, much less an elevator.

— It's all right if I go up?

The tall one, the Mutt, answers.

— Sure, Chief. The bridge is open to the public, ain't it? We don't even charge for you to walk across no more. Go ahead.

Paha Sapa is squinting into the sun.

—How?

Short, fat Jeff answers and the sudden silence of the other three is suspicious.

—Oh, any of the four cables will take you up. I prefer the one to the right of the promenade. If you fall from that one, you don't go all the way to the river—the tracks or promenade or car lanes'll break your fall.

—Thank you.

Paha Sapa has had enough of these men. He hopes that they're not typical of all New Yorkers.

Mutt speaks again.

—Think nothing of it, Sitting Bull. Say hi to your squaw for us when you get back to the reservation.

———

FOUR CABLES run the width of the river and beyond, each finding support just below the summit of its respective tower. Two of the cables rise on either side of the promenade here at the beginning of the long walk and arch up to the Brooklyn Tower, some 208 supporting cable wires, called suspenders, coming down from them, more scores of diagonal cable wires—"stays" in naval terminology—also coming down from the tower to help support the roadway. In the center of the river, coming down to the roadway, the four cables dip in that most perfect of geometric forms—a catenary curve. Paha Sapa's son, Robert, who loved math and science so much but who often seemed more poet than geometrician, once described a catenary curve to Paha Sapa as "the universe's most artistic and elegant response to gravity—the signature of God."

Paha Sapa also knows that each of the four major cables on each side ends in a giant anchorage, each anchorage an eighty-foot tower in its own right—a sight when the bridge was first built and New York was a low city—and each weighing 60,000 tons. And in each of those anchorages, all that weight of the towers, the roadway, the trains, the people, the thousands of miles of wire, and the dead weight of the cables themselves is carried, the way the flying buttresses of medieval cathedrals carry the weight of gravity from the arched interior, into anchor plates each weighing more than twenty-three tons a plate, and those plates, sitting at the bottom of a stone mass equal to a 60,000-ton pyramid, are linked to anchor bars twelve and a half feet long, which link to smaller links, which eventually lead to red-painted giant iron eyebars protruding from the huge anchorage of stone, iron, and steel, each eyebar connected to its cable, the four cables together sustaining the full weight of the bridge.

But none of that is important to Paha Sapa now. He has to decide if one of the four cables is actually walkable. He wants to talk to this Mr. Farrington.

So Paha Sapa stands at the south railing of the promenade, looking down at one of the four broad cables that runs up to the tower. At this point it dips below the level of the promenade deck and, farther back toward the New York shore, beneath the level of the bridge itself. The metal-covered and white-painted cable is not very large for something carrying so much weight—only 15¾ inches in diameter, the same size as the other three supporting cables—but he remembers that there are 5,434 wires in each major cable, each of those wires bundled and crimped in clusters of other cables within the main cables.

Big Bill Slovak loved that number—5,434. He thought there was something mystical about it. Even *wasichus,* it seemed, had their faith in spirits and signs.

Paha Sapa easily vaults over the low railing onto the cable that descends past the promenade on the right side. It's easy enough to balance on—a pipe with a diameter just under sixteen inches—but the painted and curved metal is slippery. He wishes again that he hadn't worn these uncomfortable and slick-soled cheap dress shoes.

He guesses that the cable rises about 750 to 800 feet from this point to its pass-through notch near the top of the tower about 275 feet above the river. Big Bill could have told him the exact length. Actually, he *did* tell him the exact length of the supported land span of the bridge here and its cable, 930 feet, but that span (and its cable running alongside behind him) runs behind him a couple of hundred feet to the anchorage.

Perhaps about 725 feet of rising cable ahead of him. And it rises at an angle of about 35 degrees. Not sounding very steep until you're actually *on* such a pitch or slope, Paha Sapa knows from his many years in mines and his two years at Mount Rushmore. Then a slip can be a dangerous thing.

There is a skinny cable running alongside the cable on the right side of the main cable and hanging about a foot out and perhaps three and a half feet higher than the big cable. It's a handrail of sorts, but one would almost have to lean out over the drop to hang on to it. The gap between the main cable and the "handrail" thread of steel is considerable. Paha Sapa assumes it's used more for some sort of harnesses or for hooking on gear or lowering equipment to scaffolds suspended from the main cable than as any sort of real railing.

He hops back over the railing onto the promenade deck. Several men bustling by look at him strangely but obviously assume he's a bridge worker and hurry on.

Walking back to where the rude clowns were on their scaffold hanging out of sight below the promenade deck, Paha Sapa looks at the untidy pile of material they left up on the deck. It's only the coil of extra rope that interests him. He lifts one end, stretches it, examines it. It's not what he'd choose to replace his eighth-inch steel cable to hang off Abe Lincoln's nose in his bosun's chair while carrying a steam drill but it's better than clothesline.

Paha Sapa takes his folding knife out of his pocket and cuts off an eight-foot length of the rope.

When he vaults back over the opposite railing back onto the large cable, it takes him only a few seconds to fashion a quick Prusik knot around the "handrail" cable. Bringing the doubled length of line back, he undoes his belt—wishing he'd worn his much broader workman's belt—then refastens it with the ends of the rope looped twice and knotted in a smaller Prusik knot at his right hip.

Not exactly the kind of safety margin that Mr. Borglum would okay at the work site, but better than nothing.

Paha Sapa notices a horizontal cable—almost certainly a stay against winds—connecting the handrail cables about thirty feet up this main cable and overhanging the promenade, and there are a few other such steel wire stays and tie-downs on the long, steep rise up to the tower, but he knows it will take just a few seconds to undo the two friction-hitch knots, move the rope beyond the obstacle, and tie on again. It shouldn't be a problem.

Paha Sapa begins walking briskly up the steepening incline of the cable, the rope in his right hand, occasionally pulling it taut enough to provide stability when a strong gust of wind hits him from the south.

Within a couple of minutes he's approaching the height of the tower arches that he knows from Big Bill are 117 feet above the roadway—the two center cables run between the arches to the tower—and he pauses to catch his breath and look around, pulling the Prusik knot tighter as he does so.

The feeling of exposure is somehow greater than his usual work hanging two hundred feet and more above the valley floor on the mutilated Six Grandfathers. The proximity of the rock there gives a sense, however false, of something to grab on to. Here it's just the 15¾-inch cable under his slick soles, the whole cable taut but seeming to sway a little, and the tiny handrail wire that definitely is moving against the rope and with the wind. He knows that it's a little more than 276 feet from the top of the towers to the river, but anyone falling from one of these two center cables would never get to the river—his body would crash onto the promenade deck or, from this right cable, more likely onto the train tracks far below. If he leaped really hard over or under the swaying, almost-invisible-from-below handrail cable to his right, he guesses he might make it all the way to the automobile lanes below.

He turns around and looks at Manhattan.

The city is glorious in the midmorning light, the dozens of new tall buildings gleaming white or sandstone tan or gold. Thousands of windows catch the light. He sees countless black automobiles moving along the riverside roadways and streets, many lining up to cross the Brooklyn Bridge, all looking like a line of black beetles from this height.

A small group of pedestrians has gathered at about the spot on the promenade deck where he jumped over the railing, and he can see the white ovals of their lifted faces. Paha Sapa hopes that he isn't doing something illegal—why would it be illegal?—and remembers that Mutt and Jeff, both bridge workers, told him that this is the way he could find Mr. Farrington on the tower. Of course, odds are strong that Mutt and Jeff were just making fun of an out-of-town "Chief" and a rube to boot.

Paha Sapa shrugs, turns around, and continues his climb. Even used to working at heights as he is, he finds that it's better if he focuses his gaze on the spot where the now steeply rising cable fits into a black notch near the pediment of the tower about a hundred and fifty feet above him. The wind coming up the East River from the south now is quite strong, and he has to release his gentle grip on the sliding rope for a moment to tug his cloth cap lower and tighter. He has no intention of losing a two-dollar hat to the river or having it run over by traffic on the New York–bound lanes.

Near the top, the sense of exposure increases as the great stone wall and the top of the two gothic arches come closer and closer. He finds that he's setting one foot in front of the other for balance. The angle of approach is at its steepest here. Seeing how small the openings for the two cables are, he wonders if it's even possible to get onto the top of the tower from this cable. There is an overhanging pediment that stretches about six feet beyond where both cables enter the tower, but it looks to be about seven feet high and has no steel grips or decent handholds on it. Paha Sapa would have to untie from the now freely moving thin handhold cable and leap up toward the flat overhang, hoping to get his arms over and either find something unseen to grab on to or use the friction of his hands and forearms to keep from falling backward. And if—when—he did fall, the chances of him being able to fall back onto the main cable and keep his balance there on its few inches of slippery, curved top surface are very small indeed.

But when he reaches the immense wall of giant stone blocks and overhanging pediments, he sees that if he gets down on his hands and knees, he can crawl into the square notch through which the cable and steel wire pass.

Inside in the relative darkness, stone just sixteen inches under him now, there's an aged wooden ladder to his right and sunlight above. He coils the rope over his shoulder.

Paha Sapa climbs up and out of the hole onto the top of the New York Tower of the Brooklyn Bridge.

The wind is even stronger here, blowing the tails of his clumsy suit-coat and still trying to steal his hat, but it's no factor up here on this broad, flat space. Paha Sapa tries to remember the magical numbers Big Bill recited to him about the tower tops: 136 feet wide by 53 feet across?—it was something like that. Certainly a wider expanse of segmented stone blocks up here than Mr. Borglum has left to blast and carve for the Teddy Roosevelt head at the narrowest part of the ridgeline south of the canyon where he wants to put the Hall of Records.

Paha Sapa walks easily back and forth on the top. No work crew or 93-year-old E. F. Farrington up here—the clowns tricked him after all. He hadn't really expected the old man, of course, but he thought there might be a son or grandson working up here.

He walks to the east edge and looks out at the view. The cables and their gleaming suspender wires dropping away steeply below make his scrotum contract. The cars on the roadway about 160 feet below seem much smaller, the sounds of their tires on the roadway a distant thing. Paha Sapa guesses that it's about a third of a mile to the Brooklyn Tower...1600 feet perhaps?...but the view of that tower is astounding. There is a large American flag flapping atop that tower, and he can see small human figures there, but if that's where Farrington is working...forget it. He's not in the mood to try to descend one of these four continuing cables and climb again, perfect catenary curve or not.

Looking from the south edge of the tower top, the sheer drop to the river there seeming a lot more than a mere 276 feet, he sees ferries moving to and fro, the river filled with ships, and larger ships moving or anchored in the bay beyond. The Statue of Liberty lifts her torch on an island out there.

He looks back to the west. The fairly recently completed Empire State Building rises above the other high buildings like a redwood amid ponderosa pines. Paha Sapa feels a sudden catch in his throat at the beauty of that building, of these towers—and at the hubris of a race of his species that would construct all this and put it into motion. (Eight weeks later, he'll see the Empire State Building again when he and thirty other workers follow Mr. Borglum to the Elks Theater in Rapid City to watch *King Kong*. Borglum will have seen it and have been so enthused about the movie—"the ultimate adventure!" he'll call it, "a real man's picture!"—that he'll lead a caravan of old trucks and coupes and Paha Sapa on Robert's motorcycle [with Red Anderson in the sidecar] to go see it again. Mr. Borglum will walk into the theater, for the hundredth time, without paying a cent—for some reason the Great Sculptor believes himself exempt from such petty fees as movie tickets—but Paha Sapa and the other men coerced by their boss into seeing the movie will shell out an outrageous twenty-five cents each. It will be worth it to Paha Sapa, who will look at all the images of New York at the end of the movie and think of his moments atop the western tower of the Brooklyn Bridge.)

At this moment on the morning of the first of April 1933, Paha Sapa has no thoughts of giant apes swinging from any of the buildings he's admiring. The morning has been cloudless until now, but suddenly a few moving clouds obscure the sun, sending their shapeless shadows flitting over bay, steamships, island, ferries, the southern point of Manhattan, and parts of Brooklyn. When two of these newcomer clouds diverge, Paha Sapa watches a shaft of almost vertical sunlight reach down and strike the water to the south of the bridge. The reflection is so bright that he has to raise his hand to shield his eyes.

Without warning there are men standing all around him.

Paha Sapa actually jumps in alarm, thinking that police have somehow managed to sneak up on him and are going to handcuff him and haul him away down the cable—no small feat, that.

But these are no *wasichu* police.

The last time he saw these six old men, they stood hundreds of feet tall and were each surrounded by a corona of brilliance. Now they are just old men, all but one of them shorter than Paha Sapa. They wear dress-up buckskins and moccasins, the tunics adorned with necklaces and chestplates of bones, everything augmented by the most beautiful beadwork, but the once-white deerskin has grown dark and smoky with age, as have the faces and necks and hands of the six old men.

The oldest and closest of the Six Grandfathers speaks, and his voice is now just the voice of an older Natural Free Human Being, not of the wind or stars.

—*Do you understand now, Paha Sapa?*

—*Understand what,* Tunkašila?

—*That the All, the Mystery,* Wakan Tanka *himself, shows his facets and has his avatars share their power with the Fat Takers as well as with the Sisuni and Shahiyela and the Kangi Wicasha as well as with the* Ikče Wičaśa. *This…*

The old man gestures toward the bridge tower beneath, toward the roadway far below with its moving trains and automobiles, toward the skyline of New York and the gleaming Empire State Building.

—...*this is all* wakan. *It is all a demonstration of how the* Wasicun *has listened to the gods and borrowed their energies.*

Paha Sapa feels something like anger filling him. Beneath that there is only sorrow.

—*So you are saying, Grandfather, that the Fat Takers—the Great Stone Heads who rose out of* our *Black Hills—deserve to rule the world and that we must fade away and die and disappear as the buffalo did?*

Another Grandfather, this one with his gray hair parted in the middle and a single red feather matching the intricately woven red blanket draped over his left arm, speaks.

— *You should know by now, Paha Sapa, the life you have lived should have told you, that we are not saying that. But the tide of men and their peoples and even of their gods ebbs and flows like the Great Seas on each coast of this continent we gave you. A people no longer proud of itself or confident in their gods or in their own energies recedes, like the waning tide, and leaves only reeking emptiness behind. These Fat Takers also shall know that one day. But the Mystery and your Grandfathers—even the Thunder Beings, fickle as they seem—do not abandon those they love.*

Paha Sapa looks at the face of each of the six old men. He is tempted to touch them. Each man is as solid and physical as Paha Sapa's own body. He can smell the scent from them despite the breeze—a mixture of tobacco, clean sweat, tanned leather, and something sweet but not cloying, like sage after the rain.

He shakes his head, still furious with himself and with the Grandfathers' complicated, unclear statements.

—*I don't understand, Grandfathers. I'm sorry....I've planned to...you know my plans... but I'm one man, almost an old man, by myself, and I can't...I don't...I want to understand; I would give my life to understand, but...*

The shortest Grandfather, one with all-black hair and equally all-black eyes and features as weathered and eroded as the Badlands, speaks softly.

—*Paha Sapa, why did your sculptor choose to carve the* wasichu *heads on the Six Grandfathers?*

Paha Sapa blinks.

— *The granite was good for carving there, Grandfather. The south-facing cliff meant that the men could work there most of the year and that the finished heads would receive sunlight. Also the...*

— *No.*

The syllable stops Paha Sapa in mid-sentence.

— *Your sculptor knows a sacred place when he finds it. He senses the energy there. That, not gold, is what really brought the* Wasicun *to your sacred Black Hills. They wish to put their imprint on the place just as the Natural Free Human Beings have sought their destinies there. But the future of our people is like the future of a single man . . . it is not set. It can be changed, Paha Sapa.* You can change it.

Paha Sapa thinks of the dynamite he has begun to store in his shed in Keystone and says nothing.

The fourth Grandfather, the one who looks most like an old woman, speaks, and his voice is the deepest of all.

— *Paha Sapa, think of the braids in your hair. Then think of the thousands upon thousands of braids of steel wire in the cables on this bridge and how each large cable in turn is made up totally of joined and intertwined smaller strands of braided steel — the whole stronger than any strand of steel by itself, however thick, however resilient. The twining is the secret. The twining is the* wakan.

Paha Sapa looks at the fourth Grandfather but has absolutely no idea what he is talking about. Is it possible, he wonders, for ancient spirits to go senile?

When the first Grandfather speaks again, his voice is soft but as solid and strong as the tower beneath them.

— *Wait, Paha Sapa. Believe. Trust.*

The other five's voices are like a whisper only slightly louder than the wind.

— *Wait.*

Paha Sapa puts his hands over his eyes for a second. For only the second time in his sixty-eight years, he is overcome by emotion.

— *Hey . . . you! Old man! What the hell do you think you're doing?*

When Paha Sapa removes his hand from his eyes, the six Grandfathers are gone. The shouting is coming from a white man's disembodied head rising from the solid stone.

— *I said, what do you think you're doing up here?*

The man's head is round with no cap, short-cropped hair, red-flushed face, jug ears. He grunts and pulls himself up out of the north cable hole. He's wearing a stained white coverall and some sort of web harness with a single safety strap and metal clasp wrapped around his thick waist. The man is as short as Paha Sapa but seems to be all thick muscle, including his broad chest, which he appears to be thrusting at Paha Sapa as he comes closer.

— *You heard me. How'd you get up here?*

Paha Sapa looks around as if the Six Grandfathers might still be hiding somewhere on the pediment or on one of the cables. Far below and to the northeast, a large ship blows a steam horn that sounds like a woman's scream.

— *I walked up. Are you Mr. Farrington?*

— *Walked up the* cable? *With no safety equipment? Are you* nuts?

Paha Sapa touches the short rope still curled over his shoulder. The red-faced man blinks three times.

— *What? You came up to hang yourself? Just jump off; it's easier.*

— *I used a Prusik hitch. I would have preferred better rope, but this is all the clowns had.*

— *Clowns?*

— *Mutt and Jeff. Two of the four men working on not painting the iron-work below the promenade. I asked if Mr. Farrington was working on the bridge, and they told me he was working here and that I should walk up the cable.*

— *Mutt and Jeff. Connors and Reinhardt. Jesus Christ. Prusik hitch? That's a fairly new friction knot. The Austrians just put that in their climbing manual a couple of years ago, and we use it ourselves from time to time. Are you a mountain climber?*

— *No. I work for Gutzon Borglum in South Dakota.*

— *Borglum? That crazy son-of-a-bitch? On Mount Rushmore?*

— *Yes.*

The red-faced man shakes his head. Paha Sapa can feel the anger flowing out of the other man and guesses that he is usually fairly relaxed. His eyes are bright blue and Paha Sapa sees now that the red flush and blunt red nose are normal for him, a matter of capillaries and too many hours spent in the sun rather than a sign of rage.

— *Are you Mr. Farrington, or were Connors and Reinhardt lying to me about that as well?*

— *I'm Farrington.*

—Not Mr. E. F. Farrington, obviously, but perhaps a relative? Son? Grandson?

—No, I don't know any . . . wait. I've heard that name. There was an E. F. Farrington working with Mr. Roebling when the bridge was built. . . . Master Mechanic, I think . . .

—That's right. I had a friend, dead now, who worked for Mr. Farrington and asked me to look him up if I ever came to New York. He'd be in his nineties now.

—Yeah, well, I'm Mike Farrington and no relation. But I do remember about that now. That master mechanic Farrington had an argument with some of the bosses forty years ago, not with Colonel Roebling, and left the job shortly before the bridge was opened. Listen, you can't just walk up here, you know. Prusik hitch or not.

Paha Sapa does not want to argue with this wrong Farrington. He feels suddenly weary and confused and absolutely stupid. He came to New York to fulfill a foolish promise to Long Hair and now he's come to the bridge on this even more foolish errand. And, he realizes with a sick jolt to his empty stomach, he'll miss the four o'clock appointment on Park Avenue because he'll probably be in jail. He doubts that he's brought enough money to meet bail. Mr. Borglum will fire him over the phone without even hearing his side of the story . . . and he *has* no side.

There are shouts from below the east side of the tower top and Mike Farrington walks to the edge. Paha Sapa follows listlessly.

A work scaffold is hanging beneath the north cable, about fifty feet down, and hidden from view by the nearer cable. Three men on it, all in matching coveralls with their thin harness straps clipped to a cable wire above, are waving their arms and shouting.

—Mike! Everything okay? You got a jumper there?

Farrington shouts back.

—No, it's okay. Just an old gentleman who's lost his way. Not a jumper.

Farrington turns to Paha Sapa and asks softly —

—You're nuts, but you're not a jumper, are you?

—No. And I didn't have to come all the way to the top if I wanted to jump. The jump from the roadbed level to the river would've killed me. I may be nuts, but I'm not stupid.

Farrington can't hold back the sudden flash of white teeth. He waves to the workers to continue their inspection or rust scraping or whatever they're doing there, reaches into his pocket, and pulls out a cigar and a match.

— *You want one... what's your name?*

Paha Sapa starts to say Billy Slovak and then does not. He starts to say Billy Slow Horse, but then does not. He likes this Mike Farrington even if he isn't related to Big Bill's old boss and friend.

— *Paha Sapa is my name. It means Black Hills, which is also where I live.*

— *You some kind of Indian then?*

— *Lakota. Sioux.*

Farrington flicks the match with one movement of his massive thumb, puffs the cigar alight, exhales, clamps the stogie in his teeth while he crosses his massive arms over his massive chest, grins again, and says —

— *Sioux. You're the guys who killed Custer, right?*

— *Yes. The Cheyenne helped, but we did it.*

Again the white grin and the twinkling blue eyes. Paha Sapa has never smoked, other than from the *Ptehinčala Huhu Canunpa* before he lost it on his *hanblečeya,* but the aromatic smoke from Farrington's cigar smells wonderful. He is reminded of the Six Grandfathers.

Farrington says —

— *You did, huh? With just a little help from the Cheyenne? Were you there at the Little Big Horn when it happened, Mr.... ah...Paha Sapa?*

Paha Sapa looks the younger man in the eye. He does not smile or laugh.

— *Yes, Mike. I was the last person or thing that General George Armstrong Custer saw in this life. I counted coup on him just as the second bullet hit him.*

Farrington laughs — three loud, uninhibited barks that get his maintenance crew to shouting again — and then looks more closely at Paha Sapa and quits laughing. He pats Paha Sapa on the back, not gently.

— *I believe you, sir. By God, I truly do. All right, now how do we get you down?*

— *I presume by the same cable I came up.*

— *You presume correctly, Mr. Paha Sapa. You with your little bit of clothesline and your Prusik knot friction hitch. I could get a harness from one of the boys back there, but I'm not sure you'd take it or need it. I'll walk you down. I can see a crowd's already gathered there, thirty or forty folks with nothing better to do than rubberneck on a Saturday morning, and I'm sure a couple of New York's Finest will be there.*

— New York's Finest?

— Cops, Mr. Counting Coup Paha Sapa, sir. Cops. With their clubs and handcuffs at the ready. That crowd watched you climb up here and someone's bound to have called it in or run to fetch a cop on the beat. But I'll explain to them that you're my father — or a new member of the bridge maintenance crew. Or something. Do you promise not to fall and get yourself killed on the way down? There's a goddamned Depression on, you know, and I need this job.

— I'll do my best, Mike.

Farrington looks hard at him again, the blue eyes squinting in the cloud of aromatic smoke. The crew chief clamps down harder on the cigar and the grin widens.

— I have a hunch that your best is pretty damned good, Mr. Paha Sapa. Pretty damned good.

———

Twenty-five minutes later, Mike Farrington's explanation having satisfied two bemused-looking police officers in uniform but not the jostling crowd that had gathered — more like seventy-five people than thirty or forty — Paha Sapa has shaken hands with Farrington, extricated himself from a boy in oversized tweeds and carrying a notebook who said he was a reporter, and is walking toward Broadway, into the shadow of the tall buildings again, stopping and turning frequently to look back at the towers and the bridge.

"Paha Sapa, now that you've got that out of your system, can we go get ready to keep the appointment now?"

Usually the buzz of words in his head is an annoyance to Paha Sapa, but now it makes him feel less alone in a city and world too large for him.

— Yes, General. I'll head back to the hotel, take a bath, get into a clean shirt, and we'll head down Park Avenue.

"That's the first time you've ever called me General. Or thought of me that way, as far as I know. Did something happen up there on that bridge when I wasn't looking or listening?"

Paha Sapa doesn't answer. He turns right on lower Broadway and starts walking north toward the Empire State Building and the gleaming Chrysler Building and the heart of the heart of the *wasichu* city. The day is growing warmer. Each time he looks over his shoulder, Paha Sapa sees that the Brooklyn Bridge is dwindling in the distance and partially hidden by intervening buildings, but it is never fully out of sight for long. Just as it will never again be fully out of his thoughts.

By the time he reaches Union Square, his hands are in his pockets and he is whistling "Who's Afraid of the Big Bad Wolf"—a song from a cartoon about three little pigs that won't be released until May, but which Mr. Borglum somehow got a print of (he said direct from Mr. Walt Disney himself) and projected as part of the winter Saturday-night movies that he and Mrs. Borglum host twice a month at the sculptor's studio.

Behind Paha Sapa, the bridge recedes and is obscured from time to time, but never completely disappears.

20

George Armstrong Custer

———◆———

*L*ibbie.

      I know now that you will never hear this. This or anything else I have ever said to you from here or will ever say to you. But I will talk to you anyway, this final time. This final time for both of us.

    There was that second when you leaned forward and looked Paha Sapa in the eye—looked into him and at me was my thought at the time—when your lips silently formed two syllables I was sure, then, were "Autie."

    But I am probably wrong about both the meaning of your look and of the syllables whispered below the range of Paha Sapa's (and thus my own) hearing. I know you were having difficulty seeing your guest, so it is more probable that you were simply leaning closer to have at least one clear image of the Indian who had invaded your parlor. And perhaps the syllables whispered were "oh, my" or even "good-bye."

    It was Paha Sapa's idea for us to come to New York to see you in person. He had suggested it once years before, in the mid-1920s, I believe, and I said no then and he never brought it up again. It wasn't until this past winter, when I realized that since you were approaching your 91st birthday you could die soon—a concept that had never been real to me before—that I raised it with Paha Sapa in one of our few conversations, and he agreed.

    I wanted it to be on your birthday, April 8. That seemed important to me for some reason. But Mr. Borglum was starting some very serious blasting on the possible new site for the Thomas Jefferson head that very date and he let Paha Sapa—whom Borglum knows as Billy Slovak—know that if the powderman took time off from the job that week, there would be no job for him to return to.

296

So Paha Sapa did the best he could, losing pay he could not afford to lose, and we took the long train ride to spend the weekend of April 1 and 2 in the city.

My reluctance to see you rather than merely remember you as you were when we were young and in love and then married was threefold: first, I was acutely aware that our marriage lasted a little longer than twelve years but, by the time I made up my mind to ask Paha Sapa to bring me to New York, your widowhood had gone on for fifty-seven years. Being a full-time professional widow would change anyone. Second, I did not want the arrival of this sixty-eight-year-old Indian to alarm you. I knew already through the occasional newspaper accounts that Paha Sapa encountered and shared with me that you, the most famous widow in America, were constantly being harassed by letter and in person by various publicity seekers claiming to be "the unknown" or "last" survivor of the massacre at the Little Big Horn. Charlatans all. Third and final, I confess to you now — since you will never hear this — that I dreaded seeing you as an old woman.

You were always so youthful and so beautiful in the time I knew you, Libbie, my darling. Those dark curls. That soft and mischievous smile was unlike that of any woman I had ever met. The full, firm, and — as I discovered so soon in our married lovemaking — infinitely responsive body.

How could I trade those memories for the reality of an old woman in her nineties: wrinkled, sagging, rheumy eyed, lacking hearing, sight, mobility, humor, and any glimmer of her youthful self?

That was my fear. That turned out to be too close to the fact.

The only thing that allows me to pardon myself a little from charges of cruelty here, Libbie, is the fact that I knew so well that you used to be put off and appalled by old people as well, but especially old women. There was something about a truly old woman that terrified you almost as much as the thunder that used to send you hiding under the bed in the early years of our marriage. (All of the years of our marriage seem like early years to me.)

In recent years, Paha Sapa borrowed and read all three of your published books — Boots and Saddles, *published in 1885;* Following the Guidon, *from 1890; and* Tenting on the Plains, *published in 1893 — and in one of those books, I believe it was the last one, I clearly recall this passage (a rare use of elaborate description from you, my dear) in which that fear of aging and of old women becomes all too obvious. We had ridden to this Sioux village not too long after my victory on the Washita and a group of old women, most of their husbands killed in my attack, had formed a sort of welcoming committee for us. You wrote:*

The old women were most repulsive in their appearance. Their hair was thin and wiry, scattering over their shoulders and hanging over their eyes. Their faces were seamed and lined with such furrows as come from the hardest toil, and the most terrible exposure to every kind of weather and hardship....

The dull and sunken eyes seemed to be shrivelled like their skins. The ears of those hideous old frights were punctured with holes from top to the lobe, where rings once hung, but torn out, or so enlarged as they were by the years of carrying the weight of heavy brass ornaments, the orifices were now empty, and the ragged look of the skin was repugnant to me.

I remember you talking to me in bed that night after we saw those Sioux, Libbie. You where shivering, your shoulders shaking as if you were sobbing, but there were no tears. The widowhood of these old crones was part of their ugliness, you said. They had become nothing after their warrior husbands died—merely an extra mouth to be fed, grudgingly, by the men in the band who would pay them no attention for the rest of those empty women's sad lives. "The orifices were now empty..." indeed. Empty forever, and dried up and forgotten and useless.

That was your fear then, when your complexion was still flawless and your breasts were high and firm (due, in part, perhaps, to the fact that we never succeeded in having a child) and your smile was still a girl's quick smile and your eyes sparkled with energy. So when, several years ago, Paha Sapa read some rare newspaper account of you—perhaps it had to do with an equestrian statue of me being erected somewhere, or with the 50th commemoration of my murder at the Little Big Horn—and you were quoted as saying, "I am an antique, but I do enjoy myself. I have a delightful time," I knew you were lying.

———

Paha Sapa had some personal business to attend to in New York—from what little I saw, it seemed yet another ritual to appease one of the endless list of his dead—and then he returned to the little hotel near Grand Central Terminal. The hotel obviously had been recommended to Paha Sapa, an Indian, because the clientele was largely Negro with some foreigners, also of color. But in truth, Libbie, the rooms were somewhat nicer than the one we stayed in across the street from the Brunswick that last winter we spent in New York, and while our view, you remember, had been of rooftops and alleys and water towers atop those rooftops, Paha Sapa's actually looked out on a busy and moderately attractive boulevard.

He spent no time looking at the view, but waited his turn to use the bath down the hall. Then he dressed in fresh underlinens, new socks, his best white shirt, and his one tie and rumpled suit and trousers. His cheap shoes had been scuffed up a bit during some exertion he'd expended on the Brooklyn Bridge and now he spit-shined and buffed them. They still looked cheap and uncomfortable, but one could see one's reflection in them when he left the room.

Paha Sapa had stopped at a hot dog stand on his way back from the Brooklyn Bridge, but I could tell he was still very hungry. But he had only two days in New York City and he couldn't spend all of his quarters the first day.

The walk to 71 Park Avenue was only a few blocks and Paha Sapa was almost an hour early when he got there. After looking at the tall cooperative apartment building and then at the doorman — who seemed to be looking back suspiciously — Paha Sapa put his hands in his pockets and thought about which way to walk to kill the time. He was nervous... I could tell. I thought I would be terribly nervous as well and certainly the anxiety had been building in me (in what was left of me) all during the three-day-and-night train ride east from Rapid City, but there was a strange, cold emptiness descending on me as well. It was a sensation that it might be impossible to describe to you, Libbie, so I won't try.

We were standing in front of the Doral Hotel (somewhere, in something Paha Sapa had read, someone had said that you liked to walk past this hotel when you still got out on walks, Libbie, although I can't imagine why) and that doorman was also giving us the evil eye, so Paha Sapa strolled on, crossing the street and heading east toward the river.

Thus we made several circuits, four blocks east, two blocks north, then back again, until it was time to present ourselves at the door. Paha Sapa actually stopped at one of the windows of the Doral Hotel to inspect himself. His expression did not change, but I could feel him frowning. Then he braced his shoulders and crossed the street.

It was a strange double doorway to the apartment building, somewhat like one of the air locks on Colonel Roebling's caissons as Big Bill Slovak had described them to Paha Sapa. Trapped in the little space with the burly, absurdly dressed guard — Paha Sapa was remembering a similar uniform on the guard-conductor on a Ferris Wheel at the Chicago World's Fair forty years earlier — my host repeated the fact that he had a four p.m. appointment with a resident, Mrs. Elizabeth

Custer. The doorman spoke into a brass speaking tube of the type I'd seen only on the bridge of riverboats and there came back a long, inhuman squawking. The doorman continued to squint suspiciously at us, but he told us the floor and pushed a button to open the inner door.

Before we could seek out an elevator or begin ascending the staircase, there was a nunnish flurry and rustle of black skirts and an eager or otherwise determined female motion descending that dark staircase and for a brief but thrilling moment I was sure it was you, Libbie, more spry than I had imagined you being near the end of your ninetieth year and also supernaturally aware of who was visiting and wildly eager to greet me after all these years. But when the woman's face hove into view, a sense of disappointment and reality washed over me. She was far too young to be you, although she was one of those women who go through life appearing as if they were born old. She was also scowling fiercely.

"Are you the Indian, the Mr. Slow Horse?" It was a demand and a challenge. The emphasis on certain words seemed random, an old affectation. Her voice was hoarse, as if from being raised in indignation far too many times.

Paha Sapa stepped back toward the air lock to make room for her at the base of the stairs. He did not remove his hat. He did not, I noticed, end his sentence with "ma'am" as he tended to do with lady tourists at Mount Rushmore.

"Yes."

She stayed on the bottom step to give herself physical as well as moral author-ity over Paha Sapa, but this woman was tall enough — and Paha Sapa short enough — that she needn't to have bothered with the physical and couldn't have succeeded with the moral.

"I am Miss Marguerite Merington..."

Before Paha Sapa could nod recognition of the name (which he did not, I knew, actually recognize), she swept on.

"...and I must tell you, Mr. Slow Horse, that I was totally and unequivo-cally opposed to your seeing and wasting Mrs. Custer's time and energy in this way!"

The doorman had taken a step back and not merely so that he could open the outer door while Paha Sapa held open the inner door of the air lock for the aggrieved lady. It was obvious that the doorman knew Miss Marguerite Merington and had long ago devised a strategy of keeping the maximum distance he could in such a small space.

"Well, shame on you for wasting this fine lady's time in this way is all I have

to say, *and I hope that May knows what she's* doing, *but she rarely, in my* humble opinion, *has Mrs. Custer's welf*are *in mind when she* allows *these ridiculous appointments...."*

Paha Sapa *had not tried to speak. Perhaps he, like me, was watching the outraged emphasis creep into syllables now as well as complete, if random, words.*

Then Miss Marguerite Merington *was gone, out onto the sidewalk of Park Avenue, sweeping out through the door which the doorman, wisely, held from behind on the outside as she bustled through, using the door and its window as a shield, I thought.*

"Is that Mr. Slow Horse down there?" came a shouted but still somehow softer voice from several floors above. It was not your voice, of course, Libbie. I guessed it was either your housekeeper's or, more likely since the voice held no servant's diffidence in it, that of the lady Paha Sapa and I had been writing to in order to arrange this interview, my so-called favorite niece (whom I had never met), a certain May Custer Elmer.

Paha Sapa *walked over to the stairwell and raised his face. Now he did remove his cap.*

"Yes."

"Come up, please. Come up. Take the stairs, if you are able. The elevator takes forever to react to its summons. Come up, Mr. Slow Horse!"

———

I was sure that I was ready for the encounter with your little apartment there at 71 Park Avenue—I'd read about it, or rather Paha Sapa had, including the long 1927 interview where the reporter referred to your home as "a delightful return to the elegance of the previous century," but the truth was far more powerful than that: entering your apartment was the equivalent of taking one of Mr. Wells's time machines back to 1888. Outside, through thick panes of glass on windows shut tight even on such a lovely spring day, came the bus and train and automobile honking sounds of the 20th Century; inside, 1888 in all ways. The windows, although properly clean, seemed nailed shut, and each of the little rooms we moved through smelled increasingly musty—a mixture of furniture polish, of stale air, of hidden dust, of aged things, and of aged people. Your apartment, my beloved, had an old-woman smell about it. (I remember in the early days of our marriage we each were forced to come to terms with the fact—which no one warns newlyweds about—that in such cramped, one-room-and-a-bathroom quarters, one soon must learn to live amidst all the other person's all-too-human smells. There had been something strangely exciting about that then. Now, through Paha Sapa's still-keen senses, I noted only that the apartment smelled of old women.)

There was amidst all the dark, ancient furniture, however, a proud new console radio, a gift from friends, I learned later through something Paha Sapa read. It looked anachronistic there amidst all the furniture, photographs, and paraphernalia from the previous century. The dial was dark.

I remember Paha Sapa reading years ago that for the 50th anniversary commemoration of my regiment's short-lived battle at the Little Big Horn, you'd owned no radio and thus had been invited to a nearby hotel on June 25, 1926, to listen to the radio broadcast ceremony and reenactment. Had it been the Doral across the street? I forget. The hotel had kindly offered you a deluxe room for the night but, according to published reports, you sat quite upright in your wicker chair, staring at the radio during the entire broadcast, and left—hobbling on your cane—immediately upon that broadcast's conclusion. Your only recorded comment to the actors' (one playing me) shouts and simulated hoofbeats broadcast from Montana—"Yes, that is how it would have been."

How could you possibly know, my darling? How could you possibly know what it could have been like? For all your daring trips into hostile Indian territory with me and visits to this fort or that, how could you possibly have any idea what those final minutes were like with fifteen hundred or more bloodthirsty Sioux and Cheyenne closing in on our thinning ranks? How could you possibly have any idea?

There were two more women Paha Sapa had to meet before being led into your presence in the back parlor (where the single window did indeed, just as the 1927 reporter had told us, still retain a thin view of the East River). The first, the lady who had called down the stairway to Paha Sapa, was Mrs. May Custer Elmer, our interlocutor over the past year in setting up this brief meeting. I've mentioned that the newspaper in our hometown of Monroe, Michigan, during the time of the unveiling of one statue of me or the other, once referred to Mrs. Elmer as my ("the General's") "favorite niece," but she was a grand-niece, and I had no memory of her. She was a smiling, pink-cheeked, slightly flustered middle-aged lady and did welcome Paha Sapa decently, without offering to shake the Indian's hand.

With Mrs. Elmer (who was busy telling Paha Sapa that her husband was quite the amateur astronomer) in that first room of the warren of small rooms running back to the parlor, was a Mrs. Margaret Flood, the equally middle-aged maid, who squinted at Paha Sapa (and thus at me) with suspicion as open (but much quieter) as that of Miss Marguerite Merington down in the foyer. Mrs. May Custer Elmer interrupted her description of her husband's passion for astronomy to explain that Patrick, that is, Mr. Flood, the handyman, was off running an errand today, as if that had some relevance to Paha Sapa's meeting with the dead general's widow.

And then we were in the little parlor, lit mostly by the afternoon light from the west reflected back from taller buildings and windows outside the east-facing window, and there you sat waiting, Libbie, my darling.

Except, of course, it was not you.

Being saved from the scourges of aging myself, I am not sure if any human being can keep the countenance and "selfness" of his youth and middle years so deep into old age. Perhaps men can be more successful in such indolent ambition since a few salient features—a beak of a nose such as mine, perhaps, or a mighty mustache—can stand in for the missing person the way a caricaturist's bold, cruel lines stand in for reality. But for women, alas, the ravages and betrayals of time are much more cruel.

You were seven days away from your 91st birthday on that first day of April 1933, when Paha Sapa visited you, my dearest.

Only you—the Libbie that I had known and loved and made love to and dreamt of even in my death sleep—that you was not there.

You were dressed in crepey widow's black (with some sort of cream-colored cloth at your throat, attached by a brooch from another century, my century), which seemed absurd to me fifty-seven years after the unlucky day that made you a widow.

Your hands, your lovely, soft, slender-fingered, smooth-skinned, loving Libbie hands, were now liver-spotted, tendoned, arthritis-swollen and contorted claws. The nails were yellow with age, like an old man's toenails.

You made no move to offer your hand to Paha Sapa and this relieved both of us. Even though Paha Sapa's looking-into-vision skills seemed to have waned in recent years, neither he nor I wanted to take the risk of any physical contact between him and you. At one time, years ago, when I first became aware of where and what I had become after my death at the Little Big Horn, I had fantasies of Paha Sapa going east and deliberately touching you so that my ghost-self might leave the aging Indian and dwell in and with you for the rest of our lives (yours and mine, I mean, my darling). How wonderful and intimate our silent conversations might have been over those last years. How that might have assuaged your loneliness and my own. But then I realized that I was not a ghost, nor a soul waiting to travel to Heaven (as I had preferred to think upon discovering my place in Paha Sapa's mind), and the fantasy died with that revelation.

Your face was very, very pale and the blush or whatever the makeup on your cheeks was called only made the truth of the paleness — like rouge on a corpse — more painfully obvious. All of the newspaper and magazine accounts of you over the years had stressed how much more youthful than your chronological age you looked, and based on the few photographs Paha Sapa had seen — you at age 48, age 65, age 68 — that had once been true. The smile and eyes and curls on the forehead (from dyed hair?) had indeed looked similar, if not the same. But now age had erased those vestiges of my Libbie's continuity and beauty the way an angry schoolboy might draw a wet eraser over a chalk-filled blackboard.

Your old-woman's throat was a mass of cords and cables — the Brooklyn Bridge again! — that your high, black, lacy collar did not succeed in concealing. The bone structure of your cheeks and jawline were lost to folds and dewlaps, jowls and wrinkles. I remember us — you and I — once remarking that the men on your father's side of the family, the Judge especially, resisted wrinkles far into old age. But it looked now as if you had finally taken after your mother. The few laugh lines that we — you and I — had joked about, almost celebrated, in those last months of our lives together, now possessed all parts of your face. Time had worked like a fat spider weaving its webs everywhere.

I remember, however ungallantly, that you had weighed 118 pounds that June before I left Fort Abraham Lincoln forever. Whatever you weighed now in our last real encounter, your body appeared to have collapsed inward on itself as if your bones had long since liquified, save for the bent spine so common to very old ladies and the obvious boniness of your sticklike forearms.

I would love to tell you, my darling Libbie who cannot hear me, that your eyes were still your own — blue, bright, intelligent, mischievous, alluring — but they had also undergone what Shakespeare called a "sea change," and not for the better. They had somehow darkened and seemed lost in the shadows of your deep-sunk orbital bones — the way you and I had commented on Abraham Lincoln's eye sockets near the end — and the eyes themselves seemed rheumy and unfocused.

I shall describe — and remember — no more. But these observations were made in the shadows of an April afternoon in the most indirect and already-fading light. The large, heavy, dark furniture in the room seemed to be soaking up the light. (I admit that I looked for the small signing table from Appomatox Courthouse that Phil Sheridan had given us, but it was not in this parlor and I hadn't noticed it on the way in.)

I was introduced by my "favorite cousin" May as "Mr. William Slow Horse, the gentleman with whom I have been corresponding and of whom I've recently spoken."

Mrs. Elmer waved Paha Sapa to a seat and when she herself had plopped into a chair, Paha Sapa sat us down across from you, Libbie. In the crowded room, his knees were only about four feet from yours (if one could discern where knees or any other anatomical components were in that wrinkled mass of black crepe, silk, muslin, and whatever else went into that mourning pyre of a dress).

And I confess again that in all my images of meeting you again through Paha Sapa's visit, I had never—not once—imagined another person in the room with us. Even after Mrs. Flood—"Margaret" to Mrs. Elmer—had excused herself to go about some domestic chore (or perhaps just to sit smoking in the kitchen or back stairway), the room seemed far too crowded with the three living persons and my own hovering, nonliving presence there.

I also realized at that second that I was the second ghost of General George Armstrong Custer (even though I was no ghost) to enter this room. The first ghost had been carried everywhere by Mrs. Elizabeth Custer for almost fifty-seven years and was certainly in the room with us.

When you spoke, my darling, your voice was simultaneously phlegm husky and as wispy as the spiderweb wrinkles concealing your features. Paha Sapa and Mrs. Elmer both bent forward to hear you.

"Did you have a pleasant trip to New York, Mr. Slow Horse?"

"Yes, Mrs. Custer. It was fine."

"All the way from . . . where? Nebraska? Wyoming?"

"South Dakota, ma'am. The Black Hills."

You were not leaning toward us, but I could see you straining to hear, Libbie. I could see no hearing trumpet in the room, but you were obviously having difficulties. I wondered how much of Paha Sapa's conversation you could actually hear. But there seemed to be a glint of recognition in those unfocused eyes at the sound of "Black Hills." I remembered Paha Sapa reading something you wrote in 1927: "There was a time after the battle of the Little Big Horn that I could not have said this, but as the years have passed I have become convinced that the Indians were deeply wronged."

If I'd lived, my darling Sunshine, I would have convinced you of this long before 1927. I remember Paha Sapa reading—I believe it was in your Boots and Saddles *—something to the effect that "General Custer was a friend to every reservation Indian," meaning, obviously, that I would help those who submitted to the orders of the U.S. Government, carried out by such agencies as my Seventh Cavalry, and who stayed at the agencies, ceased hunting, waited patiently for our allocations of beef for them to arrive by rail, and who tried a little farming while waiting.*

Nothing could be further from my feelings, then and later. I confess that I had and still have contempt for the reservation Indians, those who submitted under our threats and attacks and who became docile agency redskins. It was the warriors I admired—them and the women and children and old men who risked everything by going back out onto the Plains with them in a sad and doomed attempt to regain their old way of life…an attempt that was already all but impossible due to our extinction of their buffalo herds. All of us in the Seventh, from the officers down to the newest immigrant enlisted man, used to complain about the fact that the Agencies gave the Sioux and Cheyenne new repeating rifles with which to hunt the occasional game and the young men took these rifles, often superior to our own, and rode out onto the prairie to do battle with us.

We complained, but we in the Seventh Cavalry admired such behavior—we would not have wanted anything other than a fair fight—and during negotiations we soldiers tried to hide our contempt for the lesser, "tamed" Indians both on their reservations and lounging in their ill-kept tipis near the forts. They were little better than the tramps and panhandlers that Paha Sapa had passed on the streets of New York that morning.

You had been saying something.

"Have you had time to sightsee in New York yet, Mr. Slow Horse?"

Paha Sapa smiled slightly—I saw his reflection in the tall glass-covered piece of furniture holding china near you. I had not seen or felt Paha Sapa smile many times in the years I had been aware of him and of my place in him.

"I walked down to the Brooklyn Bridge this morning, Mrs. Custer."

"Oh, Auntie," interrupted May Custer Elmer, "you remember how, years ago, you used to take the taxi to the New York side of the bridge and walk partway over on the promenade and I would come from Brooklyn and meet you on the promenade deck?"

Paha Sapa had been sending his letters to Mrs. Elmer at 14 Park Street in Brooklyn.

You did not turn your face in May's direction, Libbie. You did cock your head and smile slightly, as if you were listening to pleasant music from the radio. But the radio was not on.

Mrs. May Custer Elmer cleared her throat and tried again.

"Auntie, I think you remember that I told you that Mr. William Slow Horse was in Mr. Buffalo Bill Cody's Wild West Show that you enjoyed so much. It's why we decided that you should meet with Mr. Slow Horse. Do you remember, Auntie?"

Between the very loud voice and the slow exaggeration of almost every syllable, your grand-niece was speaking to you as if you were not only old and a little deaf but also a foreigner, Libbie. But you finally quit listening to the inaudible music and looked first at her and then at Paha Sapa.

"Oh...yes. I saw you perform in Mr. Cody's show, Mr....Slow Horse, is it? Yes. I saw you perform and noticed you in the finale where Mr. Cody impersonated my husband. I remember it well....It was at the Madison Square Garden in November of eighteen eighty-six. You rode very well and your war cries were most chilling and convincing, both in the Deadwood Stage act and in the Little Big Horn finale. Yes, very convincing. Very good performance, Mr. Slow Horse."

"Thank you," said Paha Sapa.

I knew that Paha Sapa had never been to New York before and that he hadn't joined Buffalo Bill's Wild West Show until spring of 1893, shortly before the Chicago World's Fair. But whoever you were thinking of, Libbie — whichever Indian — this seemed to have broken the ice and I understand why Paha Sapa didn't correct you.

"Oh, I saw it many times after that," *you continued in that soft, husky yet sibilant whisper, turning your almost blind and formerly blue eyes first in our direction, then in the general direction of May Custer Elmer, and then toward nothing at all but the furniture.* "Miss Oakley...Little Sure Shot, you people called her in the program...became a very good friend of mine. Did you know that, Mr. Slow Horse?"

"No, Mrs. Custer, I didn't."

"What?"

Paha Sapa repeated his answer.

"Well, it is true, Mr. Slow Horse. Of course, Mr. Cody had been one of my husband's scouts long ago. Everyone in the Army knew Mr. Cody long before he opened his Wild West Circus. That November when his show premiered at the...where was it, May?"

"Madison Square Garden, Auntie."

"Oh, yes, of course...I believe I just said that. That November when Mr. Cody's show premiered at the Madison Square Garden, quite everyone was there.... General Sheridan, whom I never cared for that much, to be bluntly honest, and General Sherman, and Henry Ward Beecher...I believe that was before his scandal...was it before his scandal and the adultery trial, May?"

"Yes, Auntie, I believe so."

"Well, he was there...a strange, heavy, long-haired, and unattractive man dressed in a black cape-suit that made him look like a bag of suet. Beecher had one drooping eyelid that made him look like an idiot or stroke victim. It was hard to believe that he was the greatest speaker and evangelist and—evidently—ladies' man of that era, but so it was. August Belmont was there for the premiere of Mr. Cody's show as well as Pierre Lorillard. And I. I had complimentary tickets, of course. You and Charles weren't there, were you, May dear?"

"No, Auntie."

Paha Sapa was looking at the niece and I think both of us were wondering if May Custer Elmer had even been born by 1886. Probably. There was an arroyo of wrinkles under the lady's heavy makeup. You, Libbie, were still talking—like an old toy which, once wound up, took a long time to wind down.

"Well, it was that same autumn that our old cook and fellow traveler from the frontier days, Eliza, came to town...."

I confess that I started a bit at this. Eliza, our Negro cook—my Negro cook during the war even before I'd married Libbie, Eliza, whom my cavalry unit had liberated from slavery in Virginia and who had then followed me (and then Libbie and me) to Texas and Michigan and Kansas and points west—Eliza in New York at Madison Square Garden watching Buffalo Bill's Wild West Show and its finale where Cody pretends to be me being murdered by Indians pretending to murder me? Eliza? Only ten years after my real death?

"...She had married a Negro doctor and left us while Au...while the Armstro...while the Colonel was still alive.... Or was it a Negro attorney, May, my dear?"

"A Negro attorney, I believe, Auntie."

"Yes, yes...At any rate, I loved showing Eliza around New York that autumn and I gave her a ticket to the Madison Square Garden show.... I felt she should see it, you understand..."

For the first time in several minutes, your gaze, Libbie, returned to Paha Sapa.

"...because Eliza and I had lived through so many of the scenes depicted... not the attack on the Deadwood Stage, of course, or the Grand Review, but so many of the other scenes... and I felt sure that nothing could better call back for dear, faithful Eliza, could call back so vividly as it were, our shared experiences on the frontier as this most faithful and realistic reprsentation of a western life that has ceased to be, what with advancing civilization and all."

You paused for breath, my darling, and I paused to review Paha Sapa's memories of his brief time with Cody's show. It was, essentially, the same show that you had seen in 1886, Libbie, and which so many thousands had seen in the years after that and at the Chicago World's Fair. Cody rarely tampered with a winning formula, whether in his scouting or in his Wild West Show or in his lying about history.

"So after the performance, which I had not been able to attend—again—due to other obligations, Eliza took a card I had given her back to Mr. Cody's tent—the two had not previously met, since Eliza had left our service before Mr. Cody began scouting for the cavalry—and she reported to me later..."

And here, my Sunshine, you slipped into a cackling, Amos 'n' Andy–*exaggerated imitation of Eliza's old Virginia slave patois. (Paha Sapa owned a tiny radio that his son, Robert, had built for him and had also heard fragments of* Amos 'n' Andy *a hundred times in bars and other workers' homes, its broadcast blasted off the ionosphere by the powerful WMAQ as part of the NBC Blue Network that reached even to the Black Hills on good listening nights. When the Ruby Taylor character had almost died of pneumonia two years ago, in the spring of '31, half the men on Mount Rushmore could talk of little else.) And you, my darling Libbie, also must have been listening to it religiously, since your voice now was more the Harlem screech of Kingfish's wife, Sapphire, than of our old, slow-southern-speaking cook Eliza.*

"... 'Well, Miss Libbie, when Mr. Cody come up, I see at honce his back and hips was built pracisely like the Ginnel...* Eliza always called my husband "the Ginnel," Mr. Slow Horse, even after the war when all the officers who remained in the army were reduced in rank and Autie...my husband...retained only the rank of colonel...* 'Well, Miss Libbie,' she says, 'when I come on to Maz Cody's tent, I jest said to him: "Mr. Buffalo Bill, sir, when you done come up to the stand and wheeled around like dat, I said to myself, Well, if he ain't the 'spress and spittin' of Ginnel Custer in battle, I never seed any one that was."'"

After this relatively loud recitation of the Amos 'n' Andy *version of Eliza's Negro-ese, you cackled laughter, my darling, until you began to cough, and May Custer Elmer also laughed hard, making her broad red cheeks broader and redder, and even Paha Sapa smiled very slightly, I think (unless there was a slight vibration of a passing elevated train shaking the reflecting glass of the china cabinet). Your coughing continued until everyone else's reaction was finished, and then Margaret—Mrs. Flood—brought in a tray with a steaming teapot, once fine but now spiderweb-fissured china cups and saucers for all of us, a matching little pitcher* and sugar bowl, tiny spoons, and—on a separate dish—tiny wedges of what might possibly have been cucumber sandwiches. Since you were still coughing into a white handkerchief that seemed to have appeared from nowhere (although I had learned when I was alive and married to you that the only thing more mysterious than a woman's heart is the contents of her sleeve), Mrs. May Custer Elmer did the honor of pouring the tea. By the time she had concluded with the pouring, you had concluded with your hacking and coughing.

I knew that Paha Sapa was starving but was afraid to take a tiny sandwich wedge, not being totally sure of how such things should be eaten in the presence of the ladies. If I remember correctly, you and I, Libbie my dearest, were once, in the earliest days of our marriage, confronted with precisely such miniature-sandwich fare at one of ancient General Winfield Scott's last official soirees as head of Lincoln's army before his great age and even greater weight carried him off into History's oblivion, and that afternoon I had simply popped two or three of the tasteless little cucumber-and-bread-and-butter triangles into my mouth and washed them down with a giant swig of the general's seriously substandard wine.

You had frowned at me, but your eyes were merry in those youthful days and then, when none of the crowd was watching, you winked at me. There was no winking or conspiratorial twinkle in your eye this day, the first of April 1933, and you addressed both the cup of tea that niece May had poured and one of the tiny sandwich triangles with deadly, frowning seriousness. It's been my observation that interest in food is one of the—if not the—last things to go with the truly elderly.

It was while you were eating and chewing with such unladylike total concentration, my dearest, that I realized yet another reason that I was having trouble identifying the Libbie-you that I so wildly loved with this old-woman-Libbie in the high-backed chair opposite me: your teeth were different.

You had always had lovely teeth, but very small—each one looking like a miniature of one of those white Chiclet pieces of candy-covered gum that Paha Sapa used to discover young Robert chewing somewhere around 1906—and your perfect but tiny-toothed smile was part of your charm.

Now you obviously had full dentures. The dentist or denture maker had made no effort to match your original, lovely little teeth and these new, larger, much more aggressive substitutes changed your entire face, giving it an almost rodentlike thrust-forward and far too much exposure of the imitation teeth when you spoke or chewed.

I apologize for these unkind remarks, my darling Libbie. I make them because I know now you will never hear them.

My favorite (if unknown to me) grand-niece May cleared her throat. She was our facilitator here and she obviously believed that her aunt's mistaken belief that she had seen Paha Sapa perform in Buffalo Bill's Wild West Show (or Circus, as it had been called in New York City in 1888) was the perfect segue to the heart of our proposed discussion.

I was happy to hear this, since we had promised May that our visit would take up no more than fifteen minutes of your sacred time and energy, Libbie, and—according to the loudly hammering clock on the north wall—we had used up a little more than half that time already with our senseless chitchat.

"Auntie Libbie, perhaps you remember me mentioning that Mr. William Slow Horse wrote to us that not only was he in the re-creation of the...ah...Battle at the Little Big Horn in Buffalo Bill's show, but he was actually there. At the Little Big Horn, I mean. He was...he saw...I mean, he was there on the field with Uncle Armstrong twenty-five June that year when..."

I saw the transformation in you then, Libbie. From leaning forward to eat and sip your tea, you set down the saucer with a clank and sat far back in your high chair, your curved spine as rigid and vertical as you could make it, the expression on your face becoming guarded, protective, and neutral.

Paha Sapa had read to me an old article about your presence at an unveiling of some ridiculous equestrian statue of me in Monroe back in June of 1910: you had hobnobbed with his Immenseness, President Howard Taft, with Michigan's Governor Warner, and with countless others that weekend, but—you said to some reporter much later—what had almost finished you off (not your words, my darling) was the evening meeting at the Armory with hundreds of veterans of the Seventh Cavalry. Some unkind wit there, I think it was a humorous officer in the infantry (the same one who had made you laugh when he said that his infantry following our cavalry during the War had been fascinating, since there were no fence rails left for a fire, no pigs or chickens left for a meal, no full smokehouses left untouched, or anything else that might inhibit their hungry advance in our wake), had commented drily that reports of the massacre of me and my men must have wildly exaggerated if there were so many regimental "survivors" there that weekend. You had ignored that, but what you could not ignore was this mandatory personal meeting with hundreds of aging, toothless, white-haired, white-mustached, wrinkled old veterans in their red neckties—I had worn one, of course, and some of the men had picked up the habit then and apparently all of the grizzled old veterans thought it a good idea — all of them insisting that they knew and remembered you well and that they had been "dear friends" with the General.

Other than a few staff officers, you admitted that you remembered not a single one of these men (much less the wives and children and in-laws and grandchildren they had dragged to the unveiling of the equestrian monument there in Monroe and whom they insisted on introducing to you as if they also had been dear friends and followers and intimates with you).

But it was more than this, I am certain, that made your spine rigid and your face expressionless this first day of April 1933.

Even through the severely restricted lens of Paha Sapa's reading in recent years, I understood all too well that when it came to the topic of my death — my death and the deaths of 258 other officers and troopers of the Seventh Cavalry, including my two brothers, my very young nephew, and my brother-in-law — everyone who had taken the energy to form an opinion on me fell into either the category that considered me a megalomaniacal fool who managed to get my men, my relatives, and myself killed through sheer, arrogant stupidity, or in the opposing category wherein I, Lieutenant Colonel (still called "General" by those who loved me) George Armstrong Custer, had died following orders and in a valiant attack on the largest concentration of hostile Indian warriors in the entire history of our nation's warfare against the Indians.

Custerphobes or Custerphiles, as one otherwise forgettable editorial writer had put it some years earlier. And it was true that there seemed to be no middle ground — no one who thought I was something between those opposite and mutually exclusive poles of arrogant fool or martyred hero.

Were you forgetting important things these days in your age and illness, my darling? Had senility begun to set in behind those rheumy eyes and that wrinkled, absent expression? Is it possible that you were, even as I sat opposite you, forgetting that you had led the Custerphile contingent now for fifty-seven long, bitter years? Ever vigilant in defense against any conceivable blot on my name or record of honor, you also led the offense at times, such as in 1926 and again in 1929, when you strongly objected to C. H. Asbury, then chief agent at the Crow Agency in control of the Little Big Horn battlefield that bears my name, when Asbury considered putting up even the smallest plaque honoring the name and memory of that drunkard and coward Major Marcus Reno — who, my darling, you were certain had left me and my three companies alone on that hill to die.

All those years and decades of never faltering as you led the Custerphiles in my name, never allowing the Custerphobes a foothold or fingerhold, using your grief and widowhood and dignity as your weapons, and during that time how many faux "unknown survivors" of my so-called Last Stand had you heard from or been forced to meet with? Dozens? Scores? Hundreds?

You, my love, had gone to the 1893 World's Fair in Chicago, only seventeen years after your husband had been turned into worm meat, and there had been introduced to Chief Rains-in-the-Face, who, it was bragged by the Indians even there in Buffalo Bill's troupe, was the man who had killed me. You, my Sunshine, were all too well aware that the reason for that fat old smallpox-scarred Indian's ascendancy in the Sioux and Cheyenne hierarchy there in Buffalo Bill's Show — they had given Rains-in-the-Face Sitting Bull's old cabin to live in at the Fair, the cabin transplanted right there on the Midway Plaisance, where poor Paha Sapa first met his wife, for God's sake — was precisely the smiling, smirking Rains-in-the-Face's claim of having personally killed me in the high grass of the Little Big Horn. And when Cody introduced the smiling, pock-faced old Indian fool, you had nodded curtly, feeling the pain slashing your insides as if someone were in your belly swinging a straight razor.

No wonder you were worn out but rigidly on guard and scowling this day, this day that only Paha Sapa and I knew was our reunion, yours and mine, my darling, when Mrs. May Custer Elmer began explaining how Paha Sapa had been there on the battlefield the very day and hour and moment that I — your husband — had died.

There was a real silence when May quit talking. Paha Sapa did not break that lengthening and audibly thickening silence, nor did you, my once and former and now lost lovely girl. The heavy clock on the bureau clunked away the passing seconds. Somewhere on the East River to the south, in the direction of the Brooklyn Bridge, a large ship's horn bleated woefully.

Finally, after a full ninety seconds of our remaining six minutes had been fed to silence, you spoke even more softly than before, but with an inescapable edge in your tone that could have shaved me as cleanly as the straight razor even then slashing at your insides.

"You were there when my husband died, Mr. William Slow Horse?"

"Yes, ma'am. I was."

"How old are you now, Mr. Slow Horse?"

"Sixty-eight this coming August, Mrs. Custer."

"And how old were you then... that day... Mr. Slow Horse?"

"Eleven summers that August, ma'am. Not quite eleven that day in June."

"What do your people call the month of June, Mr. Slow Horse?"

"Different things, ma'am. My band called June the Moon of the June Berries."

You smiled then, Libbie, and the new, wrong teeth looked more aggressive than ever. An old predator's overbite, not a rabbit's.

"That name is a bit tautological, isn't it, Mr. William Slow Horse?"

Paha Sapa did not smile or blink or look away from the cold, once-blue stare aimed at him.

"I'm sorry, Mrs. Custer. I don't know that word... tautological."

"No, of course you don't, Mr. Slow Horse."

"But my guess is that it means 'redundant'—or, as my mentor, Mr. Doane Robinson, used to joke, 'repetitiously redundant'—which I guess our word for June is. The Lakota word for June is wipazunkawaštewi, *and it means more or less 'the moon in which the cherries of that moon become ripe,' and the dates for the lunar month, a moon, aren't exactly the same as those for the modern calendar month of June."*

You squinted at him through this recital, my darling, perhaps the longest speech I'd ever heard Paha Sapa give, and everything in your squint, the set of your mouth and chin, and your posture showed that you were not listening, refused to hear, and did not care.

Finally you said flatly, *"You claim to have seen my husband there on the battlefield, Mr. Slow Horse?"*

"Yes."

"Did you kill him?"

Paha Sapa blinked at that. *"No, Mrs. Custer. I didn't hurt him in any way. I didn't have a weapon with me. I just touched him."*

"Touched him? Why would you do that if you weren't attacking him, Mr. Slow Horse?"

"I was ten summers old and was counting coup. Do you know the term, Mrs. Custer?"

"Yes, I believe I do, Mr. Slow Horse. It's what Indian warriors do to show their courage, isn't it? Just touching an enemy?"

"Yes, ma'am. I wasn't a warrior, but I was trying to show my courage."

"Did you have with you a... what do you call it? A coup stick? I saw those when I traveled with my husband to Indian villages in Kansas, Nebraska, and elsewhere."

"No, I only had my bare hand."

You took a breath, Libbie, and while still sitting stiffly, leaned forward slightly, as if you were on a rusty hinge.

"Did my husband say something to you, Mr. William Slow Horse? Are you going to tell me that my husband said something to you?"

Paha Sapa and I had discussed what to say next many times. When he first suggested coming to see you, for me, several years ago, I had certain fantasies of having Paha Sapa share various secret things with you that only you and I would know, so you would understand that he was truly speaking for me. Some of the secrets seem absurd now—"Mrs. Custer, he said to remember how we went into the willows alone on the day the regiment left from Fort Abe Lincoln and what we did there…"—and unless Paha Sapa explained that my ghost was inside him, it would make no sense anyway.

We actually discussed telling you that my ghost—what Paha Sapa thought of as my ghost—was inside him. Then I could tell you, my dearest, everything that I longed to tell you. After all, we had both lived through that strange era of spirit rappings and seances before and during the War, and more than once you had wondered aloud if there was anything to these mediums and these visits from the dead.

Now Paha Sapa could have proved that there was.

Only we decided against that. It was all too…vulgar. We had finally decided (I had finally decided) that Paha Sapa would explain to you only that I, your husband, had, with my dying breath, whispered to him, a mere boy, "Tell my Libbie that I love her and always will love her." And we fully expected you to say, "Oh, and did you speak and understand English when you were ten years old, Mr. Slow Horse?" and he would reply, "No, Mrs. Custer, but I remembered the simple sound of the words and understood them years later when I did learn English."

To that end, we'd shortened the message a bit to "Tell Libbie I love her." Six simple syllables. It might seem possible, especially to a woman of ninety who had loved me all these intervening years, that I might have said that and that an Indian boy might have remembered six such syllables and finally carried them to her like six roses.

Then I heard Paha Sapa reply to you in that little room…"No, Mrs. Custer, your husband did not speak to me. I believe he was dead when I touched him."

You stared at him a long, long moment then—another minute of our short time together gone forever—and said coldly, "Then why did you come to see me, Mr. William Slow Horse? To tell me what my husband looked like in those last seconds? To tell me that he did not suffer…or that he did? Or perhaps to apologize?"

"No, Mrs. Custer. I was just curious to meet you. And I appreciate you giving me this time."

Paha Sapa stood up. I felt myself fluttering in gales of inexplicable emotions — I did not even know what they were — but you still sat there and looked calmly up at this aging Indian visitor, my love, your gaze still cold but no longer suspicious or hostile. Perhaps a little puzzled.

"If you had apologized, Mr. Slow Horse," you said to him in that whisper of a voice, "I would have told you there was no need. I realized long ago that it wasn't you Sioux and your Cheyenne friends who killed my husband… it was those cowards and Judases in his own command like Marcus Reno and Frederick Benteen who killed my darling husband and his brothers and our nephew and so many of his troopers."

Paha Sapa did not know what to say to that. I did not know what to tell Paha Sapa to say to that. He bowed and turned to leave. Mrs. May Custer Elmer hustled to show him out through the cluttered rooms.

There was a whisper from the parlor behind us and Paha Sapa turned back. You were still seated — seeming more shrunken somehow, my dearest, perhaps because you had slumped from that defiant posture and now looked only like a bent old woman — but you were beckoning Paha Sapa closer with a wiggle of one yellow-nailed finger.

He leaned over you, breathing in the scent of lilac toilet water and the deeper smell of a very old woman wrapped in her stifling layers.

You looked him in the eye then, looked us in the eye, and whispered… "Autie…" or perhaps "Good-bye" or perhaps it was a pure nonsense syllable, something choked off or irrelevant to everything that had come before.

When Paha Sapa realized that you were not going to say anything else, he nodded as if he understood, bowed again, and followed May Custer Elmer out. The housekeeper, Mrs. Flood, had bustled in behind us, carrying what looked to be medicines on a tray into the parlor for you.

Back at the hotel for colored people, Paha Sapa slept well that night. His train was leaving from Grand Central Terminal at 7:45 the next morning. Although I never really slept, there were times when I faded into the nonconsciousness of the black background which I occupied when Paha Sapa did not summon me out to the light and sound, but I did not find escape there that night.

I found myself wishing that I could have told you many things, Libbie, my darling, my wife, my life.

I wish I could have explained to you that it wasn't betrayal or cowardly officers that caused my death and that of my brothers Tom and Boston and my nephew Autie and the others there at the Little Big Horn. It was true that Major Reno was a drunk — and probably a coward — and that Benteen hated my guts (and always had) but proved his courage on the same field where Reno showed his cowardice, but none of that was relevant to my death. I know in my soldier's heart that Reno and Benteen and the others couldn't have come up to help me and my three surrounded companies; the four miles that separated us that day might as well have been the distance from the Earth to the moon. They had their own battle to fight, Libbie, my love, and no troopers could have reached us in time or to any effect other than dying with us.

There were just too many hostile Indians there, my dearest. Our best intelligence, the white agents at the Agencies, had assured us over and over that no more than eight hundred warriors in all, Cheyenne and Sioux, the Lakotas and Nakotas and Dakotas, all of them, had slipped away from the agencies to go hunt buffalo and fight. No more than eight hundred and probably far fewer than that, since such large bands rarely spent much time together — finding proper grazing for their horses was too difficult. And the sheer heaps of human excrement and other filth and garbage generated by camps of more than a few hundred Indians discouraged them from staying together long.

So we rode in expecting eight hundred and ran into . . . how many? You've heard all the figures, Libbie, my darling. They range from fifteen hundred warriors arrayed against us to more than six thousand, most coming from a village of ten to fifteen thousand men, women, and children, all of whom were willing to join in the fight — or at least in the scalping and mutilating. In the end, my darling, it turned out to be a matter of just too damned many Indians there waiting for us. It was unprecedented. It was unexpected. It was my undoing.

Even then, Libbie, we should have prevailed. Right up until the last minutes, I was sure we would prevail — even without Reno's companies or Benteen's or the supply train or the packs of ammunition.

The reason was simple: the cavalry in any solid numbers always had prevailed against Plains Indians. Our most trusted tactic was to charge any large band or village of hostiles. They might fight for a few minutes, or fight while running, but if there was a way for them simply to scatter and run in the face of a charge, they always had before. Always.

But this time they did not.

It is almost humorous when you think about it, my darling. It's precisely what you once said to me about a skittish horse you were riding in Kansas—"Horses can be dangerous, but you can always trust them to act like horses. Once you know what they're going to try to do to you, you can avoid it."

I had trusted the Sioux and Cheyenne there at the Little Big Horn to act as they had at the Washita—as Indian warriors had everywhere else the Seventh Cavalry and other regiments had encountered them. Taken by surprise by a cavalry charge, they should have fought a few minutes but then scattered as they always had before.

But this time they didn't. It was that simple, Libbie, my love.

———

If I had been able to talk to you that final day on April first, I might have explained to you that the sadness I felt was not for me, but for leading my young brother Tom (perhaps the bravest of all of us, he with his two Medals of Honor) and my non-soldier brother Boston (whom I hired as a scout at the last minute, on a whim, thinking that he would be sorry to have missed the Last Great Indian Fight), not to mention my nephew Autie, who had just turned eighteen and who came along precisely so as not to miss that promised Last Big Battle, all to that place on that day.

If I could, Libbie, if ghosts or Heaven were real, I would shake them by the hand and look them in the eye and apologize to all of them—especially to those men who'd followed me and trusted me for so long, like Lonesome Charley Reynolds and Myles Keogh and Bill Cooke—not for their deaths, for we all owe God a death (as Hamlet reminded us), but for the foolishness of my own assumptions and minor miscalculations that hot, humid June Sunday in 1876.

But I would also have reminded you of something, my darling. I would have reminded you of how much fun we had (and planned to continue to have, me earning money, at last, as a lecturer once that Final Great Indian Battle was over, and also writing my books, and perhaps some future in Democratic politics). But without worrying about our future, just remind you of how much fun we had.

I was a warrior and loved being a warrior. And you enjoyed the status and excitement of being a warrior's wife, my love… or at least of being an officer warrior's wife.

The Rebs had been the bravest enemy I would ever fight, and the hostile Indians served as a foe in the years after the War. But even then, even that last winter and spring, you and I knew that the days of an active warrior on the frontier were closing fast.

Finally, the last thing I would have told you that Saturday afternoon in your parlor of stale air was that you should have remarried. I had no doubt about that. You should have remarried as soon as you could after the Little Big Horn, Libbie, my love.

It was two years after our New York visit and totally by chance that Paha Sapa came across a newspaper quote by your "literary executor," the same accusatory and strangely syllable-stressed Miss Marguerite Merington whom we'd met briefly down in the foyer, and Miss Merington quoted you as saying around the time we met you— "One does get so lonely. But I always felt I should be committing adultery if I were to wake up one morning and see any head but Autie's on my pillow."

Well, my darling, to that I must say to you— horse apples.

The Creator designed you, more than He did most women, I believe, to be loved, to love in return, and to be a lover.

You should have found a good man as soon after June 25, 1876, as would not have seemed scandalous— an attorney would have served (as it did for our cook Eliza) or, better yet, a judge, since you always secretly wanted to marry your father the Judge— and you should have married a good man and put our life on the Plains behind you forever. No lobbying for equestrian saddles. No endless correspondence with yellow-mustached and mawkish old soldiers who write to say "I loved General Custer" but who are really saying "I would love you, Mrs. Custer, if you would let me." No writing romantic fantasies about a not-quite-true past with silly titles like Boots and Saddles *or* Following the Guidon.

You should have lived for yourself, Libbie Bacon, not for your dead husband. You should have celebrated life, not my death, and you should have become a lover again and awakened every day you could with another man's head on your pillow and your head on his. Perhaps you could still have had a child— you were 34 when I died. Stranger things have happened. You would have lived in fullness and celebrated life then, my darling.

Instead, you "lived" to serve a ghost. And there are no ghosts, my dear.

Someday I shall explain that to Paha Sapa, who thinks otherwise. I shall try to make him understand what I discovered some years ago— that I am no ghost, nor a soul waiting to go to Heaven, but only a node in his unique empathic consciousness, a sort of simulation of a self-aware memory.

It is all Paha Sapa and a twist of his odd gift of vision and always has been. There is no ghost, no "me" here, my love. There never has been.

And while I am neither ghost nor liberated soul, I have learned something about death in these years in the cradle of darkness, Libbie. I tremble to tell you that I do not think that there is anything beyond this life, my dearest, which is all the more reason I wish you had decided to live with another man and build a new life rather than choose to bury your future with me fifty-seven years ago.

But I am still glad that Paha Sapa—the loneliest man you have ever met or ever could meet, my love, a man who has lost his name, his relatives, his honor, his wife, his son, his gods, his future, his hopes, and every sacred thing ever entrusted to him—I am still glad that Paha Sapa brought me to New York on that first day of April 1933.

———

We were delayed a day and a night due to a freak spring snowstorm near Grand Isle, Nebraska, and two days after we finally got back to Mount Rushmore, the Rapid City Journal *carried this, dated April 5 and reprinted from the* New York Times—

MRS. CUSTER DEAD
IN HER 91ST YEAR

Mrs. Elizabeth Bacon Custer, widow of General George A. Custer, famous Indian fighter of post Civil War days, died at 5:30 yesterday afternoon in her apartment at 71 Park Avenue after a heart attack that occurred Sunday evening. She would have been 91 years old on Saturday. She had been in her usual health and good spirit lately and had indulged in occasional drives and short walks.

At Mrs. Custer's bedside yesterday were two nieces, Mrs. Charles W. Elmer of 14 Clark street, Brooklyn, and Miss Lula Custer, who had been summoned from her home on the old Custer farm at Monroe Mich., and Mr. Elmer.

It is expected that the funeral service will be held at West Point. Announcement of the arrangements will be made later.

For many years, almost up to the end of her long, eventful life, Mrs. Elizabeth Bacon Custer kept vividly alive the memories of the gallant cavalry commander, whose death in the Battle of Little Big Horn in Montana, in 1876, when his battalion was annihilated by the Indians, made one of the most tragic and dramatic pages of American history.

Mrs. Custer was born in Monroe, Mich., the daughter of Judge Daniel S. Bacon, where she led a peaceful and sheltered life until 1864, when she married "the boy General with the golden locks." Her youthful soldier husband, General Custer, was born in New Rumley, Harrison County, Ohio, and was graduated at West Point in 1861. At the time of their marriage, he had already served successfully and won promotion in the Civil War, after having arrived fresh from the front on the day of the first battle of Bull Run.

He was then a Brigadier General in command of a brigade of Michigan volunteer cavalry, which under his leadership became one of the most efficient and best-trained bodies of cavalry in the Federal Army. After their marriage Mrs. Custer trod the unfrequented path for a woman of open campaigning. She slept where she could, drank water that in her own words contained "natural History," and never dared confess to a headache, depression or fatigue.

She followed the General until the close of the Civil War. She was near him at Richmond, Va., when Lee surrendered to Grant at Appomattox. He was one of the officers in attendance on General Phil H. Sheridan, who bought the little table on which the conditions for the surrender of the Confederate Army were written by General Grant, and presented it to Mrs. Custer.

Indian Campaign in 1867

After the Civil War General Custer, who was still under 26, was transferred to Texas. As Lieutenant Colonel of the Seventh Cavalry, in 1867–68, he gained his first experience as an Indian fighter. For two years he was stationed with his regiment in Kentucky, and in the Spring of 1873 he was ordered to Dakota Territory to protect the surveyors of the Northern Pacific Railway while locating that line through the Indian country west of the Missouri River.

Mrs. Custer personally attended her husband on many of his most daring expeditions against the Indians. This was the era of the covered wagon, when the transcontinental trek was made by stage, canal boat, prairie schooner and afoot, and there was prairie fire and ever-lurking Indian peril to contend with.

Steamer Brought News

Finally, at Fort Abraham Lincoln, at Bismarck, N.D., Mrs. Custer waited while General Custer joined a huge expeditionary force in a campaign against the Indians that General Sheridan hoped would be decisive. Three weeks after the massacre, when General Custer with his entire command of five companies of Seventh Cavalry, numbering 207, were annihilated in about twenty minutes by the redskins, a slow-moving steamer brought the tragic news from up the river.

Following her husband's death she wrote three books on his experiences, "Boots and Saddles, or Life With General Custer in Dakota," "Tenting on the Plains" and "Following the Guidon." This was a part of her fifty years and more task of defending his memory, around which controversy flamed. She lectured up and down the country and battled for his rights in Washington. In 1926 she expressed the feeling that the old wounds had been healed.

While the widow viewed the massacre at the Little Big Horn River in Montana as a terrible tragedy, she said at one time, that "perhaps it was necessary in the scheme of things, for the public clamor that rose after the battle resulted in better equipment for the soldiers everywhere, and very soon the Indian warfare came to its end."

Before neuritis interfered with her walking she was a famous figure on the sunny side of Park Avenue as she took leisurely strolls about the neighborhood. She frequented the Cosmopolitan Club, which is near her home. She is quoted as saying that the modern club is a consolation for the widow and old maid. On her walks she was accompanied by her companion, Mrs. Margaret Flood, who, with her husband, Patrick Flood, an ex-service man, were permanent fixtures in the household.

In addition to war relics her apartment contained many Colonial treasures. One of her greatest treasures was the first Confederation flag of truce. In her hall was a long photograph showing the unveiling of a statue to her husband's memory in Monroe, Neb.

———

Good-bye, Libbie. Farewell, my darling girl. We shall not meet again.
But, as Paha Sapa has taught me without knowing he has taught me—

Toksha ake čante ista wacinyanktin ktelo.
I shall see you again with the eye of my heart.

21

The Six Grandfathers

Friday, August 28, 1936

AFTER RIDING THE ABOMINABLE TRAMCAR BACK UP THE MOUNTAIN and standing there looking down at the Hall of Records canyon while listening to Gutzon Borglum talk about blasting out the rock saved for the Theodore Roosevelt head, Paha Sapa willingly rides with his boss down on the same tramcar rather than face the 506 steps again. He's descended them once this hot August evening, and he hurts too much to do it again.

It's the pain rather than the rock dust and sweat that sends Paha Sapa straight home to his shack in Keystone. Rather than make dinner—it's almost seven p.m. by the time he gets home—he builds a fire in the woodstove, despite the remaining intense heat of the day, and heats up two big tubs of water he's pumped outside. It takes six of these big buckets to get enough water in his bathtub for a real bath, and by the time he's poured in the last two steaming tubs, the water from the first two are cooling off.

But most of it is still steaming hot as he strips off his work clothes and boots and socks and settles into the claw-footed freestanding bathtub.

The pain from the cancer has become a problem. Paha Sapa feels it creeping up from his colon or prostate or lower bowels or wherever it's advancing from—threatening to overwhelm him for the first time in his frequently pain-filled life—and stealing his strength. His one great secret ally has been his strength, quite unusual for a man of his modest weight and height, and now it is leaking away like the heat from this water or like the water itself once he pulls out the plug.

Once dressed in clean clothes, Paha Sapa goes to feed the donkeys before he feeds himself.

They are both there in their rough new pen, both Advocatus and Diaboli. Paha Sapa refills their water and makes sure they have grain to eat as well as the hay scattered around their enclosure. Diaboli tries to bite him, but Paha Sapa is prepared for that. He is not prepared for Advocatus's sideways kick and that catches Paha Sapa squarely in the upper thigh, numbing his entire leg for a moment and causing him to have to lean on the fence while fighting the nausea rising in him.

The donkeys belong to Father Pierre Marie in Deadwood, the truly ancient priest and only survivor of the three friars who taught a young Indian boy so long ago, and Paha Sapa has promised to get the animals back by Saturday afternoon. He rented the old Dodge flatbed—the same one that transported the submarine engines from Colorado—from Howdy Peterson's cousin, also from Deadwood, and Paha Sapa put fresh straw and hay in the now-fenced-in flatbed to transport the donkeys from Deadwood. He needs the truck again tonight but he plans to return it to Howdy after hauling the donkeys home early Saturday morning.

That is, if he doesn't blow himself *and* the Dodge to tiny bits tonight in the transfer of the dynamite. He plans to drive the donkeys to the site first and tie them up in the woods below the canyon, so that they don't blow if the dynamite and he and the truck do on the next trip. With that possibility in mind, Paha Sapa has already written a note asking Hap Doland, his nearest neighbor there in Keystone, to drive the donkeys home "should something unforeseen happen to me." The note is propped on his mantel. (Although he imagines that it will be the sheriff or Mr. Borglum who comes to the shack first, not Hap.)

Donkeys fed, Paha Sapa goes in to make some beans and franks and coffee for himself. He's very tired and though the hot bath distracted him, this time it has not leached away any of the pain. Paha Sapa wonders if he should have taken the Casper doctor up on his offer of morphine tablets to be dissolved and injected with a syringe.

After dinner, with the Keystone valley in shadow — the evenings are growing shorter now at the end of August — and with V-tailed swallows and terns slicing the air into chorded arcs of pale blue in search of insects and the first bats emerging to their zigzag flights, Paha Sapa starts up Robert's rackety motorcycle and drives the three miles up to Mune Mercer's cabin.

The cabin looks dark as Paha Sapa approaches and for a moment he thinks he has lost his gamble that Mune wouldn't have enough money to be out getting drunk this particular Friday night. Then the door opens and a huge, hulking form — Mune is six-foot-six and must weigh close to 300 pounds — steps out onto the rickety porch.

Paha Sapa turns off the motorcycle's little engine.

— *Don't shoot, Mune. It's me, Billy.*

The massive silhouette grunts and lowers the double-barreled shotgun.

— *'Bout goddamned time you got here, Slow Horse, Slovak, Slow Ass. You promised me the night work and money more 'n three weeks ago, goddamn your half-breed eyes.*

Mune is fair on the way to getting drunk, Paha Sapa sees and hears, but only on his private moonshine, which will probably blind him within a year if it doesn't kill him first. Paha Sapa can see now that there is the slightest lantern glow visible through the open door but that the blinds are closed tight on the front windows.

— *You going to invite me in, Mune? I've got the details about tomorrow night's job and I brought what's left of a fifth for you.*

Mune grunts again but takes a step sideways to allow Paha Sapa to squeeze through into the cluttered, filthy, and foul-smelling one-room cabin.

Mune Mercer, whose first name — probably a family name — has always been pronounced "Moon," was invariably called "Moon Mullins" during the short time he worked on the Monument as a winch man and general laborer, and, like the cartoon character, Mune is rarely seen, even on the mountain, without his undersized derby squeezed down onto his short-stubbled dome of a skull and an unlit stogie clamped in his teeth. Mune even has a scruffy and surprisingly petite mutt who, like Moon Mullins's little brother (or is he his son?), is named Kayo and, like the kid in the comic strip, sleeps in a lower drawer of a dresser next to Mune's bed. Kayo—the canine version—looks up sleepily at Paha Sapa but does not bark. Paha Sapa wonders if the mutt has also been drinking.

There are two chairs at the small rough-planked table near the sink with a short-handed pump and stove and Paha Sapa drops tiredly into one without being invited to sit. He takes out the fifth of whiskey, about a third full, and sets it on the table.

—*I see you helped your own fucking self to most of it. Some fucking gift, Tonto.*

Paha Sapa blinks at the subtlety of the insult. There's a sidekick Indian character named Tonto on a new cowboy radio drama that premiered on a Detroit radio station, WXYZ, the previous February. WXYZ is powerful enough that frequently, when the atmospherics are right, listeners with good sets or an understanding of the ionosphere can pick it up out here in the Hills. Paha Sapa has actually heard the station—and that cowboy show with the great opening music—on the earphones he had added to the little crystal set that Robert built the summer before he went into the Army, twenty years ago.

Paha Sapa smiles slightly and looks around the garbage heap of a room. The sheets on Mune's unmade bed, once white, are mostly a caked yellow now.

—*Tonto? Cute, Mune. I don't see your radio, though. How have you been listening to* The Lone Ranger?

Mune lets out a boozy breath and drops into his chair at the table. The chair groans but does not quite collapse.

—*What the fuck's the Lone Ranger?* Tonto *means "stupid" in Spanish, Tonto.*

Well, so much for subtlety.

Mune is a dimwit but was a decent winch man the few weeks he worked at Mount Rushmore. But he is a drunkard as well as a dimwit—and a drunken Mune, it turns out, is invariably a mean Mune—and although Mr. Borglum tends to look the other way when men come to work hungover on Saturdays or even Mondays, he will not abide any drinking on the job or someone like Mune Mercer, who came in hungover *every* day of the week. Out on the cliff face, men's lives depend upon the sobriety and sound judgment of the other men—especially winch men — and Mune was hungover, red-eyed, and surly until ten or eleven every morning.

When he wasn't drunk, Mune was mostly a gentle dimwit giant, and the other workers tried to cover for him — for a while — but when Mr. Borglum, who'd been traveling, finally saw the truth of the matter, he fired Mune's huge butt the same day.

So Mune had been both surprised and suspicious a week earlier when Paha Sapa came to him with the offer of a truly spectacular fifty dollars in exchange for some night work at the Monument.

Mune, mouth open and beady little eyes squinting under his derby, had cocked his giant thumb of a head to one side to show his cynicism.

— *Night work? Whaddya talking about, 'breed? There ain't no night work on Rushmore 'cause there ain't no lights for it, so there's no fucking night work.*

— *There will be a week from now, Mune — on the weekend before the president arrives on Sunday the thirtieth. You have heard the rumors about FDR coming up to the mountain, haven't you?*

— *No.*

One of the nice things about Mune Mercer is that he is never defensive or apologetic about his ignorance, which is vast.

Paha Sapa smiled then, a week ago this very night, and presented Mune with a *full* bottle of cheap whiskey, and said —

— *Well, it seems sure now that the president is coming, on Sunday the thirtieth, Mune, and there's going to be a big celebration and unveiling of the Jefferson head and Mr. Borglum wants me and you to do some night work so we can prepare a surprise he has in store for the president and for all the VIPs. And, for whatever reason, he wants this to be a surprise even for the rest of the guys working on the hill. And because we have to work alone and at night — but Mr. Borglum says it'll be almost a full moon that Saturday night — he's willing to pay us each fifty dollars.*

Mune squinted his suspicion then, just as he is doing now. Fifty dollars is a fortune.

— *Why would Mr. Borglum want me, Mr. Billy Half-breed? He* fired *me, remember? Right in front of all the fellows. Is he hiring me back for good?*

Paha Sapa shook his head.

— *No, Mune. Mr. Borglum still doesn't want a drunk on the payroll. But, like I said, he wants this to be a surprise for* all *the other workers* and *their wives, as well as for President Roosevelt and Senator Norbeck and the governor and the rest of the high muckety-mucks down below in the reviewing stand. It's a onetime deal, Mune...but it's* fifty dollars.

Mune looked more ridiculous than usual that night as he squinted beneath his derby and above his cold cigar stump until his thin slits of eyes disappeared (as they are starting to now) in folds of lashless fat.

— *Show me the money.*

Paha Sapa brought out a wad of money, almost a year's savings for him, and pulled fifty dollars from the roll.

— *What's so secret that Mr. Borglum would pay me an' a half-breed to set it up at night? He going to blow up his own fucking heads or something?*

Paha Sapa laughed politely at that, but his skin grew cold and clammy.

— *It'll be a sort of fireworks display. I guess there will be newsreel cameras there and Mr. Borglum wants to surprise everyone with a real spectacle.*

— *You sayin' that that nigger lover Roosevelt is coming at night?*

— *No. Sometime in late morning, I think. While the shadows on the faces are still good.*

— *A fireworks show in the middle of the day. That don't make no fucking sense.*

Paha Sapa shrugged, obviously as amused by the Old Man's whims and eccentricities as Mune was.

— *It's a fireworks show with quite a bit of dynamite behind it, Mune. I guess it's going to be in the form of a twenty-one-gun salute to the president...you know, like the military gives him when the band plays "Hail to the Chief"?...but with little blasts the whole length of the Monument, moving some of the stone that we're gonna have to move anyway but making it sound like like a formal cannon salute. Anyway, Mr. Borglum said I could hire you for this one night only, partially because you're not in touch with many people and won't blab, but I have other men I can hire if you don't want to do it. It's* fifty dollars, *Mune.*

— *Gimme my fifty now. In, you know, advance.*

Paha Sapa gave him only five one-dollar bills, knowing that Mune would spend it on booze in the first two days and be relatively sober by the time he, Paha Sapa, needed him the next weekend.

———

MUNE DRINKS FROM THE BOTTLE of the fifth, not offering to clean a glass to give Paha Sapa any. Seeing the state of the two glasses in the sink, Paha Sapa is glad there is no offer to share.

—I need another ten bucks.

Paha Sapa shakes his head.

—Look, Mune. You know Mr. Borglum won't pay you the rest until the job's done tomorrow night. I'm working with Jack Payne all day tomorrow on the drilling in preparation for this surprise…and since Jack already knows that something's up, I might as well give the night work to him and pay him the fifty bucks…or I should say the forty-five that's left. I know he'll show up sober tomorrow night.

—Palooka? Fuck him. You and the old man offered this job to me, you fucking sack of half-breed shit. Try to Jew me out of it and…

Mune tries to raise his bulk out of the chair but Paha Sapa stands and easily pushes him back down. The moonshine is powerful stuff and Mune has probably been hitting it since Tuesday.

—Then sober up tomorrow—I'm serious about that. If you're drunk or even seriously hungover when I come to fetch you tomorrow night, Mr. Borglum has ordered me to go get Payne or someone else. I mean it, Mune. Be stone sober tomorrow night or this fifty bucks goes to someone else.

Mune sticks out his lower lip like a scolded, sulking child. Paha Sapa thinks that if the drunken dimwit starts crying, he—Paha Sapa—will kill him. For not the first time in his life, he feels the terrible Crazy Horse joy rising in him at the thought of sinking a hatchet deep into the prescalped skull under that stupid derby.

—What time you comin' for me tomorrow night, Billy?

Paha Sapa lets out a breath in relief.

—A little before eleven p.m., Mune.

—Do I get paid then?

Paha Sapa doesn't even bother shaking his head at a question that stupid.

—In the morning. Before dawn. When we're done. Mr. Borglum may show up to check the work and pay you himself.

—Hey, you already got the money! I saw it last week!

—That was for another job, Mune. Look, I talked Mr. Borglum into giving you this last job just as my favor to you. Don't screw it up.

Mune tries to squint harder but his squint is as tight and narrow as it can go.

—Which winch will I be usin'?

—All four of them, I think. I'll check with Mr. Borglum tomorrow, but I think we'll be using all four.

—Four? There are only three winches on the face now, you stupid half-breed. I come by now and then, y'know. There're only three on the heads.

—Only three working above the heads right now, it's true. But there's the one on the backside from last year. I guess we'll be lifting some stuff from the Hall of Records canyon. Oh, and Mune?

—What?

Paha Sapa lifts his loose shirt. The long Colt revolver given to him by Curly the cavalry scout sixty years ago next week is tucked into his waistband. In the intervening years, Paha Sapa has found cartridges for it and was test firing as recently as yesterday. The nice thing about well-built weapons, he thinks, is that they're never *really* obsolete.

—Just this, Mune. You call me half-breed or Tonto once again, and I don't care how drunk you are, I'll blow your fucking dim-witted head clean off your fucking fat carcass. Is that clear, you big, stupid sack of shit?

Mune nods docilely.

Paha Sapa goes out to the motorcycle. It starts on the first kick. The long-barreled revolver is absurdly uncomfortable in his waistband so Paha Sapa tosses it onto the leather seat of the sidecar.

———

A LITTLE BEFORE MIDNIGHT, Paha Sapa drives the donkeys up to the mountain first, just as he planned. Even as he shifts the gears of the screeching hulk of a truck, he knows it is a stupid plan. He should have just put the donkeys in with the dynamite and blasting caps and made one trip out of it. If the dynamite were to go up, so would most of the town of Keystone—what are two damned, lazy old donkeys one way or the other? Paha Sapa has never had much use for anything—man or beast—that doesn't work to earn its keep in the world, and these donkeys haven't done any labor harder than hauling Father Pierre Marie's mail or groceries up the hill from Deadwood to the church and priest's cabin once a week or so.

Well, that will change tonight. The asses—and the ass of the old man currently driving them up the hill—will do some serious work for a change this night.

Advocatus and Diaboli are quiet back there during the ride. They were very unhappy when Paha Sapa lashed the clumsy slippers made out of burlap over their hooves before loading them onto the truck, but apparently the two donkeys think that they are being driven back to their real life with the priest above Deadwood—or maybe they are just sleepy, unused to being rousted from their beauty sleep once the sun goes down—and perhaps they are also pleased at all the heaps of straw and bales of hay strategically placed in the back of the slat-sided truck for their riding and dining pleasure.

Paha Sapa doesn't break it to the donkeys that the hay and straw are for the dynamite to come later.

The highway is empty. The small complex of shacks and larger buildings visible on Doane Mountain through the pines—the hoist house, blacksmith shop, compressor house—are all dark. Paha Sapa catches a glimpse of lights still gleaming from Mr. Borglum's studio, but that home is safely away from the large dirt-and-gravel parking lot where he drives the Dodge to the far end, parks in the shadows of large trees, and unloads Devil's and Advocate.

The trees now have shadows because the moon—two days away from being full—has risen above the peaks and hills to the east. The August night air is warmer than usual for this altitude and hour and the dried grasses underfoot are alive with leaping 'hoppers and other insects as Paha Sapa leads the confused donkeys thirty yards from the parking lot. The actual steep path to the Hall of Records canyon begins another hundred and fifty yards or so up the hill, but Paha Sapa is going to have to leave the donkeys here and he wants them to be quiet while he goes back for the dynamite. To that end, he not only ties them firmly to ponderosa pines with their tethers, but also hobbles them and ties on blindfolds.

Advocatus and Diaboli both kick out blindly in their irritation at this final insult to their dignity.

You ain't seen nothin' yet, thinks Paha Sapa as he hauls the two animal pack frames from the truck and cinches one onto each of the astonished animals. He also brings up the folded tarps and stacks them in the dappled moonlight.

All his life, Paha Sapa has loved the scent of pine needles underfoot at night, the aroma they release while cooling after a hot day in the sun, and this night is no different. He realizes that the pain that has been growing in his bowels and lower back the past weeks is dissipating, as is the terrible fatigue he's carried with him day and night for months now.

This is it. I'm committed. I'm actually doing this at last.

There is a freedom—almost a lightness—in this thought, and he has to remind himself, sardonically, that all he's done so far is transport two donkeys uphill for immoral purposes. There's a Mann Act, Paha Sapa knows...is there a Donkey Act?

There will be if you don't sober up, Black Hills, he snaps at himself. He knows that he has not touched a drop of whiskey or any other sort of liquor or wine or beer in more than forty years—so where is this almost drunken levity coming from?

From finally doing *what you've only thought about doing for sixty years, you tiresome moron,* he tells himself as he puts the Dodge in neutral and lets it coast out of the parking lot and downhill away from the monument before finally starting the engine.

The twenty-one crates of the best dynamite he has in storage have been set aside from the rejects and are ready to load. Paha Sapa's back has been hurting so much recently that he worried about the simple act of loading the crates—afraid his back would give way hauling the heavy crates up the ramp to the truck bed—but he has no problems at all. Each of the crates fits perfectly into the high cradle of hay bales just as he planned, and the tarps and straw set between each crate in each stack further cushion them.

Still, he lets out a breath when he's beyond the so-called city limits of Keystone. Because so many of the town's residents work for Mr. Borglum, and because tomorrow—no, today now—this Saturday, is a workday for most of them, the three backroom bars in town aren't as busy as they usually are on a Friday night, but Paha Sapa would still feel bad if a bump in this potholed, unpaved-to-begin-with road were to blow him, the truck, those bars, and twenty other structures with their cargo of sleeping wives and children to atoms.

If the nitro or dynamite goes now, he realizes as he crawls up the mountain road in low gear, it will be only him and a stretch of highway and a few dozen trees vaporized. But Paha Sapa frowns as he realizes that it's been so terribly dry this entire summer that such a blast on this part of the road will almost certainly start a forest fire that could *still* destroy all of Keystone, and the Doane Mountain and Mount Rushmore structures as well.

The twenty-one crates of dynamite and single, smaller crate of detonators don't blow during the bouncing, jolting ride up the hill.

Paha Sapa is amazed to discover not only that he expected them to, but—in some strange, inexplicable, sick way—he is a little disappointed that they haven't.

Parked in moon shadows again, he unloads all twenty-one crates and the single, much smaller box of detonators. Then he drives the Dodge quietly out of the parking lot, pulls it into an abandoned fire road three-quarters of a mile down the hill, and walks back, cutting through the woods. The almost-full moon is above the closer hills and rocky ridgelines now and keeps tangling itself in pine branches above Paha Sapa before working itself free. Its brilliance blots out the stars as it climbs higher and makes the granite cliff face and shoulders of Mount Rushmore, glimpsed to his left through the tall trees, glow a purer white in the moonlight than they do in daylight. George Washington's eyes, the oldest up there, present the perfect illusion of following Paha Sapa.

Before bringing the blindfolded and now silent donkeys back to the dynamite to load up, Paha Sapa lifts the box of detonators—supporting it against his chest with a leather strap he's rigged—and carries it up the Hall of Records canyon first.

The moonlight high on the canyon walls here looks like bold-edged bands of white paint. The shadows are very black, though, and both the approaches to the canyon and the floor of the canyon itself are littered with tree roots and then loose stones and fissures. Paha Sapa wishes that Borglum had already built that broad curving staircase he was talking about earlier in the day—yesterday now. He tries to keep to the moonlit areas, but the shadows are broad enough and black enough that once in the canyon itself, occasionally he has to use the flashlight he brought.

Once, trusting to moonlight, Paha Sapa trips and starts to fall forward onto the slightly clanking box of detonators. He stops his fall with his right arm outthrust, finding a low boulder there in the darkness.

As he carefully straightens and moves forward more slowly, he can feel the blood from his scraped and gouged palm dripping down his fingers. He can only smile and shake his head.

The rectangular test bore for the Hall of Records is invisible in the ink-black shadows thrown down that wall, but Paha Sapa can see the end of the canyon wall ahead and knows when to stop. He uses the flashlight to find the opening and, crouching in it, moves forward slowly to the end of the blind shaft. He'll be stacking the dynamite itself closer to the opening and wants to be sure that no misstep or dropped crate in the darkness could trigger these touchy detonators.

Walking back to the donkeys and waiting dynamite beyond the mouth of the narrow canyon, Paha Sapa resists the ridiculous urge to whistle. He takes a clean kerchief from his pocket, wipes the blood from his palm and fingers, and wonders at the strange sense of exhilaration rising in him.

Is this what it feels like to be a warrior going into battle?

———

— *Did you ever want to be a warrior?*

This was Robert asking his father an unexpected yet strangely overdue question. It was summer 1912, during their annual summer camping trip, and Robert was fourteen years old. They'd camped in the Black Hills many times before this, but this was the first time Paha Sapa had brought his son to the top of the Six Grandfathers. The two were sitting at the edge of the cliff, their legs dangling over, very close to where Paha Sapa had dug his Vision Pit thirty-six years earlier.

— *What I mean is...weren't most of the young men in your tribe expected to become warriors in those days, Father?*

Paha Sapa smiled.

— *Most. Not all. I've told you about the* winkte. *And the* wičasa wakan.

— *And you wanted to become a* wičasa wakan, *like your adoptive grandfather, Limps-a-Lot. But tell the truth, Father...weren't you ever tempted to become a warrior like most of the other young men?*

Paha Sapa thinks about the one silly raid on the Pawnee on which he'd been allowed to accompany the older boys — and where he hadn't even been able to hold the horses and keep them silent well enough to avoid ridicule from the others, who themselves had retreated fast enough when they saw the size of the Pawnee camp of warriors — and then he thought about how he'd rushed into the huge fight at the Greasy Grass without bringing a weapon. He realized he hadn't even wanted to hurt the *wasichus* then, on the day Long Hair and the others had attacked the huge village there, but had simply ridden with the other men and boys because he *didn't want to be left behind.*

— *Actually, Robert, I don't think I ever did want to be a warrior. Not really. There must have been something lacking in me. Perhaps it was just a matter of* canl pe.

Fourteen-year-old Robert shook his head.

— *You were no* canl waka, *Father. You know as well as I that it's never been a question of cowardice.*

Paha Sapa looked at the few clouds moving across the sky. In 1903, after Big Bill Slovak died in the Holy Terror Mine, Paha Sapa had taken his five-year-old son away from Keystone and Deadwood and out onto the plains, where the two had camped for seven days at *Matho Paha,* Bear Butte. On the sixth day, Paha Sapa awoke to find his son gone. The wagon he'd brought was still hidden in the secret place below, the horses still tethered where he'd left them, but Robert was gone.

For three hours Paha Sapa had searched up and down and along all sides of the fourteen-hundred-foot-tall hill rising out of the prairie while filling his mind with images: rattlesnake, rock fall, the boy falling, strangers. Then, just as Paha Sapa had decided that he must ride one of the horses to the nearest town to get help with the search, little Robert had walked into camp. He was hungry and dirty, but otherwise fine. When Paha Sapa had demanded his son tell him where he'd gone, why he'd been hiding, Robert had said, "I found a cave, Father. I was talking to the man with white hair who lives in the cave. His first name is the same as mine."

After breakfast, he'd asked Robert to show him the cave. Robert could not find it. When Paha Sapa asked Robert to tell him what the old man had talked to him about, the boy said only, "He said that what he told me and the dreams he showed me were our secret — only his and only mine. He said you would understand, Father."

Robert never revealed what Robert Sweet Medicine had said to him that day in 1903, or what visions he had shared. But every summer since then, Paha Sapa and his son had gone camping for a week.

Robert was dangling his long legs over the edge of the Six Grandfathers and looking at his father when he said softly —

—*Ate, khoyákiphela he?*

Paha Sapa did not know how to answer. What *did* he fear, other than for his son's life and well-being? What *had* he feared, other than for his wife's life and happiness when she was ill or for his people's future? And had that been fear or just... knowledge?

And perhaps he feared the violence of other men's memories that lay in his mind and soul like dark nodes: Crazy Horse's depressions and explosions into fury; even Long Hair's memories of joyous murders in the low light of winter sunrise with the regimental band playing on the hill behind them.

Paha Sapa just shook his head that day, not knowing how to answer the question but knowing that his son was right—he, Paha Sapa, had never been a coward, not in the usual sense—but also knowing the depths of his own failure as a father, as a husband, as a Natural Free Human Being. Paha Sapa had thought, before this summer's trip in 1912, that he might tell Robert some of the details of his *hanblečeya* on this mountain thirty-six years earlier—perhaps even specifics of the Vision the Grandfathers had given him—but he realized now that he would never do that. Beyond telling Robert that he'd gone on vision quest here, he mentioned nothing of the vision itself during this week of camping around the mountain and—interestingly—Robert did not ask.

Robert Slow Horse had inherited his mother's light skin color, hazel eyes, thin physique, and even her long eyelashes. The lashes did not make Robert look effeminate. Perhaps unlike his father, Robert was a born warrior, but a quiet one. There was none of the Crazy Horse rage and bluster in him. He allowed the bigger, older boys at his boarding school in Denver to tease him about his name or about being a "half-breed" for a while, then warned them softly, and then—when the bullies inevitably continued bullying—Robert would knock them on their asses. And he continued knocking them on their asses until they altered their behavior.

At fourteen, Robert was already four inches taller than his father. Where the height came from, Paha Sapa did not know, for Rain had been small, as had her father, the missionary minister and theologian, who had moved away from the Pine Ridge Reservation the year after his daughter's death in 1899 and died himself before the actual new century arrived in 1901. Perhaps, Paha Sapa thought, *his* own father, the teenager Short Elk, had been tall despite his name. (Even a short elk, Paha Sapa realized, was relatively tall.) He had never thought to ask Limps-a-Lot or Angry Badger or Three Buffalo Woman or any of the others around him how tall his young father had been before he'd staked himself down to die fighting Pawnee.

The Reverend de Plachette had moved to Wyoming to be near his friend William Cody for that final year of the minister's life. Cody had started a town named after himself there and built some hotels in it for the tourists he was sure would come to the beautiful West by way of the newly opened Burlington rail line. Buffalo Bill had named one of the big hotels after his daughter Irma and a road he'd paid to have built running from the town of Cody up to Yellowstone Park the Cody Road. Another sign of the aging entrepreneur's wealth was the giant TE Ranch he established along the South Fork of the Shoshone River there. Cody had driven all of his cattle from his previous properties in Nebraska and South Dakota to the ranch.

When Paha Sapa and little Robert first visited the failing Reverend de Plachette and prosperous Cody there at the ranch in early 1900, Buffalo Bill's operation was running more than a thousand head of cattle on more than seven thousand acres of prime grazing land.

Buffalo Bill, his hair white but still long and goatee still in place, had always insisted that his former employee and the boy stay with him in the big house when Paha Sapa visited, and it was that second and final visit, just before Reverend de Plachette died on the day of the first snowfall in Cody in autumn of 1900, that Cody had watched the two-year-old boy playing with some of the servants' kids.

— *Your son's smarter than you, Billy.*

Paha Sapa had not taken this as an insult. He already knew how intelligent his little son was. He'd only nodded.

Buffalo Bill had laughed.

— Hell, my guess is that he'll grow up smarter than me. *Did you see how he took that empty lantern apart and then put it back together? Didn't even break the glass. Little fellow can hardly toddle and he's already an engineer. What do you plan to do for his education, Billy?*

That was a good question. Rain had made Paha Sapa swear that Robert would go to good schools and then to a college or university somewhere in the East. Of course, she'd been sure that her father would be there to help — the old man had taught natural and revealed religion and rhetoric at both Yale and Harvard at different times — but she hadn't counted on her father dying so soon after her own death. And she hadn't counted on her father dying broke.

The schools near Keystone and Deadwood where Paha Sapa had just begun working in the mines after leaving Pine Ridge Reservation were terrible and didn't usually take Indian children anyway. The one school on the Pine Ridge Reservation was worse. Paha Sapa was saving money, but he had no idea how to buy his son an education.

William Cody had patted him softly on the back as they watched the children play.

— Leave it to me, Billy. My sister lives in Denver and I know of some good boarding schools there. The one I'm thinking of takes in boys starting at the age of nine and educates them right up to college age. It can be expensive, but I'll be more than happy to . . .

— I have the money, Mr. Cody. But I would appreciate you putting in a good word with the school. It's not every school that takes in an Indian child.

Cody had looked at the four toddlers playing on the floor.

— Who the hell can tell Robert's part Indian, Billy? I couldn't and I've been around your people for more than thirty years.

— He'll still have the last name Slow Horse.

William Cody had grunted.

— Well, maybe he's not as smart as we think he is, Billy, and he won't need a good boarding school. Or maybe other people will get smarter in the future. One way or the other, we can always hope.

———

Robert hadn't disappointed his father. The boy had essentially taught himself to read before he was four; he was reading every book

Paha Sapa could find for him by the time he was five. Somehow he learned to speak Lakota as if he'd been raised by Angry Badger's band, but he was also speaking Spanish by the time he was six (almost certainly because of the Mexican woman and her family and friends who watched him while Paha Sapa was working in the mine). By the time Robert did go to the boarding school in Denver in 1907—the trip to Denver from the Black Hills was daunting then, since there was no direct rail service, but Mr. Cody himself had driven them down the unpaved roads from Wyoming—the boy had already begun speaking and reading some German and French. He had no problem with his studies in Denver despite the fact that he'd rarely attended a real school in the Hills and that his father had been his tutor.

In truth, Robert and his father had been inseparable until that day in September '07 when Paha Sapa had looked out the oval rear window of Mr. Cody's automobile in Denver and seen his son standing with strangers in front of a red-brick building with green shutters; Robert seemed too shy or stunned or perhaps just too interested in the strange situation to think to wave good-bye. But Robert had written every week that year and in the years since—good, long, information-filled letters—and although Paha Sapa knew that Robert had been terribly homesick all of that first year (Paha Sapa had *felt* his son's aching homesickness in his own guts and heart), the boy had never once mentioned it in the letters. By January of each year they would be talking about where they would go camping together that summer.

— Did you ever bring Mother here?

Paha Sapa blinked out of his reverie.

— To the Black Hills? Of course.

— No, I mean here. *To the Six Grandfathers.*

— Not quite. We came to the Hills when she was pregnant with you and we climbed there....

Paha Sapa pointed to a peak rising to the west and south.

Robert looked surprised, even shocked.

— Harney Peak? I'm surprised you took Mother there—or even set foot on it.

— Its wasichu *name means nothing, Robert. At least to me. We could see the Six Grandfathers—and almost everything else—from up there. There was a dirt*

road that went close to the Harney Peak trailhead and none here to the Six Grand-
fathers. You saw how rough the ride in here still is.

Robert nods, looking up at the distant summit and obviously trying
to imagine his mother up there, looking in this direction.

— *Why did you ask, Robert?*

—*Ah, well, I was thinking of all the places you've taken me around here on our*
summer camping trips since I was little— *Bear Butte,* Inyan Kara, *Wind Cave,*
the Badlands, the Six Grandfathers . . .

Robert had used the Lakota words for these places, including *Matho*
Paha, Washu Niya ("the Breathing Place," for Wind Cave), *Maka Sichu,*
and so forth. Their private conversations almost always slipped in and
out of Lakota and English.

Paha Sapa smiled.

—*And?*

The smile Robert returned looked like Rain's when she had been
embarrassed.

—*And, well, I just wondered if there were religious reasons for these visits as*
well as just great places to camp— *or places important to your people.*

Paha Sapa noticed the "your" rather than "our" but said nothing.

— *Robert, when the whites summoned various* Ikče Wičaśa *and* Sahiyela
and other tribes' chiefs and holy men and war leaders to Fort Laramie in 1868, to
work out the boundaries of the Indian territories, the white soldiers and diplomats
speaking for the distant Great White Father said their purpose in mapping our
lands was "to know and protect your lands as well as ours," and our chiefs and
holy men and warriors looked at the maps and scratched their heads. The idea
of putting a limit to one's people's territories had never occurred to the Natural
Free Human Beings or to any of the other tribes represented there. How could
you know what you might win in war the next spring or lose the next summer?
How could you put a line *showing* your *land in areas that really belonged to the*
buffalo or all the animals that lived in the Black Hills . . . or all the tribes that
sheltered there, for that matter? But then our holy men began to make marks on
the wasichus' *maps showing places that* must *belong to their tribes and people*
because they were so sacred *to them*— *big loops around* Matho Paha *and*
Inyan Kara *and* Maka Sichu *and* Paha Sapa *and* Washu Niya *and* Šakpe
Tunkašila, *where we sit right now. . . .*

Robert was already grinning as Paha Sapa continued.

—*The* wasichus *were a little shocked because between just the Cheyenne and the Natural Free Human Beings, we considered just about every damned rock and hill and tree and creek and river and mesa and piece of prairie sacred in one way or another.*

Robert was laughing now—that free, easy, natural, always unforced laugh that sounded so much like Rain's sweet laughter to Paha Sapa.

—*I get it, Father. There's no place you could take me in or around the Black Hills that* wouldn't *be part of the* Ikče Wičaśa's *faith. But, still, don't you ever… worry… about me in terms of religion?*

—*You were baptized Christian by your grandfather, Robert.*

Robert laughed again and touched his father's bare forearm.

—*Yes, and that certainly took, didn't it? Actually, I don't think I've written you about it, but I often do go to various churches in Denver… not just the required chapel at school, but with the other students and some of the instructors and their families on Sunday. I especially have enjoyed a Catholic church in downtown Denver, where I've attended Mass with Mr. Murcheson and his family—especially at Easter and other Catholic holy days. I like the ritual… the smell of incense… the use of Latin… the whole thing.*

Wondering what his wife and Protestant missionary-theologian father-in-law would think of this, Paha Sapa said—

—*Are you thinking of becoming a Catholic, Robert?*

The boy laughed again, but softly this time. He looked back at the shadowing summit of Harney Peak.

—*No. I'm afraid I don't have the ability to believe the way I know you did… probably do… and perhaps the way Mother and Grandfather de Plachette did.*

Paha Sapa was tempted to tell Robert of how his grandfather had seemed to lose his faith in that year and a half after his daughter had died young. The danger, Paha Sapa knows too well, of having only one child… one child who becomes a human being's only connection to the unseen future and, oddly but truly, to the forgotten past.

Robert is still speaking.

—*… at least no religion I've encountered yet, but I look forward to seeing and learning more in different places. But I guess for right now, the only religion I can lay claim to is… Father, have you heard of a man named Albert Einstein?*

—*No.*

—*Not too many people have yet, but I suspect they will. Mr. Mülich, my mathematics and physics instructor at the school, showed me a paper that Professor*

Einstein published about three years ago, "Über die Entwicklung unserer Anschauungen über das Wesen und die Konstitution der Strahlung," and the implications of that paper, according to Mr. Mülich—the idea that light has momentum and can act like point-particles, photons, well... that's probably as close as I get to religion these days.

Paha Sapa looked at his son at that moment the way one looks at a photograph or drawing of a distant, distant relative.

Robert shook his head and laughed again, as if erasing a blackboard.

—But you know what the Catholic and Methodist and Presbyterian churches I've attended most reminded me of, Father?

—I have no idea.

—The Paiute Ghost Dance holy man you told me about a long time ago—Wovoka?

—Yes, that was his name.

—Well, his message of a messiah coming... him, I guess... and nonviolence and of how obeying his teachings would lead to the dead loved ones and ancestors returning to the world and the buffalo returning and how the Ghost Dance would induce a cataclysm that would carry away all the whites and other nonbelievers, sort of like the Tribulations and all that stuff in the Book of Revelation, sounded very Christian to me.

—That's what a lot of us thought when we heard it, Robert.

—You told me about you and Limps-a-Lot planning to hear the Prophet with Sitting Bull up at Standing Rock Agency, but Sitting Bull getting killed when he resisted arrest...

—Yes.

—But you never told me about Limps-a-Lot. Only that he died shortly after that.

—There wasn't much more to tell. Limps-a-Lot did die shortly after Sitting Bull was shot.

—But how? I mean... I know you'd thought that your honorary tunkašila *had been killed years earlier, right after you'd had your Vision and the cavalry chasing Custer's killers had burned your old village down, but you left that school the priests were running and went up to Canada to search for Limps-a-Lot when you were... gosh, you were about my age, Father.*

Paha Sapa shook his head.

—Nonsense. I was much older…almost sixteen. A visiting priest from Canada had described a man who sounded like my tunkašila. *I had to go see.*

—But still…my gosh, Father…just you riding all the way to Canada to find one man up there—and in the winter, I think you said. When you were fifteen years old. How'd you do it?

—I had a pistol.

Robert laughed so hard then that Paha Sapa actually worried the boy was going to fall off the cliff edge.

—That heavy Army Colt that you still own? I've seen that. *What'd you kill for food with* that *monstrous thing? Buffalo? Antelope? Mountain lions?*

—Rabbits, mostly.

—And you found Limps-a-Lot. After all that time?

—It wasn't so long, Robert. Less than five years after Pehin Hanska Kasata—*the summer we rubbed out Long Hair at the Greasy Grass…*

Paha Sapa paused then and rubbed his temples as if he had a headache.

—You all right, Father?

—Fine. Anyway, it wasn't so hard to find my tunkašila *once I got up to Grandmother's Country. The red-coated police told me where he was and said that I should leave and take him home with me.*

—How had Limps-a-Lot survived the attack that killed his wives and almost everyone else in your village?

—He stepped outside his tipi when the detachment of Cook's cavalry swept in at dawn and a bullet grazed him right here.…

Paha Sapa touched his forehead and felt his own scar there, the one imparted by the stock of the old Crow scout Curly's rifle. He paused a second, his finger remaining on the raised white welt that had been with him for thirty-six years. It was the first time he'd ever considered the fact that he and Limps-a-Lot had carried almost identical scars.

—Anyway, Limps-a-Lot was unconscious in the confusion, lying under the charging horses' hooves, but two young nephews carried him from the battlefield, hid him in the willows, carried him out when the smoke from the burning tipis and bodies concealed their retreat. When my tunkašila *awoke two days later, his old life and friends and wives and home—Angry Badger's* tiyospaye—*were all gone forever, and he was on a travois and heading north to join Sitting Bull's band in Grandmother's Country.*

344

— But Sitting Bull came back from Canada before he did.

— Yes. Limps-a-Lot had been ill with pneumonia when Sitting Bull took almost the last two hundred or so of his followers south — the rest had abandoned him, one family at a time, until his tiyospaye *was a shadow of its former strength of eight hundred lodges — so I found Limps-a-Lot still ill up there in a village with only eight or ten dilapidated lodges and no food, my* tunkašila *living with only a couple of dozen old men and women too frightened to come back and too lazy or indifferent to take care of him in his illness.*

— That was . . . what? Eighteen eighty-two?

— Eighteen eighty-one.

— So you brought him back, but not straight to the Standing Rock Agency.

— No, he went there later to be with Sitting Bull. First he rested and tried to recover while living with me near the Pine Ridge Agency. But he never fully recovered. And the pneumonia was not, I think, pneumonia — it never left him. I'm almost certain it was tuberculosis.

When Paha Sapa had started this story about his beloved grandfather, he'd slipped into full Lakota. Somehow, the discussion of Limps-a-Lot's final days required this, he thought, but he also knew it would be difficult for Robert to follow fully. As good at languages as his son was, Paha Sapa knew that Robert's only chance to practice Lakota was during his few summer weeks with his father and whenever they visited one of the reservations. This was a language, so beautiful and natural to Paha Sapa, in which a simple "thank you" — *pilamayaye* — translated literally to something like "feel good-me-you-made," and a request for directions to a specific house would receive a reply such as *Chanku kin le ogna waziyatakiya ni na chanku okiz'u icininpa kin hetan wiyohpeyatakiya ni, nahan tipi tokaheya kin hel ti. Nayašna oyakihi šni* — which Robert would have to work out as "Road this along northward you-go and cross-road second from-that westward you-go and house first there he-lives. You-miss you-can not." Statements involving technology became even more difficult for a nonnative Lakota speaker, so that merely asking the time became *Mazaškanškan tonakca hwo?* or "Metal-goes-goes what?" Most of all, it was a language in which everything had a spirit and volition, so that instead of saying, "It is going to storm" — a passive form that did not exist in Lakota at any rate — one said — "The Thunder Beings soon arriving-will-be." In their wonderful four years of marriage, Rain—who was sublimely intelligent and had the advantage of being with many native speakers of Lakota—never really mastered the language and often had to ask Paha Sapa what someone from the reservation had said after a rapid-fire exchange of pleasantries.

But Limps-a-Lot's spirit deserved having his final story told in Lakota, so Paha Sapa spoke slowly and in short sentences, pausing from time to time to make sure his son was following along.

—*Limps-a-Lot did not like the Standing Rock Agency, but he liked living near his good friend Sitting Bull. When Sitting Bull was killed just before the Moon When the Deer Shed Their Horns began—that is on December 17, and Sitting Bull died on December 15, 1890,* wasichu *time, my son—I believe it was only the widespread belief in the Paiute Prophet Wovoka's Ghost Dance that kept the Natural Free Human Beings there at Standing Rock from slaughtering all the* wasichu *and the tribal police as well.*

Robert was frowning to concentrate as he held up his hand almost shyly to signify a request for interruption. Paha Sapa paused.

—*Ateweye ki, émičiktunža yo—My father, excuse me, but is this because the Paiute Prophet Wovoka taught no-violence like the true-Christians?*

—*Partially, my son, because Wovoka's message, sacred to the Ghost Dancers, was "You must not hurt anybody or do harm to anyone. You must not fight. Do right always." But mostly it was because the majority of the Natural Free Human Beings there at Standing Rock—especially the Hunkpapas, who had been listening to the Ghost Dancers the longest—believed in the Ghost Dancer's prophecy that come that spring of 1891 and the greening of the grass, all the* wasichus *were going to disappear and the tall grass and the buffalos and their dead relatives would return. Most of the Hunkpapas had done their Ghost Dancing faithfully and well, dancing and chanting until they fainted. Many had their magical shirts to protect them from bullets. They believed in the prophecy. Can you understand me at this speed?*

—*Yes, my father. I will not interrupt again unless I do not understand. Please continue.*

—*After Sitting Bull was killed, the Hunkpapas had no leader. Most of them fled Standing Rock Agency. Some left for one of the Ghost Dance hiding places. Many went to be with the last of their great chiefs, Red Cloud, at Pine Ridge, where I lived at the time. I was going back to Pine Ridge, but Limps-a-Lot did not go with me. He and Sitting Bull had become good friends with the old leader of Minneconjous, Big Foot. This leader was also suffering from pneumonia that winter—or perhaps it was tuberculosis, the same as Limps-a-Lot had, since they were both coughing blood by then—and Big Foot was sure that the* Wasicun *generals were planning to arrest him, just as they had Sitting Bull. Big Foot was correct. The order for his arrest had been sent out already. Can you still understand me, my son?*

— Yes, Father. I am listening with all of my heart.

Paha Sapa nodded. He took a drink and passed the canteen to Robert, who also drank. High above them, a red-tailed hawk circled on a thermal. For one of the few times in his life, Paha Sapa did not wonder what the bird was seeing from that altitude—his thoughts were purely on Limps-a-Lot's ending-story and on how to tell it well but simply.

—Washtay. I should have stayed with my tunkašila, *but he did not want to go back to Pine Ridge with me at the time. He only wanted to join Big Foot's band of Minneconjous where they were spending the winter—it was a cold, snowy winter, Robert—at their camp at Cherry Creek, not too far from Standing Rock. I escorted Limps-a-Lot, who was coughing very badly again, to Big Foot's camp and then I left him, sure that his old friend would watch over him. About a hundred other Hunkpapas had also come to join Big Foot. I thought the camp was safe and promised to come back to check on Limps-a-Lot in a month, with the thought that I would then insist that my* tunkašila *join me at Pine Ridge for the spring. I should have stayed with him.*

I was not gone a day when Big Foot, certain that the soldiers and tribal police would be coming for him, told his people and the Hunkpapa refugees to break camp—he had decided to lead them all to Pine Ridge after all, hoping that Red Cloud, who was friendly with the Fat Takers, would protect them all.

Soon, Big Foot was so ill and hemorrhaging so badly that he had to travel on blankets laid out in the back of a wagon. Limps-a-Lot, who was also coughing blood again, rode in the wagon as well, but alongside the young man Afraid-of-the-Enemy, who was driving the wagon. On December 28, as the long line of men, old men, women—mostly old women—and a few children were approaching Porcupine Creek, they saw four troops of the Seventh Cavalry approaching.

Paha Sapa paused, half expecting to hear words from the ghost hiding in his head. None came. Nor did Robert say anything, although at the words "Seventh Cavalry," the fourteen-year-old boy had sighed like an old man. He knew something of his father's experiences with the cavalry.

— Big Foot had a white flag raised over his wagon. When the cavalry major rode up to talk—the wasichu *was named Whitside—Big Foot had to free*

himself from his blankets encrusted with frozen blood from his own bloody cough-ing. Limps-a-Lot and Afraid-of-the-Enemy and others helped the old Minneconjou stand and limp toward Major Whitside on his horse.

Whitside told Big Foot that he, the major, had orders to escort Big Foot and his people to a camp the cavalry had set up on the creek called Chankpe Opi Wakpala. *Big Foot and Limps-a-Lot and the others were sorry that they would not see Red Cloud and be under his protection at Pine Ridge, but they thought that going to* Chankpe Opi Wakpala *was a good omen. Have I told you the importance of that place, Robert?*

— I do not believe so, my father.

— You remember the story I told you years ago of how the war chief Crazy Horse died at Fort Robinson?

— Yes.

— Well, when Crazy Horse was killed there, a few of his friends and relatives took his body away. They would tell no one exactly where they had buried Crazy Horse's heart, only that it was somewhere along Chankpe Opi Wakpala.

— So that creek was sacred?

— It was . . . important. Big Foot, Limps-a-Lot, and most of the others thought that Crazy Horse had been our people's bravest leader. It seemed a good sign that they were going to the place where Crazy Horse's spirit might watch over them.

— Please go on with the story, Father.

— We learned afterward, mostly from their half-breed scout that day, John Shangreau, that Major Whitside's orders had been to . . . Did I say something amusing, Robert? You're smiling.

— I'm sorry, Father. It is just that when a boy or man in Denver says that word, I have to knock him down.

Paha Sapa rubbed the scar on his forehead. He was not wearing a hat that hot July day and the sun was making him a little dizzy. When the story was finished, he would suggest that they go in under the shade of the trees and down the hill to the campsite to begin preparing dinner.

— Says what word, Robert?

— Wašicuŋeiŋea. Half-breed.

— Oh. Well, you're not a half-breed in any case. Your mother was half white. You're a . . . quarter-breed, at most.

Mathematics had never been Paha Sapa's strong suit and frac-tions had always annoyed him. Racial fractions annoyed him more than most.

—*Please continue, my father. I shall not smile again.*

—*Where was I? Oh, yes... the scout John Shangreau knew that Major Whitside's orders were to capture and disarm and dismount all of Big Foot's band. But Shangreau convinced the major that any attempt right then to take the men's guns and horses away would almost surely start a fight. So Whitside decided to do nothing until Big Foot's band was at* Chankpe Opi Wakpala *and where the cavalry could deploy the Hotchkiss guns they had in the rear of their column. What is it? You're frowning.*

—*I don't want to interrupt again, but I have no idea what Hotchkiss guns are... or were.*

—*I saw them when I rode with the Third Cavalry in 1877... rode as the worst scout in Army history. I led them to nothing. The new Hotchkiss guns used to be brought along behind the main detachment, pulled by mules or horses. They were like the Gatling guns used in the Civil War, only faster, deadlier—they were a sort of Gatling gun cannon. The revolving Hotchkiss cannon had five thirty-seven-millimeter barrels and was capable of firing forty-three rounds per minute with accuracy out to, I remember, a range of about two thousand yards. Each feed magazine held ten rounds and weighed about ten pounds. I remember the weight because when I was twelve and thirteen summers old, I had to carry and lift and load the damned things onto the supply wagons. Each wagon carried hundreds of magazines, tens of thousands of thirty-seven-millimeter rounds.*

—*Jesus Christ.*

Robert had whispered those two words. Paha Sapa knew that the boy's mother and grandfather would have been upset at the casual blasphemy, but it meant nothing to Paha Sapa.

—*You can guess the rest of the story, my son. They reached the army tent camp at* Chankpe Opi Wakpala—*it was very cold, as I said, and the stream was frozen, the willows and cottonwood trees along it all outlined in frost. The frozen grass stood up like daggers and cut into moccasins. There were a hundred and twenty men, including Limps-a-Lot, in Big Foot's band and about two hundred and thirty women and children. But I didn't mean to give the impression that all the men were feeble old men—a lot of the warriors there were still warriors and had been at the Greasy Grass and part of the rubbing out of Long Hair. As these men looked at the cavalry and infantry drawn up the next morning, the Hotchkiss guns aimed down at them from the hilltop, they must have wondered if the Seventh Cavalry had revenge on its mind and in its heart.*

Robert opened his mouth as if ready to ask or say something, but in the end did not speak.

—*As I say, you can guess the rest, Robert. It seemed that the* wasichu *leaders—the rest of the regiment had arrived that first night at the* Chankpe Opi Wakpala *and a Colonel Forsyth had taken command—were being helpful. They'd brought Big Foot to this place in the regiment's ambulance and provided a tent that was supposed to be warmer than the tipis for the old chief to sleep in. Limps-a-Lot slept in a tipi nearby because he did not want to spend the night in a Seventh Cavalry tent. Major Whitside's own surgeon had looked at Big Foot, but there was nothing to be done for what they thought was pneumonia then—even less for consumption. Limps-a-Lot, friends later told me, was also coughing more there at that cold, windy place.*

In the morning, the bugle blew and Big Foot was helped out of his tent and the soldiers began the disarming. The warriors and old men handed over their rifles and old pistols. Not satisfied, the soldiers went into the tipis and threw axes and knives and even tent stakes onto the big pile in the center of the circle of disarmed men.

Most of the Hunkpapas and Minneconjous wore their inpenetrable Ghost Shirts that day, but not in anticipation of a fight. They'd given up their guns.

But there is always one who won't. In this case, I was told, it was a very young Minneconjou named Black Coyote. Some told me that Black Coyote was deaf and couldn't hear the commands from the soldiers and his own chiefs to put his rifle down. Others said that Black Coyote could hear all right, but that he was a stupid pain in the ass and a show-off. At any rate, Black Coyote danced around with his rifle held out, not aiming it but not putting it down with the other weapons. Then the soldiers grabbed him and spun him around and there was a shot—some thought it came from Black Coyote's rifle; others told me it hadn't. But it was enough.

You can imagine what happened next, Robert, on that sunny, very cold day near the end of the Moon When the Deer Shed Their Horns. Many of the warriors snatched up their rifles and tried to fight. Eventually the Hotchkiss guns began firing down into them. When it was over, more than half of Big Foot's people were dead or very seriously wounded . . . a hundred and fifty-three were dead on the snowy battlefield. More crawled away to die in the bushes or stream. Louise Weasel Bear, who told me the story, said that almost three hundred of the original three hundred and fifty men, women, and children who'd followed Big Foot there died at Chankpe Opi Wakpala. *I remember that something like twenty-five* wasichu *soldiers died that day. I don't know how many were wounded, but not that many more. The young woman Hakiktawin told me that most of the Seventh Cavalry soldiers had been shot by their own men or hit by shrapnel from rounds from the Hotchkiss guns striking rock or bone. I've always preferred to think that this is not the truth — that the warriors and old men and women who died there that day did fire back with some effect.*

I was not quite to Pine Ridge when I heard and I turned around and hurried to Chankpe Opi Wakpala. Limps-a-Lot had taken me to that place many times when I was a boy, simply because it was beautiful and had many legends and stories about it.

There was a blizzard. My horse died, but I kept walking, then stole another horse from a cavalry detachment I came across in the storm. When I arrived at Chankpe Opi Wakpala I saw that the Seventh had left the Indian dead and severely wounded behind, and now the bodies were frozen in strange postures and covered with snow from the storm. I found Big Foot first — his right arm and right leg were bent as if he were pushing himself up to a sitting position, his back was off the ground, the fingers of his left hand were raised and frozen as if in the act of opening, with only the little finger curled shut — and he was wearing a woman's scarf around his head. His left eye was closed but his right eye was open — the crows and magpies had not taken his eyes yet, probably because they were frozen as hard as marbles — and there was snow on his open eye.

Limps-a-Lot was lying no more than thirty feet from Big Foot. Something, probably a thirty-seven-millimeter round from one of the Hotchkiss guns, had taken his right arm off, but I found it lying nearby in the snow, rising almost vertically from a snowdrift, as if my tunkašila *were waving at me. His mouth was wide open as if he had died screaming — but I prefer to think that he was singing his Death Song loudly. Either way, his gaping mouth had filled with snow until the snow overflowed, running out in all directions like some pure, white vomit of death, filling his eye sockets and outlining his sharp cheekbones.*

I knew the wasichu *cavalry would be back, probably that same day, to take photographs and to bury the dead there, probably in a single mass grave, and I could not leave Limps-a-Lot's body there for that. But I had no shovel with me, not even a knife, and my* tunkašila's *body was frozen to the cold earth. They were as one. Nothing bent — not his arm, not his twisted legs, not even the separate arm rising from the snowdrift. Even his left ear was one with the frozen earth. With only my cold, bare hands, it was like trying to lift a rooted tree out of the ground.*

Eventually I sat down, panting, freezing, my hands numb, knowing that the cavalry detachment would be there soon and that they would take me prisoner as well—the word I'd heard was that the few Hunkpapa and Minneconjou survivors were being sent to a prison in Omaha, where they had planned to send Big Foot and all his men—and I began walking that murder field, I refuse to this day to call it a battlefield, until I found a woman's corpse with a dull, flat-bladed cooking knife in her clenched hand. I had to snap all her fingers like twigs to get the knife free. With that knife to chip away at the ice between Limps-a-Lot's frozen coat and frozen flesh and the frozen soil, I freed his body from the earth's grip in less than half an hour. I brought the severed arm with the white bone protruding as well. I propped Limps-a-Lot's body on the saddlehorn in front of me—it was like carrying a long and twisted and unwieldy, but almost weightless, cottonwood branch—and I lashed his right arm across his chest with long strips of cloth torn from my shirt.

With only that dull knife, I could not bury Limps-a-Lot in the frozen soil that day, but I took him far away from what I thought of that day as that evil field and buried him miles and miles away along the Chankpe Opi Wakpala *where it undercut a tall bluff and where larger, older cottonwoods—the kind of beautiful* waga chun, *"rustling tree," of the kind Limps-a-Lot or Sitting Bull would have chosen to stand in the center of the dancing circle—and there I made the best burial scaffold I could for my* tunkašila *up there in the branches of one of those rustling-tree perfect cottonwoods.*

But I had no robes to lay under him or to cover him with, no real weapons or tools to leave by his side. I did leave the dull knife after using it to hack off all my hair, and it was covered with my frozen blood as well as some from Limps-a-Lot. I kissed both of his hands—lifting the severed right arm toward my lips—and kissed his cold-stone of a furrowed forehead and whispered good-bye and rode the stolen cavalry horse almost all the way back to Pine Ridge before dismounting, swatting the exhausted beast on the rump, and walking the rest of the way home. It had been three days since I had eaten anything and I lost two toes on my left foot to frostbite.

The other fallen, I learned, were buried in a mass grave that very afternoon. No one knows where I left Limps-a-Lot's body and I have never returned to the secret spot.

That is all, Robert. Hecetu. Mitakuye oyasin.

So be it. All my relatives—every one of us. I have spoken.

I<small>T TAKES</small> P<small>AHA</small> S<small>APA</small> six trips back and forth with the donkeys before he gets all twenty-one crates of dynamite hidden in the Hall of Records test bore tunnel. He could have made it in five trips if he'd thought the diminutive donkeys could handle more than two crates lashed onto their pack frames at a time, but he was conservative there, and the final trip back up the canyon, a tether in each hand, is made with one donkey carrying the last crate of dynamite and the other carrying only the hundreds of feet of coiled detonation wire and other incidental things Paha Sapa will need on Sunday. He has painted the black wire a granite gray.

The night has not been hard work for Paha Sapa, at least after Advocatus and Diaboli realized—somewhere around the beginning of the third trip uphill to the canyon—that they were, at least for this one night, beasts of burden again rather than coddled priest's pets.

When he stacks the last crate inside the tunnel and covers it with the last tarp—the gray-white canvas almost indistinguishable from the granite in the quickly disappearing moonlight—one of the donkeys sneezes and Paha Sapa allows this to substitute for his own tired sigh.

Walking back down the narrow canyon, he realizes that as the moon has moved to the west, shining now through the trees on the high ridge wall to the west of the canyon, all of the ink-black shadows from his early trips are now bright stripes and trapezoids of milk-white moonlight, and all of the formerly safe areas to step are now treacherous shadows. It does not matter. He has every step of the way memorized after his seven trips up (including the first one on foot carrying the box of detonators) and seven trips back.

Remembering the long telling of Limps-a-Lot's final story to Robert, Paha Sapa is reminded of that same long-ago time in 1890 at *Chankpe Opi Wakpala*. While searching the faces of the frozen, snow-covered forms in that field for Limps-a-Lot's corpse, he had, for the first time, reached into the black place where Long Hair's ghost had resided those fourteen years, babbling away in English about his pornographic memories of his wife, and dragged that ghost kicking and screaming to a place behind his, Paha Sapa's, eyes, forcing it to watch and to look and to see, forbidding it with his own Voice of God to say nothing.

After Limps-a-Lot's burial, Paha Sapa threw Long Hair's ghost back into the silent, lightless place where it had resided until then. He did not speak to it again (or allow it to speak to him) for another eleven months, but the oft-interrupted conversation began that day. Custer's ghost was later to tell Paha Sapa that he, Custer's ghost, was certain that he'd arrived in Hell and that his punishment would be to look at such sights as the field at *Chankpe Opi Wakpala* for all the rest of eternity. Paha Sapa immediately reminded Long Hair's ghost that the snowy field and the frozen dead men, women, and children could just as easily have been at *Washita*.

It was another year before he and the ghost spoke again.

The ghost has said nothing this night. Of course, he has not spoken at all in the past three and a half years, not since the trip to New York in the spring of 1933.

Paha Sapa skirts the parking lot and cuts downhill through the woods to where he has hidden the Dodge truck. Advocatus and Diaboli seem almost too weary to climb the ramp up into the truck and then are too weary even to chew on the straw.

The moon has disappeared to the west; the eastern sky is already growing light. Paha Sapa checks his old watch. Almost five a.m. He has time to drive back to Keystone, load Robert's motorcycle into the back of the truck with the donkeys—there was room to load it with the dynamite crates earlier, but Paha Sapa was stupidly sentimental about not blowing up his son's machine if the nitroglycerine detonated—and then make the trip to Deadwood to return the two tired beasts to Father Pierre Marie and the Dodge truck to Howdy Peterson's cousin. He'd come home on the motorcycle and have time to make some breakfast for himself before coming up the hill again to start a long Saturday of work supervising the drilling of the face in preparation for tomorrow's—Sunday's—demonstration explosion for the president, honored guests, and newsreel cameras.

Paha Sapa is so exhausted that far more than the cancer hurts him this beautiful but hot morning. Everything hurts, down to the marrow of his bones. He knows that this night, Saturday night to Sunday morning, even with the moron Mune's help, he will have much more hard labor to do through the night than merely walking donkeys up a hill and canyon a few times and transferring twenty-one relatively light crates of dynamite. And he will have to start earlier to have any chance of finishing the placement of the charges and wires before sunrise, and this on a Saturday night, when everyone stays awake partying until late.

Driving the heavy Dodge truck down the bumpy road toward Keystone, flinching for no reason every time the wheels hit a deep pothole, he tries to think of a prayer asking *Wakan Tanka* or the Six Forces of the Universe or the Mystery itself for strength, but he cannot remember the words for any such prayer.

Instead, he remembers a Grandfather Chant that Limps-a-Lot taught him when he was very little and he sings it now —

> *There is someone lying on earth in a sacred manner.*
> *There is someone — on earth he lies.*
> *In a sacred manner I have made him walk.*

Then he comes out of the forest just as the sun rises over the hills to the east, temporarily blinding Paha Sapa — who has to fumble in the tangle of junk in the lidless glove compartment to find his sunglasses — and he remembers and sings a song that the Sun himself taught his people —

> *With visible face I am appearing.*
> *In a sacred manner I appear.*
> *For the greening earth a pleasantness I make.*
> *The center of the nation's hoop I have made pleasant.*
> *With visible face, behold me!*
> *The four-leggeds, the two-leggeds, I have made them to walk;*
> *The wings of the air, I have made them to fly.*
> *With visible face I appear.*
> *My day, I have made it holy.*

22

The Six Grandfathers

Saturday, August 29, 1936

THE WORKDAY PROCEEDS IN A WHITE HALO OF HEAT. THIS LAST week of August finally has seen temperatures drop out of the high nineties in the Black Hills but the carved, white-granite inward curve of Mount Rushmore continues to focus sunlight and heat like a parabolic mirror and drives temperatures back up into the triple digits for the men hanging there by hot steel cords. By ten a.m. men working on the face are taking their salt tablets. Paha Sapa realizes that he is seeing halos of white light around not just the rock noses and cheeks and chins jutting from the granite, but also around the tanned and lip-blistered faces of the other workers.

He knows this illusion is just a by-product of fatigue and lack of sleep and does not worry about it. The effect is more pleasing than disturbing as men with their pneumatic steam drills and sledgehammers and steel spikes each move within their own white nimbus, the pulsing coronas sometimes merging as the men lean close or work together.

The fatigue-induced white halos are not a problem for Paha Sapa; the pain from his cancer is becoming one.

He grits his teeth tighter and sets the pain out of his thoughts.

All this Saturday morning he has been directing Palooka Payne on drilling the holes for the five charges to be detonated in tomorrow's "demonstration blast" for the president and other VIPs. Everyone loves a good explosion. This one, as with all the demonstration blasts on public occasions, has to *look* and *sound* significant enough to give the civilians on Doane Mountain and in the valley below a sense that it is doing some work on the mountain while not being big enough to lob rocks or boulders at them.

One crew of men is rigging the extra crane arm over the Jefferson face, ready to drape the gigantic flag—sewn years ago by old ladies or FHA students or somesuch in Rapid City—to conceal Jefferson, and also rigging the ropes and cables that will lift the huge and heavy flag even while the crane swings to one side. But the flag itself will not be draped until tomorrow morning. Although there is not a breath of wind in the blazing heat of this late morning, a stiff breeze might tear the flag, tangle the cables, or otherwise ruin the draping. A special crew will drape the flag the next morning, not too long before the guests are scheduled to arrive.

The president's train is supposed to be pulling into Rapid City late this evening of the 29th, but already word is coming up the hill that the president will definitely be arriving here tomorrow, Sunday, later than originally planned; FDR has added a longer-than-originally-scheduled service at the Emmanuel Episcopal Church in Rapid City *and* a luncheon with local Democratic leaders at the Alex Johnson Hotel (still the only air-conditioned hotel in South Dakota) before coming up to Mount Rushmore in his motorcade.

This has made Borglum apoplectic. He is swearing to his son, Lincoln, to his wife, to June Culp Geitner, to supervisor Julian Spotts, to worried Democratic politicans who make the mistake of taking his phone call, to William Williamson (head of the delegation in charge of greeting the president), and to unsmiling Secret Service liaisons that President Roosevelt will *have to change his plans back* to arrive earlier, *as Borglum had directed and as Roosevelt had originally promised,* or the shadows on the faces will be in the wrong position and the unveiling of the Jefferson head will be ruined. The president's and governor's people explain to Borglum that the president has expedited his arrival as much as possible and expects to arrive no later than 2:30.

Gutzon Borglum growls at the gathered men.

—*That'll be two and a half hours too damned late. The unveiling of the Jefferson figure and the dedication ceremony are going to happen* exactly *at noon.*

Tell that *to the president! If he wants to be part of it, he'll have to get here about fifteen minutes before the unveiling.*

Then Borglum walks out of the studio where the group is gathered and takes his tramway up to the tops of the heads.

The few old-timers who've been working here since Borglum talked President Calvin Coolidge into taking a horse-drawn wagon (which broke down, forcing the president to make the rest of the trip by horse) up to this isolated spot to "dedicate the site" of the as-yet-totally-untouched Mount Rushmore on August 10, 1927, just shake their heads. They know the Boss will wait for this new president.

Between drillings, chief pointer Jim Larue informs Paha Sapa that Coolidge wore totally dude-ish new cowboy boots, fringed buckskin gloves, and a Stetson big enough to shade half of west South Dakota when he rode up the hill. Earlier in that trip, he had allowed some not-quite-local Sioux Indians to dress him up in a war bonnet that hung to his heels, and they gave Silent Cal the official name "Chief Leading Eagle"— *Wanbli Tokaha* in Lakota, which most of the white locals decided actually meant "Looks Like a Horse's Ass."

Doane Robinson, who was a big part of this wooing of Coolidge, once told Paha Sapa that the most devious thing done by the local whites was to dam up the little stream near where the president was staying at the Game Lodge in the Hills, bring down hundreds of fat, disgustingly liver-fed, stupid breeding trout from the hatchery up in Spearfish, and release these torpid creatures, a clump at a time, into the hundred yards of stream where Coolidge—who had never tried fishing before in his life—was standing uncomfortably, still dressed in suit, vest, tie, stiff collar, and straw boater, awkwardly holding the expensive trout-fishing rod Robinson and the others had given the visiting president as a gift.

Incredibly, Coolidge caught a fish in the first five minutes. (It would have been almost impossible not to, said Doane Robinson. One could have all but walked across the creek on the back of the fish released there without getting one's shoes wet.) And he kept catching these slow, fat breeding trout, released every hour on the hour from the newly built little dam just upstream. Coolidge was so delighted with his fishing prowess that he not only went fishing for hours each day he was at the

Game Lodge, but insisted on serving the dozens upon dozens of trout he caught every breakfast and dinner at the lodge.

The locals, who could taste the rotted liver from the slaughterhouse in Spearfish that these trout had been fed on for years, gamely smiled and tried to swallow as Coolidge beamed at everyone at the table and urged second helpings of *his* trout.

———

PAHA SAPA and Palooka have the five blasting holes drilled by ten a.m. and Paha Sapa has run and secured the detonator wires in their protective orange guides across the face of the cliff under the Jefferson head and the white rock now ready for the Teddy Roosevelt fine drilling. For safety's sake, he will not install the dynamite in the holes until tomorrow morning after everyone else is off the face.

But he has Palooka continue drilling for him well into the blazing noon and tells the driller to join him after the lunch break for more work.

— *What're these slots for, Billy? They're not even blast holes. They're more like...well, big slots.*

It's true. Paha Sapa has shown the driller where they're going to expand niches under rock ledges and cliff lips and in crevices all along the face of the cliff, from Washington's right shoulder to the farthest west, then east up and around the bend in the swooping saddle between Washington's lapels and Thomas Jefferson's right cheek, then down under Jefferson's chin, then east again to the left of the undifferentiated mass that is Jefferson's parted hair, beneath and to both sides of the *tabula rasa* of prepared granite ready for the carving of Teddy Roosevelt, then farther to the right into the shadowed niches between the Roosevelt granite field and the busy working face of Lincoln, then down under Lincoln's still-emerging chin and beard where scaffolds are clustered, and finally even on the just-blasted cliff face to the southeast of Lincoln's unseen left ear. With Paha Sapa supervising exact placement of these excavations, he and Palooka will be working all day on these holes.

The slots *aren't* blast holes. Palooka guesses that they're going to be support insets in the stone for still more scaffolds to join those still on the face under Washington (where his cravat and lapels continue to emerge) and under Jefferson (where more work has to be done on the neck), across the exposed granite prepared for TR, and on both sides of and beneath Lincoln's head. Those portable scaffolds that can be cranked up on pulleys will be removed by tomorrow to clear the way for the crowd's viewing, but many of the other working walkways and scaffolds rest on sturdy posts with drill holes not unlike these horizontal niches Palooka will be drilling all the rest of this Saturday.

Paha Sapa does not say that these *aren't* support holes for future scaffold pilings.

On another scaffold nearby, Howdy Peterson is beginning the honeycombing process on the lower TR carving field. This has been the procedure on the previous three faces—as blasting gets down to the last inches of clean rock before the "skin" of the faces emerges, drillers like Palooka and Howdy lean their weight into the drills (thus the scaffolds rather than bosun's chairs) to drill hundreds upon hundreds of parallel holes, honeycombing the rock. Then carvers like Red Anderson come in with their large hammers and cold chisels and break away the stone in sheets, exposing the smooth face that will later be buffed and shaped and worked as actual sculptures.

Meanwhile, back down at the hoist house—the closest to the cliff that the tourists can wander—Edwald Hayes and the other hoist operators have an example of the flaked-off "honeycomb" nailed to the wall of the hoist house and acknowledge to the curious visitor that, *Yep, we get a few of these real, actual honeycombed mementos of the mountain carving intact. Not many. They're real rare. That's why the fellows keep this one here as a sorta souvenir.* The tourists invariably ask if Edwald (or the other operators) could see fit to part with that interesting honeycomb. *Don't hardly see how I could, sir (or "lady"). Y'see, it belongs to another guy. He might be real mad if I sold it, since it's so rare and all.... 'Course, if you really want it, I might see my way clear to sell it to you and just take my chances with the owner.*

The going price for the largest honeycombs is six bucks. The tourists take off with the chunk of honeycombed granite tucked in the husband's jacket, almost running to their cars as they chuckle about the fast one they've pulled, and then Edwald or the other operator will phone up the mountain and say—*Okay, boys, send down another one.*

The honeycombed souvenirs are priced according to size—two dollars, four dollars, and six dollars—and the price is always in multiples of two, Paha Sapa knows, because moonshine in the area sells for two dollars a pint. Thousands of "rare and unique and one-of-a-kind" honeycombs have changed hands here over the years.

Borglum has driven off after his confrontation with the president's people (perhaps, the workers buzz, to go confront FDR with his be-here-on-time-or-else ultimatum), and his son is in charge, but Lincoln focuses his supervision on the crane and flag-pulley preparation over the Jefferson head and the new drilling all over the emerging Lincoln head and pays little attention to Palooka and Paha Sapa and their seemingly innocuous small-time drilling on various parts of the cliff. Lincoln knows that "Billy Slovak" has to prepare for tomorrow's demonstration blast and for much more serious working detonations in the week to come as Teddy Roosevelt's skin and head shape are finally exposed.

When the noon whistle blows (without the deeper, louder blast-warning whistle that often follows, since Paha Sapa and the other powdermen do their blasting during the lunch break and after four p.m., when the workers are off the face), Paha Sapa heads up to the winch shack to fetch his metal lunch pail—he only had time in the morning to toss in some bread and old beef—and walks into the shade of the main boom and winch building atop Jefferson's head.

It's hot in the shed but a group of men, including Paha Sapa's fellow powdermen Alfred Berg and Spot Denton, are huddled there with their lunch pails. Part of the space in the shack is taken up by a hollow five-foot-tall bust-mask of a clean-shaven Abe Lincoln, part of some earlier sculpture that Borglum did years ago and which he normally has set out along the scaffolding trail around the base of the emerging Lincoln head so that men can touch it with their hands while working there and "feel" the Lincoln that is still in the stone. Borglum ordered it brought in during the blasting.

Whiskey Art Johnson pats a place on the stone floor near the Lincoln face.

—*There's room here, Billy. Come in and set a spell, get out of the sun.*

—*Thanks, Art. I'll be back.*

He picks up his lunch pail and the little Coke bottle he keeps his water in — heated almost to boiling by now — and walks back out along the ridge and then out onto George Washington's head until the slope becomes steep enough that he feels he's about to slide right over Washington's brow to the boulders three hundred feet below. It's a comfortable place to sit, half reclining, and there's a small niche in the president's forehead, carved to give a sense of a wig, where Paha Sapa can rest his pail and bottle without worrying about them rolling over the edge.

As he munches his bread and meat, he looks to the southwest and toward the summit of Harney Peak.

Doane Robinson once loaned him a new book that said that the granite on Harney Peak was 1.7 billion years old. *Billion.* The Natural Free Human Beings have no word for billion or for million. The biggest number that Paha Sapa remembers encountering when he was with his people was in the phrase *Wicahpi, opawinge wikcemna kin yamni,* which had to do with the three thousand stars visible in the sky on a perfect viewing right.

That is funny, in a way, since most *wasichu* whom Paha Sapa has spoken with about the night sky in his seventy-one years, including Rain and her father, seem to think that one can see millions of individual stars in the night sky on a perfect, dark viewing night. But the *Ikče Wičaša* knew that there are only about three thousand stars visible even on the clearest, darkest night. They knew because they had counted them.

Once, when Robert was very young, perhaps during that first camping trip to Bear Butte when they had let the fire die down to embers shedding almost no light and were lying back watching the stars, Paha Sapa asked his son to guess how many stars the full moon was hiding behind itself, on average, as it moved across the sky through the night. Robert guessed six. Paha Sapa explained that, on average, the full moon blocked no stars, and not just because its light made the stars fade from view. He remembers Robert's little gasp from where he lay on his blanket that night and the five-year-old voice.

— *Gosh, Father, it's really* empty *up there, isn't it?*

Yes, thinks Paha Sapa now, *it is.*

He and Rain never had a real honeymoon.

They were married at her father's new mission church on the Pine Ridge Agency—already being called the Pine Ridge Reservation—that vast expanse of arid land and windblown dust east of the Black Hills in the southwest corner of what became the state of South Dakota. In the wet spring of 1894, Paha Sapa and a few Sioux friends—but mostly Paha Sapa—built the tiny wood-frame, four-room house that he and Mrs. Rain de Plachette Slow Horse moved into immediately following the ceremony in mid-June of that year. That time was warm in Paha Sapa's memory, but it had been busy and cold and wet—the roof leaked terribly—in that strange June when summer just refused to come to the Plains. Billy was not working on the reservation where Rain was a teacher in the mission school and their little house was just over the rise from where her father's larger home and the mission church sat at the crossroads of four wagon ruts; Billy, like many of the Natural Free Human Beings who'd come to Pine Ridge after the death of Sitting Bull and the slaughter at *Chankpe Opi Wakpala,* lived on the reservation but did day work as a hired hand and wrangler (although he was never good at cowboying) at various *wasichus'* ranches in the richer grazing country north of Agency land.

Most mornings, even during their "honeymoon," Paha Sapa had to be up and out and dressed and saddled up and off for the long ride to some neighboring white man's ranch by no later than 4:30.

Rain never complained. (Thinking about it later, he could not remember a time when Rain ever complained.) She always insisted on getting up in the dark with him to make his coffee and a good breakfast, then make a solid lunch that he could take with him in the battered old gray lunch pail that he still used. It was usually something better than sandwiches, but when it was a sandwich, she always took a tiny bite out of one corner of the bread. It was her way of sending her love to him in the middle of the day. For more than three decades after she died, Paha Sapa would check the corner of any sandwich he was eating that day, just out of the echo-habit of that short time when he was loved.

Rain and Paha Sapa were both virgins when they consummated their marriage in that leaky small house on the Pine Ridge Reservation. This did not surprise Paha Sapa, but much later, when they shyly spoke of it, Rain confessed that it had surprised her that Paha Sapa, who was twenty-nine when they were wed, had not "had more experience."

This was not a complaint. The two lovers learned together and taught each other.

Paha Sapa's only regret was that he had Crazy Horse's memories and Long Hair's pornographic monologues in his head when he finally carried his own bride to their marriage bed. Of the two men whose memories Paha Sapa reluctantly carried with him, Crazy Horse had been the gentler lover — when his couplings had not been merely to satisfy a hunger — and the dead warrior's illicit relationship with Red Cloud's niece Black Buffalo Woman (who was married to No Water at the time, even while Crazy Horse was technically, although not in reality, bonded with the sickly woman Black Shawl in an arranged marriage) showed moments of true tenderness. Even Long Hair's explicit recollections, once Paha Sapa had the bad luck to learn English and knew what the ghost was babbling on about, were merely examples of that most secret place of all in a human being's life — the privacy of intimacy. Through the unwanted words and images, Paha Sapa could sense Custer's real and abiding love for his lovely young wife and the couple's sincere surprise at the sexual energy that Libbie had brought to the marriage.

Still, Paha Sapa wanted no one else's sexual histories mixed with his own gentle memories and thoughts and he succeeded fairly well in mentally walling off those recollections of Crazy Horse and in ignoring the middle-of-the-night babblings of Long Hair's ghost.

So their spring 1898 trip to the Black Hills was Rain's and Paha Sapa's first time away from the reservation together, except for the nightmare weeks the previous autumn when he took Rain to Chicago for the terrible surgery.

That train trip to Chicago — the Reverend Henry de Plachette accompanying them, since the surgeon was *his* trusted friend — and the surgery had taken place not long after Rain discovered the lump in her right breast. (In truth known only to the two of them, it had been Paha Sapa who discovered it, when he was kissing his darling.)

Dr. Compton had strongly recommended removing *both breasts,* as was the custom at the time, even though no tumor was detectable by touch in Rain's left breast, but—defying both her father's and her husband's advice (for the first time)—Rain had refused. The couple had been married almost four years at this point and still no pregnancy, but Rain was determined that there *would* be a child someday. *I can nurse the baby with the remaining breast,* she had whispered to Paha Sapa minutes before they took her away to chloroform her. *The remaining one will be closest to my heart.*

The surgery seemed successful, all of the tumor was removed and no other cancer was found, but the operation took a terrible toll on Rain. She was too weak to travel. When it was certain that his daughter would recover, Reverend de Plachette returned to his church and flock at Pine Ridge, but Paha Sapa stayed another four weeks with his darling in that little boardinghouse near the hospital in Chicago.

The Lakota name for Chicago had long been *Sotoju Otun Wake,* which meant, more or less, "Smoky City," but Paha Sapa had wondered if it had ever been as dark, smoky, sooty, black, and windy as during those endless November and December weeks he spent there with his beloved. The view out the window next to their bed in the boardinghouse was of warehouses and a huge switching yard where trains screamed and rumbled and backed day and night. The stockyards were close, and the stench aggravated the constant nausea caused by Rain's medicine. Paha Sapa, refusing Rain's father's offer to pay for everything (the minister was suffering hard times after a lifetime of relative wealth), had borrowed money, an advance on his wages, from the white rancher Scott James Donovan, just to pay the room and board. He would be paying the medical bills for the next twenty-three years of his life.

And so it was that when they arrived home at the Agency on Christmas Day 1897, the train being delayed a day while a plow train cut a way through twenty-foot-high drifts southwest of Pierre, even the Pine Ridge barrens and their tiny home looked beautiful in the white snow under blue western sky. Rain vowed that this was a new start for her and for them and that she would not allow the cancer to return. (A year earlier she might have said, Paha Sapa later thought, that *God* would not allow it, but he'd watched his bride become more thoughtful about such things. She continued being the only teacher at the missionary school, she led the choir every Sunday, she taught Sunday school to the Indian children, and she had not objected or interfered when her father had asked Paha Sapa to be baptized before he could sanction their marriage. Rain still read the Bible every day. But Paha Sapa had silently watched some aspect of faith—at least the specific Episcopal faith of her father—slowly seep out of his wife, rather like the energy she never fully recovered after the surgery.)

But her happiness and high spirits did return. By spring of 1898, her light, quick laughter filled the house and Paha Sapa's soul again. They made plans for building another room on the house the following summer after Paha Sapa finished paying back rancher Donovan. In April, smiling more broadly than Paha Sapa had ever seen her smile except on their wedding day, Rain announced that she was pregnant.

The late-May trip to the Black Hills came about by accident.

For his own reasons, the rancher, Donovan, had to lay off some of his hands for two months. Paha Sapa had found no other work for that time and was just helping Reverend de Plachette with repairs around the church and school and the old house everyone called the rectory. School was out—it always dismissed by the third week in May, since the families needed the children to work, plant, and herd on their tiny plots of land. Rain's father had to return to Boston to deal with things after the death of his older brother there. Reverend de Plachette would be gone for at least a month and perhaps longer.

It was Rain who suggested that she and Paha Sapa take the church buckboard and mules and some camping equipment and go see the Black Hills. Living so near them now for four years, she had never really seen them. Her father had said that they could use the buckboard and mules. She was getting food ready for the trip even as she suggested the idea.

Absolutely not, Paha Sapa had said. He would not consider it. She was three months pregnant. They could not possibly take the chance.

What chance? insisted Rain. No more than if she stayed on the Agency. Her workload here, fetching the water and chopping wood all day and handling the work at the school and church, represented much more serious hard labor than a restful ride to the Hills. Besides, if there was a problem, they'd be closer to towns and doctors in the Black Hills than they were there at Pine Ridge. Also, her morning sickness had all but ended and she felt strong as an ox. If the mules didn't want to pull the buckboard up into the Hills, *she* would...and *still* consider it a vacation.

No, said Paha Sapa. Absolutely not. The roads were terrible, the buckboard old, all the riding and jolting and...

Rain reminded him that while he was off working at the Donovan ranch, she was driving that same buckboard twenty miles and more some days, making her deliveries to the sick and shut-ins on the rez. Wouldn't it be better if he were with her and if the next trip in the buckboard was a pleasure trip rather than just more work?

Absolutely not, said Paha Sapa. I won't hear of it. I have spoken.

They left on a Monday morning and by evening were in the south end of the Black Hills. Paha Sapa had bartered an old single-shot rifle that he rarely used (he kept the Colt revolver) with a Seventh Cavalry sergeant for an army tent, two cots, and other camping materials that took up two-thirds of the space in the back of the buckboard. Spring had come earlier than usual this year, and the fields were bright with wildflowers. The first night was so warm that they didn't even set up the tent; they slept in the back of the wagon with so many comforters and mattresses under them that they lay higher than the sidewalls of the buckboard. Paha Sapa pointed out the important stars and explained to his bride that there were about three thousand stars visible up there on this perfect viewing night.

She whispered—

—*I would have guessed millions. I'll have to tell the students next fall.*

On the second day they followed a wide and usually empty new road up into the south edge of the Black Hills proper—the hills there were gentle, rolling, and rich with high grasses, the trees clustered near the tops of these knolls—and in the midst of the seemingly endless waves of low hills, he showed her where *Washu Niya*, "the Breathing Cave," lay in a hidden and wooded little canyon. Unfortunately, a homesteading *wasichu* family, who'd gotten the land for free, had boarded up the entrance to the cave and locked the door and were charging fees for those tourists who wanted to see it. Paha Sapa could not imagine paying money to go into *Washu Niya* so they continued traveling north.

The new town of Custer, set in a broad valley, was mostly saloons, blacksmith shops, liveries, and whorehouses (with crib doxies in their tents for the miners who had little money), but they camped on a high grassy hill outside of town and went in for food and a sarsaparilla at a soda fountain with a striped red-and-white awning.

The third day, they entered the heart of the Black Hills, their two patient Christian mules pulling the loaded buckboard up steep, rutted paths used by the mining companies and mule skinners. The route of the Denver–Deadwood stagecoach was to their west. Their own mules, slow and thoughtful as they were, learned to scamper the buckboard out of the way when a heavy freight wagon came barreling down the muddy track toward them.

In some of the broad, grassy valleys before they got into the higher country, Paha Sapa showed Rain the ruts and gouges from Custer's "scientific expedition" into the previously unmapped Black Hills in 1874, two years before Long Hair's death.

Rain was shocked.

— *Those marks look like an army came through this valley* last week! *How many scientists did Custer take with him on this expedition?*

Paha Sapa told her.

Ten companies of the Seventh Cavalry, two companies of infantry, two Gatling guns pulled by mules, a three-inch artillery piece, more than two dozen Indian scouts (none of whom were really familiar with the Black Hills), gangs of civilian teamsters—some of the bearded, wild-eyed men driving their freight wagons past them that day might have first come with Custer—as well as white guides (but not Buffalo Bill Cody this time), interpreters in half a dozen Indian languages, photographers, and a sixteen-piece all-German band that played Custer's favorite tune, "Garry Owen," from one end of the Hills to the other. In all, Custer's 1874 "scientific expedition" had been composed of more than a thousand men—including President Grant's son Fred, who was drunk most of the time and whom Custer ordered to be put under arrest once for disorderly conduct—all traveling in 110 six-mule-team Studebaker wagons of the sort still being used in Custer City and Deadwood.

As Rain stared, Paha Sapa added—

— Oh, yes . . . and some three hundred beef cattle, brought down from Fort Abraham Lincoln in North Dakota, so that the men could have their steaks every night.

— Were there any . . . scientists?

— A few. But it was the two miners they brought along—Ross and McKay I think their names were—who served the purpose of the so-called expedition. They were looking for gold. And they found it. The Fat Takers began pouring into the Black Hills as soon as word got out, and word was out before Custer's expedition had left.

— But hadn't the government given the Black Hills to your people—our people—just a few years before this? At Fort Laramie in eighteen sixty-eight? And signed a treaty to that effect? And promised to keep whites out of the Black Hills forever?

Paha Sapa smiled and slapped the reins against the mules' backsides.

The narrow, new dirt road ran up through the beautiful Needles rock formations (which, more than twenty-five years later, would inspire historian-poet Doane Robinson to go looking for a sculptor) and then into narrower valleys filled with flowers and aspen and birch stretching between high, gray granite peaks. In the evening, Paha Sapa remembered a good camping spot near a stream and pulled the buckboard into the high grass and drove it half a mile from the road into an aspen grove where new green leaves were already quaking in the mild May breeze.

The dinners Rain cooked during their camping trip were excellent, better than any fare Paha Sapa had eaten around a campfire since he was a boy. And the camps were comfortable thanks to the Seventh Cavalry cots and camp chairs and folding tables.

The sun had set, the long May twilight was lingering, and the quarter moon had just risen above the high peak to their east when Rain set down her metal coffee cup.

— Is that music I hear?

It was. Paha Sapa slipped his camp knife into his belt, took Rain's hand, and they walked through the aspen forest and moon shadows up a small saddle, then down through the pine trees on the other side. When they came out through the lodgepole pines and into a scattering of aspen again, both stopped. Rain put her hands to her cheeks.

— Good heavens!

Below them was a lovely lake—large for the Black Hills—that had not been there before. Paha Sapa had heard about this from other men on the ranch but hadn't known exactly where it was located. In 1891, they'd dammed up the stream at the west end of this valley where needle-type vertical boulders rose shoulder to shoulder and named the new body of water Custer Lake. (Years later, it would be renamed Sylvan Lake.) Three years ago, in 1895, they'd built a hotel right next to the water and adjacent to the invisible dam, near the high boulders on the far west end of the lake.

Paha Sapa put his hand on Rain's shoulder.

An orchestra was playing on the broad stone-and-wood patio next to the water. Parts of the path circling the lake had been covered in fine white gravel that now gleamed in the starlight and moonlight. Festooned along the porch of the hotel, the patio, and in the trees across the lake were countless glowing Chinese lanterns. Couples in formal dress danced to the orchestra's lively beat. Others strolled on a wide lawn or up the gleaming white path or out onto the lantern-lit pier, from which canoes, paddleboats, and other little boats, many with white lanterns hanging from their sterns, held couples where the men were paddling and rowing and the women were lifting their wineglasses.

Paha Sapa felt as one does in certain dreams in which you visit your old home and find it totally different, changed, not the way it could possibly be in your world.

And even as he felt that, there came a stronger emotion, as strong as scalding water in his lungs.

Paha Sapa looked at the laughing, dancing, strolling *wasichu* couples, some of the men in tuxedos, the women in long, flowing dresses, the lamplight gleaming on their decolletages, looked at the hotel with its expensive rooms looking out over the moonlit lake and with its dining room where waiters glided like ghosts bringing fine meals to the well-dressed laughing men and women, the white husbands and wives, and he realized with a sick turning in his soul that *this* is what his beautiful wife, his beautiful young mostly *white* wife, daughter of a famed minister who had written four books on theology, experienced traveler to Europe and the great cities of America before she was twenty...*this* is what Rain de Plachette should have had, deserved to have had, *would* have had if only she had not...

—*Stop it!*

Rain's hands were on his forearms. She physically jerked him around to face her. The orchestra paused and there was the distant sound of applause drifting across the new *wasichu*-made lake. Rain's expression was fierce and her eyes burned into him.

She had read his mind. She often read his mind. He was certain of it.

—*Just* stop *it, Paha Sapa, my love. My life. My husband. That out there...*

She released his left forearm to swat away the image of the hotel, the orchestra, the dancers, the boats, the colored lanterns with a dismissive sweep of her right hand....

—*That has nothing to do with* me *and what I want and what I need. Do you understand me, Paha Sapa? Do you?*

He wanted to speak then but could not.

Rain put her hand back on his forearm and shook him with her strong, workingwoman's hands. Her grip could bend steel, Paha Sapa realized. Her fierce hazel-eyed gaze could see into stone.

—*I never wanted that, my darling husband, my dearest. What I want is here...*

She touched his chest over his heart.

—*...and here...*

She brought his hand to the upper curve of her abdomen, just below her remaining breast.

—*Do you understand? Do you? Because if you don't... then the hell with you, Black Hills of the Natural Free Human Beings.*

—*I understand.*

He put his arm around her. The orchestra started up again, playing something popular, no doubt, in New York dance halls.

Then Rain surprised him completely.

—*Wayáčhi yačhiŋ he?*

He laughed aloud, and not at the problems with her gender language, but simply in delight that she knew the words. How *did* she know the words? He did not remember ever having asked her to dance.

— *Han.* Yes.

He took her in his arms there in the aspen trees above the new lake and they danced late into the night.

By THE TIME Paha Sapa quits work at five p.m., the white halos are gone from around his coworkers and have been replaced by a pounding headache that gives him vertigo as he plods down the 506 steps to the bottom.

Everything is in place on the cliff for tomorrow's festivities except for the five actual demonstration charges. No one will be allowed on the cliff face in the morning except Paha Sapa as he rigs those charges. A skeleton crew will work from above to rig the flag on the boom arm and pulleyed cables over the Jefferson head. The rest of the final preparation in the morning will be down on Doane Mountain where the press and crowds and important personages will be gathering.

Borglum is back and waving aside those workers who are scheduled to work on the flag covering the next day, obviously about to give them their final directions. But Paha Sapa needs no final directions and he slips away to the parking lot, kicks Robert's motorcycle into life, and follows the dust cloud of homeward-bound workers down the mountain road.

A third of the way down the hill he has to swerve the motorcycle into the trees, get off, fall to all fours, and vomit up his lunch. The headache seems better after that. (Paha Sapa, who has dealt with so many kinds of pain for so long, has not had a serious headache like this since Curly the Crow scout almost split his skull open with a rifle butt sixty years earlier.)

Once home, Paha Sapa heats water for another hot bath to help rid himself of some of the pain and stiffness, but ends up falling asleep in the tub. He wakens in cold water and darkness with a jolt of terror — *Has he slept too late? Did Mune wander off to a speakeasy when Paha Sapa failed to pick him up at the appointed time?*

But it's only nine fifteen. The days *are* getting darker earlier now. It feels like midnight to Paha Sapa as he dries himself off and watches the water swirl out of the tub.

He can't face dinner but he packs some sandwiches and sets them in an old burlap bag—he doesn't want to bring the lunch pail. He realizes how stupid and sentimental this is, willing to blow himself apart but not wanting the lunch pail that Rain used to put food in for him blown apart. Stupid, stupid, he thinks, and shakes his aching head. But he leaves the sandwiches in the burlap bag.

He goes to the old blacksmith shop in Keystone, now the only gas station, and has the retarded boy there, Tommy, fill the motorcycle's little tank. It would be too absurd if his plot failed now due to running out of gas.

Driving up the mountain to fetch Mune (whose own Model T succumbed earlier this year to too many drunken collisions with trees and boulders and who is now dependent upon his equally drunkard and unemployed friends for transportation), Paha Sapa thinks of how his plot—he's only recently begun thinking of it as a plot, but that's what it is (*the Gunpowder plot!* his tired mind decides)—depends now on the idiot Mune Mercer. If Mune *has* wandered off with his idiot friends, believing more in Saturday-night whiskey than in the promised Sunday-morning fifty dollars...well, the plot is over. Paha Sapa simply cannot get the crates of dynamite from the Hall of Records canyon to the ridgeline summit or then deploy those crates on the face without the help of at least one man to run the winches.

Except that Paha Sapa has spent years of sleepless nights trying to find alternatives so that he *can* do it alone. If Mune is gone, Paha Sapa knows that he'll spend the night hauling those crates of dynamite down the canyon and around the valley and then up the 506 steps himself, one crate at a time, and then go dangling out in space without a winch handler if he has to. But he also knows the night is not long enough for that approach, even if his energy were to hold out.

So, again, it all depends on Mune Mercer. Paha Sapa finds himself chanting a prayer to the Six Grandfathers to help him with this one element that is out of his control. The prayer reminds Paha Sapa that, before noon tomorrow, he finally has to compose his Death Song.

Incredibly, miraculously, Mune is there at the appointed time and waiting outside and is even relatively sober.

The problem now is first cramming the giant into the little sidecar—in the end Mune looks like a huge cork in a tiny bottle—and then getting the little motorcycle with all that extra weight up the last mile of road to Mount Rushmore. With that final miracle granted, Paha Sapa glides the motorcycle across the empty parking lot and into the cover of trees. The moon has risen a little earlier tonight and it is even fuller.

—How come you parkin' here in the trees?

Mune's massive brow is furrowed.

—In case it rains, of course. I don't have a cover for the motorcycle or sidecar.

Mune frowns up at a sky free of all but a few light clouds. It has not rained in five weeks. But he ponderously nods his understanding.

It's only eleven p.m. and music comes from the direction of the sculptor's studio. Paha Sapa walks Mune to the base of the stairway and again the giant balks.

—Hey! I hate these fucking stairs. Can't we take the tram?

Paha Sapa presses the big man's sweaty back.

—Sshhh. This is all to be Mr. Borglum's surprise, remember? We're not using any of the power equipment. You walk up to the Hall of Records canyon winch—all the cranking's by hand tonight, remember—and I'll go around and up the canyon. Just send the wire down.....I've got all the hooks and palette cables down there. When I send the crates of fireworks up, just stack each one outside the cable shack. But be careful with them. We want the show to be for the president tomorrow, not just for the two of us tonight.

Mune grunts his understanding and starts clunking his slow way up the stairway. Paha Sapa flinches, thinking that the thud of the giant's hobnailed boots will be enough to bring Borglum or someone checking to find out what all the racket is.

The next hours are a dreamscape.

Paha Sapa has nothing to do between lifts of the dynamite crates and stands there in the shifting puzzle of moonshine and moon shadow, looking up at the black silhouette of the winch boom and shack, always waiting for Mune to change his mind, or discover that the crates so crudely stenciled as FIREWORKS — CAUTION! HANDLE WITH CARE! are actually filled with dynamite and then just run away, but that does not happen.

Finally the last crate and covering tarps are gone, the narrow steel wire comes down a final time, Paha Sapa shines his flashlight into the Hall of Records tunnel to make triply sure that he's sent everything up, and then he clips on the bosun's chair he'd stored there, whistles once, and relaxes as the cable lifts him three hundred vertical feet to the top of the ridge.

His next five hours on the cliff face with the giant Heads are even more dreamlike.

Usually when a driller or powderman has to move laterally across the cliff face as Paha Sapa must tonight, there's a "call boy" tied into a safety harness and sitting far out on the brow of the Head above the worker. It's easy work for the money, since all the call-boy has to do is to relay the workingman's shout to the cable winch operator up in his shack. Then the call boy leans far out to check on the driller's or powderman's or other worker's movement while being held in place by his harness — one wire running back to the shack, one up to the boom arm — and sometimes looking quite comical since he can be standing almost horizontal, feet on the granite, eyes facing straight down, all the while shouting further directions to the winch operator controlling the unseen worker's movement below.

Well, there are no call-boys this night.

Paha Sapa has explained the new system to Mune half a dozen times, but he went over it again before he dropped over the edge of George Washington's hair.

—*No call-boy, so we're doing it with this rope this time, Mune. I've got enough rope that it'll go with me wherever the cable does. You keep one hand on the rope here where I've rigged it to run by your chair. One hard tug means stop lowering. Two tugs means higher. One tug, pause, then another tug means swing to the right at that level. One tug, pause, then two tugs means swing to the left.*

Mune's ferocious frown of pained concentration makes Paha Sapa think that Mune appears to be trying to figure out the article on quantum effect published by Albert Einstein that Robert mentioned twenty-four years ago. Since then, everyone has heard of Einstein... except, perhaps, for Mune Mercer.

—*Here, Mune, I've got it all written out on this chart. If we get tangled up, just clip your harness onto the boom wire and walk out on George's brow a bit and look down to see what the mess is. OK?*

Mune frowns but nods doubtfully.

In the end, it all works as well as if there were a call-boy. Paha Sapa has planned the deployment of the dynamite crates and detonators (which he takes down first and stores on a safe ledge, kicking back and forth to the box like a bird returning to its nest) so that he has little lifting or descending to do, and all of that at the beginning and end of each placement. Mostly it is just him kicking and gliding, lifting and placing and wedging and then kicking off and flying sideways through the night air and moonlight again.

Then Mune cranks Paha Sapa up, they move to the next winch shack farther east along the cliff's edge, and Paha Sapa drops over on his bosun's chair with his rope in his hand and the easy dream of weightlessness begins again. Improbably, miraculously, there are no hitches, either in the cable or the plot.

Palooka has drilled the holes perfectly. The dynamite crates slip in easily and are concealed by the gray tarps. It is the placement of detonators (since the whole crate of dynamite has to go off at once, rather than single sticks or fragments of a stick) and then the placement and concealment of the long gray wires that take most of the night.

But by 4:43 a.m. they are finished. Even the second detonator box is in place and concealed—the first having already been placed there publicly by Paha Sapa in preparation for the day's demo blast—along the rim of rock running flat to the east of Lincoln's cheek.

Paha Sapa drives Mune home, pays him his forty-five dollars, and doesn't look back as he coasts the 'cycle down the long winding hill to Keystone and home as the sun is rising. For a while he worried that Mune might come to the site and talk to Borglum about the mysterious work in the middle of the night and about dynamite crates labeled FIREWORKS, but now Paha Sapa knows beyond all doubt that Mune Mercer is too stupid and too selfish to notice, care about, or talk about such things. Mune, he knows, will sleep for a few hours and then hitchhike to a speakeasy in Deadwood that's open on Sundays and then get forty-five dollars' worth of drunk.

It's another hot, sunny, windless August day.

Paha Sapa considers sleeping for an hour—except while in a hot bath, he trusts his lifelong ability to wake when he wills himself to—but decides not to risk it. After changing his shirt and splashing cold water on his face, he makes some coffee and sits for a while at his kitchen table, thinking of absolutely nothing, and then, when cars belonging to other Mount Rushmore workers in Keystone begin starting up, he washes the mug and sets it in its place in the tidy cupboard, cleans and sets away the coffee pot, looks around his home a final time — he's already burned the note he left on the mantel two nights ago regarding taking care of the donkeys if something happened to him — goes outside, kicks his son's motorcycle into life, and joins the smaller-than-usual procession of workingmen in their battered old vehicles all heading up to Mount Rushmore.

The crowds, he knows, will come later.

23

The Six Grandfathers

Sunday, August 30, 1936

PRESIDENT ROOSEVELT DOES NOT ARRIVE BY NOON, BUT GUTZON Borglum does not start the ceremony without him.

Paha Sapa is the only man on the face of the cliff, perched near Lincoln's cheek—the carving has not yet exposed the head's bearded chin—far to the right but still able to see George Washington, the flag-covered Jefferson, and the white granite slope from whence the Teddy Roosevelt head will begin to emerge. The only other men on the mountain this day are the eight workers peering over the top of the Jefferson head where the winch, boom, pulleys, and rope stays attached to scaffolds are holding the giant flag in place until it is time to swing it away and then pull it up out of sight.

The plan is for the five-charge demonstration blast to be detonated first, then an orchestra will play, and only then will the flag be removed from Jefferson's face. After that, Borglum and a few others will speak to the crowd and radio audience as the head is officially dedicated. There are no plans for President Roosevelt to speak. Just as in the original plans for the dedication of the cemetery at Gettysburg more than three score and ten years earlier, the presence of the president of the United States is mostly a technicality; others are scheduled to do the speech making.

Borglum has loaned Paha Sapa his second-best pair of Zeiss binoculars so that there will be no question that his powderman will be able to see the Boss raise and then lower the red flag as the signal to detonate the five charges, and the heavy optics bring individual faces into clear focus.

By eleven a.m., townspeople and the curious from all over western South Dakota are arriving and beginning to fill up the bleachers above and to either side of the main VIP viewing area on Doane Mountain, right where, if Borglum gets his way (and when hasn't he? thinks Paha Sapa) there will be a huge Visitors Center and fancy View Terrace and probably a gigantic amphitheater with seating for thousands, just for patriotic presentations—including, Paha Sapa is certain, elaborate programs literally singing the praises of a certain sculptor named Gutzon Borglum.

For right now, though, Borglum has had his son, Lincoln, take the bulldozer and improve the ruts leading to the center of that viewing area, below and in front of the V shape of the VIP stands and general bleachers. President Roosevelt, Paha Sapa learned just that morning, will not be getting out of his open touring car during the dedication ceremony. Even without his binoculars, Paha Sapa can see the spot where the president's car will stop, already ringed as it is by bulky microphones on stands, black cables, newsreel cameras, and areas taped off under the ponderosa pines to corral the press photographers. All the other VIPs will be *behind* FDR as he and Borglum look at Mount Rushmore during the ceremony.

Paha Sapa finds Gutzon Borglum through the binoculars and feels a sudden shock as he sees that Borglum is using his *best* pair of Zeiss binoculars to look straight at him.

Normally, Paha Sapa would be atop the ridge to set off a detonation, even one as small as the five-charge demonstration. He suggested this position along Lincoln's cheek with the argument that with all the crowds and congestion, he might have problems seeing Borglum and his flag from atop the ridge.

Borglum scowled and squinted at that.

—*Admit it, Billy. You just want a better view.*

Paha Sapa shrugged and shuffled his silent agreement at that. It was true, of course. But it wasn't the ceremony that he wanted the better view of; it was the twenty-crate explosion all along the cliff face.

He is sitting on the twenty-first crate of dynamite (they are rigged to blow in series so he should see the effects of the other twenty before this one goes) and for a terrible, clammy-sweat second, Paha Sapa is sure that Borglum can see the crate through his long-lens binoculars and now knows exactly what his powderman is up to.

But no...the gray-painted extra detonation wires are also covered with granite dust all along this Lincoln cheek ridge to Paha Sapa's position. He's sitting on a dynamite crate, but the crate is under the last of the gray tarps he's brought up to further conceal all the hidden charges. It's true that he has one detonator too many—the smaller one for the five-blast demo charge, a larger one for all the other boxes of dynamite—but he's taken care to hide that second detonator box behind the crate he's sitting on, out of sight even if Borglum were using an astronomical telescope to look up at him.

Paha Sapa pans across the rest of the arriving crowd, and when he comes back to Borglum, the Boss has turned away, the fresh and ever-present red kerchief around his neck easy enough to see amid the crowd of mostly white shirts and dark jackets. Borglum himself is all in white—or a rich cream-colored long-sleeved shirt and slacks, Paha Sapa sees—except for the large kerchief and black binoculars strung around his neck.

Paha Sapa lowers his own glasses and leans back, his sweat-soaked shirt against the strangely cool curved granite of Lincoln's emerging cheek. He's angry that his hand is shaking slightly as he removes his watch from his pocket. Another two hours, at the most, before FDR arrives and the ceremony commences.

———

THE MORNING AFTER their dance in the aspen grove across the lake from the new hotel, Rain announced that she wanted to climb Harney Peak, which was looming over them to the northeast.

Paha Sapa crossed his arms like one of the cigar store Indians that all Indians hate.

—*Absolutely not. There'll be no discussion of this.*

Rain smiled that peculiar smile that Paha Sapa always thought of as her "Ferris Wheel smile."

— *Why on earth not? You yourself said that it was a short walk—two miles or less?—and that there was no climbing involved. A toddler could do it, you said.*

—Maybe. But you're not going to do it. We're not. You're . . . with child.

Rain's laugh seemed as much in delight at the fact he'd just announced as it was making fun of his concern.

— We're going to go on lots of walks on this camping trip, my darling. And I'll be walking a lot at home during the six months left. This is just a little more uphill.

—Rain . . . it's a mountain. *And the tallest one in the Black Hills.*

—Its summit is still only a little more than seven thousand feet, my dear. I've summered in Swiss towns that sit at higher altitudes.

In rebuttal, Paha Sapa shook his head.

She moved closer and her hazel eyes looked almost blue that perfect morning. After their dancing in the aspens, they'd returned to their little campsite and Rain had gone to the back of the buckboard and started removing both the mattresses that Paha Sapa had insisted on bringing in case she "needed to lie down." Seeing her lifting them, Paha Sapa had run to grab the mattresses from her and to carry them back to the big army tent. *Why do we need these?* he'd asked innocently. At times, he had discovered, his wife could literally purr like one of the cats that stayed around the mission school and church. *Because, my dearest love, our army cots, while wonderfully comfortable, are not adequate for long periods of lovemaking.*

But still . . . in the clear May morning light, Paha Sapa was shaking his head, arms still crossed, the frown seemingly etched into his bronzed face.

Rain set her finger to her cheek as if struck by a thought.

— What if I rode Cyrus up?

Paha Sapa blinked and looked at the old mule, who, hearing his name, twitched one notched ear in recognition but did not look up from his grazing.

— Well, maybe, but . . . No, I don't think . . .

Rain laughed again and this time it was totally a laughing *at him.*

—Paha Sapa, my dearest and honored anungkison *and* hi *and* itancan *and* wicayuhe . . . *I am* not *going to ride poor Cyrus up that hill . . . or anyplace else. First of all, he wouldn't leave Daisy. And second of all, I'd look like the Virgin Mary being led into Bethlehem, minus the big belly. No, I'll walk, thank you.*

—Rain . . . your condition . . . I don't think . . . If something were to . . .

381

She held up her forefinger, silencing him. From less than a quarter of a mile away, just over the low ridge, came laughter and a woman's shout. Paha Sapa imagined the Sunday-dressed *wasichus* playing croquet or badminton on the long green lawn that sloped down to the mirror-still lake.

He also understood what his silent wife was saying. They were almost certainly much closer here to medical help should there be a problem with her pregnancy than they would be in all the months to come at Pine Ridge.

Her voice now was low, soft, and serious.

—*I want to see the Six Grandfathers mountain you've talked about, my darling. There's no easy way in to it, is there?*

—*No.*

The presence of the hotel and new man-made lake and white gravel path here in the heart of his Black Hills made Paha Sapa dizzy, as if he were living in someone else's reality or on a new and only vaguely similar planet. The very idea of there someday being roads to the Six Grandfathers made him ill.

—*I want to see it, Paha Sapa—it and a view of all the Black Hills. I'm putting the luncheon things in this old army map case you brought. Why don't you make sure that the tent is secure and that Daisy and Cyrus will be all right for the few hours we're gone?*

The view from the summit of Harney Peak (or Evil Spirit Hill, as Paha Sapa still thought of it) was incredible.

The last half mile or so of the very visible trail was across the top of one rounded granite outcropping after the other. Having no interest in scrambling up the scree- and boulder-tumbled spire to any technical high-point "summit," the two strolled out onto the north-facing rock terraces of the high shoulder of the mountain.

Yes, the view was incredible in all directions.

Back the way they had come were the Needles formations, forests, and receding grass-and-pine hills all the way to Wind Cave and beyond. To the northwest was the dark-pined and gray-rocked heart of the majority of the Black Hills. Far to the east the Badlands were like a scabbed white scar against the plains; farther north the distant marker of Bear Butte rose against the horizon. Everywhere beyond the Hills stretched the Great Plains which were—for these very few weeks in late May into early June and only then after a rainy spring such as this had been—as green as Rain had once described Ireland.

There were gray granite summits and needles and ridgelines poking up and out of the so-dark-green-they-were-black pine forests in all directions, but the Six Grandfathers was the only rising gray mass to challenge Harney Peak itself. The long summit ridge was almost literally at their feet. The last time Paha Sapa had seen the Black Hills—and especially the Six Grandfathers mountain—like this, he had been floating high in the air with the spirits of those six grandfathers.

— *Oh, Paha Sapa, it's so beautiful.*

And then, after they sat for a while on the blanket Paha Sapa had spread on the stone summit ridge—

—*All you've ever said, my darling, is that you attempted your* hanblečeya *there when you were a boy of eleven summers.*

She took his hand in both of hers.

— *Tell me about it, Paha Sapa. Tell me everything.*

And, to his great surprise, he did.

When he was finished telling her the entire tale, the entire experience, everything he had seen and heard from the Six Grandfathers, he fell silent, astounded and somewhat appalled that he had said all he had.

Rain was looking at him strangely.

— *Who else did you describe this Vision to? Your beloved* tunkašila?

— *No. By the time I found Limps-a-Lot in Grandmother's Country, he was old and ill and alone. I did not want to burden him with so terrible a Vision.*

Rain nodded and looked thoughtful. After a long moment in which the only sound was the light breeze moving through the rocks and low plants there at the summit, she said—

— *Let's eat lunch.*

They ate in silence, with Paha Sapa feeling more foreboding with each minute the silence stretched on. Why had he told his beloved—but mostly *wasichu*—wife this tale, when he had told no one else? Not Limps-a-Lot when he had the chance. Not Sitting Bull. Nor any of the other *Ikče Wičaśa* when he had had the chance over the past dozen years.

Both were watching something that Paha Sapa had never seen before, not even when he had flown with the Six Grandfathers. The high grass of the endless plains, at its absolute greenest this May morning, moved to the caress of strong breezes that were strangely absent there on the summit ridge of Harney Peak. Paha Sapa thought of invisible fingers stroking the fur of a cat. Whatever it reminded him of, he and Rain watched as the strong but distant breezes moved mile upon mile of grass, flowing ribbons of air made visible, the underside of the grass so light it looked almost silver as ripple moved on to ripple. *Waves,* he realized. Having never seen an ocean in real life, he realized he was looking at one now. Most of the plains and prairie there had, he knew, been parceled up into rich men's ranches and poor men's homesteaded parcels—the former destined to grow larger, all the latter doomed to fail—but from this summit on this day, those buildings and barbed-wire fences were as invisible as the absent buffalo and the root-chewing destructive cattle that had taken the buffalo's place.

Now, from this height, there was only the wind playing on wavetops across that perfect illusion of a returned inland sea. Then came the stately cloud shadows moving across that sea of dark grass interspersed with brilliant ovals of sunlight. *"When the sun shone through the clouds, making silvery pools in the dark sea..."* Pools *in* the sea. Where had he read that startling phrase? Oh, yes, last year in Dickens's *Bleak House,* which Rain had so enjoyed and had recommended he read, although his hours for reading, between returning from the ranch long after dark and leaving for the ranch while it was still dark, were few enough. But he loved reading books on her recommendation so that they could talk about them on Sundays and sometimes she returned the favor by reading some of his old favorites. The *Iliad* had been one such. Rain admitted that she'd had a tutor who had attempted to get her to read the *Iliad* in Greek but that the spears and blood and boasting and violent death had caused her to turn away. (But this spring, reading the same Chapman translation that had so moved young Paha Sapa in Father Pierre Marie's school amid the almost carnal scent of sunbaked tent canvas, she told her husband that she had learned, from him, how to love Homer's tale of courage and destiny.)

The picnic food was good. Rain had actually baked a pie using a campfire oven. She had also brought lemons and although there was no ice, the lemonade in carefully wrapped glasses was sweet and light to the tongue. Paha Sapa tasted none of it.

Finally, when they were packing away the plates, he said—

—*Look, Rain...I know the so-called Vision was all a hallucination... brought on by many days of fasting and the heat and fumes in the sweat lodge and by my own expectations that...*

—*Don't! Paha Sapa...don't!*

Paha Sapa had never heard her use that tone of voice with him before. He was never to hear her use it again. It silenced him at once.

When she spoke again, her voice was so soft that he had to lean toward her there on the rocky summit ridge of Harney Peak.

—*My dearest...my husband and darling boy...that Vision you were granted is terrible. It makes my heart ill. But there is no doubt that God—whatever power rules the universe—chose you to receive that Vision. Sooner or later in your life, you will have to do something about it. You have been* chosen *to do something about it.*

Paha Sapa shook his head, not understanding.

—*Rain, you're a Christian. You lead the choir. You teach Sunday school. Your father...well...You can't possibly believe in my gods, my Six Grandfathers, my Vision. How could...*

Again she silenced him, this time with the palm of her hand on the back of his hand.

—*Paha Sapa, is not another name for* Wakan Tanka, *besides "the All," also "Mystery"?*

—*Yes.*

—*That is at the heart of all our faith, my darling. Of everyone's faith, for those who can find and hold faith in their hearts. Unlike my father, I* know *so very little for certain. I understand little. My faith is fragile. But I do know—and, yes, I have faith—that at the heart of the heart of the universe there is Mystery with a capital M. It has to be the same Mystery that allowed us to find our love and to find each other. The same love that has allowed the miracle of this child growing in me. Whatever you decide to do because of this Vision, Paha Sapa, my darling, you must never deny the reality of the Vision itself. You have been chosen, my dearest. Someday, you will have to decide. What* you *will have to decide, I have no idea and I doubt if you do either. I only pray...pray to the mystery within that Mystery itself...that by the time you* do *have to decide, your life will have given you the answer as to which way to proceed. It will, I fear, be the hardest of choices.*

Paha Sapa was stunned. He kissed her hand, touched her cheek, then rubbed his own cheek roughly.

— Wovoke, the crazy old Paiute prophet I told you about, must have thought that he was chosen as well. But in the end, he was just crazy. The Ghost Dance shirts did not stop bullets. I saw that Limps-a-Lot had been wearing one, under his ratty old wool jacket.

Rain winced, but her voice was just as strong as before.

— That old man thought he had been chosen, my darling. You have been chosen. You know that and now I do as well.

The wind suddenly arrived from the plains below and arose around them, whistling through crevices in the rocks.

Paha Sapa looked into his wife's eyes.

— But chosen to do what? One man can't stop the Wasicun *Stone Giants or bring the buffalo back or return the* Wakan *— the sacred Mystery — to his people who have lost it. So . . . chosen to do* what?

— You'll know when the time comes, my dearest. I know you will.

They did not speak again on the slow walk down Harney Peak, but they held hands much of the way.

THE IMPORTANT GUESTS are arriving in the front-row stands far below.

Through the melded twin Zeiss circles, Paha Sapa can see the gleaming bald head of his old mentor Doane Robinson. He knows that Doane will be eighty years old this coming October, but the poet and historian would never miss a ceremony like this, a celebration of the next visible part of a shared reality that was once just Doane Robinson's solitary dream (however much that dream has changed).

Near Robinson in the front row is an older man who looks as if he has a bulky towel wrapped around his chin and left cheek and neck. This is US senator Peter Norbeck and Paha Sapa knows that Norbeck — along with the dreamer Doane Robinson and pragmatic congressman William Williamson — is part of the troika who actually had argued for, pushed ahead, presented to the Senate and House, found funding for, begged for, and tirelessly defended the Mount Rushmore project (often from the excesses of Gutzon Borglum himself) all the way to its current three-heads-almost-finished reality. But Senator Peter Norbeck, who had taken more verbal abuse from Borglum over the years than most men would permit from their wives, is now dying of recurring cancer of the jaw and tongue. The cancer and repeated surgeries for it have finally robbed him of his speech and turned the lower half of his face into a nightmare guaranteed to frighten children and some constituents, but Norbeck has grown a beard to hide some of these ravages and has draped this towel-scarf around the lower part of his face as if it were a normal part of his wardrobe—a second tie, perhaps, or a flashy cravat.

As Paha Sapa watches through the binoculars he's steadying with his elbow on his left knee, he sees Norbeck leaning back to say something to three men in the row behind him. Pointing toward the gang of straining reporters held back by their rope, the dying senator makes quick pantomine motions that end with an upward spiral of his fingers. All three of the politicians—plus Doane Robinson sitting three chairs to Norbeck's right—throw back their heads and laugh heartily.

William Williamson is not laughing. The congressman chosen to lead the welcoming delegation for FDR is pacing nervously back and forth in front of the stand of tall microphones.

Paha Sapa glances at his own watch—2:28. He can see that Gutzon Borglum is far too busy down there now, talking to important people, to have time to run up and stop Paha Sapa even if he were to see something out of the ordinary through his binoculars. But Borglum *does* have a telephone connection to his son, Lincoln, who's in charge of the eight men at the crane and boom atop the Jefferson head, and the official program for the dedication says that it will be Lincoln who will, with a touch of a button, detonate the demonstration blast at the drop of his father's red flag—but in reality it's always the chief powderman who sets off the shot. Paha Sapa *is* sitting far enough forward along Lincoln's cheek—also covered with a sort of towel, he realizes now, looking down at the granite he's sitting on—that he'll be able to see Lincoln Borglum's waved flag, half red, half white, when his father's second-in-command down there phones up the order to blast as a sort of backup command.

But the detonator boxes are with Paha Sapa.

For the hundredth time, he looks at the twenty sites where he's planted the dynamite crates with their detonators. His worry is the same one he's always had: that the power of the explosions will send large rocks or small boulders all the way to the crowd and reviewing stands. It shouldn't, the way he's half buried the dynamite in the spots he's chosen. Big Bill Slovak, who had briefly worked with an urban de-molition crew in Denver after leaving a Cripple Creek gold mine where unsafe practices by the owners had resulted in the deaths of twenty-three miners in one collapse, always liked to point out to the younger Paha Sapa that gravity was the real force involved when one was try-ing to collapse large structures, not the dynamite blast itself. Implod-ing rather than exploding had been the demolition crew's motto. *Give me one stick of dynamite,* Big Bill used to say on their lunch breaks down there in the Holy Terror amid the glow of carbide helmet lamps and the taste of rock dust, *and I'll bring down Notre Dame. Just take out the right parts of the right buttresses, and gravity will do all the rest.*

Paha Sapa hopes that will be true on this blast, but there is always the threat of flying debris. He's calculated for the safety of the men atop the cliff and is *almost* sure that the president and all the guests and visitors at the viewing area on Doane Mountain are safe from small flying rocks, much less the inevitable rolling boulder debris from the blast, but he still worries.

Paha Sapa realizes that he should have said to his son years ago— *I am no warrior and never will be. I lack the ability to willingly hurt people.*

It was true, he sees now. Despite the necessary fistfights he's had in his long life, including those in his early months on this job five years ago, he's never *willingly* acted to hurt or kill another human being. Even when he's fought in self-defense or to stop some racist bullying at his expense, he's done so with the least force necessary—while at the same time knowing, from both Crazy Horse's vivid memories and from the rants of Long Hair's ghost, that there are times when the *great-est force possible* is the answer.

But he knows now, as he sits on this crate of dynamite with both detonator boxes within easy reach, that he chose not to throw him-self and Gutzon Borglum out of the rising tramway bucket because he refused to kill Borglum if he had any choice left. And he does have a choice. At least for the next few minutes.

There's a ripple of noise from below, then applause, and the motor-cade is pulling into the parking area. Other vehicles pull to one side or the other but one long black touring car, men in dark suits now walk-ing ahead of it protectively, bounces down the new road and comes to a stop in front of the viewing stands with the microphones just outside the front passenger-side door.

A man gets out of the backseat of the open car and receives a wave of cheers. Paha Sapa steadies the binoculars. It's South Dakota's popular cowboy governor, Tom Berry. The governor leans over and talks to the man sitting in the front passenger seat for a few seconds and then steps back and waves to the crowd again.

Now the high school band is playing "Hail to the Chief"—Paha Sapa hears it twice, once regularly and the second, tinny time through all the microphones hooked to loudspeakers—and Franklin D. Roosevelt, still seated in the front passenger seat, of course, wearing no hat, his head thrown back, sunlight glinting on the gold frames of his sunglasses, raises an open palm and turns away from Paha Sapa and the waiting Borglum and waves at each part of the semicircle of the crowd, including both those seated and those standing. The standing crowd is relatively quiet but the VIPs on the closer reviewing platform respond so enthusiastically that the last notes of "Hail to the Chief" are drowned out. Three radio reporters are babbling wildly into their bulky microphones, but those devices aren't hooked up to the natural amphitheater's loudspeakers. All Paha Sapa can hear, delayed and overlaid like a ghostly stutter, is the somewhat tepid applause and soft cheers of the crowd. It is, after all, a mostly Republican South Dakota audience.

Then the overlapping loudspeaker squawk, emphasized by the natural echo basin of the curved cliff face above his narrow granite ledge, becomes even more garbled and irritating as William Williamson launches into his welcoming speech.

Paha Sapa pulls the smaller of the two detonator boxes closer and carefully takes the ends of the two wires, from which he's stripped back the insulation with his pocketknife, runs his thumb and forefinger up each to clean it of dust, and then threads each of them through a hole in each post and carefully wraps the excess around the two threaded terminal posts. When he's sure the contact is clean, he screws the Bakelite terminal post coverings down tight onto the wire.

"I met one of these four presidents you're about to blow up, you know. Shook hands with him. He talked to me about my graduation from West Point. Later, he met Libbie at a reception and said, 'So this is the young woman whose husband goes into a charge with a whoop and a shout.'"

Long Hair's voice in his head almost makes Paha Sapa fall off the dynamite crate. Almost three years of silence from the damned ghost and he chooses *now* to begin babbling again?

"It was Old Abe, of course. The fellow whose cheek you're leaning against. In 'sixty-two, the other officers and me serving under General McClellan in the Army of the Potomac talked seriously about marching on Washington to replace that incompetent gorilla with our choice of war dictator, Little Mac himself."

Paha Sapa paws at the air as if swatting away a gnat.

—*Be quiet. You're dead.*

"I'm just waiting to see if you're going to do this thing or if you're going to lose your nerve...again."

Paha Sapa has heard this Custer-laughter many times before. The *Wasicun* obviously did not have an especially charming laugh even in life—it sounded too much like a mischievous boy's nervous cackle—and sixty years in the grave has not improved it.

—*You can't stop me, Long Hair.*

Again the insufferable laughter.

"Stop you? I don't want to stop you, Paha Sapa. I think you *should* do this thing. *Have to* do this thing. It's long overdue."

Paha Sapa closes his eyes for a few seconds to block out the white glare, the heat, the maddening literal double-talk of the noise from below repeated in its amplified echo. He wonders if the *wasichu* ghost is trying to confuse him...trick him...or perhaps just distract him at the coming crucial moment.

"None of the above, old friend," Custer whispers to him. "I'm serious. No man—especially no man bred from a warrior people—can keep receiving these insults and injuries for so long without striking back—and striking back boldly. *Do it,* Paha Sapa. Blow these damned stone heads to hell today, right in front of the cameras and the president and God himself. It won't change a damned thing—your people will still be defeated and irrelevant and forgotten—but it's a warrior people's answer to such humiliation. *Do it,* for God's sake. I would."

Paha Sapa shakes his head, more to free himself of the voice than in reply.

Up until now he has felt no fatigue or pain while he's spent the long morning and interminable afternoon on this thin ledge, in this intolerable heat. Now the pain flows in as if Long Hair's ghost has opened a door for it. Paha Sapa is suddenly so tired he wonders if he will have the strength to crank the handle against the resistance of the detonator box's coils to charge it, or find the strength to raise the plunger against that friction and push it down.

"See what I mean, Paha Sapa? You've gone two nights without sleep and have been working on this hill three solid days and nights without a break. You're going to pass out and your body is going to tumble down the cliff here and be a footnote in the history of this dedication ceremony—the White House will send Borglum a note expressing its sadness at the terrible tragedy of the death of one of his workers—and *these damned Heads will still be here.* Blow them now. What the hell are you waiting for?"

Paha Sapa raises the binoculars. A fat man he doesn't recognize is speaking into the main microphone. President Roosevelt is smiling. Borglum is leaning casually against the president's touring car and he doesn't have his hand on the red flag yet.

When Paha Sapa speaks, it's in a stilted whisper. If someone from below is looking at him through binoculars, he does not want it to be seen that his lips are moving.

—*You're cursing, Long Hair. Didn't you promise your wife that you wouldn't curse?*

The ghost's laughter echoes in Paha Sapa's skull again, but it is not quite so grating this time.

"I did, yes. I made that vow in eighteen sixty-two, in Monroe, Michigan, shortly after Libbie and I had been introduced at a Thanksgiving party and only *one day after* she had, regrettably, seen me inebriated on a public street there in Monroe. I prayed and I admitted sin and I vowed that I would never touch liquor again as long as I lived, nor would I take the name of the Lord in vain or use ungentlemanly language ever again, no matter how frequently my occupation and mean comrades urged me to. But I did not make the pledge to Libbie that day, oh, no—I made it to my older sister Lydia, who, in good time, conveyed it to young Miss Elizabeth Bacon, who had indeed seen me in my unforgivable condition while spying out through the drapes of her upstairs window there from Judge Daniel Bacon's home. But Libbie is dead, my Indian friend, as is your own dear wife, and all our vows have expired with them."

—*Shut up. You just want me to die. You just want to be released.*

Long Hair laughs again. "Of course I do, damn you. I'm no soul waiting for Heaven, no ghost waiting to pass upward and onward, just a memory tumor of Paha Billy Slow Horse Slovak fucking Sapa. We're both tired of this life, this world. Are you just waiting for more pain and loss? What *are* you waiting for, Paha Sapa? Trigger the goddamned fucking detonator *now*."

Paha Sapa blinks at the shouted obscenities echoing in his aching skull. Has the ghost finally gone mad?

Then again, why *is* he waiting? He fully intends to set off the demonstration blast, then listen to the dedication, and only then—after detonating a single stick of dynamite to get the crowd's and cameras' attention—only then set off the twenty-one crates' worth of explosive.

But the ghost has a point... why wait?

He realizes, blushing, that it's because he wants to hear if President Roosevelt will speak after all, even though he's not scheduled to, and if he does, what he will say. He realizes that he's worked five years blasting and helping to carve this monument and wants to hear what the president of the United States thinks of it. He realizes, through fatigue as real as the granite under and behind him, that he wants the president and guests today to be proud of the work done on Mount Rushmore.

"Oh, that is so goddamned pathetic..." begins Long Hair's ghost.

Paha Sapa ignores him. Borglum has begun speaking to the president and guests and has the red flag in his hand.

The detonator boxes, chosen by Borglum himself, are made in Germany and are a little more complex than the old wire-it-up-and-push-down boxes that Paha Sapa used in the mines.

First he takes the handle of the demo-charge detonator box and cranks it four times to the right, charging it. Then he clicks the handle to the left, releasing the plunger safety, and raises that plunger against considerable friction. It is ready to send the current to the detonators in each dynamite crate.

Borglum is finishing his short talk about the combined use of explosives, drills, and chisels on the giant sculpture that is Mount Rushmore, emphasizing, as he always does, the sculptor's tools that have, in truth, done less than 3 percent of the actual work of removing rock.

Borglum turns his back on the president and the crowd and theatrically raises the red flag. Up on the ridge above the flag-covered Jefferson head, Borglum's son, Lincoln, on the phone with someone down there, raises his own red-and-white flag.

At the last second, Paha Sapa glances down to make sure it's the five-stick demo-charge detonator box that he's charged, and not the box linked by gray cables to twenty crates of dynamite. But his vision is foggy with fatigue and he has to look back through the binoculars quickly or miss the signal.

Borglum drops the red flag with a dramatic flourish, as if he's a flagman at the Indianapolis 500.

Paha Sapa pushes the plunger all the way down.

———

HE HAD NEVER FELT AS ANGRY as he did the day in May of 1917 when his son, Robert, told him that he had joined the United States Army and was prepared to go fight in Europe.

Robert had graduated from his private Denver school in December of 1916 and spent the spring months living with his father in the shack in Keystone and then in Deadwood, finishing applications to various colleges and universities, and generally being lazy. Paha Sapa had disapproved when Robert had spent too much of his savings on the almost-new Harley-Davidson J. (A rich classmate of Robert's in Denver had received the motorcycle as a graduation present and immediately smashed it up. Robert had purchased the broken 1916 machine for a few cents on the dollar, had shipped the pieces to his father's address, and spent the majority of January through April happily rebuilding it.) Despite his original disapproval, Paha Sapa had pitched in to help Robert on Sundays and other odd hours when he wasn't working in the Homestake Mine, and he had to admit to himself that he loved the quiet hours working next to his son in the shed they were using as a garage. It was the kind of mostly silent, mostly working separately, but strangely close activity that perhaps only fathers and sons could share. Paha Sapa thought of it often in the years to come.

Robert's grades—which Paha Sapa had always known were good but had little idea of *how* good—along with enthusiastic recommendations from relatively famous faculty there in Denver had, by April of 1917, earned the boy eight scholarship offers. In Robert's usual inexplicable (to his father) way of doing things, he had made separate applications to the same colleges and universities under two names, both of them legally belonging to him due to the quirks of various state and federal registrations—Robert Slow Horse and Robert de Plachette. The latter applications had stressed his connection to his late mother and white grandfather, as if Robert were an orphan, and listed the Denver boarding school as his address for the past nine years. The former applications specified his living Lakota Sioux father and listed the Pine Ridge Reservation and Paha Sapa's shack in Keystone as Robert's former homes.

By late April, Robert could inform his father that Robert de Plachette had not only been accepted by Princeton, Yale, and three other top Ivy League universities, he had received generous scholarship offers from those top schools. Robert Slow Horse, on the other hand, received scholarship offers from Dartmouth College, Oberlin College, and Black Hills State University in nearby Spearfish, South Dakota...the little town Silent Cal Coolidge's liver-fed trout had come from.

Paha Sapa was irritated at the games his son had been playing with something so vitally important as a college education, but he was also proud. Then he became irritated again when he heard that Robert, who had long stated his intention of going to school not only out of state but away from the West, was considering the lesser known of the schools that had accepted him.

— *Where are Dartmouth and Oberlin colleges, Robert? Why even consider them when Princeton and Yale have offered you scholarships?*

It was late at night and they were working on the final reconstruction touches to the Harley-Davidson J's sidecar when this conversation came up. Robert had flashed that wide, slow grin that made him so popular with the girls.

—*Dartmouth's in New Hampshire and Oberlin's in Ohio, Father. Could you hand me that three-eighths socket wrench?*

—*But what makes* them *contenders compared to the Ivy League schools?*

—*Well, Dartmouth* is *Ivy League... sort of. Founded in seventeen sixty-nine, I think, with a royal charter from whichever governor was representing George the Third at the time, chartered with a mission to educate and Christianize Indians in the region.*

Paha Sapa had grunted and wiped sweat from his face, leaving a streak of grease on his cheek.

—*And how many... Indians... have they graduated since then?*

Robert's smile was wide and bright under the hanging bare sixty-watt bulb.

—*Almost none. But I like their motto*—"Vox Clamantis in Deserto."

—*"The Voice of the Climbing Flowering Plant in the Desert?"*

—*Almost, Father. "The Voice of One Crying in the Wilderness." I can sort of relate to that.*

Paha Sapa had arched an eyebrow.

—*Oh? Do you consider your home here, the sacred Black Hills, a wilderness?*

Robert's voice had turned quietly serious.

—*No. I love the Hills and want to come back here someday. But I think that the voice of our people crying out here has gone without answer for too long.*

Paha Sapa had stopped what he was working on and turned his head toward his son at the sound of that "our people"—he'd never heard that from Robert before—but his son was frowning at the bolt he was trying to tighten.

Paha Sapa cleared his suddenly tight throat.

—*And what's the appeal of the Ohio college... what's the name... Oberlin? Do they have a catchy motto?*

—*Probably, but I forget what it is. No, I just like Oberlin's style, Father. They admitted Negroes in eighteen thirty-four or some year around there... and women before that. After the Civil War, Oberlin graduates led the way to go down and teach in the Freedmen's Bureau schools all over the South. Some of them were killed by night riders for doing it.*

—*So you're telling me that you want to go teach Negroes in the South? Do you have any idea how strong the reconstituted Ku Klux Klan is getting? Not just in the South but everywhere?*

— Yes, I've paid some attention to that. And no, I don't want to teach—in the South or anywhere else.

— What do you want to do, Robert?

It was a question that had haunted Paha Sapa much more than had Custer's ghost in recent years. His son was so bright, so good-looking, so personable, and such a fine student that—if he dropped the Indian last name that wasn't really his father's anyway—he could be *anything:* lawyer, doctor, scientist, mathematician, judge, businessman, politician. But Robert, who had always been curious about everything but who refused to focus on one single area of interest, seemed maddeningly indifferent to careers.

— I don't know, Father. I guess I'll have to go to Dartmouth for a few years. . . . It's liberal arts, so they don't demand you decide on a major of study or career path right away. In truth, I want to be just like you when I grow up, but I don't know how to do that.

Paha Sapa had frowned and stared at the top of Robert's lowered head until his son looked up.

— Let's be serious about this, Robert.

Robert's eyes—his mother's eyes—were as darkly serious as Rain's had been when she was saying something very important to Paha Sapa.

— I am *serious, Ate . . . Atewaye Ki. I want to become as good a man as you have always been.* Mitakuye oyasin! *All my relatives!*

So Robert had accepted the offer from Dartmouth in New Hampshire and had finished his motorcycle and gone on long rides down prairie dirt and gravel roads every day—and often in the moonlight—and then on April 6, one month and a day after his second inaugural, President Wilson, who had been reelected for promising to keep the United States out of the European war, went to Congress and asked for a declaration of war against the central powers of Germany, Hungary, Turkey, and Bulgaria.

Five weeks after that, Paha Sapa came home from a twelve-hour shift at the Homestake to find his son standing in the kitchen and wearing the dark khaki uniform, the high puttees, and the flat-brimmed Montana peak hat of the American Expeditionary Force. Robert calmly explained that he'd driven the few miles to Wyoming to enlist as a private in the Army, in the 91st Division and would be leaving the next day for basic training at Camp Lewis in Washington state.

Paha Sapa had never touched his son in anger. While all the white fathers he knew spanked their kids, especially their boys, whenever they got out of line, Paha Sapa had never raised a hand to Robert and almost never raised his voice. A look or slight lowering of his tone had always sufficed in terms of discipline and he had never been tempted to spank or strike his son.

That moment, in the kitchen in the shack in Keystone on May 8, 1917, was the closest he ever came to striking Robert—and it would have been no token slap: Paha Sapa would have pummeled Robert with his fists, beating him into submission as he later beat the bullies on Mount Rushmore who insisted on picking fights with him, if he hadn't forced himself to sit down at the kitchen table instead. He was so furious he was shaking.

— *Why, Robert? College? Dartmouth? Your future? Your mother's hopes for you, Robert. My hopes. Why in God's name?*

Robert had also been shaking with emotion, although which emotion—embarrassment, fear at his father's potential wrath, excitement, chagrin, nervousness—Paha Sapa would never know. He only saw the trembling of his son's always calm hands and heard the slightest hint of tremolo in the always calm voice.

— *I have to, Father. My country's at war.*

— *Your* country!?

Paha Sapa felt like jumping to his feet then and seizing his much taller son by the front of his oversized service coat, ripping the buttons off, and throwing the eighteen-year-old through the closed screen door.

But all he could do was to say again in a strangled rasp—

— *Your* country!?

He felt then that he had failed completely in showing his son Bear Butte and the Badlands and the Paha Sapa themselves, the Six Grandfathers in the sunlight, the forests of aspen and ponderosa pine, the valley meadows and grassy hills farther south and the plains where the wind became a visible thing moving its invisible hand across the hide of the world. He realized, too late, that he should have taken Robert to the valley of the stream called *Chankpe Opi Wakpala,* where the scattered bones of Paha Sapa's beloved *tunkašila* lay bleaching beneath an ancient cottonwood tree and where Crazy Horse's heart had been secretly buried so that no *wasichu* could ever disturb it.

All he could say, for the third and final time, was—

—*Your…country?*

Robert de Plachette Slow Horse had not cried, to his father's knowledge, since he was one and a half years old, but he looked as if he was going to cry now.

—*My country, Father. And yours. We're at war.*

Paha Sapa came very close to being physically ill. He gripped the edge of the kitchen table with all his strength.

—*It's a war between a* wasichu *kaiser and a* wasichu *king, Robert, with lots of other* wasichu *parliaments and prime ministers and foul-breathed old men speaking a score of languages all swept up in it. For no reason. For no reason. Do you know how many young English boys died at the Battle of the Somme, Robert…on* just the first day?

—*More than nineteen thousand dead, Father…before breakfast that first day. More than fifty-seven thousand casualties that entire first day. More than four hundred thousand soldiers from the British Empire dead or injured before the battle was over, more than two hundred thousand French casualties—and it wasn't their battle—more than four hundred and sixty thousand German casualties.*

—*More than a million men dead or wounded in one battle, Robert…for* what? *What was gained by either side when that battle was over?*

—*Nothing, Father.*

—*And you're volunteering for* that? *To join that absolute…*madness.

—*Yes. I have to. My country's at war.*

He sat down across from his father and leaned across the table.

—*Father, do you remember when I was about five and you took me to Bear Butte for the first time?*

Paha Sapa could only stare sickly at his son.

—*Do you remember that I disappeared for several hours and all that I'd tell you when I came back to our campsite was that I'd been with a nice man who had the same name as I did? Robert Sweet Medicine—you also met him. I know you did.*

Paha Sapa could not even nod or shake his head. He looked at his son as if he were already in the grave.

— Well, I told Mr. Sweet Medicine that I'd never repeat the things he told me that day, Father, but I'll break that promise and tell you this.... He told me that I was not destined to die a warrior's death. That I would never die on a battlefield or from another warrior's hand. Does that make you feel better, Father?

Paha Sapa grasped his son's wrist so hard the bones groaned.

— Why, Robert? Dartmouth? Your real life ahead of you? Why... this?

Robert looked down a moment and then met his father's gaze.

—A couple of months ago when we were working on the Harley, you asked me what I wanted to do... with my life. I didn't answer. I've been afraid for years to tell you the truth. But I've known for years what I want to do, must do*.... I want to be a writer.*

The words made no real sense to Paha Sapa. All he could see was the campaign hat, now laid on the table, the black eagle with the spread-wings buttons on the coat, and the bronze disks on the high khaki collar of the uniform jacket—the disk on the left with the embossed letters U.S. and the disk on the right showing the crossed rifles of the infantry.

—A writer? Do you mean like a journalist? A newspaperman?

—No, Father. A novelist. You love to read.... You read novels all the time. I learned my love of books and of Dickens and of Cervantes and of Mark Twain and of all the others from you*, Father. You know that. I'm sure that Mother would have led me to books in the same way; she was a teacher, I know, but she wasn't there and you* were*. I want to be a writer... a novelist... but to write about something, I have to have* lived*. This war, this so-called War to End All Wars, as obscene as it is—and I know it's obscene, Father, just as you do: I know it has no more glory in it than a terrible train wreck or auto accident... but it will be the major event of this century, Father. You know that. How will I ever know who I* am *or what I'm made of or how I'll react under fire—perhaps I'm a coward, I* have *no idea* now*—but how will I know any of these things or learn about myself unless I go? I have to go. I love you, Father—I love you beyond all words in any language I know or could ever learn—but I have to do this thing. And I* swear *to you* on everything sacred to both of us *— on Mother's grave and the memory of her love for both of us —that I *will not fall in battle.*

And he had not. He had been as good as his—or Robert Sweet Medicine's—word.

After ten months of training, the 91st Division was shipped first to England and then to France in the late summer of 1918. The little blue unfolding army-issued envelope-letters with Robert's tight script filling each page arrived weekly, without fail, just as they had for all his years away at school.

August 1918 was filled with even more training near Montigny-le-Roi.

Paha Sapa bought a large map which he affixed to the kitchen wall.

In September, Robert's division marched to the front and the letters began listing addresses such as Void, Pagny-sur-Meuse, and Sorcy-sur-Meuse, and Sorcy.

Paha Sapa bought a pack of children's crayons and made red and blue circles on the wall map.

That September and October, Robert and his division fought in the reduction of the German St.-Mihiel salient, then in the ferocious Meuse-Argonne offensive, then regrouped in places with such horribly familiar names as Flanders and Ypres. Robert wrote of amusing little incidents in the trenches, about the sense of humor of the western-states young men he spent time with, of the habits and manners of the French and Belgians — on October 26, in a place called Chateau-Rumbeke, King Albert of the Belgians phoned the division's head-quarters to express his welcome to the Americans. Robert reported that although it was a rainy, hot, steaming, flea-bitten, rat-biting night in the Allied trenches, the men of the 91st were thrilled to death by the king's welcoming phone call.

Later, Paha Sapa would learn how terrible the fighting in the so-called Ypres-Lys Offensive from October 30 to November 11, 1918, really was. Robert had been in the midst of the worst of it. His commanding officer wrote a letter of praise and commendation to go along with three medals that the private-promoted-to-sergeant would receive in that time. He was not touched by shell or wire or bullet or poison gas or bayonet.

At eleven a.m. on the eleventh of November 1918, an armistice was signed in a railroad car at Compiègne and a cease-fire went into effect. All of the opposing armies began to pull back from their front lines. The last Allied soldier to die on the Western Front was reported to be a Canadian named George Lawrence Price, killed by a German sniper at 10:58 a.m. that day.

The 91st Division moved back into Belgium to wait for demobilization and shipment home. Robert wrote of how beautiful the early-winter countryside was there, despite the ravages of four years of war, and how he was seeing a young lady in the village during his free time, communicating with her and her parents and sisters through his high school French.

What was later called the Spanish flu first broke out at Fort Riley, Kansas — General Custer's and Libbie's old stomping ground — and soon spread around the world. A strange mutation of a more common influenza virus, it was most deadly among the young and physically fit. The actual number of people killed by the influenza virus could never be certain, but some estimated up to 100 million people — a third of the entire population of Europe and more than twice the number of all the soldiers killed in the Great War.

Robert died of pneumonia — the most common cause of death among the young with this influenza — in an army hospital near his billet south of Dunkerque and was buried in the Flanders Field American Cemetery along with 367 of his comrades near the village of Waregem in Belgium.

Paha Sapa received the news on Christmas Eve 1918. Two more letters, following their slower and more circuitous route, arrived from Robert after the death notice, each letter celebrating the beauty of Belgium, his delight at seeing the young (unnamed and possibly not the same) lady, the pleasure he was receiving from the books he was reading in French, his profound gratitude just for surviving the war while suffering nothing worse than a slight cough he was fighting, and his eagerness to see his father when the 91st Division demobilized in earnest in February or March.

———

PAHA SAPA KNOWS that something is horribly wrong just by the *sound* of the first explosion.

The five charges he set for the demonstration explosion, one quarter of a stick of dynamite each, buried in deep holes in the raw rock beneath the slight rim ridge running from Washington past Jefferson, have been primed to detonate in such rapid series that they will sound almost simultaneous to the onlookers below — BAM,BAM,BAMBAMBAM. The demonstration blast was designed to make some enjoyable noise and kick up a maximum of granite dust with the minimum of loose stone actually moved through the air.

But this explosion is far too loud. It *feels* too serious, the vibration flowing into Paha Sapa through the rock beneath him and through the curved vertical stone of Abraham Lincoln's cheek and vibrating his teeth and bones and aching internal organs.

And it's too solitary.

Paha Sapa looks up to see his worst fear realized.

This is the "look up" blast he's buried just to the right of George Washington's cheek and it's taken a large gouge out of the cheek itself.

Paha Sapa looks down and sees the wrong detonator, the gray wires rather than black leading from it. He hears rather than sees the commotion in the sound-shocked side of Doane Mountain below as the newsreel cameras swing on their tripods and as everyone from the youngest child to the president of the United States raises a shocked gaze to the area of the mountain where several score tons of granite have just been lifted into the air in a mighty cloud of dust.

There's nothing Paha Sapa can do. The charges have been rigged in deliberate series, but the electrical charge has already been sent to the fuses of all twenty-one detonators.

He has not meant for this to happen yet. Long Hair's ghost distracted him just when…

The second, third, fourth, and fifth blasts go off simultaneously. George Washington's right eye socket explodes outward and the first president's brow cracks, slumps, and falls, taking the aggressive beak of granite nose with it.

The third blast has taken the mouth and chin and launched Model T–sized chunks of granite far, far out into the thick August air. The fourth explosion blows Washington's right cheek, what was left of his mouth, and part of the left brow into the air. The fifth blast brings the teetering debris of the previous four sliding and crashing down.

Chunks of rock larger than Paha Sapa strike and scar Abraham Lincoln's face above and below and beside the Lakota powderman's partially shielded roost. Below, people are screaming, the screeching microphones and loudspeakers still echoing the reality.

Jefferson flies apart more efficiently than Washington, which is appropriate for the third in line in any profession rather than the first.

But most of the five explosions here happen behind the huge flag that is still draped there, making the Jefferson Head seem like a firing-squad victim who's chosen a large blindfold.

Paha Sapa didn't want this to happen when the flag was still in place. It's a major reason why he was willing to wait.

My country, Father. And yours. We're at war.

Paha didn't believe that then and doesn't believe it now, when the country is *not* at war, but he had no intention of destroying the giant flag so patiently sewn by little old ladies and high school girls in Rapid City.

Incredibly, the thin fabric actually muffles the explosions a tiny bit. Then, faster than the eye can follow, the giant flag is torn to shreds as ton after ton of pulverized rock flies outward and upward in an expanding cumulus cloud of gray dust and flame.

The flag tatters are burning.

Jefferson's prodigious jaw goes first, sliding in fragments toward the heap of old boulders far below. *Let gravity do the work, Billy, my lad.*

By the time the flag shroud is burned and blasted away, Jefferson's nose and eyes and brow and entire left cheek are gone, pulverized. And now the unthinkable is happening.

After Lincoln Borglum's eight workers were to have swung the boom arm of the crane away, even while cranking up the flag on its various ropes and guy wires, the plan was for them to head for the 506 steps. The workers were finished for the day and Borglum wanted to introduce his son to President Roosevelt before the party broke up for good.

But now Lincoln Borglum and his men seem to be trying to do something—crank up the flag? Reach the other charges before they detonate?

No time for any of those things, but with a surge of nausea and terror, Paha Sapa sees the small black figures still wrestling with the crane boom arm when an explosion blasts that thick boom high into the air and sends flames from the burning flag fragments over the whole top of the now-shattered Jefferson head. Through the granite dust and real smoke he can see the tiny figures running, falling…is that a man falling with the flag fragments and blackened boulders?

Paha Sapa prays to every God he knows that it is not.

Then all five crates of dynamite in the Theodore Roosevelt field of granite go off.

This throws the most rock of all at Paha Sapa and toward the crowds below. He has buried the dynamite crates deep in their niches—the idea, with each head, was not just to destroy what is there, but to deny Borglum or any future sculptor from ever finding enough rock for any future carving, and this goal has now been achieved, for the Washington and Jefferson heads as well as the shattered gray sheet that was the prepared field of granite for the TR carving. The good rock is gone. The shards of brow, ear, fragment of nose left of Washington and Jefferson will be ruins forever, but there is not enough rock for any more carving. And now none at all for the entire Teddy Roosevelt site.

Amid the noise and rock-shrapnel and burgeoning dust cloud, Paha Sapa has seized the borrowed binoculars to get a last glance of Gutzon Borglum and the guests on Doane Mountain.

Paha Sapa has calculated wrong. Rocks larger than his fist, larger than his head, are ripping through pine trees and aspen foliage to crash among the crowd like so many meteorites from space.

Those who were standing have already fled like victims at Pompeii or Herculaneum, running across the parking lot, forgetting their cars in their panic. Those trapped in the closer reviewing stands are huddled on the wooden planks, husbands trying to shield their wives from falling debris, the white cloud almost to them now, and heavier rocks from the TR granite field blast beginning to fall. Paha Sapa sees Senator Norbeck standing, his towel blown away by successive shock waves and his cancer-ravaged jaw and chin and neck looking like a bloody preview of things to come for the others.

And the president…

Paha Sapa's bowels clench at the thought.

He had almost forgotten, until the presidential touring car with its special hand controls pulled up, that President Franklin Delano Roosevelt is a cripple, unable even to stand without steel braces locking his wasted, withered legs in place and unable even to pretend to walk without someone next to him bearing his full weight. The president of the United States *can't* run.

But in the three seconds he looks down there, before the expanding dust cloud and the final explosions eliminate his view forever, Paha Sapa sees a Secret Service man who was looking toward the reviewing stand and crowd, his back to the seated president and to Mount Rushmore, turn and leap into the driver's seat of the powerful touring car, jam its gears into reverse, and roar backward away from the falling debris and approaching cloud, almost running over Governor Tom Berry as he does so. The roar of the car's engine is audible even amid the explosions and screams and avalanches of rock. The president's head is still thrown back almost jauntily, his smile replaced by a look of great interest if not wonder (but not horror, Paha Sapa notices), his eyes still fixed on the death of his four stone predecessors on the cliff above.

Gutzon Borglum, on the other hand, stands where he was, legs apart, his fists on his hips, staring at the approaching cloud of grit and dust and flying rock like a pugilist whose turn it is to await his opponent's blow.

The Abraham Lincoln Head explodes above and around Paha Sapa.

Reacting from some atavistic survival instinct, he throws himself flat on the narrow ridge even as the cliff comes apart above and beneath him.

Lincoln's heavy brow comes loose in one piece and falls past Paha Sapa, just feet away, with a horrible mass greater than a house, heavier than a battleship. The pupils of Lincoln's eyes—carved granite rods three feet long that give the appearance of a real eye pupil glinting from a distance below—go firing across the valley like granite rockets, one cutting through the mushrooming dust cloud to pierce Borglum's studio like a spear.

Lincoln's nose also severs in one piece and takes off a seven-foot stretch of the ledge just inches away from Paha Sapa's outstretched and wildly gripping fingers.

The next two blasts deafen Paha Sapa and throw him six feet into the air. He lands half off the ledge, legs dangling over hundreds of feet of empty, dust-filled air, but the bleeding fingers of his left hand find a rim and he grips and grunts and scrambles back up amid the pelting of rock bits and blasts of unspeakable noise. His shirt and work pants have been ripped to shreds. He is bleeding in a hundred spots from rock splinter strikes, and his right eye is swollen shut.

But he is alive and—illogically, treacherously, hypocritically—he fights to stay on the collapsing ledge amid the chaos and to *stay* alive.

How can this be?

The final crate of dynamite is inches from his face. It should have gone off with the others. Has the delay fuse in the detonator been damaged?

Paha Sapa's survival instincts tell him to shove the crate off the ledge before it does explode. Let it join the exploding, sliding, roiling, dust-clouded chaos below. In that fraction of a second, Paha Sapa confronts the full extent of his cowardice: he'd rather die from being hanged in a few weeks than be blown to atoms right now.

But he does not push the crate over the edge of the avalanching cliff.

Instead, Paha Sapa tears his nails as he claws the boards off the top of the crate. He has to know why it hasn't detonated.

The reason, he sees through the enclosing, choking dust, is that there is no dynamite in the crate—not a single stick—although there was the night before when he hid this final crate here and carefully attached the interior detonator and detonator box wires.

There is just a single slip of paper.

Paha Sapa sees his name written on it and the few sentences scrawled beneath, the words not quite legible in the swirling dust, but the handwriting quite recognizable. There is no doubt as the dust occludes everything and shuts off Paha Sapa's breathing as well as vision. The note is written in his son Robert's bold but careful script.

The ledge beneath him gives way.

———

PAHA SAPA SNAPS AWAKE.

Sleeping, dozing…impossible! A second Vision? No. No. Absolutely not. Just a dream. No. How could…one can't fall asleep in the middle of…three nights with no sleep, the long days of work, the heat. Long Hair's ghost babbling, lulling him. No, not possible. Wait, what has he missed?

The Will Rogers twang of Governor Tom Berry is just wrapping up. The loudspeaker echoes off itself and the three intact Heads, the intact rock field where TR is meant to rise. Borglum begins to speak. The red flag is in his hand again...no, for the first time.

Paha Sapa wonders if he has died. Perhaps Hamlet was right—to sleep, perchance to dream. Ay, there's the rub. Death would be welcome if it were dreamless, but to live this over and over in dreams...

Borglum is explaining that we—the royal we, the unnamed sixty workers and he—use dynamite to clear the surface rock but do all the actual carving by hand.

My ass, thinks Paha Sapa. He looks down. The cables are not connected to the detonators. The dream hangs on him like a wet, dead chimpanzee. His head pounds with pain and he feels as though he might have to vomit over the rim of the ledge...the ledge that crumbled under him only seconds ago. The vertigo still inhabits his inner ear and belly.

Borglum is raising the red flag.

Paha Sapa threads the wires, wraps them, presses down the Bakelite covers. His scarred, blunted hands have done this a thousand times, and he allows them to do it now without his intervention. The only intrusion he allows his mind is to check the color of the cables. Black. The demonstration charge. Wired, the voltage cranked up in four turns to the right, safety clicked left and off, plunger raised against the drag of coil. Paha Sapa keeps his right hand on the plunger and raises the binoculars with his left hand.

Unlike in the dream, Gutzon Borglum does not turn his back on the president or wave the red flag dramatically, as if he were a flagman at the Indianapolis 500. Borglum's left arm is along the back of the president's car seat, his body half turned toward the president, eyes lifted to the cliff, as he casually lets the flag drop.

BAM, BAM, BAMBAMBAM.

Paha Sapa has no physical memory of pushing the detonator box plunger, but it is pushed, the charges fired as fused.

To Paha Sapa's blast-deafened ears, these quarter-charge reports are more like rifle shots than dynamite blasts. The amount of rock blown out is purely symbolic, the dust cloud negligible. But the audience below applauds. Oddly, President Roosevelt offers his hand to Borglum and the two men shake as if the outcome of the blast had been in question.

There is movement above Paha Sapa. Lincoln Borglum and his workers have swung the boom, lifted the flag. Thomas Jefferson ponders the blue sky. The sounds of the real applause and the delayed and overlapping amplified applause pitter-patter on the stone faces above and around Paha Sapa.

Borglum has leaned close to the microphone again. His tone is imperative; he is giving the president of the United States a direct order:

—*I want you, Mr. President, to dedicate this memorial as a shrine to democracy; to call upon the people of the earth for one hundred thousand years to come to read the thought and to see what manner of men struggled here to establish self-determined government in the western world.*

Applause again. Everything sounds very, very far away to Paha Sapa, whose hands are threading and wrapping the bare leads of the gray-painted cable to the terminals of the second detonator box. Borglum's phrasing—"to call upon the people of the earth"—sounds familiar, derivative, to Paha Sapa as he cranks the detonator four times to the right, building the charge. Yes, he knows…it echoes the translated opening to the Berlin Olympic Games earlier this month: *I call upon the youth of the world…*

And it is just like Borglum to mention not the faces he's not even finished carving, but the "shrine of democracy" and all its reading material tucked away in the Hall of Records that's now just a test bore in the unknown canyon behind the heads.

One hundred thousand years of *wasichu* domination of the Black Hills. He pulls the detonator plunger up against its friction until it clicks into place. Ready.

FDR was not scheduled or invited to speak—Paha Sapa cannot remember if Abraham Lincoln had been invited to speak at Gettysburg (Robert could tell him), but he knows that the sixteenth president hadn't been the *main* speaker, and now this thirty-second president was not invited to speak at all—but, overcome with emotion or politics (just as Paha Sapa expected), Franklin Delano Roosevelt reaches out and pulls the heavy circle of the microphone closer.

The familiar tones from radio, the reassuring cadence—still sounding as if it is on radio due to the speakers and echoes—blasts up and out from Doane Mountain to Mount Rushmore and then to the world.

———*...I had seen the photographs, I had seen the drawings, and I had talked with those who are responsible for this great work, and yet I had no conception, until about ten minutes ago, not only of its magnitude, but also its permanent beauty and importance.*

...I think that we can perhaps meditate on those Americans of ten thousand years from now...meditate and wonder what our descendants—and I think they will still be here—will think about us. Let us hope...that they will believe we have honestly striven every day and generation to preserve a decent land to live in and a decent form of government to operate under.

The applause is louder now and Paha Sapa can hear it before the speakers echo it around him. There are some cheers from the mostly Republican crowd. Paha Sapa lifts the binoculars again and catches FDR turning away from the beaming Borglum and waving that oft-parodied wave to the crowd, the magnificent head back, the grin locked and lacking only the cigarette holder and cigarette to make it whole. Paha Sapa sees that poor Senator Norbeck's towel has slipped—the dream tries to slide in with its sickening reality—but the cancer-mauled creator and protector of Mount Rushmore is smiling a corpse's smile.

Time seems to twist out from under Paha Sapa. Has he dozed again? Is he going mad? He lifts the sun-heated binoculars.

Borglum is leaning almost casually against the touring car. The sun has heated that metal as well and Paha Sapa can see how Borglum is using his white sleeves to protect his arms against the burning steel (is it bulletproof?) of the car's black door. More VIPs are milling around the automobile now and frowning Secret Service men hold some back.

The microphone has been removed—or, rather, radio announcers are babbling into theirs, but the speakers here are not carrying their broadcasts—so there is no way that Paha Sapa can hear what the president and the Boss are saying. But he does.

Roosevelt's voice is relaxed, satisfied, genuinely curious.

— *Where are you going to put Teddy?*

Borglum half turns and points to the left of Paha Sapa as he explains that the TR head will go in that lighter-granite area between Jefferson and the emerging Lincoln head.

— *I have it all planned out in my studio.*

Borglum is inviting the president up to the studio—right then. It would be like Borglum to expect the president of the United States to accept the impromptu invitation and to hang around while Borglum grills some steaks for everyone later.

Roosevelt is smiling and speaking.

—*I will come back someday to look this over more fully.*

Borglum is smiling and nodding, obviously believing FDR. Paha Sapa knows his boss, literally inside and out. How could someone *not* want to return to Mount Rushmore? Besides, there are so many more dedications ahead—the Abraham Lincoln head, probably next year in 1937, then Teddy Roosevelt, of course, by 1940 if Borglum's schedule is kept to (and Paha Sapa knows that Borglum also expects Franklin Roosevelt to remain president for three or four more terms, at least), and then the Hall of Records before 1950 or so...

Paha Sapa looks up, squinting into the sunlight. Lincoln Borglum and his men have folded the huge flag away, secured the boom arm and pulleys, and have left for the staircase. Lincoln had better hurry if he wants to be introduced... the fringes of the crowd are breaking up, the VIPs have left their seats, the president's Secret Service men and aides are clearing a path for the automobile.

This is the time, Paha Sapa realizes. Now. This second.

The detonator box is between his knees, the plunger still raised.

He is still sitting that way an hour later when he raises his head, lifts the binoculars, and looks down.

Almost everyone is gone. The president's car is long gone. The parking lot is almost empty. The reviewing stand is being dismantled.

There's motion above Paha Sapa and he looks up to see Gutzon Borglum dropping toward him. Of all the hundred or so workers who've learned to move across the face and faces of Mount Rushmore, no one floats with a lighter or surer touch than Gutzon Borglum.

The Boss drops to the ledge and steps out of the bosun's chair and safety harness. He looks down at the detonator box still secured and armed between Paha Sapa's knees.

—*I knew you wouldn't do it. Where did you hide the dynamite crates?*

Keeping his right hand on the plunger, Paha Sapa points out the various hiding places on and under and around the various faces.

Borglum shakes his head—he is wearing his broad-brimmed hat, the red kerchief is still around his neck—and sits on the ledge, propping one powerful forearm on his knee.

Paha Sapa has to fight the hollowness in him in order to speak at all.

—*How long have you known what I was going to do?*

Borglum shows his nicotine-stained teeth.

—*Don't you know? I've always known what you were* planning *to do, Paha Sapa. But I've also always known you* wouldn't *do it.*

The statement makes no sense but Paha Sapa has the urge to ask the Boss how he learned his, Paha Sapa's, true name. The detonator is still fully charged. The plunger is still raised.

—*Paha Sapa, you remember our meeting in the Homestake Mine. The handshake?*

—*Of course.*

Paha Sapa's voice sounds as weak and hollow and defeated as he feels.

—*You're so damned arrogant, Old Man Black Hills. You think you're the only person in the world with the gift you have. Well…you're not. You got those bits of my past when we shook hands that day—I felt them flow into you—but I got bits of your past and future. This day has been as clear to me as our shared memories of you counting coup on Custer or the face of your* tunkašila.

Paha Sapa looks at Borglum and blinks and tries to understand this but cannot. Borglum laughs, but not cruelly, not out of some victory. It's a tired but strangely satisfied sound.

—*You know, Paha Sapa, that doctor you snuck off to see in Casper is a damned quack. Everyone knows that. You need to see my doctor in Chicago.*

Paha Sapa has no reply to that. Borglum looks up at the Washington head, then at Jefferson, then at the white field of granite that will be Teddy Roosevelt.

—*I think the president was really impressed. Now I've got to go beg the Park Service for another hundred thousand dollars so that I can finish everything. They'll think that I'm lying when I say I can get everything done with only a hundred thousand bucks, and they'll be right…but it'll keep us going.*

Borglum cranes his red-kerchiefed neck to look up at Abraham Lincoln looming over them.

—*One of the things I saw that day in the mine, Paha Sapa, is that in nineteen forty-one I'll…well, we'll see if that comes true. I believed in all the rest, but I don't have to believe in that if I don't want to. Shall we take those damned contact wires off now?*

Paha Sapa says nothing as Borglum undoes the wires from the detonator box terminals. The Boss tosses the gray-painted cables aside and then sets the detonator box gently next to the other one. In his place, Paha Sapa might have tossed the detonator over the side of the cliff, but the boxes are expensive and Borglum is a man who watches every penny when he can. Not in his own life, of course, but for the Mount Rushmore job.

With the detonator harmless, Paha Sapa finally can speak again.

—*Are the police on the way, Mr. Borglum? Waiting below?*

Borglum looks at him.

—*You know there are no police waiting, Paha Sapa. But I need you to tell my son where all the crates of dynamite are. Are they usable on the job?*

—*Most are. I have some more crates in the shed next to my house that aren't so good. Someone should check those and get rid of them.*

Borglum nods. He pulls a second and smaller red handkerchief from his pocket and mops the sweat from his forehead.

—*Yeah, Lincoln will take care of those too. We'll check the sticks in these boxes and store them up in the powder shed for now. You going to take a little vacation…go away for a little while?*

Paha Sapa understands nothing.

—*You'll let me go?*

Borglum shrugs. Paha Sapa realizes, not for the first time, how powerful the sculptor's hands, forearms, shoulders, and personality are.

—*It's a free country. You're overdue for a real vacation. I'm gonna have the boys work on the Lincoln head here through September and start the serious honeycombing for Teddy Roosevelt in October. But when you come back, I'll have a job for you.*

—*You have to be kidding.*

The quality of Borglum's grin and gaze shows that he is not.

—*I don't think you should be powderman anymore, Old Man, although I know it'd be all right if you were. I thought maybe you should work with Lincoln on supervising the drilling and bumping on the TR head, then work with the second team to start the serious work on the Hall of Records and the Entablature. We'll talk about it when you get back from vacation.*

They stand then, both men easy on the narrow ledge with nothing between them and two hundred feet of clear air other than their experience and sense of balance. The long August day is shading into a golden evening that — suddenly, sharply, inexplicably — feels more like the benediction of autumn than the constant test of endlessly blazing summer.

Borglum is slipping into his bosun's chair and safety strap and Paha Sapa looks up to see a second bosun's chair dropping down for him on its almost invisible steel wire.

24

Along the Greasy Grass

September 1936

PAHA SAPA HAS THE SIDECAR LOADED AND IS READY TO LEAVE at dawn, but Lincoln Borglum and a work crew show up early to check out the extra stored dynamite and transport it elsewhere. The younger Borglum knows what's going on and acts embarrassed, almost apologetic, but powdermen Clyde "Spot" Denton and Alfred Berg, as well as Red Anderson, Howdy Peterson, Palooka Payne, and the other men carrying the crates out to the waiting truck are just confused.

It's Red who asks the question.

— *Where you goin', Billy?*

Paha Sapa tells the truth.

— *Home.*

He's dug up the coffee can from the backyard so he has all his remaining money in the sidecar. He's also loaded everything else he'll need for the rest of his life—some food for the trip, a change of clothes, the oversized leather jacket Robert left for him when he went in the Army, and the loaded Colt revolver.

Lincoln Borglum offers to shake hands and although it confuses Paha Sapa, he sees no reason not to do it. Then he kicks the motorcycle alive and drives down the hill to the highway that runs through Keystone.

First he stops at the blacksmith shop to fill the bike's gas tank. Gene Turnball, bustling around with his one dead eye, says chattily—

—Didja hear that Mune Mercer killed hisself last night?

Paha Sapa pauses in the act of checking the oil.

—Mune? How?

—He was blind drunk over to Deadwood when he left Number Nine and drove a car off that bad curve above the Homestake. Flinny said it rolled over an' over for three, four hundred feet before it come to a stop on the talus there. Mune wasn't even throwed out—and it was a topless roadster—but it took his head clean off.

—Mune didn't have a roadster. He didn't have any car.

—That's true. He stole it from his drinkin' buddy at Number Nine, that big Polack who works in the mine, you know who I mean, the mean one with the sister who's real popular at Madame Delarge's, and Flinny said the Polack's really pissed off about it.

Well, thinks Paha Sapa as he pays his thirty cents and drives out of town for the last time, *my little conspiracy claimed a life after all.*

Instead of heading down to Rapid City, Paha Sapa drives west and then north through the Black Hills a final time. This takes him past Mount Rushmore, and he pauses just once, west of the Monument at the point where the road curves and only George Washington's head is visible almost straight above the highway. Paha Sapa has always thought that this was the best view of the Monument.

Except for some lumber trucks, the roads are almost empty all the way to Lead. The air is cooler today—it's not just the speed of his passage, he's sure, since the old motorcycle rarely gets above forty miles per hour—and somehow the sunlight has shifted from end-of-summer to early-autumn illumination in just a day. From Lead he takes the canyon down to Spearfish and the sound of the Harley-Davidson J's little engine pangs echoes off the steep canyon walls on either side.

Beyond Spearfish (where Paha Sapa always imagines the fat trout in the hatchery having nightmares of Calvin Coolidge's return), he heads north toward Belle Fourche but turns left on unpaved Highway 24 before he gets to that little town. The tiny white sign that tells him that he's entered Wyoming is illegible because of the rifle bullet holes and shotgun pellet splatters.

He's come this way rather than heading straight to Montana be-cause he wants to see *Mato Tepee*—what the *wasichu* have named "Dev-il's Tower"—again. He brought Robert there on one of their summer camping trips when the boy was eight.

The 867-foot promontory with its broad, flat top and deeply ribbed sides—it looks like a fossilized tree stump in the scale of the *Wasichu Stone Giants*—is most sacred to the Kiowa, who call it *T'sou'a'e* or "Aloft on a Rock," but all the tribes have borrowed the Kiowa's story of how the giant bear chased seven sisters to the top of the tree stump after the *wagi* of the stump said "Climb on me" to them. Once the girls were on the ordinary stump, the stump began to grow, the gigantic bear pawing and clawing wildly at them, leaving the vertical grooves that one could still see on the huge rock formation.

Of course, the girls could not come down while the bear was there (and the bear would not leave), so *Wakan Tanka* allowed the seven sis-ters to ascend into the sky, where they became the seven-star formation known by *wasichus* as the Pleiades. (Although some Kiowa insist to this day that the sisters became the seven stars of the Big Dipper. Kiowa, Paha Sapa has always thought, make up in imagination what they lack in consistency.)

Paha Sapa and Robert visited *Mato Tepee* in 1906, the year President Teddy Roosevelt anointed the tower as America's first national monu-ment. Not only the Kiowa but the Lakota, Cheyenne, Arapaho, and Crow tribes formally objected to this, but the Park Service—which controlled all access to the formerly sacred site—hired an anthropolo-gist who proclaimed (Paha Sapa remembers reading the announce-ment in the Rapid City *Journal* just two years earlier, in 1934), "It is extremely unlikely that any one tribe has been in the area of Devil's Tower National Monument for a sufficiently long time to have occu-pied an important place in their lives or their religion and mythology."

Paha Sapa smiled at that and could imagine how Limps-a-Lot would have laughed aloud at the idea. Not only did that stone tower go back generations in most of the tribes' storytelling—Limps-a-Lot had told Paha Sapa and the other boys no fewer than ten differing stories about the seven sisters and the place—but that anthropologist had not appre-ciated, as Limps-a-Lot and even Robert had, how *quickly* the Natural

Free Human Beings and other bands could create new mythology about any new habitat they found themselves in and then insert that mythology—or new view of reality—as central to their thinking.

There is, shockingly, a gate on the dirt road leading to the tower now and a man in a park uniform and WWI campaign-style hat demanding fifty cents for entry. But Paha Sapa turns around and drives away. He saw enough of the tower as he approached and he'll be damned if he'll pay the same price to see a rock outcropping that looks like a giant tree stump as he once paid to get into the World's Fair.

He has to backtrack a bit to take county roads that are no more than two ruts in the prairie north to intersect Highway 212 in Montana. Here on the ruts there are no signs at all to notify him when he has left Wyoming and entered Montana somewhere beyond a town (consisting of one store with a gas pump) called Rockypoint.

Paha Sapa stops at a dirt crossroads to buy a Coca-Cola where one building in the midst of endless prairie and distant hills shows how empty this part of Wyoming-Montana truly is. All the money from the coffee can bank, the bills now wedged in his back pocket, makes him feel rich.

The boy behind the counter is a dull-seeming *wasichu* and when he takes Paha Sapa's nickel, he leans across the splintered wood counter and whispers conspiratorially—

—*Hey, Chief, you wanna see something really intrestin'?*

Paha Sapa drinks the Coca-Cola in one head-back glug. The day's driving and all the dust that is Wyoming have made him thirsty. The boy had whispered, so he whispers back—

—*Don't tell me...a two-headed calf.*

—*Naw, better'n that. This is history-like intrestin'. Nobody but us who live here know about it.*

History. Paha Sapa is a sucker for history. Also, he realizes, he is a victim of it. (But so is everyone else.)

—*How much? And how long will it take to see it?*

—*'Nuther nickel. And it's just a couple minutes walk, ten tops.*

Feeling rich in his last days, Paha Sapa slides two nickels across the counter, one for history and the second for another cold Coca-Cola.

It's actually about a fifteen-minute walk behind the store. The boy seems to have a coordination problem and walks like a poorly handled marionette, arms and legs all akimbo, booted feet lurching out at random, but he manages to lead Paha Sapa across a field where two bulls watch them with lethal intent in their eyes, then over a barbed-wire fence and up a small hill with a few pine trees at the top, then down a slope toward a broad low-grass valley.

— *There she is. Somethin', huh?*

For a moment Paha Sapa thinks it's the retarded boy's idea of a joke, but then he sees the old tracks and gouges in the lowest part of the valley, the old wagon wheel ruts stretching from the low ridge on the eastern horizon to an even lower ridge far to the west.

The boy puts his thumbs behind his suspenders and becomes an avatar of civic pride.

— *Them's General George Armstrong Custer's wagon ruts, Chief. From when he brought the Seventh Cavalry through here a long, long time ago with wagons, cattle, cannons, extra horses, even had his wife along, I hear tell.... Hell, it musta been a real circus. Wouldn't ya've liked to have seen it?*

— *It was worth the nickel, son. That Custer sure did get around.*

Paha Sapa drinks the last of his second Coca-Cola and hurls the bottle out across the Spanish bayonet and other spindly shrubs toward the distant wagon ruts.

The kid screams— *Hey!*— and goes running after the bottle, bringing it back up the hill like a faithful if slightly glowering, uncoordinated, and dumber-than-usual Labrador retriever.

— *That's a penny deposit, Chief.*

———

PAHA SAPA CAMPS that night just off the road in a high, wooded plateau in the forty-mile empty stretch of Montana between Epsie and Ashland. He's certain that this long north-south pine-covered plateau will be a national forest, if it's not already, and that it will be named after Custer.

He's brought no tent, but folded on the floor of the motorcycle's sidecar is a ground tarp and another, waterproof tarp to rig as a lean-to if it rains. This night is warm and cloudless. The moon is just past full and, although it rises late, it ruins his star counting. He realizes that this is the same full moon by which he's recently danced weightless across the face of Mount Rushmore, placing his dynamite charges. That event seems more lost in history to him than the Custer wagon ruts he paid good cash to see. Somewhere north in the forest of pines or the adjoining high prairie, coyotes begin howling. Then a single, deeper, more terrifying howl—it sounds like a wolf to Paha Sapa, although Montana has fewer and fewer wolves these days—and all the coyotes fall silent.

Paha Sapa remembers Doane Robinson discussing the ancient Greek maxim of the *agon*—of how life separates everything into categories of equal to, lesser than, or greater than. The coyotes honor the *agon* with their craven silence. Paha Sapa knows how they feel.

Seeking more pleasant if still painful thoughts, he remembers how the full moon looked over the huge black silhouette of *Mato Tepee* when he and Robert camped there in the summer of 1906, and how late he and his eight-year-old son talked into those nights. Perhaps that was the summer when Paha Sapa fully realized how gifted his son truly was.

When he sleeps this night, Paha Sapa has a single dream. In the dream, he is on the ledge at Mount Rushmore again, with Abraham Lincoln's head exploding and disintegrating around him, the ledge under him crumbling, but this time he can read the note in the otherwise empty dynamite crate.

It is Robert's handwriting, of course, and the message is short—

Father—

I would have caught the Spanish Flu even if I'd gone to Dartmouth or stayed home with you. As it was, I was with brave friends of mine at the end and I fulfilled my destiny of meeting the loveliest of all girls. The flu would have found me anywhere. The girl might not have. It's important that you understand that. Mother agrees with me.

Robert

Paha Sapa is weeping when he awakens from the dream. Later, he is not sure whether it was seeing Robert's signature again that made him weep in his sleep or the painfully, malignantly hopeful "Mother agrees with me."

————

HIS MORNING DRIVE west through low, rolling hills dotted with scrub pine and intervals of low-grass prairie too dry to support cattle soon takes him into the Northern Cheyenne Reservation. All reservation Indians, in his experience, are sullen and suspicious of outsiders—he certainly was during his years at Pine Ridge—and the ancient Cheyenne clerk when he stops at the only store in Busby to buy bologna confirms that experience, even though the Cheyenne and Sioux have gotten along better than most. Just beyond Busby, he knows, he'll be entering the large Crow Agency for the rest of his trip (the rest of his life, he thinks and bats the pathetic, sorry-for-himself thought aside), and the Crows and Lakota have *not* gotten along, historically speaking. He knows that reservation sullenness will turn to open animosity in Crow country and hopes that he won't have to stop anywhere there.

A little clerkly sullenness doesn't matter to Paha Sapa. He's only about thirty miles from his destination. He can carry out his plan long before the sun goes down. For some reason, it's important to him that it still be daylight.

But a few miles beyond Busby, the Harley's engine seizes and stops. Paha Sapa parks it in the low grass off the road, sets out the ground tarp, and slowly strips the engine down to its component parts; he is in no hurry and working on the motorcycle always reminds him of the hours and nights and Sundays he spent rebuilding this machine with Robert.

Hours pass as Paha Sapa sits in the sunlight next to the gray-painted motorcycle, carefully setting out the pieces on the tarp in their proper order and relation to one another: intake valves, rocker arms, the delicate springs, the spark plug (fairly new), the heads of the intake ports, the cylinder heads themselves, then the camshaft…placing each in its proper spot, ready for rebuilding even if he were blindfolded as Robert must have learned to field-strip his Model 1917 American Enfield bolt-action rifle, learning each piece by feel as well as by sight, taking care not to allow dust to gather on the oiled and greased pieces or to get into the interior.

The problem is with the right cylinder of the little 61-cubic-inch V-twin engine. The rod bearing between the piston connecting rod and the crankshaft has burned out and split in two.

Paha Sapa sighs. There was a rudimentary garage, another former blacksmith shop, attached to the cluttered and smelly one-room general store back in tiny Busby, but even if the garage were still a blacksmith shop, he couldn't engineer his own bearing. He'll need a replacement.

His highway map shows no town at all ahead of him, westward into hostile Crow country as he still thinks of it, so he replaces the parts he can, sets the broken bearing, piston, and connecting rod in a bag in the sidecar, and pushes the motorcycle the four miles back to Busby in the grasshopper-leaping heat. Two old cars pass him, both driven by Indian men, but neither stops to offer help or a ride. They can see that he's an outsider.

Back in Busby — Paha Sapa sees a few houses off to the north of the highway, no trees, and guesses the population of Busby to be somewhere around a hundred souls — the mechanic in the general store-garage is the same old man who grudgingly sold him the bologna earlier. The Cheyenne has to be in his eighties and admits, when asked, that his name is John Strange Owl but quickly informs Paha Sapa that he will answer only to "Mr. Strange Owl." Mr. Strange Owl studies the parts that Paha Sapa has set out on the only clean expanse of the filthy garage bench and solemnly reports to Paha Sapa that the problem with the machine is a burned-out and broken rod bearing. Paha Sapa thanks him for the diagnosis and wonders when he might get a replacement. Mr. Strange Owl has Paha Sapa wait while the old Cheyenne confers with two other old men and a teenager who've been hollered in to help deal with the crisis.

All right, Mr. Strange Owl announces at last, for something as exotic as this Harley-Davidson J V-Twin machine, they'll have to send not just to Garryowen or the warehouse at Crow Agency or even to Hardin, but all the way to Billings to get a bearing. And since Tommy don't go to Billings except on Friday mornings, and this being Tuesday and all, they won't get the bearing back 'til Friday evening, probably around suppertime, and Mr. Strange Owl closes up exactly at five, every day, no exception, and never opens the store or garage on Saturdays or Sundays, no matter how much folks around Busby fuss and want him to, so it'll be Monday, September seventh (today is the first of September), before Mr. Strange Owl and young Russell and maybe John Red Hawk here, who owned a motorsickle once, can get around to working on it.

Paha Sapa nods his understanding.

— *Is there a bus that comes through here? I'm just going thirty miles or so to the Little Big Horn battlefield.*

— What the hell do you want to go to a battlefield for? Nothing there. Not even a restaurant.

Paha Sapa smiles as if sharing in the understanding of how totally foolish that goal would be.

— Is there a bus, Mr. Strange Owl?

There is. It comes through every Saturday on its way from Belle Fourche to Billings. It doesn't stop at the old battlefield, though. Why would it? But it takes on mail at Crow Agency headquarters, just down the road from the battlefield.

—Do you think anyone here would like to earn a dollar by driving me to the Little Big Horn sooner than Saturday?

There is much earnest conversation about this, but in the end the three old men decide that Tommy Counts the Crows is really the only one who can or would want to drive anyone to the battlefield, and that would have to be during his regular run to Hardin and Billings on Friday, three days from now, and Tommy will probably have to charge three dollars for that, not one dollar, and does Mr. Slow Horse want to sell the broken motorcycle for…oh, say…ten dollars? Odds are good, the Northern Cheyenne old men and boy agree, that the Harley-Davidson can't be fixed at all. A burned-out bearing's a terrible thing and who knows what trouble it's already caused in the rest of that old engine? Mr. Strange Owl might see his way clear to paying the ten dollars for the broken motorcycle *and* have Tommy Counts the Crows drive the Lakota stranger to Crow Agency for only one dollar, not three.

Paha Sapa suggests that he pay the three dollars to use some of Mr. Strange Owl's tools and to rent space inside the closed garage on Friday evening after Tommy Counts the Crows gets back with his bearing. Mr. Strange Owl thinks that three dollars for the use of his tools is fair, but the rental of the garage space and use of its electric lights would require another two dollars.

Impressed by the old fart's negotiating ability, Paha Sapa asks—

—Do you know, by any chance, Mr. Strange Owl, if the Lost Tribe of the Israelites happen to have wandered to this place and settled in Busby, Montana?

The three old men and teenager do not understand this query at all but it's evident in the looks they exchange that they've already decided that their uninvited Sioux guest is crazy.

Paha Sapa confirms the diagnosis by laughing.

— *Never mind. I agree to pay the five dollars for the use of the tools and garage space and lights on Friday night.*

Mr. Strange Owl's loud, wheezing voice reminds Paha Sapa of the kind of bellows that once worked in this very space when the garage was a blacksmith shop.

— *And don't forget the price of the bearing itself, plus, of course, the dollar to Tommy for fetching it all the way from Billings.*

— *Of course. Is there any place here I might be able to stay the three nights before Tommy goes to get the bearing in Billings?*

This conference among the three old and one young Cheyenne is much shorter than the earlier ones. No one in Busby, it turns out, wants to board a Sioux, Paha Sapa is told without a hint of apology, not even for cash money, but Mr. Strange Owl informs him that there is a creek just down the road with some cottonwoods if Mr. Slow Horse would like to camp there. There'll be no charge for the campsite. But Mr. Slow Horse has to promise not to shit or piss in or near the creek, because, you know, people in Busby use that water.

Paha Sapa makes a solemn promise to avoid shitting or pissing within fifty yards of their stream and gathers his tarps, jacket, canteen, and leather gladstone valise from the sidecar. He buys an extra loaf of bread and a flashlight from Mr. Strange Owl in the general-store side of the garage. He noted the creek bed—almost dry this time of year—and the picket line of dying cottonwoods as he went over the tiny bridge both while driving west and then when pushing the motorcycle back east earlier today. It's not even a half-mile walk, and he has hours before sunset.

Walking west toward the lowering sun, Paha Sapa knows in his heart that the sensible thing to do is just keep walking—hitchhike if anyone will stop for him on the Crow reservation to the west, but just keep walking if no one does. It's only twenty-five or thirty miles to the battlefield. He can walk through the cool of the night, taking a little care to watch for snakes that come out to soak up the warmth of the dirt and gravel on the road, and be at Greasy Grass by tomorrow afternoon. He's walked farther than that in one spell of steady day-and-night walking many, many times in his seventy-one years and in conditions far worse than this straight road in the pleasant weather so early in the Moon of the Brown Leaves.

But for some reason, Paha Sapa can't stand the thought of leaving Robert's beautiful gray-with-brown-and-orange-trim-and-lettering motorcycle behind to the mercy of Mr. Strange Owl and Mr. Red Hawk and the invisible but threatening Tommy Counts the Crows. And he wonders if the Crows Tommy counts are the flying kind or the sullen reservation kind.

You'll be leaving the motorcycle behind somewhere *in a few days anyway,* says a more sensible and less sentimental part of his mind.

Yes, somewhere. But at the battlefield. And at a place of his choosing, not at the burned-out bearing's choosing. He's come this far with Robert's beloved machine, across many miles and almost twenty years of time, and he wants to travel with it the rest of the way.

———

By RIGHTS, Paha Sapa should have been restless during his three nights and three days of waiting, so close to his purpose and destination yet so stranded here near a no-place named Busby, but a perverse part of him welcomes the time spent relaxing and thinking and reading along this dried-up excuse for a creek. (What little water there is in the mostly dry streambed lies in puddles and hoofprints — someone around Busby runs cattle — and those few circles of brown stagnant water, it is obvious, have already received their share of excrement and urine. But bovine, not human, so Paha Sapa can understand Mr. Strange Owl's and the residents of Busby's concern. For drinking water and for his morning coffee, Paha Sapa has to hike back to the Busby store and pay Mr. Strange Owl two bits to fill his two small canteens at their pump.)

Paha Sapa has found a sheltered place, out of sight of the highway, and rigs his ground tarp and overhead tarp so that he can quickly close up the latter when the rain comes (and his bones tell him it is coming). He makes sure that the site is up and out of the streambed itself so that there will be no surprises if the rain turns into a gully-washer. Anyone who has lived in the West for more than a week, he thinks, would take such precautions.

This thought reminds him of the flooding everywhere that rainiest-in-his-life month of August in 1876, and with that memory comes the wave of guilt and emptiness at the loss of the *Ptehinčala Huhu Canunpa,* the most sacred Buffalo Calf Bone Pipe of his people. The despair and shame are as fresh as if he had lost the pipe yesterday.

And how does he feel after this most *recent* failure?

In 1925, on the recommendation of Doane Robinson, he read a poem called "The Hollow Men" by a certain T. S. Eliot. He still remembers the final two lines of that poem and they seem to fit his state of mind—

> *This is the way the world ends*
> *Not with a bang but a whimper.*

Doane Robinson told him that the bang and whimper in the poem related to the failure of Guy Fawkes's Gunpowder Plot, whenever that was in English history. (Suddenly he imagines Robert's voice, the tone always enthusiastic, never pedantic, whispering excitedly—*Sixteen oh five, Father. Fawkes and some friends attempted to blow up Parliament, but the barrels of gunpowder were found in the vaults under the House of Lords before Fawkes could set them off, and the final whimper was his, you see, whimpering as he was tortured. His sentence was to be tortured and hanged and drawn and quartered, the hanging first and only to the point where he was almost but not quite dead, but he cheated them from the drawing-out-his-bowels-while-he-was-still-alive part by jumping from the gallows and breaking his own neck.*)

— *Thank you, Robert*...

Paha Sapa whispers to his absent son—

— *I needed that to cheer me up.*

But joke as he may, he knows that he is one of the Hollow Men now.

Having silently promised his beloved *tunkašila* that he would protect the sacred *Ptehinčala Huhu Canunpa* with his life, he lost it instead...while fleeing some fat, flea-bitten Crows.

Having promised Limps-a-Lot, Angry Badger, Loud Voice Hawk, and the other *wičasa wakan* that he would return with word of his Vision, he failed to return in time...failed even to tell them about the Vision. To this day he has never revealed the details of the *Wasichu* Stone Giant Vision to a single human being other than his wife.

Having promised his beloved wife on her deathbed that he would watch over and care for their son always, swearing to her that he would make sure that Robert became educated and would be happy as a man, he allowed the boy to go into the army and then to war and to die young in a strange land among strangers, his gifts and potential untapped.

Having promised himself that he would deny the *Wasichu* Stone Giants their destiny of rising from the sacred soil of the Black Hills and wiping out the buffalo while stealing the gods, past, and future of the *Ikče Wičaśa* and other tribes, Paha Sapa has totally failed at that as well. He couldn't even manage to dynamite some fucking rock.

There is nothing left to fail at.

Or almost nothing. A week earlier, knowing that he could fail yet a final time, Paha Sapa went to Deadwood and purchased new cartridges for the Colt revolver, then test-fired twelve of them in a remote canyon. Even gunpowder, he knows, becomes weak and useless with age.

> *This is the way the world ends*
> *Not with a bang but a whimper.*

But he is tired of whimpering. And it is past time for the bang.

———

ON THURSDAY EVENING it begins to rain and by midnight it has become the downpour Paha Sapa has been warned about by his aching bones and sinews. He's rigged the tarps well, high on a spot above the highest watermark of the old stream, the lean-to's opening facing away from the wind, and the sweet geometry of the two tarps rigged on ropes well out from under the tall cottonwoods where lightning might strike or where heavy rotted-out limbs will fall at the slightest push of wind, and Paha Sapa stays comfortably dry between his blankets as the storm rages through the night.

He's using this last luxury of the flashlight he bought from Mr. Strange Owl—at twice the price of any flashlight—to read Henry James's *The Ambassadors*. Paha Sapa has been checking this book out of the Rapid City library—doggedly, between reading other books—for almost ten years now. He simply *can not get through it*. It's not just the meaning of

James's book that eludes Paha Sapa, it's the meaning of *individual sentences themselves*. The story itself seems so insignificant, so overblown, so petty and obscure, that Paha Sapa has actually wondered if Henry James tried to hide his complete lack of a tale to tell behind these wandering, convoluted, grammatically and syntactically indecipherable sentences and flurries of words and paragraphs seemingly unattached to thought or human communication. Trying to decode this thing reminds Paha Sapa of his first weeks of confusion and overload while trying to learn to read under the tutelage of the Jesuits at the Deadwood tent school, especially under the patient, never-frustrated guidance of Father Pierre Marie, who—Paha Sapa now realizes with a shock—must have been only around twenty years old when he taught Paha Sapa and the other boys.

But why, Paha Sapa asks himself as the storm attacks his tarp, has he persisted with this one unreadable novel when he's read hundreds of others so easily? Just give it up.

But Robert admired Henry James and loved this book, so Paha Sapa has continued checking it out of the big library in Rapid City, returning it each time with no more than a few pages conquered. His struggle to finish this book reminds Paha Sapa of what he heard about the battles in the Great War, at least before the Americans (including his son) entered the war near the end: so much life's energy and so many artillery shells expended for such terribly small patches of murky ground gained.

But the real problem, he thinks as he switches off the flashlight (although he could continue reading by the constant lightning flashes if he wished to), is that he still has to return the book to the library. It's why he put it in his valise in the first place. He's not a thief.

Somewhere between here and the Custer battlefield, he has to find a place to buy an envelope and then find a post office. All logic dictates that Mr. Strange Owl's store should serve both purposes out here, alone as it is in the prairie, but it does not. When Paha Sapa asked to buy a large envelope and a stamp, Mr. Strange Owl stared at him—again—as if the Sioux were crazy.

The lightning flashes, the thunder rolls, and the creek rises, but Paha Sapa sleeps dry and dreamlessly in his well-lashed lean-to, with only the echoing whimpers of tortured Jamesian sentences to disturb his sleep.

ON FRIDAY MORNING the storm is gone and the skies are clear, although the air feels cooler than early September. Paha Sapa packs up his camp and hangs out the tarps in the sunlight to dry while he takes a walk north along the meandering stream.

It strikes him that his world has gotten smaller the older he's become. When he was a boy, before Greasy Grass and the hard part of his life, Angry Badger's *tiyospaye* had wandered together from the Missouri River in the east to Grandmother's Country in the north to the Grand Tetons and west, then south along the Platte River to the Rocky Mountains, south almost to the Spanish town of Taos, east back a long loop through Kansas and Nebraska, back to the heart of the heart of the world near the Black Hills.

Paha Sapa remembers the sight of the *tiyospaye* on the move, usually with several other bands for safety's sake, the warriors ranging ahead on their ponies, the old men and the women walking, the younger children playing and ranging wide to either side of the march, the *travois* being pulled by the older nags and dogs. Often they would come to a grassy hilltop and see thousands of buffalo stretching off for miles. Other times they would cross a rise to see a mountain range in the mists of distance, knowing that those white peaks in summer would be their destination soon. There were no boundaries to the world of the *Ikče Wičaśa* then....

"It's because you murderous Sioux had killed or chased out all the other tribes."

Paha Sapa stops in surprise. The voice in his head is louder than usual.

—*I thought you'd gone away.*

"Where would I go? Why would I go? And why are you going where you're going? Not for me, I hope. It makes no difference to me where you end things."

—*I'm doing nothing for you, Long Hair.*

Custer's irritating laughter echoing in his head, Paha Sapa glances over his shoulder to make sure that none of the local Northern Cheyenne are watching him talking to himself. There is only a single black cow on a nearby hill, watching with that placid, stupid, trusting expression that can only be called bovine.

"Well, good. We were talking about how you Sioux, you peace-loving Sioux who, I'm sure historians will soon be saying if they aren't already, fought only to defend their lands and families, used to go to war against everything that moved on two legs. And killed everything with four legs as well. Your warfare was as indiscriminate as your old habit of driving hundreds of buffalo off a cliff to enjoy a liver or two."

It is true, Paha Sapa thinks. He has to smile. The Indian's enemy, *this* enemy, knows them—knew them—better than do their *wasichu* so-called intellectual friends. Every spring and summer and fall, the warriors in Angry Badger's *tiyospaye* would paint themselves and ride out to go to war for no more reason than it was time to go to war. A Natural Free Human Being male without someone to fight was simply not a natural free human being. Warring against other tribes and against strangers sometimes seemed necessary, but if it wasn't necessary, which it so often wasn't, the fighting would have been pursued anyway. It was necessary for its own sake. It was a break from the women and their talk and the smells and sounds and banality of life in the village, in the lodge, that almost all men looked forward to. It was a test of courage and fighting ability that could be found nowhere else. Most of all, of course, it was fun.

But even as Paha Sapa acknowledges these things to himself, he realizes that Custer is not finished with his rant.

"When the Army called your leaders to that first peace powwow at Fort Laramie in eighteen fifty-one, you Sioux kept talking about territory you'd owned forever but which in reality you'd just taken away from the Arikara and Hidatsa and Mandan on your way west from Canada and Minnesota. You bragged about territory that had belonged to you forever but which really had belonged to the Crows and Pawnee just a few years earlier. You Sioux were a ruthless, relentless invasion machine."

— *We didn't take all the land away from the Cheyenne.*

"Not for want of trying, my red friend. Besides, you liked teaming up with the Cheyenne and Arapaho to kill the Pawnee and the Ponca and Oto and Missouri, all the weaker tribes."

— *They were weak. They deserved to die or lose their lands. That was the thinking then.*

"It still is, Paha Sapa. At least among us whites. Look at that Hitler fellow you were reading about when we went to New York three years ago. He knows the price of weakness—his and his enemies' both. But your so-called Natural Free Human Beings have lost the balls to live and die that way—through your own courage, taking what you want from those too weak to keep it. You're all fat, slow reservation Indians now, wearing cowboy hats, working for *wasichus,* and waiting for handouts."

Paha Sapa has no reply to that. He thinks of his own decades working for the Fat Takers. He thinks of the brash, ambitious, confrontational energy that Gutzon Borglum exudes, breathes in and exhales, and that he knows in none of his own kind any longer, including himself.

"When Mitchell and Fitzpatrick called that original eighteen fifty-one meeting at Fort Laramie, they had to deal with the Cheyenne who killed and scalped two Shoshones whom the Cheyenne had specifically given safe passage to so they could get to the council..."

The ghost's voice bores on like one of the pneumatic steam-powered drills that Paha Sapa has listened to most days of his life through the past five years.

"So when Mitchell helped calm things down and convinced the Cheyenne to say they're sorry and to pay the Shoshones their blood price of knives and blankets and tobacco and colored cloth—all stuff the Cheyenne had received from the whites as bribes just weeks earlier—the Cheyenne couldn't help but insult the Shoshones again at the peace banquet by serving boiled dog."

Paha Sapa has to smile.

— *Yes, the Shoshone never developed a taste for dog.*

"But you did, didn't you, my friend?"

Paha Sapa remembers well the feasts when he was a boy and the joy of spooning through the kettle with the other boys, searching for the dog's head. It was a delicacy. Just the memory makes him salivate.

"Eaten any of your neighbors' puppies in Keystone recently, Paha Sapa?"

— *What are you doing, Long Hair? Trying to make me angry?*

"Why would I do that? And what are you going to do if I am trying to provoke you...shoot me? Speaking of which, why the Little Big Horn? Why not here? One Montana river or creek is as good as another, isn't it? And this way at least someone will get the use of the motorcycle. Old Mr. Strange Owl looks like a nice fellow to me...for a Northern Cheyenne, I mean. That greedy old bastard was probably there at the Little Big Horn as a greedy young bastard, fighting alongside your relatives and stealing from my brothers' mutilated bodies on the day you all killed me."

Paha Sapa realizes that the ghost *is* trying to make him angry. He has no idea why.

The ghost-voice continues.

"I have a question for you, Mr. Black Hills. Why didn't you self-proclaimed Natural Free Noble Human Beings When Others Aren't Human At All ever rub out—or try to rub out—the Nez Percé or Flatheads or Ute or Plains Cree or Piegan or Bannock or Blackfoot?"

— All the others were too far away or too high in their mountains—although we did try to wipe out some of them—but the Blackfoot are just too tough. They're scary people, Long Hair. The men will kill you just to take your teeth to gamble with, rolling them on a blanket like dice, and the women will chop off your ce and hang it on their lodge pole as a children's toy.

The ghost laughs again.

Paha Sapa returns to the campsite, folds up the dry tarps, closes his valise, and walks back to the town of Busby.

———

HE'S ON THE ROAD by midnight.

Poor Tommy Counts the Crows, assigned by Mr. Strange Owl to make sure that Paha Sapa did not steal anything, had fallen asleep by ten p.m. Paha Sapa made sure the tools were returned to their right places and left the young man sleeping, pushing the rebuilt motorcycle a hundred feet down the road before kick-starting it to life.

The electric headlamp was new to motorcycles in 1916 and Paha Sapa has repaired but never replaced the original one on Robert's machine. The beam it casts is flickery and not very bright at the best of times. On the road headed west tonight, he would have turned it off completely and navigated by moonlight, except that a solid cloud cover has moved in and the moonlight is too diffused to drive by. It's still bright enough, however, for Paha Sapa to see that the Crow houses he's passing on either side of the road tend to be tumbledown hovels and shacks...not so very much different, he decides, from the majority of tumbledown hovels and shacks he saw on the Northern Cheyenne reservation or, for that matter, on Pine Ridge and the other Sioux reservations in South Dakota.

—Long Hair? General? You still here?

"You can call me Colonel. What do you want now? To tell me how tumbledown the shacks and hovels are here in Crow country?"

—No. I wanted to explain to you why I didn't push the plunger down on Mount Rushmore. But the shacks did make me think of it.

"I know why you didn't push the plunger down on Mount Rushmore, Paha Sapa. You lost your nerve. But do you have another explanation?"

—The cemetery on Pine Ridge Reservation... the one at the Episcopal mission church and school. The cemetery where Rain and her father are buried.

The ghost says nothing. The purr and putter of the Harley-Davidson J's rebuilt engine, working perfectly now, is the only sound in the night. It's cool enough that Paha Sapa is wearing the long leather jacket Robert left him.

Paha Sapa considers not continuing—this ungrateful ghost does not deserve a conversation, much less an explanation—but after a while he goes on:

—Every once in a while some boys... men too, I think... on the reservation would sneak into the cemetery at night and carry out some vandalism there. Most of the crosses and headstones were made of wood, of course, so they just kicked those apart, but a few of the larger headstones—the Reverend de Plachette's, for instance—were of stone, and the vandals took crowbars or sledgehammers to the stone, smashing it as much as they could, tipping over what they couldn't smash.

The ghost's voice sounds weary.

"You didn't want to be just another cemetery vandal."

— When I heard both Borglum and the president say that the Mount Rushmore heads would be there for a hundred thousand years, I could imagine the vandalized and broken fragments of the heads being there that long. Every culture honors its dead leaders—you're honored at this place we're headed. The thought of being like those vandals who come to the cemetery out of their stupidity and frustration and urge to destroy other people's remembrances because they're unable to create anything themselves... it felt wrong.

"Very noble, Paha Sapa. So you'll let the *Wasichu* Stone Giants stand astride your sacred Paha Sapa and prairie rather than be a vandal."

— *Your* Wasichu *Stone Giants have already risen and done what they did to us, Long Hair. Vandalizing Borglum's life's work wouldn't have changed that. Look on either side of the road.*

The headlight flickered and danced, illuminating little. But visible in the cloud-filtered moonlight were more shacks with packed dirt for front yards, a huddling of shacks in lieu of a community, filth where high-grass prairie had once grown.

"I know. I came this way in my last days alive, remember? I remember this prairie glistening after morning rains. I remember the flowers stretching from horizon to horizon here, just as the buffalo herds did. You Indians were always filthy in your ways, Paha Sapa. We could smell your garbage heaps from twenty miles away. The only thing that made you look and seem noble was the fact that you could keep moving, leaving your buffalo-run heaps of rotting carcasses and giant mounds of stinking garbage behind you. Then we came and you ran out of room."

— *Yes.*

It's not the truth of it, or at least not all the truth, but Paha Sapa is too weary to argue.

———

HE REACHES A HARD ROAD—paved—before two a.m. and has seen signs to the battlefield from his road from Busby and now more directing him south along this paved highway. One way or the other, the Custer battlefield is less than a mile to the south and then back a mile or two the way he has come.

The town of Garryowen—obviously named after Custer's and his regiment's favorite song—appears to be composed of two houses along the road to the south, and the placed called Crow Agency looks to be composed of three buildings along the road to the north. He turns right and drives the eleven miles north to the little town of Hardin—small, but big enough to have a five-and-dime and a post office. The motorcycle's tires sound strange to him as they hiss and hum on pavement.

———

HE DOES NOT GET BACK to the battlefield until almost eleven a.m.

433

Not wanting to be arrested for vagrancy in Hardin (and, as a strange Indian hanging around a *wasichu* town in the middle of the night, Paha Sapa knows this is a real possibility even with his motorcycle to show he's not a hobo freshly hopped from a freight train and with a pocket full of money to back up that argument), after finding the five-and-dime and post office in the darkness, he drove back out of town and down by the river, rolling out of sight behind willows, and lay on the tarp until sunrise. Why he felt he had to do what he is going to do at the battlefield in the daylight rather than in darkness was a mystery even to him, but he knew he was not going out there at night.

Perhaps, he thought wryly as he lay there counting the few stars that deigned to show themselves between the slow-moving clouds, this Indian who has spent most of his life carrying a ghost from that battlefield is afraid of ghosts after all.

Sunrise was a cloudy, milky affair and the air was far cooler than normal for the fifth of September, the breeze chilly enough to send Paha Sapa rummaging in his gladstone for a sweater to slip on under Robert's wonderful, perfectly aged and faded leather jacket. Unlike Mr. Strange Owl's emporium in Busby, both the five-and-dime and post office were open on Saturday here in Hardin, but the latter did not open until nine thirty. Before he finally weighed, stamped, and handed James's *The Ambassadors* to the postal clerk for mailing back to the Rapid City public library, he had put in a dollar, although he was certain that the overdue fines would be much less than that. Leaving town, he suddenly realized that he was ravenous. He saw Indians—Crow men with their black cowboy hats and distinctive Crow way of walking, half cowboy and half ruptured duck—going into a diner on Main Street. Paha Sapa parked the motorcycle diagonally at the curb alongside the old Model T's and various jury-rigged attempts at ranch-worthy pickup trucks and went in to have breakfast. He ordered two eggs (sunny-side up), steak (medium rare), pancakes on the side, toast, orange juice, and asked the waitress—also a Crow, but not as sullen as most he'd known—to keep the coffee and maple syrup coming.

"A hearty meal for the condemned man?"

Paha Sapa jumped at the sudden sound of the voice in his ear and looked around. No one was near. Paha Sapa's lips didn't visibly move as he answered.

—Something like that. I'm hungry.

"Have you composed your Death Song yet?"

A wave of guilt flowed over Paha Sapa. Lakota warriors were not fanatical about singing their death songs when they had little time to do so before the end—sometimes the death songs were composed by relatives and friends and chanted after the man's death—but Paha Sapa had no relatives or Lakota friends left alive and he felt that he'd be betraying Limps-a-Lot, who believed in such things, if he didn't at least try. Often he wondered if Limps-a-Lot had found time to chant his own Death Song before the Hotchkiss guns had opened up.

No personal death songs had occurred to Paha Sapa and none did now in the glow of the largest breakfast he'd eaten in years and five cups of coffee. The only song that came to mind had been one that Limps-a-Lot himself had shared when Paha Sapa was nine or ten years old:

Wi-Ä‡a-hÄ‡a-la kiÅ‹ he-ya

pe lo ma-ka kiÅ‹ le-Ä‡e-la

te-haÅ‹ yuÅ‹-ke-lo e-ha pe-lo

e-haÅ‹-ke-Ä‡oÅ‹ wi-Ä‡a-ya-ka pe-lo

The old men
say
the earth
only
endures.
You spoke
truly.
You are right.

It sounded good. If he thought of nothing else between here and the battlefield only some fifteen miles south, he might try chanting that in his last seconds.

But now he whispered to the ghost—

435

— *Not yet. I'll think of something.*

The ghost's reply was low and—Paha Sapa realized to his surprise—serious.

"Next to 'Garry Owen,' I was always partial to 'The Girl I Left Behind Me.' I had the regimental band play it the day we rode out from Fort Abraham Lincoln that last time. It always made some of the troopers and all of the watching, waving wives blubber."

— *Let me get this straight, Long Hair. You want me to chant "The Girl I Left Behind Me" as my Death Song?*

"Why not? It sort of applies to both of us, although Rain left you behind rather than the other way around. I left Libbie behind—we both knew it could happen, although I don't think either one of us really believed it—but she never abandoned me. All those years alone as a widow…"

Paha Sapa was in a good mood from the giant breakfast—certainly the best breakfast he'd eaten since Rain had died—and he didn't want it spoiled by morose thoughts, his or his ghost's.

— *Well, I don't have a regimental band with me today, so I don't think I'll try "The Girl I Left Behind Me."*

Then, without thinking about it, he whispered—

— *Are you frightened, Long Hair?*

Paha Sapa half-expected the irritating boyish laughter, but it did not come.

"Of the bullet in the brain…*your* brain…no. Not at all. But since you asked, what I'm frightened of is that this magic forty-five-caliber bullet might put you out of *your* misery forever but won't kill *me*—since I am, after all, only a ghost. Imagine still being conscious and thinking and aware, through what's left of *your* senses, after they bury your dead and rotting body in the ground…down there in the darkness and loam, with the worms, for how long until the last of your brain is consumed and…"

—*All right, all right. Do you want me to leave a note asking that my remains be cremated?*

Paha Sapa meant it as a joke, although he was feeling a little ill after the helpful cascade of images, but Long Hair's ghost evidently took him seriously.

"I'd appreciate it, my friend."

Paha Sapa shook his head, noticed that other men in other booths *had* noticed him whispering to himself, left a very large tip, paid his check, and went back to the restroom—the first indoor plumbing he'd had at his disposal in many, many weeks (his shack in Keystone had an outhouse) and a great luxury.

"A hearty bowel movement for the condemned man."

— *Oh, do shut the hell up. I beseech you.*

Paha Sapa thought that he had never used the word *beseech* aloud before, and he felt ridiculous doing so then. But the ghost of General (Colonel at the time of his death) George Armstrong Custer did shut up long enough for Paha Sapa to enjoy the miracle of indoor plumbing.

The restroom was very clean.

———

IT IS LATE MORNING when he turns off Highway 87—a modern two-lane highway busy with trucks and dark cars—back onto the gravel road he took from Busby. The entrance to the battlefield park runs off to the right of this smaller road. There is a sort of gate at the entrance to the park or monument or whatever it's become, but no one is there, and Paha Sapa is relieved at that. He spent enough of his life's savings on the huge breakfast.

Paha Sapa has almost no sense of recogntion as he rides his son's motorcycle down the narrow strip of road along the ridge where Custer died. Below is the Greasy Grass—what *wasichus* still call the Little Big Horn—and he can see the giant cottonwoods where the hundreds of lodges of the Sioux and Cheyenne had stretched out of sight around the bend in the valley to the south.

The ghost's self-imposed silence has not lasted long.

"I do have one regret."

— *Other than getting yourself and a third of your regiment killed, you mean?*

Paha Sapa feels sorry he's thought that even as he thinks it. It's too late in the game, as the Mount Rushmore workers and baseball players might say, for petty jibes.

The ghost doesn't seem to have heard.

"I just wish I'd had a chance to drive — ride — whatever you do — this motorcycle you and your boy rebuilt. I rode a bicycle once, but it's not the same."

Paha Sapa has to chuckle.

— *I can see the whole Seventh Cavalry on Harley-Davidsons.*

"We'd need leather jackets. And some sort of new insignia."

— *Skulls, perhaps.*

They arrive at what a small sign announces as LAST STAND HILL. Paha Sapa parks the motorcycle and starts to take the valise with him but then thinks better of it. He's put the Colt into a canvas bag with a shoulder strap, but he leaves that in the valise. This isn't the place. There are three cars parked here: two old Fords and a fancier Chevrolet. He sees a few people in summer linens moving among the white crosses and headstones on the grassy hillside.

Paha Sapa stops at a stone monument put up not long after the battle here. The names of the Seventh Cavalry dead are listed on a bronze plaque burnished gold by age and touch.

"Are we tourists today, Mr. Paha Sapa?"

— *I thought you might want to see where you fell.*

"I don't, especially. Besides, my bones aren't buried there. They moved me to West Point. Libbie's buried there next to me."

Paha Sapa looks down across the hillside, opening his vision to the ghost within him. The headstones, not all with names, were set where the men's mutilated bodies were found and buried where they fell.

Why did he ride up the couloir onto the bluffs with the warriors that day? He can't really remember. To count coup? Why? As a young *wikasa wakan* in training, he hadn't even cared about such things...or so he'd thought.

Paha Sapa goes back to the motorcycle and drives south along the ridgetop, the gravel road barely wider than a walking path. There are no other cars here beyond Last Stand Hill. In ten minutes, the slowly moving motorcycle covers the three or four miles that separated Custer and his men from the rest of the Seventh Cavalry — and rescue. But Reno and Benteen didn't attempt a rescue, Paha Sapa knows; they merely listened to the shooting go on and on to the north and then, horribly, fall silent. They had their own problems to deal with.

A little sign by a walking path says WEIR'S ATTEM TO RESC E C TER. Someone has shot the missing letters out with a high-power rifle. Paha Sapa drives on to a gravel parking area where an intact sign reads RENO AND BENTEEN MONUMENT AND BATTLEFIELD.

The ghost's whisper is almost inaudible even coming from inside Paha Sapa's head.

"Libbie fought until she died to keep Reno from having a monument or mention anywhere on the battlefield. As soon as she died, they gave him one."

— *Do you care?*

"No."

This time, Paha Sapa leaves the gladstone in the sidecar but takes the canvas bag, hitching the strap easily over his shoulder. In the bag is some bread, bologna, and the loaded Colt.

He walks across the broad crown of the hill toward the cliffs and valley.

"You're hurting terribly, aren't you, Black Hills?"

Paha Sapa considers not answering but decides he will. What harm can it do now?

— *Yes. The cancer has its grip on me today.*

"Would you...do this thing...just because of the cancer? I mean, if you hadn't failed at Mount Rushmore?"

Paha Sapa does not answer because he cannot. But he hopes he would not be here with the Colt just because of the pain and disease. It bothers him a little that he'll never know.

Almost out of sight of the parking lot, he finds a smooth place to sit. The grasses here come up almost to his shoulder when he's sitting in them. The clouds are breaking up some now, allowing patches of sunlight to move across the rolling hills and curving valley below, and everywhere the grasses are moving in languid thrall to the wind.

"Benteen and Reno had a better hill," says the ghost, his tone calmly, coolly professional rather than wistful or envious. "I could have held out here all day and night with my men...if I'd had *this* hilltop."

— *Does it matter?*

There comes the faintest echo of sad laughter. It's as if the ghost is already leaving him. But not quite yet.

439

"Paha Sapa, did you see those ravens? They followed us down the road. All the way in."

Paha Sapa saw them and sees them now, perching on a rail twenty yards away on a splintered old fence that runs from the parking lot, perhaps delineating the end of the park boundary. The two ravens are watching him. Watching *them*.

He doesn't like this. Who would? Ravens are symbols of death for the Lakota, but then most things are in one story or another. Some say that it's the ravens that carry the *wanagi* of dead people up to the Milky Way to begin the spirit-journey there. Others, including Limps-a-Lot, did not believe this.

He tries to remember the Lakota word for raven. Was it *kagi taka* or *kangi?* He can't recall. He's losing his own language.

It doesn't matter now.

Paha Sapa sits cross-legged in the grass and takes out the heavy revolver. It smells of gun oil and warm metal. He's left one chamber empty under the hammer so he doesn't accidentally blow his foot off—advice from a Seventh Cavalry Crow scout who's been dead for more than fifty-five years—but a loaded chamber revolves into place as he thumbs the hammer back.

He has decided that he's not going to draw this out. No Death Song nonsense. No ceremony. He's decided on the right temple and sets the muzzle there now.

"Wait. You promised me … about the cremation."

Paha Sapa lowers the pistol only slightly.

—*I wrote it out. On a napkin. In the bathroom at the diner.*

"I don't believe you."

—*Where were you? Dozing?*

"I don't pay attention to everything you do, you know. Especially at times like that. Where is it? Is it somewhere people will find it?"

—*It's in my shirt pocket. Will you* please *shut up a minute? Just one minute.*

"Show me the note."

Paha Sapa sighs—truly irritated—and carefully lowers the hammer. He removes the napkin from his shirt pocket and holds it in front of his own eyes, thinking that Custer is being a shit to the last second of his unfairly extended existence. The note in pencil begins "My Wishes" and is only one sentence long.

—*Satisfied?*

"You misspelled *remains*—it's not *manes*. There's an *I*."

—*Do you want me to go back to town to the diner and get the pencil I borrowed from the waitress?*

"No."

—*Good-bye, Long Hair.*

"Good-bye, Paha Sapa."

Paha Sapa lifts the revolver, cocks the hammer back, and sets his finger on the trigger. The sun is warm on his face. He takes a deep, sad breath.

—*Mr. Slow Horse!*

It's not the ghost; it's a woman's voice. Paha Sapa is so startled that he almost pulls the trigger by accident. Lowering the cocked hammer and then the pistol and looking over his shoulder, he sees two women moving in his direction through the tall grass.

His body was turned away from them such that it's probable that they did not see the pistol. He hurriedly slips the Colt into the canvas bag and awkwardly gets to his feet. Everything in him cries out in the pain of rising.

—*Mr. Slow Horse! It is you, is it not? The motorcycle was Robert's, I know. I've seen the photograph a thousand times. He gave it to me. I saw the photograph of you but did not get to keep it.*

The women are dressed in expensive and stylish dresses and wide-brimmed hats. The older of the two looks to be in her late thirties and her accent seems to be French. The younger woman, who bears some resemblance to the first, can't be older than seventeen or eighteen. Her eyes are a brilliant hazel.

Paha Sapa is very confused. He looks back toward the road and sees a long, sleek 1928 Pierce-Arrow sedan stopped there. The sun has come out from beneath the fast-moving clouds and turns the expensive white automobile into something too dazzlingly beautiful for this world. There's a mustached man standing by the car and Paha Sapa realizes stupidly that the man is a chauffeur.

The older woman is still speaking.

— ...so we did not arrive at the Mount Rushmore until yesterday, and Mr. Borglum was very gracious, very sorry that we had missed you. All of our letters and telegrams had gone astray, you see, since we had been trying to reach you via the name William Slow Horse de Plachette, the name and the Keystone address Robert gave us in his delirium—and the returned letters said "undeliverable"—and we also wrote the mission on the Pine Ridge Reservation. But Mr. Borglum said you would be here at the Custer Battlefield, so I told Roger to drive like the very wind, and here we are and...oh!...you are Mr. William Slow Horse, are you not? Paha Sapa to your friends and family?

He can only gape stupidly. The Colt in its canvas shroud lies heavy at his feet. Finally he can make noises that simulate speech.

— Borglum? Borglum didn't know where I was going. Borglum could not have told you.... No one knew where I was...

He stops, beginning to understand what the woman has said.

Her voice, with the accent, is almost musical.

— Oh, yes. He was quite certain about where you were headed...is "headed" the right word? He even told us that you would be at this second hill, not the first, where the big monument is.

Paha Sapa licks his lips. He cannot tear his gaze from the two women's faces. On the fence far behind him, one of the ravens makes an accusatory noise.

— I'm sorry, miss. I'm...confused. What did you say your name is? You say you knew my son?

The woman blushes and for a second looks angry at herself, or perhaps as if she wants to cry.

— I am so sorry. Of course. You never received my letters...we know that now. Nor the telegrams the past months.

She holds out her hand. She is not wearing gloves.

— I am Madame Renée Zigmond Adler de Plachette. Your...what is the phrase in English? Yes. Daughter-in-law. I married Robert in November of nineteen eighteen...November fourteenth, to be precise. My father, Monsieur Vanden Daelen Adler of Belgium, was, of course, concerned about the marriage because Robert was...

She pauses. Paha Sapa prompts.

— An Indian?

Madame Renée Zigmond Adler de Plachette laughs softly.

— No, of course that was no problem. No problem whatsoever. It was that he was a…the word in English escapes me…a gentile. Yes, gentile. We are Jewish, you see, from one of the oldest diamond-cutting families of Jews in all of Belgium. But in the last few years… Well, you understand the situation growing in Germany and Europe, Herr Hitler and all…so Father is moving his business and our family to Denver and New York. To Denver, you see, because Flora's fiancée, Maurice, has always wanted to start a—how do you say it?—a beef cows ranch, and of course to New York because of Father's diamond business, since he was, it is not immodesty to say, the preeminent diamond cutter and then diamond merchant in Belgium and he hopes to build the same reputation here in America. Flora and I have come ahead in order to… Oh, my! Oh, dear!

She puts her hands to her cheeks.

—I have been so excited to meet you, my dear Mr. Slow Horse. I am chattering on like, how do you say it? A house aflame. My dearest apologies for forgetting to introduce…My darling Flora, I apologize to you as well.

She speaks in quick French or Belgian to the waiting, silent young woman with the so-familiar hazel eyes and then turns back to the stunned, numb Paha Sapa.

—Monsieur Slow Horse, may I present to you our daughter, my dear Robert's and mine, and your granddaughter, Mademoiselle Flora Daelen de Plachette. Her fiancée has stayed behind in Brussels to help my father with the last of the business there but should be joining us next month in…

But the young woman has extended her hand, and all sound fades away as Paha Sapa stares at that hand. The shape and form and length and delicacy of the pale fingers—and even the mildly bitten nails—are so totally familiar to Paha Sapa that they make his old man's heart hurt.

He takes her hand, that hand, *her* hand, in his.

And it is as if the bullet has been fired after all.

Bright lights explode in his skull. There is a final blinding flash, a terrible sense of all boundaries collapsing, a rushing in and flowing out, a terrible tsunami of noise that drowns all thought and sensation, and he is falling forward toward the astonished women…falling… falling…fading…gone.

25

HE HEARS THE RAVEN WINGS FLAPPING AND FEELS THE TALONED impact as one raven snatches up his *nagi* spirit-self and bears it and what is left of him aloft, away from the high-grassed earth.

The spirit of Paha Sapa's first reaction is anger. He realizes that he has come to not believe in any continued existence after death, and now that that existence is proven to him—as the raven rises higher with its mate beside it and Paha Sapi's *nagi* in its talons, flying toward the clouds and sky and Milky Way where Paha Sapa's spirit will have to walk forevermore—he realizes that he doesn't want to walk, even reunited with his ancestors, in the Milky Way. He wants to stay on the high-grassed Earth and talk to this woman who says she is his daughter-in-law, his lost son's wife, and with the young woman who looks so much like his darling Rain that seeing her made his heart hurt so much it felt as if he'd been pierced by a barbed war arrow.

Paha Sapa suddenly realizes that he can see, but not through his own eyes. He is being carried by the raven and he *is* the raven.

It is a new and frightening experience. Paha Sapa has flown by magic before, but it has always been a lifting-up sort of flight—rising like a balloon as a boy with arms spread wide, being lifted in one of the Six Grandfathers' giant palms, floating upward in the magical car of Mr. Ferris's fine Wheel—and this flapping, hurtling, forward-motion-through-the-air sort of flying is breathtaking.

The raven glances below and Paha Sapa sees the battlefield falling far behind and farther below. The white Pierce-Arrow looks as tiny as a white bone lying in the grass.

He would like to have looked at that 1928 Pierce-Arrow closely, perhaps taken a ride in it. Even while flying to the afterlife in the sky, Paha Sapa thinks that his Belgian daughter-in-law's family must be very rich to afford such a fine car.

The raven looks to its left and Paha Sapa sees the other raven flying there, its feathers so black they seem to drink the sunlight, its pinion muscles working easily. The other raven's eye looks nothing like a human being's eye: it is perfectly round, surrounded by small white beads of muscle that look to Paha Sapa like the *sintkala waksus* sacred streamed stones he sought out for his sweat lodge ceremony during his *hanblečeya,* and the round raven eye is an inhuman amber in color, a predator's color, more like a wolf's eye than a man's. But behind that unfeeling raven's eye, Paha Sapa catches just a second's glimpse of the dancing blue of Long Hair's bright eyes—the same blue eyes the young Paha Sapa looked into sixty years ago at the second of Custer's death. So Long Hair's *nagi* spirit-self is also being borne aloft.

Paha Sapa wants to shout to the Custer-carrying raven—*I told you you were a ghost!*—but his spirit-self has no voice.

And yet the blue human eye behind the round raven eye seems to blink at Paha Sapa in a final, bemused farewell just before that raven breaks off in its flight and heads north while Paha Sapa's continues east and a little south. Whatever Long Hair's destiny is after being finally released to real death—and Paha Sapa can only hope that it includes Libbie—it lies elsewhere and Paha Sapa will never know it.

Paha Sapa's raven climbs and climbs and climbs until the horizon curves downward at both ends and the blue sky here above the clouds becomes almost black. The stars are coming out.

But then the raven ceases climbing. They are not going to the Milky Way. Not yet.

The raven looks down and Paha Sapa is not surprised to see the Black Hills dark in its surrounding heart muscle of red-ringing rock, the tiny island in the endless ocean of autumn-brown grass. *Wamaka-ognaka e'cantge*—the heart of everything that is.

Suddenly he is surprised as the raven begins to descend.

He is surprised again to see that the great sea has suddenly surrounded the Black Hills again, obscuring all sight of the land beneath the waters. He wonders if he is about to be punished by having to view yet again the Vision of the *Wasichu* Stone Giants rising from the Black Hills and exterminating the buffalo and his people's way of life.

No.

There are no voices in his head, no Six Grandfathers speaking to him this time, but he suddenly understands that the great waters he sees with *Wakan Tanka's* bright beam of light shining on them are the tides of time.

The raven folds its wings and dives, becoming in the graceful awfulness of that ancient motion the ultimate predator swooping down on its not-yet-visible but already hapless, helpless, and infinitely hopeless victim, and then the diving raven, wings still folded back flat against its ebony body, crashes beak-first and unblinkingly into the tidewaters of time. The water is as cold as Hell.

———

IN AN INSTANT the waters are gone. The skies are blue and cloudless. The raven flies steady and even some thousand feet or so above the earth. But everything is…different.

Paha Sapa sees *Matho Paha,* Bear Butte, ahead to the left, but the butte itself looks different. It is, he remembers in his son's high, happy voice, a *lacolith:* an intrusive body of igneous rock, uplifting earlier sedimentary layers that have largely eroded away. This intrusion is of magma forcing itself into cooler crustal rock during the Eocene period. Paha Sapa has no idea when the Eocene period was, but he clearly remembers Robert telling him that Bear Butte shares a similar geological history with the Devil's Tower in Wyoming and with the Black Hills themselves.

But now the butte rises in a changed landscape.

The nonvoice in his mind informs Paha Sapa that he is looking at his beloved Black Hills and Great Plains sometime between 11,000 and 13,000 years before Paha Sapa was born. It is late summer, early autumn, but the air is cooler, and as the raven descended, Paha Sapa sees total snow cover on the Grand Tetons and Rocky Mountains to the west. Those peaks are usually shed of all but the tiniest remnants of snow by the end of August or early September, but now they are a wall of white rising in the west.

Paha Sapa's educated eye sees other things that are subtly wrong. There are too many trees on the plains and foothills and some of those trees are tall species of pines and firs that do not grow near Bear Butte.

The grasses on the prairie are taller and greener than any Paha Sapa has seen even in spring, much less near the end of summer. They have not been grazed down anywhere.

The raven passes over a river and Paha Sapa knows at once that there is too much water in the river for this time of year and that the water rushing there is a milky blue, filled with fine dusty particles carried from remnants of glaciers in the west and north.

Glaciers.

The raven flaps, moving at miraculous speed, swooping up, then down, and Paha Sapa's spirit soars with it.

The animals!

On the plains, the buffalo graze by the million, but there are other grazers there as well, and not just antelope and deer. The bison themselves look larger, with longer horns, but moving in herds nearby are tiny rawhide-colored horses of a kind Paha Sapa has never seen. These are not a tended herd as in his boyhood days, not horses descended from those who escaped the Spaniards a century or two earlier, but smaller, wilder, strange-looking horses that belong to this place 11,000 to 13,000 years before his time.

Moving between herds of bison and smaller herds of the wild horses comes a line of elephants.

Elephants!

The raven gracefully circles only a few hundred feet above the family group of pachyderms. Not circus elephants—these are some sort of mammoth, although not as woolly as the one he saw pictures and bones of with Rain in a display at the Chicago World's Fair. The mammoths' ears seem small but the males' tusks are long and curving. A baby elephant, no more than six feet tall at the shoulder—what does one call a baby elephant? — holds its mother's tail as the giants pound gently across the springy turf. As the herd approaches the river, the lead male trumpets and somewhere in the pine forests on the other side of the river, another mammoth trumpets back.

And a lion coughs. Farther away, wolves howl.

If Paha Sapa had his body, he would cry now.

He sees a pride of lions, half hidden by low foliage, lazing near the river. They are just...lions...as one would see in the Denver Zoo, but also not like that at all. They are free, majestic, unagitated, in their own environment. A lioness is doing the work, stalking slowly toward small groups of antelope and horses drinking at the river's edge.

A shadow passes over the raven — *his* raven — and the black bird banks away in some panic. The cause of the shadow is a huge bald eagle high above, circling to watch the lion cubs below. Paha Sapa wonders — Would an eagle, even one this size, be so brazen as to try to pluck even the smallest of lion cubs out from under the careful watch of its parents?

He's lived long enough to know that anything that eats flesh will kill and eat anything else if it gets the chance. Sometimes, Paha Sapa knows, the killing, even among the mostly utilitarian birds and big animals, is more for the joy of killing than for the eating.

Paha Sapa glimpses other large animals he can't even identify — something like a very-long-necked camel; then something else, broad-legged, long-necked, and small-headed and almost as large as a small bison, moving through the undergrowth toward the trees with the comical slowness of a sloth.

Paha Sapa wants to think he's dreaming but knows too well that this is no dream. The camels, the sloths, herds of strange small horses, the lumbering mammoths, as well as the stalking lions and jaguars and oversized grizzlies, are all real in this world, whenever in the past this world is. It is a Vision but not a dream.

Perhaps spooked by the eagle's presence, his raven flies south past Bear Butte to the Black Hills, climbing all the time. Mount Rushmore does not exist. The Six Grandfathers mountain is intact and untouched.

But before the raven left the prairie and plains and forest and river, Paha Sapa had caught a final glimpse of something strange—a small group of human beings approaching from the north. They were not *Ikče Wičaša* or any other tribe or band he might recognize: their faces were hairy, they wore rude, thick animal skins, and they carried spears far cruder than anything the Plains Indians would make.

Were they his ancestors or his ancestors' ancestors or just strangers? But he was sure that they were just arriving from the north after having wandered for many years across lands just revealed by retreating seas and glaciers.

And—of this he was certain without having any idea how he was certain—within a few generations of these hairy men's arrival in this New World, all the large predators and most of the large prey he had just seen with such joy—the lions, the camels, the mammoth elephants, the giant sloth, and even the horses—would be hunted to extinction here and everywhere in North America.

For the first time in sixty years, Paha Sapa sees the truth behind the truth of the *Wasichu* Stone Giants Vision.

The Fat Takers, in their elimination of the bison, were just finishing a trend that Paha Sapa's ancestors and their earlier cohorts had begun in earnest 10,000 years ago—wiping out all the large, great species that had evolved here on this continent.

The elders of the *Ikče Wičaša*—turned into bowlegged cowboy imitators now in Paha Sapa's day—may meet in solemn, play-pretend council and the arthritic old men may spend days in sweat lodges while preening in the old clothes and beads and feathers of their recent ancestors and flattering themselves that in *their day* they were spiritually superior, their tribes serving as protectors of the natural world, but...in truth...it was they and all those who came before them, their much-revered ancestors and these hairy strangers who may not have been ancestors at all, who wiped out forever these beautiful species of mammoth elephant and camel and lion and shrub ox and cheetah and jaguar and sloth and the giant bison that made today's grown buffalo look like calves, not to mention the native species of small, hardy horses that had evolved and been wiped out here by man long before the Spanish brought over their European varieties.

The raven flies very high now, and Paha Sapa's heart feels very low.

Beneath them, the sunlit ocean-sea tides of time have flowed in again, surrounding the Black Hills, then slowly ebbed away.

The raven dives again.

———

Even from a height where the horizon begins to curve, Paha Sapa sees that he is descending into some near-future of his own era. He also knows (without knowing how he knows and without having anyone to ask) that it is still Saturday, the fifth of September — although in what year or century or millennium or epoch, he does not know.

In the Black Hills, the four heads of Mount Rushmore gleam like bald men's scalps in the sunlight. Farther south there is another, whiter granite gleam, as if another mountaintop has been mutilated, but the raven does not bank that way, and Paha Sapa cannot see where the raven does not look.

Bear Butte is where it should be, although even from great altitude it is obvious that the majority of pine trees on its lower slopes and ridgelines have been burned away. This does not concern Paha Sapa; prairie fires have swept across *Matho Paha* in numbers known only to the All, if Mystery chooses to count such things.

But the *wasichu* cities and towns are much larger — Rapid City, Belle Fourche, Spearfish, even tiny Keystone in the Hills — and between the sprawling towns sunlight glints off windows on uncounted ranches, outbuildings, warehouses, and homes and new constructions.

The raven flies north just as it did a few minutes and 11,000 years earlier.

Paha Sapa sees that the Great Plains have been sliced into geometric parcels even more than in his lifetime. In this not-so-far-away future, at least one of the highways is a broad four lanes, two in each direction with a brown-grass median in between, similar in design to photographs he's seen in newspapers of such a futuristic highway design in Germany that was first called the *Kraftfahrtstraße* in 1931 when the first four-lane section was completed between Cologne and Bonn but which Hitler is now — in Paha Sapa's lifetime just ended — enthusiastically calling the *Reichsautobahn,* which Paha Sapa translated as something close to "Freeways of the Reich." The German chancellor is putting his Depression-lashed men to work building more such *autobahns* all over Germany, and the *New York Times* has opined that not the least use of such a four-lane-highway system could be to move troops rapidly from border to border.

This new *autobahn,* stangely ringing the north part of the Black Hills within the very grooves of the ancient "Race Track" of Lakota lore, is filled with more automobile and truck traffic than Paha Sapa has ever seen or could have imagined. Even New York City in 1933 was not this insane with rushing vehicles. And the automobiles and trucks and indefinable shapes rushing east and west along the four long, curving lanes are painted a full spectrum of bright colors that catch the sunlight.

Having come of age in an America where railroads—the Iron Horse to Limps-a-Lot and the other Natural Free Human Beings a generation earlier than Paha Sapa's—were invariably the fastest way to travel, Paha Sapa finds it hard to believe that these *autobahns* will soon bind America together. (Unless, Paha Sapa thinks with a stab of insight, there is soon to be another installment in the Great War not long after his death, with Germany winning this time and occupying the United States.)

But it's not Germans who occupy the prairie beneath him, he acknowledges as his raven swoops lower, but cattle.

Cattle, those stupid, filthy things that evolved in Europe or Asia or somewhere and that are now filling the plains beyond any prairie's capacity to provide for them. When Paha Sapa was working (badly, he knew, because he never learned to be a good cowboy) for rancher Donovan, he'd smile when he heard Donovan and the other old-timers in the area talking about the "grand old traditions" of ranching in the West. The oldest of those traditions were fifty to seventy-five years old.

But in this near-future, even if it's only twenty or thirty or fifty years from this lovely early-September day in 1936 when Paha Sapa has died, he sees that the cattle have continued to do what cattle do: cropping the grass to its roots and overgrazing until the desert is returning to the North American plains; befouling with their excrement every stream and river they can reach while breaking down the streambeds and riverbeds with their odious weight; leaving their trails everywhere in the desertified dust that was once noble grasslands to the point that from the high altitude Paha Sapa's raven flies, a water tank in a thousand empty acres of disappearing grass now looks like the hub of a wheel with a radius of five miles or more and tan-white spokes of cattle trails.

And to protect their sacred, stupid cattle, the *wasichu* ranchers (and their faithful Indian companions) have wiped out the few remaining predators — the last wolves, the last grizzly bears, the last mountain lions — and declared war on such other species as prairie dogs (the overriding myth is that cattle break their legs in the burrow holes) and even the lowly coyote. Paha Sapa imagines that he can see the sunlight glinting off the millions of brass cartridge casings ejected in the killing-on-sight of all these species whose crime was getting in the way of…cattle.

The air on this fifth day of September in its unnumbered future year is…very warm. It feels like late July or early August to Paha Sapa, embedded as he is in the raven's exquisitely tuned senses. When they were high, he'd seen that there was no snow at all left on the summits of the Grand Tetons or the Rocky Mountains to the west and southwest, not even in that range that Paha Sapa visited as a boy which the Ute had alliterately named the Never No Summer Range.

There will be full, hot, snowless summer there now, even deep into autumn.

Swooping in a circle above the river, Paha Sapa can see that the partitioning of the plains does not stop with the new *autobahn* circling its four-lane-way north of the Black Hills from Rapid City or by the much busier (and paved!) web of state roads and county roads and fire roads and ranch driveways, or even with all the squares and rectangles and trapezoids of ranch land fenced off with barbed wire — and that is *all the land* as best he can see — but now the high- and green-grassed plains of his earlier vision and even of his childhood years have been carved into geometric shapes by the relentless overgrazing of the cattle.

On one side of the barbed-wire fences the raven swoops over, letting the wind carry it, the grass is low and unhealthy and missing its most beautiful varieties of botanic species, but on the other side of the wire, the more heavily grazed side, it is essentially dirt.

The hoofprints and cattle wallows and trails—bison never followed one another in single file, but stupid cattle invariably do—are bringing back the desert.

Paha Sapa once heard Doane Robinson talk to a group of physical scientists about the danger of desertification, but the threat seemed far away in the bring-in-more-cattle-and-people 1920s. Now he can see the results. Those parts of the Great Plains of the United States of America that didn't blow away in the dust storms during the Great Depression have now been overgrazed, overtrod, overpaved, overpopulated, and overheated—for whatever reason the climate feels so warm—to the point that the deserts are returning. When his raven rises, Paha Sapa can see the once-blue river running brown with cattle shit and mud from its cattle- and erosion-collapsed bare banks.

The voice that is not his son's but which sounds much like his son's whispers to him without words.

In the old days, even in the thousands of years after the ancestors and others before the *Ikče Wičaśa* had wiped out all of the top predator and grazing species except for the bison, the great prairies of tall grass and short grass that spread from the Mississippi River all the way to the Rocky Mountains stayed healthy due to the interaction of natural forces.

Bison, unlike cattle, stampeded and wandered great distances in a way that spread the grass seeds of the now-missing healthy tall grasses. Their hooves, so unlike cattle hooves, actually helped plant the seeds. The buffalo grazed the grass in a way that did not chew down to the roots and kill the plants as cattle do, and they never grazed in one place for a long period of time. Their manure enriched the grasses that gave cover and a home to a thousand species no longer present.

The grasslands needed fire to replenish themselves. Lightning provided that replenishment, with no men—Indian or Fat Takers—to stop those fires, but even after the Natural Free Human Beings spread across the plains, they had the habit of annually lighting prairie fires themselves.

So did the Assiniboin and the River Crow, the Northern Arapaho and the Shoshone, the Blackfoot and Bloods and Plains Cree. So did the old, lost tribes whom first the Sioux and then the Fat Takers' diseases had rubbed out—the Mandan and Hidatsa and Santee and Ponca and Oto and Arikara.

These peoples had burned the prairie regularly for their own reasons, sometimes for reasons lost to time, sometimes to flush game—and sometimes just for the fun of seeing the flame and destruction—but the fires had always helped to keep the varied prairie grasses and flowers and plants healthy and renewed.

All that is gone now, especially in this not-so-far future the raven is showing him.

All the thousands of interacting species here have now come down to two—man and his cattle. The Fat Takers and their fat, stupid meat beasts, both constantly bred for more fatness.

Oh, birds still migrate over and past this new world where the grasses no longer grow, but even the species of birds are disappearing faster than human beings can note their passing. The destruction of the wet places, the driving out of all variety among the grasses and four-legged beings of the prairie, and the draining and grazing and paving over of the birds' mating places...yes, there are still species of birds to be found, but they tend to be of the thieving, scavenging, garbage-begging, back-alley species like magpies. They are the equivalent of the few remaining wild animals: scruffy coyotes eking out an existence on the edge of men's and cattle's dusty world, their sad countenances suggesting they know that the deserts are inexorably approaching.

His raven turns south and climbs for the sky again, and Paha Sapa hopes that it will not descend again. He welcomes death.

Let the time tides flow in and out as they always have; why must he—Paha Sapa—have to see the ravages of what men have done and will continue doing to the world and themselves?

He senses rather than sees that the time tides have, again and again, turned bloodred on both rims of the horizon as other Great Wars have raged. Perhaps men love their cattle so much, he thinks glumly, because men so much love slaughter in great numbers.

The raven has reached the icy upper air and it pauses there, hanging motionless on some unseen thermal. The stars are coming out in the darkened sky of day again, and the horizon has again bent itself like a warrior's bow.

Paha Sapa, the cynic and unbeliever for so much of the last part of his now-departed life, manages the sincerest prayer he has ever prayed.

Please, O Wakan Tanka—my mediating Grandfathers—the All, the Mystery none of us will ever understand—O please, God, show me no more. I have died; please let me be dead. For my part in what you have shown me, I am heartily sorry. But punish me with no more Visions. My life has been saddened and stunted with Visions. Let me die and be dead, O Lord God of My Fathers.

Merciless, the raven swoops downward once again.

———

For a few moments there are no sounds or images, no motion or sensation, only knowledge.

His granddaughter, Mademoiselle Flora Daelen de Plachette, soon to become Mrs. Maurice Dunkleblum Ochs when her fiancée finishes up the closing-out of her grandfather's business in Brussels and joins her in America, is pregnant.

This seventeen-year-old beauty who could have been his darling Rain's twin, Flora is pregnant with Paha Sapa's (and the absent Monsieur Vanden Daelen Adler's) great-grandson, who shall be named Robert. The happy couple will have four more children, all of whom will survive childbirth and childhood, but it is Robert's soul whom Paha Sapa touched with his vision-forward ability when he took his granddaughter's hand the second before his stroke. And it is Robert's future that bore him forward into time as surely as these ebbing, flowing ocean tides of time below him now.

Born in 1937, Robert Adler Ochs will become both scientist and writer; his popularized science books and TV series will be enjoyed by millions of people. His specialty shall be physics, but as was true of his grandfather from America, the first Robert, this Robert will become an expert in other sciences such as geology and the environment and meteorology of Mars and of other planets. Robert Adler Ochs will be a guest in Mission Control in Houston in July of 1969 when men first walk on the moon, sitting with other scientists all acting like children released from school on a snow day.

Of Robert Ochs's three children, his middle child—Constance (who will publish under her married name, C. H. O. Greene)—will most continue her father's tradition of excellence in science and writing. Born in 1972, Constance Helene Ochs Greene will be a major researcher well into the middle of the 21st Century and beyond. Her trio of specialties—her broad interests so rare in the continued age of specialization in the sciences—will be climate change, genetics, and ethnology. Her book *The World We Made, the New World We Can Make* will sell more than twenty million download copies worldwide.

But in a changed world.

And that actual change in the real world is the goal behind Constance Greene's three bestselling books and behind the more than two hundred papers she will publish in scientific journals during her lifetime. Her special interest...no, her passion, her dream, her mission, her goal, her reason for being...will be Pleistocene megafauna rewilding of the Great Plains of North America.

Even when she someday will be an honored and elder scientist leading an international effort that will see rewilding projects in more than thirty nations, it is always the Great Plains of North America that will continue to command the majority of her love and attention.

And there are enough details to command the attention of ten thousand Connies—ten thousand Constance Helene Ochs Greenes.

As the overgrazed and overburdened and variety-starved prairies are finally dying for good in the 21st Century, the ranches failing even after countless subsidies from the government and after a thousand attempts at "diversification" of what constitutes "ranching," the deserts returning to where they have not been for hundreds of thousands of years, the small and midsized towns emptying out, the human population disappearing, the last dregs of economy in the region vanishing just as quickly, Dr. Constance Helene Ochs Greene will spend most of her long life being part of a solution that offers a new birth not only to many species of animal and plant life, but to entire groups of people as well.

Perhaps it is Connie Greene's voice that Paha Sapa hears during this final descent of his *nagi*-carrying raven. Or perhaps it is again the soft voice of the oldest and wisest of the Six Grandfathers. Or perhaps it is Limps-a-Lot's wise whisper or the soft voice of his most darling Rain.

More likely, it is all of their voices that Paha Sapa will hear next.

THE RAVEN SWOOPS LOW over the Black Hills. Borglum's four *Wasichu* Stone Heads are there in place, looking slightly grayer with time. Either they have not turned into striding stone giants or the day of their striding and Taking of Fat has passed.

Even while the raven circles on high thermals, Paha Sapa can see that some eight miles to the west and south of Mount Rushmore there is another mountain turned to sculpture. This one is larger and newer, the granite more brightly white.

The voices of those he has loved and worshipped and will love in the future whisper in his ear.

This is Crazy Horse and his horse. Unlike Rushmore, where the heads are just part of the great rock mass, this entire mountain has been sculpted. The scale of blasting and sculpting is larger in every way.

After so many years in the mines and on mountaintops of making as precise measurements and estimates of measurements as humanly possible, especially of sculpted or soon-to-be-sculpted rock, Paha Sapa cannot help but make such estimates now.

The three presidents' heads that Paha Sapa worked on were each about sixty feet high. Crazy Horse's head in this new, giant sculpture looks to be almost ninety feet high.

But where the four presidents on Mount Rushmore were designed to be only heads with the occasional hint of shoulder—say the jacket lapels on Washington and the roughed-out knuckles of Lincoln holding a lapel (not yet started when Paha Sapa left forever)—here the entire upper body and both arms of Crazy Horse have been released from the mountain by explosives and then sculpted and bumpered down to smooth, white stone. And beneath Crazy Horse is his horse, the animal's stylized, artistically maned head pulled down and turning back in dynamic motion, as if powerfully reined in, the horse's left leg raised and bent and finely finished from its muscled chest to its fragile shank and hovering hoof.

Paha Sapa sees that Crazy Horse's left arm is rigidly extended above the elaborately carved mane of the stallion and that the war leader is pointing with one finger.

The whole sculpture is 641 feet wide and 563 feet tall.

As the raven circles on the powerful thermals rising from the sun-heated stone—the air on this future fifth day of September is even hotter than in the previous vision-future—Paha Sapa can see that the carving of Crazy Horse's face bears almost no resemblance to what the man looked like in life. That can be forgiven, he thinks, since Crazy Horse never allowed a photograph of himself to be taken or a portrait to be painted.

What is less forgivable, to Paha Sapa's large-sculpture-trained eye, is that the quality of the carving and sculpture here is far inferior to Gutzon Borglum's work. The entire pose is strained and awkward and clichéd and Paha Sapa can see almost none of the nuance that Borglum and his son worked so hard to achieve in their brute-force, pneumatic-drill efforts to evoke even the slightest shadings and tiniest minor hints of the dead presidents' facial muscles and furrowed brows and most subtle expressions.

This huge, blocky, gesturing hero-Indian and his strangely European-feeling stone doodle of a prancing horse look to Paha Sapa—in comparison to Borglum's work—as if they have been carved out of a bar of Ivory soap by a bored schoolboy with a dull knife.

Without asking the voices within him, he knows that the Sioux and Cheyenne and other nearby tribes hate this thing. He doesn't know all their reasons for hating it and does not want to know. In a real sense, he does not *need* to ask; he already knows within himself. He only wishes he had another chance at this new target with his twenty-one crates of dynamite.

If he had a voice now, Paha Sapa would scream—*You brought me forward in time again to see* this? *Will this punishment never end?*

But he has no voice.

Still, the raven leaves the giant cartoon of Crazy Horse behind and turns north and gains altitude again, flapping and coasting its way out of the Black Hills and past Bear Butte again, onto the Great Plains.

———

THE CHANGES HERE are obvious and immediately visible.

The endless curving ring of *autobahn* is still there, but it looks aged and gray and there is little traffic on it. The cities and towns are much smaller. Rapid City looks to be a third the size it was in Paha Sapa's day, much less in the mindless sprawl he just saw in his second vision. Spearfish is all but gone. Deadwood and Keystone and Casper and Lead, he realizes, *are* gone—there are no *wasichu* towns at all in the Black Hills when the raven flies north.

He has no idea what kind of catastrophe has caused this disappearance of so much and so many but his spirit-skin goes cold considering the possibilities.

The real shocks are still ahead.

Just north of the strangely empty *autobahn,* all former signs of habitation and what the *wasichus* invariably called civilization simply cease.

As the raven loses altitude, Paha Sapa can see that the state and county highways are…gone: blown up, broken up, plowed under, or simply overgrown. Only the vaguest traceries of straight lines, overgrown with healthy plants, give a hint of where all those dividing lines were.

He realizes that all the ranches are also missing. No single war or natural catastrophe could cause that, could it? Removing buildings and leaving not even the foundations, while the *autobahn* and smaller versions of Rapid City and other towns remain to the south and east? No, not war or plague or some natural catastrophe could account for that. This emptying-out of an entire region has to be the result of a purposeful, planned migration and of a careful deconstructing and removal of the works of man built here over a century and more…but to *what* purpose?

Why would the *wasichus* concievably unbuild and remove the ranches, barns, roads, power lines, sewer lines, stock tanks, fences, vehicles, cities, small towns, dogs, pigs, chickens, cattle, and other imported species—including themselves—that they had taken almost two centuries to seed the earth here with?

Paha Sapa realizes as the raven continues to descend that a tall fence runs parallel to the *autobahn* for as far as the raven's eye can see in both directions. The raven takes care to land not on that fence, but on a nearby old wooden fence post with no wire attached.

That is something else that is missing beyond this point, Paha Sapa realizes — fences. Barbed wire. All the fences that sliced the prairie through all of the 20th Century and then resliced and resliced it again into ever smaller shapes are . . . gone.

There is a sign on the fence and while Paha Sapa has no idea if the raven with its small but wily brain can read it, Paha Sapa can.

DANGER — HIGH VOLTAGE

Twenty yards to their left is an elaborate double gate with a cattle guard of round bars as the flooring. Paha Sapa guesses that the gate is automated. (This is the future, after all.)

The sign on the gate makes much less sense to him than did the high-voltage warning.

P.M.R.P. Tracts 237H — 305J
Access with Permits Only
Warning: No Food, Shelter, or Services for the Next 183 Miles
Warning: Dangerous Animals
Warning: Human Contact May Be Hostile
Permit Holders Proceed at Your Own Risk
U.S. Dept of the Interior and Sec. of U.S.P.M.R.P.

The raven hops off the fence post and soars over the fence as if it does not exist. Bear Butte is within this wild area. Paha Sapa can see where there has been a winding road in to the rising butte, perhaps a parking lot and visitors area, maybe even a visitors' center with restrooms or some sort of small museum.

They are all gone now, their former presence indicated only by a preponderance of weeds where the concrete and asphalt and foundations have been broken up.

The plant life is rich and varied both on and around Bear Butte. In Paha Sapa's day there were mostly ponderosa pines on the hill itself, as well as some scrubby junipers. Now there is a profusion of pine and fir on the butte itself. The prairie at the base of the butte was mostly yucca and low, sparse grasses in Paha Sapa's time: now it is rich with diverse plants, many of them unidentifiable to Paha Sapa's eye.

He sees faded ribbons — prayer flags — and patches of once-colored cloth filled with tobacco hanging from the branches of the scrub oak and other deciduous trees that grow along the creek at the base of the butte. This doesn't make much sense. The offerings are Sioux or Cheyenne...but don't the electrified fence and gate sign five or six miles back suggest that all this is off-limits to most people?

The raven takes wing again, flying north along its now-familiar route to the river where Paha Sapa lost his band's sacred *Ptehinčala Huhu Canunpa* sixty years ago and where most of that band and Paha Sapa's extended family were wiped out by elements of Crook's cavalry.

The day is even hotter down here than it was in the Black Hills but the land beneath the raven's wings is not desert. Far from it.

The grasses are even richer and taller here than near Bear Butte. Paha Sapa saw only tiny patches of true tallgrass prairie as a child; now it extends east and west and north for as far as the raven's eye can see from five thousand feet. Its bending in the wind that has come up is slower and more sinuous even than the Hand of God stroking of the world's fur he remembered from the shorter grass prairie beyond his village.

He has no idea how the ancient tallgrass prairie could have returned.

Fire. Bison herds. Burning. Time.

The voice in his *nagi* spirit-ear is Rain's, his great-granddaughter Constance's, Limps-a-Lot's, Robert's, and the wisest of the Six Grandfathers'.

Paha Sapa is moved to tears he cannot shed, but he still does not understand.

The raven swoops, clears a grassy hilltop by only fifty feet, and Paha Sapa sees.

Buffalo. Bison. Filling the valley. Filling the hilltops to the north. The herd stretching off east and west and north for miles. Thousands of buffalo. Tens of thousands. Hundreds of thousands. More.

The raven banks west toward the river.

The mountains so far beyond to the west — seen only by the raven's magical predator's eye — are totally without snow now. Not even the peaks have a dash of white. The river is narrower, its level much lower, obviously not supplied by melting snow from those now-dry distant peaks. But the water that remains is clear and dark and looks clean enough to drink without worry; even in Paha Sapa's day there were compelling reasons not to drink from a local stream.

The raven circles and Paha Sapa gasps—or makes an equivalent *nagi* spirit–sound to a gasp.

The wildlife here near the river is extensive. And large.

Besides the bison herd that stretches on to three of the horizons, there are running herds of small, tan horses. Not the same as the tiny horses he saw from 11,000 and more years ago, but similar. Very similar.

—*Przewalski's horses.*

Paha Sapa has no idea who Mr. Przewalski is, but he likes his horses—tiny, tough, wild, black-maned, as alert as any wild prey. And he absolutely loves the sound of the sweet voice.

A line of camels comes out of the deciduous forest to drink.

—*Bactrian camels from the Gobi Desert to stand in for the extinct* Camelops hesternus—*Western Camel—that evolved here and was so successful in the Pleistocene. But it's amazing how similar the DNA is.*

Paha Sapa has not the slightest clue as to what DNA is or was, but he could listen to this voice forever. He wants it to never stop.

—*There were four species of* Proboscidea *here during the Pleistocene, Paha Sapa—*Mammuthus columbi, *the prevalent Columbian mammoth;* Mammut americanum, *the American mastodon;* Mammuthus exillis, *the Dwarf mammoth—not quite so common—and your and my old friend* Mammuthus primigenius, *the Woolly mammoth we saw reconstructed at the Chicago World's Fair.*

Paha Sapa weeps silently at that.

—*After much testing, we decided that the genotype of the endangered Asian elephant was the closest to our missing friends. And it adapts well to the warming climate across the Great Plains. But there are several thousand African elephants here as well—if only to save them from the environmental disasters in Africa over the past thirty years.*

Elephants? Paha Sapa thinks just as a group of them comes out of the high, blowing grass of the low hills and lumbers down toward the river. One of the smallest wants to run down ahead of the herd, but the mother—or at least one of the females—restrains the youngster with the gentle curve of her trunk.

A cluster of drinking Bactrian camels and groups of pronghorn antelope scatter at the approach of the elephants. But they scatter along the east side of the river.

On the west side, a large pride of lions crouch to drink.

—*From southern Africa. The last of their kind. But they are doing wonderfully well here. The prides in the PMRP's eastern tracts beyond the Missouri River number in the thousands now. For some reason it makes it a more popular area. There are only four hundred trekker permits given out for that area each year and we get more than a million requests.*

Trekker? Paha Sapa mentally repeats to himself.

A jaguar has just emerged from the tall grasses beyond the river, then effortlessly disappears again. Paha Sapa wonders if he actually saw it. Something like a very large sloth is watching the jaguar from the trees. The sloth's curved claws are long and black. The plants along the river—whose banks are no longer tumbledown from cattle—grow in almost shocking variety. The grass here looks like a manicured lawn in places.

—*One of the side effects of diversified grazing.*

Hundreds of yards upstream, a bald eagle is circling, looking for carrion or fish. Paha Sapa's raven does not react as if threatened this time. Paha Sapa thinks—*The one constant. There are always eagles.*

But the raven rises again anyway, turning southeast. The tour must be over. Paha Sapa wants to shout; he wants to weep; but most of all, he wants to hear the chorus of beloved voices once again. But he knows his tour is over.

—*It's not over yet, Paha Sapa. You haven't even seen the best part yet.*

A minute later he glimpses them through the raven's incredible eyes. A tiny scattering of white marks there, miles away and miles below in that river valley. Then a tiny scattering of white triangles there, miles away and miles below in the opposite direction, along a tallgrass prairie ridgeline.

The raven banks right and swoops toward the ridgeline.

Dear All, thinks Paha Sapa. *Dear* Wakan Tanka. *Let this death-dream be real.*

Out in the valley this side of the white triangles, boys watch over a small herd of horses. These are the largest versions of the strange, wild horses Paha Sapa has just seen running wild across the prairie. They are pony sized but not docile. The boys here obviously have to be on their toes to keep these small herds of captured horses captured.

The raven continues rising toward the ridgeline.

It is a small *tiyospaye,* no more than twenty lodges, but the tipis are tall and well made, the tipi poles made of stripped lodgepole pines of just the right length — like the fingers of a hand — the first three poles making a star and the star shape making a vortex of powerful light for those who will live within its welcoming power. If arranged correctly, the full ten poles of each tipi represent the universe's deepest morality — the *ohokičilapi* of mutal respect toward all things — and the ten *ohokičilap* poles are arranged correctly and covered with the clean, bright hides of buffalo with the hair scraped off properly. The lodges are arranged in circles as commanded to the Natural Free Human Beings by Bird Woman and by the Six Grandfathers, so that people's homes will repeat the sacred-hoop pattern of the universe itself.

There are people moving around the *tiyospaye* as the raven lands atop a tipi pole, and Paha Sapa sees that the men and women are wearing handmade clothing similar to that he wore as a boy…similar, but not a museum re-creation. Many of the skins and hides are the same, antelope and deer and buffalo, all scraped smooth, softened by women's chewing, but there are other textures and colors he cannot identify. He sees a war shield propped against a tipi and realizes with a shock that the hide of the shield is made of elephant skin.

An older man walks by, someone important, Paha Sapa guesses based on the beadwork on his moccasins and the perfection of his fringed tunic and trousers, but on this warrior's shoulders and head are the hide, mane, and roaring jaw of a lion.

Paha Sapa would blink if he had eyelids.

These are Natural Free Human Beings. Paha Sapa can hear through his raven's ultrasharp ears as the people speak in a soft, oddly accented Lakota. Then Paha Sapa realizes what the Lakota accent reminds him of — Robert's slight accent when he learned the language from his father. Perhaps some of these men and women were English speakers before they adopted Lakota. Or perhaps the dialect has just changed over time, as it does in every language.

Then something strange happens.

Four boys are sitting on a log nearby, tossing knives at a circle drawn in the dirt in a game Paha Sapa knew well as a boy, when suddenly there are soft musical notes in the air.

One of the boys excuses himself from the game, reaches into a pocket on his deerskin trousers, and answers something that must be a telephone but that is no larger or thicker than a playing card. The boy speaks for a minute—still in smooth Lakota—then folds away the impossible phone, returns it to his pocket, and comes back to the game.

—*Have you seen enough to understand, Paha Sapa? It took us years before we understood that the ecosystem of the Pleistocene Megafauna Rewilding Project would be worthless unless we rewilded the most central of all the late-Pleistocene megafauna predators—man. But this time, there will be no mass extinctions because of our presence. Herd population management applies not just to the four-leggeds. And Connie was the first among us to see who deserved the choice—the right—to live in the PMRP Reserves, as long as they did so by the rules of the epoch they had come to live in. The children's phones . . . well, some things cannot be denied, in any culture, and it was agreed that they were an important safety feature. Adults may choose to live among jaguars, lions, and grizzly bears, but children should be able to phone for help. Even so, the phones work only within the confines of the preserve and the children must give them up when they turn fifteen if they want to remain living in the preserve.*

Paha Sapa knows that he's dreaming now but it's all right. Like Hamlet, what he always feared most about death was the possibility that one might still dream.

But this is all right.

The raven launches itself into the air and flaps for altitude, circling first to gain height and then heading southwest.

Once airborne, Paha Sapa sees something to the northeast that he missed before. A ribbon of silver steel running along the east-west river valley and silver-and-glass glinting carriages moving slowly beneath the ribbon.

Paha Sapa knows at once what it is. He has seen pictures of the *Wuppertal Schwebebahn*—the monorail in Wuppertal, Germany, built and opened sometime around 1900. Just as with that *Schwebebahn,* he can see the sleek carriages hanging *under* the thin rail line here, the view unimpeded from the mostly glass-walled cars. With his raven-vision, he can see the silhouettes of the passengers even from miles away and from thousands of feet higher. Some are seated; some are standing. It reminds Paha Sapa of the joyous passengers in the 1893 Ferris Wheel.

— *Three hundred trekker permits and a few commercial safari camps, of course, carefully regulated, but more than forty-two million people a year—tourists—pay to ride through all or part of the Great Plains Pleistocene Megafauna Rewilding Preserve. It's become North America's preeminent tourist attraction. But it's time for you to go home, Paha Sapa. As much as we hate to see you go.*

Paha Sapa feels right now much as he felt that day on the Ferris Wheel on the Midway of the Great White City—the first hours he spent with Rain.

He thinks—*I don't need to go. I'm already in a better version of Heaven than my people or Rain's father could ever concoct. But if it's time to go to Heaven, I'm ready.*

The voices' collective laugh sounds a bit like Robert's, much like Rain's, only a little like Limps-a-Lot's, some like a lady's he's never met, and not at all that much like the Six Grandfathers'. The last words they will ever say to him are odd.

— *Go to Heaven? Like hell. That baptism went to your head, Paha Sapa. There's too much work left undone.*

———

THE RAVEN FLIES DUE WEST and then north by west.

The ocean of time flows in, covering everything below like low clouds, and the shafts of sunlight on the water seem to move with the flying bird. Paha Sapa tries to remember the sentence he likes from *Bleak House,* but he is not able to form coherent thoughts.

The sea of time ebbs away. The low, rolling hills below are brown and tan and brown again, the only green in the meandering river valley with its picket line of old cottonwoods.

The raven does not swoop this time; it drops in a near-vertical high-speed dive that terrifies Paha Sapa.

No... I cannot... I'm not ready... I don't...

Ravens listen to no one. It does not slow as it continues its mad dive toward the brown hill with its high brown grass.

The impact is terrible.

———

THEY LIED.

As much as they love him—and he knows they do—they lied.

This *is* Heaven.

Paha Sapa is lying on the top step of the stairs leading down to the Great Basin near the Columbian Fountain in front of the main Administration Building in the White City, with his head in Rain's lap and with Rain looking down at him with concern. He does not even care that other people have gathered around.

His lips are dry, but he whispers up to his concerned darling—*Tokša ake wancinyankin ktelo.*

"I will see you later." It's the phrase he taught her just two hours ago in the Ferris Wheel and it is their bond of betrothal. Both know it. Neither have acknowledged it yet.

—*Oh, Monsieur Slow Horse, we are so relieved.*

It is not Rain speaking but the older woman. The mother.

His daughter-in-law. Madame Renée Zigmond Adler de Plachette. (How strange to meet someone with his darling's last name.)

And the woman on whose lap his head is resting is not twenty-year-old Rain but his seventeen-and-a-half-year-old granddaughter, the only-just-pregnant and engaged-to-be-married Mademoiselle Flora Daelen de Plachette.

Paha Sapa tries to sit up but three pairs of hands push him back down.

The mustached chauffeur—Roger—has joined them, Paha Sapa realizes. Roger has brought water in—amazingly—a crystal pitcher. He offers a crystal glass with—more amazingly, impossibly—real ice in it and Paha Sapa obediently sips the iced water. It tastes wonderful.

Roger helps him to a sitting postion, and while the ladies are standing and brushing off dried grass and briars, the chauffeur whispers something in French or Belgian or, more likely, Irish, and surreptitiously hands Paha Sapa a small silver flask. Paha Sapa drinks.

It is the first whiskey he has drunk since he was seventeen years old, and it is by far the best he has ever drunk.

Roger helps him to his feet while both the ladies ineffectually paw and push and pull at him with their little white hands. Paha Sapa sways but, with Roger's help, stays standing.

—*I was sure I was dead. Certain I'd had a stroke.*

Roger says in an American-enough accent now—

—*Sunstroke, more likely. Better get in out of the sun.*

Paha Sapa can hear the unspoken "old timer" at the end of that. He just nods.

His son's strangely middle-aged wife, Renée (he hopes to God that they'll be on a first-name basis soon), says—

—*Monsieur... I am sorry, I must become used to the American expression... Mister Slow Horse...*

—*Please call me Paha Sapa. It means Black Hills, and it's my real name.*

—*Ah, oui... yes... of course. Robert did tell me this. Mr. Paha Sapa, we are staying at the... oh, I can't think of the name of it, but it appears to be the only decent hotel in Billings... Roger knows the name... and if we leave now, we could have lunch together in the dining room there. We have much, I think, to talk about.*

Paha Sapa's answer is said from a great distance but sincere.

—*Yes, I would like that.*

—*And, of course, you need to get out of the sun at once. You must ride with us. Roger, would you please give Monsieur... Mister... Paha Sapa a hand back to the car.*

Paha Sapa stops Roger's helpful hand before it can touch him. He looks at his son's wife.

—*It's just Paha Sapa, Mademoiselle... may I call you Renée? It's such a pretty name, and it reminds me of one I love dearly.*

Madame Renée Zigmond Adler de Plachette blushes fiercely and for a second Paha Sapa can clearly see the beautiful young nineteen-year-old girl with whom his romantic son fell in love. He realizes that the marriage must have been just days before the influenza and overwhelming pneumonia descended on Robert, and he also knows that there is a long and serious story—possibly having to do with the father's and family's horror that she married a gentile—behind her having never contacted him before this.

He wants to hear it all. He says softly—

—I'll follow you into town on the motorcycle. It's Robert's, as you know, and I don't want to leave it here. I'll be all right. Just keep an eye on me in the mirror, Roger, and if I start driving or acting goofy again, you can stop for me.

The chauffeur grins under his mustache and nods. The four begin walking back toward the road and parking area.

— Oh, monsieur... sir... you have forgotten this.

His granddaughter is holding out the canvas shoulder bag with the Colt revolver in it. If she is surprised by the heaviness of the bag or if she has peeked inside, she says and shows nothing.

— Thank you, mademoiselle.

They discuss logistics again and then the small procession is moving, the long white Pierce-Arrow turning around in three tries and the Harley-Davidson J putt-putting along behind it.

As they pass Last Stand Hill on the left, Paha Sapa stops, lets the motorcycle idle while the sedan moves on ahead of him. Looking at the stone monument and the white headstones dotting the hillside, he suddenly realizes — *My ghost is gone.*

It is not an altogether pleasant sensation. As he realized only yesterday, George Armstrong Custer had been married to his Libbie for twelve years when he died; Paha Sapa had been married to Rain de Plachette for four years when she died. But Paha Sapa and Custer's ghost were together for sixty years, two months, and some days.

Paha Sapa shakes his head. The pain in him seems to have receded a bit.

He looks to the southeast, toward the distant and quite invisible Black Hills and all he has left behind there...and all he might yet see and do there.

When he whispers the next words, they are not offered to the bones or memories buried on this battlefield hill in Montana, but to those people he has loved and fought against and lived with and worked alongside of and held close and seen slip away and lost forever and found again in sacred places elsewhere, not close to this place, and yet also not so very far away from this place.

— Toksha ake čante ista wacinyanktin ktelo. Hecetu. Mitakuye oyasin!

I shall see you again with the the eye of my heart. So be it. All my relatives — every one of us!

Epilogue

Gutzon Borglum's vision of Mount Rushmore was never completed.

Besides specific plans to finish carving elements of Washington's, Jefferson's, and Lincoln's upper bodies, including coats and lapels, with Abraham Lincoln's left arm and hand grasping his lapel to be finished in some detail, Borglum also insisted on the necessity of completing the long-planned Entablature and the Hall of Records, which had already been begun.

Originally, as part of Borglum's search for money and official support in the late 1920s, the Entablature was to be a huge area of the mountain to the right of the four heads, words chiseled onto a flattened, clean white surface in the shape of the Louisiana Territory, each letter of each word taller than a man. It was (according to Borglum's insistence and early announcements) to have carried an appropriate passage to be written by Calvin Coolidge. Borglum had begged Coolidge to compose this message when the president was there at the first dedication of the Mount Rushmore site in 1927, and Coolidge had reluctantly promised to do so.

The ex-president began slowly composing his message to people a hundred thousand years in the future after he'd left office in 1929, and in 1930 he'd completed the first two paragraphs, which were released to the world's press by Gutzon Borglum. The world's press almost hurt itself laughing and criticizing Coolidge's stilted Entablature Message.

In private, Coolidge was furious because these two paragraphs *were not the paragraphs he had written*. With typical arrogance, Borglum had taken the liberty of rewriting them before releasing them to the press.

Despite the ex-president's privately expressed anger, Borglum had begun the actual carving on the Entablature site, blasting and carving in a giant 1776 where the first paragraph would go. Coolidge then withdrew from the whole affair. Despite pleas from the Mount Rushmore Commission, the ex-president refused to write another word. In the following year, 1931, the retired president asked a friend, Paul Bellamy, who was visiting Coolidge at the ex-president's home in Massachusetts, just how far Bellamy thought the distance was "from here to the Black Hills." Bellamy opined that he thought it must be about fifteen hundred miles.

"Well, y'know, Mr. Bellamy," said Coolidge while drawing on his cigar, "that's about as close to Mr. Borglum as I care to be."

Coolidge died in 1933. Undaunted, Borglum brought his Entablature idea to the Hearst newspaper chain in 1934, suggesting that there should be a national contest, open to all Americans, to write the Entablature "manuscript." Borglum was willing to offer cash, medals (designed by himself, of course), and a college scholarship to the winner.

The National Park Service, which was overseeing the Mount Rushmore Project by then, thought it was a terrible idea and so did Borglum's and Mount Rushmore's most faithful and successful backer, South Dakota's Senator Peter Norbeck. Borglum ignored their warnings and concerns and went ahead with the national contest, convincing FDR to be on the judging committee along with First Lady Eleanor Roosevelt, Interior Secretary Harold Ickes, nine US senators, and a sprinkling of other notables. The Underwood Typewriter Company agreed to donate twenty-two new typewriters as prizes.

In 1935, the judging committee, including President Roosevelt and the First Lady, made its recommendation for five finalists. Borglum didn't like them and tossed them all out. The grand prize was finally won by a young Nebraska man named William Burkett, and the money and scholarship allowed Burkett to attend four years of college during the depths of the Depression. Burkett was so grateful that he asked to be buried in the unfinished Hall of Records, where, in 1975, the Park Service installed a seven-foot-tall bronze plaque bearing the full script of his winning Rushmore Entablature Contest essay. The Park Service denied his request.

The Hall of Records and the giant carved stairway leading to it were central parts of Gutzon Borglum's design for the Mount Rushmore "Shrine to Democracy," and he started serious work on the entrance tunnel in the winter of 1938–39. Both the noise of the jackhammers in the confined space and the incredible amount of fine dust kicked up made work in the tunnel dangerous and almost unbearable. Borglum pressed on.

In the summer of 1939, Congressman Francis Case, on behalf of the appropriations committee, personally looked into working conditions inside the advancing Hall of Records entrance hallway and reported that working conditions there were nearly impossible and that the odds for the workers contracting silicosis and then suing the government were too high.

Work on the Hall of Records ceased forever with the blowing of a whistle on a July afternoon in 1939. After workmen left the mountain in 1941, it was discovered that mountain goats had taken up residence in the 14-foot-wide-by-20-foot-high tunnel that ran 75 feet into the mountain.

The Theodore Roosevelt head, the fourth and last figure to be completed on Mount Rushmore, was officially dedicated on the night of July 2, 1939, nine years after the George Washington head had been unveiled. That night was the first time the Mount Rushmore faces were fully lighted—however briefly—and Borglum did so first by skyrockets and aerial bombs and then by a battery of twelve powerful searchlights being switched on. Singer Richard Irving sang Irving Berlin's brand-new song, "God Bless America." Although President Roosevelt did not attend, some 12,000 guests turned out for this dedication of the final head, and silent-movie cowboy star William S. Hart and a group of "Sioux Indian dancers in full regalia" added excitement to the evening.

Borglum announced that he had years, if not decades, of work still ahead of him at Mount Rushmore. Much "bumping"—refining of the facial features by specialized pneumatic hammers—remained, and he still had to blast out and carve the upper bodies, Lincoln's hand, and so

forth. Nor had he given up hope on the Hall of Records; he was looking at improved ventilation and other work safety features to put into
place as soon as the funds flowed again.

In February of 1941, Borglum had begun a new charm offensive
with FDR and Congress—insisting to the president that funding had
to be improved so that the "Shrine of Democracy" could be fully finished, as he had promised Roosevelt in 1936, during the president's time
in office. Borglum set off for Washington to argue for increased funding—as he had every spring for the past fourteen years—and this
time his wife, Mary, went with him. They stopped off in Chicago so
that Borglum could give a speech and while there, Borglum saw a spe-
cialist about a prostate problem he'd been having.

The doctor recommended surgery and Borglum decided to get it
out of the way immediately so that he could lead the spring work rush
back at Mount Rushmore.

A series of blood clots from the surgery kept Borglum in the hospital for two weeks, and on February 28 a messenger arrived with the
crushing news that President Roosevelt was cutting all non-defense
spending to the bone and would no longer approve moneys for projects such as Mount Rushmore.

On March 6, 1941, exactly one week after he received the news from
Roosevelt and after a series of embolisms created by more blood clots,
Gutzon Borglum died in the Chicago hospital.

Many of the workers who'd labored on Mount Rushmore for almost fifteen years thought that Borglum's body should be interred in
the unfinished Hall of Records hallway tunnel, but the Park Service
would not consider such a thing. Borglum's remains were temporarily interred in Chicago and then moved to Forest Lawn Cemetery in
Glendale, California, three years later. A memorial service for Borglum
was held for the workers and local friends of the boss in Keystone's
white-steepled Congregational church.

The Park Service, Congress, and the Mount Rushmore Commission were ready to shut down work that very week, but the Mount
Rushmore workers petitioned the commission to appoint Borglum's
son, Lincoln, as the new director and to go on and "complete the work
as to his father's wishes."

The commission agreed, but it was only a token gesture. With only $50,000 in funds remaining, the twenty-nine-year-old Lincoln Borglum focused the last months of work on finishing up some of the fine details on Teddy Roosevelt's face and doing some final touch-ups of George Washington's collar and lapels.

That last summer season of work went very well and seemed, at least to a visiting outsider, like all the other productive summers of work, with baseball games by the Rushmore team, horseplay coming down the 506 steps on Friday, Saturday night dances, free Sunday afternoon motion pictures at Lincoln Borglum's place, and lots of hungover men not receiving to-MAH-to juice after climbing the 506 stairs on Monday morning.

But it wasn't the same, and every man still working on the project knew it. Nothing in the increasingly alarming world in the autumn of 1941 seemed quite the same.

The last whistle blew and the last pneumatic drill and bumper fell silent on Mount Rushmore on October 31, 1941.

———

THE STORY OF PAHA SAPA'S SON Robert's Jewish-Belgian father-in-law, Monsieur Vanden Daelen Adler, was later told in the 1955 book *Survival of a Belgian Jewish Diamond Cutter* and was turned into the low-budget 1959 movie *Diamonds or Death,* starring Macdonald Carey as Adler and Ruth Roman as Adler's wife ("Zigmond" in real life, "Suzanne" in the film) with the twenty-five-year-old Maggie Smith, in only her second film role, playing "Renée." The film, never released on VHS or DVD, is known today to historians for the wonderful deep-focus photography by Paul Beeson and by its moody, totally inappropriate-to-the-subject score by jazz trumpeter Dizzy Reece. Some *Star Trek* fanatics are aware of the film due to the brief and rather awkward appearance in it of actor Leonard Nimoy (credited in the movie as "Leonard Nemoy") as the Nazi sidekick to the Gestapo officer "Heinrich" who was so obsessed with stopping the Adler family from fleeing Belgium. ("Heinrich," overplayed by Henry Rowland, had been an uncredited Nazi officer in the infinitely superior *Casablanca* seventeen years earlier. Nemoy-Nimoy had only four lines in the movie, but his atrocious German accent with those four lines somehow is well-known to serious *Star Trek* fans.)

In reality, diamond cutter turned diamond merchant Vanden Daelen Adler had one of the greatest success stories of any Jew seeking to get his family out of Belgium before World War II.

When the war broke out in 1939, Belgium had a population of around nine million people, some 90,000 of them Jews. More than 80,000 of these Jews were concentrated in the two major cities of Brussels and Antwerp. More than three-fourths of Belgian Jews before the war were self-employed, with the majority of these involved in diamond cutting or the selling of diamonds. The diamond trade in the port city of Antwerp was almost completely in Jewish hands.

Germany invaded and occupied neutral Belgium in May of 1940. Thousands of Jews fled Belgium during the invasion and thousands more were deported to France (where they would soon fall under German control again), so that by November of 1940, there were an estimated 55,000 Jews remaining in the country. Reports of the number of Belgian Jews killed during the war vary greatly, ranging from an American prosecution exhibit at the Nuremberg War Crime trials that "approximately 50,000" Jews deported from Belgium were killed in Auschwitz-Birkenau gas chambers between April 1942 and April 1944, to claims by some Belgian historians that "more than half of the Jewish population of Belgium survived the war" to arguments by even more recent revisionist historians that "Belgium lost virtually none of its native Jewish population." The so-called Anglo-American Committee of Inquiry announced in 1946 that, out of a total of 5.7 million European Jews who perished during the war years, 57,000 were Jews from Belgium. One Jewish historian later put the number at 26,000. No two historians seem to agree.

As one of the first wealthy Belgian Jews to take the rise of Hitler seriously and then take early action, Monsieur Vanden Daelen Adler's plan was to get all of his extended family out of continental Europe by October of 1936.

It helped that in 1936 the four most important diamond exchanges in Belgium (of which about 80 percent of the merchants were Jews) united in the *Federatie der Belgische Diamantbeurzen* diamond federation. Vanden Daelen Adler was elected the first chairman of that federation.

If he'd wanted to, Adler could have easily stolen diamonds or cash for his purposes, but instead he used his own wealth, which was considerable (almost $1 million in 1936, equivalent to more than $15 million today). He had a list of 124 family members whom he thought he could get out of Europe in 1936: the majority of these family members outside of Belgium were in France (from whence his family had emigrated to Belgium in the 1780s), but some were in other European countries, including Germany. Adler saved 85 of them. The rest, for various reasons, refused to leave.

In 1936, immigration laws in England, the United States, and most other countries were designed to keep Jews — even wealthy Jews — out, but Vanden Daelen Adler had been working for three years bribing officials and greasing those rules. Those family members he could not get to England or the United States (where he sent his elderly mother, two sisters, his daughter, his granddaughter, and her future husband), he managed to get to Latin America. Adler did not trust any place in Europe as being safe from the Nazis, and in 1936 he was having second thoughts about England. He did help twelve of his relatives and in-laws gain secret passage to Palestine, although it was a risky trip. Adler later admitted to his biographer that, in spite of his later success as a diamond merchant in the United States, he wished he himself had emigrated to Palestine so that he could have helped create the state of Israel.

Adler's position as chairman of the *Federatie der Belgische Diamantbeurzen* in those final months of his preparations for the family exodus helped immensely. No one in Antwerp or Belgium questioned his many trips to England, the United States, or other countries. And — except for some rare stamps — diamonds are the most portable form of wealth known to humankind.

Vanden Daelen Adler would later say that his proudest achievement, after having saved eighty-five members of his extended family (not including himself), was that after doing so, he arrived in the United States with less than a hundred dollars left from his original wealth of almost $1 million. By 1940, Adler's new diamond business in the United States had regained most of his fortune but he spent a large part of that wealth to buy guns and other weapons for Palestine after the war to help create a Jewish state.

Adler died of a heart attack in 1948, just three weeks after Israel came into existence.

———

Dr. Robert Adler Ochs, born in Denver, Colorado, in 1937, was once quoted as saying, "My profession is physics; my religion is humanity."

It's true that Ochs began blending his brilliant career in physics and his ability to explain science to the public at a relatively young age. His first book, *The Existential Joys of Physics,* became a modest bestseller and an alternate Book-of-the-Month Club selection in 1960, when Ochs was only twenty-three years old. His 1974 book, *Mankind and Mystery: Science Looks at the Cosmos,* remains one of the top five bestselling popular science books in publishing history. In the late 1970s, Ochs's discursive, almost casual BBC series *Man, Mystery, and Science,* using Jacob Bronowski's technique (from his series *The Ascent of Man*) of just chatting conversationally while stepping from place to place around the world to look into the history and humanity of physics and other science through the ages, was — Dr. Carl Sagan once admitted — one of the prime inspirations for the later hit American series *Cosmos.*

Of the nine books that Robert Ochs published during his decades as a working physicist and science populizer, the one he admitted to being most proud of was a small, privately published and circulated volume entitled *Conversations with My Tunkašila.* In this little book, Ochs told of the "summer vacations" from the time he was fourteen until he was twenty-two that he spent visiting his Oglala Sioux great-grandfather in the Black Hills of South Dakota. In the early years, the two would go camping together, despite his great-grandfather's advanced age.

Conversations with My Tunkašila created quite a stir among some of Ochs's academic friends around the world, since — besides long discussions about Lakota beliefs and attitudes about courage and life — the physicist's elderly *"tunkašila"* had explained how knowledge of astronomy had given his Sioux peoples what the old man called *Wakan Wašt'e,* "the cosmic powers of good."

The old man had described new constellations hidden within known constellations, such as *Wičinčala Šakowin,* "The Seven Little Girls," and how, when that constellation reached a precise point in the summer sky, the Natural Free Human Beings would gather at *Hiŋaŋ Ḳaġa Paha*, Harney Peak in the Black Hills, to welcome back the Thunder Beings. Ochs also cited his *tuŋkašila* on how to find and track the movement of the oval constellation *Lo Iŋaŋḳa Očaŋḳa*, the Race Track, and telling of how his people would, when *Lo Iŋaŋḳa Očaŋḳa* reached a precise position in the spring sky, gather together at *Pe Ṡia*, the spiritual center of the Black Hills (a location the old man would not reveal, but which Robert Ochs hinted was where his beloved *tuŋkašila* had built his cabin), for what Ochs's Lakota great-grandfather called the *Oḳišat'aya wowahwala*, or "Welcoming back all life in peace."

There were dozens of other astronomical observations, all relating to specific geographic points such as Devil's Tower in Wyoming (where the summer solstice was celebrated) to Bear Butte in South Dakota to various former winter camps of the Natural Free Human Beings in Nebraska and western South Dakota. Each celebrated a subtle shifting of certain stars within known constellations and each was tied to some ancient ceremony. But what astounded the astronomers who read Ochs's privately distributed book was that his old great-grandfather had revealed cosmologies and levels of astronomical observations known by the Plains Indians that had never been guessed at by ethnographers, historians, or scientists.

And everything in the night sky and on earth, as young Robert Ochs's *tuŋkašila* revealed, was connected, more than symbolically or ceremonially, with what the old man called the *Caŋgleška Wakaŋ*, or "Sacred Hoop."

Scientists in a dozen fields, who had long been sure that the Sioux, Cheyenne, and other Plains tribes had *had* no serious astronomy, were forced to revise their beliefs and textbooks based on Dr. Ochs's short little privately published book.

It was in the last summer that Ochs visited his so-called *tuŋkašila*, when Robert was twenty-two years old, that he published his revolutionary doctoral thesis, *Revised Variations in Velocity Shear Induced Phenomena in Solar and Astrophysical Flows Due to Quantum Effects*. He dedicated the thesis to his great-grandfather.

Dr. Ochs retired in 2007, at the age of seventy, and is currently a professor of physics emeritus at Cornell University and a leading consultant on the James Webb Space Telescope, the successor to the

Hubble telescope that will go into solar orbit far beyond the moon, currently scheduled for launch no earlier than 2013.

———

DR. CONSTANCE GREENE, born in 1972, the paleo-ecologist, environmental expert, and ethnologist once called "the twenty-first century's female Leonardo" by *Time* magazine, credits some of her interest in the human aspects of various Pleistocene rewilding efforts around the world to camping trips she took with her father, Robert Ochs, when she was a girl.

In a BBC interview she did in 2009, Dr. Greene—known as Connie not just to her students and friends but to most of her peers around the world—said:

> When I was ten years old, my dad took me camping to a place in South Dakota called Bear Butte. You're not allowed to camp on or near the butte unless you're Native American, but somehow my dad got permission, so we camped near the summit of that interesting lacolith. Except for rattlesnakes, there was no danger up there, so Dad let me wander by myself a lot as long as I stayed within shouting range. There was this one afternoon— it was raining, I remember, and I met...I mean I had this dream about...at any rate, at age ten, I suddenly saw that if we were ever going to bring back the big predators to the world, in other nations as well as in the dying American West, the rewilding—it was already a term that I'd heard from my father and his friends—the rewilding would have to have a human component. Indigenous peoples should have a choice. You can't just...I mean, you *can't*...keep a culture alive by trying to freeze it in stasis while you're embedded deep within a different culture. It's impossible. It ends up amounting to dressing up a few days a year, chanting old chants that few believe in any longer, and doing dances that your great-great-great-great-grandparents did, too often to get a few bucks from tourists. It doesn't work. But if we were really going to set aside these millions and millions

479

of acres and hectares of land and reintroduce the closest genetic cousins to the megafauna top predators and
other extinct species that evolved there originally, that
used to live there, that used to own the damned place...I
thought, why not the original people too? Why not give
them a choice? I thought it was a good idea at the
time—I was ten, remember, but my mom and dad had a
weird habit of listening to me—and so did all my relatives.

———

PAHA SAPA never worked for Gutzon Borglum again, although it is said
that the two remained friends until the end of Borglum's life.

One piece of advice that Paha Sapa did take from his former boss
was to consult with Borglum's doctor. It turned out that the 1935 diagnosis of cancer by the "quack in Casper" had been false. In January of
1937, Paha Sapa underwent surgery for a long-term and very painful in-
testinal obstruction. The surgery was successful, there was no tumor or
malignancy, the obstruction never returned, and Paha Sapa remained
relatively pain free for the rest of his life.

Sometime in 1937, Paha Sapa moved to a remote place deep within the Black Hills and built a small but comfortable home there. He
was not a recluse; he traveled frequently to visit his grandson, his later
grandchildren, and old friends such as Borglum. But after World War
II, word got out among the *Ikče Wičaśa* that there was an old man in the
Black Hills with the *name* Black Hills, and some people—at first it was
just other old men, but later it was more and more *young* men—made
the long trek into the Hills to visit with this Paha Sapa, trade stories,
and, increasingly, to ask questions about the Old Days.

Somehow the legend grew that this old man had carried the ghost
of Long Hair Custer with him for sixty years.

More and more young Lakota men—and then young Lakota
women—came to visit Paha Sapa, traveling first from the nearby Pine
Ridge Reservation, then from the Rosebud, then Lower Brule, Crow
Creek, Yankton, Cheyenne River, and Standing Rock reservations.
Then, almost shockingly, young and old Cheyenne and Crows and even
Blackfoot from their reservations way over in the northwestern corner

of Wyoming and Montana. When members of tribes from California and Washington state began visiting the old man — tribes Paha Sapa had never even heard of — he laughed and laughed.

Paha Sapa did turn away data-hungry ethnologists, Native American apologists, and at least one media-famous founder of the American Indian Movement, but he always had time to sit and talk and smoke a pipe with any young person or old person without, as the *wasichu* like to say, an agenda. Many of the Natural Free Human Beings who visited him during the summers of those last years remember his curious great-grandson Robert, and how the boy had a gift — unusual for *wasichus,* they said — of knowing how to listen. The old man also often had other great-grandchildren around or was planning a trip to Denver or elsewhere to visit *them.* Even when the elder's arthritis became very painful near the end, he would neither complain nor curtail such travel.

Many of those who visited Paha Sapa in those last decades remember that one of his favorite phrases was — *Le aŋpet'u waṣte!* This is a good day.

One of the younger Lakota visiting heard that and asked Paha Sapa if he didn't mean to say Crazy Horse's and the other old warriors' famous old saying "This is a good day to die!" but Paha Sapa only shook his head and repeated *Le aŋpet'u waṣte!*

A good day to live.

Paha Sapa died at his home in the Black Hills in August of 1959. He was ninety-three years old.

As per his wishes — found written in pencil on an old napkin he'd kept — Paha Sapa was cremated, and the majority of his ashes were buried next to his wife, Rain, at the old Episcopal Mission Cemetery on Pine Ridge Reservation.

But, as per those same wishes, some of Paha Sapa's ashes were taken by a few of his friends and relatives, including his great-grandson Robert, and either scattered or buried somewhere along the small river called *Chankpe Opi Wakpala* where, it is said, the heart of Crazy Horse and the bleached bones of the old-days *wičasa wakan* Limps-a-Lot, whose wisdom was taught so widely and so well by Paha Sapa in his last years, also lie there undisturbed in places secret, sacred, and silent except for the sound of the wind moving on the face of the high grass and amid the leaves of the *waga chun* trees.

Acknowledgments

THE AUTHOR WISHES TO ACKNOWLEDGE the following sources for information used in *Black Hills:*

A Terrible Glory: Custer and the Little Bighorn: The Last Great Battle of the American West by James Donovan © 2008, published by Little, Brown and Company; *The Custer Myth: A Source Book of Custeriana,* written and compiled by W. A. Graham, © 1953, published by Stackpole Books; *Troopers with Custer: Historic Incidents of the Battle of the Little Big Horn* by E. A. Brininstool © 1952, published by the University of Nebraska Press; *Custer's Fall: The Native American Side of the Story* by David Humphreys Miller © 1957, published by Meridian, the Penguin Group; *Crazy Horse and Custer: The Parallel Lives of Two American Warriors* by Stephen E. Ambrose © 1975, published by Anchor Books, a division of Random House; *Custerology: The Enduring Legacy of the Indian Wars and George Armstrong Custer* by Michael A. Elliott © 2007, published by the University of Chicago Press.

I'd like to make special mention of *Killing Custer: The Battle of Little Bighorn and the Fate of the Plains Indians* by James Welch (with Paul Stekler) © 1994, published by W.W. Norton and Company. I was privileged to meet Jim Welch and his wonderful wife, Lois, at the Salon du Livre in Paris in the 1990s and always looked forward to seeing them again. His death in 2003 at the age of sixty-two was a shock and a loss to us all.

Other sources to acknowledge include *The Black Hills After Custer* by Bob Lee © 1997, published by the Donning Company; *Exploring with*

Custer: The 1874 Black Hills Expedition by Ernest Grafe and Paul Horsted © 2002, 2005, published by Golden Valley Press, an imprint of Dakota Photographic; *1876: The Little Big Horn* by Robert Nightengale © 1996, published by Robert Nightengale through DocuPro Services; *The Custer Album: A Pictorial Biography of General George A. Custer* by Lawrence A. Frost © 1964, published by the University of Oklahoma Press; *With the Seventh Cavalry in 1876* by Theodore Goldin © 1980, privately published; *Custer and His Times (Book 4)* edited by John P. Hart © 2002, published by Little Big Horn Associates; "Carbine Extractor Failure at the Little Big Horn" by Paul L. Hedren © Summer 1973 issue of *Military Collector and Historian; Archaeology, History, and Custer's Last Battle* by Richard A. Fox © 1993, published by the University of Oklahoma Press.

Reference material for Elizabeth ("Libbie") Custer include *The Custer Story: The Life and Intimate Letters of General George A. Custer and His Wife Elizabeth* edited by Marguerite Merington © 1950, published by the University of Nebraska Press; *Elizabeth Bacon Custer and the Making of a Myth* by Shirley A. Leckie © 1993, published by the University of Oklahoma Press; *Touched by Fire: The Life, Death, and Mythic Afterlife of George Armstrong Custer* by Louise Barnett © 1996, published by Henry Holt and Company; *Boots and Saddles, or: Life in Dakota with General Custer* by Elizabeth B. Custer © 1885, reprinted 1969, published by Corner House Publishers; *General Custer's Libby* by Lawrence A. Frost © 1976, published by Superior Publishing Company. It should be noted that frequently cited dates for Elizabeth Custer's death, including Wikipedia and multiple printed sources, are wrong. Mrs. Custer died on April 4, 1933, and her obituary appeared in the *New York Times* on April 5 of that year.

Material referred to for the Lakota and Indian side of the Battle of the Little Big Horn and other details include *Crazy Horse: A Lakota Life* by Kingsley M. Bray © 2006, published by the University of Oklahoma Press; *Black Elk Speaks: Being the Life Story of a Holy Man of the Oglala Sioux as Told through John G. Neihardt* © 1932, published by University of Nebraska Press; *Counting Coup and Cutting Horses: Intertribal Warfare on the Northern Plains, 1738–1889* by Anthony McGinnis © 1990, published by Cordillera Press; *Mother Earth Spirituality: Native American Paths to Healing Ourselves and the World* by Ed McGaa (Eagle Man) © 1990, published by HarperSanFrancisco, a division of Harper Collins; *American Indian Myths and Legends* selected and edited by Richard Erdoes and Alfonso Ortiz © 1984, published by Pantheon Books; *Black Elk: The Sacred Way of a Lakota* by Wallace Black Elk and William S. Lyon © 1990, published by HarperSanFrancisco, a division of Harper Collins; *Bury My Heart at Wounded Knee: An Indian History of the American West* by Dee Brown © 1971, published by Bantam Books by arrangement with Holt, Rinehart & Winston; *Where the Lightning Strikes: The Lives of American Indian Sacred Places* by Peter Nabokov © 2006, published by Penguin Books; *My People the Sioux* by Luther Standing Bear © 1975, published by the University of Nebraska Press; *The Tipi: Traditional Native American Shelter* by Adolf Hungrywolf © 2006, published by Native Voices Book Publishing Company; *Lakota Belief and Ritual* by James R. Walker (edited by Raymond J. DeMallie and Elaine A. Jahner) © 1980, 1991, published by University of Nebraska Press in cooperation with the Colorado Historical Society; *Lakota Star Knowledge: Studies of Lakota Stellar Theology* by Ronald Goodman © 1992, published by Sinte Gleska University; *Stories of the Sioux* by Luther Standing Bear © 1934, published by University of Nebraska Press.

The author wishes to acknowledge *An English-Dakota Dictionary* by John P. Williamson © 1992, published by the Minnesota Historical Society Press; *Lakota Dictionary* compiled and edited by Eugene Buechel and Paul Manhart © 2002, published by University of Nebraska Press; *Reading and Writing the Lakota Language: Lakot'a Iyapi nahaŋ Yawapi* by Albert White Hat Sr. (edited by Jael Kampfe) © 1999, published by the University of Utah Press.

For help in searching the Black Hills area and the Dust Bowl period, the author wishes to acknowledge *Exploring the Black Hills & Badlands—Summer & Autumn 2008* © 2008, an official publication of South Dakota's Black Hills, Badlands, & Lakes Association; *Deadwood: The Golden Years* by Watson Parker © 1981, published by University of Nebraska Press; *The Worst Hard Time* by Timothy Egan © 2006, published by Mariner Books, a division of Houghton Mifflin Company. And a very special thanks to Dr. Dan Peterson and his wife, Barbara, from Spearfish, South Dakota, who introduced me to so many of these historical and hidden places in and around the Black Hills.

ACKNOWLEDGMENTS

Materials referenced for the carving of Mount Rushmore include *The Carving of Mount Rushmore* by Rex Alan Smith © 1985, published by Abbeville Press Publishers; *Mount Rushmore* by Gilbert C. Fite © 1980, published by the Mount Rushmore History Association; *Mount Rushmore's Hall of Records: The Little-Known Story of the Memorial's Sealed Vault and Its Message for Future Civilizations* by Paul Higbee © 1999, published by the Mount Rushmore History Association (originally published in *South Dakota Magazine*); *Gutzon Borglum: His Life and Work* by Robin Borglum Carter © 1998, published by the Mount Rushmore History Association; *Mount Rushmore Q&A: Answers to Frequently Asked Questions* by Don "Nick" Clifford © 2004, self-published.

The author would especially like to thank Mr. Clifford, who was a Mount Rushmore worker from 1938 to 1940, for his time and conversation at the Memorial site.

For reference material relating to the 1893 Chicago World's Fair, the author wishes to acknowledge *The World's Columbian Exposition: The Chicago World's Fair of 1893* by Norman Bolotin and Christine Laing © 1992, 2002, published by University of Illinois Press; *The Chicago World's Fair of 1893: A Photographic Record* with text by Stanley Appelbaum © 1980, by Dover Publications; *The Devil in the White City: Murder, Magic, and Madness at the Fair That Changed America* by Erik Larson © 2003, published by Crown Publishers; *Images of America — Chicago's Classical Architecture: The Legacy of the White City* by David Stone © 2005, published by Arcadia Publishing; *The Great Wheel* text and illustrations by Robert Lawson © 1957, published by Walker & Company.

A special thanks here to the members of the Dan Simmons Forum at dansimmons.com for their help on the long and amusing chase through original newspaper accounts and other printed materials to discover which way Mr. Ferris's original wheel rotated.

Of all the myriad Internet and other materials accessed, none was more useful in finding details of the building of the Brooklyn Bridge than my old favorite, *The Great Bridge: The Epic Story of the Building of the Brooklyn Bridge* by David McCullough © 1972, published by Simon and Schuster.

Finally, a sincere thank you to Maka Tai Meh Jacques L. Condor for taking the time to read and comment on this manuscript.

About the Author

Dan Simmons is the award-winning author of several novels, including the *New York Times* bestsellers *Olympos, The Terror,* and *Drood*. He lives in Colorado. For more information about Dan Simmons, visit www.DanSimmons.com.